INDEPENDENT LEGIONS
PUBLISHING

INDEPENDENT LEGIONS PUBLISHING

THE BEAUTY OF DEATH II
DEATH BY WATER

Edited by Alessandro Manzetti and Jodi Renée Lester

ISBN: 978-88-99569-73-0

1° edition paperback November 2017

THE BEAUTY OF DEATH II

DEATH BY WATER

Edited by Alessandro Manzetti and Jodi Renée Lester

Water does not resist. Water flows. When you plunge your hand into it, all you feel is a caress. Water is not a solid wall, it will not stop you. But water always goes where it wants to go, and nothing in the end can stand against it. Water is patient. Dripping water wears away a stone. Remember that, my child. Remember you are half water. If you can't go through an obstacle, go around it. Water does.

—Margaret Atwood

TABLE OF CONTENTS

JOANNA PARYPINSKI

THE DEEPEST PART OF THE OCEAN

WHEN I looked up from my algebra homework, I saw him standing in the dining room—barefoot, dripping a steady *plink, plink, plink* of rainwater onto the hardwood floor.

"Grandpa?"

He acknowledged me with a shaky wave and a raise of his mad Einsteinian eyebrows, stretching the jowls of his sourdough face, which ran wet with tiny tributaries winding through his wrinkled cheeks, while his sodden flannel shirt clung to his bird bones and melted into the antediluvian brown trousers that ended high above his bare ankles, above the gnarled and hairy feet daggered with fungus-yellow toenails that stood in the puddle he had created.

"I almost had her this time," he said with a shake of his fist, the gesture of foiled conquest.

"Had who?"

He yanked the golf cap from his head and waved it irritably, scattering drops of water like shards of glass, said, "The mermaid," and took a step away from his little puddle, succeeding only in dragging it into a river that followed him toward me, and "I saw her in a raindrop." He paused, his eyes flickering with revelation, looked down at his small puddle on the floor. "Hallo, are you in there?"

I thought if I ignored him he might wander off—after all, it wasn't my job to babysit Grandpa—and I was very much concerned at the time, as most teenagers are, with the bare minimum expectations of my familial role. Instead he came up to my couch, pushed my legs off one end, and sat down, soaking the cushion beneath him. He smelled like mildew.

"Hey!" I said, "I'm trying to work, here!"

"Emily, dearest. Don't you ever play outside anymore?"

I snapped my textbook closed, careful to leave my pencil in the right spot, too anxious to lose where I was. "Not when there's a tsunami outside."

"Pah. You never seen a tsunami," he said. "Where I grew up, we had *real* tsunamis. Great terrible waves that roared out of the ocean like dragons. Houses knocked down like cards. This? This is just a little rain."

I looked out the window, at the flag whipping into a frenzy as rain turned to television static, as a flash of lightning burst like a migraine.

God, I hated this weather.

There's not much you can do about it, though, when you live in San Francisco, and the rain drones on relentlessly as an army, and you can't hear your own thoughts rattling around over the tempest that batters and bruises your raw nerves—when the sky is a seething black mass of artificial night. God. I'm all strung out again thinking about it, here in the darkness. My anxiety was bad before, worse after Grandpa's stay with us, after what happened, but I'll get to that.

Sad thing is, I'm not even calmed anymore by the whispery exhalations of the tide. Back then I could stand and listen to the waves, the sea, the sound of the midnight oracle portending moonlit movements and crashing elegies against the broad-shouldered beach, but now I know what might break the surface (so I've taken a preemptive strike instead, gone below).

A while later, my mother burst inside in a whirl of rain and wind behind the shield of her umbrella, her typically coiffed hair fallen in spidery disarray over her face. "Poseidon's fury," she grumbled, then spotted us. "Dad! You're getting the sofa all wet. Emily—how could you let him sit there?"

She forced him to go change his wet clothes, at least, before he caught his death. He ambled dutifully up the stairs, and my mother said, "Come on, Emily. Help me out. Can't you look after him when I'm not here?"

"He's an adult, isn't he? I can't tell him what to do."

My grandfather had come to stay with us not long after my grandmother died. Heart failure. She'd been a lovely, tiny lady, the daintiest person I ever knew, with pinprick little eyes, but she was surprisingly strong, able to lift heavy flowerpots and muscle her way through stirring thick dough. She was always there, a solid presence, until one day she wasn't, and we could feel the very physicality of her absence—not just a lack but the inverse of a presence. Mind you, Grandpa didn't take it well, or at least my mother told me he wasn't well, and so he came to stay with us.

"He's forgetful," she said, sounding somehow ashamed.

But he didn't seem forgetful to me—odd, fanciful, full of whimsy, but not forgetful. He told me stories of his childhood as sharply as if they had happened yesterday, not sixty years ago.

I couldn't help but be contrary. What else do you expect of a fourteen-year-old girl? Even when I agreed with my mother, I simply felt compelled to argue. "What happened to respecting my elders?"

She looked at me sharply, then more softly. "Respect is more complicated than that."

DO YOU want the truth? I couldn't stand to see my grandfather like that. Here he was, the man who had raised my mother, who had dozens of stories about life in the tiny Japanese village where he grew up, making mischief with his friends, getting drunk on fishing trips, his brief stint as a naval officer. You could see the sea in his eyes, hear the roar of the coast in his voice. Now he was reduced to a rambling senior wandering around barefoot, purposeless, and in the way of selfishness I worried less about his mental state and more about me, about what would become of me when I was too old to tie my shoes—would I, too, someday become such an obsolete creature, force my grandchildren to look after me like a child myself, void of dignity?

So I tried to avoid him, tried to avoid the thought of impending mortality—turning antique, toothless. Hah. What did I know of growing old? What did I know of death? What did I know of the deep loneliness that comes when you've been ripped away from your partner of more than half a lifetime?

MY FATHER always came home in the middle of the night. He worked odd hours, so I got used to hearing the creak of heavy footsteps ghosting down the midnight halls—the shadow outside my bedroom door—his indistinct presence, there without a face. On weekends, he materialized on the couch as if he had always been there, feet propped on the ottoman, a bowl of chips perched on the slight bulge of his stomach, a bottle dangling from one hand over the edge of the armrest. Our conversations weren't really conversations back then: he would eye me skeptically, suspiciously, and ask how school was going with the tone of a mildly curious interrogator, and whatever my answer, he would nod slowly and return to the television.

"It's because he has no imagination, the poor bastard," my grandfather told me once. "That's why he's always in front of the tube."

Was the problem, I wondered, that my grandfather simply had too much imagination? Was it that he could no longer quite disentangle the threads of reality from his own woven works? I couldn't imagine my father going senile—he was simply too matter-of-fact. And you know what? He never did go senile. He died at sixty-eight, still doing puzzles and answering *Jeopardy!* questions with lightning precision, when a swift-moving cancer swept through him like the tide, sweeping him away before my eyes.

For a while I was terrified of my own mind, which was already prone to flying, dancing, skittering lizard-like from one horrible possibility to the next—an anxious mind. "Getting away from me," that's what my mother called it: "Your imagination's getting away from you again, Em." Maybe that. Maybe it's overcoming me. In the end, though, I couldn't keep it contained, and I guess it didn't really matter.

A lack of imagination won't save you, either—in the end.

THE SWEET sleepy silence that falls in the wake of endless rain is like a cool wash of balm easing over shattered nerves, those tender spots like spoiled fruit, and in that wake a gleaming bepuddled world, puddles slick and gray and gathering at the edges where the road dips down to receive the curb. Amid that dreamy lonesome *after*, after the storm, I couldn't find my grandpa anywhere, and here I was supposed to be looking after him.

When I did find him—which wasn't that hard, mind you, he was just down the street—he was standing in a puddle up to his knees. A puddle that should only have been a few inches deep, a puddle nearly flush with the ground. A whisper of a puddle.

But there he was, up to his knees in it. Like he was in a hole, and the dull light made him strange, colorless, sunken.

When he saw me, he pointed—"She's down there! I saw her!"

It's amazing how quickly the mind accommodates impossible things, for in a moment I was no longer contemplating the spatial disparity (where oh where were his legs, were they gone, were they *gone*?) but instead worrying over what a neighbor might think if they looked out their window right now and saw us standing in the drowned street like fools.

He looked up again to see me gaping at him like a fish, and when he looked back down he seemed disappointed. "Oh, cock and balls," he said. "I think we've scared her off."

Have I mentioned that my grandfather was delightfully crude? Every time he swore, it was with such imaginative gusto, you could hardly blame him for being profane around children. He made curse words sound as wholesome as apple pie.

He stepped out of the puddle, drawing one pale leg, saggy and dripping, from the inch of water that could not conceivably have contained it, that had swallowed it into some elsewhere, and planting his bare foot on the pavement. His trousers were rolled up to his knees. He didn't unroll them until we were inside, and when he did they were ribbed with angry horizontal lines.

"Grandpa," I said, "Look. I know you're older than I am, and all, but I really don't think you should be walking around like that. It's not cool, you know?"

What? You expected an eloquent speech? Give me a break; I was fourteen.

We sat at the dining room table where a lightbulb in the overhead fixture had burned out, leaving us in an uneven half-light that crawled eerily over my grandfather's face.

"May I tell you about her?" he said.

"Who?"

He hitched up his pants and said with a shrug in his voice, "It would be a lie if I said I'd never loved anyone other than your grandmother."

"*What?*' I was appalled—I didn't want to hear it, this mocking of his marriage, this reminder that he wasn't just a stock grandfather with stock stories but a real human being.

"Before I ever met her, I fell in love with a mermaid."

"You...?"

"It was after the worst storm I'd ever seen. Ripped and raged through that piss-little fishing village, bringing the sea with it. A nasty bitch of a wave caught me and threw me, tossing and tumbling. I nearly drowned. Eventually I found myself a bit worse for wear on a flooded road, and that's where I found her, stranded. At first I thought it was a corpse, but bodies tend to bob to the surface—she floated just below. When I looked down, damn it all to hell and back again, I saw the most beautiful creature staring back at me. Black hair like silk, face pale like the moon, eyes deep as the ocean, breasts—"

"Grandpa!"

He put up his hands in surrender. "Well, she was beautiful. With a silver tail and everything, though I couldn't see where it ended. It was long, I'll tell you that. She said she had come from the deepest part of the ocean. I was smitten. If you haven't felt those pangs of desire yet, Emily, you will soon I'm sure. Well, we had ourselves something of an adventure, swimming through the debris-ridden road to get her back to the ocean where she belonged. When we got there, damned if I wanted to let her go! I knew we couldn't be together, but I imagined building a great wonderful fish tank, big enough for her to live in, big as a house!

"Instead, she told me to follow her. *Down.*

"I'll tell you this: I considered it. But in the end, I couldn't do it. What an ass was I, Emily! I let her go. But I came back to see her a few times more. We met at the beach, and sometimes I told her stories, and sometimes she sang songs that could tear your heart out—hypnotic songs. Hers is a voice I'll never forget. It haunts my dreams.

"Have you ever been in love, Emily?"

Love? There I was, talking to my grandfather about love, something I never talked about with my parents, with my friends, with anyone, really, and my weird old grandpa who smelled like a pungent cheese, limburger perhaps, who put the paper against his forehead in the morning to pretend he could divine the day's news telepathically, who tottered around with his arms akimbo and asked me if he was a good dancer when I played my music through the television speakers, was asking me about love, the deepest and most precious, most secret feeling in the world to me then. I would have been less mortified if he'd asked me about my period. Anyway, what did I know of love? I didn't even realize at the time that there are different sorts of love—not just the romantic kind, the mermaid kind, but the peculiar type of fondness you feel for your wacky grandfather, that you don't even understand until he's gone.

"Okay, Grandpa. How could she survive in the deepest part of the ocean?" I said. "And how does she see? It's like pitch black down there."

"I'll tell you this—I'll be damned if she wasn't imbued with her own inner light," he said, a smile coming over him from across the ages. "Like you in that way."

LUCKY FOR me, I was due for another obsession right about then. I was always prone to pendulums of obsession and apathy, between studying a new subject fervently for hours, insatiable, mad-minded, and then spending an entire Saturday on the couch watching my dad flip channels. My previous interests had been magic, astronomy, butterflies, and detective stories, each one giving way to the next. While I didn't know it at the time, I had finally found an obsession that I would never grow out of.

"The abyssopelagic zone is aphotic, meaning no light penetrates that deep," I read to my grandfather from the book I had checked out at the library. The cover was faded and soft with wear, the pages filled with illustrations of the ocean, of alien creatures, horror movie creatures: dragonfish, vampire squid, goblin shark. Fish with teeth. "Imagine if you could swim down with her and see all that."

"She comes from a very different world than we do, I'll tell you that," said Grandpa, wagging his finger in a way that told me he was about to impart some old-man wisdom. "We must always try to meet people from different worlds. If you don't, you'll never learn anything new."

My grandfather, too, seemed to come from a different world—one that I could never visit, an irrecoverable world, and he was right, because he taught me about things, like love, even if he taught them sideways.

"What are you two reading about?" my mother asked as she peered over my shoulder in a way I always hated, like she was spying on me.

"Where the mermaid lives."

I'll never forget the way she yanked me away from the dining table, up to my bedroom, put her finger in my face, and told me sharply I was not to listen to my grandfather's stories. "If you indulge him, he'll only get worse. I know your imagination gets away from you, but you can't believe his nonsense."

"What if it isn't nonsense?"

She looked at me scornfully.

"It *is* nonsense. He's an irrational old man who barely knows up from down, and I won't have you follow him down that rabbit hole. Stop enabling him." It was only later that I understood the crack in her voice. Here I thought she was just being a cold bitch, but really, when I look back now, I realize her voice was so hard and brittle because she was terrified that more and more of her father was going to slip away into the ether, that she would lose him before he was physically gone. I know because that's how I felt, years later, when my mother was diagnosed with Alzheimer's. Gradually she forgot my name, lost track of where she lived, looked around familiar places with childish bewilderment. It was a slow, cold, remorseless metaphysical death. But of course I didn't comprehend that when I was a kid. All I felt was the fire of teenage spite at adults who behave callously because they can, because they're adults, not because they're human beings with their own complex inner lives that I couldn't yet fathom.

THE FOLLOWING Monday was gray and oppressively humid; a fine mist of almost-rain hung suspended in the air, and Grandpa had gone out without me.

I thought he might include me now that he had told me the truth, for I believed at that point that it must be the truth after all, no matter what my mother tried to convince me, and, thinking we might go out mermaid hunting together, I actually geared up—put on my rainboots, teased through my jackets to find one that was waterproof. But Grandpa went out on his own, leaving as surreptitiously as the wind, so what did I do?

I followed him.

I followed him into the sodden, heavy afternoon, keeping enough distance between us that he wouldn't turn around and see me.

You know why I didn't go up to him, why I followed in secret? Because he didn't invite me along. The pain of betrayal unfolded in me like a ripe flower, and I followed, feeling small and inadequate.

He paused to peer in every puddle, in every puddle finding nothing, and we continued in this way for, oh, maybe an hour, weaving through marshy grass and narrow winding switchback streets that sloped into rainwater seas, before he stopped at a dirty creek on the edge of a wooded hill. At one end, the gaping black mouth of a sewer outfall disgorged a slow stream of brown water into the abysmal brook.

Rolling up his pants and removing his shoes, Grandpa waded into the shallow water, which came up just over his spider-veined calves, and made his way to the dark orifice, gateway to an underground realm of sewage, decay, and magic.

He called echoingly into the dank throat of the tunnel. By now I was cold and tired. The light gray of afternoon was sinking into a darker, duskier gray of secret twilight. It was time to bring Grandpa back, I thought—or, my anger having long since chilled to a wet, muddy, dull and uncaring resentment, maybe I should just leave him here, leave him to rot in the sewers.

Then she arrived.

At first she was just a dark shape swimming out of the tunnel, swimming from darkness into the muted tones of overcast evening: a woman rising slowly out of the water, long black hair like seaweed struggling down her shoulders, naked from the waist up—water glistening on her pale, almost silvery breasts. They embraced. Grandpa's back hitched and shuddered with tears of grief, joy, relief, and when her bony arms twined around him, caressed his back, I saw long pointed fingers like crab claws, the skin turning silvery-black as the talons tapered to their points.

They were too distracted to notice me creeping closer, close enough to see her face—pearlescent, with cheekbones sharp enough to cut flesh.

"I knew it! I knew it, I knew it was you. But—why did you have to abandon me?" Grandpa croaked. "I looked everywhere for you."

"I was waiting," she said in a dreamy voice like sunshine sparkling on seashells, like dark music. "Waiting for the right time."

"Thank God you're here," my grandfather murmured. "You're real. I thought I was going—crazy."

She began humming rather than reply, and the sound took on ethereal tones, warbled as if coming through water. I might have closed my eyes and fallen asleep to the tune but that she stopped suddenly, leaving us with harsh silence. What made her stop?

She had seen me.

From over my grandfather's shoulder, her eyes snapped to me: two round silver fish-eyes, cold with blank inhumanity. Slowly her black lips peeled back in a wide curved expression that looked like a grin but wasn't—no, it was an inverted grin, upside-down and terrible to reveal rows of jagged needle like teeth that reminded me of the stupid hungry mouth of an anglerfish.

Still holding on to him, she began to sink into the water, bringing Grandpa with her, and what was even worse, somehow, was that he didn't fight; he let her drag him down; perhaps he wanted to go with her into the dark forgetful depths where he could pretend not to remember the love he still felt for my grandmother, the pain he still felt over her absence. Together, they disappeared into the murky water.

After tearing off my rainboots and throwing my jacket behind me, I waded in after them. The creek should have been maybe three feet at its deepest, but when I looked down I saw them far below me, maybe ten feet down, vanishing into an impossibly vast greenish abyss, the mermaid's arms still wrapped tightly around my grandfather.

I dove.

The dirty water burned my eyes as I fought my way down. If words could travel through water, I would have shouted for my grandfather to break him out of the spell she had over him, which was not love, I could see that now, it was love's wicked cousin, the bastard child of jealousy and lust.

My chest ached, desperate for breath, suffocating, and still they were too far below me, and still the burn in my eyes, this time from tears, and still the belief I could catch up to them if only—if only I could swim faster—but we were deep, too deep, and I would have to retreat to the surface soon, which was high above now, nearly lost in the darkening water.

The last glance I had of my grandfather—finally he looked up and saw me swimming above them, a moment that seemed to clear his head, and he tried to swim up to me but the mermaid gripped him more tightly, still grinning that cavernous sharp-toothed not-grin, and for the first time I noticed her tail, long silvery and slimy, tapering slowly but never quite reaching a point, a tail that vanished into the abyss far below them, impossibly long, and in the moment after my grandfather and I locked eyes for the last time and I saw the apology within them, and the fear, a great dark shape rose up from the end of the mermaid's tail, a behemoth of darkness that unhinged its monstrous jaws to envelop the two creatures sucked quickly, now, toward it, sucked away into the mindless ravening abyss.

WHEN I broke the surface, gasping and shuddering, I stood in the creek for long moments sucking rotten air, deliriously convincing myself I would dive back again as soon as I caught my breath. But when I did, I discovered that the creek was only a few feet deep; even in the middle, it came up only as far as my waist. There was nothing down there. He was gone.

In the years that followed, I always kept an eye out for him, just in case—in fish tanks, in puddles, in ponds. Still, I knew I wouldn't find him. I knew where she had taken him: to the deepest part of the ocean.

So that was where I went.

As you can guess, that particular fascination, obsession, call it what you will—it never left me. Lately I've been studying abyssal zone ecosystems in a submarine stationed 20,000 feet below the surface of the Pacific, where there is no light and nothing remotely familiar, only the freakish bioluminescent creatures that glide through the somnolent deep.

A few hours ago I saw something outside the window of the sub…something familiar. Something that's got me all strung out again.

It was my grandfather. Pale, his nearly translucent skin glowing with ghostlight, made visible in the black emptiness—floating dreamily past, gazing in at me with round silver eyes, his pale fleshy legs replaced by a long, long tail.

I shouldn't have done it, I know, but I put on a diving suit and went out against protocol, swam out into the black silent abyss, the weight of thousands of tons of water crushing down on me. He drifted out of sight, and I followed deeper, surrounded by the pale snowfall of the deep sea, the excretions of the world above falling forever.

When I looked back, I couldn't see the sub anymore.

He had lured me out into the vast darkness of the ocean with only the small light on my helmet to guide me through the nothing, with only the light of his luminous skin to draw me forward like an untethered astronaut floating through space. But I had to see him again, to know that he was real, to know that I wasn't going—well, crazy.

Even after half a lifetime of studying, I realize, in the end, that I still don't know anything. What do I really know of the mysteries in the endless deep? What do I know of death? All I have is you, whoever you are, the person in my head, my imagination, and who knows where that will lead me this time—what dark impossible corridors of madness might lie at the bottom of the sea where the hungry giants live?

LUCY TAYLOR

YOU WILL COME TO NO HARM IN WATER

"LILLIAN, WE'RE going to miss the plane."

Martin Wallace tapped his Rolex while his wife perused a display case in Bobby Twin Elks Loan and Pawn just west of Albuquerque. "That one, please," she said to the elderly Navajo behind the counter, "let me see it."

The old man rummaged in the case and handed her a white medallion with a hole drilled near the top to accommodate a leather cord. Lillian asked what it was made from.

"Bone. Whale maybe."

She turned it over several times, her face rapt with the kind of child-like delight Martin had once found charming.

He paced the aisle. "Lillian, we have to leave."

"Just a moment."

He was starting to wonder if she were actually trying to make them miss their flight and what other evasive tactics she might use to spoil their trip. His trip, really. An idea of a second honeymoon to renew the spark in their rocky five-year marriage and forestall any ideas of divorce she might secretly be harboring. He'd found the number for a high-priced divorce lawyer and some incriminating texts from same. The discovery had shocked and angered him; he'd thought Lillian too needy to instigate divorce. And though he said nothing, this changed things, made him rethink his long-range plans for their marriage.

Now, as she dillydallied, he clenched his fists in frustration. How she vexed him, this handsome woman with vivid azure eyes, a foxy face and, in his astute opinion, an insufficient chin. Her habitual expression of uncertainty put him in mind of some small prey animal peeking fearfully out of its den with an eye to predators. One of those women requiring a male escort through life, who felt the need of a man to protect and cherish her. That he'd been chosen for this role he found a source of never-ending irony.

Now she flashed a winning smile he made no effort to return and showed him the medallion.

"It was meant for me to find here, don't you think?"

"Undoubtedly," he said. "You should buy it."

And although he found the object singularly unattractive, he understood why his wife, who had a superstitious bent, would want to own it. On one side, inked into the bone in the manner of scrimshaw, was written in ant-sized script a promise Lillian would probably like to tattoo on her heart, "You Will Come to No Harm in Water," and on the reverse, a primitive rendition of a fish skeleton against a background of an ever-narrowing spiral. Above the curved lines representing ribs, a single bulbous eye stared out with malevolent intent. Unlike the skeleton it belonged to, the eye seemed alive and menacing.

He gave the item back to Lillian, then wiped his hand discreetly on his jeans.

She put the medallion around her neck and trotted over to admire herself in a mirror. An unease crept over Martin that he tried to dispel with the sound of his own voice. He asked the Navajo how he came to acquire the piece.

"Pawn," the old man said, regarding Martin as one might a poorly made reproduction of an ancient Anasazi pot. "Spanish girl come in, said her grandpa was a fisherman in the Gulf and wore this all the time. When he died, she found it in his tackle box. Told me she'd come back for it one day, but that was years ago. I knew she never would."

"Gramps didn't drown, I hope?" said Martin as Lillian shot him a look. He slid his arm through hers, guiding her toward the door and into the bright, scalding day. Over her shoulder she called back to the shopkeep, "You don't know what this means to me!

I'm terrified of water and where we're headed is in the middle of the ocean."

WELL, NOT exactly the middle, but close enough, he thought, when they were belted in, the Southwest jet taxiing on the runway while Lillian death-gripped the armrests. He pried one hand loose, squeezed it reassuringly and put her fingers to his lips. Her skin smelled of lavender hand lotion, yet somehow, beneath the fragrance, a subtle foulness clung, the faint stench of rotting sea life.

When he forced himself to kiss her fingers, he felt his stomach clench. "It's going to be a wonderful trip," he said, more to himself than her. "A new beginning for us both. You'll see."

Her eyes were tightly shut and she didn't respond. He felt an unexpected flicker of desire as the old, eroticized resentments rose in him along with his cock.

He'd been in love with her once, he was sure of it. When they'd met at a New Age church in Santa Fe—her seeking the kind of solace some find in sex or spirituality or a lurid combination of the two, his ambitions simpler, to find an easy mark—he'd recognized her name and experienced an almost orgasmic shivering. The heir to an ice cream empire, her family name was plastered on tubs of Marsha-Mellow and Chunky Cherub around the world, her father a sickly octogenarian unlikely to last out the year. And she, a made-to-order prize beset with wealth and phobias.

But now the bloom was off the Chocolate Cherry, frail zombie-Daddy still clinging to shreds of life, their marriage more a series of staged skits between bouts of heavy drinking on Lillian's part and cruel, covert punishments on his. Nothing so vulgar as physical violence, of course. He preferred a more nuanced approach, tormenting her with silence, making her fret and guess about how she had displeased him. With the threat of divorce looming, however, he'd decided to reverse course and become again the loving spouse, to deluge her with hot sex and mindfuckery, to unbalance her completely. To that end, he'd found a jewel of a tropical island, one of those semi-private ones frequented by the über-rich where Lillian was most at home. Add to that a barge-sized bed, strong drink spilled into goblets the size of cannonballs, and bouts of mad, inebriated sex. How better to reignite marital passion and regain her trust.

But her fear of the water *was* a minor problem.

She'd confessed this fear soon after they were married, when he'd suggested a South Pacific cruise. Wishing to explore her weaknesses for later use, he'd peppered her with questions. "Did you watch someone drown or almost drown yourself? Parents pitch you into the deep end of the pool?"

Her answer had grated on his patience because, like Lillian herself, it was both nonsensical and vague. She'd told him that, as a young child, her parents took her to the tony resort of Sea Island, Georgia.

"We went out in a glass-bottomed boat," she'd said. "At first I loved it. Seeing all that underwater life, the bonefish and the barracudas, the bright blue mahi mahi with their big, domed foreheads. It all seemed magical until it changed, and I saw something different. I realized the ocean I thought I knew was only a disguise, a camouflage for something unimaginable and awful, an endless nothingness, a void. I only saw it for a second—that's all it would allow—but for that instant, it was like looking through a telescope at a secret universe that despises us and means us only harm. I realized this is why the oceans were created. To conceal what's really underneath. An ocean of the dead."

"The nightmares of an over-stimulated child," he'd said with false assurance, for in truth he found her tale disturbing on so many levels, not least of which that she was clearly mentally unwell. "I know boats. My father had a Chris-Craft Commander he docked in Bimini." (In truth his father was a petty thief whose entire knowledge of the ocean came from *Sea Hunt* reruns.) "One day I'm going to take you on a boating trip. It'll be wonderful, you'll see!"

Her face had taken on a ghastly sheen, as though he'd outlined his plan to sodomize the bogeyman with a sharp stick up the anus. It was that same look on an older face that he saw now, the scrunched brow and cadaverously pallid skin, the twitchy corner of her mouth, as she dozed next to him on the plane.

Inevitably, his gaze was drawn to the amulet around her neck. The rawness of the tiny pictograph, the gleam of the bone, even the promise of protection, all held a kind of primitive allure. Knowing how much it meant to her, for a moment he almost coveted it himself.

IN EMERALD Key, they spent the first week at the island's posh resort—luxurious cottages and doting staff who knew when to be invisible, a helicopter ferrying guests to and from the airports in Nassau and Freeport. He made a point of spoiling her, praising her wit, her charm, her not inconsiderable talent for debauchery. Decadence was cultivated as an art, fine wine and Kama Sutra sex and rutting in the full moonlight, a cocaine-laced tryst with a unicorn from Melbourne whose cell number he obtained discreetly and tucked away for future use. The spell he'd cast when they first met was rewoven with strands of tenderness and cruelty and passion, and she gorged on it, grew bovine and louche feasting on the poison of his tainted adoration.

By week's end, she was sufficiently compliant to let him rent a thirty-five-foot Viking motor yacht complete with lavish master cabin and well-appointed bar, lacking nothing except the convenience of a swim platform. But after all, he told her, neither of them was going in the water.

At first they only explored the coastline near the shore, but later he motored far out into the sea and anchored in deep water. Here, with Shakespearean aplomb, he professed remorse for his sometimes less than chivalrous behavior, a bravura performance that drew tears and promises of lifelong fidelity from them both. In fact, so real was the performance and delivered with emotion so apparently heartfelt, that later, when they tangled in a sweaty heap upon the deck, he experienced a moment of what might have been real love, as intimate and potentially lethal as the onset of an aneurysm. But love, he reminded himself, though sometimes as intense as lust, was also just as fleeting, and he regained his good sense in short order.

Now, while she showered, he leaned on the rail, dazzled by the sunlight on gleaming green swells. A wind was coming up, the water becoming choppy. Below he noticed something odd, a few pebbled, undulating patches, jellyfish perhaps or some detritus dumped into the sea by those indifferent to ecology. They clotted near the stern, slapping the hull with a sound like liver flipped into a pan. He found a mini-bottle in the pocket of his trunks, uncapped it, drained the contents, and flung the empty. Havoc ensued. What he'd thought to be a few distinct animals turned out to be an enormous school of tiny fish that, when the projectile struck, exploded into a chaos of seething, agitated life.

Repulsed, he turned away as Lillian came up from the galley, freshly dressed in cut-offs and a wisp of a red tee, the amulet starkly white against her sun-burnt cleavage. As she tottered across the deck, drink in hand, he noted that the severe lines in her face had softened noticeably—Bacardi, he thought, better than Botox.

She gazed toward the horizon, a blurred seam where sea and sky merged into a single chalky band. In the west, a band of clouds impersonated snow-clad peaks.

"Sip?" she said, lifting the paper cup toward his mouth.

"No thanks."

"Aren't you drinking today?"

He feigned dismay. "You make it sound like a moral failing. Don't worry I'll catch up. It's our last night. I intend to drink my share tonight and more."

She let her free hand rove down his chest. "Actually, it may be better if the captain's sober, so he can navigate."

"Right now all I want to navigate is you."

She threw her head back, her smooth bare throat like something from a nature show, gazelle giving itself to a lion. A stimulating image—as if on cue, he hardened.

"My love," he said and swept her up into his arms—she, laughing with delight at this show of male prowess, her gaze enamored, lips parted in expectation of a kiss—and in a move intended to be seamless, an action choreographed to perfection in the dungeons of his mind, he pivoted and tried to heave her violently out over the rail—her face a parody of passion, now gone rubbery with horror—as he opened up his arms. Instead of falling, she clamped her arms around his chest, so that, far from the graceful uncoupling he'd foreseen, they seesawed as a single off-kilter beast whose lower half pedaled air, piteously screeching, while its upper half engaged in a frenetic jig of thrusts and grunts intended to jettison the part unwanted.

Her strength was unexpected, terrifying. He raised a fist to batter her away, but doing so required him to take his free arm off the rail and lean far forward. He felt the fulcrum shift. His bare feet lift off the deck, a high-wire act gone hideously wrong. She lost her grip and dropped, but took with her the tipping point, so that he flipped and plunged headfirst. The water, already churning from her entry, gulped him down.

When he surfaced, she had made it to the anchor line, where she held on for dear life, screaming, "What did you do? What the fuck have you done?" until something even greater than his betrayal took precedence. She looked around frantically. "Where's the ladder?"

He jerked his head in cold disdain. "Up there. You happy now? If you hadn't pulled me over with your stupid stunt, I'd be up on deck and I could lower it down to you. This is all your fault."

"What are you talking about? You did it! You threw me off the boat on purpose! You tried to kill me!"

"Prove it," he said, "it's my word against yours." Then, out of habit, he added, "Anyway we both know it's only your imagination," and almost laughed, so ill-timed was the oft-used line, so absurd and awful their predicament. Without a swim platform or a ladder within reach, there was no way back onto the boat.

When he explained their only hope was for him to swim to shore, she wept and begged him not to go. "Don't leave me here! You can't! Who knows what's in this water? What if there're sharks?"

"Give them a swift kick in the snout and try not to lose a leg."

"Oh God!"

The boat lifted on a swell. The anchor line grew taut, forcing her to reposition her hands, which he could tell were already slipping. She looked above her helplessly. "What if the rope breaks? What if it can't hold me?"

"It holds a fucking five-ton boat. I expect it can hold you."

She risked taking one hand off the rope to finger the medallion and, with that small gesture, he realized there was one thing left to do. He swam toward her. She cringed as though he were a monster, as though he meant to drown her here and now.

"I want this." He grabbed the leather cord around her neck. "I'm the one who has to swim for miles. I need this this more than you do." He expected her to fight him, felt disappointed when she bent her head so he could more easily remove it. "You've already taken everything," she said, "my pride, my self-respect. You might as well have that, too."

He slid the cord over his head, and the medallion dropped onto his chest, the skeleton and ghastly eye now nestled in his chest hair.

Lillian wiped brine and tears from her eyes. "You threw me off the boat, Martin. Why?"

For once he had the luxury of total honesty. "Because you're rich. Because I could."

MANY MILES into what seemed an endless swim, he wondered if this was why the swarms of sleek, incessant fish pursued him—because it was their nature, because they could. Or perhaps the current was merely sweeping them in the same direction and, like him, they obeyed the sea's imperative. There were hundreds, thousands of the tiny things, glistening anchovies and spike-nosed ballyhoos. When, he dived below, they massed above his head in an inky, undulating carpet. Within their ranks, he occasionally glimpsed massive creatures, too, monsters cumbersome and massive whose shadows darkened the sea floor.

Yet nothing that he saw or thought he did was as terrifying as the changes to his breathing. The inhalations seemed sporadic and ill-timed. He barely needed to surface, but stayed below for far too long. When he came up, it was more to try to orient himself to land than to satisfy the urge to breathe.

As afternoon turned into dusk, he swam with grim determination, battling rising swells and hordes of hovering fish, until his feet brushed bottom and the water heaved him up onto a broad stretch of sand and coral. Before him stretched just what he'd hoped for—a beach deserted save for flocks of restless gulls and hillsides thick with vegetation. He'd come ashore on the lee side of Emerald Key, a few miles south of the resort. He flopped onto his back, content, as a pleasurable lassitude invaded him.

He decided to shelter among the trees that night and make his way at leisure to the resort tomorrow, where he'd report the tragic accident and help organize a rescue party for his wife that surely would arrive too late. He would be understandably vague about the location of the boat and was already rehearsing in his head the circumstances of their calamity. Love-making that led to some contorted pose he'd be too much the gentleman to describe in any detail, a tragic lunge or ill-timed thrust and both ending up in the drink.

She was probably already dead.

Although he wanted desperately to sleep right where he lay, the tide was coming in, the waves already lapping at his legs. He forced himself to his feet and staggered toward a group of palms, but only made it a few yards before collapsing to his knees. He realized the long swim amid the teeming fish had quite undone him. His breath was ragged, limbs quivering and cramping. Worse, several of the tiny fish, trapped in the lining of his trunks, were making frenzied efforts to escape and choosing exits not intended for that purpose. Maddening as it was, he couldn't find the energy to remove them.

He lay half-conscious in the fading light, until the sound of a vehicle approaching jolted him alert. A jeep roared up the beach, passed him by at a rapid clip, then slammed to a halt, reversed. He recognized the resort's gold diamond logo on the doors. The driver, a dark-skinned woman with sleek coils of braided hair, jumped out and ran to him. Behind her came an Asian speaking into a walkie-talkie.

The woman knelt and gazed into his eyes, her face maternal, oozing empathy. "Sir? Mr. Wallace? Are you Martin Wallace?"

Her voice was an exotic lullaby, reminding him how desperately he longed to sleep. He would have done so, too, except that suddenly, without warning, she slapped him hard.

"Stay with me, Mr. Wallace. We've called an ambulance."

He tried to think what he must do, but he felt muddled, drugged, as though in the pristine ocean air wafted strange hallucinogens.

The man and woman got on either side of him and helped him to his feet.

"You're a hero, Mr. Wallace," said the man and moved as if to clap him on the back, then felt him trembling and thought better of it.

He tried to ask how they knew to look for him, but his best attempt produced only coughing and the wet rasp of a clogged gutter.

They leaned him up against the Jeep, then Lullaby, with the vicious right, was crooning in his ear, "We've great news, Mr. Wallace." Her smile gut-punched him; it was too ebullient, a nightmare mouth full of teeth and tongue.

Her partner chimed in. "Your wife's alive! She made it," and caught Martin when his knees buckled.

He tried to speak, produced a gurgling wheeze. "What happened? How?"

"Your wife said after you two jumped in to take a dip—" here Safari Hat looked away, embarrassed—"Hey, you forgot the ladder wasn't down, you'd be surprised, it happens. But no swim platform on the boat, that's a lawsuit waiting to happen, take my word. You swam for help, that took some guts, but you know what she did? Climbed the anchor line with her hands and feet. Said she fell back into the water a dozen times, her hands are cut to hell, but she got onboard and radioed for help." He paused to draw a deep breath that Martin would have killed for. "Your wife has grit, Mr. Wallace. She told the guys who rescued her you were what kept her going, the reason she didn't give up. She said you took something important from her, but now she has it back."

He fought to breathe. A whistle warbled in his throat like the prelude to a death rattle.

"Sir, you'd best lie down."

"Help. Me." He wanted her to help him remove the amulet, but the leather cord had shrunken during his immersion and refused to stretch or break.

You will come to no harm in water *(but you will suffocate in the air.)*

The woman took his arm. "Sir, I know this is a shock. If you'll just sit—"

He shook her off. Only a few yards away, waves glossy as obsidian unfurled along the shore. He took off in a stumbling shamble toward the water. As he threw himself face-first, the sea rushed out to meet him, sucked him in with its long carnivorous tongue and mercifully dragged him under.

Where his starving lungs felt saturated, not with air or water, but the absence of requiring either, so his descent felt less like a languid dive than a violent spiral through the innards of an angry god.

Nor was he alone in his debasement, for swarms of fish accompanied his fall, darting so close he could feel the whisper of their gills and knife-like scales, the kisses of their red and puckered mouths. They fought over the tattered chum that swirled behind him, competing with each other for the soft organic morsels, racing to devour the juiciest nuggets: a crimson pinch of stubbled throat, a nipple or a lip (he couldn't tell), eyelashes drooping from a toothy overbite like a surreal mustache.

And even then he felt that parts of his anatomy still belonged to him, and these he hoped to salvage from the slaughter, for where he was going wouldn't he need something of himself? It was the smallest fish and their savage cohorts, the jellies, that foiled his feeble efforts. The tiny ones sucked out marrow, bile, and eyeballs and scoured the creased and furrowed niches where the body held itself aloof, those private crannies meant to be exempt from excavation, while the jellies were more devious and savage, they impersonated beating hearts and pulsed imperiously inside his gaping chest. Still others, hellish creatures not of any world he knew, gave off a ghastly inner luminescence, the better to display the contents of their bellies—cunning, decorative items like teeth and tiny gall stones, a waxy smidgeon from a ruptured ear. In one, he spied an entire cerebellum, barely masticated, that might well have been mistaken for crenellated brain coral if not for the blooms of dark, arterial blood that still spewed forth.

When a disk of vertebrae drifted past embedded in a patch of flesh and chest hair and carved to imitate some kind of grotesque charm, he recognized it as something that was once his own and tried to reach into the mass of fish to claim it, this remnant from a familiar part of Hell. Toyed with by the memory of what it meant to have hands, he grabbed for it and missed and missed again, seizing only emptiness. His descent slowed but didn't stop, his consciousness a tiny moon orbiting an unseen monster, ternal in this hidden ocean, never to be harmed.

DONA FOX

WALKING ON WATER

GROWING UP on a farm, you learn that animals die. It hardens you up and prepares you for people dying. Readies you for all the death you're eventually going to face. It's not hard to watch a chicken, running around the yard, fluffing its feathers, scratching the dirt like an idiot one minute, getting its cold-eyed head chopped off across a bit of stump the next. You'd laugh along with me to see its body running in a circle as if looking for its missing head, loose neck flopping, blood splashing.

It's a bit harder when the butcher truck comes to kill the pigs. Right there by the barn. You try not to remember their soft brown eyes. Eyes just like mine, as if a human was trapped in a pig's body. No amount of pillows over your head can block their frantic squeals—they know what's coming.

Harder to bear still, a quick glimpse in the dark often revealed Daddy, whiskey drunk for courage, staggering to the lake with a wriggling gunnysack and a hammer. Frantic, Annie would hunt for her pups for days. I never let myself know the litters so I could take it all in stride.

Old Blue had been my daddy's dog, a collie. I learned to walk hanging on to his hair. Daddy said Old Blue deserved to go on his own terms. Blue chose his spot, in the shade under the holly trees beside the house, and watched us from there until he died. We buried him there.

Late the night we buried Blue, I heard Daddy stumbling down the stairs. He shut the door, as he did when he was drunk for courage, too hard for stealth, but there was no new batch of puppies to drown in the lake, no new batch of kittens to twist their little necks. I slipped out of bed and crept down the stairs barefoot meaning to follow him. Stepping carefully in the dark under the holly trees, I lost him.

I figured I'd go check the barn.

When I came out from under the trees that surrounded our house, moonlight lit the farm. Now I could see where I was stepping and I could see a line drawn in the dirt, a line that swayed from side to side as if a snake had passed there. I followed the curving path of the line and it led me to the barn.

Daddy hung from the pulley at the gable end. He was still swaying so he couldn't have been there long.

I ran inside the barn and climbed up into the haymow. I reached out, pulled him in, and loosened the rope around his neck.

"Fuck off. Go to Hell." It was the Daddy voice. The one I obeyed in fear, without question. The Daddy who killed.

He clawed his way to the edge of the open haymow door and slid back over the edge. I watched his body fall and jerk as the rope tightened around his neck again.

That was late Friday. He was still there when Jeffy and I went to school on Monday.

Mama was already gone by then so I told my favorite teacher, Miss Palmer.

THE AXE was under my mattress, ready for morning. I smelled fresh-brewed coffee as I crept down the stairwell. My uncle was pouring amber liquid into his thermos. His own blend of half-'n'-half as he had the job of raising us until Mama could be found.

I know she didn't go far.

Now, out of eight, counting my daddy, there's just my Uncle Bert, Jeffy, and me. Our three older brothers signed up for the service together laughing and joking. At least we're in different branches, makes us safer, better odds they told Mama, like betting on different numbers. Uncle Bert says they haven't written, he means sent money, for months.

I think Mama gets the letters instead.

Uncle Bert's no farmer. All the animals had long been auctioned off, even Annie, though I'd considered her my dog. Uncle Bert said no sixteen-year-old girl wants a dog nowadays anyway. Shows what he knows.

"Will you be late tonight, Uncle Bert?"

He jumped, "What the hell, where'd you come from? Don't sneak up on me like that."

"Are you going to be late getting home?"

"Why?" He narrowed his eyes and I noticed how puffy his face had become. "Kids at school talking about the phenomena? The lights. Are you scared?"

"No. I'm not scared. They're nothing new. I'm thinking about dinner. Should we eat whatever we can find, or what?"

"Yeah, yeah, I'll probably have to work. You kids go ahead, eat what you want." He looked around the kitchen, "There's food, right?"

"Yeah, Uncle Bert, there's still bread."

"I'll bring something. Yeah, I'll swing by the store on my way home. And, here, just in case, I don't know." He pulled a few dollars from his pocket and tossed them on the table. "Just so you have some money, you know."

I didn't know. We don't live anywhere near a store.

"Yeah, good. Thanks, Uncle Bert."

He grabbed me and squeezed me too hard, too long. He petted my head so fierce it felt as if he were trying to pull me into his heart. We probably could have gone and lived in better circumstances with my favorite teacher, Miss Palmer. She'd helped me out in the past, and she told me, anytime, she would always be there for me, but times like this I felt he needed us. And this was our home, the last place I'd seen Mama.

I was afraid he was going to start crying again. He pushed me away, nodded, and slipped the thermos under one arm. He patted his pocket for his keys and stumbled out the door. He'd already had one cup of coffee.

The truck engine ground and stopped. Ground and stopped. Oh, please, please, start. It caught. The sound of the gears being tortured followed.

The noise of the engine faded as I tiptoed up the stairs. But Jeffy was already awake. He trailed me and the axe to the ridge where three of the five trees stood; the three planted when our older brothers were born were much larger than the two holly trees by the door that were planted for Jeffy and me.

"What are you doing, Amy?" Jeffy was still in his T-shirt and gray-white boxers with the mud stains from yesterday.

I used my math, planned and calculated, "You need to stand right there," I marked a spot in the dirt with my toe. "Don't move and I mean, don't move or I'll kill you. Really. Understand?"

He nodded hard.

The first tree was John's. My oldest brother. The first time the axe struck the wood I felt as if it sunk into my own heart. But I wouldn't stop. I wouldn't think about what the trees symbolized. I pushed up my sleeves.

I went at the trees like a machine, calculating, planning, positioning my little brother in safe spots, watching the trees crash so the sun could shine unimpeded over the ridge onto the house where I believe my mama has gone to live. It's a beautiful house with an ornate fountain; only the lake and the green field with gray stone markers lay between us.

Some say it was a mistake to place a graveyard so close to the lake. I've watched it all my life and I'm sure they're right. The lake has become a roiling boiling cauldron of the dead. How could the gases not build; the lights not be seen for miles. How could it not call out, to demons, perhaps, or simply the dead from other planes, alien spaces, to dance among us as Daddy danced on the end of his rope?

Perhaps it was nothing alien at all, but a quite natural visitation of swamp gas from the rotting bodies in their graves that then spread out like fog over the lake, picking up any bit of light. It was just that lately the lights had become more prevalent, more solid, and began to disturb me more deeply as my emotions rose to the surface with my years. I couldn't keep an eye on the globules for the trees. The trees that weren't really my brothers.

Now the town folks have seen the lights and I want to keep a better watch. I feel a duty, living here, so close. Perhaps my daddy had felt it, too; maybe that's why he fed the lake so well.

My second brother was Phillip, the first born of the twins. The thought of Mama and Daddy when they were young, together, buying the two trees for the twins puts a sad lump in my throat. I don't know how old the trees were when they bought them, but this scot pine had been in the ground for nineteen years. A guilty chill passed over my skin.

For the first time, I felt eyes on me; I looked around, expecting to see someone standing behind me. Of course, there was no one there. I looked to the barn, to the open mouth of the haymow. The pulley at the gable end hung empty. I hardly ever saw Daddy swaying there and then it was mostly at night. I laughed.

"What, Amy? What's funny?" Jeffy didn't look up from his game in the dirt.

"Nothing, I thought I heard Daddy's old truck. That maybe Daddy was here again somehow. Daddy." There, I said Daddy three times, as I did when I was a kid and I was scared. I'm not scared now, they're just trees, and they're dead. I'm just cutting down dead trees.

Phillip's tree was very tall. A man's hand could cover the stump, once I cut the pine down, so the job wasn't going to take me long. I struck my axe into the tree. The pitch wept. I had to pause; pitch doesn't run in dead trees.

I heard a sound on the other side of the ridge, down in the tall grass around the lake. Not Jeffy, he was right here, irritatingly close. He was making spaceship sounds, swooping his hands around my legs.

I tried to tell myself there was nothing down there, that it must be John's tree, still settling. But I should have checked over the ridge before I felled the first tree. I hadn't thought to check.

I peered over the edge of the ridge, listening now, too. Relieved that I saw nothing squirming to get free from under the tree. There was no movement in the grass. Except…off to the left, down the path Daddy's boots had beaten on his way to the drownings, a twisted figure was crawling up the bank. I blinked.

It was gone. I think.

I was overheated, sweat running into my eyes. I was feverish now to finish this task. I wielded the axe again and the tree swayed precariously for a moment then plunged to the ground. The branches cracked and the trunk bounced as it slid down the bank. I squinted and I could make out the tips of the branches just skimming the surface, like a Jesus bug, walking on the humid surface of the lake.

Jeffy was at my side, "Let me count, let me count." His fingers crawled across the pitchy stump.

"There's nineteen." I knocked him away. "You're getting pitch all over your hands. You go in the house and wash with the borax." I pulled him down to the ground and rubbed his sticky fingers in the dirt. "Better yet, don't come back out here until you can't see a speck of dirt on your hands." I gave him a shove. He stumbled toward the house.

I drove the axe into the tree.

I heard Jeffy sob. I turned around. His shoulders shook. Damn.

I left the axe in the tree.

I put my arm around him and dried his tears with the bottom of his T-shirt, "I'm sorry, I didn't mean anything." Sniffling, he went into the house; I turned back to the ridge.

A wreck of a woman stood between Andy's tree and me. Her eyes were empty, her blue face a mosaic of mossy puzzle lines, some of the pieces missing, a few just now falling off. I wouldn't have known her at all but she was wearing Mama's good church dress. She held her stomach in with a half-fingered hand. She was wheezing and gasping as if the air I was breathing could no longer satisfy her needs.

"No harm in cutting down John and Phillip's trees, those boys is with me now, but it's not Andy's time." Gently, she removed the axe from the wound in Andy's tree.

"Mama." I moved forward, to put my hands on her, to kiss her cheek.

She jerked away, but not quick enough, my lips had barely grazed her. The chill settled in my teeth. My cheekbones ached. I saw the graveyard with roots that fed into the water.

I looked down and saw my brothers dancing on the lake. I longed to join them.

I heard a voice behind me. Uncle Bert gripped my shoulder and leaned on me, "Andy's injured; he's coming home. Money's tight; all the same, I'm anxious to see him."

I stared at the wound I had made in Andy's tree.

"Me, too, Uncle Bert."

Mama was gone; she must have gone over the ridge while the demons' songs distracted me.

ANDY'D CHANGED. The wheelchair tracks didn't take long to roll straight over the ridge and down into the murky water. It looked like Uncle Bert had tried to save him. They sank and died together, Uncle's sleeve bound up in Andy's wheel. I hadn't heard a sound that night, but I woke up soaked and screaming from my dreams.

I went to live in the town across the lake with Miss Palmer, my favorite teacher, the one I'd gone to when my daddy hung himself. Jeffy went somewhere else.

Miss Palmer dressed me up like a city girl and took me to church on Sunday. I didn't fit in and I'm not sure I belonged in a religious setting. I'll always believe it was my sinful thoughts that brought the demons down on us that Sunday.

Sister Moore led the girls up to the choir loft for Sunday school. She stood in front of the short wall that separated the loft from the main church below. As she recited the lesson, she rocked in hypnotic circles, it would be so easy for her to lean back too far, tip over the little partition, and hurtle to the floor below. Thick support hose that didn't begin to hide the wormy purple veins strangled her stout legs. She balanced precariously on coal black heels that choked her swollen feet. The lenses in her glasses were bifocaled and thick as a serving dish.

She stumbled on the edge of the carpet. She slipped on the painted wood floor.

Mrs. Moore's lips barely moved when she talked. I could only count the hairs in her mustache for so long before boredom settled in and a little voice began to frolic in my mind. *One push. Just one shove, push the old biddy over the edge. Do it. Now. One push.* I could feel the act gathering as my muscle juices built up, my body was getting ready to rise, and then I felt the tingly needle of anticipation, that preceded the heady rush as if I were pushing her, as if it were actually happening. Like pushing Daddy out of the haymow.

I let the feeling tantalize me, ride me. I could feel my palms sticking on her shiny purple Sunday dress. She would topple so easily.

I could picture the panic and the horror on all their little faces. They didn't grow up on a farm as I did. I'd seen so many dead things. Maybe she wouldn't die. Not right away. What would happen if I pushed her? I folded my hands and crushed them between my knees. I was saved from damnation when the organist struck the first chords announcing the end of Sunday school. We lined up, marched single file, and joined the main congregation downstairs for the morning service.

I slid into the pew beside Miss Palmer, shut my eyes, and began to swing my legs.

The Devil and his demons placed the spires on your churches; baptized children in His name. I kicked the bottom of the hymnal lodged in the holder on the back of the pew in front of me in rhythm to the words beating through my head. *The Devil and his demons placed the spires on your churches; baptized children in His name...baptized in His name...children in His name...Devil (kick) demons (kick) baptized (kick) children. Your Daddy...Uncle Bert...they had to be stopped...*

I opened my eyes and quit kicking the back of the pew in front of me. Where the heck were these thoughts coming from? I knew they weren't my own thoughts. I looked around the church, the whisper still damp in my ear.

The congregation was in silent prayer. Every cell phone was respectfully turned off. Brother Johnston's bald head glowed at me tenderly; it wasn't he, he hadn't spoken. Miss Palmer stood beside me with her eyes only half-closed, always slyly checking to see who might be watching her.

I smoothed down my skirt and was rethinking my irreverent slouch when the double doors at the back of the chapel opened and the air became warm and so humid it was like being in a pan of water.

I can't say why I didn't scream and run or at least duck under the pew. Maybe television has inured me to the fantastic, the strange, and the peculiar. Even the monstrous. Perhaps I thought it was a joke at first or that we were being filmed. Or perhaps I'd finally gone mad. I certainly had the right.

In any case I just sat there, a TV-trained immobile spectator while a swarm of the aliens, demons, or followers of the revivalists, more likely that's what they were, preceded by the two more recognizably human of the bunch, the ones I came to know as the leader and his pale wife, passed down the aisle and up over the altar, leaving the carpet rumpled and soaked in their wake.

They surrounded and incorporated Brother Johnston. He didn't scream. He actually chuckled; which probably led me further into believing there was nothing wrong, a few of the parishioners even laughed with him. But when the damp and misshapen monsters backed away, Brother Johnston was gone, just gone. I figured later that must have been when he became part of them, because from that time on they knew my name, my sorrows, and my weaknesses. But they weren't there to give me comfort as he'd been.

Thus, they came into what had been Miss Palmer's church, and relativity changed; it was her church no longer, this new leader became the host.

It all seemed normal at the time. Even the fact I never heard him speak; his words rang only in my mind. In retrospect, there were so many oddities, which should have sent me as far from him as I could find a means to travel.

I was unable to discuss his physical appearance with anyone; my tongue tied as soon as I tried to describe what I saw when I looked at him. If I tried to write or type a description of him, my fingers stumbled. Any attempt to take a photo of him came out blank. I attempted signing and my arms went wild. I had to assume everyone else's experience of him was as intoxicating as mine.

Miss Palmer began to keep strange hours. I followed her to the church one night and watched her with the leader; both of them were flirting and laughing. The light from the full moon hit the stained glass and glorified them both. My heart broke outside another, plainer, window; his wife fumed in the choir loft.

Miss Palmer came home in the morning, glowing. "You're going to be baptized. The leader and I are preparing the program together, choosing the songs, and some bits of poetry."

"Not Bible verses?" I said.

She stared at me for a moment, a line between her eyebrows. Then she smiled, "No, just some bits of poetry."

Her period of delight went on for a week then one morning she came home subdued.

"What's wrong?" I touched her hand. She was cold and damp. The early morning light showed the tiny green lines that crisscrossed the whites of her eyes.

She put her hand on my forehead. "You're skin's burning. You're sick. Let's get you in a cold bath."

I raved in the bath; I tried to warn her about demons and drowning.

She put me to bed in a thin gown beneath a cool cotton sheet.

After she left I tried the door. She'd locked it.

"Miss Palmer, let me out. Talk to me."

I heard her crying on the other side of my door.

That night she came to me, her skin pearlescent, she was leaving again.

"Miss Palmer?"

She pushed me to my pillow; a damp handprint shimmered on my shoulder.

On her return, she locked herself in her room. This time her sobs were so plaintive I pulled a chair up to her door and waited for the night to pass. Her cries ceased, light came in the windows, but the door never opened.

Finally, I broke it down. All manner of damp footprints covered the floor. It was obvious she'd been drawn out the window. A streak of brackish water marked a wicked path down the side of her bed, across the floor, and over the windowsill.

I ran to the church.

They enfolded me. *You're our child now. We're baptizing our children today.*

They pressed a goblet of green honey wine to my lips and held back my head.

The dangling horizon, quicker to the sight than Earth's sky should ever dare to droop suspended at the twelve tiny figures in a shadow box. Gray cotton on the cardboard above, a tiny mirror denoting the black lake before me, icy, hungry. My bare feet tentative in the frozen blades of silver.

We stood in the cemetery.

The lake was different now for they were in power.

The breeze mocked the thin white gowns of the initiates calling the rose to our cheeks. We blinked into the wind, licked the dryness from our lips, and struggled to hide our shame with slender arms as the rough muslin inflamed our virgin skin.

Then he was ready, arms everywhere, bare below his several knees, ghost of a tremble in his hand, *One rule that must be obeyed. Do not open your eyes in our water. You will not know what you will see.*

The ceremony had come to an ellipsis…

Holding for the first sight of my teacher, this had started out as Miss Palmer's affair after all, she'd spent too many darknesses with him sweating, apparently over which melodies would be sung and when. Laughing together, they'd chosen the poetry that would roll across his golden tongue.

Someone knew where she was…someone surely knew.

Hanging his head, the leader rubbed his neck and closed his eye, as was his wont.

A dust devil blew by us playing with a bit of burlap.

The cold families huddled, whispered, and glared at me; the orphan farm girl, conversant with swamp gas and death.

My fellow initiates hugged their chill arms even as the leader's wife was warming, steam rising from her skin.

We shall begin. One rule; do not open your eyes in our water.

The leader worked his way through all the others. He dunked, they gasped and choked and took great gulps of the lake that then became a vital piece of them; the core that spread its roots within as they bobbed back up soaked and shaking with the cold, water running down their exquisite forms as if they were [still human] fountains, now accepted by our hosts.

My time came, still no Miss Palmer, so he went ahead and plunged me under. His [webbed] fingers outstretched, cupped over the top of my head, he thrust me into the water. I held my mouth clamped against the lake.

Weeds became conversant with my thighs, wrapped around my ankles, and yanked me urgently away.

The leader's hand squeezed my head one last time as if to say, *No choices, no choices.*

I chose to open my eyes and I knew what I saw.

I drowned in the visions and that was my choice, too. You won't find scrapes on my palms and fingertips. I don't have torn or broken nails. I didn't change my mind and go back to be revived.

This carpet of bones is awkward for escaping; they make tiny tick tick sounds I can hear even in the bottom of the lake as I flee through the dark water, no time to kick them from beneath my feet.

I avoid the roller coaster paths created by both man and nature. Here dangerous chunks of cement jut from the slimy bed into the water. Roots of fallen trees thrust up a hazardous impediment just over there. Weeds thrive in the rich soil, fed as it is by the graveyard, ropey weeds that encircle and explore a car, a tricycle, an empty wheelchair.

I hear someone calling my name, as if there were anyone left who knew of me, who cared.

I lie down on the familiar bones; press my cheek against a smooth ivory bowl.

The water turned colder as it leached my heat. The surface beneath me grew harder as inertia drew the softness from the planes where my body and the bones made contact.

As time passed, moss covered my face and the roots made of me a home. Police cars cruised by periodically, searchlights illuminated the water and scanned the old farm and the graveyard. In the echoes above the lake, I no longer hear my name. I am an orphan, broken and abandoned. I chose that.

ERIC J. GUIGNARD

A JOURNEY OF GREAT WAVES

THE AMARANTHINE pull of the ocean is a marvelously ominous sensation, thinks Kei, the tugging from the surf like little tendrils dragging back what it can from piebald sand into the maw of the briny void. The pulling, too, gives her thought of some urgent love a mother must have for its newborn; the instinct is deep-set as any lightless fathom below, of a maker reaching desperately to its lost child. Such is the ocean as our own progenitor that we are drawn to her from birth, screaming and obtuse at the sea's allure until it snatches us back finally into the same great womb from which we were born.

So here the tide creeps forth, surge by surge, reaching for Kei with those very same tendrils. She lets them caress her feet, her bare calves, tasting, tempting, and a shiver comes with it. She moves through spume, searching the wreckage, but with no great interest.

It is not flesh and blood but the heart which makes us mothers and daughters. This proverb comes to her suddenly, and Kei remembers her grandmother, *Sobo* Youko, repeating it often. Last week in English class, Kei's teacher, Ms. Onuma, claimed the quote to have derived from an old German poet.

Baka bah oom, *Ms. Onuma, those will always be Grandmother's words, not some rich lord's from two centuries ago.* Of course, if she answers that on next Monday's exam, she'll fail...such is American high school.

A seagull squawks. A dolphin leaps. The air is warm and drowsy. Kei feels old and young at the same time, already grown weary in the yearning body of a teen. She does not understand how her classmates can be so *kuso* happy all the time; there is only one thing left that brings her joy, one person, and that person languishes in illness...

Today, more wreckage than ever clogs the shore, leavings of the ruinous tsunami from far away, and questions fill her mind: Is it due to the maternal bond that she searches these castaway things, the sea offering gifts and baubles as to a child...or is it all but taunts? Kei escaped the ocean once before and now, perhaps, the ocean sends her reminders of whence she came, where she'll return, for what else has an islander to expect?

The beach is filled by flattened soccer balls and scuffed plastic bowls and gasoline cans riddled with rust. Unmated sneakers weep strands of seaweed. There are shattered planks, blobs of hemp and sodden foam, a clammy metal drum, waterlogged books, fishing buoys, a dog's carrier filled with muck, tires encrusted with mussels and barnacles and sea stars; the enormous steel hull of some lost vessel stabs up from the tide, broken at mid-ship, though even halved it seems to tower upward a hundred feet, while millions of empty water bottles with the Japanese writing of her homeland clutter the sand like worshippers at the great altar of ruin. A couch cushion that is cross-hatched black and delicate gold molders—the pattern reminds her of home, of her "old" home, her "real" home. There is much more, and part of her aches to discover anything in the brine of that life she lost.

But the sun is waning, and she has a new home, on a new island, and knows she'll be missed, will be worried over if she does not soon return, though before she puts her back to mother ocean to retrace steps over the pigweed-lined banks, up three carved stone steps, and through a screen of satin leaf trees, she spots one more sea-swept gift languishing on the beach: a small porcelain doll with black cloth hair and the bright kimono dress of an imperial *ojou* or a haughty *no kimi.*

Kei pauses, bends to look closer at the doll. Its face has a slight knowing smile, one corner of tight red lips pulled higher than the other corner. Its eyes are…red, painted red as its lips, red as bright pooling drops of blood. The doll is beautiful and strange at the same time, cast off, as she herself feels, and she touches it. The doll feels somehow warm, fleshy. But isn't that so of any waterlogged thing, beach-landed and cooking days under a long sun? There's a familiarity to the doll also, although it's any toy that could have been replicated a thousand times over.

Without warning a voice cries in her head, and it sounds as she imagines her own mother's voice once to have sounded: *Throw it back! Throw it as far as you can, Kei-Kei, and run away, run, run!*

But that's silly, and Kei has long grown weary of others telling her what to do, even if such a demand were coming from an instinct within herself, some ghost of a memory, as irrational and hysterical as that instinct or memory may be. Another voice—this one emotionless and sensible—argues immediately that such a throw would be pointless. She'd have to hurl the doll a hundred yards beyond the pull of the tide, otherwise the surf would just return it back to shore, and then what would be the point?

Kei brushes sand off it, the doll's silver and scarlet kimono still damp on one side, but islanders are used to dampness: the ocean has a way of pervading the broadest of walls, the thickest of blankets. Damp is in the air, it is all around, it is life. Otherwise, the doll is unmarred from its oceanic voyage.

She brings it home.

"THANK YOU," Leolani says as she takes the porcelain doll. Her smile seems too big to fit any child's face, less so one waning under the illness she suffers.

"A gift from the sea," Kei replies. "My grandmother used to collect these. She was your great-aunt."

"Of course I know that! Because we're second cousins."

"How'd you get so smart? I did not understand great-aunts and distant cousins when I was your age."

Although that is not true; heritage has always been important in her family, and Sobo Youko drilled her frequently with relationships and ancestral names. But Kei will say anything to see the smile return to Lani's face.

"I was born in the year of the rat, so Mom says that makes me extra clever."

"It must be true." Kei nods to the doll. "What will you name her?"

"Hmm...I think she wants to be called *Obaasan.*"

"Old grandmother?"

"Yes, like the oldest of all the other dolls."

"That's funny. Have you been learning Japanese?"

Lani shrugs. "I just thought it, like somebody said the name in my mind."

Kei furrows her brow, and that haunting voice of her mother comes again: *Throw it back into the sea! You were wrong to take it...*

"I guess she doesn't look very old, but you don't look old either, and you're almost an adult." Lani giggles. "You are Obaasan Kei!"

Kei can't help it, she giggles too. Lani's joy is infectious.

Oba Hana's call for dinner sounds from the dining room.

"Walk or be carried?" Kei asks.

"It's only the house. I can walk."

"And you'll be running again in no time. Should Obaasan stay with the others?"

"Of course, it's where she belongs if she's their old grandmother."

"Of course."

Kei sets the new doll above Lani's bamboo-and-velvet bed, into an alcove made from the shelves of rich koa slabs, between a pink panda, long-stained from spit and apple juice, and a baby-blue child in pajamas, praying with a Zen expression on its face. There are others. Lani is old enough to no longer play with the dolls, but not so old as to forget the comfort they provide late at night.

The girls make their way across the small house to a dining nook, where Kei's aunt and uncle await. Oba Hana is really her mother's cousin, which makes her "once removed," but Kei thinks of her as an aunt, feels closer as an aunt is a maternal figure, not a cousin. *Oji* Tommy's a California poster boy who served in the Navy and now charters diving excursions around Honolulu.

"Who's ready for boiled asparagus and steamed peas?" Oba Hana asks.

"Yuck, no," Lani cries.

"Okay, double servings then for Leolani?"

"Are we really having that?"

"Just kidding, Dad grilled burgers."

"Yay!" The relief on Lani's face is palpable.

They eat in a room that is snug and warm, adorned with Oba Hana's watercolor art and the surfboard of Oji Tommy's youth, facing a picture window that is aptly named, as what Kei sees through it is no less fantastic than any picture ever made.

Oranges and browns and mauves tangle in leaves, and the sky is a jungle of overgrown clouds as much as the island is overgrown by shifting bracken. The sun sets low behind a purple ocean, the waters seeming to devour it like a piece of great red fruit, its own weight the very thing that pulls it farther and farther down into the maw of the waves. Tall palm trees silhouette the glass like fingers of an extraordinary animal trying to reach inside, dreaming, perhaps, of life as their own. Hoary bats dart by, chittering love songs, and lazy drops of rain begin to fall.

And if Kei squints very hard, she can still see the beach, filling by each crashing wave with more of the tsunami's debris: soggy wicker baskets and sun-stripped rowboats; crushed sandals and tires marred by shark bites; dolls and bloated bodies, sometimes difficult to tell apart. It's overwhelming at times.

What will be done with all that rubbish, that wreckage, those memories? Eventually it must be taken away, disposed of, *abandoned.*

They feel sorry for her, everyone does. It is something that cannot be helped. It is nature that she was cast adrift...*It is Obaasan come to claim her family...*

Kei winces at the strange thought.

"How was the beach?" Oba Hana sounds slightly hesitant to ask, but it's a thing that cannot be unsaid. "Anything interesting, or just rubbish?"

"Mostly scraps and trash, the hull of a freighter. I'll never use a plastic water bottle again. The beach is drowning in them."

Oba Hana's eyes soften. The laugh lines at her mouth pull taut. "Does seeing the wreckage hurt?"

Kei bites her lip. "Yeah...I keep expecting to find a photograph or one of Sobo Youko's oil-paper umbrellas."

"But you're drawn to it anyway, you have to sort through it all?"

The word barely comes out. "Yeah..."

"It's so hard, dear. No one wants their grief to return years later, and yours has come to literally surround you. But still, I worry when you're down there—"

"Kei found me a doll!" Lani interrupts.

"I did," Kei grabs on to Lani's excitement, happy to change the subject. She hates when Oba Hana talks about her being a worry, like a guilt she's responsible for. "It reminded me of Sobo Youko's dolls."

Oba Hana snorts. "What doll would not remind you of her collection? She had near ten thousand."

"This one wore a kimono."

"Ah, her favorite."

Kei loses herself in recollection for a moment, the rows upon rows of her grandmother's dolls: porcelain, cloth, china, corn husk, leather, bone. Sobo Youko kept so many, and each with its own story, like their ancestors. Already her memory grows hazy as to keeping them separate. *But Obaasan, Obaasan, why did it seem familiar?*

Oji Tommy breaks the silence. "I sailed off the coast of Haleiwa today, and there was a house floating in the distant waves. No kidding, an entire house, its windows and tile roof perfectly intact."

"Some homes float because they have walls made of foam instead of wood," Lani says importantly, "to save money."

"I never heard that before."

"I saw it on Discovery channel."

"Wow, you teach us new things every day, baby."

Lani smiles, and so Kei smiles. It fills her with joy.

She thinks again of Sobo Youko's words: *It is not flesh and blood but the heart which makes us mothers and daughters.*

If that is true, Leolani is truly Kei's heart, for it is not relations that define us, but the love we bear those relations. How often had Sobo Youko drilled such words into her, rapping her knuckles to pay attention? How often does she see herself in Lani? How long can she bear the pain?

"How long?"

The question startles her, as if Oji Tommy has read her mind, parroting her thought. But when she looks up, he's speaking to her aunt.

Oba Hana replies, "Four years since March…I still can't believe it."

"There are websites tracking the disaster, the Tōhoku Tsunami's debris," Oji Tommy adds. "It took that long to reach us, four years, after running the coast of Alaska and Oregon. All that wreckage is swirling in a big pool; what doesn't wash up on Hawaii's coast will head back home to Japan and then circle around the Pacific again. The currents, you know, it'll spin around us forever."

Her clothes, her memories, floating in the ocean until the end of days...

Oba Hana had proved Sobo Youko's words true about the heart which makes us mothers and daughters; she'd taken in Kei four years ago, when no one else was left. And before that, it'd been Sobo Youko who'd fostered infant Kei, when Kei's parents drowned in a sinking ferry.

Sobo Youko had been full of love and the most regal of poise, but so too had she been filled with bitterness and small-minded judgment.

It is because Hana married a gaijin—a foreigner—*that their daughter fell frail.* So once said Sobo Youko in her crisp, emotionless voice.

Sour old bitch. So once replied Oba Hana in her fury.

Cruel words on both sides, though the dispute was long ago. There is no grudge any longer; the tsunami took care of that. The tsunami took care of everything Kei knew, everything she'd worried about, everything she'd disliked, everything that had not fit into her life then of twelve years; as it was useless, so was it taken, but at the cost, too, of all she loved, all she desired, all she cherished, all of it crushed by the sea, sent to swirl forever in that great sink.

Yet she wonders: *Would Sobo Youko have ever recanted, given time changed her ways? Found the joy that Lani gives?* Would her heart have ever swelled to know that family goes on, regardless of circumstance? Or would she have ticked off her fingers the number dead, the number remaining, until all her brood joined each other under the waves?

"Want to play a board game?" Oji Tommy asks Lani as they finish eating.

"Yay, which one?"

"Whatever you want, baby."

"How about Clue, but only if Kei can play."

"Set it up," Kei replies. "While I help your mom clean up."

They leave, and Oba Hana clears dishes to the sink, where Kei wipes away crumbs and mustard blobs.

The rain begins to hasten, rattling upon the roof like tapping at a door to come inside. A moan of thunder sounds from faraway.

"Are you feeling okay?" Oba Hana asks Kei. "You seem so—"

"I'm happy, of course," Kei lies. It's not bad on Honolulu, but neither is it where she belongs.

"You say 'of course' like Lani says it, not dismissively, but like it's something that should be assumed and not discussed further."

Though she bristles, Kei forces a smile. "I *am* happy, it's just different than before. You and Oji Tommy have done so much."

"Lani loves you being with us, she's always wanted a sister."

"And a pony, and a unicorn."

"Don't make fun, every girl wants one of each, not to mention a prince to whisk us away."

And all I wanted was a mother...

"You know my childhood was also in Japan, in the Setagaya Ward," Oba Hana says. "Before I came here with my parents, uprooted from all I loved so my father could earn an extra nickel in the seafood markets."

"Sobo Youko complained often about your dad. Said he splintered our family by leaving the homeland."

"Yes, she'd say such things. I remember your grandmother too well—she was *Oba* Youko to me, spoiled and stuck in her ways. I remember her doll collections, filling up shelves on walls and old display cabinets that were inlaid with ivory slabs and memories, as old as Grandmother's Grandmother's Grandmother, she said."

That brings a cheerless smile to Kei's face, wistful in truth. "Sobo Youko loved her dolls more than anything."

"More than anything but her family. Family was always foremost, venerate one's ancestors, foster your heirs, and such."

"Except those who leave for new countries."

"That is true," Oba Hana says with a laugh. "When I was a bit younger than you now, fifteen or fourteen, I stayed at Oba Youko's house for two weeks. I'll never forget how she dressed every day in those *tsukesage* kimonos. They're very...modest."

"Because, heritage," Kei and her aunt say together and giggle. Leolani inherited that giggle from her mother. It's endearing.

"Did your grandmother take you to the *Ningyo Kanshasai* festival?" Oba Hana asks. "The doll appreciation ceremonies?"

"I'd go alone to watch the dolls burn."

"I'm surprised your grandmother let you attend alone. It's not a place for children."

"Yet it's filled with children giving funerals to their dolls. I watched them pay last respects to their toys and then set them to fire."

"Still, that she let you…"

"Sobo Youko did not know everything I did," Kei says with a wry smile. "She took her naps."

Oba Hana elbows Kei gently. "Hey, I take naps too. Should I worry?"

"There's nothing here to sneak off to, only the beach. At the festivals, I just found it…*comforting* to know one's doll could surpass fabricated flesh. Weird, I know."

"The great dollhouse in the sky," her aunt quips. "I remember Oba Youko believed dolls hold memories and are filled with souls. You cannot just throw one away, that would be like discarding a child. There are great spiritual repercussions for not disposing of them honorably, of course."

"Of course," Kei says with a mock. It strikes her, not for the first time, that her aunt has lost all hint of homeland accent.

A gust of wind howls outside, soft and sad, pushing through curtains of rain. Through the picture window the sea has blackened but for moonlit crests of froth, slobbering like the spit of fleeting mad dogs.

"The festival is Shintō tradition," Oba Hana says. "It provides homage to used dolls. Families share thanks for the joy brought by their toys, and priests give rituals to release the dolls' spirits before cremating them."

"Sobo Youko never gave a funeral for any of her dolls."

"She'd never burn her own dolls, because they always had a place in her heart, in her house. Your grandmother wanted to save them all forever, as she wanted to save all her family forever, to keep everyone together under one roof, locked in old traditions, ancient customs. The world moves forward, but not for her."

"I'd bring her gifts of dolls sometimes, when I'd find them. That'd make her happy. Sobo Youko was not often happy."

"Oh, I know." Oba Hana sighs. "She loved her kimono dolls most, like herself, the ones of heritage."

Yes, Kei thinks. *Like the doll I found today...*

And a memory is triggered, a day in Japan, at the last Ningyo Kanshasai festival, when the priests had called forth those spirits from the dolls, ready to cast them into the furnace, to release them, and how silly it all seemed. Kei walked by the altar, looking at each, dreaming of their doll lives, the way she dreamed of her grandmother's dolls; she spoke to them, played with them, watched them slumber, while alone in the large *shoin-zukuri*-style mansion as her grandmother napped or wrote letters to distant cousins.

The kimono-clad figure with black hair and red eyes had *whispered* to her of a girl needing a doll, a doll needing rescue from the flames...Kei had taken it from the pile, while mourners bowed their heads in prayer. Once she'd got home, an uneasy misgiving began tingling in her thoughts at having swiped the strange porcelain doll with red eyes. But she'd presented it to her grandmother so as to curry favor; that was before the night of the tsunami...before the night that all she'd loved was taken by the sea.

That doll was Obaasan...

But Kei's sensible voice, emotionless and rational, argues immediately that of course many dolls would appear the same: *What is a doll but a replica of something real? And what is real, but has a million duplicates, a million ilk?*

What are we, *but a replica of our own forebears?*

And the voice returns of her mother: *Throw it back, Kei-Kei!*

And she wonders in reply: *Do the dead mourn the living?*

The rain is falling harder now, battering their tin roof like *taiko* drummers pounding *chū-daikos* in epic song, all booms and peels. The waves crash in and out, adding to the cacophony, the rhapsody. The wind moans, echoes of ancient gods at eternal war.

She almost does it, almost flees to Lani's room to take the doll and hurl it back into the waves, but Oba Hana breaks the moment.

"Hot weather storms are the worst," she says absentmindedly, toweling plates with painted rose vines snaking along each lip. "Would you mind checking the windows? We don't need water getting in tonight."

Kei does, and afterward the dread has passed, and she joins Lani and her uncle playing games in the den, where any one of six friends again plot to murder Mr. Boddy.

THAT NIGHT Kei dreams of the dead, the drowned worlds of the spirits that dwell far beneath the waves, farther even beneath the muck of the seafloor, the worlds of darkness that the tides orbit, cold and soundless. They climb from their clamshell sepulchers, wearing funeral garb of the abyss, long white fingers like flitting tendrils reaching for her, surge by surge as the current pulls them along, and her, by equal measure, sucked down to meet their spectral grasp, down to depths without end. She knows it's where she belongs.

Obaasan is amongst them in all her ageless splendor, wearing the kimono robe of her realm, hued by wisps of plankton and swirling gyres. Each upward stroke of thin arms illuminates the darkness from which she rises with glittering brine like a universe of flashing stars. She is beautiful, she is magnificent. She is dreadful.

The distance between Kei and the drowned grows less. There is no sound, her vision dims as she descends. A chill takes hold, a sense of arctic ice that has never known light. She is weightless, yet she sinks, while Obaasan rises, rises without form, like a bottle of myrtle-green ink dropped into water; the fluids do not mix, yet neither can they entirely separate.

The distance grows less still. Grandmother Youko is behind, and there are her brothers, Oji Toshio, and Oji Bunta, and Oji Nori, all drowned, all taken by the sea. Grandmother's mother is there, and her mother before, and their husbands and sons and their wives and cousins.

We are all cousins, Kei thinks. *We are all family to Obaasan, born from her womb, and she has come to collect us home, to our true home at the bottom of the ocean…*

Goddess, demoness, mother, it does not matter. A vision overlaps the dream, or perhaps it is the dream itself, of a drowned girl's doll sunk long ago upon the silt. Obaasan clothes herself in that doll much as a hermit crab puts on new shells, for without form she cannot leave the sea to reclaim her family.

A sound like crying comes to Kei, and she cannot understand, so deep are they beneath the waves that all is dead, even noise, but then she suddenly rises from the depths, faster and faster, and the cry is louder, a shriek now, and Kei wakes, damp.

Lani's late-night cries are something Kei's grown accustomed to, but this is a different sound, a wail of terror, not of pain from illness.

The house is rocking gently, like a ship on waves.

She leaps from her bed, thinking only of the girl, and runs to Lani's room, followed by her aunt and uncle.

"Earthquake?" Oba Hana asks, out of breath, but no one responds.

Water pours from under Lani's closed door. The house rocks harder.

Kei takes the knob. It is wet. She turns it, hearing the click of tumblers, then the squeal of hinges, then a monstrous whoosh as the door is forced open from behind, and seawater pours forth in an impossibly rushing, swirling green torrent.

Oba Hana screams. Oji Tommy buckles from the flood, falling, dragged down the hall. Kei feels the pull too, but she holds on to the doorknob, grips it tight with both hands, and her feet are yanked out so that she glides atop the water, like a ribbon dragged skimming over a pond.

Lani cries again, gurgling, while the depth of water falls away, the bottled surge dispersing through the house like the crest of a wave that has overturned itself and diffuses rapidly. Kei can find footing again. She stumbles in, splashing. Water pours down into Lani's bamboo-and-velvet bed, filling it; the water falls from above, from the koa-shelved alcove. Lani's caught under this deluge, unable to escape the bed, imprisoned by the frailty of her body, cornered by fear, ambushed by Obaasan.

Obaasan...

Oba Hana pushes past, seizing Lani from her bed and they stumble away, as Kei stares at the doll.

The pink panda, the Zen child, the others are gone, swept away, there is only the porcelain doll she found washed up on the beach, its eyes twinkling red like jewels lost from a sunken galley, its hair black and long, snaking out like tentacles rising up from the depths, its kimono pulled open to release the jet of water, pouring out where a mother's breasts would be.

A roar comes from the doll, while outside the house there is a roar, too. Obaasan's slight, knowing smile is grotesque, somehow turned upward to reveal hints of shark teeth. It is no less strange a thing than the torrents gushing from behind its robes, the doll calling to the sea, and calling, too, for its children to come home.

The house shakes more, Lani stumbles. The storm has worsened. The wind shrieks, the rain smashes their roof.

"Kei!" A voice yells for her. Dimly she recognizes it as Oji Tommy. "Where are you?"

She reaches to seize the doll and is almost buffeted away by the force of the ocean. Obaasan still feels fleshy, how Kei first found it, but no longer warm. The doll's chill stiffens her fingers.

She holds the doll outstretched in front of her like she would a yowling cat.

Her aunt and uncle's voices run over each other.

"We must go—"

"We'll flood!"

"—up the mountain!"

The floor seems to fall from under her as water rises, the walls of Lani's room pull apart. The salt of the ocean splashes in her face, stinging her eyes, mixing with tears, or perhaps it is also seawater she cries, cries for her loss. Regret and sorrow and fear are all sharp sensations, and the sting of each is the same. The pull of each is the same, tugging us down into its dismal riptides...She breaks free, escaping the room.

The voice of her dead mother joins the others, prompting her escape: *Keep running, Kei-Kei, you must flee!*

She ignores them all. Kei has long grown weary of others telling her what to do, even if such a demand were coming from some instinct within herself to get away, to gain safety. It is her fault she took Obaasan from the sea, her fault Obaasan is pulling the sea back to it. There might be time, if she hurries.

Yes, run, that sensible voice says. *Run to me...*

She races down the hall through water that rises to her knees, across the house, the roar louder and louder in her ears, and she reaches the front door and wrenches it open, and she makes it outside where rain strikes her face so hard it is like a hundred hands trying to slap her into submission.

She sprints through the screen of satin leaf trees and expects the ocean will come into view, and then she'll go down three carved stone steps and across the pigweed-lined banks to the shore, and it will be over...

But she is stopped, for the ocean in all its might is already running to her. A tsunami wave grows, rising a hundred feet into the air, or perhaps higher, reaching for the stars as if to drown even them. And there upon the water's crest is Obaasan, in all her beauty, her great kimono robes twining through the foam and swirls of green and black waves.

Kei has time to wonder—to hope—that her aunt and uncle and Lani may reach higher ground, but she doubts it...doubts it very much, and for what does it matter?

It matters not at all, whispers that emotionless and sensible voice in her head, the voice of Sobo Youko and the voice of Obaasan; they are very calm, very curt in such a matter. *It is not flesh and blood but the heart which makes us mothers and daughters...*

And no greater heart is there than Obaasan's.

The doll opens its arms to the sea, to accept its return, and so the sea takes it and its children, and Kei wonders at the leavings of her own existence that will someday be cast back to land, fragmented and mysterious as tsunami wreckage, while she churns downward, swirling and spinning amongst the currents forever to the home she has always known.

LUCY SNYDER

ANTUMBRA

I WOKE in the afternoon gloom to the sound of my twenty-year-old stepsister Lily dragging something heavy and wet up the back patio steps through the kitchen door. The smell of blood and brine smothered me the moment I sat up.

I swore to myself and called down to her: "What did you do?"

"You'll see," she sing-songed.

"Pleasant mother pheasant plucker." I lay back on the sweat-stained sheets for a moment to gather my focus. Four hours of sleep wasn't enough to keep my head from spinning, but it was all I could seem to get these days. The cells in my body kept waiting for the moon to move, despite all my meditating to try to tell them that the big rock blotting the sun wasn't going anywhere.

I kept having nightmares from everything I saw in the months after the Coronado Event. In the worst dream, I was sitting in my bedroom when an earthquake hit. The walls would crack, revealing not drywall and wood but rotten meat, and cold blood would pour in, flooding everything. The red tide would sweep me off my bed and press me up against the ceiling. My stuffed toys turned into real animal carcasses floating by my head. I'd be struggling to breathe in the two inches of air between the gore and the plaster when I would feel something grab my ankle. And then I'd wake up.

I was a high school senior when it all happened. Back then I was so focused on prom and graduation and other such bullshit that I didn't notice the first reports on CNN that an astronomer named Gabriel Coronado had spotted a large, dark object hurtling toward the Earth at barely sublight speeds. But the science geeks at my school started talking about it, so the rest of us finally paid attention. Some of the religious kids said it was going to be the end of the world. But everyone else figured it would be like one of those big-budget movies where they send a heroic team of astronauts up with good old American nukes to blow the comet/asteroid/spaceship to smithereens before it reaches the Earth.

I think NASA and the Pentagon tried to pull some kind of mission together. Or at least that's what they told the media to try to calm people down. Their astrophysicists told them the big black object out there was going to pass by, so they probably figured they just had to keep people from looting and committing mass suicide.

And it did miss us by half a million miles. But it was so huge and moving so fast it jerked the Earth and moon in its gravitational wake like a couple of hobos spun around in the wind from a speeding semi. When the storms and earthquakes and wildfires from meteor strikes passed, the Earth and moon were locked in a new static orbit.

Our city was in permanent lunar eclipse, which was far better than the relentless daylight some parts of the world suffered if you didn't consider the massive flooding we got from being stuck at high tide. The ocean invaded our city, and Cat 5 hurricanes blasted us every spring because of all the hot air blowing in from the lightside. But at least we weren't broiling.

After ten years of living in the antumbra, my body still hadn't adjusted to the new normal. All my cycles were screwed up. Sometimes I'd bleed twice in a month, and then half a year would pass before I kicked another egg. At least I had my life, which was more than about four billion people could say. And I mostly had my health, even if I was turning into a bona fide lunatic.

Lily, on the other hand, was thriving like apocalypse was that special vitamin she'd been missing as a kid.

"Are you sleeping, are you sleeping, sister June? Sister June?" she sang off-key from the kitchen. "I got something for you, I got something for you, yum yum food! Yum yum food!"

"Okay, okay, I'm coming." I crawled off the bed, pulled on a T-shirt, and stumbled downstairs.

Lily stood peacock proud in gore-soaked clothes beside a massive hunk of *something* that she'd dragged in on a sled of black trash bags and flattened cardboard. The coppery smell of blood and the bay stink made my eyes water. It was cylindrical, maybe four feet long and two feet in diameter. I didn't see any bones in the ruby-red flesh. The black skin of the thing was covered in fur, like that of a seal or otter, except for where it had a double row of naked purple suckers as big as saucers.

"Where did you get this?" I asked her, frowning down at the massive hunk of tentacle.

"It didn't come from a people!" Lily exclaimed, as if that was the alpha and omega of all my possible questions. "Will you cook it? It's all bitter raw."

"I'm glad it wasn't a person." We'd had a long talk when she was nine about how it was wrong to eat people. I'd mostly done it to convince her to stop biting neighborhood kids she didn't like. Later, she saw a TV show about dolphins and decided that anything that could communicate was a person. Cats and dogs became people to her, and that was just as well. She got hungry for meat and bones a whole lot during her growth spurts and I couldn't watch her all the time. "But where did you get it?"

"It came up from the sea." She shrugged. "Hungry. Tried to eat people. I helped the Robichaud guys kill it."

I frowned at her. "And what were you doing with the Robichaud brothers?"

Lily crossed her sinewy arms behind her and rocked side to side like a guilty preschooler. She licked her lips with her impossibly long tongue, running it briefly over her chin. "Just helping."

"Helping" my ass. Christ. Well, at least I'd gotten Doc Freeman to give her an IUD. I stared down at the tentacle. The doctor would give us good trade for organs from a creature like this. I didn't know what the hell she did with them, but apparently monster parts were useful to someone's research somewhere.

"It's a shame you only got this," I said. "Doc Freeman would have liked more."

"I got more!" Lily smiled, her sharp teeth gleaming in the fluorescent light, and pointed behind me. "In there. An eye and a brain-thing. In ice, like she said."

I followed her point to the dining room table, and saw a stained Styrofoam picnic cooler that had been duct-taped shut. "Oh. Sick. Good job, sis."

The tentacle passed muster with the food safety scanner; it was a little radioactive, but so was every damn thing since the Coronado Event. The planet got hit with about a billion space rocks following in the big black's wake, and they were loaded with uranium and God knew what. Maybe some of the rocks came from planets the big black smashed, worlds that had their own strange forms of life. That would explain a whole lot about what was happening to the Earth.

Doc Freeman had given us the scanner in exchange for a crate of scotch we salvaged from a drowned mansion. It had saved us from being poisoned probably a dozen times. Well, saved *me*, anyhow; nothing ever seemed to make Lily sick these days.

She helped me cut the tentacle into thick steaks. I wrapped half and put them in the freezer, threw two on our electric grill, and put the rest in the fridge. Thanks to good loot trades, we were pretty well fixed for hydrogen fuel cells, so we didn't have to be too stingy with electricity. I could deal with all the humidity and mildew that came with giving up our air conditioning for the sake of the grow lights for our indoor herb garden, but the thought of drinking warm beer was just too much to bear.

The mystery meat grilled up nice and tender with some wine, soy sauce, and what was left of our scallions; if I closed my eyes I could pretend it was a filet mignon. But my memory of what beef really tasted like was hazy. The light from the corona around the moon screwed up my sleep, but it wasn't enough to grow grass for cattle. We had to get corn and wheat from penumbra states like Nebraska, if we could get them at all.

"Watermelon." Lily was gazing mournfully at her clean-licked plate. "I want watermelon."

"Maybe soon," I said. "Doc said the caravan should be back in a month or two."

She stared down at her blood-crusted nails. "Dirty. I should wash?"

"Yes, you should."

Lily gazed at me with her big orchid-purple eyes, looking every bit the changeling my stepfather claimed she was the day he walked out our door and stole my Mustang. I'd worked three summers straight to save up for that car. I borrowed a boyfriend's van and ran after the bastard to get my property back, make him take responsibility for his daughter for just once in his lousy life. But he got himself killed trying to steal fuel before I could catch up to him.

My mom had already died in the epidemic after the meteorite storm; before her throat closed up, she'd made me promise to look after Lily. She probably knew Lily's dad would bail on us sooner or later. I was fifteen when they met, and I knew right away what she saw in him. Dude needed an inseam zipper. They married before anyone knew about the big black, of course; otherwise she'd have found a guy with survival skills. Mom was never dumb on purpose. But she was making good money selling real estate, so what else did she need a man for back then?

Lily was eight when I met her, and already full of bad habits from her dad's mix of spoiling and neglect. He was vague about who her mother was. I guess she must have been a hot mess for anyone to award custody to a slackerjack like him.

My stepsister never seemed exactly normal brain-wise, but she looked human enough when she was young. That all changed after her dad was gone. She got the same fever that killed my mom, but the worst it did was make her teeth fall out. A new set grew in, almost reptilian, and needle-sharp. Her eyes changed, and she started getting muscles that made some people mistake her for a boy.

We met Doc Freeman when I took my sister to the city's free clinic to make sure she was okay. The doc took a real interest in Lily, and by extension me, and got us medicines and such when we needed them. I once asked the doc why she was fascinated with Lily, and she went off on this long lecture about virally induced mutations and epigenetics and evolution. I only understood some of what she was telling me, but the take-home was that Lily's blood might be useful for making vaccines or serums that the labs on the darkside were creating. The darksiders were making all the best stuff these days; they had to, or else they'd have nothing to trade with the countries that could still grow food.

"I need a shower." Lily licked her lips again, staring at me like I was something she wanted on her plate. "Shower with me."

Dread and anticipation coiled inside me. I knew what she wanted. And I knew I should say no. Touching her was wicked, but I'd been doing it for years. It started after we left my hometown to try to find a better place. For months it was just the two of us and miles of dark and cold and wet wreckage. We were both going crazy from fear and hormones, and when she crawled into my sleeping bag and kissed me that first time, it seemed like the best way to take care of her. That's what I told myself, anyhow.

We weren't alone in the world anymore...but it wasn't like the Robichaud boys ever wanted to spend any time with *me*. They and everybody else just had eyes for Lily. Sure, a couple of the other guys in the neighborhood regularly inquired after my swallowing abilities and generously offered me the use of their boners. But all that hot romance aside, they seemingly thought soap was just something you stuck in a sock to use as a weapon.

"Okay," I said. "Let's take a shower."

Ten minutes later, I had two fingers knuckle-deep inside her as the warm water beat down on us.

"Ah! There. Yes," she said, digging her nails into my shoulders.

I stroked her inside the way she liked...and realized something was missing. "I can't feel your cord."

"Pulled it," she gasped.

"What?" I took my hand away, horrified.

"Pulled it out." She frowned up at me, clearly annoyed that I was interrupting sexytimes with something so boring.

"Why?"

"Don't like it." She was starting to look as pissed off as I felt.

"You'll get pregnant without it!"

"So?" She crossed her arms over her breasts.

Rage surfing on thirteen years of frustration crested inside me. It felt like I was having to explain one of the basics to her all over again: don't bite people, don't run with scissors, don't eat rotten meat.

"So we can't have a fucking baby, are you stupid?" I yelled.

Lily snarled and chomped me on the shoulder, hard. I hollered and shoved her off me. She hit her head on the moldy tile wall, cursed me and punched me in the stomach. I tumbled out of the tub, tearing the old vinyl shower curtain down with me, and landed in a heap on the hairy floor beside the toilet. Blood was spilling out of the bite wounds on my shoulder.

My stepsister stared down at me, looking scared and confused.

"Jesus." I sat up, shook off the dirty curtain and touched the skin around the bite to try to see how deep it went. It was the worst one she'd given me yet, and my flesh was already swelling up and turning purple. "You and your fucking spit venom. You really get on my last nerve sometimes, you know that?"

I GOT myself bandaged up with some tape and gauze pads. Lily hovered around asking if she could help, but I was too angry to do anything but tell her to sit on the couch downstairs and stay out of my way. I got dressed, grabbed the Styrofoam cooler, and hauled it over to Doc Freeman's office. Stabbing pains were shooting down my whole right arm by the time I got there and blood had soaked through the gauze into my T shirt.

"Oh! That doesn't look good," the doctor said as she came out of the exam room. She was wearing a crisp white labcoat and freshly shined boots, as usual; I never could figure out how she always managed to look so put together and professional considering all the nasty stuff she had to handle. I was lucky to make it through a day of scavenging without getting a new hole in my clothes.

I could hear a faint motor whine as her artificial eye focused on me. The whole upper left of her face was cybernetic; the rumor was that she'd been hit with a pea-sized meteorite, a cosmic bullet to the skull, but her family was rich and got her to a reconstructive neuroengineer right away.

"It doesn't feel so good." I set the cooler down on the receptionist's desk.

"Lily?" Doc Freeman asked.

"Lily." I nodded.

"Well, let's take a look." She helped me take my shirt off and the sodden bandages nearly came with it. "Oh, she got you good, didn't she? What happened?"

"I found out she pulled out her IUD. I told her she can't have a baby. *We* can't."

"Oh my." The doctor began to clean my wound with betadine. "You realize she *can*, though, right? She's allowed. She's an adult; it's her choice."

I craned my neck to stare back at her incredulously. "I cannot believe you're saying that. She's a fucking child. A *dangerous* child. You *know* that. She's got no business having a baby."

"You're worried you'd end up with childcare duties?" Doc Freeman injected me with antibiotics, then followed it with a shot of the antivenin she'd made after the first time I reacted badly to one of Lily's bites. Making venom in her saliva glands was a fairly new trick; lucky for me the doc figured out what was going on right away.

"Of course I'm worried!" I replied. "Even assuming the baby took after the dad and not Lily, I couldn't handle her *and* her kid."

"Still. She's an adult. As are you. You can always leave her to fend for herself."

"No." I squeezed my hands into fists on my lap. "That's what her father did. I won't do that to her."

The doctor silently wrapped my shoulder in fresh gauze.

"Can you honestly look at me and tell me that you think having a baby is in Lily's best interest?" I asked. "Medically, psychologically? Can you say that? And would it be any good for the baby? C'mon, look at me—this is how she deals with being told 'no.'"

The doctor sighed. "Much as it would be interesting to see the result of her pregnancy…no, I can't say it would be in her best interest."

"Can you help me out here?"

"What do you want me to do?" The doctor looked angry. "Sterilize her against her will?"

"No. I just…I just want to keep her out of trouble. Is that so wrong? I just want a little control here."

The doctor's expression was unreadable. "I can give you all the control you can take. But that, my dear, will cost you."

I gingerly slipped my bloody shirt back on. "I've got something in the cooler over there that might be worth it to you."

The doctor went to the Styrofoam container and cut the tape off with a pair of surgical scissors. I hopped off the exam table and followed her over, curious. She lifted the lid off and exposed a multi-pupilled gray eye the size of a cantaloupe and a brain that was twisted like a giant cruller.

Something dark passed over her features for just a fraction of a second, but then she smiled. "*Very* interesting. And where did these come from?"

"Something that crawled out of the sea today."

"Ah. I heard about that. I went to investigate but the carcass had already been thoroughly butchered."

She replaced the lid and went to the safe where she kept her most valuable bits of biotechnology. "Bear in mind that what I'm about to give you is not a medical device. It was developed for the military, and was not perfected. Do you understand?"

"As in, it might not work?"

"Yes."

"So what are the side effects?" I didn't ever worry that she was giving me something dangerous; my gut told me there was no way she would do anything that might hurt Lily. My stepsister was too important to her. But I didn't want her to get sick if it wasn't even going to work.

"Not well documented, I'm afraid. Headaches, vertigo, confusion, and nausea are reported to be the big ones."

"What is it, this device?"

"Here." She handed me an unlabeled blister pack containing two gel capsules, one red and one clear. Each was filled with some kind of glittery fluid.

"These both contain synchronous cerebronanobots," she said. "The clear is for the controller, and red is for the target. Both the controller and the target take the capsules orally. Then, once the nanobots have entered the bloodstream and successfully crossed the blood-brain barrier, they take up residence in the frontal and temporal lobes. Once they've synched, the controller should begin to have empathic access to the target's mind and can, at least in theory, exercise some control. You replace your target's superego with your own, if you succeed."

"Wow." I uncertainly took the blister pack from her hand. "That's pretty heavy stuff."

"It is. But I expect she'd pull another IUD or cut out a subdermal implant. The only other option would be for you to bring her here for hormone shots every three months. I doubt she'd be very cooperative. The nanobots are all I have to offer you."

"YOU GAVE me some kind of new infection," I told Lily when I got back to the house.

"I sorry." Tears rolled down her cheeks. She always got extremely remorseful for a few days after she bit me.

"Doc Freeman gave us pills to take." I held up the blister pack.

She made a face. "Don't like pills."

"Well, I don't like them either. But we both have to take them."

I poured us two glasses of water and broke the capsules out of their blisters.

"Down the hatch." I handed her the red one.

"Why mine diff'rent?"

"Because the infection didn't make you sick." I'd thought my lies out carefully on the walk back to our house. "Because you're a carrier, and I'm not."

"Oh. Okay." She took the capsule from my hand and swallowed it down with a gulp of water.

After a quick, silent prayer to a god I no longer believed in, I swallowed mine down as well.

We settled onto the couch to watch her favorite cartoons, and she laid her head on my good shoulder. I waited to see what would happen. For the first hour, nothing was different. But then came a faint buzzy feeling in my head, an electric warmth, a melting sensation. I realized that I could feel how my own shoulder felt against her cheek.

Before I fully realized what was happening, she was in my lap, kissing me, pulling my jeans off. I couldn't even summon the clarity to wonder where my will had gone. We fucked for hours in the blue light of the television; in the morning, we ate bitterly raw steaks straight from the refrigerator and stumbled out, hand-in-hand, to go see the Robichaud boys.

Hours melted into days melted into weeks. It was all dreamtime for me, an erotic nightmare from which there was no waking.

I came back to myself, briefly, in a room in a flooded mansion. I was alone, sitting on a rotting red velvet couch beneath a chandelier dripping with algae, but I could hear Lily moaning in the room above me. I could feel the webbed claws clutching her, the strange appendages slithering into her as she writhed, and I tried to stand, to stop what was happening, but the orgasm took her and my mind went with it, down, down into the murky water.

I didn't surface again until months later in a flooded laboratory. I found myself blinking in a fluorescent glare, holding Adam Robichaud's blond head under the water; I'd already drowned him. Lily was up on what looked like a dentist's chair, naked, panting hard, her distended abdomen rippling. I realized my mind was no longer bound to hers, and the sudden absence filled me with cold loneliness. Doctor Freeman stood behind her, smoothing her hair away from her face, whispering encouragements to breathe.

Lily wailed as the baby began to squeeze through. First the head, then an arm that was jointed in too many places…

"Oh God," I whispered when I got a good look at the infant.

"Oh, June, excellent, you're back with us." Doc Freeman caught the baby as it slithered out, deftly keeping her hands clear of the snapping mouth. "I am afraid I told you to take the wrong capsule. I just couldn't have you interfering in my work any longer. But as you can see, everything has turned out well in your absence."

"What…?" I began.

"I made a people!" Lily grinned at me, glowing with maternal pride. She looked happier than I had ever seen her.

"Yes you did!" Doc Freeman smiled back at her. "And this little fellow is quite hungry. Keep breathing, my dear!"

The doctor sloshed past me and set the newborn down on Adam's floating corpse. The little creature latched onto his naked back with its sucker mouth and began to devour his flesh.

"Welcome to *Homo freeman*," the doctor said. "The first of his kind, and certainly not the last."

"Oh!" Lily gasped. Her belly rippled again.

"Three more to go!" the doctor called. "Keep breathing and pushing!"

I took a step toward them, and felt a sharp cramp and heavy pressure in my own belly. It was not a sympathy pain. Terror filled me as I looked down and saw my nine-month bump.

"Once your nephews are all born, I expect it'll be time to induce you, dear June. Your child will not be as exotic, I'm sure, but she'll come in handy just the same."

I turned and tried to flee, but my nephews' alien father rose up out of the water, looking like a cross between a frog god and the worst fever hallucination I'd ever had, and clutched me to its clammy torso.

"Save your strength," Doctor Freeman called. "Believe me, you'll be needing it soon enough…"

STEPHEN GREGORY

THE DROWNING OF COLIN HENDERSON

COLIN HENDERSON was swept off the deck of the *Thisbe* on the night of the fourteenth of January 1966. There was a fearful storm which had come on suddenly, and the trawler was working hard to beat her way into the safety of the Menai Strait. Henderson went on deck to secure a shifting crate, when an extraordinarily heavy wave collapsed across the ship. He went overboard in a welter of white and green foam.

Weighted down by his boots and his waterproof jacket, Henderson was kept up on the surface of the sea for only a matter of seconds. He saw the lights of the *Thisbe* for a moment before she wallowed and vanished behind the swell. The sky was black. There was no moon. A torrent of spray whipped from the wave tops beat into his face, and he was hurled upwards on the peak of a huge sea before tumbling into a cavernous trough. Then he went under. One final cry for help was checked and swallowed in water. The weight of his clothes and the might of the storm pressed him downwards and he was engulfed.

It was strangely quiet. Henderson watched his hands working in front of his face. They gestured slowly, the fingers opening and closing. They seemed very white with short clean nails. There was darkness shot through with streams of bubbles. It was green and black and silver, with his hands working. A noise of whistling had begun. His neck was hurting. He was aware of being upright and was grateful for this. His legs were lost in darkness, it was only black below him, there was no marbling of silver. The whistling became a long sustained shriek. The light faded. Still his hands, like someone else's hands, continued to move so slowly. The noise grew. A chaos of bubbles blew into his face and then it was green and still. Two things happened together as Henderson died: the shrieking stopped, for a blissful second there was silence, and a marvelous silver blue bubble as big as a cauliflower sprouted from his mouth. For an instant it was joined there. His chest was clenched with pain. Then the bubble was plucked from his lips. It swam away and disappeared in the green distance. He was a dead man.

It was midnight. The storm raged on the surface and the *Thisbe* crept towards shelter. Henderson moved downwards through the darkness. He spun gracefully with the current so that his arms were raised above his head while his legs were moved in a gentle dance. Sometimes he turned head over heels and continued like this, downwards and eastward. A bubble broke from his mouth. It caught in his yellow jacket for a long time and stayed there like a silver pocket watch. As Henderson turned again, the bubble moved on and was trapped in his hair. The bubble spun upwards and shrunk to nothing. His eyes remained open. They did not stare. They were fixed in a level gaze, one eyebrow lifted and held by the frown on his forehead. Henderson's mouth opened and closed as though he were singing. Then a hand would move to his face and brush away an imaginary cobweb. It was peaceful, after the storm on ship. The silence was broken by the mumbling of deep water.

When dawn broke, Henderson surfaced at the mouth of Malltraeth Bay. He rose into a gray daylight with his face turned up. The storm had become a heavy driving sea into land. The dead man rolled in the waves. His hair stuck and shivered like the seaweed in a tidal pool. His mouth ran with water. There was salt in his eyebrows and eyelashes. If he could see, there was the level land of Anglesey and to the southeast the mountains rose behind Caernarfon. It became lighter and Henderson bobbed through a gentle sea. His heels in the heavy boots touched land while his stiffening fingers clutched at the movement of weed. There was a cormorant fishing. It beat its way out of the water when the yellow jacket creaked. A cloud of gulls fell into the waves and looked at the man. One bird jabbed its beak once into Henderson's beard and flapped away, screaming. The gulls moved off to the sands of Malltraeth.

All morning he swam slowly in the shallow water. It was warmer and there was a clear sky. He turned over when the swell came, his face pressed into the green clean sea. Into the bay as the tide pushed on. There was rubbery weed before the bottom cleared to a firm hard sand. The tide stopped and waited. The sea held. The man lay on the sand with his face to the sky. When the sea retreated, Henderson remained, like a man asleep. He lay on the sands in his yellow jacket and boots, with his hair drying in salt sunlight. White lips. Seaweed skin. Empty eyes. A throat full of brine. A dead man.

Crabs collected at his fingernails and tested the flesh. It was very soft. They began to feed there. The heron came and was afraid. Curlews fled with a skyful of sad songs. Only a pair of crows stopped to see and soon they saw it was safe to stay. Their heavy beaks broke open the skin on Henderson's cheeks.

But a man came, attracted by the yellow jacket. And soon they carried Henderson from the estuary

It was the fifteenth of January 1966. A woman arrived to see the dead man. They had cleaned his face and put powder where the crows had been. Henderson had closed his eyes and his mouth. They asked the woman: "Is this man Colin Henderson, of the *Thisbe*?"

"Yes," she said, and she touched her husband's lips.

DANIEL BRAUM

THE FOURTH BELL

THE FOURTH bell's pitted metal left me no doubt the crusty old thing had to be from a shipwreck. It wasn't only larger than the dozens of other bells on Terrence's work table, it was categorically different.

I had returned from the hospital last night to find Terrence had moved his work area, and Gerald's massive ten-foot square tank, right smack into the middle of our living room and I still wasn't used to it. Early evening sun streamed through the ceiling-to-floor glass windows, turning the views of our sprawling property and the Long Island Sound beyond into giant rectangles of dirty, orange-tinted light. The room was full of wonderful things from the life Peter, Terrence, and I had built. Without Peter, the way the cavernous space dwarfed everything only added to the oppressive weight on my chest. Terrence was my best remaining friend on this earth; my brother, my partner, my creative soul mate, my chosen family, and I knew he was all torn up inside just like I was, but nothing I did or said seemed to reach him.

Gerald floated motionless in the center of his tank. His eight sucker-covered arms dangled in what I took to be boredom and resignation but his eyes were alive and watching us. Flags, a Ouija board, waterproof maps, chess pieces, and children's blocks with letters on them littered the bottom of the tank. Terrence picked up one of the smaller bells and held it to the glass. Gerald remained motionless. I know Terrence wanted a response but the only sign Gerald was even alive was the minute ripple traveling along the thin fin-like skin on the contour of his pink-gray head.

Terrance slammed the bell on the table and huffed through the pages of one of the oversized old books held aloft in front of him by one of the mechanical arms from our last project.

"I don't think he likes you very much," I said as diplomatically as I could.

"Of course *it* does," Terrence said without looking up. "Doesn't matter anyway."

I hated his refusal to use Gerald's name.

The sunlight cast August's glow on the miasma of mechanical parts, tools, and equipment that covered every available inch of tabletop space in the room. A dust-filled ray illuminated the nest of spider-like mechanical legs, wire-laden circuit boards, and other disassembled pieces and remains of our last project that surrounded the tarnished World War II-era dive bell languishing in the far corner.

Gerald gracefully brought his arms together and jetted to the bottom of the tank. He gathered the letter blocks and brought them to the side of the tank nearest Terrence. I marveled at how adeptly he tumbled them over and over with the tips of those four-foot tentacles. He could turn any color or squeeze into the tiniest space, though this usually meant he was all fed up. He glanced at me, then put the last block into place; his tablespoon-sized eyes saying everything I needed to know, though they didn't need to.

D-I-E T-E-R-R-E-N-C-E, the blocks spelled.

He waited for Terrence to look, then quickly changed them to read "Hi Terrence."

If Terrence noticed, or even cared, he didn't show it. He struck at the seven bells he had arranged in front of him with a thin copper rod. I expected their sounds to be sharp or at least cleaner, but each tinny ring sounded as if it had traveled from faraway through some muffling impediment. Peter's face sprang into my mind. His tortured face, sucking in those last gurgling breaths. Closing my eyes never helped.

Terrence fervently struck the bells again in a different sequence.

I hated that he had moved Peter's worktable into the living room and claimed it as his own. The table had always been covered with the latest schematics and plans the three of us were working on. The old books and all the bells were new additions. The largest bell, the old crusty one, sat fourth in Terrence's current lineup and felt like even more of an intrusion than the rest of the miasma.

Terrence brushed his sandy hair out of his eyes and squinted as the mechanical arm moved the book he was trying to read closer to him. Despite the beginnings of worry lines and creases his face was still boyish and had never lost that rascal charm. After the crash, he'd taken to wearing vintage rock T-shirts and old jeans. He had been planning to dress like that at Peter's funeral until I informed him in no uncertain terms that I'd drag my ass out of the hospital if I had to and dress him properly myself, but there never was a funeral. At least not one that we were told about. Peter's "long-lost" family had come out of the woodwork upon the news of his death and promptly set about trying to lay claim to his share of our fortunes. There was no way we were going to let those vultures get their hands on anything of Peter's. Cutting us out of the funeral and not even letting us know where they had buried him was their way of punishing us.

Terrence claimed his newfound wardrobe was his version of Einstein's same-black-suit-everyday thing. I knew it really had to do with a yearning for when the three of us were young and together and everything was easy. Today he had on a Rolling Stones shirt. Peter had loved the Stones. Terrence couldn't even name four songs by them.

"You know, it wouldn't hurt to *try* being—"

"It's not a pet," Terrence said. "Pampering isn't going to help figure out which seven bells I need."

"Need for what?"

"To make it right for…"

He knew if he said "make it right for Peter" one more time I was going to slap him.

Peter was gone. Terrence hadn't been right there, forced to watch his pained last moments of life, unable to help like I had.

Maybe if he started being nicer to those of us left in his life it would help, otherwise he wasn't making anything right.

Gerald moved the querent around on the Ouija board and changed the blocks so they spelled incomprehensible phrases.

"What are you doing, Gerald?" I asked.

He ignored me.

"See what I mean," Terrence said. "At least when Peter was spacing out we still knew he was contributing to the plan."

The plan. It was always all about a *plan* for him. Ever since we were kids Terrence was at his happiest when embroiled in some *plan*. Peter, Terrence, and I, the three little geniuses. All grown up, out of school, and in this great place of our own where we made one plan after another happen. Without Peter we weren't the same, nothing was. I know that's the way things go. Everyone dies in the end. Everything changes but Terrence wasn't right.

He worried me. And he hadn't even been the one who watched Peter, trapped upside down in the car, in that ditch. Gasping for air. Drowning out in the middle of the desert. I hated this was how I remembered him.

Gerald tapped the letter block *S* against the glass. I knew it was his shorthand for "smile."

Terrence scowled.

"I know you don't want to hear it but think about it, maybe if you were nicer he might just decide to help," I said.

"Nicer doesn't matter," Terrence muttered. "I don't even think he knows."

I didn't know what Terrence was after with his books and bells. But if Gerald didn't know I had no doubt he could figure it out, one way or another.

No one could replace Peter. Not even someone as special as Gerald. With Gerald I thought we would be three again and that maybe things would sort of feel the same. He could pick the exact scores of cricket matches in advance and had something to do with a new project Peter had been dreaming up right before the crash. Peter's Australian contact had no shame and demanded an exorbitant sum to part with Gerald but money was never an issue. We had all the money we could ever want but no amount could give Terrence and me what we wanted most.

I LAST saw Peter in New Mexico. I try to remember how happy he was that night, out in that desert canyon testing our latest project. He had pinpointed the spot as having the largest concentration of Gila monsters and we had carefully driven off the road and found our way in. From the front seats of our rented SUV we watched our rover walk on its mechanical legs, maneuvering around the bases of tall cactus and granite outcroppings of rock like one of those robots fire departments sent into burning buildings. The rover's top was loaded with antennae and dishes pointing up that detected cosmic rays, its underbelly crammed full of temperature sensors to track the fat nocturnal lizards Peter had come for. Night air tinged with the clean scent of desert brush and dry earth gently blew through the open windows.

A smile bloomed on Peter's face as he watched the data come up on his tablet. He loved the mandala patterns it formed. Seeing him happy was a rare thing. Too often his face was solemn and stern. That's when I knew he had his birthplace, Mumbai, on his mind which had been happening more and more lately; all his recent paintings depicted the faraway city in one way or another. I knew his family was out there somewhere but that was all. Any direct mention of either subject caused him to shut down.

I wanted to remember him overcome with joy, that joy particular to an inventor seeing his invention manifested for the first time. The joy as he watched the rover move over the sand and listened to the whir of the motors in its joints and grind of metal on metal as antennae and sensors rotated.

"It's working," I said. "It's locked onto some star now for sure."

"It tracks all celestial objects not just the stars," Peter said. "I can't believe how many lizards it detected already."

Peter hunted in the back seat for his watercolor pad and aquarelle pencils. He set his tablet on the dash, propped the pad on the steering wheel. Instead of sketching he began writing in his distinctive flowery handwriting. I glanced at the pad and saw something about cricket match scores, and a phone number next to the words "Darwin Australia." As usual he was on to something new even before what we were working on was complete.

The data coming from the rover bloomed into a mandala on Peter's screen. The shape was a graphic representation of how the movement patterns of the nocturnal Gila monsters corresponded to all those celestial objects in the night sky, even the ones we couldn't see with our eyes. I couldn't see it yet but I knew there had to be an application for biology or maybe astro-science. Peter came up with the ideas, Terrence handled the lion's share of building them, but it was my job to figure out who we could sell them to and for what.

Peter was no help. He said he had dreamed it up so he could use the shapes of the plotted data in his paintings but now he was sketching an octopus and what looked like a dive bell next to his scrawl. All his inventions ultimately were born from his desire to create art. We all loved him for that. His purity. The integrity with which he created. I worried that Terrence secretly resented him for it as well.

I noticed the breeze had ceased. Something kinetic waited in the stillness. A fat rain pellet splattered on the back of our rover as a rumble I felt in my chest punctured the night's quiet. Before I could voice my confusion the dry earth transformed into spattering mud from the downpour that had not existed a mere second ago. The rumble became a roar. Something hit our car. A wall of water. We were in a flash flood. Foaming, roaring, spraying water lifted us and sent us careening along the canyon floor. I saw one of the rover's mechanical legs in the maelstrom and managed to click my seatbelt as we spun end around end. The water took us where it pleased, knocking us against cacti and brush until we lurched to a halt against a boulder. Peter's tablet flew into the windshield. We strained against our seatbelts. I felt the current pushing, tilting, willing us with its elemental force in the other direction. Something gave and we spun free of the boulder. Down became up. My stomach heaved. We flipped and dropped into a ditch on the side of the road with a crunch. My head hurt. The window was spider-webbed. We were upside down but all right. I looked over at Peter and we both cracked a pained laugh. Then the water poured through the windows. The way we were tilted Peter was lower than me; his hair and forehead already submerged. I struggled to break free of my belt and reach him. I tasted my own blood and the belt held me fast. Water rose to above his nose and he began to gasp for breath. The water stopped before it reached me. I waited there bleeding, trapped upside down with my drowned friend. Sometime in the night the water receded. It wasn't until morning before someone found us.

GERALD WAS tapping on the glass trying to get my attention. Terrence was in the middle of speaking. I tried to banish the image of Peter's lifeless body hanging upside down with his head underwater.

"...I just need to pin down the locations," Terrence said. "I feel like the bells know. They call to each other."

"Terrence. They're bells."

I expected rage or sarcasm for questioning him, but before me was just my friend. My sad friend wearing a T-shirt of a band he didn't know or like. My friend who was struggling just like me.

"I don't know how I know," Terrence said. "I just do."

One of the old books on the table was open to a page with a drawing of a boy reaching into a man's pocket. Beneath it was another drawing of a hand reaching into the silhouette of a man's head. Hand-drawn staves annotated with music notes and notations surrounded the drawings.

I glanced at the fourth bell. I didn't like the way it made me think of a shipwreck. Shipwrecks meant drownings.

"How do you know you need seven?" I asked. "And how do you know you have the right seven?"

D-O N-O-T L-I-S-T-E-N, Gerald had spelled with the blocks.

"I'm not incompetent," Terrence said, that awful rage surfacing again. "Are you going to trust the octopus over me? Are you going to question everything I do or do you want to help?"

"You know I want to help. I'll always help you. What do I have to do?"

"Okay. Good. Just listen. I'll try to show you what I mean."

Terrence struck the seven bells again with that copper rod. The sounds were hollow, even more muted than before. Terrence bobbed his head and kept looking back and forth from me to the bells. After a moment it was clear nothing was happening. For Terrence's sake, I really wanted whatever he was doing to work.

He muttered something about Peter always getting it right and went back to flipping through the big book the mechanical arm was holding.

A tiny shadow moved across the worktable. Then about a dozen rounded, almost triangular, fish-like shapes followed. Only nothing was casting them. Gerald jetted to the corner of his tank nearest us. He rolled and unrolled his arms while patterns of green and purple pulsed along his skin.

The little school of shadows moved back and forth on the table then disappeared. My ears filled with the rasp of dozens of whispers all speaking at once. Then there was only one voice. Peter's voice.

"Do not go to Lin-Kasai," it said.

I waited to hear more but there was nothing. Terrence continued to flip through his book in frustration. Hearing Peter's voice had me shaken.

"I can't figure out if I should look next in Argentina or—"

"You didn't see or hear any of that?" I asked.

Before he could answer, the items in Gerald's tank lifted from the bottom. A cloud of blocks and chess pieces and map markers swirled around Gerald floating motionless in its center.

"Are you doing that?" Terrence screamed at him.

There was no way for Gerald to spell no. I could feel his fear. Everything ceased moving and fell to the bottom. Gerald quickly began arranging them. He marked a location and a route to it with plastic pawns on a map of Long Island.

"Hmmm. A change of heart?" Terrence said. "What's gotten into him?"

"Go easy. He almost got pummeled by that cloud of stuff flying around in his tank. Did your bells do that?"

"I think so. They all have neat tricks. I just can't figure out exactly what they are."

"Neat tricks, huh?"

Gerald was messing with his blocks again. I expected another round of Die Terrence.

I W-A-N-T T-O H-E-L-P, Gerald spelled. W-A-N-T T-O C-O-M-E.

"But you can't," Terrence said.

I wanted Gerald to come with us too. Terrence had begun a dialog and addressed him directly. That was something, and at least some kind of a start. I'd take it.

IT TOOK us all night to find the place. I don't know why. It wasn't terribly faraway. An industrial park in Hauppauge. I'd been in a nearby park last summer where they manufactured the blades for a hydrofoil we had created. This whole area was deserted. We walked through an alley that led into a square formed by the convergence of several alleys. A circular fountain that had gone dry long ago remained in the square's center, a lonely reminder that people used to frequent here. A garbage dumpster partially concealed a door on the other side.

We walked across and rolled the dumpster away from the door.

The words Silversmith and Ironworks adorned the wall in faded black paint.

The opening refrain of the song "Gimme Shelter" blared from Terrence's pack.

He fished his phone out. Gerald filled the screen. His suckers were alive with motion as he formed words with the blocks.

"Who is filming him?" I asked. "How's he calling you?"

"I don't know," Terrence said. "He's using the arm? Doesn't matter. He's just trying to piss me off."

Gerald moved his head right up against the camera so his eye filled the screen.

"You can't come," Terrence yelled and turned his phone off.

I hated watching him like this. He pushed the old door open and I followed him inside. Light streamed in from the doorway and spaces between the rows of boarded windows high up on the left wall. Empty black iron cauldrons big enough for a person to bathe in and discarded dirty white molds were in a heap in the center of the floor. From the look of the thick layer of dust and all the debris no one had passed this way in ages. Terrence picked up one of the molds. Inside the block of dirty plaster was a concave half-hourglass shape.

"A bell," he said. "They're all molds for bells."

I found something profound about the empty shape. I knew if I could just corral my thoughts I could share them with Terrence. What I was driving at was something he needed desperately to know. But I found no words and couldn't form a cogent train of thought.

Terrence was picking up molds and inspecting them. I crossed to the other side of the floor and into a small square room that was once an office area. A map of the world covered its back wall. Different colored pins marked towns and cities. Lines were drawn in marker between them indicating supply lines or delivery routes or who knows what. One lone pin was marked at the tip of South

America. Lin-Kasai was written in black marker next to it in a familiar scrawl.

"I think you ought to see this," I called to Terrence.

A star had been drawn around the pin on the town of Playa Portencia. The map indicated it was not far from our home on the North Shore, in fact it showed to be only a few beaches over. Granted I spent most of my time working, but I'd never heard of it. Next to the star was written:

"You'll find me here. Bring the bells."

The handwriting was unmistakably Peter's flourishing scrawl.

PETER'S PARENTS had buried him but wouldn't tell us where. That was all I knew to be true. Everything else, the handwriting on the map and Gerald sending us to the foundry, there had to be an explanation for.

Playa Portencia was a fishing town, a real throwback to what life on Long Island used to be like. Too few of them remained. The fishing boats were out for the day, except for a large freighter on the horizon, bound for some port unknown or maybe heading into the seaport in the city. A hot wind whipped spirals of sand along the asphalt parking lot. Terrence and I trudged to the rocky shore, the bells snugly stashed in his backpack. Saltwater tide pools were everywhere between the rocks of all shapes and sizes covering the beach. At the shore about a dozen wooden docks stretched into the water. Three quarters the way across was a square concrete foundation the size of a child's desk. It looked like the base for a statue or monument.

Someone bumped into me as I maneuvered on some rocks to avoid dipping my feet in a tide pool.

"Sorry," I said.

He looked nothing at all like a fisherman; he was older than me, but young and oh so thin. His shock of dark hair was flipped to one side, like a fifties rocker.

"I wasn't looking, sorry man," I repeated.

He pointed to the freighter just barely visible on the horizon.

"That's the *Amaranth*," he said.

I called to Terrence to look. He was already at the concrete, bent down and reading from a placard set in it. I looked back to the skinny man but he had vanished.

"Here lies Peter Ramacoord. Beloved son," Terrence read.

"It also says that this is a historic site. A merchant ship was claimed by the rocks here long ago."

He stood there in silence. I wanted to ask him if the name of the ship was the *Amaranth* but he was having a moment; thinking about Peter, I hoped, which was what he had needed to do for so long. Then he placed his pack on the concrete and took out the bells. A thin silver flute. A small brass one that looked like the kind they rung for a butler in the movies. The old iron one he placed in a groove in the concrete as if it were made for it.

For some reason this made Terrence laugh. It was the first levity I'd seen in him for a while, but it was a nervous laughter. I didn't like it.

"Terrence, what was the name of the merchant ship?"

"I had it right all along," he said, ignoring me. "I was just in the wrong place."

I moved so I could read the placard myself but then he rang the first bell.

I winced; part of me expecting an explosion of sound or something. There was nothing. Terrence fell to his knees, his body shaking as if responding to something physical. The fourth bell rocked back and forth in its concrete cradle. I could see it and all the bells vibrating but I heard nothing.

I noticed a faint ting, an almost imperceptible sound, like the first patter of a sparse rain on grass. Someone was standing at the shore by one of the docks, sketching in a pad. I knew that pose. I knew those black jeans and that tattered T-shirt. Peter.

A realization was dawning on me how this had come to be. The idea was just aching to be born in my mind, along with my thoughts about the molds in the foundry, something about the distinction between the living and the dead and between the past and the future, but I could not grasp it long enough to give it voice.

"Reach for it," Peter said. "Let all misconceptions and misunderstandings fall away like negative space and see the creation."

Though he was by the shore I heard his words in my mind clearly as if he were right in front of me. I wasn't sure if he were speaking to me or about something he was drawing.

"I've got it," Terrence shouted to me. "I've figured it out. They're not bells they're keys."

He didn't see Peter.

The wind whipped the waves into spray. The ephemeral vortexes of mist unlocked my answers. I knew what I had to say to Terrence. I knew how to make this all right.

"You always were the smart one," I said. "I knew you would figure it out. They're not keys to open. But to close. We're here to say goodbye. To lock our memories, our love for him in our hearts. That's the way things go. That's what we do, that's all anyone can do when you lose—"

"No. The bells *open* doors. I figured it out. We figured it out. Just think of what we can do with this."

"Terrence, I really think we should stop and think this over."

"No," he said. "I have all the bells and I know what to do."

A big wave rolled in and erupted into a cloud of spray and foam. The water gurgled and became a patch of bubbles. When it cleared something big was there. At first I thought it was a boulder or dislodged seaside rocks, but it was metal. A brown metal orb patched up with different colored metal plates, climbing from the sea on eight robotic legs. Our rover's mechanical legs. It was our dive bell. Gerald's head peered from the glass porthole in its center. Seawater sluiced off its sides as it stood on four legs. The other four waved in the air, pincers at the end clacking open and closed. Terrence laughed and I wished it were with the amazement and joy I felt. His face looked anything but happy.

Gerald had no voice. No blocks to spell with but the meaning of his suit's outstretched arms was universal. Stop.

Terrence looked at him and smiled. He held up the fourth bell and said, "No."

"I'M SICK of you," Terrence said. "You *think* you're Peter but you're not. And I'm not surprised. I knew you were building it. I let you."

Gerald moved toward him. His mechanical legs whirring and clicking as he inched closer.

Terrence raised the fourth bell higher. Its crust fell away revealing a finish that was solid black. Its odd gloss looked like it would shine and reflect light, but it didn't; it was as if it were a piece of night cut in the shape of a bell. I knew I couldn't let him ring it.

I ran to him and grabbed for it. Terrence pivoted. I slipped on wet rock and fell into a tide pool. I heard a crunch, crunch, crunch and the whir and hiss of motors and hydraulics. Gerald had closed the distance from the shore and was upon Terrence reaching for him with his mechanical arms.

Terrence rang the bell before Gerald's arms could restrain him. I winced again, but I heard no sound. Gerald snaked two of his arms around Terrence's waist and lifted him. With his two others he tried to pry the bell from Terrence's grasp. I knew the strength of those motors. He should have been able to snatch it away like that, but was unable. Terrence held on.

"He only wants to help," I said. "He knows you need to stop. You treat him like he's nothing."

"He is nothing," Terrence cried. "Nothing like Peter at all."

"Of course he is nothing like me," a familiar voice said. "He has way too many legs."

Peter had come from the shore. Terrence saw him now. They stood side by side in their black jeans and rock T's. A smile grew on Terrence's face. We were all together again.

"You're back," Terrence said. "You've come back to us. I knew you would."

He was all choked up and fighting not to cry.

"No. I'm not back. I've only come for these," he said. "They're much too dangerous to have around."

Peter reached for the bells. As his hand neared them one by one they disappeared. Something changed. I couldn't pinpoint what. It was the relief akin to the removal of an annoying background hum or the fixing of a flickering fluorescent light. It was hard to say what was different but I felt the relief from a pressure I hadn't realized was present. Only the fourth bell, the bell that Terrence held, remained. I knew it too needed to disappear. I knew once it too was gone the weight I'd been carrying around would be lifted, and danger would be averted.

"Don't do this, Peter," Terrence said to him. "Don't you miss us?"

Peter smiled. Terrence smiled too. Seeing them standing there next to the mechanical hulk Gerald wore, smiling together, provided some comfort. This was my family.

Things were going to be all right again. Everything was going to be okay.

Terrence closed his hand around the top of the black bell and thrust it at the glass faceplate of Gerald's dive bell. Gerald's arms grasped for him but Terrence pounded, pounded, pounded away.

The plate cracked, spider-webbed, and broke open. Water poured out sending Gerald onto the rocky beach. He convulsed on the rocks, his tentacles reaching for a tide pool. Terrence put his foot down, blocking Gerald's path to shore. He pushed the empty shell of Gerald's suit and it fell.

"Do something," I screamed to Peter and ran to them.

Peter only reached for the fourth bell. As his hand neared it both he and it disappeared. Gerald crawled for the shore. I ran into Terrence and did my best to tackle him. He met my charge, punched me, and flung me off him.

A big wave crashed on the shore and enveloped Gerald. As it pulled back to sea, Gerald was gone. I stood and ran for the water and dove in. I hit my head on a rock. Sharp edges cut my hands and arms. I tried to swim. The current took me. Waves battered me. I pulled myself forward. With the last of my air I called for Gerald before everything went black.

I WOKE up to the all too familiar blips and chirps of a hospital room.

"Don't worry," Terrence's voice said. "I'm with you. I'm working on something to make this all right."

I meant to protest but whatever drugs they had me on took me.

AFTER MY concussion healed Terrence returned to take me home. My stitches itched and I wanted them out. The living room was back to the way it was. No worktable. No tank. Nothing to indicate Gerald had ever been with us.

"I'm working on something," Terrence said gently. "When you are up to it do you want to go visit Peter's grave?"

"Gerald's gone," I said.

"I'm sorry," he said. "I think I can find him."

He was happy. He was embroiled in a plan again. Angry as I was, there was some comfort in seeing him content. But I knew he was wrong. No memorial, no visiting of Peter's grave, no machine Terrence could dream up was going to help this time. Gerald was gone. Peter was not coming back. The water had taken everything.

SIMON BESTWICK

THE TARN

A LATE Saturday afternoon, November '83; the gray sky above was nearly black, rain streaming down as I walked a field of wilted yellow grass. To my right, the motorway, cars rushing by, their head lamps little yellow coals, lorries rumbling past in a mist of rainwater churned up by their wheels, their lights like blazing eyes.

Below, to my left, a housing estate; up ahead, an old mill—red bricks sooted black, windows boarded, outline ragged with neglect—and, just before that, the tarn.

Lots of old mills had them. Tall grass and rushes grew around it, but I could see the water, flat and gray like lead, still but for the rain. I looked at it for nearly half a minute, then took a deep breath and started walking again, praying I was wrong.

The sodium lights along the motorway were coming on. Some glowed dull red, warming up; others shone orange. They made me think of my nan's old coal fire; I wanted more than anything to be there again, or at least indoors, warm, out of this, with no reason to look in that water. But most prayers go unanswered, and as I reached the water's edge, I saw mine hadn't been any exception.

She was facedown, about two feet from the bank. Her little blue duffel coat hung open, spread like wings in the water; her dark hair spilled out around her head, waving like weeds. Real weeds, I noticed, clung to her—a thick strand lay across her back, another knotted round her ankle like a tiny noose.

HER NAME was Maisie Donovan. She'd gone to a local playground that morning; when her dad went to get her for lunch, she was gone, and none of her friends knew where.

My cousin Geoff was a police constable back then, and asked if I'd help with the search. I was out of work and glad of the chance to do something useful. So were quite a few other lads. There was a sense of community in Salford then; still is. We'd spread out, reeling off her parents' description of Maisie, till finally someone on that housing estate had remembered seeing her heading up towards the old mill.

I knew there was nothing to be done as soon as I saw her, but waded in anyway. It wasn't deep. I pulled her out, tried to give her the kiss of life with no success, then covered her with my jacket and ran for the nearest phone.

"Bad business," Geoff said later. I was in the back of an ambulance with a red blanket round me, holding a mug of hot sweet tea—I'd been close to hypothermia when the police arrived. A doctor knelt beside the body; blue lights played across the ground and the faces of the crowd that had gathered.

"The hell was she doing up here?" I said, teeth chattering, and spat again. I couldn't get the taste of her mouth—stagnant water, rotten weeds—out of mine.

"God knows," he said. "You know kids, Bill. What were we like, that age? She went off wandering, went too close, fell in. Nasty, but that's how it happens."

That's how it happens. Not much of an epitaph for a child. But the truth, or so it seemed then. And that was where it should have ended, but it didn't.

I WAS laid up for a week after that; got a cold that turned into a chest infection. Smoking ten B&H a day probably didn't help. I went to bed and didn't get up. My dad said I should be up and looking for work, but Mam shushed him. Looking back, I expect it was more than just physical: today they'd talk about PTSD or depression, but back then, you just put your head down and carried on.

I suppose that's why I went back to the tarn. There were flowers there, most of them withered and dead, and the same cold gray water. I was wrapped up warm, but shivering; when I touched my face it was hot. I should probably still have been in bed.

I started back the way I'd come, but looked back once. It's still the most desolate thing I've seen. Bitter sky and ragged grass, the dull crag of the mill, the chill dead water of the tarn. But then I saw something the other side of the water, across from where I'd found Maisie.

Something glistened on the grass and earth by the bank. Plastic? I touched it, then snatched my fingers away to rub them clean; it was still sticky. A foot-wide trail of clear mucus, hardening like resin. I sniffed my hand: rotten weeds, dead fish. I thought of a slug's track, or the slime that covered a frog.

A WEEK later, another child drowned in a fishing pond: Stephen Philipson, a ten-year-old from Irlam way—again, on an afternoon of heavy rain. Mam tried to hide the newspaper, but I saw.

I went out, down the pub. It was a weeknight, quiet, but I saw Geoff sitting by the fire. I bought two Scotches and took them over.

"Cheers, our kid," he said. "How you doing?"

I shrugged.

"You heard, then?"

"What about?"

"The other kiddy."

"Oh. Yeah."

"Nasty business. 'Specially after the one you found."

"Another accident?"

Geoff looked round. "Keep this to yourself, all right?"

"Okay."

"Pathologist was eighty, ninety percent sure what happened to the Donovan girl was an accident. But this new one—it's exactly the same there, too."

"What is?"

"He wasn't sure. Said they looked a bit like finger marks, but weird sort of shape—probably caused by something else, but no idea what."

I saw what he was getting at. "On both of them? You mean

someone—"

"No, I do *not*, and neither does anyone else. Officially. Got it?"

"Right."

"But unofficially—keep an eye out, our kid."

"Okay." I hesitated, but had to ask. "What's so weird about the marks, anyway?"

Now *he* hesitated. "You didn't get this from me. They were a bit like fingers, pathologist said—bloody *long* fingers. But—well, if some sick bastard *had* done it, you'd have thought they'd have grabbed the kids from behind. Pushed them in, held them under."

I thought again of Maisie Donovan, facedown in the tarn.

"But the pathologist said it was like they'd been grabbed from the front. As if someone in the water had pulled them in."

Someone in the water, or under it.

I KEPT an eye out, as he'd asked: watched the playgrounds for anyone staring at the kids. I made a point of looking at people's hands, to see how long their fingers were. My cough came back, even worse. I didn't sleep well.

Then a third child drowned: another boy, this one eight years old. They found him in a park duck pond—again, in the rain. Geoff didn't want to tell me, but I pestered him until he did—yes, he'd had the same marks as the other two.

Maisie kept coming back at odd moments—the memory of her, I mean, as I'd found her. I had some idea that if she *had* been murdered, catching the swine might make it stop.

As at the tarn, a heap of dead flowers lay where it had happened. I paced around the duck pond and stopped at the far end: it was thick with rushes, and at the bottom of a grass slope. At the top of the slope was a set of iron railings, bent wide enough to let something more or less man-sized slip through.

I saw something else, too: a wide strip of grass, leading down from the railings to the rushes, had been flattened, and was matted with some clear substance. I touched it and a piece broke off: it was like a very thin resin, and it smelt. Like dead, rotten fish.

I went on up to the fishing pond after that. It was a big, square-shaped pool with a busy main road along one side, a quiet side road by another, and blocks of council housing by the other two. I checked the banks and verges, but couldn't find anything, and then it started raining again.

I was tired; I walked up the path to the side road, which was where I saw a patch of something dry and shiny on the pavement. Just over the road, there was a big patch of waste ground, where an old factory had been pulled down about nine or ten years before.

I went over, in among the damp trees, walked lumpy, overgrown ground till I found a small pool of water. There was dried slime on the grass on either side: a trail led away from the pond, through high grass and nettles. Farther off was the motorway, and even farther up was the old mill.

BY THE time I got home, I was practically on fire and my lungs felt scorched when I breathed. I went straight to bed and lay sweating, the room spinning around me. And that was when I remembered a story of my nan's.

Nan knew lots of creepy old stories about Salford: she'd loved telling them to us, and we'd loved hearing them. But the one I remembered was Jinny Greenteeth.

Jinny Greenteeth, Nan had said, lived in the water—the River Irwell, to be exact, which runs right through Salford. She had long green hair like waterweed, and lay waiting for children to come too near the bank. When they did, she grabbed them, and pulled them in to drown.

But that was just a story—and anyway, Jinny Greenteeth had lived in the Irwell, not in an old mill tarn.

Except that—well, *nothing* lived in the Irwell in those days. They've cleaned it up now, but we used to say it looked like a pint of Guinness. So what would you do? You'd go looking for a new home. Swim upstream, or, if you could, climb out of the water and find somewhere else.

Like maybe a pond, or a tarn. And, maybe, you'd burrow into the mud at the bottom and hibernate. Then wake up and…

Wake up and what?

Feed. On whatever it was you fed on.

If I hadn't been so feverish, I'd have laughed it right off. But by the time I fell asleep, it seemed to make a lot of sense.

GEOFF CAME around the next day, after Dad had gone to work. I was better than before, but still coughing like hell.

"There's been another," he said.

"Where?"

"Never mind that now. The hell did you think you were doing, hanging round crime scenes like some bloody ghoul? You were seen."

"You were the one who told me—"

"To keep an eye out, not play at whatever you're playing at. Hanging around playgrounds, for Christ's sake? They'll think you're a bloody kiddy-fiddler."

"I'm not!"

"*I* know that. Well, leave off with it. Stay home, stay in bed, and get a bloody job while somebody'll still employ you."

I wanted to ask where the latest death had happened, but knew he wouldn't tell me. It didn't matter. I'd already worked out that the two ponds were the nearest bodies of water of any size to the tarn—the one I'd seen on the waste ground had been only two or three feet wide. They'd be easy to reach by something crawling through the grass on its belly.

Rain spotted against the window.

After Geoff had gone, and Mam had gone out shopping, I got dressed, then hunted in the kitchen till I found a near-empty bottle of Ben Shaw's Lemonade. I emptied and rinsed it, pulled on Dad's heavy raincoat, and slipped out.

I REACHED the field beside the old mill about an hour later. The sky was darkening: it wouldn't be long.

I hid in some bushes, waiting for it to come, or go.

The wind blew; the sky above blackened. Rain spotted, then quickened: first a drizzle, then heavier, till it came down in rods.

I put my hand in my coat pocket, wondering what the right moment would be, and how I'd know it, watching the tarn.

Thunder rumbled; the old mill stood black against the sky.

And then I heard it; a croaking sound that rose and fell in pitch. It became almost tuneful after you'd listened for a while, and the more you listened, the more you heard.

I was almost at the edge of the tarn before I realised what I was doing. Had it known I was there and decided to deal with the threat? Or, perhaps it had decided to lure another victim straight to its nest, and I'd simply been the closest? I don't know what the range of its hypnotic call was, how far away Maisie Donovan or the rest were when they'd heard it. Perhaps some heard it more clearly than others. And children would be the most susceptible: fewer defences, less sense of danger to temper their curiosity.

I could see something in the water now: a low hump, beachball sized, covered in what looked like wet green waterweed. It had two fat pale spots, that blinked as I came closer. I understood what was happening, but I kept walking.

My hand was still in my pocket, though, and as I reached the bank of the tarn I pulled the bottle out. The thing in the water shifted, gathering itself; its ridged, saw-toothed back broke the surface.

I tried to twist the screw-top lid. It was stiff and wouldn't move, but at last I felt it turn, as two thin, bony arms, ending in webbed, clawed, impossibly long-fingered hands, reached out from the surface of the tarn.

THE REST is…fitful. I remember a long eelish tail coiling round my legs, and sometimes, in nightmares, a blurred face: something between a frog and a deep-sea fish, but at the same time almost human.

Someone saw me heading towards the mill and called Geoff. He came down planning to tear me off a strip; instead he found me in the tarn, half dead.

I was in hospital for a month after that, and nearly died twice. Pneumonia, together with the poison that had saved me: a solution of paraquat from my dad's allotment, poured into that old Ben Shaw's bottle.

There were no more drownings, anyway.

I still live in Salford, and I've a family of my own. The Irwell doesn't look like a pint of Guinness anymore: they say it's clean now. But I wouldn't know. I never go down there, and I don't let my kids go near it either.

See, they never found anything in the tarn. Just a long, slimy trail, leading away. I want to believe it crawled away to die, but the past doesn't die. It only waits.

PETER STRAUB

THE BALLAD OF BALLARD AND SANDRINE

1997

"SO, DO we get lunch again today?" Ballard asked. They had reached the steaming, humid end of November.

"We got fucking lunch yesterday," replied the naked woman splayed on the long table: knees bent, one hip elevated, one boneless-looking arm draped along the curves of her body, which despite its hidden scars appeared to be at least a decade younger than her face. "Why should today be different?"

After an outwardly privileged childhood polluted by parental misconduct, a superior education, and two failed marriages, Sandrine Loy had evolved into a rebellious, still-exploratory woman of forty-three. At present, her voice had a well-honed edge, as if she were explaining something to a person of questionable intelligence.

Two days before joining Sandrine on this river journey, Ballard had celebrated his sixty-fifth birthday at a dinner in Hong Kong, one of the cities where he conducted his odd business. Sandrine had not been invited to the dinner and would not have attended if she had. The formal, ceremonious side of Ballard's life, which he found so satisfying, interested her not at all.

Without in any way adjusting the facts of the extraordinary

body she had put on display, Sandrine lowered her eyes from the ceiling and examined him with a glance brimming with false curiosity and false innocence. The glance also contained a flicker of genuine irritation.

Abruptly and with vivid recall, Ballard found himself remembering the late afternoon in 1969 when, nine floors above Park Avenue, upon a carpet of almost unutterable richness in a room hung with paintings by Winslow Homer and Albert Pinkham Ryder, he had stood with a rich scapegrace and client named Lauritzen Loy, his host, to greet Loy's daughter on her return from another grueling day at Dalton School, then observed the sidelong, graceful, slightly miffed entrance of a fifteen-year-old girl in pigtails and a Jackson Browne sweatshirt two sizes too large, met her gray-green eyes, and felt the very shape of his universe alter in some drastic way, either expanding a thousand times or contracting to a pinpoint, he could not tell. The second their eyes met, the girl blushed, violently.

She hadn't liked that, not at all.

"I didn't say it was going to be different, and I don't think it will." He turned to look at her, making sure to meet her gaze before letting his eye travel down her neck, over her breasts, the bowl of her belly, the slope of her pubis, the length of her legs. "Are you in a more than ordinarily bad mood?"

"You're snapping at me."

Ballard sighed. "You gave me that *look*. You said, 'Why should today be different?'"

"Have it your way, old man. But as a victory, it's fucking pathetic. It's hollow."

She rolled onto her back and gave her body a firm little shake that settled it more securely onto the steel surface of the table. The metal, only slightly cooler than her skin, felt good against it. In this climate, nothing not on ice or in a freezer, not even a corpse, could ever truly get cold.

"Most victories are hollow, believe me."

Ballard wandered over to the brass-bound porthole on the deck side of their elaborate, many-roomed suite. Whatever he saw caused him momentarily to stiffen and take an involuntary step backward.

"What's the view like?"

"The so-called view consists of the filthy Amazon and a boring, muddy bank. Sometimes the bank is so far away it's out of sight."

He did not add that a Ballard approximately twenty years younger, the Ballard of, say, 1976, dressed in a handsome dark suit and brilliantly white shirt, was leaning against the deck rail, unaware of being under the eye of his twenty-years-older self. Young Ballard, older Ballard observed, did an excellent job of concealing his dire internal condition beneath a mask of deep, already well-weathered urbanity: the same performance, enacted day after day before an audience unaware of being an audience and never permitted backstage.

Unlike Sandrine, Ballard had never married.

"Poor Ballard, stuck on the *Endless Night* with a horrible view and only his aging, moody girlfriend for company."

Smiling, he returned to the long steel table, ran his mutilated right hand over the curve of her belly, and cupped her navel. "This is exactly what I asked for. You're wonderful."

"But isn't it funny to think—everything could have been completely different."

Ballard slid the remaining fingers of his hand down to palpate, lightly, the springy black shrub-like curls of her pubic bush.

"Everything is completely different right now."

"So take off your clothes and fuck me," Sandrine said. "I can get you hard again in a minute. In thirty seconds."

"I'm sure you could. But maybe you should put some clothes *on*, so we could go in to lunch."

"You prefer to have sex in our bed."

"I do, yes. I don't understand why you wanted to get naked and lie down on this thing, anyhow. Now, I mean."

"It isn't cold, if that's what you're afraid of." She wriggled her torso and did a snow angel movement with her legs.

"Maybe this time we could catch the waiters."

"Because we'd be early?"

Ballard nodded. "Indulge me. Put on that sleeveless white French thing."

"Aye, aye, *mon capitain*." She sat up and scooted down the length of the table, pushing herself along on the raised vertical edges. These were of dark green marble, about an inch thick and four inches high. On both sides, round metal drains abutted the inner side of the marble. At the end of the table, Sandrine swung her legs down and straightened her arms, like a girl sitting on the end of a diving board. "I know why, too."

"Why I want you to wear that white thing? I love the way it looks on you."

"Why you don't want to have sex on this table."

"It's too narrow."

"You're thinking about what this table is for. Right? And you don't want to combine sex with *that.* Only I think that's exactly why we *should* have sex here."

"Everything we do, remember, is done by mutual consent. Our Golden Rule."

"Golden Spoilsport," she said. "Golden Shower of Shit."

"See? Everything's different already."

Sandrine levered herself off the edge of the table and faced him like a strict schoolmistress who happened momentarily to be naked. "I'm all you've got, and sometimes even I don't understand you."

"That makes two of us."

She wheeled around and padded into the bedroom, displaying her plush little bottom and sacral dimples with an absolute confidence Ballard could not but admire.

Although Sandrine and Ballard burst, in utter defiance of a direct order, into the dining room a full nine minutes ahead of schedule, the unseen minions had already done their work and disappeared. On the gleaming rosewood table two formal place settings had been laid, the plates topped with elaborately chased silver covers. Fresh irises brushed blue and yellow filled a tall, sparkling crystal vase.

"I swear, they must have a greenhouse on this yacht," Ballard said.

"Naked men with muddy hair row the flowers out in the middle of the night."

"I don't even think irises grow in the Amazon basin."

"Little guys who speak bird-language can probably grow anything they like."

"That's only one tribe, the Pirahã. And all those bird sounds are actual words. It's a human language." Ballard walked around the table and took the seat he had claimed as his. He lifted the intricate silver cover. "Now what is that?" He looked across at Sandrine, who was prodding at the contents of her bowl with a fork.

"Looks like a cut-up sausage. At least I hope it's a sausage. And something like broccoli. And a lot of orangey-yellowy goo." She raised her fork and licked the tines. "Um. Tastes pretty good, actually. But..."

For a moment, she appeared to be lost in time's great forest.

"I know this doesn't make sense, but if we ever did this before, *exactly* this, with you sitting over there and me here, in this same room, well, wasn't the food even better, I mean a *lot* better?"

"I can't say anything about that," Ballard said. "I really can't. There's just this vague..." The vagueness disturbed him far more than seemed quite rational. "Let's drop that subject and talk about bird language. Yes, let's. And the wine." He picked up the bottle. "Yet again a very nice Bordeaux," Ballard said, and poured for both of them. "However. What you've been hearing are real birds, not the Pirahã."

"But they're talking, not just chirping. There's a difference. These guys are saying things to each other."

"Birds talk to one another. I mean, they sing."

She was right about one thing, though: in a funky, down-home way, the stew-like dish was delicious. He thrust away the feeling that it should have been a hundred, a thousand times more delicious: that once it, or something rather like it, had been paradisal.

"Birds don't sing in sentences. Or in paragraphs, like these guys do."

"They still can't be the Pirahã. The Pirahã live about five hundred miles away, on the Peruvian border."

"Your ears aren't as good as mine. You don't really hear them."

"Oh, I hear plenty of birds. They're all over the place."

"Only we're not talking about *birds*," Sandrine said.

1982

ON THE last day of November, Sandrine Loy, who was twenty-eight, constitutionally ill-tempered, and startlingly good-looking (wide eyes, long mouth, black widow's peak, columnar legs), formerly of Princeton and Clare College, Cambridge, glanced over her shoulder and said, "Please tell me you're kidding. I just showered. I put on this nice white frock you bought me in Paris. And I'm *hungry*." Relenting a bit, she let a playful smile warm her face for nearly a second. "Besides that, I want to catch sight of our invisible servants."

"I'm hungry, too."

"Not for food, unfortunately." She spun from the porthole and its ugly view—a mile of brown, rolling river and low, muddy banks where squat, sullen natives tended to melt back into the bushes when the *Sweet Delight* went by—to indicate the evidence of Ballard's arousal, which stood up, darker than the rest of him, as straight as a flagpole.

"Let's have sex on this table. It's a lot more comfortable than it looks."

"Kind of defeats the fucking purpose, wouldn't you say? Comfort's hardly the point."

"Might as well be as comfy as we can, I say." He raised his arms to let his hands drape from the four-inch marble edging on the long steel table. "There's plenty of space on this thing, you know. More than in your bed at Clare."

"Maybe you're not as porky as I thought you were."

"Careful, careful. If you insult me, I'll make you pay for it."

At fifty Ballard had put on some extra weight, but it suited him. His shoulders were still wider far than his hips, and his belly more nascent than actual. His hair, longer than that of most men his age and just beginning to show threads of gray within the luxuriant brown, framed his wide brow and executive face. He looked like an actor who had made a career of playing senators, doctors, and bankers. Ballard's real profession was that of fixer to an oversized law firm in New York with a satellite office in Hong Kong, where he had grown up. The weight of muscle in his arms, shoulders, and legs reinforced the hint of stubborn determination, even perhaps brutality in his face: the suggestion that if necessary he would go a great distance and perform any number of grim deeds to do what was needed. Scars both long and short, scars like snakes, zippers, and tattoos bloomed here and there on his body.

"Promises, promises," she said. "But just for now, get up and get dressed, please. The sight of you admiring your own dick doesn't do anything for me."

"Oh, really?"

"Well, I do like the way you can still stick straight up into the air like a happy little soldier—at your age! But men are so soppy about their penises. You're all queer for yourselves. You more so than most, Ballard."

"Ouch," he said, and sat up. "I believe I'll put my clothes on now, Sandrine."

"Don't take forever, all right? I know it's only the second day, but I'd like to get a look at them while they're setting the table. Because someone, maybe even two someones, does set that table."

Ballard was already in the bedroom, pulling from their hangers a pair of white linen slacks and a thick, long-sleeved white cotton T-shirt. In seconds, he had slipped into these garments and was sliding his sun-tanned feet into rope-soled clogs.

"So let's move," he said, coming out of the bedroom with a long stride, his elbows bent, his forearms raised.

From the dining room came the sharp, distinctive chirping of a bird. Two notes, the second one higher, both clear and as insistent as the call of a bell. Ballard glanced at Sandrine, who seemed momentarily shaken.

"I'm not going in there if one of those awful jungle birds got in. They have to get rid of it. We're paying them, aren't we?"

"You have no idea," Ballard said. He grabbed her arm and pulled her along with him. "But that's no bird, it's *them*. The waiters. The staff."

Sandrine's elegant face shone with both disbelief and disgust.

"Those chirps and whistles are how they talk. Didn't you hear them last night and this morning?"

When he pulled again at her arm, she followed along, reluctance visible in her stance, her gait, the tilt of her head.

"I'm talking about birds, and they weren't even on the yacht. They were on shore. They were up in the air."

"Let's see what's in here." Six or seven minutes remained until the official start of dinner time, and they had been requested never to enter the dining room until the exact time of the meal.

Ballard threw the door open and pulled her into the room with him. Silver covers rested on the Royal Doulton china, and an uncorked bottle of a distinguished Bordeaux stood precisely at the mid-point between the two place settings. Three inches to its right, a navy-blue-and-royal-purple orchid thick enough to eat leaned, as if languishing, against the side of a small square crystal vase. The air seemed absolutely unmoving. Through the thumb holes at the tops of the plate covers rose a dense, oddly meaty odor of some unidentifiable food.

"Missed 'em again, damn it." Sandrine pulled her arm from Ballard's grasp and moved a few steps away.

"But you have noticed that there's no bird in here. Not so much as a feather."

"So it got out—I know it was here, Ballard."

She spun on her four-inch heels, giving the room a fast 360-degree inspection. Their dining room, roughly oval in shape, was lined with glassed-in bookshelves of dark-stained oak containing perhaps five hundred books, most of them mid-to-late nineteenth and early twentieth century novels ranked alphabetically by author, regardless of genre. The jackets had been removed, which Ballard minded, a bit. Three feet in front of the bookshelves on the deck side, which yielded space to two portholes and a door, stood a long wooden table with a delicately inlaid top—a real table, unlike the one in the room they had just left, which was more like a work station in a laboratory. The real one was presumably for setting out buffets.

The first door opened out onto the deck; another at the top of the oval led to their large and handsomely furnished sitting room, with reading chairs and lamps, two sofas paired with low tables, a bar with a great many bottles of liquor, two red lacquered cabinets they had as yet not explored, and an air of many small precious things set out to gleam under the parlor's low lighting. The two remaining doors in the dining room were on the interior side. One opened into the spacious corridor that ran the entire length of their suite and gave access to the deck on both ends; the other revealed a gray passageway and a metal staircase that led up to the captain's deck and cabin and down into the engine room, galley, and quarters for the yacht's small, unseen crew.

"So it kept all its feathers," said Sandrine. "If you don't think that's possible, you don't know doodly-squat about birds."

"What isn't possible," said Ballard, "is that some giant parrot got out of here without opening a door or a porthole."

"One of the waiters let it out, dummy. One of those handsome *Spanish-speaking* waiters."

They sat on opposite sides of the stately table. Ballard smiled at Sandrine, and she smiled back in rage and distrust. Suddenly and without warning, he remembered the girl she had been on Park Avenue at the end of the sixties, gawky-graceful, brilliantly surly, her hair and wardrobe goofy, claiming him as he had claimed her, with a glance. He had rescued her father from ruinous shame and a long jail term, but as soon as he had seen her he understood that his work had just begun, and that it would demand restraint, sacrifice, patience, and adamantine caution.

"A three-count?" he asked.

She nodded.

"One," he said. "Two." They put their thumbs into the round holes at the tops of the covers. "Three." They raised their covers, releasing steam and smoke and a more concentrated, powerful form of the meaty odor.

"Wow. What is that?"

Yellow-brown sauce or gravy covered a long, curved strip of foreign matter. Exhausted vegetables that looked a little like okra and string beans but were other things altogether lay strewn in limp surrender beneath the gravy.

"All of a sudden I'm really hungry," said Sandrine. "You can't tell what it is, either?"

Ballard moved the strip of unknown meat back and forth with his knife. Then he jabbed his fork into it. A watery yellow fluid oozed from the punctures.

"God knows what this is."

He pictured some big reptilian creature sliding down the riverbank into the meshes of a native net, then being hauled back up to be pierced with poison-tipped wooden spears. Chirping like birds, the diminutive men rioted in celebration around the corpse, which was now that of a hideous insect the size of a pony, its shell a poisonous green.

"I'm not even sure it's a mammal," he said. "Might even be some organ. Anaconda liver. Crocodile lung. Tarantula heart."

"You first."

Ballard sliced a tiny section from the curved meat before him. He half-expected to see valves and tubes, but the slice was a dense light brown all the way through. Ballard inserted the morsel into his mouth, and his taste buds began to sing.

"My God. Amazing."

"It's good?"

"Oh, this is way beyond 'good.'"

Ballard cut a larger piece off the whole and quickly bit into it. Yes, there it was again, but more sumptuous, almost floral in its delicacy and grounded in some profoundly satisfactory flavor, like that of a great single-barrel bourbon laced with a dark, subversive French chocolate. Subtlety, strength, sweetness. He watched Sandrine lift a section of the substance on her fork and slip it into her mouth. Her face went utterly still, and her eyes narrowed. With luxuriant slowness, she began to chew. After perhaps a second, Sandrine closed her eyes. Eventually, she swallowed.

"Oh, yes," she said. "My, my. Yes. Why can't we eat like this at home?"

"Whatever kind of animal this is, it's probably unknown everywhere but here. People like J. Paul Getty might get to eat it once a year, at some secret location."

"I don't care what it is, I'm just extraordinarily happy that we get to have it today. It's even a little bit sweet, isn't it?"

A short time later, Sandrine said, "Amazing. Even these horrible-looking vegetables spill out amazing flavors. If I could eat like this every day, I'd be perfectly happy to live in a hut, walk around barefoot, bathe in the Amazon, and wash my rags on the rocks."

"I know exactly what you mean," said Ballard. "It's like a drug. Maybe it is a drug."

"Do the natives really eat this way? Whatever this animal was, before they serve it to us, they have to hunt it down and kill it. Wouldn't they keep half of it for themselves?"

"Be a temptation," Ballard said. "Maybe they lick our plates, too."

"Tell me the truth now, Ballard. If you know it. Okay?"

Chewing, he looked up into her eyes. Some of the bliss faded from his face. "Sure. Ask away."

"Did we ever eat this stuff before?"

Ballard did not answer. He sliced a quarter-sized piece off the meat and began to chew, his eyes on his plate.

"I know I'm not supposed to ask."

He kept chewing and chewing until he swallowed. He sipped his wine. "No. Isn't that strange? How we know we're not supposed to do certain things?"

"Like see the waiters. Or the maids, or the captain."

"Especially the captain, I think."

"Let's not talk anymore, let's just eat for a little while."

Sandrine and Ballard returned to their plates and glasses, and for a time made no noise other than soft moans of satisfaction.

When they had nearly finished, Sandrine said, "There are so many books on this boat! It's like a big library. Do you think you've ever read one?"

"Do you?"

"I have the feeling…well, of course that's the reason I'm asking. In a way, I mean in a *real* way, we've never been here before. On the Amazon? Absolutely not. My husband, besides being continuously unfaithful, is a total asshole who never pays me any attention at all unless he's angry with me, but he's also tremendously jealous and possessive. For me to get here to be with you required an amazing amount of secret organization. D-Day didn't take any more planning than this trip. On the other hand, I have the feeling I once read at least one of these books."

"I have the same feeling."

"Tell me about it. I want to read it again and see if I remember anything."

"I can't. But…well, I think I might have once seen you holding a copy of *Little Dorrit*. The Dickens novel."

"I went to Princeton and Cambridge, I know who wrote *Little Dorrit*," she said, irritated. "Wait. Did I ever throw a copy of that book overboard?"

"Might've."

"Why would I do that?"

Ballard shrugged. "To see what would happen?"

"Do you remember that?"

"It's tough to say what I remember. Everything's always different, but it's different *now*. I sort of remember a book, though—a book from this library. *Tono Bungay*. H. G. Wells. Didn't like it much."

"Did you throw it overboard?"

"I might've. Yes, I actually might have." He laughed. "I think I did. I mean, I think I'm throwing it overboard right now, if that makes sense."

"Because you didn't—don't—like it?"

Ballard laughed and put down his knife and fork. Only a few bits of the vegetables and a piece of meat the size of a knuckle sliced in half remained on his plate. "Stop eating and give me your plate." It was almost exactly as empty as his, though Sandrine's plate still had two swirls of the yellow sauce.

"Really?"

"I want to show you something."

Reluctantly, she lowered her utensils and handed him her plate. Ballard scraped the contents of his plate onto hers. He got to his feet and picked up a knife and the plate that had been Sandrine's. "Come out on deck with me."

When she stood up, Sandrine glanced at what she had only briefly and partially perceived as a hint of motion at the top of the room, where for the first time she took in a dun-colored curtain hung two or three feet before the end of the oval. What looked to be a brown or suntanned foot, smaller than a normal adult's and perhaps a bit grubby, was just now vanishing behind the curtain. Before Sandrine had deciphered what she thought she had seen, it was gone.

"Just see a rat?" asked Ballard.

Without intending to assent, Sandrine nodded.

"One was out on deck this morning. Disappeared as soon as I spotted it. Don't worry about it, though. The crew, whoever they are, will get rid of them. At the start of the cruise, I think there are always a few rats around. By the time we really get in gear, they're gone."

"Good," she said, wondering: *If the waiters are these really, really short Indian guys, would they hate us enough to make us eat rats?*

She followed him through the door between the two portholes into pitiless sunlight and crushing heat made even less comfortable by the dense, invasive humidity. The invisible water saturating the air pressed against her face like a steaming washcloth, and moisture instantly coated her entire body. Leaning against the rail, Ballard looked cool and completely at ease.

"I forgot we had air conditioning," she said.

"We don't. Vents move the air around somehow. Works like magic, even when there's no breeze at all. Come over here."

She joined him at the rail. Fifty yards away, what might have been human faces peered at them through a dense screen of jungle—weeds with thick, vegetal leaves of a green so dark it was nearly black. The half-seen faces resembled masks, empty of feeling.

"Remember saying something about being happy to bathe in the Amazon? About washing your clothes in the river?"

She nodded.

"You never want to go into this river. You don't even want to stick the tip of your finger in that water. Watch what happens, now. Our native friends came out to see this, you should, too."

"The Indians knew you were going to put on this demonstration? How could they?"

"Don't ask me, ask them. *I* don't know how they do it."

Ballard leaned over the railing and used his knife to scrape the few things on the plate into the river. Even before the little knuckles of meat and gristle, the shreds of vegetables, and liquid strings of gravy landed in the water, a six-inch circle of turbulence boiled up on the slow-moving surface. When the bits of food hit the water, the boiling circle widened out into a three-foot, thrashing chaos of violent little fish tails and violent little green shiny fish backs with violent tiny green fins, all in furious motion. The fury lasted about thirty seconds, then disappeared back under the river's sluggish brown face.

"Like Christmas dinner with my husband's family," Sandrine said.

"When we were talking about throwing *Tono Bungay* and *Little Dorrit* into the river to see what would happen—"

"The fish ate the books?"

"They'll eat anything that isn't metal."

"So our little friends don't go swimming all that often, do they?"

"They never learn how. Swimming is death, it's for people like us. Let's go back in, okay?"

She whirled around and struck his chest, hard, with a pointed fist. "I want to go back to the room with the table in it. *Our* table. And this time, you can get as hard as you like."

"Don't I always?" he asked.

"Oh," Sandrine said, "I like that 'always.'"

"And yet, it's always different."

"I bet *I'm* always different," said Sandrine. "You, you'd stay pretty much the same."

"I'm not as boring as all that, you know," Ballard said, and went on, over the course of the long afternoon and sultry evening, to prove it.

After breakfast the next morning, Sandrine, hissing with pain, her skin clouded with bruises, turned on him with such fury that he gasped in joy and anticipation.

1976

END OF November, hot sticky muggy, a vegetal stink in the air. Motionless tribesmen four feet tall stared out from the overgrown bank over twenty yards of torpid river. They held, seemed to hold, bows without arrows, though the details swam backward into the layers of folded green.

"Look at those little savages," said Sandrine Loy, twenty-two years old and already contemplating marriage to handsome, absurdly wealthy Antonio Barban, who had proposed to her after a chaotic Christmas dinner at his family's vulgar pile in Greenwich, Connecticut. That she knew marriage to Antonio would prove to be an error of sublime proportions gave the idea most of its appeal. "We're putting on a traveling circus for their benefit. Doesn't that sort of make you detest them?"

"I don't detest them at all," Ballard said. "Actually, I have a lot of respect for those people. I think they're mysterious. So much gravity. So much *silence.* They understand a million things we don't, and what we do manage to get they know about in another way, a more profound way."

"You're wrong. They're too stupid to understand anything. They have mud for dinner. They have mud for brains."

"And yet…," Ballard said, smiling at her.

As if they knew they had been insulted and seemingly without moving out of position, the river people had begun to fade back into the network of dark, rubbery leaves in which they had for a long moment been framed.

"And yet what?"

"They knew what we were going to do. They wanted to see us throwing those books into the river. So out of the bushes they popped, right at the time we walked out on deck."

Her conspicuous black eyebrows slid nearer each other,

creating a furrow. She shook her beautiful head and opened her mouth to disagree.

"Anyway, Sandrine, what did you think of what happened just now? Any responses, reflections?"

"What do I think of what happened to the books? What do I think of the fish?"

"Of course," Ballard said. "It's not *all* about us."

He leaned back against the rail, communicating utter ease and confidence. He was forty-four, attired daily in dark tailored suits and white shirts that gleamed like a movie star's smile, the repository of a thousand feral secrets, at home everywhere in the world, the possessor of an understanding it would take him a lifetime to absorb. Sandrine often seemed to him the center of his life. He knew exactly what she was going to say.

"I think the fish are astonishing," she said. "I mean it. Astonishing. Such concentration, such power, such complete *hunger*. It was breathtaking. Those books didn't last more than five or six seconds. All that thrashing! My book lasted longer than yours, but not by much."

"*Little Dorrit* is a lot longer than *Tono Bungay*. More paper, more thread, more glue. I think they're especially hot for glue."

"Maybe they're just hot for Dickens."

"Maybe they're speed readers," said Sandrine. "What do we do now?"

"What we came here to do," Ballard said, and moved back to swing open the dining room door, then froze in mid-step.

"Forget something?"

"I was having the oddest feeling, and I just now realized what it was. You read about it all the time, so you think it must be pretty common, but until a second ago I don't think I'd ever before had the feeling that I was being watched. Not really."

"But now you did."

"Yes." He strode up to the door and swung it open. The table was bare, and the room was empty.

Sandrine approached and peeked over his shoulder. He had both amused and dismayed her. "The great Ballard exhibits a moment of paranoia. I think I've been wrong about you all this time. You're just another boring old creep who wants to fuck me."

"I'd admit to being a lot of things, but paranoid isn't one of them." He gestured her back through the door. That Sandrine obeyed him seemed to take both of them by surprise.

"How about being a boring old creep? I'm not really so sure I want to stay here with you. For one thing, and I know this is not related, the birds keep waking me up. If they are birds."

He cocked his head, interested. "What else could they be? Please tell me. Indulge a boring old creep."

"The maids and the waiters and the sailor guys. The cook. The woman who arranges the flowers."

"You think they belong to that tribe that speaks in bird calls? Actually, how did *you* ever hear about them?"

"My anthropology professor was one of the people who first discovered that tribe. The Piranhas. Know what they call themselves? The tall people. Not very observant, are they? According to the professor, they worshipped a much older tribe that had disappeared many generations back—miracle people, healers, shamans, warriors. The Old Ones, they called themselves, but the Old Ones called themselves **We**, you always have to put it in boldface. My professor couldn't stop talking about these tribes—he was so full of himself. *Sooo* vain. Kept staring at me. Vain, ugly, and lecherous, my favorite trifecta!"

The memory of her anthropology professor, with whom she had clearly gone through the customary adoration-boredom-disgust cycle of student-teacher love affairs, had put Sandrine in a sulky, dissatisfied mood.

"You made a lovely little error about thirty seconds ago. The tribe is called the Pirahã, not the Piranhas. Piranhas are the fish you fell in love with."

"Ooh," she said, brightening up. "So the Pirahã eat piranhas?"

"Other way around, more likely. But the other people on the *Blinding Light* can't be Pirahã, we're hundreds of miles from their territory."

"You *are* tedious. Why did I ever let myself get talked into coming here, anyhow?"

"You fell in love with me the first time you saw me—in your father's living room, remember? And although it was tremendously naughty of me, in fact completely wrong and immoral, I took one look at your stupid sweatshirt and your stupid pigtails and fell in love with you on the spot. You were perfect—you took my breath away. It was like being struck by lightning."

He inhaled, hugely.

"And here I am, fourty-four years of age, height of my powers, capable of performing miracles on behalf of our clients, exactly as I pulled off, not to say any more about this, a considerable miracle for your father, plus I am a fabulously eligible man, a tremendous catch, but what do you know, still unmarried. Instead of a wife or even a steady girlfriend, there's this succession of inane young women from twenty-five to thirty, these Heathers and Ashleys, these Morgans and Emilys, who much to their dismay grow less and less infatuated with me the more time we spend together. 'You're always so distant,' one of them said, 'you're never really *with* me.' And she was right, I couldn't really be with her. Because I wanted to be with you. I wanted us to be *here.*"

Deeply pleased, Sandrine said, "You're such a pervert."

Yet something in what Ballard had evoked was making the handsome dining room awkward and dark. She wished he wouldn't stand still; there was no reason why he couldn't go into the living room, or the other way, into the room where terror and fascination beckoned. She wondered why she was waiting for Ballard to decide where to go, and as he spoke of seeing her for the first time, was assailed by an uncomfortably precise echo from the day in question.

Then, as now, she had been rooted to the floor: in her family's living room, beyond the windows familiar Park Avenue humming with the traffic she only in that moment became aware she heard, Sandrine had been paralyzed. Every inch of her face had turned hot and red. She felt intimate with Ballard before she had even begun to learn what intimacy meant. Before she had left the room, she waited for him to move between herself and her father, then pushed up the sleeves of the baggy sweatshirt and revealed the inscriptions of self-loathing, self-love, desire and despair upon her pale forearms.

"You're pretty weird, too. You'd just had your fifteenth birthday, and here you were, gobsmacked by this old guy in a suit. You even showed me your arms!"

"I could tell what made *you* salivate." She gave him a small, lop-sided smile. "So why were you there, anyhow?"

"Your father and I were having a private celebration."

"Of what?"

Every time she asked this question, he gave her a different answer. "I made the fearsome problem of his old library fines disappear. *Poof!,* no more late-night sweats." Previously, Ballard had told her that he'd got her father off jury duty, had cancelled his parking tickets, retroactively upgraded his B- in Introductory Chemistry to an A.

"Yeah, what a relief. My father never walked into a library, his whole life."

"You can see why the fine was so great." He blinked. "I just had an idea." Ballard wished her to cease wondering, to the extent this was possible, about the service he had rendered for her father. "How would you like to take a peek at the galley? Forbidden fruit, all that kind of thing. Aren't you curious?"

"You're suggesting we go down those stairs? Wasn't *not* doing that one of our most sacred rules?"

"I believe we were given those rules in order to make sure we broke them."

Sandrine considered this proposition for a moment, then nodded her head.

That's my girl, he thought.

"You may be completely perverted, Ballard, but you're pretty smart." A discordant possibility occurred to her. "What if we catch sight of our extremely discreet servants?"

"Then we know for good and all if they're little tribesmen who chirp like bobolinks or handsome South American yacht bums. But that won't happen. They may, in fact they undoubtedly do, see us, but we'll never catch sight of them. No matter how brilliantly we try to outwit them."

"You think they watch us?"

"I'm sure that's one of their main jobs."

"Even when we're in bed? Even when we…you know."

"Especially then," Ballard said.

"What do we think about that, Ballard? Do we love the whole idea, or does it make us sick? You first."

"Neither one. We can't do anything about it, so we might as well forget it. I think being able to watch us is one of the ways they're paid—these tribes don't have much use for money. And because they're always there, they can step in and help us when we need it, at the end."

"So it's like love," said Sandrine.

"Tough love, there at the finish. Let's go over and try the staircase."

"Hold on. When we were out on deck, you told me that you felt you were being watched, and that it was the first time you'd ever had that feeling."

"Yes, that was different—I don't *feel* the natives watching me, I just assume they're doing it. It's the only way to explain how they can stay out of sight all the time."

As they moved across the dining room to the inner door, for the first time Sandrine noticed a curtain the color of a dark camel hair coat hanging up at the top of the room's oval. Until that moment, she had taken it for a wall too small and oddly shaped to be covered with bookshelves. The curtain shifted a bit, she thought: a tiny ripple occurred in the fabric, as if it had been breathed upon.

There's one of them now, she thought. *I bet they have their own doors and their own staircases.*

For a moment, she was disturbed by a vision of the yacht honeycombed with narrow passages and runways down which beetled small red-brown figures with matted black hair and faces like dull, heavy masks. Now and then the little figures paused to peer through chinks in the walls. It made her feel violated, a little, but at the same time immensely proud of the body that the unseen and silent attendants were privileged to gaze at. The thought of these mysterious little people watching what Ballard did to that body, and she to his, caused a thrill of deep feeling to course upward through her body.

"Stop daydreaming, Sandrine, and get over here." Ballard held the door that led to the gray landing and the metal staircase.

"You go first," she said, and Ballard moved through the frame while still holding the door. As soon as she was through, he stepped around her to grasp the gray metal rail and begin moving down the stairs.

"What makes you so sure the galley's downstairs?"

"Galleys are always downstairs."

"And why do you want to go there, again?"

"One: because they ordered us not to. Two: because I'm curious about what goes on in that kitchen. And three: I also want to get a look at the wine cellar. How can they keep giving us these amazing wines? Remember what we drank with lunch?"

"Some stupid red. It tasted good, though."

"That stupid red was a '55 Chateau Petrus. Two years older than you."

Ballard led her down perhaps another dozen steps, arrived at a landing, and saw one more long staircase leading down to yet another landing.

"How far down can this galley be?" she asked.

"Good question."

"This boat has a bottom, after all."

"It has a hull, yes."

"Shouldn't we actually have gone past it by now? The bottom of the boat?"

"You'd think so. Okay, maybe this is it."

The final stair ended at a gray landing that opened out into a narrow gray corridor leading to what appeared to be a large, empty room. Ballard looked down into the big space, and experienced a violent reluctance, a mental and physical refusal, to go down there and look further into the room: it was prohibited by an actual taboo. That room was not for him, it was none of his business, period. Chilled, he turned from the corridor and at last saw what was directly before him. What had appeared to be a high gray wall was divided in the middle and bore two brass panels at roughly chest height. The wall was a doorway.

"What do you want to do?" Sandrine asked.

Ballard placed a hand on one of the panels and pushed. The door swung open, revealing a white tile floor, metal racks filled with cast-iron pans, steel bowls, and other cooking implements. The light was a low, diffused dimness. Against the side wall, three sinks of varying sizes bulged downward beneath their faucets. He could see the inner edge of a long, shiny metal counter. Far back, a yellow propane tank clung to a range with six burners, two ovens, and a big griddle. A faint mewing, a tiny *skritch skritch skritch* came to him from the depths of the kitchen.

"Look, is there any chance...?" Sandrine whispered.

In a normal voice, Ballard said "No. They're not in here right now, whoever they are. I don't think they are, anyhow."

"So does that mean we're supposed to go inside?"

"How would I know?" He looked over his shoulder at her. "Maybe we're not *supposed* to do anything, and we just decide one way or the other. But here we are, anyhow. I say we go in, right? If it feels wrong, smells wrong, whatever, we boogie on out."

"You first," she said.

Without opening the door any wider, Ballard slipped into the kitchen. Before he was all the way in, he reached back and grasped Sandrine's wrist.

"Come along now."

"You don't have to drag me, I was right behind you. You bully."

"I'm not a bully, I just don't want to be in here by myself."

"All bullies are cowards, too."

She edged in behind him and glanced quickly from side to side. "I didn't think you could have a kitchen like this on a yacht."

"You can't," he said. "Look at that gas range. It must weigh a thousand pounds."

She yanked her wrist out of his hand. "It's hard to see in here, though. Why is the light so fucking weird?"

They were edging away from the door, Sandrine so close behind that Ballard could feel her breath on his neck.

"There aren't any light fixtures, see? No overhead lights, either."

He looked up and saw, far above, only a dim white-gray ceiling that stretched away a great distance on either side. Impossibly, the "galley" seemed much wider than the *Blinding Light* itself.

"I don't like this," he said.

"Me, neither."

"We're really not supposed to be here," he said, thinking of that other vast room down at the end of the corridor, and said to himself, *That's what they call the "engine room," we absolutely can't even glance that way again, can't can't can't, the "engines" would be way too much for us.*

The mewing and skritching, which had momentarily fallen silent, started up again, and in the midst of what felt and tasted to him like panic, Ballard had a vision of a kitten trapped behind a piece of kitchen equipment. He stepped forward and leaned over to peer into the region beyond the long counter and beside the enormous range. Two funny striped cabinets about five feet tall stood there side by side.

"Do you hear a cat?" he asked.

"If you think that's a cat...," Sandrine said, a bit farther behind him than she had been at first.

The cabinets were cages, and what he had seen as stripes were their bars. "Oh," Ballard said, and sounded as though he had been punched in the stomach.

"Damn you, you started to bleed through your suit jacket," Sandrine whispered. "We have to get out of here, fast."

Ballard scarcely heard her. In any case, if he were bleeding, it was of no consequence. They knew what to do about bleeding. Here on the other hand, perhaps sixty feet away in this preposterous "galley," was a phenomenon he had never before witnessed. The first cage contained a thrashing beetle-like insect nearly too large for it. This gigantic insect was the source of the mewing and scratching. One of its mandibles rasped at a bar as the creature struggled to roll forward or back, producing noises of insect-distress. Long smeary wounds in the wide middle area between its scrabbling legs oozed a yellow ichor.

Horrified, Ballard looked hastily into the second cage, which he had thought empty but for a roll of blankets, or towels, or the like, and discovered that the blankets or towels were occupied by a small boy from one of the river tribes who was gazing at him through the bars. The boy's eyes looked hopeless and dead. Half of his shoulder seemed to have been sliced away, and a long, thin strip of bone gleamed white against a great scoop of red. The arm half-extended through the bars concluded in a dark, messy stump.

The boy opened his mouth and released, almost too softly to be heard, a single high-pitched musical note. Pure, accurate, well defined, clearly a word charged with some deep emotion, the note hung in the air for a brief moment, underwent a briefer half-life, and was gone.

"What's that?" Sandrine said.

"Let's get out of here."

He pushed her through the door, raced around her, and began charging up the stairs. When they reached the top of the steps and threw themselves into the dining room, Ballard collapsed onto the floor, then rolled onto his back, heaving in great quantities of air. His chest rose and fell, and with every exhalation he moaned. A portion of his left side pulsing with pain felt warm and wet. Sandrine leaned against the wall, breathing heavily in a less convulsive way. After perhaps thirty seconds, she managed to say, “I trust that was a bird down there.”

“Um. Yes.” He placed his hand on his chest, then held it up like a stop sign, indicating that he would soon have more to say. After a few more great heaving lungfuls of air, he said, “Toucan. In a big cage.”

“You were that frightened by a kind of parrot?”

He shook his head slowly from side to side on the polished floor. “I didn’t want them to catch us down there. It seemed dangerous, all of a sudden. Sorry.”

“You’re bleeding all over the floor.”

“Can you get me a new bandage pad?”

Sandrine pushed herself off the wall and stepped toward him. From his perspective, she was as tall as a statue. Her eyes glittered. “Screw you, Ballard. I’m not your servant. You can come with me. It’s where we’re going, anyhow.”

He pushed himself upright and peeled off his suit jacket before standing up. The jacket fell to the floor with a squishy thump. With blood-dappled fingers, he unbuttoned his shirt and let that, too, fall to the floor.

“Just leave those things there,” Sandrine said. “The invisible crew will take care of them.”

“I imagine you’re right.” Ballard managed to get to his feet without staggering. Slow-moving blood continued to ooze down his left side.

“We have to get you on the table,” Sandrine said. “Hold this over the wound for right now, okay?”

She handed him a folded white napkin, and he clamped it over his side. “Sorry. I’m not as good at stitches as you are.”

“I’ll be fine,” Ballard said, and began moving, a bit haltingly, toward the next room.

“Oh, sure. You always are. But you know what I like about what we just did?”

For once he had no idea what she might say. He waited for it.

“That amazing food we loved so much was toucan! Who would’ve guessed? You’d think toucan would taste sort of like chicken, only a lot worse.”

“Life is full of surprises.”

In the bedroom, Ballard kicked off his shoes, pulled his trousers down over his hips, and stepped out of them.

"You can leave your socks on," said Sandrine, "but let's get your undies off, all right?"

"I need your help."

Sandrine grasped the waistband of his boxers and pulled them down, but they snagged on his penis. "Ballard is aroused, surprise number two." She unhooked his shorts, let them drop to the floor, batted his erection down, and watched it bounce back up. "Barkis is willin', all right."

"Let's get into the workroom," he said.

"Aye aye, *mon capitain.*" Sandrine closed her hand on his erection and said, "Want to go there on-deck, give the natives a look at your magnificent manliness? Shall we increase the index of penis envy among the river tribes by a really big factor?"

"Let's just get in there, okay?"

She pulled him into the workroom and only then released his erection.

A wheeled aluminum tray had been rolled up beside the worktable. Sometimes it was not given to them, and they were forced to do their work with their hands and whatever implements they had brought with them. Today, next to the array of knives of many kinds and sizes, cleavers, wrenches, and hammers lay a pack of surgical thread and a stainless steel needle still warm from the autoclave.

Ballard sat down on the worktable, pushed himself along until his heels had cleared the edge, and lay back. Sandrine threaded the needle and, bending over to get close to the wound, began to do her patient, expert stitching.

1982

"OH, HERE you are," said Sandrine, walking into the sitting room of their suite to find Ballard lying on one of the sofas, reading a book whose title she could not quite make out. Because both of his hands were heavily bandaged, he was having some difficulty turning the pages. "I've been looking all over for you."

He glanced up, frowning. "All over? Does that mean you went down the stairs?"

"No, of course not. I wouldn't do anything like that alone, anyhow."

"And just to make sure...You didn't go up the stairs, either, did you?"

Sandrine came toward him, shaking her head. "No, I'd never do that, either. But I want to tell you something. I thought *you* might have decided to take a look upstairs. By yourself, to sort of protect me in a way I never want to be protected."

"Of course," Ballard said, closing his book on an index finger that protruded from the bulky white swath of bandage. "You'd hate me if I ever tried to protect you, especially by doing something sneaky. I knew that about you when you were fifteen years old."

"When I was fifteen, you did protect me."

He smiled at her. "I exercised an atypical amount of restraint."

His troublesome client, Sandrine's father, had told him one summer day that a business venture required him to spend a week in Mexico City. Could he think of anything acceptable that might occupy his daughter during that time, she being a teenager a bit too prone to independence and exploration? Let her stay with me, Ballard had said. The guest room has its own bathroom and a TV. I'll take her out to theaters at night, and to the Met and Moma during the day when I'm not doing my job. When I *am* doing my job, she can bat around the city by herself the way she does now. Extraordinary man you are, the client had said, and allow me to reinforce that by letting you know that about a month ago my daughter just amazed me one morning by telling me that she liked you. You have no idea how god-damned fucking unusual that is. That she talked to me at all is staggering, and that she actually announced that she liked one of my friends is stupefying. So yes, please, thank you, take Sandrine home with you, please do, escort her hither and yon.

When the time came, he drove a compliant Sandrine to his house in Harrison, where he explained that although he would not have sex with her until she was at least eighteen, there were many other ways they could express themselves. And although it would be years before they could be naked together, for the present they would each be able to be naked before the other. Fifteen-year-old Sandrine, who had been expecting to use all her arts of bad temper, insult, duplicity, and evasiveness to escape ravishment by this actually pretty interesting old guy, responded to these conditions with avid interest. Ballard announced another prohibition no less serious, but even more personal.

"I can't cut myself anymore?" she asked. "Fuck you, Ballard, you loved it when I showed you my arm. Did my father put you up to this?" She began looking frantically for her bag, which Ballard's valet had already removed to the guest rooms.

"Not at all. Your father would try to kill me if he knew what I was going to do to you. And you to me, when it's your turn."

"So if I can't cut myself, what exactly happens instead?"

"*I* cut you," Ballard said. "And I do it a thousand times better than you ever did. I'll cut you so well no one will ever be able to tell it happened, unless they're right on top of you."

"You think I'll be satisfied with some wimpy little cuts no one can even see? Fuck you all over again."

"Those cuts no one can see will be incredibly painful. And then I'll take the pain away, so you can experience it all over again."

Sandrine found herself abruptly caught up by a rush of feelings that seemed to originate in a deep region located just below her ribcage. At least for the moment, this flood of unnamable emotions blotted out her endless grudges and frustrations, also the chronic bad temper they engendered.

"And during this process, Sandrine, I will become deeply familiar, profoundly familiar with your body, so that when at last we are able to enjoy sex with each other, I will know how to give you the most amazing pleasure. I'll know every inch of you, I'll have your whole gorgeous map in my head. And you will do the same with me."

Sandrine had astonished herself by agreeing to this program on the spot, even to abstain from sex until she turned eighteen. Denial, too, was a pain she could learn to savor. At that point Ballard had taken her upstairs to the guest suite, and soon after down the hallway to what he called his "workroom."

"Oh my God," she said, taking it in, "I can't believe it. This is real. And you, you're real, too."

"During the next three years, whenever you start hating everything around you and feel as though you'd like to cut yourself again, remember that I'm here. Remember that this room exists. There'll be many days and nights when we can be here together."

In this fashion had Sandrine endured the purgatorial remainder of her days at Dalton. And when she and Ballard at last made love, pleasure and pain had become presences nearly visible in the room at the moment she screamed in the ecstasy of release.

"You dirty, dirty, dirty old man," she said, laughing.

A few years after that, Ballard overheard some Chinese bankers, clients of his firm for whom he had several times rendered his services, speaking in soft Mandarin about a yacht anchored in the Amazon basin; he needed no more.

"I want to go off the boat for a couple of hours when we get to Manaus," Sandrine said. "I feel like getting back in the world again, at least for a little while. This little private bubble of ours is completely cut off from everything else."

"Which is why—"

"Which is why it works, and why we like it, I understand, but half the time I can't stand it, either. I don't live the way you do, always flying off to interesting places to perform miracles…"

"Try spending a rainy afternoon in Zurich holding some terminally anxious banker's hand."

"Not that it matters, especially, but you don't mind, do you?"

"Of course not. I need some recuperation time, anyhow. This was a little severe." He held up one thickly bandaged hand. "Not that I'm complaining."

"You'd better not!"

"I'll only complain if you stay out too late—or spend too much of your father's money!"

"What could I buy in Manaus? And I'll make sure to be back before dinner. Have you noticed? The food on this weird boat is getting better and better every day?"

"I know, yes, but for now I seem to have lost my appetite," Ballard said. He had a quick mental vision of a metal cage from which something hideous was struggling to escape. It struck an oddly familiar note, as of something half-remembered, but Ballard was made so uncomfortable by the image in his head that he refused to look at it any longer.

"Will they just know that I want to dock at Manaus?"

"Probably, but you could write them a note. Leave it on the bed. Or on the dining room table."

"I have a pen in my bag, but where can I find some paper?"

"I'd say, look in any drawer. You'll probably find all the paper you might need."

Sandrine went to the little table beside him, pulled open its one drawer and found a single sheet of thick, cream-colored stationery headed *Sweet Delight.* An Omas roller-ball pen, much nicer than the Pilot she had liberated from their hotel in Rio, lay angled atop the sheet of stationery. In her formal, almost italic handwriting, Sandrine wrote *Please dock at Manaus. I would like to spend two or three hours ashore.*

"Should I sign it?"

Ballard shrugged. "There's just the two of us. Initial it."

She drew a graceful, looping S under her note and went into the dining room, where she squared it off in the middle of the table. When she returned to the sitting room, she asked, "And now I just wait? Is that how it works? Just because I found a piece of paper and a pen, I'm supposed to trust this crazy system?"

"You know as much as I do, Sandrine. But I'd say, yes, just wait a little while, yes, that's how it works, and yes, you might as well trust it. There's no reason to be bitchy."

"I have to stay in practice," she said, and lurched sideways as the yacht bumped against something hard and came to an abrupt halt.

"See what I mean?"

When he put the book down in his lap, Sandrine saw that it was *Tono Bungay.* She felt a hot, rapid flare of irritation that the book was not something like *The Women's Room,* which could teach him things he needed to know: and hadn't he already read *Tono Bungay*?

"Look outside, try to catch them tying us up and getting out that walkway thing."

"You think we're in Manaus already?"

"I'm sure we are."

"That's ridiculous. We scraped against a barge or something."

"Nonetheless, we have come to a complete halt."

Sandrine strode briskly to the on-deck door, threw it open, gasped, then stepped outside. The yacht had already been tied up at a long yellow dock at which two yachts smaller than theirs rocked in a desultory brown tide. No crewmen were in sight. The dock led to a wide concrete apron across which men of European descent and a few natives pushed wheelbarrows and consulted clipboards and pulled on cigars while pointing out distant things to other men. It looked false and stagy, like the first scene in a bad musical about New Orleans. An avenue began in front of a row of warehouses, the first of which was painted with the slogan MANAUS AMAZONA. The board walkway with rope handrails had been set in place.

"Yeah, okay," she said. "We really do seem to be docked at Manaus."

"Don't stay away too long."

"I'll stay as long as I like," she said.

The avenue leading past the façades of the warehouses seemed to run directly into the center of the city, visible now to Sandrine as a gathering of tall office buildings and apartment blocks that thrust upward from the jumble of their surroundings like an outcropping of mountains. The skyscrapers were blue-gray in color, the lower surrounding buildings a scumble of brown, red, and yellow that made Sandrine think of Cézanne, even of Seurat: dots of color that suggested walls and roofs. She thought she could walk to the center of the city in no more than forty-five minutes, which left her about two hours to do some exploring and have lunch.

Nearly an hour later, Sandrine trudged past the crumbling buildings and broken windows on crazed, tilting sidewalks under a domineering sun. Sweat ran down her forehead and cheeks and plastered her dress to her body. The air seemed half water, and her lungs strained to draw in oxygen. The office buildings did not seem any nearer than at the start of her walk. If she had seen a taxi, she would have taken it back to the port, but only a few cars and pickups rolled along the broad avenue. The dark, half-visible men driving these vehicles generally leaned over their steering wheels and stared at her, as if women were rare in Manaus. She wished she had thought to cover her hair, and was sorry she had left her sunglasses behind.

Then she became aware that a number of men were following her, how many she could not tell, but more than two. They spoke to each other in low, hoarse voices, now and then laughing at some remark sure to be at Sandrine's expense. Although her feet had begun to hurt, she began moving more quickly. Behind her, the men kept pace with her, neither gaining nor falling back. After another two blocks, Sandrine gave in to her sense of alarm and glanced over her shoulder. Four men in dark hats and shapeless, slept-in suits had ranged themselves across the width of the sidewalk. One of them called out to her in a language she did not understand; another emitted a wet, mushy laugh. The man at the curb jumped down into the street, trotted across the empty avenue, and picked up his pace on the sidewalk opposite until he had drawn a little ahead of Sandrine.

She felt utterly alone and endangered. And because she felt in danger, a scorching anger blazed up within her: at herself for so stupidly putting herself at risk, at the men behind her for making her feel frightened, for ganging up on her. She did not know what she was going to have to do, but she was not going to let those creeps get any closer to her than they were now. Twisting to her right, then to her left, Sandrine removed her shoes and rammed them into her bag. They were watching her, the river scum; even the man on the other side of the avenue had stopped moving and was staring at her from beneath the brim of his hat.

Literally testing the literal ground, Sandrine walked a few paces over the paving stones, discovered that they were at any rate not likely to cut her feet, gathered herself within, and, like a race horse bursting from the gate, instantly began running as fast as she could. After a moment in which her pursuers were paralyzed with surprise, they too began to run. The man on the other side of the street jumped down from the curb and began sprinting toward her. His shoes made a sharp *tick-tick* sound when they met the stony asphalt. As the ticks grew louder, Sandrine heard him inhaling great quantities of air. Before he could reach her, she came to a cross street and wheeled in, her bag bouncing at her hip, her legs stretching out to devour yard after yard of stony ground.

Unknowingly, she had entered a slum. The structures on both sides of the street were half-collapsed huts and shanties made of mismatched wooden planks, of metal sheeting and tarpaper. She glimpsed faces peering out of greasy windows and sagging, cracked-open doors. Some of the shanties before her were shops with soft drink cans and bottles of beer arrayed on the window sills. People were spilling from little tarpaper and sheet-metal structures out into the street, already congested with abandoned cars, empty pushcarts, and cartons of fruit for sale. Garbage lay everywhere. The women who watched Sandrine streak by displayed no interest in her plight.

Yet the slum's chaos was a blessing, Sandrine thought: the deeper she went, the greater the number of tiny narrow streets sprouting off the one she had taken from the avenue. It was a feverish, crowded warren, a *favela*, the kind of place you would never escape had you the bad luck to have been born there. And while outside this rat's nest the lead man chasing her had been getting dangerously near, within its boundaries the knots of people and the obstacles of cars and carts and mounds of garbage had slowed him down. Sandrine found that she could dodge all of these obstacles with relative ease. The next time she spun around a corner, feet skidding on a slick pad of rotting vegetables, she saw what looked to her like a miracle: an open door revealing a hunched old woman draped in black rags, beckoning her in.

Sandrine bent her legs, called on her youth and strength, jumped off the ground, and sailed through the open door. The old woman only just got out of the way in time to avoid being knocked down. She was giggling, either at Sandrine's athleticism or because she had rescued her from the pursuing thugs. When Sandrine had cleared her doorway and was scrambling to avoid ramming into the wall, the old woman darted forward and slammed her door shut. Sandrine fell to her knees in a small room suddenly gone very dark. A slanting shaft of light split the murk and illuminated a rectangular space on the floor covered by a threadbare rug no longer of any identifiable color. Under the light, the rug seemed at once utterly worthless and extraordinarily beautiful.

The old woman shuffled into the shaft of light and uttered an incomprehensible word that sounded neither Spanish nor Portuguese. A thousand wayward wrinkles like knife cuts, scars, and stitches had been etched into her white, elongated face. Her nose had a prominent hook, and her eyes shone like dark stones at the bottom of a fast, clear stream. Then she laid an upright index finger against her sunken lips and with her other hand gestured toward the door. Sandrine listened. In seconds, multiple footsteps pounded past the old woman's little house. Leading the pack was *tick tick tick.* The footsteps clattered up the narrow street and disappeared into the ordinary clamor.

Hunched over almost parallel to the ground, the old woman mimed hysterical laughter. Sandrine mouthed *Thank you, thank you,* thinking that her intention would be clear if the words were not. Still mock-laughing, her unknown savior shuffled closer, knitting and folding her long, spotted hands. She had the ugliest hands Sandrine had ever seen, knobbly arthritic fingers with filthy, ragged nails. She hoped the woman was not going to stroke her hair or pat her face: she would have to let her do it, however nauseated she might feel. Instead, the old woman moved right past her, muttering what sounded like *Munna, munna, num.*

Outside on the street, the ticking footsteps once again became audible. Someone began knocking, hard, on an adjacent door.

Only half-visible at the rear of the room, the old woman turned toward Sandrine and beckoned her forward with an urgent gesture of her bony hand. Sandrine moved toward her, uncertain of what was going on.

In an urgent, raspy whisper: *Munna! Num!*

The old woman appeared to be bowing to the baffled Sandrine, whose sense of peril had begun again to boil up within her. A pane of greater darkness slid open behind the old woman, and Sandrine finally understood that her savior had merely bent herself more deeply to turn a doorknob.

Num! Num!

Sandrine obeyed orders and *nummed* past her beckoning hostess. Almost instantly, instead of solid ground, her foot met a vacancy, and she nearly tumbled down what she finally understood to be a staircase. Only her sense of balance kept her upright: she was grateful she still had all of her crucial toes. Behind her, the door slammed shut. A moment later, she heard the clicking of a lock.

BACK ON the yacht, Ballard slipped a bookmark into *Tono Bungay* and for the first time, at least for what he thought was the first time, regarded the pair of red lacquered cabinets against the wall beside him. Previously, he had taken them in, but never really examined them. About four feet high and three feet wide, they appeared to be Chinese and were perhaps moderately valuable. Brass fittings with latch pins held them closed in front, so they were easily opened.

The thought of lifting the pins and opening the cabinets aroused both curiosity and an odd dread in Ballard. For a moment, he had a vision of a great and forbidden room deep in the bowels of the yacht where enormous spiders ranged across rotting, heaped-up corpses. (With wildly variant details, visions of exactly this sort had visited Ballard ever since his adolescence.) He shook his head to clear it of this vision, and when that failed, struck his bandaged left hand against the padded arm of the sofa. Bright, rolling waves of pain forced a gasp from him, and the forbidden room with its spiders and corpses zipped right back to wherever had given it birth.

Was this the sort of dread he was supposed to obey, or the sort he was supposed to ignore? Or if not ignore, because that was always unwise and in some sense dishonorable, acknowledge but persist in the face of anyway? Cradling his throbbing hand against his chest, Ballard let the book slip off his lap and got to his feet, eyeing the pair of shiny cabinets. If asked to inventory the contents of the sitting room, he would have forgotten to list them. Presumably that meant he was supposed to overlook his foreboding and investigate the contents of these vertical little Chinese chests. *They* wanted him to open the cabinets, if *he* wanted to.

Still holding his electrocuted left hand to his chest, Ballard leaned over and brought his exposed right index finger in contact with the box on the left. No heat came from it, and no motion. It did not hum, it did not quiver, however delicately. At least six or seven coats of lacquer had been applied to the thing—he felt as though he were looking into a deep river of red lacquer.

Ballard hunkered and used his index finger to push the brass latch pin up and out of the ornate little lock. It swung down on an intricate little cord he had not previously noticed. The door did not open by itself, as he had hoped. Once again, he had to make a choice, for it was not too late to drop the brass pin back into its latch. He could choose not to look; he could let the *Sweet Delight* keep its secrets. But as before, Ballard acknowledged the dread he was feeling, then dropped his hip to the floor, reached out, and flicked the door open with his fingernail. Arrayed on the cabinet's three shelves were what appeared to be photographs in neat stacks. Polaroids, he thought. He took the first stack of photos from the cabinet and looked down at the topmost one. What Ballard saw there had two contradictory effects on him. He became so light-headed he feared he might faint; and he almost ejaculated into his trousers.

TAKING CARE not to tumble, Sandrine moved in the darkness back to the top of the staircase, found the door with her fingertips, and pounded. The door rattled in its frame but did not give. "Open up, lady!" she shouted. "Are you *kidding*? Open this door!" She banged her fists against the unmoving wood, thinking that although the old woman undoubtedly did not speak English, she could hardly misunderstand what Sandrine was saying. When her fists began to hurt and her throat felt ragged, the strangeness of what had just happened opened before her: it was like…like a fairy tale! She had been duped, tricked, flummoxed; she had been trapped. The world had closed in on her, as a steel trap snaps shut on the leg of a bear.

"Please!" she yelled, knowing it was useless. She would not be able to beg her way out of this confinement. Here, the Golden Shower of Shit did not apply. "Please let me out!" A few more bangs of her fist, a few more shouted pleas to be set free, to be *let go, released.* She thought she heard her ancient captor chuckling to herself.

Two possibilities occurred to her: that her pursuers had driven her to this place and the old woman was in league with them; and that they had not and she was not. The worse by far of these options was the second, that to escape her rapists she had fled into a psychopath's dungeon. Maybe the old woman wanted to starve her to death. Maybe she wanted to soften her up so she'd be easy to kill. Or maybe she was just keeping her as a snack for some monstrous get of hers, some overgrown looney-tunes son with pinwheel eyes and horrible teeth and a vast appetite for stray women.

More to exhaust all of her possibilities than because she imagined they possessed any actual substance, Sandrine turned carefully around, planted a hand on the earthen wall beside her, and began making her way down the stairs in the dark. It would lead to some spider-infested cellar, she knew, a foul-smelling hole where ugly, discarded things waited thug-like in the seamless dark to inflict injury upon anyone who entered their realm. She would grope her way from wall to wall, feeling for another door, for a high window, for any means to escape, knowing all the while that earthen cellars in shabby slum dwellings never had separate exits.

Five steps down, it occurred to Sandrine that she might not

have been the first woman to be locked into this awful basement, and that instead of broken chairs and worn-out tools she might find herself knocking against a ribcage or two, a couple of femurs, that her foot might land on the jawbone, that she might step on somebody's forehead! Her body all of a sudden shook, and her mind went white, and for a few moments Sandrine was on the verge of coming unglued: she pictured herself drawn up into a fetal ball, shuddering, weeping, whimpering. For a moment this dreadful image seemed unbearably tempting.

Then she thought, *Why the FUCK isn't Ballard here?*

Ballard was one hell of a tricky dude, he was full of little surprises, you could never really predict what he'd feel like doing, and he was a brilliant problem-solver. That's what Ballard did for a living, he flew around the world mopping up other people's messes. The only reason Sandrine knew him at all was that Ballard had materialized in a New Jersey motel room where good old Dad, Lauritzen Loy, had been dithering over the corpse of a strangled whore, then caused the whore to vanish, the bloody sheets to vanish, and for all she knew the motel to vanish also. Two hours later a shaken but sober Lauritzen Loy reported to work in an immaculate and spotless Armani suit and Brioni tie. (Sandrine had known the details of her father's vile little peccadillo for years.) Also, and this quality meant that his presence would have been particularly valuable down in the witch-hag's cellar, although Ballard might have looked as though he had never picked up anything heavier than a briefcase, he was in fact astonishingly strong, fast, and smart. If you were experiencing a little difficulty with a dragon, Ballard was the man for you.

While meditating upon the all-round excellence of her longtime lover and wishing for him more with every fresh development of her thought, Sandrine had been continuing steadily on her way down the stairs. When she reached the part about the dragon, it came to her that she had been on these earthen stairs far longer than she had expected. Sandrine thought she was now actually beneath the level of the cellar she had expected to enter. The fairy tale feeling came over her again, of being held captive in a world without rational rules and orders, subject to deep patterns unknown to or rejected in the daylit world. In a flash of insight, it came to her that this fairytale world had much in common with her childhood.

To regain control of herself, perhaps most of all to shake off the sense of gloom-laden helplessness evoked by thoughts of childhood, Sandrine began to count the steps as she descended. Down into the earth they went, the dry firm steps that met her feet, twenty more, then forty, then fifty. At a hundred and one, she felt light-headed and weary, and sat down in the darkness. She felt like weeping. The long stairs were a grave, leading nowhere but to itself. Hope, joy, and desire had fled, even boredom and petulance had fled, hunger, lust, and anger were no more. She felt tired and empty. Sandrine leaned a shoulder against the earthen wall, shuddered once, and realized she was crying only a moment before she fled into unconsciousness.

In that same instant she passed into an ongoing dream, as if she had wandered into the middle of a story, more accurately a point far closer to its ending. Much, maybe nearly everything of interest, had already happened. Sandrine lay on a mess of filthy blankets at the bottom of a cage. The Golden Shower of Shit had sufficiently relaxed, it seemed, as to permit the butchering of entire slabs of flesh from her body, for much of the meat from her right shoulder had been sliced away. The wound reported a dull, wavering ache that spoke of those wonderful objects, Ballard's narcotic painkillers. So close together were the narrow bars, she could extend only a hand, a wrist, an arm. In her case, an arm, a wrist, and a stump. The hand was absent from the arm Sandrine had slipped through the bars, and someone had cauterized the wounded wrist.

The Mystery of the Missing Hand led directly to Cage Number One, where a giant bug-creature sat crammed in at an angle, filling nearly the whole of the cage, mewing softly, and trying to saw through the bars with its remaining mandible. It had broken the left one on the bars, but it was not giving up, it was a bug, and bugs don't quit. Sandrine was all but certain that when in possession of both mandibles, that is to say before capture, this huge *thing* had used them to saw off her hand, which it had then promptly devoured. The giant bugs were the scourge of the river tribes. However, the Old Ones, the Real People, the Cloud Huggers, the Tree Spirits, the archaic Sacred Ones who spoke in birdsong and called themselves **We** had so shaped the River and the Forest, which had given them birth, that the meat of the giant bugs tasted exceptionally good, and a giant bug guilty of eating a person or parts of a person became by that act overwhelmingly delicious, like manna, like the food of paradise for human beings. We were feeding bits of Sandrine to the captured bug that it might yield stupendous meals for the Sandrine and Ballard upstairs.

Sandrine awakened crying out in fear and horror, scattering tears she could not see.

Enough of that. Yes, quite enough of quivering; it was time to decide what to do next. Go back and try to break down the door, or keep going down and see what happens? Sandrine hated the idea of giving up and going backward. She levered herself upright and resumed her descent with stair number one hundred and two.

At stair three hundred she passed through another spasm of weepy trembling, but soon conquered it and moved on. By the four hundredth stair she was hearing faint carnival music and seeing sparkly light-figments flit through the darkness like illuminated moths. Somewhere around stair five hundred she realized that the numbers had become mixed up in her head, and stopped counting. She saw a grave that wasn't a grave, merely darkness, and she saw her old tutor at Clare, a cool, detached Don named Quentin Jester who said things like, "If I had a lifetime with you, Miss Loy, we'd both know a deal more than we do at present," but she closed her eyes and shook her head and sent him packing.

Many stairs later, Sandrine's thigh muscles reported serious aches, and her arms felt extraordinarily heavy. So did her head, which kept lolling forward to rest on her chest. Her stomach complained, and she said to herself, *Wish I had a nice big slice of sautéed giant bug right about now*, and chuckled at how crazy she had become in so short a time. Giant bug! Even good old Dad, old LL, who often respected sanity in others but wished for none of it himself, drew the line at dining on giant insects. And here came yet another proof of her deteriorating mental condition, that despite her steady progress deeper and deeper underground, Sandrine could almost sort of half-persuade herself that the darkness before her seemed weirdly less dark than only a moment ago. This lunatic delusion clung to her step after step, worsening as she went. She said to herself, I'll hold up my hand,

and if I think I see it, I'll know it's good-by, real world, pack Old Tillie off to Bedlam. She stopped moving, closed her eyes, and raised her hand before her face. Slowly, she opened her eyes, and beheld...her hand!

The problem with the insanity defense lay in the irrevocable truth that it was really her hand before her, not a mad vision from Gothic literature but her actual, entirely earthly hand, at present grimy and crusted with dirt from its long contact with the wall. Sandrine turned her head and discovered that she could make out the wall, too, with its hard-packed earth showing here and there the pale string of a severed root, at times sending in her direction a little spray or shower of dusty particulate. Sandrine held her breath and looked down to what appeared to be the source of the illumination. Then she inhaled sharply, for it seemed to her that she could see, dimly and a long way down, the bottom of the stairs. A little rectangle of light burned away down there, and from it floated the luminous translucency that made it possible for her to see.

Too shocked to cry, too relieved to insist on its impossibility, Sandrine moved slowly down the remaining steps to the rectangle of light. Its warmth heated the air, the steps, the walls, and Sandrine herself, who only now registered that for most of her journey she had been half-paralyzed by the chill leaking from the earth. As she drew nearer to the light, she could finally make out details of what lay beneath her. She thought she saw a strip of concrete, part of a wooden barrel, the bottom of a ladder lying on the ground: the intensity of the light surrounding these enigmatic objects shrank and dwindled them, hollowed them out even as it drilled painfully into her eyes. Beneath her world existed another, its light a blinding dazzle.

When Sandrine had come within thirty feet of the blazing underworld, her physical relationship to it mysteriously altered. It seemed she no longer stepped downward, but moved across a slanting plane that leveled almost imperceptibly off. The dirt walls on either side fell back and melted to ghostly gray air, to nothing solid, until all that remained was the residue of dust and grime plastered over Sandrine's white dress, her hands and face, her hair. Heat reached her, the real heat of an incendiary sun, and human voices, and the clang and bang and underlying susurrus of machinery. She walked toward all of it, shading her eyes as she went.

Through the simple opening before her Sandrine moved, and the sun blazed down upon her, and her own moisture instantly soaked her filthy dress, and sweat turned the dirt in her hair to muddy trickles. She knew this place; the dazzling underworld was the world she had left. From beneath her shading hand Sandrine took in the wide concrete apron, the equipment she had noticed all that harrowing time ago and the equipment she had not, the men posturing for the benefit of other men, the sense of falsity and stagecraft and the incipient swelling of a banal unheard melody. The long yellow dock where on a sluggish umber tide three yachts slowly rocked, one of them the *Sweet Delight.*

In a warm breeze that was not a breeze, a soiled-looking scrap of paper flipped toward Sandrine over the concrete, at the last lifting off the ground to adhere to her leg. She bent down to peel it off and release it, and caught a strong, bitter whiff, unmistakably excremental, of the Amazon. The piece of paper wished to cling to her leg, and there it hung until the second tug of Sandrine's dirty fingers, when she observed that she was gripping not a scrap of paper but a Polaroid, now a little besmudged by contact with her leg. When she raised it to her face, runnels of dirt obscured portions of the image. She brushed away much of the dirt, but could still make no sense of the photograph, which appeared to depict some pig-like animal.

In consternation, she glanced to one side and found there, lounging against bollards and aping the idleness of degenerates and river louts, two of the men in shabby suits and worn-out hats who had pursued her into the slum. She straightened up in rage and terror, and to confirm what she already knew to be the case, looked to her other side and saw their companions. One of them waved to her. Sandrine's terror cooled before her perception that these guys had changed in some basic way. Maybe they weren't idle, exactly, but these men were more relaxed, less predatory than they had been on the avenue into Manaus.

They had their eyes on her, though, they were interested in what she was going to do. Then she finally got it: they were different because now she was where they had wanted her to be all along. They didn't think she would try to escape again, but they wanted to make sure. Sandrine's whole long adventure, from the moment she noticed she was being followed to the present, had been designed to funnel her back to the dock and the yacht. The four men, who were now smiling at her and nodding their behatted heads, had pushed her toward the witch-hag, for they were all in it together! Sandrine dropped her arms, took a step backward, and in amazement looked from side to side, taking in all of them. It had all been a trick; herded like a cow, she had been played. Falsity again; more stagecraft.

One of the nodding, smiling men held his palm up before his face, and the man beside him leaned forward and laughed into his fist, as if shielding a sneeze. Grinning at her, the first man went through his meaningless mime act once again, lifting his left hand and staring into its palm. Grinning even more widely, he pointed at Sandrine and shouted, "*Munna*!"

The man beside him cracked up, *Munna!,* what a wit, then whistled an odd little four-note melody that might have been a birdcall.

Experimentally, Sandrine raised her left hand, regarded it, and realized that she was still gripping the dirty little Polaroid photograph of a pig. Those two idiots off to her left waved their hands in ecstasy. She was doing the right thing, so *Munna*! right back atcha, buddy. She looked more closely at the Polaroid and saw that what it pictured was not actually a pig. The creature in the photo had a head and a torso, but little else. The eyes, nose, and ears were gone. A congeries of scars like punctuation marks, like snakes, like words in an unknown language, decorated the torso.

I know what Munna *means, and* Num, thought Sandrine, and for a moment experienced a spasm of stunning, utterly sexual warmth before she fully understood what had been given to her: that she recognized the man in the photo. The roar of oceans, of storm-battered leaves, filled her ears and caused her head to spin and wobble. Her fingers parted, and the Polaroid floated off in an artificial, wind-machine breeze that spun it around a couple of times before lifting it high above the port and winking it out of sight, lost in the bright hard blue above the *Sweet Delight.*

Sandrine found herself moving down the yellow length of the long dock.

Tough love, Ballard had said. To be given and received, at the end perfectly repaid by that which she had perhaps glimpsed but never witnessed, the brutal, exalted, slow-moving force that had sometimes rustled a curtain, sometimes moved through this woman her hair and body now dark with mud, had touched her between her legs, Sandrine, poor profane lost deluded most marvelously fated Sandrine.

1997

FROM THE galley they come, from behind the little dun-colored curtain in the dining room, from behind the bookcases in the handsome sitting room, from beneath the bed and the bloodstained metal table, through wood and fabric and the weight of years, **We** come, the Old Ones and Real People, the Cloud Huggers, **We** process slowly toward the center of the mystery **We** understand only by giving it unquestioning service. What remains of the clients and patrons lies, still breathing though without depth or force, upon the metal work table. It was always going to end this way, it always does, it can no other. Speaking in the high-pitched, musical language of birds that **We** taught the Pirahã at the beginning of time, **We** gather at the site of these ruined bodies, **We** worship their devotion to each other and the Great Task that grew and will grow on them, **We** treat them with grave tenderness as **We** separate what can and must be separated. Notes of the utmost liquid purity float upward from the mouths of **We** and print themselves upon the air. **We** know what they mean, though they have long since passed through the realm of words and gained again the transparency of music. **We** love and accept the weight and the weightlessness of music. When the process of separation is complete, through the old sacred inner channels **We** transport what the dear, still-living man and woman have each taken from the other's body down down down to the galley and the ravening hunger that burns ever within it.

Then. Then. With the utmost tenderness, singing the deep tuneless music at the heart of the ancient world, **We** gather up what remains of Ballard and Sandrine, armless and legless trunks, faces without features, their breath clinging to their mouths like wisps, carry them (in our arms, in baskets, in once-pristine sheets) across the deck and permit them to roll from our care, as they had always longed to do, and into that of the flashing furious little river-monarchs. **We** watch the water boil in a magnificence of ecstasy, and **We** sing for as long as it lasts.

LISA MANNETTI

THE DOUBLE LENS

A woman must have money and a room of her own if she is to write fiction.
—Virginia Woolf

"Abbot and Bessie, I believe I gave orders that Jane Eyre should be left in the red-room till I came to her myself." "O aunt! have pity! Forgive me! I cannot endure it—let me be punished some other way! I shall be killed if—"
—Charlotte Brontë, *Jane Eyre*

What do you know about this mendacity thing? Hell! I could write a book on it! Don't you know that? I could write a book on it and still not cover the subject? Well, I could, I could write a goddam book on it and still not cover the subject anywhere near enough!!—Think of all the lies I got to put up with!
—Tennessee Williams, *Cat on a Hot Tin Roof*

Truth? I do not know what the truth is anymore.
—William Styron, *Sophie's Choice*

Without words said, a wave of understanding rippled through the crowd. Oceania was at war with Eastasia! The next

moment there was a tremendous commotion. The banners and posters with which the square was decorated were all wrong! Quite half of them had the wrong faces on them. It was sabotage!
—George Orwell, *1984*

APRIL 1975

It was hard to say where all the trouble began, but one of the things Sue remembered most clearly was lying in bed in her fourth-floor walk-up apartment on East 83rd Street in Manhattan one night reading *Helter Skelter.* It scared her so badly (well-written as it was), she not only slept with the lights on for a week, she had to put the book aside every few hours and read something *sane. Mrs. Dalloway, To the Lighthouse, Orlando*—Woolf, she knew, had bouts of insanity and may have been mad when she walked carrying a large stone into the depths of the Ouse River, but her talent was enormous and she was someone a bright young 22-year-old woman who wanted to be a writer (a significant writer, like Woolf herself) could admire. Charles Manson—he was a crazy cultist—and no one around him and his decidedly unmerry band of follower-monsters was safe, that was for sure. Imagine, Sue thought: Manson thought he could ignite a race war he called Helter Skelter and take over the world and had ordered the brutal murders of seven people in Los Angeles back in '69. She remembered the headlines and she shuddered.

Sue Munsinger (oh how she loved that secret meaning of her name based on British dialect: Sue "Must Sing" it meant) knew she herself needed just what Woolf insisted (and in the seventies, Virginia was seen not just as a feminist prototype, but prophetic) women *must have* to write: Money and a room of one's own. Well, Sue had the room (shabby to the point, she often joked, that cockroaches weren't a problem because after however many millions of years of evolution, *they'd* been smart enough to avoid even taking a twelve-month lease on the studio apartment) and she had a salaried job—it just didn't pay very much.

The glamour factor, Sue supposed, was in part the reason her job didn't pay all that well. (*Don't be euphemistic* she wrote in her journal, *it's hard to live on $160 a week.* But at least she hadn't had to ask her parents for money to make up the rent or pay the light bills. Still, it wasn't *The New Yorker*, but she was a fact checker at the brashly sophisticated, trendy *New World Manhattan Magazine* and there *were* perks (concerts, movies, movie premiers, records, books—oh, the books!) and a certain amount of hob-nobbing with the well-known staff writers and getting fast, up-close glimpses of the famous: Truman (Capote), Andy (Warhol), Tennessee (Williams). Even if she couldn't call them by their first names to their faces, she could refer to them as *if* she could when she talked to her old college pals, and who would be the wiser? It was her first job out of school and she had a terrific boss and technically she was not a secretary; she had a title, "editorial assistant," and an apartment. What she didn't have was time to write fiction. Not at a job where she was expected to work forty hours a week but where in fact she routinely put in huge amounts of unpaid overtime and certainly not at workday's end when the job was done and she was dead-dog tired.

Sometimes she chided herself that it was really her own fault she wasn't concentrating enough on her poetry or fiction because in part, she knew, she was looking for a boyfriend (someone to love) after the betrayal she experienced when Tom Smith dropped her three weeks after they graduated from a good university in southern Connecticut. She didn't tell herself, even though he'd been ham-handed, he was adolescent and had a mean streak; no, she blamed herself. Then to compensate for the loss, she tried working harder and, as she frequently reminded herself, the job *was* fun. Well, there were some nervy moments. She'd been totally relieved when she didn't have to actually phone Paul Newman to check a quote about his latest film (*Slapstick*) because she'd had a crush on him since she was about twelve and didn't think she could actually speak to him over the phone. Not even incoherently. It never occurred to her she'd probably talk to an assistant's assistant, she was just glad the writer of that particular piece had done the checking himself and provided a short memo/transcript so the quote was deemed by the editorial powers good to go.

Not all the fact-checking jobs were simple. One rainy Tuesday morning a long, involved feature story came in from one of the British writers (the editor-in-chief really liked the Brits and, as a group, they seemed not only fun-loving and slightly zany—one rode a bicycle in the aisles of the open-plan newsroom-style office on occasion—but very bright and well-educated, too. And oh boy, she often told herself, those accents were terrific. Sexy, too.). This particular piece had been assigned by her own boss to a thirty-something dark-haired *bon vivant* named Antony Barr-Thorpe and it was about a large and growing religious cult called the GeoPeople Society. Everybody knew cults were on the rise: The Hare Krishnas wore saffron robes and chanted, and the Moonies were a front for the aggressive, political Unification church and it was never a good idea to buy the flowers or incense sticks or cheapjack (as Tony called it) they sold in the process of soliciting millions one buck at a time, and Sue had no problem getting quick verification of those facts from newspaper articles and the AP/UPI wire services on that sort of general statement. Before lunchtime, she was having trouble, though. According to what Tony Barr-Thorpe had written, that while the GeoPeople Society (run by a woman who was known as Mother Taranch) presented themselves as a group who wanted to save the planet and its people and were involved in a lot of good-works projects from drug rehab to disaster relief to working for world peace and democracy, those organizations were shells: They were, in fact, a totalitarian cult whose members practiced mind control and a host of other human rights abuses on the members who'd been sucked in *and* on outsiders they deemed "enemies." Tony's sources for the article were people who'd left GPS and according to the piece they were getting harassed like crazy: frivolous, expensive law suits (just like Moonies, this so-called church had millions and millions of dollars), they were being surveilled, their friends and loved ones were told lies about them (everything from the fact that they had venereal disease and worked as male or female prostitutes to the fact that they ran kiddie porn rings). The damages and fallout were horrific. The article came with proof in the form of pages and pages of stolen secret documents that showed the higher-ups from Mother Taraneh on down were the only ones in the know and that she and her select cronies were scamming for money and power. The newbies and low-level members came on board because they bought into a lot of the Joni Mitchell-type, anti-paving-paradise-and-putting-up-parking-lots, Earth Day philosophy and a heady dose of self-help claptrap that was supposed to make GP happier, healthier, wealthier and wiser.

"Tony," Sue said, "I've tried calling these numbers and I don't get through...nobody's even answering so that I can fact-check," she told him over the phone that first morning. And how am I going to get the officials to talk about this stuff—even though in the piece they're just denying what you've written?" There were disclaimers and quotes throughout the article that said the GPS had no such policies, that their aims were beyond reproach and that the information Tony ferreted out was bogus. People, their spokespersons maintained, flat out lied. She lit a cigarette and tapped the eraser end of a pencil while she listened.

"Look, love, their headquarters are right up there near Broadway. And their number's listed right in the Manhattan white pages. Just call, get someone on the phone...except for their inane slogan, they're going to deny it all anyhow...," Tony said.

"*GeoPeople Society: Earth, Its People, and the World...,*" Sue repeated. She glanced down at the galleys, the reporter's words spinning up at her and felt a rill of anxiety well up inside her. "Tony," she said, "this is going to sound slightly bonkers, but what if they come after *me*?"

"You, you're just a fact checker. My bum is on the line." He laughed.

"HELLO, I'M Susan Munsinger with *New World Manhattan Magazine*, and I'm fact-checking an article we're planning on publishing. I just want to ask a few questions, and confirm a few details, okay?"

"Well..."

"So the spiritual leader of your group is Mother Taraneh, correct?"

"Yes."

"And she models herself after Mother Theresa?" Sue went on.

"Mother Taraneh does not have to model herself after anyone," the woman on the other end of the line said. "Her own name means song, and through her own inner joy she is spreading God's truth—"

"But she dresses like Mother Theresa—with the royal blue stripe on the hem of her veil and—" Sue said, plowing on.

"Our holy Mother does her own good works."

Sue didn't want to antagonize her, but she couldn't resist. "Well, she's not going into leper colonies with food, is she?"

"There's no leprosy, as you know, here in the United States."

"What about worldwide?"

"We take care of people everywhere."

Sue said, "We've obtained insider information that in fact your organization does not tell new recruits everything and that they don't find out what they're really signing up for until months—sometimes years—later, and have paid over a lot of money."

"Not true," the pleasant-sounding woman who refused to give her name said. "And all the money donated by our parishioners comes from their hearts because they believe in the Mother's goodness."

"But don't you offer them free personality tests?"

"Yes, but it's so they can begin to open their minds to universal truth."

"You believe that psychology and psychiatry are all wrong, actually harmful, and so you use a machine, a sort of lie detector called the 'Emotional Response Analyzer' to—"

"—It's our version of the confessional and it's a religious artifact, a holy rite." The woman's voice was cold, supercilious, Sue thought.

Sue sped on. "We've heard that certain former members, like Marie Caswell for example, say they were forced into a virtual prison on one of your properties upstate, had no contact with friends or family, and could not even make phone calls or write letters."

It was the only question the anonymous woman even came close to answering. She shouted into the phone. "Marie Caswell is an OED. She's an embittered liar who was asked to leave because she was committing criminal acts and we refused to cover up for her!"

Sue felt a momentary confusion. Wasn't the OED the Oxford English Dictionary? "Pardon me," she said, "OED?"

"Official Enemy Declared!"

"Oh. Right. Well, one more thing. We've learned that Charles Manson—the convicted mass murderer—was affiliated with GPS. Can you tell me about that? Was he a member of the organization in California?"

"Charles Manson!" The voice was a shriek and Sue heard the

line click.

"Hung up on me," she said.

JUNE 1975

The next thing she knew, there *were* cockroaches in her apartment and she was out of a job. Sue Munsinger was heartbroken. She wrote in her journal, "Virginia Woolf speaks of the 'great interval of nothingness' after her own mother died, and I feel the same kind of numbness, the sense of being bereft."

Her boss had been on maternity leave and she felt terrible about what happened to Sue. "It's not because you weren't good at what you're doing," she said. The ostensible reason was that a big Australian newspaper magnate was taking over the magazine and they were cutting down on overhead by letting go of the lower level editorial staff members. But Sue—as far she could determine from checking the masthead (where just about everyone except janitors was listed by name each week in the front of the magazine)—was the only one who lost her job. Sue tried to figure out what she might have done wrong. She did have a glass of wine with lunch more often than she should have, she thought. But then, they'd just given her a ten-dollar-a-week raise just before she got the boot. So that didn't make sense—beyond her own guilt, she amended inwardly. But why should she feel guilty? There were writers who showed up for staff meetings after three-martini lunches. Because she did feel guilty. She did. No matter how many times the shrink told her that her own perceptions were what counted.

Her parents had paid for her to see a psychiatrist. Lots of sympathy (even if it's not free, Sue thought). She read a lot, she went on long walks, but her days were becoming more and more unstructured and formless. What had Virginia Woolf written in her own diary?

A battle against depression, rejection (by Harpers of my story) routed today (I hope) by clearing out kitchen; by sending the article (a lame one) to N.S.; and by breaking into P.H. two days, I think, of memoir writing. This trough of despair shall not, I swear, engulf me. The solitude is great.

Sue couldn't find another job. She went on plenty of interviews, but money was tight everywhere in publishing and there was nothing.

SUE MUNSINGER had also tried to throw herself into writing poetry and fiction—but every attempt felt half-hearted. And the rejections, even from the smaller magazines here and in the U.K. that paid in copies were depressing. At least Virginia Woolf and her husband owned Hogarth Press and *she* had an outlet for her work. She had a husband, Sue thought. She had a girlfriend, too. And God knows, Sue tried to put on a brave face, but it was all wearing thin. Very thin.

FEBRUARY 1976

The sort of dusky day, cold and damp, like looking up through lake water. A hint of sleet in the air. Sue was lying under the covers on the daybed that was supposed to be a couch during business hours or when one entertained in evenings (not that she had anyone to entertain) when very distinctly she heard the doorknob to her apartment turning. She'd been trying to push herself to get up and get dressed and get going because she had an appointment with Dr. Anselm in less than two hours. She peered through the half gloom. Was the handle actually turning? Her mind shut down with terror and she felt a rising sword of adrenalin paralyze not just her midriff, but her arms and legs. She couldn't move, couldn't croak out, "Who's there?" Was the "police lock"—a sturdy iron bar that fitted into the floorboards—in place? She heard her neck creak as she turned stiffly to look. It was—it was. Then she heard light footsteps moving away from 4 B and going down the grubby hallway. She swallowed, but the fear remained.

"I THINK someone tried to get into my apartment," Sue told Dr. Elizabeth ("Call me Betsy") Anselm that afternoon.

"Did you call the police? Tell the super?"

Sue shook her head. Her heart was thudding. "This might sound a little crazy," she said, "but my parents phoned me and said they got an anonymous phone call where the person—a young sounding guy—said to them 'My name is Jeff Van

Ketterman and I used to work with Sue at *New World* and are you aware she was let go because she has a drinking problem? I thought you'd want to know, because I heard she's seeing a doctor, but maybe she needs more help than anyone—including Sue—realizes.'" She twisted a Kleenex in her hands. She hadn't started crying yet, but tears were frequent during the sessions. "Then they hung up before my parents could even answer."

"Do you know this guy?"

"I do, but I don't think it was him—"

"Why not?"

"Well for one thing he was an assistant in the Art Department, and I don't think I spoke to him more than once or twice the entire time I worked there. And—this is going to sound paranoid, but I get the feeling someone watches me, and watches when I come and go. Someone followed me home when I was carrying two bags of groceries from Gristedes the other night. And twice when I left the apartment for interviews when I came back in it seemed like my papers and things were gone through."

"What do you mean, Sue?"

"Well, I had the rejection letters for my stories that I've gotten in the top right-hand drawer of my desk and they were in the order I've received them and when I went to file the last one yesterday, they weren't in sequence anymore."

"Couldn't you have accidentally disarranged them yourself?"

She shook her head. "I don't think so."

"How much drinking are you doing?"

"Well, when I cook myself a decent meal—I mean more than just a sandwich or a plate of eggs, I have a glass or two. A few—"

"Just my point. You could have very easily moved the letters yourself—"

"But books and things. Disappear or get moved. There are odd clicks on my phone— " She took a deep breath. "There was a journalist—a woman who wrote about a weird cult called Scientology a few years ago and they went after her hammer and tongs—and I think the GPS may be after me."

"But why? You were just a fact checker like you told me?" Betsy smiled.

"It's in their official policy—doctrine—they ruin anyone who has anything against them. They conduct actual campaigns, they sue people, they—"

"But you only spoke to them. Have they gone after the writer? The magazine?"

"I don't know," she said, glancing down. "But they could be keeping it on the Q.T. I mean someone is reading my diary," Sue said. "I found a smudge, a thumbprint—like a person who's been eating a Hershey Bar in several places and—" She paused. "And the pages they were reading, they were all about how much it scared me that Charles Manson and his cult used to creepy-crawl houses when people they wanted to victimize slept. They did it and left traces to scare people, get them off balance. I also wrote about worrying about having wine at lunch sometimes when I worked at *New World*—even though everyone did. I wrote about how phobic I am about cockroaches." She took a deep breath. "And now, suddenly, after more than a year in my place, I have them."

"The main thing is how you perceive all this...why do you think you'd be so important to them?"

Sue was embarrassed. "Maybe they're trying out new scare tactics, ways to intimidate," she said. "Maybe they're 'practicing' on a little fish—someone no one else would pay attention to. Like murderers who kill prostitutes and drug addicts because they won't be missed..."

"You do have a great imagination," Betsy laughed.

Sue smiled weakly. "Thanks. You know, at least I feel safe here. The GPS despises all psychiatrists." She didn't tell Betsy that she'd found an empty Vlasics jar (it wasn't hers, it wasn't because she didn't eat pickles—she'd always hated them) under her kitchen sink—way in the back of the cabinet, out of the light and under the pipes. That was two days after she'd written the entry in her own diary about Virginia Woolf cleaning *her* kitchen and Sue was straightening shelves and neatly lining up supplies like Brillo pads, dish sponges and Comet bleach and she'd seen the first of what would become many cockroaches. Now she kept packets of what she called "separate" cockroach sponges just to squash them against walls or—even if she didn't see them in the bathroom when she went in to pee—to wipe the toilet ring before she sat down.

Over and over she wondered: Was someone creepy-crawling the apartment? Reading her diary? Calling her parents? Loosing vermin on her? Trying to drive her crazy? Was she imagining all this? She wondered, she really did wonder, but there was no answer.

MARCH 1976

"...There is something worse than death, with its promise of release and slumber. There is dust rising, endless days, and a hallway that sits and sits, always full of the same brown light and the dank, slightly chemical smell that will do, until something more precise comes along, as the actual odor of age and loss, the end of hope," Virginia Woolf wrote.

She was tired, she loved that phrase, "There is dust rising," and the words were swimming up at her, but she was afraid to turn off the reading light. Sue felt she was in the same kind of funk Woolf experienced. She hated hanging (dishabille) in her old bathrobe, barefoot, hair unwashed, nails grimy in the apartment, but she hated going out more. Every time she left (the grocery store, a walk in the slushy gray streets, to the corner bar for a drink) she was sure someone was going through her things in the apartment. She called the police once and the earnest young officer who stood with one elbow leaning on the kitchen counter holding a pen and notepad (quickly put into his shirt pocket) had shrugged. "Nothing's missing? Who could get in? I mean if your super has a key and he's coming in, why would that be? Nothing's defaced—I mean no writing on the walls, right? Nothing's ever been broken—"

How could she tell him that she'd come in very suddenly one night and found an open lipstick near the mirror (it wasn't her lipstick! She never wore red or used Maybelline!)—as if someone had planned to write something and left in haste. Would they write "Pig" or "Die" or "Rise" as they'd done in the Manson murders? It occupied her thoughts all the time.

She was alone, lonely, isolated. She was dependent on her parents' good will and money and the jokes asking about when she was going to give up and come home to live didn't sound so much like jokes anymore. Her mother had taken to sending her larger checks for food when she saw Sue had lost a lot of weight. "I have my savings," she told her, "I'm just not hungry."

IN THE psychiatrist's reception room Sue sat waiting for the start of her appointment, leafing through the glossy pages of *Time* magazine. There was a short, boxed sidebar piece about how the Scientologists had broken into all kinds of government offices—including the IRS and the United States post office. She flipped back, intent on reading the main article, but she was called into Betsy's office.

Her hands were trembling. Before she could even sit down or say hello she said, "Now I've really got to wonder if the GPS is targeting me." Tears came into her eyes. "Every short story and poem I sent out for the last month to every single magazine came back unopened this morning. A huge stack—all the envelopes were crammed and wrinkled and stuffed into my mailbox. How could that happen? How?"

"Postage?"

Sue shook her head. "No, they had plenty…something is happening. I know it's them. I'm sure there was enough postage, I always check."

When she got home, she looked at the pile of clasped manila envelopes. Not a single one was stamped.

March 28th, 1976

From the diary of Sue Munsinger:

Betsy is suggesting—oh so gently—that it's not a bad or terrible thing, that it's not my fault, but perhaps the loneliness, the isolation has gotten to me and I'm losing it. Perhaps, she says, the meds aren't enough. Maybe I need a rest for a while—somewhere. My parents couldn't pay for that, and I don't want them to. It's too embarrassing, too shameful.

Virginia was really lucky. She didn't have to worry so much about rejection because she and Leonard owned their own publishing house. Except for one short item I posted in New World, I've never had a single thing accepted. Nowhere. Can't get a job, no money for graduate school. The weirdest part is, I never wanted to be a journalist or an editor. I wanted to be a famous writer. I wanted to write my heart out (like Salinger says, "Are all your stars out?") in peace and calm and tranquility. A sort of Emily Dickinson who became famous after she died. See? I was always worried that if I did become famous it would go to my head and I'd screw up. Start taking drugs, drink myself to death. But I thought I really, really care about writing and if I can write well enough, I can achieve a kind of everlasting life that way. If I could just keep trying. If I had money and a room of my own. But the room, I now realize, is mental space—not a studio apartment in Manhattan. The money is your own earnings—not weekly checks from your parents in upstate New York attached to short (worried but loving) notes. Christ. It all hurts so goddamn much. Losing Tom, the job at New World, the sense of betrayal, the instant tears that start and then won't stop.

I think about this hideous, grinding half-life inside the gray walls of my mind. Walls that rise like the dust that dispirited Virginia Woolf. I went out for coffee this morning, because the goddamn cockroaches can have this dump as far as I'm concerned. And when I came back, the window on the fire escape was open and the book of Woolf's letters was open. Maybe it's a sign. She wrote to her beloved Leonard of her incipient madness: "I don't think any two people could have been happier....It's not your fault. You've done everything for me....I can't go through another of those times....I can't concentrate....I can't fight any longer. I'm spoiling your life."

You see, Mom and Dad? Like Virginia Woolf, I can't even write this properly. And like her Leonard, you've also been so incredibly good to me. I'm costing you a fortune, I'm miserable, I can't go on ruining your lives.

Dad, do you remember the time I wanted to wade in the Esopus River (that tributary of the Hudson up in Ulster County) and you told me no one wades there—there's white water and rapids and I cried. From the bridge where we stood it looked so peaceful. All that green, all that lush foliage. And it was so quiet except for the gurgle and trip of the water over the stones.

I've set out all my work for you and Mommy. All the stories (some of them are good, I know it) and all the poems. Maybe you can find a home for them someday. I like to think you might or that at least they'll give you some comfort.

I told Betsy that one of the things I couldn't understand was how when people were in the GPS cult they could be made to feel that all the good things they ever did could be wiped out with a single transgression. Now I know, because I feel utterly worthless. A failure. And nothing is going to make any of this right. The loss of hope as Virginia writes.

I really thought someday I might achieve what she did, that my work might stand for something. But I can't face rejection, the blank days and roiling anxieties, the apathy and the sadness that are worse than death. I can't face going to a madhouse.

Virginia Woolf lifted a large stone, put it in her pocket, and on March 28th, 1941 she walked into the Ouse River in Sussex England.

Did she think about the silver flow of cold water around her, climbing up her shoes and stockings and billowing her skirt, her dark hair? Did she think about how even if life held no prospect for change, the current would carry her? Did she think about the sound—knowing it would be for the last time—she would hear birdsong and rushing wind?

I will think of you, and of those things as I stand along the grassy banks of the Esopus, and I will think of her, and how her work lives on and I will carry two stones.

MARCH 29TH, 1976

Memorandum from special psych ops agent Betsy Anselm to Director of Special Services, GPS:

As per directive dated March 21st, 1976, you may report to Mother Taranch that we can now show that facts such as sleep deprivation, loss of job, isolation, scare tactics, infiltration of home, surveillance, etc., created a state of heightened suspicion and a prolonged feeling of desolation and hopelessness. It can certainly be tried with variations of acts and intensity on subjects who are deemed even more important OEDs and who through word or deed undermine our policies and our organization.

Unquestionably, "Operation Virginia" was a resounding success.

DANIELE BONFANTI

THE GORGE OF CHILDREN

SPRING – AOSTA VALLEY

The river is born from a vertical chasm in the wall of the glacier, like silver blood pouring out of a gash. Thick water out of darkness through the shimmer of the sun on the green ice and into the light of a cloudless Alpine sky. It is four meters wide here, but it will grow, fast and hungry, as it feeds on all the streams cascading down the steep walls of the valley.

Two kayaks are already in the water, a big man with jughead ears and a woman with wavy blonde hair escaping her helmet: both warm up lazily, ferrying smoothly through the creases to the other shore, or paddling upstream in the narrow near-bank eddy, then elegantly peeling off into the current with firm, high-bracing strokes, to hop downstream five or six waves and spin back into the eddy.

Together with a tall man in civilian clothes, camera strapped across his chest, a third paddler is lingering on the stony bank with his tomato-red creek boat—a Burn III with the airbrushed logo of his sponsor Zermatt Watches—on his shoulder, and his black, carbon fiber paddle held in his other hand like a lance. He closes his brown eyes, slowly inhaling the breeze caressing his curly hair—the sun on his face, the voice of the water rustling in his ears. When he opens them again, he looks at the photographer and smiles.

"You should be on the water with us, mate. You would have home-field advantage, too." Pleasant, measured cockney accent; tenor voice.

The answer is deadpan: "And who would drive the van?"

The kayaker chuckles. "Come on—you, me, Léa, and Iancu! We're like the four fuckin' knights of the Apocalypse, aren't we?"

"You'll have to content yourself with the Three Musketeers today, Sean."

Sean squeezes his eyes. "Ha. And what about D'Artagnan?" Then raises an eyebrow, "Really, Cedric. You're missing out on this one. It will be great."

"I'm sure, but I told you: I don't do that shit anymore, not after the Congo…I've got family."

"Well, me too."

"As a matter of fact, you used to. Then guess what? Your knockout fashion model wife left you with Mister Safety and your baby son—who calls *him* dad, if I'm not mistaken—'cause she cried her onyx black eyes out all night long each time you were out on an expedition, waiting for *that* call."

"Thanks for the memo. Ever the friend."

"No problem, you can always count on me."

Sean quietly shakes his head. "Anyway…come on. One of the few places on the surface of this planet where *nobody's ever been*. And it's right there," he vaguely hints downriver with his chin. "Doesn't that make you hard?"

Cedric shrugs. "A little, yes."

"And it's not that dangerous; you know it."

"One hundred percent is a pretty high body count for a rapid, in my book."

"*Two* is a pretty low number in mine. They were both unprepared and had poor timing. Perhaps they were just unlucky, too. Anyway, they weren't us."

"Still. You have *no idea* what you'll find in there. Could be a siphon big enough to swallow you and your boat whole. Not even your Swiss sponsor is going to pull you out from there, you know? Could be anything. And I can't afford a risk like that."

"You're exaggerating. You saw it. It's just the Elbow, you can't really see that turn and…Oh, right, we had this argument already."

"Twice," he smiles. He pounds a hand on Sean's paddle

shoulder, causing the action-cam–rigged helmet dangling from his hand to swing a little. "Go. I'll be right there with this when you exit the gorge," he lovingly pats his Leica. "Remember to say 'cheese.' I'll do my best to make you presentable. Luckily, you have Léa in the party, so at least some pictures will be nice." He squeezes his shoulder. "And be careful, man."

"Don't worry, mate, child's play. After all, it is called the *Gorge of Children*, isn't it?"

Cedric squints, deep crow's feet carved by wind and sun. "You *know* why it's actually called that, right?"

"Come to think of it, no. Graceful name, though."

"Too bad it's because they used to make human sacrifices there. *Child* sacrifices."

"You're shitting me."

"I can't believe you didn't know. It was half the reason *ADAM* bought my story in advance."

"Oh. And the other half were the magic words 'Sean Williams,' right?"

"More like the words 'first integral descent of the Dora de Pulaz, including the fucking Elbow.'"

"You know you're a crappy person, right? My very worst friend." He smiles, showing large, white, slightly uneven teeth. "Anyway, *children*?"

"Yep. They were—"

"Sean!" It is Léa, calling from the river, her voice throaty. "So? Shitting your pants?"

Sean turns to answer her, widening his smile even more, "No, it's just our dear Cedric here is telling me only now that we may meet the ghosts of dead children in there."

Her eyebrows rise over wide, green, almond-shaped eyes. "Fuck, man, you didn't know?"

He shrugs. Then he looks back at Cedric with inquiring eyes.

And Cedric says, "Nobody wants to see Léa angry, so, the short version: before Augustus conquered and enslaved them, there was a tribe called the Salassi here in the Aosta Valley, one of the last to hold out against Roman domination. Tough guys. Well, this river was a god in their pantheon, and the gorge was its number one place of worship. The town of Pre de Pulaz, just beyond the gorge, is built upon the ruins of a Salassi village; you can still see some of them, I'll take you, it's interesting stuff. Aulo Murena, the

Roman general who led the conquest, wrote that they believed the god's core resided in the gorge, and they had to present him with a gift each spring equinox if they wanted to keep him content and prevent him from getting out and laying waste to the village. Prosaically, it was probably related to their fear of spring overflows. Yet, you know what those gifts were..."

"Children."

"Yep. According to Aulo Murena, they had to give the god 'a son' each spring."

"That's—"

"Sean!" Léa, again.

"Coming, coming!" and he quietly moves in her direction, looking back once just to say, "See you there, mate."

ICY BUCKETFULS against their faces. Sharp water tries to snatch them away, to pull them below. Black, blurred rocks beneath a thin veil, barely surfacing between one wave and the next. One centimeter of polyethylene separating them from the maw of the roaring beast.

They move among walls of water that crumble and resurrect, only to collapse again

They are very different paddlers. Iancu dominates his wild boat with utter strength, his impressive back, shoulders, and arms conveying all their might to his paddle that keeps pushing and pulling and working. Léa carves her way through the waves with grace; though solid, her strokes seem to barely touch the water, caressing it, while her hips do most of the work, giving the right chine to the right current at exactly the right time. Sean is something in between, aggressive but gentle; one with his boat, and grinning, he makes it look almost easy.

What they have in common is that feeling: blood loaded with electricity as it fuels muscles, all senses overloaded and otherworldly keen, on. Alive.

And not one of them is *fighting* the river—that would really be a one-way battle and they well know: they are trying to go along with its will. The difficult part is understanding it, while avoiding being submerged in the process.

Sean is in the lead. His eyes dart around, looking for secret lines in the middle of that heartbreakingly beautiful, white inferno. The banks are no more than fifteen meters away, both sides, but they could as well be on another planet.

He punches through a hole, rides a pourover; beside him, the gray rocky walls flow by, rising higher and looming. Ahead, they overhang so much that they almost touch, high up where they end, about eighty meters above, and only a narrow strip of light—blazing—remains.

A quick stern draw, skirting a nasty sieve—bared, broken, foaming teeth of stone ready to chew on him—but then the river horizon vanishes just before him, too close; he raises his paddle and waits for the right moment to hit the lip with a high, vertical stroke, pulls back his blade as he pushes with his hips—and his boat is floating in the air with its front rocker well forward while he rotates ahead and meets the surface with a precise stroke, pushing with his feet against the bulkheads, in full control of his bow.

An unexpected flower of water blooms underneath, though, hurling him sideways—right into a three-meter hole, and suddenly there is a front of water running dizzyingly toward him; too late to do anything but raise the paddle high and hold his breath. The impact is a harsh slap that turns the world black, generating a whirl of bubbles.

Sean's red boat is capsized, thrashed by the frenzied hands of the river.

The blade of his paddle appears.

Underwater, his lips contract in a devilish sneer; they open to trace a silent, gurgling battle cry.

He surfaces, his body holding on to the paddle that escaped one hand. A thrust of the back completes the eskimo roll, and his fingers run to recover and seize the shaft of the paddle.

Breathing hard, he takes in the scenario around him from this new point of view.

They are inside the gorge now; the notorious Elbow getting nearer, fast.

And he was right. As their scouting from upriver promised, the rapid is not that bad—still a full big-water grade V, sure—and it is actually lots of fun, with many standing waves and huge cushions along the edges.

Gigantic arches of stone overlook them, like the nave of a cathedral, keeping all gazing eyes away.

A great peace. Warped by the rumble of the river, growing in texture with the reverberations.

Their three boats stand out, bright colors against white water and dark shadows, getting darker toward the gloom of the Elbow.

They become off-key details, their yellow and their red, while sliding and hopping toward obscurity for a few more seconds.

Then, they vanish.

HIS LEICA ready, Cedric is perched like a sniper on a rock, the waves that engulf it spraying him liberally.

He aims upriver, the length of the gorge beyond the Elbow: a completely white seething of foam, with big fleeting bulges and sharp crests, a huge water dome in the middle and not one visible rock.

Despite the biting breath of the river, a drop of sweat runs down his temple, through his thin blonde hair.

A thrill.

But then there are colors, materializing out of the black and into the white, and his shutter begins to click as they jolt up and down and slither over, around, and into the seams, the holes, and the waves.

They vanish again behind the gurgling dome, reappear on its right—looking so small and fragile so close to it—and are out of the gorge in thirty seconds, passing right under Cedric who, with a celebratory, "*Epic!*" immortalizes their triumphant…

Why are their faces like that?

Grim, pale. Sean barely turns to look at him on the rock, then his gaze goes back ahead, distant, and he keeps paddling like a machine.

Cedric frowns as Léa's yellow Braaap passes by. She looks faraway just like Sean, and Cedric must yell, "Everything all right, guys?"

She dignifies him with a quick look, and nods, her lips taut and unmoving.

FIVE KILOMETERS downriver. Cedric takes one shot while Léa boofs the last drop; another, just perfect, as she rides the blade-like seam of currents where the Dora de Pulaz finally ends its tormented rush, joining the shiny waters of its bigger sister, Lady Dora Baltea.

Then he runs toward the take-out, a wide smile on his face

and a bottle of Blanc de Morgex in his hand.

The first one to reach the landing place is the Romanian behemoth.

"Guys! You did it!" the photographer greets him.

Iancu nods.

And nothing more. He lays his paddle behind the cockpit, unfastens his spray skirt, and in a couple of seconds he is standing on the slippery rocks of the bank. He lifts his blood-red Director as though it were made of paper and loads it on his tattooed shoulder, covering Cedric in its shadow, already moving quiet steps toward the trail leading to the road.

Cedric's lashes blink fast over puzzled eyes.

Now Léa and Sean are disembarking, too.

Cedric gallantly pulls her boat out of the water when she is out, asking her, "Are you guys all right? How was it?"

She shows a weary smile, rubbing her flat, too-small nose. "Couldn't be better."

Sean is silent beside her, action cam notably missing from his helmet.

"What happened?" Cedric asks, pointing at where it should be.

"Torn off during a roll..."

"Hell, that sucks, I was looking forward to see—"

Sean is walking already, following Iancu's steps. "It was too dark anyway."

Léa moves, too, leaving her boat behind for Cedric to be the gentleman mule.

Cedric protests, "But how was it? Come on, guys, tell me how it was at the Elbow! Then we'll celebrate." He tentatively waves his wine bottle.

Léa turns back, without stopping. "Wonderful. It was wonderful."

SUMMER – LAKE COMO

"Dying like that, someone like Iancu. It's fucked up. I mean..."

The dark-eyed brunette who spoke, holding Cedric's arm, shakes her head.

Velvets drapes and burning candles. Crysanthemums, gerberas, and lilies, mixing sweetness in the heavy air. Several people scattered in the living room, dressed in black, talking in murmurs.

The couple stares at a big framed picture on the wall. A piercing deep blue sky and blinding white snow, separated by the curvy line of a fantastic cornice, jutting out several meters from the ridgeline. Iancu is skiing next to the edge of it, a high plume of white powder tracing a perfect semiparabola glittering like a spray of diamonds. His smiling face is almost as bright under an orange mask.

“I know exactly what you mean, honey. You do all kinds of dangerous stuff, you flirt with death all the time in the most spectacular ways—and people keep telling you you’ll get killed, and you don’t really care. That’s why it’s fun. Then you doze off driving home from the post office ’cause you’ve worked your ass off on a roof all day, and you go down into the fucking lake.”

“Yeah, that’s the gist of it. What does it all mean?”

“Meaning, ha. Come on, Marta. Still looking for meaning, at your age?”

Marta does not answer, but asks, “Are they still looking for the body?”

“They say it’s useless by now. Very deep, strong currents…and the bottom is basically a huge mass of quicksand.”

“But then…”

A sad smile. “Marta, lots of people saw the accident. He went down, didn’t come up.”

She sighs. “I know. It’s just…to think he’s still down there…,” vaguely gesturing backward to the deep scar filled with cold water outside the window.

He shrugs, “All bodies of water are graveyards, honey. People have two options if they want to take a swim: delude themselves or live with it.”

She looks back, through the French window to the balcony overlooking the lake. Léa and Sean are there, deep in conversation, almost as if they’re arguing, but inaudible beyond the double glass. “Aren’t you joining your friends?”

He turns, and sighs. “You’re not coming?”

“I’ll say hello later. Now, I’m sure I’d be a third wheel.”

He quickly kisses her on the cheek. “Thanks.”

On his way, he grabs two beers from a refreshment table.

They are so absorbed in their exchange they fail to notice him approaching, and when he opens the door, a scrap of Léa’s words is taken in together with a humid gust of Breva wind, smelling of sweet decay, of maceration: "...still having those nightmares, and—"

She almost jumps when she sees Cedric, and stops mid-sentence with her orchid lips parted on the next word.

He offers a melancholic smile. "Guys. Am I glad to see you both." He raises the bottles of Bereta, they clink together. "You know, despite all the trappings of death his family put together in there, I'm sure he'd have wanted us to remember him with beer."

Their lips wear small smiles, now. But deep circles under their eyes make them grotesque. "Sorry, not in the mood," croaks Léa.

"Maybe later, mate," nods Sean, swallowing drily.

Cedric shrugs. "What were you two talking about?"

A quick look between them. Guilty?

Léa coughs and says, "Nothing. Iancu. What else? This sucks."

Cedric looks into her large, green, almond eyes that, despite their gorgeous brightness, look in need of sleep, but stays silent. He steps to the rail, lays his hands on the wrought iron, and watches the lake.

The water looks like it has been scattered with sequins, blinking in the ponderous afternoon sun above four hundred meters of darkness. Its crown of mountains encloses it heavily, severely, with their bright green oaks and chestnut woods and their gray, high, jagged profiles of limestone two thousand meters above.

"He loved it here. The lake stole his heart the first time he saw it. Once he told me the only thing that cheered him up when he had to go back to everyday life, and everyday work, was that he knew he would wake up and come out here drinking a beer." He uncorks one, adding hop bitterness to the musk of the lake, raises it, and before taking it to his lips he whispers, "To you, man."

AUTUMN – CORSICA

"This is where we found her backpack."

The young woman with Léa's green, almond eyes and orchid lips, but different hair and some years more, points at a sort of alcove beneath a thick myrtle bush without looking at it.

Her eyes are on the sea.

Cedric follows her gaze, along a barely tracked trail through the impenetrable scrub above the precipitous cove, a *calanque* sculpted by water and wind and ages into a phantasmagoria.

The trail vanishes quickly into a low thicket—quivering in a cold breeze that spreads about the dense, balsamic texture of a conflagration of aromas—but its destination looks quite obvious: at the tip of the V-shaped inlet, a sea-cave gapes at the bottom of the cliff of red granite. A fifty-meter wide, twenty high, naturally arching ceiling where human faces and animal muzzles of stone hang upside down, their laughter and snarling frozen in time.

The crystal waters become dark underneath, where they are swallowed, in a deep breath.

The woman speaks in a throaty voice, much like her sister's, but hers sounds raw and broken. "That route was so important to her."

"Don't talk like that, Claudette. Don't use the past."

She turns to look at him. The saddest smile on Earth. "She's not coming back, Cedric."

"But..."

"I don't need to see a body. I just know. She was my little sister." Her eyes go back to the cave.

Cedric does not insist, and just follows her gaze again. "*Gravité*. Her masterwork," Cedric comments, following the invisible route along that arch, right on the jagged line dividing light from shadow, vertical from horizontal, from one side of the cave to the other, until it touches the water again.

She lightens up, just for a second. "It is."

"Hate to ask, Claudette, but...was she having one of her mood swings lately?"

She shakes her head. "No. For the past three years—since she opened *Gravité*—she's been well, didn't even need her meds anymore. She used to say whenever she felt...you know...she could take the bike, ride here from home, and come down here—do the route and 'be born again.'" She frowns. "Still, there was *something*. But different. I haven't seen her much this year, I've been in Marseille for work, but when I saw her she looked, I don't know, tired...troubled about something?" She shakes her head. "Anyway, I'm sure she just fell. It's as simple as that."

Cedric looks at the dark, unanswering threshold down there. An involuntary, uncontrolled fall from that ceiling, even into water, could be less than nice. Kill? Unlikely. Stun, injure? Likely—and then the sea will do the rest.

Claudette turns again, looking him in the eye. “So, is your mind still set? You won’t find her, you know.”

Cedric nods, taking the trail. “I have to look anyway.”

Winter – Aosta Valley

Dear Sean,

Man, I’m just so glad I’ll be seeing you next month for the snow-trail in La Thuile.

Since I came back from Corsica (hell, it’s been three months already) I’ve been losing sleep. I wake up at night and just sit at the window and look outside at the snow and the mountains for hours, listening in my head to the operas we both loved. Her sister said she’d been troubled about something lately, you know? And thinking back I can’t shake off the feeling that last time I saw her she looked *scared* to me, that there was something wrong (I keep feeling like I almost get it, but then it goes away, and it’s driving me nuts) and that she wanted to say something to me, but didn’t dare. Can you imagine? Léa scared of something? Léa *not daring*?

Hell, she managed to be both the strongest and the frailest woman I’ve ever met.

But she didn’t do any of this to *prove* anything to anyone, not even herself, as I know you and I did sometimes. She was just happy there, hanging solo from an overhang with her fingertips wedged in some crack, and the sky below.

I keep thinking about the light that switched on in her face in those moments—the light that curled back up inside her beautiful eyes the rest of the time. That was a sight to behold.

It’s been a shitty time (to say the very least) and I’m looking forward to spending some quality time with you, during the race (if you can keep my pace), and especially after, during the third half, and having a beer or two (or three) and being depressed together.

Hugs,

Cedric

~

Sorry, mate. I was just about to write you that unfortunately I cannot make it. I won’t be there in La Thuile.

Looking forward to next time.

Sean

SPRING AGAIN – AOSTA VALLEY

Un uom nell'onda!—*a man in the wave! shouts the choir, over frenzied strings like that stormy lake, over Alaide's exquisite panic*—Ciel! Soccorso!—*in Renata Scotto's enchanting voice, as her beloved dives in vain, trying to rescue the friend he just ran through, pushing him into the water*—and then the phone rings, shattering the sublime chaos of the scene behind Cedric's closed eyelids.

Turning down the volume on the hi-fi, he answers, "Hello?" with a slightly furry tongue.

"Hi, Cedric, it's Asha."

Five years back. Zermatt Watches' advertising photo shoot. Those legs, those unending legs as she walks like a tantric goddess in a bathing suit, the Matterhorn ridiculously huge and perfect behind her, shining white and wounding the sky, deep. And Sean, stomping his beer mug down on the table, and, with a white mustache of foam, pulling down his sunglasses to show goggling eyes while he says, "Who's that*?" "You don't know Asha Nagpal?' "I'm going to. Bloody hell, I'm going to marry her."*

"Asha! Wow, it's been a long time."

"It has indeed. Sorry I sort of vanished after Sean and I..."

"Never mind. I get it. How's life treating you?"

"Well, I'm a bit tired. Always flying here and there for fashion shows, and...and I'm sounding like the most spoiled and ungrateful woman in the world, aren't I?"

"Well, I wouldn't say *the* most."

Chuckle, like crystal jingling.

"But tell me, something you needed besides hearing my beautiful baritone?"

Another tiny chuckle, then a shadow can almost be heard thickening the wire. "It's Sean." An electric discharge through his spine, black closing in at the edges of his visual field (*that* call?), but while he croaks, "Something hap—" she's quick to add, "No, no, nothing happened. I'm just a little worried."

"Why?" The black edges aren't going away.

"I've driven them to the airport this morning, little Rick and him, and...he was strange. I've been so glad he wanted to take the boy for a trip there, but...I don't know how to explain it, but he looked...haunted." There is something ominous in the ensuing silence. "I was wondering if you can...I don't know...Thing is, it may sound absurd, but I had the same feeling when my dad got cancer and he wouldn't tell us. I'm worried, Cedric. I was wondering, since you're seeing him tonight, could—"

Swallowing, "Tonight?"

"Yes..." She sounds puzzled. "Right?"

"Here?"

Now her voice wavers. "For the snow-trail, there in La Thuile? He's going to run with you, isn't he?"

Men lie to their wives all the time. Let alone ex-wives. Friends are supposed to cover for them. But.

"Actually, Asha, he told me he couldn't come."

"But..."

"Maybe he's planning to surprise me?"

"That can't be...He told me he made arrangements for Ricky to stay with your family during the race, sleeping there."

"But no...Marta and the girls are in Liguria, visiting her parents..." Heart rushing, heat creeping up the neck to the ears.

"Something's wrong, Cedric. Sean's never lied to me. *Never.* I'm scared. Oh, God, and my Ricky...What's happening?"

Boom, boom inside the chest. Cedric tries to level his voice, sound confident. "Stay calm, Asha. I'm sure it's all right. Which flight did they take?"

"They departed from Heathrow at ten this morning. I think they must have landed in Milan about noon."

A quick glance at the wall clock: three hours ago. "I'm calling him on the mobile."

"I've just tried, it's turned off."

"Okay, okay. I'll..." Then his gaze spots the flier magnetized on the fridge. A picture of a runner in the middle of a vast snowfield glittering under Orion, an ice-blue full moon surfacing beyond frozen peaks, and the writing FIRST EDITION: LA THUILE SNOW-NIGHT-ULTRATRAIL, 54 KM +3400m D, and *the date*: 21 MARCH, CELEBRATING SPRING WITH SWEAT (AND BEER)!

"Cedric?"

"I'm..." But his eyes are now on another picture. *His own* picture on the cover of the last June issue of *Adventure, Discovery and Mystery* framed on the wall. The picture of three specks of color coming down a completely white seething of foam, with big fleeting bulges and sharp crests and a huge dome. Sean, Iancu, and Léa appearing just beyond the Elbow, inside the Gorge of

Children.

You know *why it's actually called that, right?*

"Cedric, talk to me, you're freaking me out!"

He sounds like he cannot believe what he is saying when he answers, "I think I know where they are."

SEAN IS already there.

As Cedric runs down the steep, rocky trail, his friend is standing almost on the brink of the high bank, unmoving, looking down the Dora next to the upstream end of the gorge.

His son Richard lies close to him, a few steps farther from the drop.

"Sean!"

The four-year-old does not move as his father turns back, his face streaming with tears, his eyes wide and bloodshot.

Cedric slows down without halting, raising both hands, palms forward. "Sean, for God's sake, what have you done to him?"

"It's…it's just Xanax. I didn't want him to feel anything. But I couldn't do it anyway." He opens his arms, lets them fall weakly. "I just couldn't…you understand? He's my child." And he moves one step on the slippery, dark rock, closer to the raging water—just three meters beneath. "But maybe…"

Slow breaths. "Now calm down, man. I'm here to help you."

The crazed man strongly shakes his curly head. "But you can't! Nobody can!" Another half step toward the water. Cedric stops.

"Talk to me, Sean. It's me, right? Your very worst friend. There's no need for…," he gestures at the river. "That. Right?"

A hysteric laugh. "Can't help me on this one, mate."

Cedric's feet almost imperceptibly slide a little forward. Now about five meters divide the two men. "Sean. It's all in your head."

A little forward, again; knees slightly bending, muscles tightening.

"It keeps calling, you see? Every night, *every single bloody night.* It will slay the whole town if I don't do it. Thousands will die. It…it showed me things." He squeezes his eyes closed, as if to drive those visions away. "And yet I couldn't. Maybe it will accept—"

But Cedric has already leapt, and when his friend opens his eyes again, he is upon him, grabbing and tugging back and head-butting Sean at the same time.

Sean's head falls back while his eyes go white, but when Cedric pulls him away from the edge he struggles hard.

And now they are dancing in a circle on the edge of the roaring dragon, the sprays slapping them wildly.

"Don't stop me, please don't stop *meee*!"

Sean's right hand finds Cedric's left, grabs his little finger, bends it backward until it snaps.

A cry of pain, and half the strength holding Sean is gone.

With a jolt, Sean throws himself backward and he is loose, Cedric falling from the backlash, hitting the rock hard on his back—just a glimpse: Sean stumbling toward the edge—and for a couple of seconds, or maybe more, everything is black.

Air, again, flushing down his choking lungs. Breath, breath. Pain throbbing in the hand.

Richard? He is there, sprawled beside him on the rock, his eyelids fluttering.

Sean is gone.

A sharp tip of pain digging in his back, Cedric scrambles to his knees and right hand, crawls to the edge.

Sean is hanging there, one hand gripping a small overhead handhold, the other pressing against the rock from below. His feet—already soaked, a shoe gone—graze the waves.

Cedric reaches down. "Grab my hand!"

Sean looks up. He smiles, his eyes grateful. "Look after my son, mate. Maybe it will accept me, after all." And he lets go of the handhold.

"*Sean! Nooo!*"

But his body is already hurled about like a puppet by the hands of the river, and it does not even seem to belong to a living thing while appearing and disappearing among the folds of water as it enters the gorge. Just a worthless object. It lasts just a few seconds, then he is gone.

THE TRAIL runs along the upper lip of the gorge. Here, the crevice is so narrow it could be leapt over.

Cedric, holding the chemically sleeping Richard in his arms, follows it at full speed while a hammer keeps driving spikes into his back with every stride.

The path snakes its way on rocks, through huge larches whose roots have formed a gnarled staircase covered in a bed of dry needles.

The river roars beneath, amplified in a resounding weaving of echoes, a deep rumble vibrating through rocks, bones, and belly.

But there is another noise now, harsher, of something breaking—of tons of rocks falling, growing into a deafening thunder. Cedric stumbles at the shockwave, hitting the ground with his knees in his attempt to protect the child, while the earth keeps quaking for some seconds.

Then he scrambles to his feet and runs, badly staggering, his leg stiff, blood soaking his blue jeans. He passes the ninety-degree turn of the Elbow and keeps going.

And something is moving beneath, down there.

Blood pumping in his ears, his legs twitching and his lungs scratching, he keeps running. Then, an opening in the woods: the trail begins its descent near the exit of the gorge.

The town of Pre de Pulaz appears, its outskirts gathered around the black-roofed, pointed bell tower of a stone church. People are swarming into the streets, staring upriver.

Between Cedric and the town, something is coming out of the gorge.

And the townsfolk begin to scream.

Not only water, though it moves like it.

A winding waterspout as wide as the whole river, made of water and scaly flesh, like the body of a snake, with no head but a wave crest crowned by a ring of twitching, black, curved thorns—claws?—each as big as a tree; and a long tongue, or proboscis, or tentacle, protruding from the center of it.

There is Sean in that proboscis—half of him.

His upper body juts out of the appendage, his arms limp, like a broken doll, and yet his eyes are open wide and alive. He is screaming while the thing sucks him in—but no. It is not sucking him in: the following second, already several meters downriver and close to vanishing inside the waves, Sean's disarranged body is spat out into the billows.

Then, more water comes out of the Gorge of Children—a mountain of water which is more than water. It is its body. Now it is clear, the waterspout was only a head: the creature is the river. And its bulk now hides head, man, and everything else, as the rumbling mass plunges down toward the town where everybody is running away from the banks. But the wave is huge and the river overflows, sweeping away cars and uprooting trees and devastating the first houses, already grabbing the slower runners.

Their cries cannot be heard over the roar.

Not even when they see the clawed waterspout rearing up beside the church, taller than its puny bell tower, and they know it has come to take them all.

RAMSEY CAMPBELL

RAISED BY THE MOON

IT WAS the scenery that did it for him. Having spent the afternoon avoiding the motorway and enjoying the unhurried country route, Grant reached the foothills only to find the Cavalier refused to climb. He'd driven a mere few hundred yards up the first steep slope when the engine commenced groaning. He should have made time during the week to have it serviced, he thought, feeling like a child caught out by a teacher, except that teaching had shown him what was worse—to be a teacher caught out by a child. He dragged the lever into first gear and ground the accelerator under his heel. The car juddered less than a yard before helplessly backing towards its own smoke.

His surroundings grew derisively irrelevant: the hills quilted with fields, the mountains ridged with pines, the roundish moon trying out its whiteness in the otherwise blue sky. He managed to execute most of a turn as the car slithered backwards, and sent it downhill past a Range Rover loaded with a family whose children turned to display their tongues to him. The July heat buttered him as he swung the Cavalier onto a parched verge, where the engine hacked to itself while he glared at the map.

Half the page containing his location was crowded with the fingerprints of mountains. Only the coast was unhampered by their contours. He eased the car off the brown turf and nursed it several digressive miles to the coast road, where a signpost pointed left to Windhill, right to Baiting. Northward had looked as though it might bring him sooner inland to the motorway, and so he took the Baiting route.

He hadn't bargained for the hindrance of the wind. Along the jagged coastline all the trees leaned away from the jumpy sea as though desperate to grasp the land. Before long the barren seaward fields gave way to rocks and stony beaches, and there weren't even hedges to fend off the northwester. Whenever the gusts took a breath he smelled how overworked the engine was growing. Beside the road was evidence of the damage the wind could wreak: scattered planks of some construction which, to judge by a ruin a mile farther on, had been a fishmonger's stall. Then the doggedly spiky hedge to his right winced inland, revealing an arc of cottages as white as the moon would be when the sky went out. Perhaps someone in the village could repair the car, or Grant would find a room for the night—preferably both.

The ends of the half-mile arc of cottages were joined across the inlet by a submerged wall or a path that divided the prancing sea from the less restless bay. The far end was marked by a lone block of colour, a red telephone box planted in the water by a trick of perspective. His glimpse of a glistening object crouched or heaped in front of it had to be another misperception; when he returned his attention to the view once he'd finished tussling with the wheel as a gust tried to shove the car across the road, he saw no sign of life.

The car was panting and shivering by the time he reached the first cottage. A vicious wind that smelled of fish stung his skin as he eased his rusty door shut and peered tearfully at the buildings opposite. He thought all the windows were curtained with net until he realised the whiteness was salt, which had also scoured the front doors pale. In the very first window a handwritten sign offered ROOM. The wind hustled him across the road, which was strewn with various conditions of seaweed, to the fish-faced knocker on a door that had once been black.

More of the salt that gritted under his fingers was lodged in the hinge. He had to dig his thumb into the gaping mouth to heave the fish head high and slam it against the metal plate. He heard the blow fall flat in not much of a passage and a woman's voice demanding shrilly, "Who wants us now?"

The nearest to a response was an irregular series of slow footsteps that ended behind the door, which was dragged wide by a man who filled most of the opening. Grant couldn't tell how much of his volume he owed to his cable-knit jersey and loose trousers, but the bulk of his face drooped like perished rubber from his cheekbones. Salt might account for the redness of his small eyes, though perhaps anxiety had turned his sparse hair and dense eyebrows white. He hugged himself and shivered and glanced past his visitor, presumably at the wind. Parting his thick lips with a tongue as ashen, he mumbled, "Where have you come from?"

"Liverpool."

"Don't know it," the man said, and seemed ready to use that as an excuse to close the door.

A woman plodded out of the kitchen at the end of the cramped dingy hall. She looked as though marriage had transformed her into a version of the man, shorter but broader to compensate and with hair at least as white, not to mention clothes uncomfortably similar to his. "Bring him in," she urged.

"What are you looking for?" her husband muttered.

"Someone who can fix my car and a room if I'll need one."

"Twenty miles up the coast."

"I don't think it'll last that far. Won't they come here?"

"Of course they will if they're wanted, Tom. Let him in."

"You're staying, then."

"I expect I may have to. Can I phone first?"

"If you've the money you can give it a tackle."

"How much will it take?" When Tom's sole answer was a stare, Grant tried, "How much do you want?"

"Me, nothing. Nor her either. Phone's up the road."

Grant was turning away, not without relief, when the woman said, "Won't he need the number? Tommy and his Fiona."

"I know that. Did you get it?" Tom challenged Grant.

"I don't think—"

"Better start, then. Five. Three. Three. Five," Tom said and shut the door.

Grant gave in to an incredulous laugh that politeness required him to muffle. Perhaps another cottage might be more welcoming, he thought with dwindling conviction as he progressed along the seafront. He could hardly see through any of the windows, and such furniture as he could distinguish, by no means in every room, looked encrusted with more than dimness.

The few shops might have belonged to fishmongers; one window displayed a dusty plastic lobster on a marble slab also bearing stains suggestive of the prints of large wet hands. The last shop must have been more general, given the debris scattered about the bare floor—distorted but unopened tins, a disordered newspaper whose single legible headline said **FISH STOCKS DROP**, and was there a dead cat in the darkest corner? Beyond two further cottages was the refuge of the phone box.

Perhaps refuge was too strong a word. Slime on the floor must indicate that it hadn't been out of reach of the last high tide. A fishy smell that had accompanied him along the seafront was also present, presumably borne by the wind that kept lancing the trapped heat with chill. Vandalism appeared to have invaded even this little community; the phone directory was strewn across the metal shelf below the coin box in fragments so sodden they looked chewed. Grant had to adjust the rakish handset on its hook to obtain a tone before he dragged the indisposed dial to the numbers he'd repeated all the way to the box. He was trying to distinguish whether he was hearing static or simply the waves when a man's brusque practically Scottish voice said, "Beach."

"You aren't a garage, then."

"Who says I'm not? Beach's Garage."

"I'm with you now," Grant said, though feeling much as he had when Tom translated his wife's mnemonic. "And you fix cars."

"I'd be on the scrap heap if I didn't."

"Good," Grant blurted, and to compensate, "I mean, I've got one for you."

"Lucky me."

"It's a Cavalier that wouldn't go uphill."

"Can't say a word about it till I've seen it. All I want to know is where you are."

"Twenty miles south of you, they tell me."

"I don't need to ask who." After a pause during which Grant felt sought by the chill and the piscine smell, the repairman said, "I can't be there before dark."

"You think I should take a room."

"I don't tell anybody what to do. Invited you in as well, did they?"

The man's thriftiness with language was affecting Grant much as unresponsive pupils did. "Shouldn't they have?" he retorted.

"They'll do their best for you, Tom and Fiona. They need the cash."

"How did you know who they were?"

"There's always some that won't be driven out of their homes. A couple, anyway."

"Driven."

When competing at brevity brought no answer, Grant was about to add to his words when the man said, "You won't see many fish round Baiting anymore."

Grant heard the basis of a geography lesson in this. "So they've had to adapt to living off tourists."

"And travellers and whatever else they catch." The repairman interrupted himself with a cough that might have been a mirthless laugh. "Anyway, that's their business. I'll be there first thing in the morning."

The phone commenced droning like a fly attracted by the fishy smell until Grant stubbed his thumb on the hook. He dug the crumpled number of the holiday cottage out of his jeans and dialled, rousing only a bell that repeated itself as insistently as the waves for surely longer than his fellow students could have disagreed over who should answer it, even if they sustained the argument with a drink and quite possibly a toke to boot. No doubt they were expecting him to arrive ahead of them and set about organising as usual. He dropped the receiver onto its prongs and forced open the arthritic door.

He might have returned to his car along the sea wall, the top of which was nearly two feet wide, if waves hadn't been spilling over much of its length. There appeared to be little else to describe to any class he would teach; rubble was piled so high in the occasional alleys between the cottages that he couldn't even see behind them. The bay within the wall swarmed with infant waves, obscuring his view of whatever he kept glimpsing beneath them: probably the tops of pillars reinforcing the wall, except that the objects were irregularly spaced—the tips of a natural rock formation the wall had followed, then, although the string of blurred shapes put him in mind of a series of reflections of the moon. He was no closer to identifying them by the time he reached the Cavalier.

He manhandled his suitcase through the gap the creaky boot vouchsafed him and tramped across the road. He was hesitating over reaching for the knocker when the cottage door sprang open. He was bracing himself to be confronted by the husband, which must be why the sight of the woman's upturned face was disconcerting. "Get in, then," she exhorted with what could have been intended as rough humour.

Perhaps she was eager to shut out the wind that was trying all the inner doors, unless she wanted to exclude the smell. More of that lingered once Grant slammed the door than he found inviting. "Let's have you up," the woman said.

She'd hardly set one shabbily slippered foot on the lowest of the narrow uncarpeted stairs that bisected the hall when she swung round to eye him. "First time away?"

"Nothing like."

"Just your case looks so new."

"My parents bought me a set of them when I started college."

"We never had any children. What's your name, anyway?" she added with a fierceness he hoped she was directing at herself. "You know ours."

"Bill Grant."

"Good and strong," she said, giving him a slow appreciative blink before stumping shapelessly upwards to thump the first door open with her buttocks. The rumpled sea widened beyond the small window as he followed her into the room. He'd passed a number of framed photographs on his way upstairs, and here above the sink was yet another gray image of a man, nondescript except for the fish he was measuring between his hands. As in the other pictures, he was her husband, Tom. His presence helped the furniture—a barely even single bed, a barren dressing table, a wardrobe no larger than a phone box—make the room feel yet more confined. "Anything like home?" Fiona said.

It did remind him somewhat of his bedroom when he was half his size. "Something," he admitted.

"You want to feel at home if you go anywhere. I know I would." Having stared at him as though to ensure some of her meaning remained, she reached up to grab his shoulders with her cold swollen hands as an aid to squeezing past him. "We'll call you when it's time to put our snouts in the trough," she said.

He listened to the series of receding creaks her descent extracted from the stairs, and then he relieved his suitcase of the items he would need for an overnight stay, feeling absurdly as if he was preparing for a swift escape. Once he'd ventured across the tiny strident landing to the bathroom, a tiled white cell occupied by three dripping sweaters pegged on a rope above the bath and by a chilly damp that clung to him, he sat next to his pyjamas on the bed to scribble notes for a geography lesson based on Baiting, then sidled between the sink and the foot of the bed to the window.

It seemed his powers of observation needed work. The whitish rounded underwater blobs were closer together and to the middle of the sea wall than he remembered, unless any of them had indeed been a version of the moon, which was presently invisible above the roof. Perhaps he would soon be able to identify them, since the waves were progressing towards relative calm. He left his bulky bunch of keys on the windowsill before lying down to listen to the insistent susurration, which was occasionally interrupted by a plop that led him to believe the sea was less uninhabited than the repairman had said. He grew tired of craning to catch sight of whatever kept leaving ripples inside the sea wall, and by the time Fiona called "Ready" up the stairs, an invitation reminiscent of the beginning of a game, he was shelving towards sleep.

He must have been near to dreaming while awake, since he imagined that a face had edged out of hiding to watch him sit up. It might have been dour Tom's in the photograph, or the moon that had crept into view above the bay, possibly appending at least one blob to the cluster along the sea wall. "I'll be down," Grant shouted loud enough, he hoped, to finish wakening himself.

He wasn't expecting to eat in the kitchen, on a table whose unfolding scarcely left room for three hard straight chairs and a stained black range crowned with bubbling saucepans and, beneath a small window that grudgingly twilighted the room, a massive stone sink. He'd thought a fishy smell that had kept him company upstairs was carried by the wind, but now he realised it might also have been seeping up from the kitchen. He was exerting himself to look entertained when Tom frowned across the table at him. "She ought to have asked you to pay in advance."

"Oh, Tom, he's nothing but a youngster."

Grant was a little too much of one to appreciate being described that way. "Can I give you a cheque and a card?"

"And your name and address."

"Let's have you sitting down first," Fiona cried, stirring a pan that aggravated the smell.

Grant fumbled in the pocket of his jeans for the cheque book and card wallet. "How much am I going to owe you?"

Tom glowered at his soup bowl as though ashamed to ask. "Thirty if you're here for breakfast."

"Of course he will be, Tom."

"If he isn't sick of it by then."

Grant wrote a cheque in his best blackboard handwriting and slid it with his guarantee card and driving licence across the table. "Grant's the word, eh?" Tom grumbled, poking at the cards with a thick flabby forefinger whose nail was bitten raw. "She said you were a student, right enough."

"I teach as well," Grant was provoked into retorting. "That'll be my life."

"So what are you planning to fill their dim little heads with?"

"I wouldn't mind telling them the story of your village."

"Few years since it's been that." Tom finished scrutinising the cheque and folded it twice to slip into his trousers pocket, then stared at or through his guest. "On a night like this there'd be so many fish we'd have to bring the nets in before dawn or have them snapped."

"Nights like this make me want to swim," Fiona said, and perhaps more relevantly, "He used to like taking the boat out then."

She ladled soup into three decidedly various bowls, and watched with Tom while Grant committed his stained spoon to the viscous milky liquid. It explained the smell in the kitchen and tasted just not too strongly of it to be palatable. "There are still fish, then," he said, and when his hosts met this with identical small-eyed stares, "Good. Good."

"We've given up the fishing. We've come to an arrangement," said Tom.

Grant sensed that was as much as he would say about it, presumably resenting the loss of his independence. Nobody spoke until the bowls were empty, nor indeed until Fiona had served three platefuls of flaccid whitish meat accompanied by heaps of mush, apparently potatoes and some previously green vegetable. More of the meat finished gently quivering to itself in an indistinguishable lump on a platter. Grant thought rather than hoped it might be tripe, but unless the taste of the soup had lodged in his mouth, the main course wasn't mammalian. Having been watched throughout two rubbery mouthfuls, he felt expected to say at least, "That's good too. What is it?"

"All there is to eat round here," Tom said in a sudden dull rage.

"Now, Tom, it's not his fault."

"It's people's like his." Tom scowled at his dinner and then at the guest. "Want to know what you want to tell the sprats you're supposed to be teaching?"

"I believe I do, but if you'd like—"

"About time they were told to stop using cars for a start. And if the poor deprived mites can't live without them, tell them not to take them places they don't need to go."

"Saints, Tom, they're only youngsters."

"They'll grow up, won't they, if the world doesn't conk out first." With renewed ire he said to Grant "They need to do without their fridges and their freezers and their microwaves and whatever else is upsetting things."

Grant felt both accused of too much urban living and uneasy about how the meat was stored. Since no refrigerator was visible, he hoped it was fresh. He fed himself mouthfuls to be done with it and dinner generally, but hadn't completed the labour when he swallowed in order to speak. "At least you aren't alone, then."

"It's in your cities people go off and leave each other," muttered Tom.

"No, I mean you aren't the only ones in your village. I got the idea from your friend Mr. Beach you were."

Tom looked ready to deny any friendship, but it seemed he was preparing to demand, "Calling him a liar, are you?"

"I wouldn't say a liar, just mistaken," Grant said, nodding at the wall the cottage shared with its neighbour. His hosts merely eyed him as though they couldn't hear the renewed sounds beyond the wall, a floundering and shuffling that brought to mind someone old or otherwise incapacitated. "Rats?" he was compelled to assume.

"We've seen a few of those in our time," said Tom, continuing to regard him.

If that was meant for wit, Grant found it offered no more than the least of the children he'd had to teach. Some acoustic effect made the rat sound much larger as it scuffed along the far side of the wall before receding into the other cottage. Rather than risk stirring it or his hosts up further, Grant concentrated on downing enough of his meal to allow him to push away his plate and mime fullness. He was certainly full of a taste not altogether reminiscent of fish; he felt as though he was trying to swim through it, or it through him. When he drank a glass of the pitcher of water that had been the solitary accompaniment to the meal, he thought the taste was in there too.

Fiona cleared the plates into the sink, and that was the end of dinner. "Shall I help?" Grant had been brought up to offer.

"That's her work."

Since Fiona smiled indulgently at that, Grant didn't feel entitled to disagree. "I'd better go and phone, then."

He imagined he saw a pale shape lurch away from the window into the unspecific dimness—it must have been Fiona's reflection as she turned to blink at him. "He said you had."

"I ought to let my friends know I won't be seeing them tonight."

"They'll know when you don't, won't they? We don't want the waves carrying you off." Wiping her hands on a cloth that might have been part of someone's discarded garment, she pulled out a drawer beside the sink. "Stay in and we'll play a few games."

While the battered cardboard box she opened on the table was labelled Ludo, that wasn't quite what it contained. Rattling about on top of the familiar board inside the box were several fragments of a substance Grant told himself wasn't bone. "We make our own amusement round here," Fiona said. "We use whatever's sent us."

"He's not your lad."

"He could be."

The scrape of Grant's chair on the stone floor went some way towards expressing his discomfort. "I'll phone now," he said.

"Not driving, are you?" Tom enquired.

"Not at all." Grant couldn't be bothered resenting whatever the question implied. "I'm going to enjoy the walk."

"He'll be back soon for you to play with," Tom told his wife.

She turned to gaze out at the dark while Tom's stare weighed on their visitor, who stood up. "I won't need a key, will I?"

"We'll be waiting for you," Fiona mumbled.

Grant sensed tension as oppressive as a storm, and didn't thank the bare floorboards for amplifying his retreat along the hall. He seized the clammy latch and hauled the front door open. The night was almost stagnant. Subdued waves smoothed themselves out on the black water beyond the sea wall, inside which the bay chattered silently with whiteness beneath the incomplete mask of a moon a few days short of full. An odour he no longer thought it adequate to call fishy lingered in the humid air or inside him as he hurried towards the phone box.

The heat left over from the day more than kept pace with him. The infrequent jab of chill wind simply encouraged the smell. He wondered if an allergy to whatever he'd eaten was beginning to make itself felt in a recurrent sensation, expanding through him from his stomach, that his flesh was turning rubbery. The cottages had grown intensely present as chunks of moon fallen to earth, and seemed less deserted than he'd taken them to be: the moonlight showed that patches of some of the windows had been rubbed or breathed or even licked imperfectly clear. Once he thought faces rose like flotsam to watch him from the depths of three successive cottages, unless the same face was following him from house to ruined house. When he failed to restrain himself from looking, of course there was only moonlit dimness, and no dead cat in the general store. He did his best to scoff at himself as he reached the phone box.

Inside, the smell was lying in wait for him. He held the door open with his foot, though that admitted not only the infrequent wind but also more of the light that made his hand appear as pale as the receiver in it was black. His clumsy swollen fingers found the number in his pocket and held the scrap of paper against the inside of a frame that had once contained a mirror above the phone. Having managed to dial, he returned the paper to its niche against his unreasonably flabby thigh and clutched the receiver to his face with both hands. The fourth twosome of rings was parted by a clatter that let sounds of revelry at him, and belatedly a voice. "Who's this?"

For longer than a breath Grant felt as if he was being forced to stand up in class for a question he couldn't answer, and had to turn it back on the questioner. "It's Ian, isn't it?"

"Bill," Ian said, and shouted it to their friends. "Where have you got to?" he eventually thought to ask.

"I've broken down on the coast. I'm getting the car fixed tomorrow."

"When are we seeing you?"

"I told you, tomorrow," Grant said, though the notion felt remote in more ways than he could name.

"Have a drink for us, then, and we will for you. Won't we, you crew?"

The enthusiasm this aroused fell short of Grant, not least because he'd been reminded of the water accompanying dinner, a memory that revived the taste of the meal. "Don't get too pissed to drive tomorrow," Ian advised and made way for a chorus of drunken encouragement followed by the hungry buzz of the receiver.

Grant planted the receiver on its hook and shoved himself out of the box. Even if Baiting had boasted a pub, he would have made straight for his room; just now, supine was the only position that appealed to him. As the phone box shut with a muted thud that emphasised the desertion of the seafront, he set out along the top of the submerged wall.

It was broad enough for him to feel safe even if he wobbled—luckily for his career, however distant that seemed, teachers didn't have to be able to swim. He wouldn't have minded being able to progress at more than a shuffle towards the landmark of his car blackened by the moonlight, but the unsynchronised restlessness flanking him made him feel less than stable, as if he was advancing through some unfamiliar medium. The luminous reflection of the arc of cottages hung beneath them, a lower jaw whose unrest suggested it was eager to become a knowing grin. The shape of the bay must be causing ripples to resemble large slow bubbles above the huddle of round whitish shapes along the middle of the sea wall. He still couldn't make them out, nor how many images of the moon were tracking him on or just beneath the surface of the inlet. The closer he came to the halfway mark, the larger the bubbles appeared to grow. He was within a few yards of them, and feeling mesmerised by his own pace and by the whispers of the sea, when he heard a protracted stealthy wallowing behind him. He turned to find he had company on the far end of the wall.

It must be a swimmer, he told himself. Its glistening suggested it was wearing a wet suit rendered pallid by the moon; surely it couldn't be naked. Was the crouched figure making a joke of his progress? As it began to drag its feet, which struck him as unnecessarily large, along the wall, it looked no more at home on the path than he felt. Its head was bent low, and yet he had the disconcerting impression that it was presenting its face to him. It had shuffled several paces before he was able to grasp that he would rather outdistance it than see it in greater detail. He swung around and faltered just one step in the direction of his car. While his attention had been snared, another figure as squat and pale and dripping had set out for him from the opposite end of the wall.

He was paralysed by the spectacle of the pair converging effortfully but inexorably on him, the faces on their lowered heads indisputably towards him, until a movement let him peer in desperation at the farthest cottage. The front door had opened, and over the car roof he saw Tom. "Can you come and help me?" Grant shouted, stumbling towards him along the wall.

The cottages flattened and shrank his voice and sent him Tom's across the bay. "No need for that."

"There is," Grant pleaded. "That's in my way."

"Rude bugger."

Grant had to struggle to understand this meant him. It added itself to the sight of the advancing figure pallid as the underside of a dead fish. The closer it shuffled, the less it appeared to have for a face. "What are they?" he cried.

"They're all the moon brings us these days," Tom said, audibly holding Grant or people like him responsible, and stepped out of the cottage. He was naked, like the figures on the wall. The revelation arrested Grant while Tom plodded to the car. Indeed, he watched Tom unlock it and climb in before this sent him forward. "Stop that," he yelled. "What do you think you're doing? Get out of my car."

The Cavalier was no more likely to start first time for a naked driver than it ever did for him, he promised himself. Then it spluttered out a mass of fumes and performed a screeching U-turn. "Come back," Grant screamed. "You can't do that. You're polluting your environment."

No doubt his protests went unheard over the roaring of the engine. The sound took its time over dwindling once the coastline hid the car. The squat whitish shapes had halted once Grant had begun shouting. He strode at the figure crouched between him and the cottage and, since it didn't retreat, with as little effect at the other. He was repeating the manoeuvre, feeling like a puppet of his mounting panic, when that was aggravated by a burst of mirth. Fiona had appeared in the cottage doorway and was laughing at him. "Just jump in," she called across the water.

He didn't care how childish his answer sounded if she was capable of saving him. "I can't swim."

"What, a big strong lad like you?" Her heartiness increased as she declared "You can now. You can float, at any rate. Give it a try. We'll have to feed you up."

Beyond the spur of the coastline the sound of the car rose to a harsh note that was terminated by a massive splash. "That's the end of that," Fiona called. "You can be one of my big babies instead."

Grant's mind was refusing to encompass the implications of this when Tom came weltering like a half-submerged lump of the moon around the bay. Grant dashed along the sea wall, away from Fiona and Tom. He was almost at the middle section when he saw far too much in the water: not just the way that section could be opened as a gate, but the pallid roundish upturned faces that were clustered alongside. They must be holding their breath to have grown clear at last, their small flat unblinking eyes and, beneath the noseless nostrils, perfectly round mouths gaping in hunger that looked like surprise. As he wavered, terrified to pass above them, he had a final insight that he could have passed on to a classroom of pupils: the creatures must be waiting to open the gate and let in the tide and any fish it carried. "Don't mind them," Fiona shouted. "They don't mind we eat their dead. They even bring them now."

An upsurge of the fishy taste worse than nausea made Grant stagger along the wall. The waiting shape crouched forward, displaying the round-mouthed emotionless face altogether too high on its plump skull. Hands as whitish and as fat jerked up from the bay, snatching at Grant's feet. "That's the way, show him he's one of us," Fiona urged, casting off her clothes as she hurried to the water's edge.

She must have been encouraging Grant's tormentors to introduce him to the water. In a moment fingers caught his ankles and overbalanced him. His frantic instinctive response was to hurl himself away from them, into the open sea. Drowning seemed the most attractive prospect left to him.

The taste expanded through him, ousting the chill of the water with a sensation he was afraid to name. When he realised it was the experience of floating, he let out a howl that merely cleared his mouth of water. Too many pallid shapes for him to count were heaving themselves over the wall to surround him. He flailed his limbs and then tried holding them still, desperate to find a way of making himself sink. There was none. "Don't worry," Fiona shouted as she sloshed across the bay towards him, "you'll soon get used to our new member of the family," and, in what felt like the last of his sanity, Grant wondered if she was addressing his captors or Tom.

GREGORY L. NORRIS

DROWNING

SHE WAS different than the others, *beautiful* in a manner that defied the word's conventional definition. From the instant Homer's eyes locked with the specialized tank, and hands in heavy gloves peeled back the protective layers of sphagnum, and she was born back into this modern world after dying untold centuries in another, his heart reacted with powerful emotion. Homer Callison fell in love with the dead woman from the bog.

"Careful—*careful*," he barked, his façade disguising the truth. "Exposed to air, these bodies absolutely fall apart."

The museum's Downshire liaison held up his gloved hand. "No worry, sir. She's pickled properly in bog acid. We've seen to everything. She'll be as lovely in New York as in the shadow of Drum Keenagh Mountain. And as intact."

Homer exhaled through his nostrils and nodded. "Let me see the rest of her."

The liaison—Aileene or Aelwife, Homer couldn't exactly remember the man's name given the upsurge of energy and heat within his blood—rolled back the peat. Downshire Woman, as she was referred to in the museum's communiqués, lay supine in the suspension with hands folded over stomach in a funereal pose. She floated atop a layer of sphagnum, the barest smile frozen upon her lips. Highly acidic water, the bog's low temperature and lack of oxygen had preserved the dead beauty's skin. Calcium phosphate in those same conditions had dissolved her bones and eroded her right leg from the knee down. The left formed a gnarled club, almost to the shin.

His entire body reacted in tiny electric prickles, the pins and needles from sleep. Only Homer was awake.

"*Magnificent,*" Homer sighed.

"That she is, a true beauty," said Aileen or Aelwife. "A rare find, indeed."

The sallow yellow-green tint of the bog water in the tank glowed around the mummified corpse. Homer's gaze wandered over Downshire Woman's angelic face, the swell of her breasts, and the rough weave of her clothing visible through the solution. Pinned to the tunic was a trio of black beads, glass or polished volcanic stone, Homer assumed. Long seconds later, Homer blinked. He didn't realize he'd held his breath until the last sip of air began to boil in his lungs.

"Done," Homer said. "I'll be returning to the States and taking her with me."

The liaison's smile sharpened. "Now, wait a minute, Mister Callison. There are one or three finer details yet to discuss."

The briny stink of the surrounding landscape registered for the first time in multiple short breaths. With it came the fear she wouldn't be theirs, *his*. Homer's heart galloped. He choked down a dry swallow and then got right into the other man's face.

"I don't care about details—name your price. I'm authorized to pay you on behalf of the museum."

The man—his name was neither Aileen nor Aelwife but Aberdeen—nodded. "As you wish."

"Now. Immediately. See to it."

Homer tipped his gaze back to the makeshift glass sarcophagus and gasped. Downshire Woman's eyes were open and aimed at him. He blinked and understood it was the glass beads he'd focused upon, not her eyes. Those were tightly shut, submerged in a solution of bog acid powerful enough to dissolve bones. The depths would forever separate them, more so than even the centuries between his life and her death.

A stiff wind rose, bitter with the lingering chill of the early spring and the sea located close to the bog; the sea, which had created the conditions here. Homer shuddered. The sensation of being watched persisted. He realized the origin owed to Aberdeen and his men, the peat harvesters who'd discovered the sad beauty from another time. Jealousy replaced the flicker of unease. A storyline played out in Homer's imagination in which he was her liberator.

"Sir?" Aberdeen repeated.

"Yes, whatever is required."

"So you'll be overnighting in the village?"

Homer looked higher. The darkening gray palette overhead threatened more rain. "No," he said and then reconsidered haste. The trek through what felt like miles of Sitka spruce, lodge pine, and European larch stretched longer before them, especially with Downshire Woman's fragile remains in tow.

The first drops of a cold downpour pelted the bog. Some struck the open pools with empty, plunking notes. Haste? Beyond Drum Keenagh and the Downshire, even greater distances awaited. The whole of the Atlantic, in fact.

"Yes, but I'll depart the moment I've secured transportation."

Aberdeen ordered his men into action through grunts. A wooden cart used for hauling peat appeared. A glass seal was placed over the sarcophagus. Rough hands maneuvered Downshire Woman's resting place up, onto the cart, and under cover of a burlap tarp.

Homer, she called to him, only none but he heard the dreamy song of her voice. *Please don't leave me, Homer!*

"I won't, my love," Homer answered.

Aberdeen turned to him. "You say something, Mister Callison?"

"No, now get on with your work. I'm not paying you to—"

"Thus far, you haven't paid us anything," Aberdeen said through that slippery smile.

THE RETURN trip to the village of Hill Hampstead passed with maddening slowness. Aberdeen and his men had packed her in peat, as instructed, but Homer imagined the beauty jostled with every bump, and suffered knotted insides and sore feet as he walked beside the horse-drawn cart.

His room at the Rampion Inn was on the second floor at the top of a narrow staircase. There was no question his find, his *beauty*, would not travel to the room with him. A new anxiety possessed Homer on the final leg of the journey. She wasn't cargo or livery to be stacked with dried goods and other supplies.

Rain hammered Hill Hampstead and robbed the world of its

color, as the bog had his beauty. Beautiful Downshire Woman. His—

Homer's next breath came with difficulty. From somewhere nearby, a woman's sob reached through the rain's sharp staccato. The entire world wept around him through the rain's tears. Not even the blanched gold of lit windows representing dry rooms drove out the sorrow or the growing chill.

LAMB STEW and potatoes sat mostly untouched on his plate. Homer pushed the food around with his fork. The change of clothes clung to his flesh with an awkward, itchy fit. His mind drifted back to the locked door of the downstairs office where she rested, waited.

"Is the meal not to your liking?"

Homer blinked out of his trance to see the barmaid hovering close, too close. "No, everything is quite satisfactory, thank you."

She flashed a look that spoke of disbelief in his statement. Homer cut into a chunk of lamb, dragged it through the glop of beige gravy, and choked down the gamy morsel. The food wasn't unpalatable; by all rights, he should have been ravenous following the arduous hike to the bog and the even slower return to Hill Hampstead. Food and other comforts, however, eluded him. Downshire Woman consumed his thoughts and desires. Dare he think it? Even his secret lusts.

Homer pushed the plate away and reached for his billfold. On his way toward the stairs, he diverted to the sealed office and tested the door. Though locked, his anxiety worsened. Homer leaned his forehead against the door and whispered, "I am here, my love. You are not alone."

HE BOOKED return passage to New York onboard the luxury liner, due in Queenstown. Homer paced his room, unable to sleep. The cold April rain beat against the inn's eaves and windows. He struggled to breathe. It was, he thought, a condition like drowning while also still very much alive.

And then for the first time the notion struck him: most of the bodies recovered from the brine…hers was not the norm. Unlike Kreepen Man, discovered in 1903, Rendswühren Man, exhumed in Germany in 1871, Camnish Woman and Gallagh Man long decades before, Downshire Woman's pose—seeming at rest—ran counter to other findings. Bog bodies in Denmark, Germany, Ireland, and Scotland fell into one of two categories: victims of accident or murder. Those who'd stumbled to their deaths or were dragged there. But not the beauty locked behind the office door. According to her repose, she appeared to have gone to her life's end in the bog willingly.

Happily even, judging by her tranquil expression.

Homer closed his eyes. When he opened them, three black dots formed between the blinks, each perfectly round like the beads pinned to Downshire Woman's clothing.

SHE SOON visited him when, at last, he drifted into a state not quite asleep.

"You will not leave me, my love," she sang in a voice that seduced him fully, and sent ribbons of electricity jolting through his consciousness.

Homer opened his eyes and saw that she was stretched across the lumpy mattress beside him in her funereal pose. The bedclothes were damp. Tiny creatures born of the swamp undulated over and about her—segmented worms with hard shells, things with multitudes of short, skittering legs, pallid nightmares with unblinking amphibian eyes.

Homer gasped himself awake in the dark room. Rain lashed the Rampion Inn. In the darkness, he tested the blanket beside him—dry. Only a dream. Still, as raindrops pelted the windows, he sensed her there, somewhere in the shadows. The dream's revulsion evaporated. He began to sweat. The collar of his nightshirt tightened.

She called his name. "*Homer.*"

He sat up, aware of his thirst, his erection. Three black circles formed in the dark space before his eyes, reverse full moons that shone with a sinister kind of light.

"I hear you," he said, though Homer couldn't tell if he spoke with his lips or thoughts. "Yes, my beauty. My love…"

And then he felt the water engulf him, acidic and black, filled with primordial creatures. Homer clawed at his throat for breaths that refused to come. He was drowning, sinking. But he stopped caring, because she appeared to him in a vision that bloomed among the dark moonlight, alive as she once had been. Flowers, not sphagnum, wreathed her body, which glowed with an aura of sallow yellow color.

"Who are you?" he thought/asked. The words resonated with a hollow ripple, like notes of rain falling into stagnant puddles. He realized he could breathe again, though not exactly.

"I am...," she said.

He floated beside her and rested against the young beauty, conscious of the cold in her touch when she unfolded her hands and wrapped them around him in embrace.

"I am *yours*."

Homer exhaled. The vision shorted out. Instead of dark circles, he now stared at a section of pale white rectangle glowing in the bald illumination of an electric light. He sucked in a deep breath and woke fully. For a terrible instant, he had no idea where he was. Turning around, recognition dawned.

He stood outside the locked office door, hunched on bare feet and clad only in his nightshirt. For another second or so longer, the euphoria at having been with her in the bog persisted. Then an absence even deeper filled Homer, and the embarrassment at having wandered out of his room in a state of undress while in the throes of a somnambulant spell didn't register.

Homer leaned against the door and pressed his cheek against the wood. Cold worked through his sweaty skin. He could almost see her through the door. Almost.

"I'm here," he whispered.

Then he remembered her pledge and realized the opposite was true.

He was *hers*.

Hers, and Homer found himself strangely at peace with the notion, even selling himself on the belief that he would be okay when she went on display and others fell enamored with her beauty. He would see her daily. Nightly. She would no longer be lost to the bog, alone. And neither would he.

"Mister Callison?" a voice asked—the Rampion Inn's keeper, Mister Donnelly.

Homer peeled his face off the door and straightened. "I was checking to make sure the door was secured."

"Aye, you were," said Donnelly.

Though he made no direct contact with the other man's eyes, Homer gleaned Donnelly's expression from the periphery.

"What's in there is priceless," he said, and continued on his way past Donnelly to the staircase.

Donnelly be hanged, by morning he and his acquisition would be on their way to Queensland for the next long leg of the journey back to New York. Homer mopped his face with the back of his hand and entered his room. He imagined her in the bed beside him, wreathed in flowers. But when he shut his eyes and attempted to sleep, she again crawled with unwanted visitors from murky, stagnant pools, and the damp nightshirt clung to his flesh, making it impossible to drift off.

THE GIANT stretched across Cork Harbor, a sight unlike any seen before. Homer's inner voice urged him to absorb its majesty—he was part of history on that April day, witness to the amazing. Only that modern miracle of science and industry didn't interest him. His concern was foremost with miracles from the past.

"Be careful," he snapped at the four workers hired to transport Downshire Woman from dock to stateroom.

At the onset, the crate wrapped in thick folds of burlap had been consigned to cargo. But special consideration from the museum—and Homer's demands, made clear through several biting remarks—sealed the arrangement. The crate could not be trusted to survive intact in cargo, and that was the end of the argument. The men carried it amidships, through C Deck, to Homer's first-class suite.

The room was designed in the Queen Anne style, with scalloped ceilings and exquisite rosewood paneling. The bed was far better than that at the Rampion Inn; better than any in New York, Homer discovered after tipping the men and locking the stateroom's door.

Sleep claimed him almost immediately. Only sleeping felt more like falling, falling, through days and centuries. When he struck the icy water, she was waiting.

SHE WAS alive. Young, though she moved with a manner that suggested far greater years and experience. Beautiful, so beautiful, but there was an edge to the maiden's looks, a sharpness. She would always possess men's hearts, and so they plucked hers at the very peak of blossoming. Carved out her heart and filled the gap with common earth. A blood sacrifice to the

Three who ruled from the summit of Drum Keenagh whose names men had forgotten but still dreamed of; the Three who could destroy a harvest, and had—or grant bounty through bloodshed. She was lonely, and her looks were a curse. They tore out her heart and offered it to the Three in the hope they would be blessed.

Homer watched, a disconnected observer standing on the edge of the bog, aware of the sphagnum shifting beneath his feet. Spongy, almost not there, but there enough to register, he watched as the filthy men who'd done the deed lowered her corpse into the water. And again, he was struck by the smile frozen on her lips, as though their filthy hands somehow released her, as though she understood that living was the curse; that through death, she would be blessed forever and made immortal.

Something glinted above the bog. Homer struggled to break focus with the image of Downshire Woman as she sank into the brine. He gazed up and cold rushed through his core, deeper than bones or marrow. Soul? Suspended in the overcast sky above the bog, there but not fully like the carpet of sphagnum beneath his soles, were three perfect black circles. The sinister orbs hovered behind the clouds, ghostly and colossal afterimages. Three obsidian moons had jumped down from orbit to levitate above the mountain.

No, not moons. Homer felt the truth slither across his prickling epidermis with the unmistakable sensation of being watched. Three giant black eyes stared down through the clouds.

The eyes shifted.

Toward him.

Homer jolted awake in the darkness, unsure of where he was. The trio of obsidian eyes hovered in the darkness, their focus trained upon him. The eyes closed, and he grew conscious of a different sensation, that of a beating heart, one so powerful that it shook his surroundings.

He remembered his location and faced the direction of the pulse. The crate. The mummified corpse from the bog, beautiful Downshire Woman. Homer's heart quickened in counterpoint for different reasons.

He slid out of bed, slipped against the burlap-covered crate, and absorbed the vibrations rippling through the stateroom.

"I'm here, beloved," he whispered.

Then he realized the pulses weren't from heartbeats. The colossus had set sail and was steaming across the Atlantic, headed toward New York.

SHE WOULD become not only his work but his life. In a daze, Homer dressed in the one good suit he'd brought with him—midnight blue, fashionable and prestigious. He knotted his tie, tied the laces of his new wingtips, and wandered out of his stateroom for the first time since arrival, to D Deck. He was ravenous and soon discovered why: the whole of April the thirteenth had passed by while Homer slumbered. He hesitated leaving her, his new reason for being, but Homer sensed his world was soon about to change and the occasion needed to be marked if not exactly celebrated. Besides, the museum had spent a small fortune booking his passage home from Ireland. They would expect their money's worth.

He chose the First-Class Dining Saloon over the Café Parisien, drawn to its immensity. The saloon stretched between the second and third funnels and was, he assumed, the smoothest ride available onboard the luxury liner, judging by the absence of any vibration working up through floor tiles crafted to resemble Persian carpet.

The table and chairs were made from oak, the style Jacobean. Opulence and newness filled the space, along with the clink of glasses and the scrape of silverware across plates. Homer sat alone at the table and drank in the debauched gluttony around him—a ten-course meal that began with oysters and then featured consommé Olga, poached salmon in a mousseline sauce with cucumbers, filet mignon, roast duckling with apple sauce, creamed carrots, roast squab and cress, cold asparagus vinaigrette, pâté de foie gras served with celery, Waldorf pudding, and, finally, French ice cream.

Homer hesitated. He was surrounded by hundreds of souls but also alone. Alone, until the beautiful young woman approached the table where he sat by himself and, without waiting for an invitation or for Homer to pull out her chair, took a seat.

They faced one another across the table.

"Eat," she urged.

He couldn't be sure that her lips moved. From the periphery, he noted the three black circles pinned to her tunic.

As the courses arrived Homer ate like it was his last meal. Ate, like she had according to his vision from that long ago night before they tore out her heart and sacrificed her to the Three.

At one point, Homer realized the chair across from him was empty. He wiped his mouth on the linen napkin and nodded.

HE MADE it to the deck. The chill in the air instantly cut through clothes and skin and attempted to settle into Homer's marrow. The Atlantic rolled past far beneath, an oily black abyss that stunk of brine and fish. From the rail, Homer buried his eyes into the dark depths and revisited the bog, where she had willingly gone, a smile fixed upon her lips. New York no longer loomed at the end of the horizon, too distant to be seen. If he looked up, Homer knew Drum Keenagh would tower before him, with three empty eyes perched above its time eroded summit.

The Three were close, watching.

"I will honor her," he whispered. "Guard over her, my beauty, my life. I will keep her company, and love her for all time."

Homer closed his eyes and exhaled. His next conscious thought came at 11:40 as the behemoth's starboard bow struck the iceberg, shocking him out of the trance.

THE ORDER was given. Lifeboats were uncovered. A distress rocket sailed up, detonating somewhere far short of the unfeeling stars that speckled the cold night sky. More explosions followed from rockets and the vessel herself, which rapidly filled with water.

"Women and children first!" crewmen called, and Homer's only thought was for her.

He attempted to reach her but was impeded by the throng of passengers streaming out of staterooms and cabins. So many people, announced by screams as terror thickened and sweated through the corridors. Then the doomed *Titanic* itself, holding its head low in shame, held him back. The luxury liner was not unsinkable as trumpeted, and seemed to concede the truth by aiming its bow beneath the icy water.

Tears clouded Homer's eyes. "No," he said. And then he shouted the pledge, even as the ship was coming apart around him. "I won't leave you!"

THE FIRST lifeboat was lowered containing only twenty-eight souls though it was capable of carrying sixty-eight. Water surged into the ship. The tilt on the behemoth's deck grew steeper, steeper.

Homer stood frozen, barely aware of the hands of the two crewmen who dragged him away from C Deck and from reaching her. Around him, bodies scrambled to board the last of the lifeboats scurrying away from the *Titanic*. There was no way those few craft could hold the multitudes.

The word passed quickly through the crowd in angry shouts—"*Every man for himself!*"

An eighth distress rocket exploded overhead. Homer looked up. The flash waned. He blinked. Three obsidian circles superimposed across the insides of his eyelids.

She was down there, submerged again beneath the icy water. As men began to dive from the deck, swimming toward the flotilla of escaping lifeboats, Homer closed his eyes and waited.

A deafening crack of thunder split the luxury liner in two, and then he was falling. Homer struck the water. The last rational spark of his inner voice told him to surface, to swim—swim for his life toward the boats, because there was still a chance. But then he heard her voice, beckoning to him from the depth.

"You promised to be with me, my love. *Forever.*"

Homer opened his eyes. Far below, a spark of yellow-green light broke the darkness. It sank quickly out of sight.

I'm coming, Homer thought.

Then he exhaled the last sip of air from his lungs and breathed in the briny water.

MICHAEL BAILEY

UNDERWATER FERRIS WHEEL

THE LANKY gentleman in the pinstriped suit and moth-eaten neck ruffle staggers forward. He holds a card for you to take: COME RIDE THE UNDERWATER FERRIS WHEEL.

THERE IS a mixed scent of caramel corn, candied apples, corndogs, and spilled beer as Cate waits her turn in line with her son. The trailer has a sign lit with small yellowing bulbs, which works cordially with the other food trailers to light up the otherwise dark path of sweets, meats, and deep-fried foods on sticks.

She lets go of Ian long enough to dig in her purse for money.

"Large cotton candy," she says to the man leaning over the counter.

"Stick or bagged?" he says, pointing to the prefilled plastic bags of rainbow clouds lining the inside of the trailer.

In back, a man wearing a hairnet spins pink silk onto a cone of white paper.

She takes in the smells of hot sugar and oil.

"Stick," Cate says, and then adds a couple corndogs to the order.

She turns to her son to see if he wants ketchup or mustard or both, but he's gone. The couple standing in his place looks past her to the menu.

"Ian?"

She expects him at the ticket counter because he wanted more rides, not food, and he isn't there, nor is he wandering around the carny games across the promenade.

The others in line don't seem bothered that he's disappeared.

Cate holds a twenty-dollar bill instead of her son and no longer is she hungry, the appetite for junk food replaced with a gut-wrenching feeling of losing him. The man leaning through the window balances a pair of hefty golden corndogs in one hand, the other expecting money. She hands him the bill, not remembering having taken the cotton candy.

"Ma'am?"

He holds her food, calling for her as she calls for Ian.

"Did you see a boy," Cate says to the couple, her hand waist high to estimate height, "blonde hair, red and white striped shirt?"

Ian had chosen his outfit to match the tents he'd seen from the road when they were first setting up the carnival, she knew, because he had pestered her the entire week to go.

Shaking their heads, they take her place as she steps out of line.

Hundreds fill the food court and labyrinth of walking paths.

"Ma'am?" the man calls again.

She no longer cares about the food or the money. She holds on to the cotton candy like a beacon, hoping Ian will see the pink light and come running from out of the darkness.

"ONE MORE ride, after we eat something," Mom says.

She drags him through the crowd, making her own path. Behind them, Ian's wake is swallowed by kids able to ride the bigger rides (by themselves); drunken men stumbling around and yelling, hanging off each other, beers sloshing over plastic cups (even though Ian knew there's this place called the beer tree where they're supposed to drink); and other kids—Ian's age—dragged around by their parents.

Heavy metal music blasts from speakers hidden around the rides, and then pop music, and then what the older kids at school call dub step, and then country. The music changes as rapidly as the scenery, fading in and out as they make their way from the rides to the food court.

He has enough tickets clenched in his fist for two rides, but his mom wants to go with him on the Ferris wheel after they eat and that will eat all ten that are left.

"One last ride," she had said, meaning either the marvel of their day would soon end, or they'd be going to the stupid adult stuff, like seeing the animals, or going to the building with all the paintings and quilts, or to the place with the judged fruits and vegetables and jarred stuff, which they could see any other day by going to the grocery store.

And they still hadn't played any games.

"Step up, son," says a man who isn't his father. He holds a softball that's supposed to be tossed into a tilted basket without bouncing out. "It's easy," he says, tossing the ball underhand, and it *is* easy because it stays in the basket, and he wasn't even looking at it.

"You can win one of these to take home."

Stuffed animals bigger than real animals hang from their necks.

"Can we play games?"

"After we eat, maybe."

Maybe means no most times.

The man with unkempt hair and brownish teeth leans out of the booth. Three baskets are lined behind him, no one else playing his game.

"Free game for the boy," he says.

"Mom!"

"There are no free games," she says, pulling him along.

The man puts his hand to his heart.

"Honest. One free toss."

"Please, Mom?"

"A gift from me to you," the man says. "No money involved, I promise. Let the boy win something to take home. One free throw."

They stop.

A bright disc of moon shines onto them.

Ian already knows he wants the dragon. It's red and about two feet long and has a forked tongue hanging out of its mouth.

The man wanting him to win the stuffed animal is within what his mom had warned as "grabbing distance," holding out a yellow dimpled softball like they have in the batting cages. He tosses another behind his back, which spins in midair and lands in the basket.

"One," says his mom.

"There we go! Step up to the counter here, but don't lean over, and simply toss it in."

He throws another spinning ball and makes it in, and Ian thinks he might have it down. It just takes some backspin and needs to brush the upper, back portion of the basket.

Ian takes the ball, tries to copy the technique. The throw looks similar, but the ball hits the bottom of the basket and comes shooting out.

"Good try! I think you almost have it down." He holds out another yellow ball. "One more go at it."

"That's how they work," his mom whispers to him. "See?"

"One more for the boy."

"No thank you," she says.

The man in the booth sets the ball on the counter. "Try it again. No gimmicks. I want to see the boy get one in. You can try it, too," he says, placing a ball in front of her as well.

This time his mom's the one smiling, but her teeth are much whiter. She hesitates and drops Ian's hand.

"One more," she says.

She picks up the ball and throws it underhand, but doesn't put any spin on it so it bounces back at her and she he has to pick it off the ground.

"The boy's going to do it," the man says. "I have a good feeling about this one."

Ian takes his turn and again concentrates. He needs to throw it like last time, but not as high. Softly, he lets it roll off the tips of his fingers and there's plenty of backspin. It hits the basket in the right spot, nearly rolls out, but remains inside.

"He's a natural," the man in the booth says, crouching behind the counter.

Ian points to the dragon, but the man stands upright with a goofy smile. His prize is a cheap metallic-looking pinwheel tacked to the end of a straw that matches his shirt.

"Ah, you want the dragon," he says. "You gotta work your way up to that one by trading up from the smaller prizes."

He hadn't noticed the various price levels until now.

"That's how they work," his mom says.

YOU FLIP the card in your hand to find the other side black. The white side, with the message about the underwater Ferris wheel, contains only the invitation to ride it and nothing more. The lanky man in the pinstriped suit is gone. You took the card and read the words and sometime in between, the man resembling a makeup-less clown vanished into the crowd, his pinstriped coattails consumed by kids holding balloon animals.

CATE WANDERS, but not far. She doesn't want to stray from the food court because Ian can't be far and he's not prone to exploring on his own. She nearly steps onto a lone ticket, remembering Ian's longing for one final ride, and retrieves it from the ground.

LIKE MONEY in his wallet, Ian counts the red tear-off tickets to make sure there are still ten. He lets them accordion out, the last ticket lapping a puddle of a spilled soda. He holds his mom's hand as she drags him around. It would be much easier to count them if he had his other hand. He tugs and his mom tugs back to let him know she's in control and that counting won't be very easy.

He's not even hungry, but they pass through ever-changing music and laughing and cheering and the shrill of those flipping cages on the Zipper, kids screaming through the fast loop of the Ring of Fire—yellow and red bulbs flashing in circular patterns as the coaster cycles, first clockwise, then counterclockwise—and the mesmerizing vertical array of green, white, and blue bars of light on the Graviton as it spins like a flying saucer dreidel.

A tongue of tickets trails behind as he counts. He folds them, one onto the next, with the flip of his index finger and thumb. He gets to five when a Goth girl he recognizes from school bumps into his shoulder and jars them loose.

They stop at a path of pavement to let a medic golf cart pass, and that's when Ian notices what he thinks is a clown. He doesn't resemble the colorful clowns with the big feet and honking noses and painted faces, and he's not one of those clowns seen around the park squeak-tying balloons into poodles and pirate swords. This one's unremarkable, except for the scrunched doily thing around his neck. He looks like someone from an old black and white photograph, like the ones hanging on his grandma's wall: pictures of his grandparents' parents. He thinks of this because the man is not smiling—lips pressed in a flat line—like old people in old photographs, dressed in what he thinks is an old black suit and jacket.

And he stares, eyes not moving away.

The cart is suddenly gone, the world no longer paused. A soft tug on his hand tells him they're moving again and Ian looks at his feet for only a moment because someone's stepped on his laces and he nearly stumbles. Looking back, the man is gone, the crowd alive in his place.

"You've never had cotton candy before, have you," his mom says.

Ian shakes his head no, although she doesn't see him do it.

"When I was your age, I loved cotton candy," she says over the noise. "Me and your father used to go to the Brendan Carnival every year when it was still around."

When Dad was still around.

She always started conversations this way, always talking about what they did as a couple before Dad died, before a non-drunk driver clipped his car and drove him off the cliffs and into the ocean where he drowned.

"Your father always liked the candied apples. He had a sweet tooth. Sometimes we'd share the...I'm not sure what it was called, but it was multicolored popcorn in these little rectangular shapes wrapped in plastic; each clustered section of color was a different flavor, like orange or cherry or grape, kind of like caramel corn but different. I haven't had that in years."

The symphony of carnival noise dulls the closer they get to the food court, the lights brighter, and the stench of puke, beer, and cigarette smoke lingering, yet overpowered by Chinese food, barbeque, and deep-fried everything.

"Wait until you try the corndogs. Your father used to love those, too."

Nine tickets. There are only nine.

"Mom, we need to get another ticket to ride the—"

"No rides until after we eat. Here, this one looks good."

They stop in front of a trailer lit up in yellow bulbs and the entire thing glows. One of the smaller bulbs in the word SNACKS is missing, like his tenth ticket.

YOU ATTEMPT to follow him, but he weaves in and out of the

multitude of people as if gliding over ice: a glimpse of a coattail, a pinstriped leg, night-black hair. He is quickly absorbed into crowds of parents and children and ages in-between. The wind picks up and you drop the card, which flaps along the ground like a dead butterfly. It flips over and along the ground as easily as it flipped in your hand, and you can read the words in a strobe-like flutter of black and white—the invitation for the ride.

CATE TURNS a boy around, but it's not Ian.

She calls his name again and then sees him standing in front of a game booth fifty feet away. Warmth flushes through her body as she remembers to breathe, the thought of losing Ian more than she can handle. Losing a husband is one thing, but losing their only son who resembles him so undeniably…

"Ian!" she says, willing her voice to reach him.

He turns just then, but not in her direction, and her heart drops.

Running to him, she continues to call his name, jouncing shoulders against those in her path and nearly trampling people over entirely. A baby stroller built for two trips her and she falls and scrapes her knee, rises, and keeps going, somehow never losing grasp of the lone red ticket and the cotton candy she points to the sky. Ian passes in and out of view, as if projected against the throng of fairgoers from a spinning shadow lamp.

"Ian!"

One moment he's there, another he's not.

A flash of silver and the pinwheel he no longer wants falls to the ground. A gangly man leans over to pick it up—one of the carnival folk, perhaps. He's the only immobile person in the multitude and wears a black pinstriped suit, as out of place in the crowd as would be a dandelion disguised in a bouquet of yellow roses. An aged neck ruffle strangles his throat and he smiles as she approaches.

He offers the pinwheel, but she doesn't want it. She wants her son.

Cate looks around him frantically.

"Did you see the boy who dropped that?"

The silence tells her he's mute. He stares at her, expressionless, his face drained of both color and emotion.

"I'm looking for my son, Ian. He dropped this," she says, taking it from him, "and you just picked it up. Did you see where he was going?"

He doesn't point, nor does he say anything. He simply takes his finger and spins the cheap toy on the stick and magically reveals a card from one of his shirtsleeves. The man stands there a moment before facing the ocean pier.

HE TUGS on his mom's hand, but she doesn't tug back to let him know she's still in control. Glancing up, Ian finds that he's not holding his mother's hand at all, but the hand of a tall man with long arms that dangle well past his knees. He can't remember ever letting go, but he must have, and somehow grabbed this man instead. Clammy fingers curl around his own. It's the man who isn't a clown, the old photograph man he saw before.

Ian jump-startles and the man let's go.

He isn't scary because he doesn't wear a fake face like regular clowns who pretend to be happy or sad or sometimes mad. He has a normal face.

He hands Ian a card.

"Are you supposed to be a mime?"

He doesn't say anything.

"I read a story once about a mime and he never said anything, either. He would pretend to be stuck in invisible boxes and climb ropes that weren't really there. But he wore makeup and had a white face and black lips like Charlie Chaplin. I don't know who that is, but my mom says he looked like Charlie Chaplin."

He shows Ian the rest of the cards, which are bound together with a rubber band. His dad used to do card tricks, so Ian knows what to do. He's supposed to take a card and look at it without showing and hand it back. Ian's card is a stained joker with worn edges and a crease down the middle. The joker wears a jester hat and rides a unicycle and looks drawn in scribbles of pen.

Before handing it back, the cards are splayed before him, at least two dozen. They are all different. About half are standard playing cards of different makes, some old, some new; mixed within are handmade cards like the joker, along with some baseball cards, a library card, credit cards, and a few driver's licenses from different states.

Ian hands the card to him facedown and watches as it's shuffled into the deck over and over again, and in lots of different ways. The unsmiling *carny*—his mom would call him—bends the cards and bends them back like his dad used to, and shuffles them flat in the air with his thumbs and then reverses the cards in an arc to slide them in place—what his dad deemed "the bridge."

He hands the deck to Ian.

"I pick one?"

The man doesn't say anything.

Expecting his card to be on top because the back looks similar, Ian lifts a three of diamonds, which looks as though someone with shaky fingers drew the number with black crayon and then smudged three red diamonds on the card with lipstick. The one after it isn't his card either, but a jack of clubs. He flips over the next card with stats printed on the back and it's a rookie card for someone who used to play on a team called the Royals; over the player's face is a smiley face sticker with the eyes scratched out. The next card is a VISA. The next is a king of hearts from a standard Bicycle deck, followed by a ripped-in-half five-dollar bill with a spade drawn in Sharpie over the president's face, and then a seven of clubs, and then another hand-drawn card.

Confused, Ian hands the deck back to him.

The man wraps a rubber band around the cards and slides them into his suit pocket.

"What's the trick?"

The man holds out his hand, as if peddling for money.

That's how they work, his mom would say.

Three of the fingers curl until he's pointing at Ian's pinwheel.

As if on cue, a cool breeze spins the cheap metallic flower around, which Ian didn't want anyway; he had wanted the dragon but they didn't have enough money to pay for more games, even though he would have given up food to pay for a few more tosses into the basket so he could win the bigger prize. Dad would have let them play. If he hadn't died, they'd have enough money to play more games and ride more rides and really have fun.

Ian gladly gives it to him. In the process, the man who looks sort of like a clown clumsily drops it as part of a gag and they both fetch for it on the ground. Lying next to the cheap toy is Ian's joker card, which the trickster silently places into his pocket with the others.

He pulls out another card, but this time it's not one of the strange playing cards; it's a business card with a black side that reflects the moon and a white side that absorbs its light. A trade for the pinwheel, it seems. Printed on the white side is an invitation.

YOU HAND the carnival worker five red tickets and he lets you past the chain and through the gate. A set of aluminum steps leads to a grated path to the ten-story wheel. Every angle of metal is lit by long neon lights and flashing bulbs that cycle in hypnotic patterns. The cart awaits—the slightly rocking yellow one with the number eight on the side. You are alone for the ride as you were in line, the carnival empty. A mechanical click and the wheel moves. The world drops with the wind at your back. You elevate in a reverse motion with the giant silver axle as you rotate around. Rods and lights and the other carts fall as you rise. At the peak, black water rises from the pier, and for a moment you float above it all, nothing but sky and water and the thin line between. The entire lit wheel is cast against the water, appearing as though there are riders beneath the placid surface revolving horizontally, perhaps looking up to you in the stars. You see your reflection on the water, and then you free-fall fly, arms stretched outward, the wind at your face. The water rising.

COME RIDE THE UNDERWATER FERRIS WHEEL

Cate reads the card a second time, and when she looks up from it, the man in the pinstriped suit is gone, like her son.

"Ian!" she calls.

She parts through people on her way to the water's edge, which seems so far away. Why would he go to the pier? Somehow she knew he'd be there, and somehow the man with the moth-eaten neck ruffle knew. He was leading her to the—

Your father and I would always ride the Ferris wheel, she had told Ian in the car. That's where she'd find him. She couldn't stop talking about it on their way to the carnival. *It was always the last thing we did before going home*, she had said.

Running takes the air from her lungs and pierces her side but she spots him at the base of the ride, gazing up in wonder. She spins him around to find his eyes glossy and terrified.

"THERE'S NO underwater Ferris wheel," Ian tells the water.

There's only the reflection of the *real* Ferris wheel.

"The card's a lie."

He walks along the planks, peering over the side to the black water. If there *was* an underwater ride, he'd at least see some kind of glowing light from below.

One last ride, his mom said.

Suddenly, his stomach aches empty and craves a corndog now. He doesn't remember ever letting go of her hand while in line but he must've let go at some point and grabbed the hand of the clown who wasn't really a clown—the man with the bad card trick who gave him the stupid invitation to see something that wasn't even there.

Mom had warned him to stay close and not to wander.

Ian knew the park and could find his way around easily enough, but finding his mom would be like finding his dad's body, which the people looking for him couldn't do after he went over the cliff. Even if he found his mom, she'd be mad and they'd leave early. They wouldn't ride the Ferris wheel as their last ride like she remembered doing with Dad. Ian only had nine tickets anyway because he dropped one. He holds them to the light, counting again to make sure.

THE PLACID water breaks, enveloping you as you ride the yellow cart beneath the surface. Round you go as the un-reflection of the Ferris wheel above glows through a watery blur. As you come round, you see them gathered on the pier. A woman and boy embrace and it feels like home.

MARGE SIMON

THE OLD WOMAN AND THE SEA

MAMA STOOD boning fish in her kitchen. She wiped her forehead with the back of her hand. It left a trail of silver scales that matched the streaks in her hair. The bones were piled on faded newspapers she'd never read. She couldn't see the tiny print, only the headline: FAMINE. But that was somewhere else, it had to be. There would always be plenty of fish. Her son James often said that, like his father before him. "Fish are like the news, something to get by on."

Where the famine was, she didn't know. They had no close neighbors, no visitors. James always made sure to pay the bills, he was good with figures. All this was done by mail, though no postman had come for many days. James usually left his boots on the porch, but not this time. She dropped the knife when she saw his face.

"Bad news?" James shook his head and slumped in a chair. He stared off at something distant. *He'll tell me when he's ready, he always does,* she told herself. Mama returned to the fish, arranged a row of neat fillets and covered them with a plate. There were a few potatoes left. They would do, if he had brought the shrimp. She didn't want to bother him right then, but she had to ask. When she got no response, she touched his arm.

"Don't," James pulled away. "They're gone." She heard this but didn't understand. It was something bad, she knew that much. "I thought they were my friends, Mama." He put his head on his arms. "They left us here to starve!"

She clicked her tongue. "Then we'll have to wait," she said. "Can't make chowder without shrimp. She paused to look over at him. "Your friends—they're coming back, aren't they?" James shook his head and covered his eyes.

Mama wrapped the fish bones and scales in the last piece of newspaper. She thought about asking him to get more papers, but not now. No, now was the time for wine. She kept some old wine bottles in the cabinet under the sink. She selected one, wiped it off, and set it on the table. He looked up at her. She uncorked it and poured his mug to the brim. He pushed it away. Heaving a sigh, she picked it up and tasted it.

"It is a good wine, son. You are not going to join me?"

"Why should I, Mama? What's to celebrate? We're going to die, don't you see?"

That night, she fried the fillets and a few of the last potatoes. They ate in silence. James took the bottle and went outside to sit on the porch. He was still there in the morning, having dozed off. The bottle was empty.

Mama baked two loaves of bread with the last of the flour Thank goodness they had a gas stove. The electric hadn't been working at all. She couldn't remember how long ago it had stopped, but it didn't really matter. They always went to bed early. Maybe James forgot to pay the bill last month. She kept meaning to mention it to him, but he didn't seem to care if she was talking to him or not.

After a lunch of bread and cheese, Mama brought out her Bible. "Listen to this, James. 'Master, we toiled all night and took nothing! But at your word I will let down the nets. And when they had done this, they enclosed a large number of fish, and their nets were breaking.'—that was from Luke." She stopped and looked at him over her glasses. His eyes were closed.

"And here, listen to this from John where Jesus said to the fishermen, 'Cast the net on the right side of the boat, and you will find some.' So they cast it, and it turned out they were not able to haul all of it in, because of so many fish. Well, son? You see how clear the good book makes things?" James remained as he was. Smoothing her apron, she knelt before him at eye level, shaking his arm for attention. "Now then, James, all you have to do is take the boat out again. Give it one more try, son. Have a little faith, for the Lord will provide."

James' eyes flew open. "Get off my back, Mama! Screw your sweet Jesus! You quote that stuff at me—you have no idea what this means, do you? No fish left. Or if any are, they're fucking polluted! Don't you see, your God has forsaken you, me, probably the world—I don't know. It's like this all over, don't you read the papers?"

"We don't have any news anymore, James. And besides, you know my poor weak eyes. I'm not good with reading, except for the Lord's word."

"Yeah, and your Lord's word is worth crap." He sat up, digging around in his jeans. "Here, Mama, here's the key! You think there's fish in that goddamn ocean, you go find them yourself." He flung the key at her. It bounced off the stove and onto the floor. Wordlessly she picked it up and placed it on the shelf by the door.

The next day, he'd taken all the bottles from under the sink. Some were on the kitchen table. Two lay empty on the floor and he was passed out on the sofa. Her fish knife had slipped from his hand. There was a bloody stain on the rug and blood on his wrists.

"James! What? Why—??" Mama checked his wrists, but the slashes weren't as deep as they'd seemed. She washed and bandaged them while he moaned and mumbled nonsense. For her, it was unthinkably horrid—seeing him like this—her James, her honest, dependable son.

Blinking back tears, Mama gripped the edge of the sink. Didn't her own mama save her and her brother from a fire, so very long ago? She remembered it had to do with something her father had done. He was a drunk, that's what her mama said. He died in that horrible blaze. After that, they'd moved to this little fishing village. Though times were hard, they'd managed to make ends meet without him. It was here that she'd met Samuel. Their son looked so much like his father. She'd had such hopes for her James, even though Sam died when he was just a child.

She squared her shoulders and lifted her eyes. "Time to do something now! It is up to me, isn't it? The Lord helps those who help themselves, as the good book says. There are plenty of fish out there, I know it, and I'll prove it to him. That'll bring him to his senses."

The hat her Samuel always wore was still on the same hook by the door. It was too big, but she pushed it down on her head anyway, saying a silent prayer. She'd take it out herself, the boat that James refused to use again. He'd been so proud of it from the start. He'd worked on the docks and saved every penny, doing outside jobs. He'd taken her out in it once, proudly showing her the dials with little needles that meant a gauge for gas and speed and some other things she couldn't remember. He even let her have a try at the wheel. That was fun, like driving a car—though she never learned to do more than steer one, never got her license. No need, of course. This was a small town, the store was just down the road. Then he wanted her to try the throttle. He'd laughed when she was so fearful of pushing it up to a higher speed. This time she wouldn't be afraid.

Even though it was early morning, the air was heavy with heat. She noticed this because there used to be a nice breeze blowing from the sea this time of year. But then, she didn't get around outside for a walk like she used to. There was also an absence of gulls, which was puzzling, but she gave it little mind. It wasn't far to the docks where the boat was moored. James was right about one thing, the other boats were gone. She smiled to herself. *Of course they are gone, they are all away fishing.* James had to be mistaken all along. Untying the boat was a struggle. She finally got it loose from its moorings and dropped the rope to climb aboard, banging her shins in the process.

It wasn't a large boat, but to her it appeared almost as long as their house. Maybe longer, she wasn't sure. He'd painted a blue stripe around the sides, christened it *Lady Luck* with a bottle of wine. That was such an exciting day! They'd invited the neighbors and even bought a keg of beer to celebrate.

James awoke at the sound of the motor turning over in the distance. His head was pounding. Scratching his chest, he got up for a glass of water. As he drank, he glanced out the window. He dropped the glass and bolted out the door. By the time he'd reached the dock, she'd remembered to pull out the choke and the engine caught. He grabbed the rapidly uncoiling rope she'd left on the dock and it whipped several times tautly around his arm. "Mama! Stop! There's not enough gas!"

But Mama was on a mission now. She didn't hear his screams

as he was yanked into the water. Eyes on the horizon, she swung the *Lady Luck* around, jammed it down full throttle. The craft seemed to be pulling to the right, so it was a struggle to make it stay on course, but she put all her strength into keeping it from reeling sideways. By and by, she hit a current that compensated some. She realized then that she was very thirsty. Water! She'd forgotten to bring any fresh water. Well, the Lord would surely provide.

A few minutes later, she remembered she'd not brought bait, or set the lines out. She muttered to herself, fanning her face with Samuel's hat. Noon came and went.

"Oh yes, my Samuel—your dear father, James—he was such a fine man. Hah! Ran off with our pastor's daughter, that little hussy! Of course, I never told you about it, James. The shame of it. A braggart and a fool he was! Well, I'll show him. I'll show you too, son! I can do this."

The heat of the sun pounding down steadily for hours was making her head fuzzy, and she was so terribly thirsty. Besides that, the throttle was still up at full, but the boat wouldn't go any faster. Something must be wrong. Finally she looked around, thinking the boat had snagged on something. She noticed the line, though it did appear more like a rope—maybe she had set a line and forgotten?—but it was taut to the right side of the boat.

The Lord has answered her prayers. It must be a big fish—a huge fish, enough to feed them for days! She could salt it down and it will stay edible, she knew how to do that. Setting the throttle to idle, she pulled in the rope. It took all her strength, drawing it hand over hand, but at last she saw what was caught on the rope. It was a dreadful thing. The face was contorted, mouth open, eyes wide—one leg skinned and dangling, the other wasn't there at all.

Mama cradled his head in her lap. She hummed a lullaby, the one that was his favorite as a baby. All the while, a single fin made circles around the boat. She spotted it and pushed his lifeless shoulders up.

"You see that, James? I told you there were fish in the sea, but you wouldn't believe. I told you to have faith. Just look out there! The Lord provides."

The motor coughed and sputtered a bit before it died.

CAITLÍN R. KIERNAN

IN THE DREAMTIME OF LADY RESURRECTION

How I, then a young girl, came to think of, and to dilate upon, so very hideous an idea?
—Mary Wollstonecraft Godwin Shelley (October 15th, 1831)

"WAKE UP," she whispers, as ever she is always whispering with those demanding, ashen lips, but I do not open my eyes. I do not wake up, as she has bidden me to do, but, instead, lie drifting in this amniotic moment, unwilling to move one instant forward and incapable of retreating by even the scant breadth of a single second. For now, there is *only* now; yet, even so, an infinity stretches all around, haunted by dim shapes and half-glimpsed phantasmagoria, and if I named this time and place, I might name it Pluto or Orcus or Dis Pater. But never would I name it purgatorial, for here there are no purging flames, nor trials of final purification from venial transgressions. I have not arrived here by any shade of damnation and await no deliverance, but scud gently through Pre-Adamite seas, and so might I name this wide pacific realm *Womb,* the uterus common to all that which has ever risen squirming from mere insensate earth. I might name it *Mother.* I might best call it nothing at all, for a name may only lessen and constrain this inconceivable vastness.

"Wake up now," she whispers, but I shall rather seek these

deeper currents.

No longer can I distinguish that which is *without* from that which is *within.* In ocher and loden green and malachite dusks do I dissolve and somehow still retain this flesh and this unbeating heart and this blood grown cold and stagnant in my veins. Even as I slip free, I am constrained, and in the eel-grass shadows do I descry her desperate, damned form bending low above this warm and salty sea where she has lain me down. She is Heaven, her milky skin is star-pierced through a thousand, thousand times to spill forth droplets of the dazzling light which is but one half of her unspeakable art. She would have me think it the totality, as though a dead woman is blind merely because her eyes remain shut. Long did I suspect the whole of her. When I breathed and had occasion to walk beneath the sun and moon, even then did I harbour my suspicions and guess at the blackness fastidiously concealed within that blinding glare. And here, at this moment, she is to me as naked as in the hour of her birth, and no guise nor glamour would ever hide from me that perpetual evening of her soul. At this moment, all and everything is laid bare. I am gutted like a gasping fish, and she is flayed by revelation.

She whispers to me, and I float across endless plains of primordial silt and gaping hadopelagic chasms where sometimes I sense the awful minds of other sleepers, ancient before the coming of time, waiting alone in sunken temples and drowned sepulchers. Below me lies the gray and glairy mass of Professor Huxley's *Bathybius haeckelii,* the boundless, wriggling sheet of *Urschleim* that encircles all the globe. Here and there do I catch sight of the bleached skeletons of mighty whales and ichthyosauria, their bones gnawed raw by centuries and millennia and aeons, by the busy proboscides of nameless invertebrata. The struts of a Leviathan's ribcage rise from the gloom like a cathedral's vaulted roof, and a startled retinue of spiny crabs wave threatful pincers that I might not forget I am the intruder. For this I *would* forget, and forswear that tattered life she stole and now so labours to restore, were that choice only mine to make.

I know this is no ocean, and I know there is no firmament set out over me. But I am sinking, all the same, spiraling down with infinite slowness toward some unimaginable beginning or conclusion (as though there is a difference between the two). And you watch on worriedly, and yet always that devouring curiosity to defuse any fear or regret. Your hands wander impatiently across copper coils and spark tungsten filaments, tap upon sluggish dials and tug so slightly at the rubber tubes that enter and exit me as though I have sprouted a bouquet of umbilici. You mind the gate and the road back, and so I turn away and would not see your pale, exhausted face.

With a glass dropper, you taint my pool with poisonous tinctures of quicksilver and iodine, meaning to shock me back into a discarded shell.

And I misstep, then, some fraction of a footfall this way or that, and now somehow I have not yet felt the snip that divided *me* from *me.* I sit naked on a wooden stool near *Der Ocean auf dem Tische,* the great vivarium tank you have fashioned from iron and plate glass and marble.

You will be my goldfish, you laugh. *You will be my newt. What better part could you ever play, my dear?*

You kiss my bare shoulders and my lips, and I taste brandy on your tongue. You hold my breasts cupped in your hands and tease my nipples with your teeth. And I know none of this is misdirection to put my mind at ease, but rather your delight in changes to come. The experiment is your bacchanal, and the mad glint in your eyes would shame any maenad or rutting satyr. I have no delusions regarding what is soon to come. I am the sacrifice, and it matters little or none at all whether the altar you have raised is to Science or Dionysus.

"Oh, if I could stand in your place," you sigh, and again your lips brush mine. "If I could *see* what you will see and *feel* what you will feel!"

"I will be your eyes," I say, echoing myself. "I will be your curious, probing hands." These might be wedding vows that we exchange. These might be the last words of the condemned on the morning of her execution.

"Yes, you shall, but I would make this journey myself, and have need of no surrogate." Then and now, I wonder in secret if you mean everything you say. It is easy to declare envy when there is no likelihood of exchanging places. "Where you go, my love, all go in due time, but you may be the first ever to return and report to the living what she has witnessed there."

You kneel before me, as if in awe or gratitude, and your head settles upon my lap. I touch your golden hair with fingers that have scarcely begun to feel the tingling and chill, the numbness that will consume me soon enough. You kindly offered to place the lethal preparation in a cup of something sweet that I would not taste its bitterness, but I told you how I preferred to know my executioner and would not have his grim face so pleasantly hooded. I took it in a single acrid spoonful, and now we wait, and I touch your golden hair.

"When I was a girl," I begin, then must pause to lick my dry lips.

"You have told me this story already."

"I would have you hear it once more. Am I not accorded some last indulgence before the stroll to the gallows?"

"It will not be a gallows," you reply, but there is a sharp edge around your words, a brittle frame and all the gilt flaking free. "Indeed, it will be little more than a quick glance stolen through a window before the drapes are drawn shut against you. So, dear, you do not stand to *earn* some final coddling, not this day, and so I would not hear that tale repeated, when I know it as well as I know the four syllables of my own beloved's name."

"You *will* hear me," I say, and my fingers twine and knot themselves tightly in your hair. A few flaxen strands pull free, and I hope I can carry them down into the dark with me. You tense, but do not pull away or make any further protest. "When I was a girl, my own brother died beneath the wheels of an ox cart. It was an accident, of course. But still his skull was broken and his chest all staved in. Though, in the end, no one was judged at fault."

I sit on my stool, and you kneel there on the stone floor, waiting for me to be done, restlessly awaiting my passage and the moment when I have been rendered incapable of repeating familiar tales you do not wish to hear retold.

"I held him, what remained of him. I felt the shudder when his child's soul pulled loose from its prison. His blue eyes were as bright in that instant as the glare of sunlight off freshly fallen snow. As for the man who drove the cart, he committed suicide some weeks later, though I did not learn this until I was almost grown."

"There is no ox cart here," you whisper. "There are no careless hooves, and no innocent drover."

"I did not say he was a drover. I have never said that. He was merely a farmer, I think, on his way to market with a load of potatoes and cabbages. My brother's entire unlived life traded for only a few bushels of potatoes and cabbages. That must be esteemed a bargain, by any measure."

"We should begin now," you say, and I don't disagree, for my legs are growing stiff and an indefinable weight has begun to press in upon me. I was warned of these symptoms, and so there is not surprise, only the fear that I have prayed I would be strong enough to bear. You stand and help me to my feet, then lead me the short distance to the vivarium tank. Suddenly, I cannot escape the fanciful and disagreeable impression that your mechanical apparatuses and contraptions are watching on. Maybe, I think, they have been watching all along. Perhaps, they were my jurors, an impassionate, unbiased tribunal of brass and steel and porcelain, and now they gaze out with automaton eyes and exhale steam and oily vapours to see their sentence served. You told me there would be madness, that the toxin would act upon my mind as well as my body, but in my madness I have forgotten the warning.

"Please, I would not have them see me, not like this," I tell you, but already we have reached the great tank that will only serve as my carriage for these brief and extraordinary travels—if your calculations and theories are proved correct—or that will become my deathbed, if, perchance, you have made some critical error. There is a stepladder, and you guide me, and so I endeavor not to feel their enthusiastic, damp-palmed scrutiny. I sit down on the platform at the top of the ladder and let my feet dangle into the warm liquid, both my feet and then my legs up to the knees. It is not an objectionable sensation and promises that I will not be cold for much longer. Streams of bubbles rise slowly from vents set into the rear wall of the tank, stirring and oxygenating this translucent primal soup of viscous humours, your painstaking brew of protéine and hæmatoglobin, carbamide resin and cellulose, water and phlegm and bile. All those substances believed fundamental to life, a recipe gleaned from our dusty volumes of Medieval alchemy and metaphysics, but also from your own researches and the work of more modern scientific practitioners and professors of chemistry and anatomy. Previously, I have found the odor all but unbearable, though now there seems to be no detectable scent at all.

"Believe me," you say, "I will have you back with me in less than an hour." And I try hard then to remember how long an hour is, but the poison leeches away even the memory of time. With hands as gentle as a midwife's, you help me from the platform and into my strange bath, and you keep my head above the surface until the last convulsions have come and gone and I am made no more than any cadaver.

"Wake up," she says—*you* say—but the shock of the mercury and iodine you administered to the vivarium have rapidly faded, and once more there is but the absolute and inviolable present moment, so impervious and sacrosanct that I can not even imagine conscious action, which would require the concept of an apprehension of some future, that time is somehow more than this static aqueous matrix surrounding and defining me.

"Do you hear me? Can you not even *hear* me?"

All at once, and with a certitude almost agonizing in its omneity, I am aware that I am being watched. No, that is not right. That is not precisely the way of it. All at once, I know that I am being watched by eyes which have not heretofore beheld me; all along there have been *her* eyes, as well as the stalked eyes of the scuttling crabs I mentioned and other such creeping, slithering inhabitants of my mind's ocean as have glommed the dim pageant of my voyage. But *these* eyes, and this spectator—my love, nothing has ever seen me with such complete and merciless understanding. And now the act of *seeing* has ceased to be a passive action, as the act of being *seen* has stopped being an activity that neither diminishes nor alters the observed. I would scream, but dead women do not seem to be permitted that luxury, and the scream of my soul is as silent as the moon. And in another place and in another time where *past* and *future* still hold meaning, you plunge your arms into the tank, hauling me up from the shallow deep and moving me not one whit. I am fixed by these eyes, like a butterfly pinned after the killing jar.

It does not speak to me, for there can be no need of speech when vision is so thorough and so incapable of misreckoning. Plagues need not speak, nor floods, nor the voracious winds of tropical hurricanes. A thing with eyes for teeth, eyes for its tongue and gullet. A thing which has been waiting for me in this moment that has no antecedents and which can spawn no successors. Maybe it waits here for every dying man and woman, for every insect and beast and falling leaf, or maybe some specific quality of my obliteration has brought me to its attention. Possibly, it only catches sight of suicides, and surely I have become that, though *your* Circean hands poured the poison draught and then held the spoon. There is such terrible force in this gaze that it seems not implausible that I am the first it has ever beheld, and now it will know all, and it shall have more than knowledge for this opportunity might never come again.

"Only tell me what happened," you will say, in some time that cannot ever be, not from *when* I lie here in the vivarium you have built for me, not from this occasion when I lie exposed to a Cosmos hardly half considered by the mortal minds contained therein. "Only put down what seems most significant, in retrospect. Do not dwell upon everything you might recall, every perception. You may make a full accounting later."

"Later, I might forget something," I will reply. "It's not so unlike a dream." And you will frown and slide the ink well a little ways across the writing desk toward me. On your face I will see the stain of an anxiety that has been mounting down all the days since my return.

That will be a lie, of course, for nothing of this will I ever forget. Never shall it fade. I will be taunting you, or through me *it* will be taunting your heedless curiousity, which even then will remain undaunted. This hour, though, is far, far away. From when I lie, it is a fancy that can never come to pass—a unicorn, the roaring cataract at the edge of a flat world, a Hell which punishes only those who deserve eternal torment. Around me flows the sea of all beginnings and of all conclusion, and through the weeds and murk, from the peaks of submarine mountains to the lowest vales of Neptune's sovereignty, benighted in perpetuum—horizon to horizon—does its vision stretch unbroken. And as I have written already, observing me it takes away, and observing me it adds to my acumen and marrow. I am increased as much or more than I am consumed, so it must be a *fair* encounter, when all is said and done.

Somewhen immeasurably inconceivable to my present-bound mind, a hollow needle pierces my flesh, there in some unforeseeable aftertime, and the hypodermic's plunger forces into me your concoction of caffeine citrate, cocaine, belladonna, epinephrine, foxglove, etcetera & etcetera. And I think you will be screaming for me to come back, then, to open my eyes, to wake up as if you had only given me over to an afternoon catnap. I would not answer, even now, even with its smothering eyes upon me, in me, performing their metamorphosis. But you are calling (*wake up, wake up, wake up*), and your chemicals are working upon my traitorous physiology, and, worst of all, *it* wishes me to return whence and from when I have come. It has infected me, or placed within me some fraction of itself, or made from my sentience something suited to its own explorations. Did this never occur to you, my dear? That in those liminal spaces, across the thresholds that separate life from death, might lurk an inhabitant supremely adapted to those climes, and yet also possessed of its own questions, driven by its own peculiar acquisitiveness, seeking always some means to penetrate the veil. I cross one way for you, and I return as another's experiment, the vessel of another's inquisition.

"Breathe, goddamn you!" you will scream, screaming that seems no more or less disingenuous or melodramatic than any actor upon any stage. With your fingers you will clear, have cleared, are evermore clearing my mouth and nostrils of the thickening elixir filling the vivarium tank. "You won't leave me. I will not let you go. There are no ox carts here, no wagon wheels."

But, also, you have, or you will, or at this very second you are placing that fatal spoon upon my tongue.

And when it is done—if I may arbitrarily use that word here, *when*—and its modifications are complete, it shuts its eyes, like the sun tumbling down from the sky, and I am tossed helpless back into the rushing flow of time's river. In the vivarium, I try to draw a breath and vomit milky gouts. At the writing desk, I take the quill you have provided me, and I write—*"Wake up," she whispers.* There are long days when I do not have the strength to speak or even sit. The fears of pneumonia and fever, of dementia and some heretofore unseen necrosis triggered by my time *away.* The relief that begins to show itself as weeks pass and your fears fade slowly, replaced again by that old and indomitable inquisitiveness. The evening that you drained the tank and found something lying at the bottom which you have refused to ever let me see, but keep under lock and key. And this night, which might be *now,* in our bed in the dingy room above your laboratory, and you hold me in your arms, and I lie with my ear against your breast, listening to the tireless rhythm of your heart winding down, and *it* listens through me. You think me still but your love, and I let my hand wander across your belly and on, lower, to the damp cleft of your sex. And there also is the day I hold my dying brother. And there are my long walks beside the sea, too, with the winter waves hammering against the Cobb. That brine is only the faintest echo of the tenebrous kingdom I might have named *Womb.* Overhead, the wheeling gulls mock me, and the freezing wind drives me home again. But always it watches, and it waits, and it studies the intricacies of the winding avenue I have become.

She rolls through an ether of sighs—
She revels in a region of sighs…
—Edgar Allan Poe (December 1847)

FRAZER LEE

TO TAKE THE WATER DOWN AND GO TO SLEEP

"THE TANK is a safe space in which to heal your psyche, Mr. Roberts."

Roberts looked at the gunmetal gray cylinder, and frowned.

"It doesn't look all that safe to me."

"*Senz-dep* is state-of-the-art, I assure you," the white-coated doctor boasted. "Admittedly, we had a few acoustic issues with the second-gen, but this is the third. You'll feel like you're floating in space—without the inconvenience of actual space tourism."

"Not to mention the expense."

The white-coat just smiled. Whatever his clients had paid, Roberts guessed it might equal the price of a return ticket to the outer atmosphere.

"Your profile is not uncommon. You are at mid-life. Even high-functioning staff have a blip on their record somewhere, and the mid-to-late forties are the usual co-ordinates."

"A mid-life crisis barely accounts for the shakes, does it? For the insomnia and the night sweats? For the recurring…dreams." Roberts shuddered. It felt cold in the lab.

"That's all this is—a blip. Your employers wish you to continue unabated. To go back into the…corporate world and close those deals."

Roberts felt movement at his side and looked down to see his hand shaking again. His limb felt distant, adrift somehow. He reached across with his other hand and gripped his wrist, ever tighter until the shakes subsided.

"One step at a time," the white-coat said, making a quick note of something on his tablet. "If you'd like to remove your robe, we'll help you into the tank."

Roberts had to peel his hand away from his wrist, he was gripping it so tightly. The sensation returned to his palm then spread out, pins and needles pricking his flesh all the way to his fingertips.

He tried not to tremble when they helped him up the metal steps.

From his vantage point atop the metal walkway, he felt as though he was looking at an aspect of some black ocean through an observation window. He jolted, recalling the last time he had looked down at the sea. Nausea swam over him, making a clammy jelly of his body. His knees gave way and he reached out for the handrail. The white-coats caught him, shouldering his body weight.

"I…I don't like the look of the water."

"It's fine."

"It looks cold."

"It's not. I assure you it is calibrated to the ideal temperature for relaxation."

Roberts found the prospect to be less than relaxing. He shivered again, uncontrollably now.

"Easy breaths now, Mr. Roberts. In through the nose, and out through the mouth."

The breathing helped balance his equilibrium, though he still felt sick to his core.

"Ready now?"

He wasn't. But neither was he going to give the white-coats any excuses to patronize him further.

The water was lukewarm and pleasant as he stepped inside. His attendants instructed him to stand still for a few moments while they attached little suckers to his skin at strategic points on his forehead, upper body, and chest. The suckers were anchored to wires, which would data-mine his body while he was in the tank. They felt invasive—almost as though they would be probing his physique for weaknesses.

The lid closed. Roberts watched the white-coats' faces disappear behind the tank's outer shell. He focused on the little glass observation porthole set into the lid just a couple of feet above his face. Then that too went dark as the white-coats activated the electronic window-tint. He lay in now total darkness and listened to his breath. All other sounds were absent, so each inhalation and exhalation had the volume and intensity of an oncoming freight train. He blinked, and the afterimage of the little observation window made a halo of light flicker before his eyes.

He breathed. And, drifting into darkness, he felt his body descend.

OPENING HIS eyes he saw that he was back at the porthole in his cabin aboard the *Serendipity*.

Raw emotion washed over him, burning hot and freezing cold; then back again. He was trembling, and knew now that exact moment was when the shakes had really set in. He could see the moonlit ocean through the porthole, could smell the brine and the rum in the plastic cup on the sill beside him. His face was wet with sweat, and from the tears that would not stop coming. His chest ached from the mere act of breathing and his mouth was dry from longing for the taste of her. He remembered reaching for the drink, and how he fumbled, knocking it over. It splashed against the occasional table beneath the porthole.

Cursing, he stumbled to the en suite and turned on the lamp. It flickered momentarily before bathing the black-and-white tiled space in sickly yellow light. He caught sight of his clammy reflection in the mirror and quickly looked away, unable to make eye contact with himself. He crossed to the sink and opened the faucet labelled Salt-Cold. He ran his finger under the salt water, thinking all the while about how the pumps below decks would be bringing the water up from the ocean beneath.

He vomited then.

Barely able to close the faucet, he staggered backwards into the cabin and slumped onto the bed. Closing his eyes he heard the deafening roar of the ship's foghorn, blasting through his skull like—

ROBERTS OPENED his eyes in the dark and heard the thunder of his flailing limbs. Numb, he could not even feel the impact of his hands and feet against the extremities of the isolation tank. He could only hear it.

There was a hiss, and the sound of muffled, panicked voices. Rubber-gloved hands were around him, lifting him from his dark cradle and out into the artificial light. It was like being ripped from the womb.

He screamed.

THE *SERENDIPITY* was vast—more like a floating town than a mere ocean liner. Navigating its labyrinthine corridors and decks would test the orienting skills of even the most experienced traveller. Roberts had once again found himself deciphering one of the wall-mounted schematics when he became aware of another lost soul, standing beside him.

"Third time I checked this thing, and I'm still lost."

Her voice was warm, with that effortless East Coast delivery. A country girl who had become a city woman. He made eye contact and found her smiling at him. Her eyes were bright blue, her pale face framed by wisps of scissor-cut hair. Her dress was on-trend but with an edge that was all her own.

"Where were you headed? Maybe we can work it out together?"

"Nearest bar. I'm parched."

"Me too. Now we simply have to work it out."

She laughed. A shrill, honest sound.

Roberts leaned closer to the map, tracing his index finger of his right hand along the corridor marked YOU ARE HERE.

"I think this stairwell will save us doubling back to the main one." He tried to sound like he knew what he was talking about. He hoped he did. "There's a deck bar two floors up. I think."

"If you're right, I'll get you a drink," she said.

He held out his hand. "Andy Roberts," he said.

She shook his hand. Her skin was soft and slightly cold to the touch. Poor circulation, maybe she was a smoker. A good grip, though. She had strong shoulders and a posture that anchored them to her center of gravity.

"Isla Guthrie."

"I know."

"Shall we walk?"

He nodded and let her take the lead.

"I enjoyed your keynote today."

"Really? What was there to enjoy?"

Now she sounded defensive. Deliberately abrasive.

"Your statement about the hierarchy of belief, for example."

"Thank you. I was very nervous."

"Well, it didn't show. The way you spoke about your father was very moving. You could feel it in the room."

"I think that was just the rocking motion of the ship. But it's very kind of you to say."

"I think your father would be justifiably proud of you."

"I hope you're right."

She lowered her gaze. Roberts knew her father's suicide had hit her hard. He blinked away an image from the press report of Professor Guthrie—facedown in his swimming pool. The tabloids had had a field day with that one—"Climate Change Professor Drowns Himself."

"You made it personal," he ventured. "The demonising of your father by the press, the anguish you suffered after his death. I had no idea about the social media abuse. The…threats. And the way the funding was pulled when the news corporations took issue. That beggared belief."

"It did." She sighed. "Our glorious leaders just want us to scurry away. Like rats!" She laughed, bitterly. She mock-whispered, "If this was the RMS *Titanic*, I think all the climate change deniers would be below decks."

"But so long as experts like you keep speaking out…"

She kissed her teeth. "The truth is an iceberg, Mr Roberts. A vast bloody iceberg that we are expending all our energy to circumvent."

"But we're just going 'round in circles?"

"Exactly." Her expression softened a little. "You get it, at least."

"TIME TO get back into the tank, Mr. Roberts."

He found it easier to face the black water this time. A sense of expectant calm washed over him as he lowered his body into the lukewarm fluid and lay back. The silhouettes of the attendants moved darkly across his field of vision, becoming indistinct through the viewing window as they sealed the door above him. He regulated his breathing, just as he had been instructed, and closed his eyes.

Floating, and still, he drifted through the dark.

A LIGHT breeze blew across the deck as the ship churned on through the ocean. Only the hardiest of smokers had braved the elements. Roberts saw some of their faces, lit by the spectral glow of e-cigarettes or the condensed torchlight of cigars and traditional cigarettes. His nostrils caught the scent of something more herbal, and probably illegal, before it drifted away.

Isla returned with their drinks, offering his glass to him with a lopsided smile. He sniffed at the mojito, luxuriating in the playful collision of citrus scent and the salt-rimmed glass.

"To finding the bar," she said, raising her glass.

"To finding each other," he replied.

She laughed. That glorious, unguarded sound. How formal she had been at her keynote earlier—the audience hanging on her every word. Her laugh demonstrated how desperately she must be to cut loose after all the ceremony of the conference.

"You're bold. I'll give you that."

"I'm sorry if…"

"Oh no. I like it. You're stiff, as well as bold. But a couple of these babies should loosen you up a bit."

She stared at him, daring him with those wicked-blue eyes. He stared back. She clinked her glass against his, and he began to raise his drink to his lips. Without taking her eyes off his, she reached out with her free hand and grabbed his wrist to stop him from taking a drink. She leaned closer to him and licked the salt from the rim of his glass. Making appreciative noises, she licked her lips, then took a gulp of her own drink. Only then did she release his wrist from her grip. He looked at her, open-mouthed, and she laughed again.

Roberts sipped his drink, his lips on the exact same spot from which she had licked the salt. The ice-cold tang of the mojito slid across his throat, quenching the fire that had taken hold of him. She watched him from the darkness, amused, and drained the rest of her drink. He was still working on his, but she went inside to get another anyway. Roberts crossed to the guardrail, carrying his drink. He felt a shudder of vertigo as he looked down at the waves, lapping at the black hull of the ship as it cut through the water. The sea was choppy, and as the water hit the sides of the vessel a few stories below, it plumed frothy white and kicked up spray. He let the droplets hit his face, enjoying their cool touch. A few drops coated his lips with their fine spray and he licked at them. More salt before another sip of triple sec and lime. He closed his eyes and turned, putting his back to the guardrail. Listening to the sea, and the deep throb of the ship's engines, he threw back his head and finished his drink. When he opened his eyes, Isla was standing before him. She wore a look of drunken dismay.

"Bastard bloody bartender says I've had enough."

"Maybe you have?"

"Maybe I fucking haven't," she retorted. "Looks like it's your round after all."

He sighed. No point in arguing. She clearly wanted oblivion, and who was he to deny her?

"Same again?"

"Same again."

She swatted at him as he passed, her fingers curling into the lapel of his jacket. He stopped, and felt her lurch against him. The warmth of her breath hit his neck—a heatwave of sensation in miniature. She blinked at him and pressed her lips to his. Biting his lower lip, she pulled away momentarily, then kissed him hard, and deep. He reciprocated, his hands finding her waist and pulling her closer to him. She tousled his hair with her fingertips as they explored one another for the first time. Then, she slid slowly away from him.

"Thirsty work," she said, staggering back a little with the slight movement of the vessel.

He led her to a vacant table away from the guardrail.

"Take a seat while I get you another," he said.

"Oooh, what a gentleman," she chuckled.

He was about to reply when she smacked him hard on the ass.

"Not too much of one, I hope," she drawled after him as he headed for the bar.

Roberts cleared his throat and straightened his shirt, amused at the way he felt like an underage drinker trying to appear less inebriated than he was. Those days were long over. But he was having fun playing the part.

The barman nodded his welcome as Roberts approached the bar.

"What can I get you?"

"Two mojitos," Roberts replied.

Leaning across the bar, Roberts spoke quietly, almost conspiratorially. "If you could mix one of them with less booze, that'd be great."

The barman paused, then nodded once more, this time with a knowing twinkle in his eye.

Taking the drinks outside, Roberts held the weaker one in his right hand so he wouldn't forget which was which. Approaching the table, he saw that Isla was no longer there. Glancing across the deck, he saw that the other patrons had gone too. Perhaps she had got talking to someone else and they had retreated inside, away from the rising wind. He was about to do the same when he glimpsed a figure, just visible beyond a column-like ventilation funnel.

Roberts followed the curve of the guardrail around to the other side of the funnel, and found Isla. He took a moment, admiring the feline curve of her body beneath her dress, then approached her—holding out the drink in his right hand. She took it, gratefully, and had a sip. Her look of pleasure turned to one of confusion.

"Is yours okay?"

He made a show of taking a drink from his glass and nodded. "Sure is."

"Hmmm." She took his glass and swapped it with her own. "Bastard," she said, and Roberts felt sure he had been rumbled. But she went on, cursing about the barman, and he knew he was off the hook after all.

"If the bar staff is incapable of mixing drinks, then I will," she proclaimed.

Roberts saw that she was already pouring some of her drink overboard. She then added a large slosh of his stronger drink to her own. She took another sip and smacked her lips.

"Better," she said. "Where were we? Oh yeah, we were kissing!"

Her riotous laughter was infectious, and Roberts laughed along with her.

He stood, and she swayed, talking and laughing until their

glasses were empty again. Roberts placed his tumbler on the table and turned to look at the sea. It was a black curtain, shimmering dark as it reflected the stars above. The air was cool and accentuated the effects of the alcohol as it chilled his face. Looking at the point where the stars met the sea, Roberts wondered how many people had gazed at the same dark vista over the centuries. The water rolled and churned; an ever-moving black skin coating the unfathomable entity of the ocean. He felt isolated and insignificant in the midst of such vastness. The engine throbbed on, its funerary drone echoing his melancholia. He turned to Isla for succour—to partake of her effervescent warmth in the unrelenting cold of the sea air.

But she was gone.

"WHO IS Isla?"

Roberts glanced down at the white-coat from the stairwell that led to the tank. He realised he didn't like the man's eyes. They were oddly lifeless.

"Why do you ask?"

The white-coat grinned. Roberts didn't much like his face either.

"We heard you mention the name a few times during your last session. Ambient mics picked it up, that's all."

Roberts had heard them laughing from inside the tank, unaware, or uncaring, that he could still hear them. He'd heard how they'd taken to calling the *Senz-dep* tank a "flirtation tank." Sarcastic bastards—they thought themselves so clever. He had obviously mentioned more than Isla's name while he was under. Well, he wasn't going to give them the pleasure.

"I'll let you know if I remember," Roberts said.

The white-coat nodded and made a note on his tablet.

"You look eager to be back in the water, Mr. Roberts."

Roberts hesitated, and realised he already had one foot poised at the entrance to the tank.

"Good," the man continued, "that shows real progress. We practically had to carry you in there last week."

"I'm beginning to feel…better," Roberts said.

"Well, let's not get ahead of ourselves, shall we?" the white-coat said.

Roberts noticed that the man was staring at his arm. He

looked down and saw he was trembling again. He reached out and leaned against the cool metal of the tank for support. He longed to be back in the water, and the quiet dark.

"ANOTHER. GET me another."

"I think the barkeep was right. Maybe you *have* had enough. Come on, I'll walk you to your cabin."

"Ah, ah. You just want to take advantage of me."

"Want? Yes. Intend to? No."

"Oh, I forgot, you're a gentleman. Infuriating gentleman." She laughed at her own joke. "I might just take advantage of *you*, you know. But you have to get me another drink first."

Roberts sighed, with a smile. "Sweet oblivion, huh?"

She just smiled back at him, licking her lips.

The barman was wearing his game face. "I'm sorry, sir, we're closing up here."

"Can I get a couple of drinks to take back to…our cabin?"

The barman's eyes twinkled again. He appeared reluctant, then saw the cash that Roberts had surreptitiously dropped on the bar.

"I'll have to pour them into plastic cups. House rules."

"Understood," Roberts replied. "I'll just go get her."

The drinks would be the lure to get Isla away from the bar so the staff could close up for the night.

He pushed open the heavy glass door that led out to the sun deck. He had to use both hands to open it against the force of the buffeting wind. He felt the wind whip across his face, cold and salty with spray, as he made his way across the deck. It was deserted. He moved around the side of the ventilation funnel, but Isla wasn't there. He called her name—twice, because the first time the wind ripped the word from his lips. Moving around the deck to where the farthest tables and chairs were situated, Roberts saw movement.

Walking closer, he heard the clanking of a metal rivet against a flagpole and realised the movement he had seen was the shadow of a flag that was flapping in the wind.

"DID YOU see her come back this way?"

The barman shrugged. "Nope. No one came through here."

"Maybe while you were clearing up?"

"Maybe. I had to grab some fresh ice for your takeouts. Did you check the restrooms?"

Restrooms. That must be it.

"Hey, do you still want to take your drinks? I have to lock up."

"Sure, thanks."

Roberts picked up the nightcaps and left the bar, following the slight curve of the corridor that led to the ladies' room. He couldn't knock with his hands full, so he tapped with the toe of his shoe against the door. Nothing. He was thinking about poking his head through the door, when a woman pulled it open. He startled and spilled some of the drink on his cuffs.

"Sorry, I…"

The woman's apologetic look quickly turned to one of suspicion, to see him loitering outside the ladies' bathroom. She was wearing a maid's uniform—collar unbuttoned. She was clearly off duty.

"Oh, no harm done. Say, I think my friend went inside. She didn't feel so good. Could you—would you mind checking on her for me?"

"Didn't see anyone else in there." That suspicion was still there, written in her glance. Then she sighed. "Okay, I'll check."

She returned moments later. "All the stalls are unoccupied. You sure she was in here?"

Roberts nodded.

"Well, I hope you find her," the woman replied, sounding like she really didn't.

Roberts took a sip from one of the drinks.

I hope I find her.

He looked at the other, the ice melting from the warmth of his hand.

I never will.

He held up the plastic cup and stared through its depths at the floor.

His shadow spilled across the carpet like blood from a wound and he lurched towards it, tumbling farther in until it enveloped him. The ship tilted, and he with it. He let go of both drinks, expecting to hear them clatter against the floor, or the wall. Breathless moments passed, in darkness and in silence.

Instead of the splashing of spilled drinks, he heard the crash of a wave and felt ice cold water sucking him down and through its tumult. He spun, nausea gripping at his throat, and the intensity of his downward spiral made him feel as though he was at the centre of a tornado. A howl escaped his throat, the futile eye of an implacable hurricane. Then, the black world upended, and he felt a wall of water at his back. The echo of his howl hung in the close air around him. He tried to move, but his body felt oddly heavy and numb. As he writhed in the water, he came to a realisation. He was back inside the tank, but upside down. The water was holding him aloft, and he was gazing down at the little viewing hatch.

Even now, the hatch was descending, elevator-car-like, far below. He watched it in disbelief, as it became no more than a pinprick of muddy light at the extreme of his visual spectrum. And between it and his unblinking eyes was a fathomless void of cold, thick blackness. The sheer, incredible volume of distance almost stopped his heart. The total perspective of it made his mind spin and his ears ring. And in that awesome void, Roberts felt something shift. Something massive. It was as if a wall was flexing, unlocking, and slowly uncoiling itself in the dark fathoms beneath him. The vibration of its movement hummed through every fibre of his body—a dark song from which there was no shelter, no escape.

Come deeper.

The voice was a depth charge, shattering his psyche.

Come deeper, now.

Roberts felt the water at his back pushing him farther down. He tried to resist, but the enormous pressure on his spine was unyielding.

"Oh Jesus."

What is Jesus?

Roberts' mind raced. If only he could find the words, he might keep hold of the last fragile shred of his sanity.

"A story, I guess," he gasped. "He died for our sins."

All of them? the voice boomed. *There are so many.*

The behemoth breathed then—a sound like children dying—and uncoiled some more. Roberts felt it beneath him, closer and heavier than ever. It was so immense that he couldn't even begin to make out its surface shape. But it gave off an aura of terrible loneliness and despair. Roberts felt warmth at his groin as his bladder emptied itself. A fog of tears clouded his eyes.

Overwhelming melancholy entered and filled him. He blinked, a reflex action to help him see better through the fog, and he saw his own outline in the black before him. The shape had a sheen, and he realised he was looking into a huge, single black eye. Its curved surface looked onyx-hard, and as it drew nearer still, the effect was like looking into a vast scrying mirror.

He saw himself then, on the sun deck, that night on the ship—with Isla. He saw her pupils widen as she realised who he was. What he was. She looked accepting of him—almost welcoming.

So it's to be you then, her eyes seemed to say.

—as though she wanted to die. To be reunited with her dead father in the deep. Facedown in the water.

He saw himself take her head in his hands and snap her neck in a single, swift, practised movement. Just as he had done before, many times. The act had taken only a fraction of time, and in its execution, he had snuffed out all that Isla had left. To live, to laugh, to love. And to change the world. Roberts' clients could not risk that. They had so much to lose.

He watched himself upending her body with practised efficiency. Saw how easily he tipped her over the guardrail and into the ocean. He watched himself lean over the rail, and saw the white froth that was her grave marker. As the ship churned on, it dissipated and faded from view. Roberts saw himself straighten his clothing as he took a few breaths.

He had chosen the perfect spot for the hit.

The funnel, and its shadow, obscured him from view both on the sun deck and the walkway above. Any potential witnesses had long since abandoned ship for their warmer quarters belowdecks, but it was wise to make sure—there were still staff around. Roberts had known the barkeep would have his back turned while he fetched some fresh ice—precisely the reason why he had requested some, well aware that the buckets had been emptied at last orders.

His charade with the staff member at the ladies' bathroom was the final curtain on his evening's performance. If and when security personnel asked any questions, it would be made clear that Isla's handsome and mysterious drinking partner had been anxiously searching for her. The barman would back this up. And Isla's fragile mental state coupled with excess alcohol would no doubt be enough to result in an open verdict of probable suicide—or at least death by misadventure. Case closed, encrypted bank transfer executed, and job done.

His clients would be satisfied. They would pack him off on a long vacation, somewhere hot and languid. Until the phone rang again and he was called to his next assignment.

He felt movement at his side and looked down to see his hand tremble, for the first time. The uncontrollable muscle spasms heralded the beginning of a sickness that would creep in to devour his sanity and his soul. And the trembling now worsened, making a danse macabre of his nerve endings.

He felt the mirror eye on him again, and Roberts snapped back into the tank. The unbearable pressure was still at his back, and the dark leviathan uncoiled before him. He heard a series of clicks from deep within its monolithic body—as loud and urgent as a bullet belt discharging in a Gatling gun. He tried to swallow, but his throat was ash. The giant thing laughed then—the sound of a world ending and a new, drowned world just beginning.

Willing his limbs to move, Roberts managed to free his throbbing forearm from the wall of pressure. He tapped on the side of the tank, then hammered at it with his fist.

But no one was listening.

PAOLO DI ORAZIO

PERISCOPE OF THE DEAD

ALFRED WOKE up suddenly from a sort of mental nothingness, maybe an anesthesia, or some other inexplicable state.

A green field was before him.

He was seated on a little chair placed on a large, smooth carpet of grass. Alfred found himself in a garden he did not recognize at all. Under the sun. On a warm and pleasant day.

The place was not his home. It was *somewhere*. Quiet. Pacific. Clean. Perfect.

He could not say if someone had brought him or if he had gone there by himself. Not so important.

He realized he was alone. Alone, with the sound of his breath inside his head. His head, like an empty room with all the world's noises closed out. All of them, except the soft, slow breathing at the center of his blank thoughts.

This was the way Alfred came back to the light from a blind past.

Without the voices.

THE VOICES inside his head.

Alfred remembered them now, and nothing else about himself. Even his name. He had no memory about his own name. He searched inside himself. But he saw nothing. Alfred remembered only the voices, the invisible crowd, faceless passengers of the deeper mind. Those weren't simple sounds, but human voices for sure. The chilling buzzing choir of Alfred's unfamiliar guests: Whispering people he never saw, never met, never knew, but always talking to him, sometimes to each other. But now that he was awake, they were unexpectedly mute, leaving Alfred in peace. A curious occurrence.

Maybe, if he had asked himself where they were, he could evoke them again. So, Alfred tried not to ask and focused only on the actual state of his body and mind. Maybe that allowed him to keep his obsessive guests out of his damn skull.

UPON THE green grass, ten footsteps away from where he was sitting, he saw a tall and long hedge, an unmeasurable corral of roses and flowers of every kind and shape. Raising his eyes, Alfred could see the sharpened ends of dozens of lances, also making a square enclosure, running along the hedge, all around that little park. The rich crown of trees hid the distant park borders, and the line of sharpened points appeared occasionally over the green front.

"Oh, good God of mine. I am in prison."

After seeing the lances all lined up, like a never-ending gate of black nails, Alfred saw no way out. Nobody could escape without getting slashed to death.

So he turned his head slowly, and finally discovered he was not alone.

He saw other people sitting or walking or standing across the park, a clean garden in front of an old mansion, a huge Victorian building with a gray roof, red bricks, white windows, and big smokestacks. Alfred didn't know those people at all, nor that house. Men, women. They wore his same clothes. White pajamas. Because everybody belonged to that place. They were looking down at the ground, or staring at the trees, scrutinizing the blue sky, smiling in silence, too. If not sleeping on a bench, they moved very slowly, almost paralyzed in their quiet positions.

"They look at nothing," said Alfred.

Then he wondered if they could be the ones who had talked for years and years inside his head, but quickly he drove that question away. He would not risk waking his head-chatterers again.

"Good morning, Alfred," said a nurse, who appeared from nothing. Her presence immediately canceled his fear of the voices. "Welcome back," she added.

The woman had just bent over to greet him close to his ear, with care and sweetness.

The scent of her lipstick stung Alfred's nose.

Then he understood.

He was not in jail.

Worse.

He was in a mental hospital.

No policemen around.

Only nurses.

Insane people everywhere. Living dummies for housemates.

A fountain with cupids and stone fishes at the center of the garden splashed water jets toward the top, then falling down again with grace into the basin making permanent arches. Alfred counted the eight jets twice. The water seemed to call and call.

So strange.

"Alfred, can you tell me who I am?"

So he learned his own name. *Alfred.* He thought about it. The name was good. He liked it. He accepted it. "Oh, miss. I am sorry. I don't think I can."

"Are you sure?" asked the nurse, sadly.

"Yes, miss, I am sure."

The man's answer sounded so dramatic to her. Alfred read that in her face.

"How do you feel?" she asked.

"Fine, thank you."

"Maybe a little weak?"

"Maybe. I just…I just can't tell."

"Alfred, I guess you want to know why you're here," said the nurse with a tremor in her sweet voice.

"I think…did something happen to me, miss? But I can't imagine…I simply can't ask."

"Sure, Alfred. Something happened," said the nurse, nodding. But the man did not understand why her voice was so unsteady. "But now you are safe, in here. I promise. Do you remember anything you want to tell me?"

Alfred stared at the woman's eyes. Bright hazel, almost asking *why*—not *what*—washed in tears that did not fall. Then, he looked at her curly red hair. Her strong arms covered with freckles. Her large hips. No doubt. Alfred hadn't met this woman before. However, he smiled at her while she softly caressed his face with the tips of her fingers. "No, miss. I don't remember anything at all."

"Do you understand what this place is?" asked the nurse putting her hand in her pocket—wanting to hide it for having touched the patient.

"I guess this is a hospital. It seems like a great house for fools. So I must have some trouble with my mind. Because I feel no pain, but I have no memories," said Alfred clearly. He did not mention the only thing he desperately remembered of his past: the voices in his head. Something he shouldn't talk about.

"Can you tell me today's date? The year?"

Alfred seemed to search for something above the horizon. "1975?"

He got no answer.

"We will take care of you, Alfred. I'd like you to tell me anything you want, anything you have in mind. Please, write down or let us know every memory that might come back to you. It's very important. You have a room and a bed, I'll show it to you later. And a doctor, of course. You're not alone."

"Thank you, miss."

They stood there looking in each other's eyes.

Alfred smiled again. Seeing her and not hearing the voices inside his head was so fine. He felt good.

Even though this place was a cage, Alfred enjoyed a sort of peace. The red-haired nurse was beautiful. She was perfect, in that quiet place. Maybe, somehow, he'd done something to keep away, to cancel forever the crazy voices. That's why Alfred did not tell her about them.

"Do you still hear those voices in your head?" asked the nurse after a long pause.

Alfred's heart stomped inside his chest. *She already knew about the voices. Why?*

There was no reason to be dishonest now. Alfred did not lie. "Oh no, miss. They're silent now."

"Do you think they are only silent, or are they absent? It's a big difference."

"I can't figure that out."

"Okay, Alfred. I'll let you rest, now," said the nurse, looking at her own watch with a rapid arm movement—quite nervous. "I'll come back in a half an hour for dinner."

"Thank you, miss. Can I stay here?" asked Alfred gently.

The nurse answered as she walked across the park, toward the mansion, "Sure. You can have a walk or have a talk with someone, too. Just do what you want."

Alfred stood there, watching her leave. Her hips swung. She walked like a soldier. Fast and martial, deadly feminine. Alfred smiled. The voices did not come back. And the nurse's body filled his mind up with all of her curves.

Oh, God, thank you.

No more voices.

Only a real, wonderful woman.

"MY NAME is Shana," said the nurse beside Alfred.

Alfred was looking at himself in the bathroom mirror. Her reflection overlapped his own.

He really didn't recognize his features, but felt so happy to realize that he could touch with his hands what he saw in the mirror. Alfred loved his own face. It wasn't a young face, but a new amazing discovery. He smiled at himself and at the woman's image looking at him through the silvery glass.

It seemed strange to Alfred, but the madhouse rules dictated that she had to follow him *everywhere*. That was comic and tragic, too. Almost irritating, in the beginning, but more and more pleasant as Alfred did all the things he had to do. Alfred soon started to feel a romantic wave flowing between them. Some kind of maternal feeling, more than anything else. He did not remember if he was married. Even the running water confused his mind. Alfred had no fear at all. He had Shana, now.

She helped him wash his hands.

"Such a wonderful name. I like it," he said watching her soaping and washing his hands.

"Dry your hands, now, Alfred," said Shana giving him the clean white towel.

Alfred did not do what he was asked, instead he watched the water going away slowly down the drain below him. He did not catch the towel immediately. Shana thought he had totally forgotten how to wash his hands, along with his other daily activities. She saw him, perhaps, looking down at his image on the soapy water left in the sink.

"How long have I been here?"

"Alfred, your towel," she said, as Alfred's brow furrowed.

"Oh, thank you," he said, when she caught his wet hands with the white towel.

"You look like a child again," said Shana smiling.

Alfred laughed softly. The water was going away, now, down to the dark underground. The sink was almost empty. He could only see an ambiguous shadow of his face painted on the thin veil of water. Something disturbed his mind, but he let it go. Shifting his glance to Shana, he noticed she had stopped smiling at him, and a sudden sparkle of hate appeared in her eyes. She turned her face to the wall, drying Alfred's hands with the towel. Then, she folded the towel and took Alfred's arm to lead him to the dining room. With no words.

DINING ROOM, 7:30 p.m.

Dozens of patients were eating at the tables. Like greedy animals.

The sound of forks, spoons, plates, and vulgar mouths.

Voices.

Somebody screamed.

Somebody laughed.

Everybody talked.

Alfred heard everything. He was back inside his old living nightmare for a while.

It seemed just like he was walking through the voices in his head. Tears came to his eyes and rolled down his cheeks. His heart slammed several times beneath his ribs—like a door shaken by the wind. He felt his knees bending, but Shana was holding him steadily by the arm until she put him in an empty chair among the other patients.

NO ONE looked at him. And Alfred would not look at his housemates eating and drinking with such disturbing noises.

It happened immediately.

Inside the vegetable broth. Liquid and transparent as tea.

A neon lamp was over his head. So, Alfred searched for his own reflection on the hot soup, breathing in its disgusting steam.

But Alfred saw something weird he'd already seen in the bathroom before.

"Who are you?" he said to the soup.

"Who are you," replied the man to his right, upset. It was an old man with rotten teeth and a yellowish beard. Alfred glanced at him, his eyes open wide. The man went crazy. "Take your eyes off me," he screamed. "Don't stare at me! Don't you! Go away, go away," he cried.

Alfred was struck by the anger of that twisted man. "Please, don't shout at me, sir," said Alfred kindly.

The man's bulging eyes, lit up with rage. Or fear.

Two assistants came along. The old man grabbed and threw Alfred's plate at him. Then he rose up and fell on the floor. The assistants helped him stand up again.

"Take him away," cried the old man in fear. "Take that shit away," he cried again.

Nurse Shana hurried over there. Alfred sat with his face dripping broth. He was astonished. "Are you okay?" the nurse asked.

"Thank you, Shana. Yes, I am," Alfred said, and let the red-haired nurse clean his face.

"Look at his eyes, please look," cried the old man restrained by the two assistants.

"Okay, Alfred. Let's go back to your room," Shana said.

Alfred was terrified.

As much as that man was.

DR. MARK and Shana were beside him, inside his room.

Dr. Mark was polite. Alfred couldn't remember having seen him before. The way he wasn't actually sure if he'd ever seen Shana, too. However, Dr. Mark treated him as if they were long-time acquaintances. That room, too, gave sensations and vibrations of intimacy to Alfred's senses. Everything was familiar to him. It meant he has been there a long time. But he couldn't say how long. Of his own past life, he remembered only the voices in his head. For a moment, he wished the voices could tell him who he'd been before entering this place and, over all, why he was here. Maybe they could have revealed it. He was certain they knew all about that. Maybe it would have been a serious risk to evoke them. Would the silence be better, or discovering the truth? And how dramatic and terrible was the truth about what happened? Dr. Mark's gentle voice broke this chain of questions.

"Welcome back, Alfred. I am happy to meet you."

Welcome back? Maybe Alfred had been there in the past? Even Shana welcomed him that way. *Welcome back*. From where?

"Shana had made me aware of your return to consciousness. Congratulations, Alfred. You fought a good battle."

"What was I battling, Doctor?"

The man in the white coat smiled. His face was calm and reassuring. With that beard, he looked like a Greek deity. "The bad things that drove you in here. And I am happy to see the results of the good we did for you."

"So, I'm free? I'm going home?"

"We would love it so much if you could do that, Alfred, but you're not completely cured yet. I invite you to make yourself at home here. Where you're not alone. You have more than a family in this house."

Alfred nodded and smiled, forcing himself to hide any signs of sadness from his face.

"Alfred," Mark asked gently. "Can you tell me what happened in the dining room?"

"That man spun out of control because I stared at his face. But I said nothing to him," Alfred said.

"He told us you have something scary in your eyes. All I see is the look of a lost person who is now going to find himself again," the doctor said.

"Thank you for your kind words, Doctor," Alfred murmured. "I feel good, now. I'm at peace. I am not angry with that man. Really. I guess it was just a misunderstanding, a moment of irritability."

"We think the same, Alfred. That old Steve's a pretty delicate patient. Well, Alfred, it's late. Now we all ought to go to sleep. See you tomorrow."

By the time Alfred said back to him *see you tomorrow*, Mark was already out of the room. Shana had already softly shut the door, leaving him alone.

Alfred did not tell them what he saw on the water from the sink before dinner. Or on his plate in the dining room.

He wouldn't do that.

Maybe he should have.

NOW THAT Shana had taught him how to wash himself, Alfred wanted to go to the bathroom. But he had no urgency. He only felt a strong emotion. A sort of fear mixed with curiosity. He was alone, so he could do it.

He entered the bathroom. He found the courage and opened the faucet wide. Plugged the drain and waited till the water filled the sink. Put his hands and leaned his weight on the edge of the sink, looking at himself in the mirror. Stopped the water, shut his eyes, and took time in silence. Listened to the silence inside his head. The shadows of the night were accomplices of that moment. He counted a dozen breaths. Finally, the body of water was ready, flat and still. Slowly, Alfred bent his head down and opened his eyes to look at the water below, beneath his face.

Then, he looked at himself in the mirror once again.

After he looked at the water a second time…it was looking at him.

HE WAS in the garden again, as he'd been the day before, the day of his awakening. Nothing really changed. Same lawn, same fountain, same hedge, and same sharp-pointed fence.

And the quiet, the silence in his head. A brand new certainty came over him: Those voices weren't gone, but they were silent. And they were silent because they belonged to real people. They weren't the effect of a mind's circuit breaker, or nightmares flowing over from slumber into consciousness. Yes. Absolutely. They were *people*.

Alfred massaged his head staring at the blue sky, searching for sutures. He thought that Dr. Mark might have surgically extracted the voices from his brain. But Alfred did not find skull holes, or any cuts or scars. His fingers read the skin beneath the hair perfectly, untouched. That's why Alfred could be sure that the voices were still inside his head, but in silence. They kept quiet as a consequence of the medicine, or do they keep hidden so as not to be caught? Or, even simpler, did they get tired of talking?

Voices had been buzzing inside his head ever since he was a child. By the time he realized that his own head had turned into a hive of unknown presences, and was not just a messy box of thoughts, it was too late. He couldn't tell, in that green oasis with flowering bushes and trees, how it had begun. Nor the reason why the voices had brought him here—if it had even been their fault.

He stood up to walk to the fountain. Slowly. The other patients also wandered like him. They measured the other patients' steps and trajectories so they wouldn't collide with each other. After the accident at last night's dinner, Alfred tried not to look at anyone. Instinct was the only way to avoid battles with the other patients. The sound of water in the fountain attracted him with an inexplicable and undeniable strength. As if inside that ornamental structure there would be an answer.

The voices. They kept quiet. Or were they only *looking at* him? Were they waiting to see what he'd do? Did they fear something or, instead, in secret, were they planning a deadly ambush? Reaching the fountain, called by the moving water, Alfred tried to cross his own past life.

The voices talked to him, talked among themselves.

Continuously.

At first, one lonely voice, from which popped out a second, and a third. One man, two women. The three, just like they were in a sunny square, attracted more passengers who stopped there and started chattering with them about different things. Everybody grouped around Alfred's hearing. The group became a larger and larger discussion crowd. The matters were a storm of vague points at first, then they turned to focus heavily on Alfred's life.

In a few months, Alfred was able to recognize every single voice, and match the relationships among the talking presences. Couples, families, friends, single people, relatives. Everybody confluent in his mind. Later, Alfred could guess that the voices were from different times and places. His brain started to work just like a radio device running through the stations; the difference being that the voices had chosen Alfred as a forced listener. The voices themselves, all anxious to talk to him, interfered with Alfred's passive listening.

From buzzing chattering, the crowd of voices turned into a kind of vocal court.

The voices controlled him. Judged him. Pondered everything Alfred thought and did. They recommended things, projects, words to say and even their exact etymology, places where he had to go. Alfred's consciousness, at last, became a mute cobblestone path, walked by a mixed public of recognizable strangers. Soon the voices started to pressure him—what to do, what to say, anything: *Eat. Sleep. Wake up. Shut up. Lie. Tell him you won't go*...Not for his benefit, just things chosen by them. The requests were repeated over and over, till Alfred could have satisfied each of them one by one. "*Alfred go to your garage and say this*," "*Alfred go to that city and bring flowers to that lady but don't tell her who the sender is*," "*Alfred you've got to sweep away all the leaves from the street*," "*Alfred, Miss Smith. Go to Miss Smith's shop, not the market*," "*Alfred, call Uncle George*," "*Alfred, bring money to that family*," "*Alfred, send three postcards.*" The unknown voices drove him to people he barely knew, some he never met, to fulfill the assignments. These people reacted in different ways. One was frightened, another thanked him, one hugged him, one sent him away. Alfred couldn't tell anybody he'd been hired by a voice in his head.

But soon, after the specific chores, the voices turned into a hellish burst of different commands impossible to obey at the same time: *"Sleep"* with *"Wake up"* and *"Go out"* with *"Stay home"*; or "*Eat*" with *"Spit out what you're chewing"* and *"Get dressed"* with *"Get naked."* They did it on purpose.

The command storm had different intensities. When chaos got placid, Alfred could take a breath and listen to the single voices. Of course, his thoughts could not speak to the mind squatters. Alfred had only to *receive*, to undergo, to listen. So, as he was lost in the almost total aphasia and apathy, every single voice was so clear and clean to reveal a peculiar sonic background made of ambient noises and additional passing voices that stigmatized the places and times from which they were talking.

Alfred knew that one always spoke from a barber shop in New York, in the 1930s. Another one, a woman named Lorena, spoke from a wool mill out of London. Abraham was a dealer in Monaco. Pier, a little child, spoke from a school in Paris. About these and many others, Alfred would learn all the clues to identify them.

He leaned on the edge of the stone fountain, thinking about all of the voices. He frightened a bird that was drinking among the water jets, making it fly away. Water inside the fountain was a continuous movement of bubbles, rings, and splashes. The blue sky shone on the liquid surface. For Alfred, it was easy to find beneath his eyes, the outline of his body projected on the water.

The face he saw reflected down, for the third time, was not himself.

Alfred closed his eyes.

Then he watched again.

It was still there below.

Alfred touched his own face.

The reflection on the water did the same.

The night before, Alfred had found his own face in the mirror. He knew the face.

It was not the same face he now saw reflected on the water.

"Who are you?" Alfred asked.

The shape on the water could not answer.

In his head, the voices, all of them, were silent.

THAT NIGHT, on the water in the sink, Alfred saw an old woman's face looking at him instead of his own reflection. He'd never seen her before. Her features did not bring any memories from his past life. She hadn't been in previous water reflections either. But two men and a young boy with a shaved head had been: The boy was on the broth. In Alfred's room, there was a little mirror. He left the sink and went to the mirror. The cool silence of the hospital. Alfred found the mirror lying on the desk. He looked at himself in the mirror and recognized his own face. He smiled at himself, then went back to the bathroom.

The reflection on the water was still the old woman's face. It was a living image. Staring at it with attention, Alfred could see the temple vein pulsing, the trembling and blinking of the eyelids and, suddenly, in an amazing gesture, her tongue quickly wet her lips. The woman looked at him. Followed him with her glance.

"Look at my hand, woman," he whispered.

Alfred swung his hand, and the woman, from underwater, silently followed the shifting hand with her eyes. To the right, then to the left, and then Alfred brought it down near the water. Suddenly dropping his fist, Alfred pretended to punch her head, and the woman's face startled. She reacted just like a real person about to be punched. Instead, Alfred's fist did not touch the water. He moved the little mirror closer to the water. He bent down to see if the little mirror captured the woman's image on the water. Well, Alfred saw that the woman on the water appeared in the little mirror. Just like a real, living face inside the sink. From there, the woman looked at Alfred's eyes, frowned, with a resolute stare.

"You're one of the voices," Alfred said before turning out the lights and going to bed.

"Yes. You are one of the voices and now none of you are talking. Mute. And now you are all looking at me," Alfred said in the dark, looking at nothing.

MORNING.

Alfred woke up from a long, deep sleep, without remembering any dreams. He felt no sensations of his body or mind, refreshed after sleeping, and his brain looked like a clean blackboard with some random chalk cloud left to remind him of the basic elements of his human being. He had to piss. He stood up lazily and had the weird idea of surprising someone new on any puddle of water, any way, anywhere. He raised the toilet lid. On the water, as always, instead of his own face, Alfred found a man who was looking at him. Alfred smiled. He didn't know what to do. But soon, the idea…

"I'm, sorry, man. I guess it's not a polite thing to do, and I don't have it in for you, but…if you stay down there…" Alfred dropped his pajama pants and underwear. "As you wish. I warned you."

The face below, inside the toilet, a man of forty in a black jacket, white shirt, and tie, pretty elegant, started vibrating and distorting under the splashing jet of urine. Alfred even saw him try to cover his face with both hands, but for him there was nothing he could do. Before his bladder was completely empty, Alfred pissed on the floor. So there, on the amber puddle, appeared now not Alfred's face, once again, or the man in the jacket's face, but that of a bride under a veil. Her makeup and hairstyle were typical of the 1920s. That face, just like all the ones seen by Alfred, did not remind him of anyone at all. Alfred flushed the toilet, and with the water the man in jacket and tie was swallowed away. As the water formed again, Alfred looked at it and saw a new guy, a messy-haired man with a dirty T-shirt. He smiled at Alfred with rotten and bent teeth. His eyelids half shut made him look like an idiot.

"On every pool of water, a different person. They're back again. They are *the voices*."

Alfred got a notebook.

He filled it up with rich descriptions of people he was seeing in every liquid reflection instead of his own face.

"SHANA, THE voices have not gone away," Alfred confessed.

"Are they talking to you again?" the nurse asked.

"No, miss. They aren't. But now they are showing themselves to me."

"What do you mean? Can you see their faces? When you arrived here the first time, you didn't tell us about faces, only voices."

Alfred paused before answering. The cool morning breeze made him feel alive. "Yes, I see them," he said. He did not specify how. He guessed that would seem too crazy. Alfred feared that the doctors would do something bad and painful to him.

"Who are they?" Shana asked.

"Men, women, children. I think they were the same people who talked to me for years. They talked to me till the day I woke up in here. However," Alfred added, "as you asked me the other day, I wrote down in a notebook every stranger I've seen up until now."

"Good. Then I'll take a look at your notes."

"Of course, miss. I tried to write everything in detail."

"Do you want to know why you woke up in here? Do you still remember nothing before your recovery?"

"I remember…" Alfred brought a hand to his face to hide his eyes. He wanted to cry. "I only remember the crowd of voices. A lot of orders and orders and orders."

Alfred cried, at last. Shana wrapped her arm around his shoulders. In the mansion's garden, sitting on the bench, they were alone and distant from the fountain and other people.

"Then, suddenly, I woke up in here. In my head I could no longer hear their voices," Alfred said, putting his hand down from his eyes and looking at Shana beside him.

Alfred's eyes were full of tears.

Shana's face was marked with tears.

But her face was blurry. Split.

Because of the tears' film in Alfred's eyes, he was seeing a stranger's face overlapping Shana's, just like a motion picture projected over her head.

And from her eyes, moreover, three little faces rolled down her cheeks, that Alfred saw brushed away when she dried her face with the back of her hand. "We thought," Shana whispered, "we had healed you, Alfred." Her features were deformed by resignation. She was beautiful no more. "I think I ought to tell Dr. Mark, dear Alfred. Before you hurt yourself or somebody else again," the nurse proclaimed standing up.

"No, miss. Please," Alfred begged. "I won't hurt anyone."

Feeling a waterfall of sadness rumbling inside himself, Alfred looked at Shana hurrying toward the mansion, face in her hands. She was crying.

Tears.

Water.

Faces.

"DOCTOR, ARE you sure there is no other way?" Shana asked.

Dr. Mark answered, staring at the two doctors on Alfred, shaken on the table by an incessant wave of electric convulsions. "Nurse, this is 1975. Medical science has made massive progress since the end of the war. Shock treatment is the best cure against schizophrenia."

"What if he could already be healed? I mean, if the real problem was something different?"

"There is no other possibility than the one we know. Maybe a resemblance between auditory and optical phases. This new hallucination form is the same mental disease with a different way of expression. Alfred is not healed at all. Evidently, the first shock cycle hadn't generated the expected results. Alfred's mental disorder seems to be stronger than we believed."

"He'll never be healed, I guess," Shana whispered, crying softly.

"I think I agree with you, nurse."

"I'm sorry, Alfred. I am so sorry," Shana whispered, crying.

HE WAS sitting at the same old chair of his awakening, in the garden. Three days after his brand new shock treatment. Four hundred and fifty volts.

He forgot once again how to wash, how to dress himself. He didn't know where he was, what day it was. Neither did he remember receiving the first of the new series of shock treatments. He only knew he was awake and so confused. His muscles were a mass of extreme tiredness.

"May I have a glass of water?" he asked Shana, who was standing in silence beside him.

"Of course, Alfred. I'll be back in a while."

Alfred had no awareness of the treatment to which he had been submitted. Every session removed the most recent previous moments. Alfred knew he was under *some* therapy. And whatever that was, the cure made him unhappy. He felt empty. Erased. Violated.

Shana returned with a plastic cup. "Here it is, Alfred. Sorry for the delay."

"No…no problem, miss. Thank you," Alfred murmured. He was able to grip the cup with his shaky hand and keep it pretty steady. Alfred was sure he'd never seen this woman before, even though he thought he loved her. There was something magic between them.

"I read your notes, Alfred."

"My handwriting is not so good," he said smiling.

"You'll regain it soon."

"We have lot of time for that, don't we?"

"All the time we need," Shana said biting her lower lip.

"I am the periscope of the dead," Alfred said.

"Yes. I got it in your notebook. But, please, tell me…how can you claim a thing like that?"

"I don't know. They come from every time, especially the deep past. I saw ancient men of every race, soldiers from the last century, and a saint, the name of whom I can't remember, dressed like a friar."

"Don't you think they could be a simple projection of your mind? Maybe faces you saw in your life or that you saw around here?"

"No, miss," Alfred said. "As you read from my notes, I saw children's faces on the water. And in here we are all old people. The ones I see on the water aren't shadows from my mind. I am not insane. They are real, they come up to the water, inside every body of water. And they have chosen me, someone to watch in the world."

"Can you say why?"

"I guess I can't. I don't know. Maybe they feel alone. Maybe each of them do not have someone who loves them. Who remembers them. Maybe one day Dr. Mark will figure it out."

"I really hope so," Shana said bringing Alfred to her chest.

"Now...you can go, Shana," Alfred said when she loosened the hug.

"Are you sure?"

"I am fine, thank you."

"So I'll be back in half an hour for dinner."

"Half an hour for dinner," Alfred lied, smiling.

He wanted to be alone. He had to.

The garden, the fence with those tall, sharpened points. The roses, the trees. And the fountain. He would never be gone from here. Only suffering and pain waited for him.

He watched the water.

The sun shined too bright, unbearable for his eyes. Inside his head, silence ran in the form of his breath. The moment was crucial.

Once again, inside the cup, on the water in the cup, there was not the reflection of his face.

There was another man's face. Alfred knew all the faces he got pretty well. This man he had not seen before.

Alfred drank him.

Alfred drank that face.

And he saw the man screaming in despair, as his liquid face slid into Alfred's mouth.

Bad pain in the pit of his stomach.

As if he'd swalloved a stone.

Dark lightning.

WHEN ALL of the patients had grouped in a circle around him, several minutes of torment had passed. Shana was returning to fetch him for dinner, but found him folded on the ground tormented by abdominal cramps, his face pushed into the grass, biting the earth. The nurse called out for help. Then she leaned on Alfred, who burned with fever, covered in sweat. The patients enlarged their circle, looking at Shana and Alfred like astonished and frightened babies.

"Alfred, honey, what's wrong with you?" Shana asked in tears, turning him on his back.

"Your water..." Alfred wheezed.

"It's the water's fault?"

Alfred nodded, blinking fast and staring at some point in the sky.

Dr. Mark came along, with two assistants and a stretcher.

Immediately, Shana said, "He only drank a cup of water."

ALONE IN his room, lying on the bed, Alfred had another spasm.

He turned on his side and a mass of blood poured from his stomach onto the floor. He didn't seem frightened by that. The puddle exploded in every direction, and the gleaming pools of blood stretched themselves under the bed. The lamp on the night table was on, so Alfred could see the red puddle shining under his glance, dimmed by pain. Alfred thought he could see his shape reflected by the red fluid. His stomachache stopped fast. When Alfred's sight became clear again, instead of his own face, he found a woman staring at him from the puddle of blood. "Mother," he cried out.

His mother.

It was really her face on the red blood instead of Alfred's.

Crying in silence, the man stretched his hand down toward the blood on the floor.

"Oh, mother of mine."

Tears fell down into the red.

Alfred saw that his hand was not reflected on the bloody surface as he moved it toward his mother's face. As if the blood itself was colored glass between mother and son. Or a hole in the floor showing a room full of plasma right under the bed. The woman moved her lips as she said something that her son could not hear. Alfred plunged his hand into his blood and touched his mother's face. It felt as if his fingers had really done it. Then he pulled his hand back. He gazed at it, painted in warm fluid, turning it back and forth. Thinking he'd actually touched the woman. With trembling fingers that dropped red into red, he tried one more time.

Again, the hand went down and reached the woman's face. She grabbed Alfred's hand and put it gently on her cheek. She closed her eyes enjoying the caress, while her son felt on his palm the real consistency of her skin beneath the blood.

The touch ignited in Alfred's mind his book of memories. His mother stared at him, austere looking. The hazel of her eyes was altered through the transparent red, but she could see everything, both Alfred and his room above her.

As if the scarlet puddle of blood was a skylight to the world.

Alfred began to see every moment of his life. And what he could see in the end was frightening. Unbelievably frightening.

So, his mother knew that her son had finally discovered his infinite fault.

"Oh, Mother," cried Alfred. "Please, forgive me. I wouldn't hurt you. It's the voices' fault. They told me to do it. I just obeyed their command."

The woman slowly closed her eyes, to show God-like compassion and forgiveness. When she opened them again, their judging light had given way to the old sweetness that Alfred had known ever since he was a child, until the voices arrived and took him forever. The reason the voices had chosen Alfred remained encrypted among the unfathomable forces of the hereafter's plans.

The woman strongly grabbed Alfred's wrist and pulled her son to her, forcing him to go down, to get close.

"Oh, Mother. Really, can I?"

She only smiled, a spell of love and desire.

Alfred jumped off the bed, diving into the puddle, led by the woman who withdrew deeper to make room for him. Alfred held his breath and dove deeper into the red, his open eyes matching his mother's, her sweet smile, her timeless love.

She embraced him.

He kissed her mother's lips.

She smiled, eyes closed.

He felt ashamed for that unnatural gesture but, in that liquid space, human morality could only stay at air level just beyond the surface.

All around, Alfred could again see every face he'd already met and heard taking shape in that place where he was levitating with his mother. They coagulated, gaining features. Fluctuating, the crowd got closer and closer, forming a circle.

Closer and closer.

Alfred tried to get free from his mother's embrace. He feared he would be crushed by the nearing crowd. All of them arriving in groups and fleets.

As he saw them get closer, like a moving wall of dead that

finally had him, Alfred realized he couldn't go back to the surface.

He could not re-emerge.

All of those faces.

The voices.

All of the hands that blocked him.

His room's light, up there, above him, filtered by the red.

Someone turned it off.

Forever.

They got him in the dark.

In Dr. Mark's office.

The light of the room trembled. Shana looked at the ceiling with tears in her eyes. She knew what the flickering lights meant. Her stomach was tied in knots as she spoke to the doctor.

"I think you got too involved in Alfred's case. I can't load you with all of this pain. You're so precious to me, Shana."

"Oh no, sir. I want to stay with him to the end. I have forgiven him. He has no faults."

"You know if Alfred remains in here, he'll have to go on with the shock treatment and remain in isolation. I don't want him to rot in a common prison. They would kill him."

"I'll be strong, Doc. Though I strongly believe Alfred is not a schizophrenia case. He's my brother, after all. I know him even if he doesn't know who I am anymore."

"I think so, Shana. But, please, go back home and take two weeks off. Alfred is with his new family, now."

"Dr. Mark, Alfred's gone."

"Untie him, unplug the electrodes, and bring him back to his room. But remember, we must say he killed himself in his bed. So cut his wrists. The whole world must not think our methods are inhumane."

The two assistants went back to Alfred's body.

Dr. Mark, elbows on desk, thought about nothing for a while.

Until dusk.

Until Alfred's voice whispered inside his head, "Thank you, Doctor. Thank you all the same."

The doctor's hands trembled.

DENNIS ETCHISON

WET SEASON

MADDEN WATCHED the black crowd on the other side of the moving gelatin wall, as rainwater poured down in translucent sheets over the windshield. He did not listen to the patternless tattoo. Instead he followed with his eyes the group of black shadows floating past the car.

"I…I shouldn't have made you come, Lorie," he said at last to the black figure next to him.

She turned from the window, her lidded eyes not disapproving. "That's enough, Jim. I wouldn't have felt right, otherwise."

Madden pressed his chin to his chest, squeezing his eyelids shut. He cleared his throat and rubbed his eyes, and his fingers came away moist.

Again his wife spoke, very quietly. "You…were very close to her, I suppose. James, I only wish there were something…Forgive me if I'm crude. But I only wish I could have gotten to know her better. That she might have become, in time, my little girl as well."

He pressed her cool hand.

"It was—just—all the mud around her—" He bit his lips and started the engine and roared up the cemetery road, spinning out and spattering mud as he went.

THE FORD geared to a slippery halt under the wet sycamores.

Bart stood at the end of the cracked driveway, behind the main house, propping open the sagging screen door to his apartment.

Through mist Madden saw the controlled, mildly pleasant line shaping his mouth, leaving the face somber in a new and ill-fitting mask.

"Forget about the rug," said Bart. "It's filthy anyway."

"We're so sorry to do this to you, Bart." Madden's wife brushed water from her clothing. "But we thought the twins were really too young to, well, exactly have their faces rubbed in it."

Bart smoothed a hand over his protruding, black-T-shirted belly. "The kids are in the bedroom. Rain must have got 'em drowsy. Left them staring out the window, counting drops or something," he added gently to Madden, testing a smile.

"Let me see to them." Madden's wife started across the room.

The men waited until she was gone.

Bart faced him. "Come over here and have a drink."

"No."

"Really, boy, really now. You know how I mean it. Come on."

At once Madden felt his joints chilled and tired. "No, Bart. I…I don't need it." He lowered himself to the sofa that was bulging and splitting like a fat man's incisions.

Bart watched the misty screen door and compared it to the pale Scotch and water in his hand. Twice he shaped his lips to stillborn beginnings. He shook his head and said nothing.

"You look at the hole, and the mud," Madden began finally in a low voice, "and you think of…that human being there in a box, being lowered into the ground, and you wonder how it can be that—that a part of your body, a piece that has come from you like an arm or leg, can be cut off, killed and buried away, and you never being able to feel with it again.

"But you know, I worked with a man once who had lost an arm in the Korean War; and he said he could close his eyes anytime and suddenly it was there again, the nerves were restored and he could feel down into his fingertips. But when he opened his eyes to see why he hadn't touched what he was reaching for, his eyes told him there was nothing there anymore."

Rain began to tap erratically on a metal vent somewhere in the roof.

"And you know, I can still see the world through my little girl's eyes, feel it as she felt it, even...even though she's been cut off me, like one of my sense organs. I still *feel* her, feel *through* her, and my nerves, my ganglia just won't listen to the goddam facts."

Outside, water continued to fall and fall illogically, relentlessly, in what seemed to be the result of a vast macrocosmic defrosting.

Giggling, the twins came out of the bedroom.

Madden saw them and smiled wanly from the sofa. The two little boys acknowledged him peripherally and grinned, grasping their mother's hands more securely.

"How did it go, boys?" inquired Madden, generating concern, and immediately hated his own detachment. *You are my sons, now,* he thought, *my only sons, and I should hold you tight against me—*

"We had fun, Da-da. We had samiches."

"An' we tooka nap an' went out an' played an'—"

Why, noted Madden wearily, *they're actually speaking directly to me....She almost never lets them do that. What is this, some kind of show for Bart?*

"Out? But it didn't let up today, did it, Bart?" he said.

"Well, uh," the dark man gestured firmly to Madden, "they—" and he dropped his voice, ready to spell out words before the children, "they begged to go out. You brought them in their raincoats and, you know, it was one of those things. For a few minutes is all. Made 'em real happy. God knows I have no practice in child-rearing. Jesus, Jim, I hope they didn't catch anything."

"Tad and Ray never catch colds," stated Madden's wife, smiling her wide, smooth, peculiar kind of smile. "You did fine, Bart."

Madden watched his wife. Svelte in the gray light, she snaked an arm around each of her children's shoulders.

"We'd better go," she said. "It's Sunday and I have Women's Guild meeting tonight."

"Thanks, Bart. I mean it more than I can say."

They walked together, heads down, to the door. Sunday comics section for her hair and Lorelei and the giggly children clamored down the shiny, fragmented driveway.

Bart gripped his arm, looking deep into his eyes and nodding.

"You know I know. I can't say it. But I remember the Sunday

we buried Mama." Hearing it said now, Madden felt no longer a memory of pain but a bond with manhood. "Just so's you know I know." And a slap caught Madden between the shoulder blades and sent him into the rain.

To a car where a somehow strange woman and children waited.

HE SWITCHED off the ignition and sat very still, staring into the liquid pattern on the windshield.

"Ready, children?" asked Mrs. Madden, not looking to the back seat, taking her purse into her lap.

From the back seat came giggling.

Madden lay his head back to let his eyes trace the headliner of the car. Half a minute earlier, shutting off the wipers, he had caught himself hypnotized as the twin arcs of the wiper blades melted away. Now, the motor silenced, he listened to the sound of endless beads beating their pattern into the top of the automobile.

In the back seat, there was whispering like the swishing of cars down an empty street.

"Let's go, children," prompted their mother. "There'll be plenty of time for secrets when we get in the house."

Abruptly Madden snapped to. He focused his eyes from the windshield to the woman next to him, attuned his ears from the drumming overhead to the whisper of cloth on plastic as the children slid across the back seat. He touched the handle of his wife's door; it was cold. Almost as cold as his hand.

Behind him, someone giggled.

OUTSIDE THE picture window, premature dusk settled along the block like silent black wings.

"Won't...won't you eat something?" asked Mrs. Madden tenuously. She leaned into the living room, spoon in hand and spoke in silhouette from the yellow kitchen doorway.

He cleared his throat. "What?" Madden's five fingertips moved involuntarily to the pane. The glass was cold.

"Well," she intoned maternally, "you should have something. It's almost dark. Let me turn on the—"

"It's all right, Lorelei." *For God's sake,* he thought, *don't patronize me. Not now.*

Chilled and fatigued to the marrow, he sat in the newly rearranged and alien living room and tried to release his senses from the pain of here-and-now. He shut his eyes and tried to let his thoughts blow with the storm on down the blurred panorama of empty street.

She puttered for a time in the kitchen and Madden, curiously detached in the dark and the overstuffed chair, noticed again her effortless, liquid movements. The way she had of gliding over a floor as though it were polished glass, her legs flowing out and back with each step in a charming suggestion of no gristle or bone. No deliberate, angular bend to Lorie's arm, no; in her, stirring and pouring out and rinsing away became a Siamese rubber-arm ballet.

"Your soup is in the oven, keeping warm. And the twins are tucked in, so don't—I mean, they shouldn't give you any trouble."

Mrs. Madden paused in silhouette, then glided behind the enormous sagging hand that enclosed her husband.

"Lorie," he swallowed. Away in the bright kitchen, an electric clock hummed.

She sat on the armrest.

"Lorelei, do you ever…think about the decision you made ten months ago?" He tried to stop his teeth from chattering. "I mean—"

Her arms reached a pale circle around his shoulders. "You are the finest father my boys could possibly have. And I…" And she smoothed his hair with her oddly flat hands and did not finish. "Do you need to talk, Jim? The Guild meeting—"

Yes, he thought, pressing his eyes tightly shut until shards of gray light fired inside his eyelids, *yes, I need something. I hear your words but they're only words, I need more than talk, I need you warm against me, I need to live—*

He drew her into his lap. And at once it struck him.

She was *not* warm. Her skin was cold, cold almost as—

He pushed her away.

"Jim, I'm sorry. Is there something I can do for you?"

"No." He stared ahead into the night-filled room. "They're waiting for you already. There isn't anything you can do for me."

Picking up coat, purse and overshoes, Mrs. Madden pulled back the front door to a sheet of rain. A reminder about the soup, and she entered the falling sea.

THE TELEPHONE refused to warm in his hands.

A sputter and crackle of rain and whispers on the wires between and across town, a mile away, a phone purred to life.

And purred. And purred.

"Yeah?"

"Hello, Bart. What am I interrupting?"

"Jimmy? That you, boy?"

"I hope I'm not interrupting anything."

"No, no. Listen. Lorie gone to her meeting?"

"That's right."

"Then you're alone." Pause. "Everything all right over there?"

"Yes. Aw, look, I shouldn't have called."

"You wanna talk, Jim?"

"I guess. No....Bart, is someone coming over tonight? You going out?"

"In this weather? Look, is everything all right?"

Pause. "Uh, Bart, I wonder...I just wondered if...aw, never mind, I shouldn't have bothered you."

"Look. You wanna come over here? We could talk, if you want."

"Can't leave the kids."

"They're asleep, then, and you're alone over there. You want me to come over? Talk or something until Lorie gets back?"

Pause. "I have no business bothering you."

"Crap. Look, I'll come over, okay? We can talk, you know, like we used to."

"I'm pretty bad company tonight, I'm afraid. And the weather. Sure you want to?"

"My idea, isn't it? And look, how can you turn down a lonely ol' bachelor like me? See you in ten minutes."

"Thanks very much, Bart," but he had hung up.

MADDEN WAITED on the back porch, listening.

Far down in the darkness, the throaty thrumming of the frogs met with the rushing of running water.

All about his thin figure, dirty streams dripped from the roof to mingle with puddles at his cold feet, to slip on down over the slanting yard, to join larger tributaries that splashed their way through the thorny shrubbery of the ravine to feed at last with violent churning into the shrouded riverbed far below.

From in front, Madden heard wet brakes grip to a splashing stop. Shivering, he turned inside.

The two men sat across from one another in the living room, two men who knew each other best of all in the world. There was only a pale-moth glow from the kitchen. They spoke, and they did not speak, and from time to time Bart laughed and sipped from the brandy snifter in his lap.

"...But then they threw the next game to the motherin' Angels," Bart was saying.

"Yes," said Madden.

Bart rose and ambled to the black picture window.

Abruptly Madden was aware that his brother had stopped talking.

Madden stared with him. He saw his brother frown. *Do you feel it too?* he thought. Vaguely illumined beneath the street lamp was Bart's car, leaning against the curb, weathering the storm. Idly, Madden had a vision of the rain pouring off the metal top, streaming over the rolled-up windows and down into the innards of the door, where the handle and lock mechanism were.

"Jimbo. God damn it."

Madden watched him. "What's wrong?"

Bart drained his glass. "I don't wanna say it. I don't even know I'm right. Or if I oughta say it."

"It's all right—I can talk about Darla. Probably it would do me good." He massaged his face, trying to relax. "I know I have to face—"

"No. That's not what I'm talking about." Bart pivoted from the window and the rain. "Listen to me, kid. *Do you feel it?*'

"Feel what?"

"Something, about this house, this town. I don't know how to say it. But can't you feel it?" Bart glared into the empty brandy glass.

"Something like what?" Madden lounged back into the cushion, ready to listen. *Now,* thought Madden, *this is the way. It won't prove a thing unless he says it first.*

"Damn," breathed Bart. He turned back to the night and lit a cigarette. "Maybe I'm going off the deep end. Look. Can I ask you a question?"

"Shoot."

"Something about this house. I don't know. The way it smells now, the way the chairs creak when I sit down, the color of the *light*, for God's sake, like the room is underwater or something. And all since she moved in." The cigarette reflection burned in the window. "Naw. Man, you're the one needs to talk at a time like this. I'm supposed to cheer *you*."

"So you're cheerin'. Shoot."

"Look, it's just that—haven't you noticed anything, well, different about the place since Lorie and her kids moved in? That it isn't really yours anymore? I mean, it's like every person has a rhythm, a pattern to his everyday life. You go into a man's bedroom, it *smells* like him, the bed bends a certain way when you sit on it, because it's been shaped to fit every angle and bulge just right over the years. And you go into the kitchen, the way the dishes are piled up in the sink tells you more about the guy than a look at his diary, if you know what I mean. It's like the house soaks up what you are, the way you feel about life, and everything in the house gets to feeling the same way, too. And not only the place, but the woman he marries: she seems to fit right in, fit him, and the house…and that's part of it, too, Jimbo. She's—and I know I'm steppin' way over the bounds on this, but dammit, man, she's *not you*, you know? Let me ask: don't you notice anything unusual about Lorie?"

Madden shut his eyes impatiently. "She's an unusually attractive woman, if that's what you mean."

"No. But then I promised myself not to bring up any of this with you, at least not for a long time…

"But it isn't just this house. Hell, we both grew up in Greenworth, I knew every turn in the river like the lines on my hand years before the government moved in. And it's changed now, somehow. First, it was just the way the trees started growing crooked along the banks, but lately the whole town seems, I don't know, *funny*. The way the air smells, the paint on the houses…I don't know. I just don't know. But I'll tell you this: if I were blindfolded and left here, I'd never in a year guess this was the same town we grew up in."

Outside, the moon slipped for a moment through a pocket of clouds, washing Bart's face fishlike-pale by the window.

"Bart. What is it?"

"I wish I could be sure, kid. Maybe you should forget it. I pray to God *I* could. Jim, do you know how many storms like this we've had in Greenworth in the last twenty-five years?"

Madden stirred.

"I'll tell you: three, before two years ago. And not one raised the river more than a few inches. But in two years, five big ones. Here." Bart spilled his coat pocket onto the coffee table. "What the hell—I spent yesterday in the library looking things up, I don't know what for. Something made me do it. But God, I've gotta show you."

Madden reached to the lamp.

Little white slips of paper fluttered in Bart's hands. For the first time in his life Madden saw his brother trembling.

"God!" he laughed nervously. "Help me, will you, Jim? Here are the pieces to a crazy jigsaw, it doesn't make any sense, but something in the back of my head keeps me from getting any sleep lately. Here, look, read it all and then tell me I'm nuts and send me home, but *do something!*'

"'Deaths by drowning, County Beach: this year and last, total 31. Previous two years' total, 9.' What's this for?"

"Don't stop now." Bart fumbled at the liquor cabinet.

"'Total rainfall in inches, adjacent counties last year, up 300%.'"

"See! It's spreading."

Another slip of paper. "'New residents in Greenworth, past 24 months: Broadbent, Mr. and Mrs. C. L.; Marber, G.; Nottingham, Mr. and Mrs. Frank R....'" Madden leaned forward intently.

"There's two dozen more."

He scrutinized his brother's now twisted face. "So?"

"So? So you're right, they're nothing separately, but put them all together—Let me ask you: Lorie never told you where she moved from when she came here, did she?"

"Now that you bring it up, no. But what—?"

"Listen to this. Last night I got out the phone book and dialed these new listings. Twenty-one are married couples. And every woman—" Bart emptied his glass. "Every woman is in the Women's Guild."

Ice water poured into Madden's stomach. "So?"

Bart jerked forth a folded clipping. "This was in the *Gazette* when one finally moved in twenty months ago."

Madden fingered the newspaper photo of "Mr. and Mrs. Peter Hallendorf, newly established real estate broker and his lovely bride."

"Use this." A pocket magnifier hit the coffee table.

She *was* lovely. There in the enlarged dots was a face that was—"I don't see—"

Bart's shaking finger jabbed at the indistinct eyes, the mouth.

At first he didn't see it. Just that her eyes were softly, lethargically lidded.

Bart snatched a framed photograph from the bookcase and tossed it to his lap.

And there.

There were two sets of lidded eyes, two wide, smooth, peculiar smiles, side by side. They might have been sisters.

Madden groped. At the bottom of his consciousness, the pressure was rising now and he felt his finger giving way in the dike.

"Jim," grunted Bart. "I called the Community Center this evening. They never heard of it. *There is no Women's Guild!*

"And now. Just one more question. I hate to remind you, boy, but you've got to have all the pieces in front of you." Bart leaned over him, breath coming fast and pungent. "Tell me again how it was your little girl died."

Madden bit his knuckle. "Man, I don't know what you're driving at. Please—"

"Just say it!"

"She...she, you know. She drowned—in the—bottom of the tub." He fought up out of the chair.

Both men faced each other, white-faced.

"Goddam," breathed Bart, turning back to the darkness. "Goddam me for saying it."

WALKING IN the wet, Madden knew at last that he could leave the house behind and give himself up to the storm. Slimy, tangled brush grabbed at his sopping clothes, but he did not think of it and slid down the ravine to the churning riverbed. In the glistening night he saw the swelling rush muddying over collapsing banks, and he remembered the first and worst storm, two seasons ago: how the ravine filled steadily to the brim, spilling up over the backyard; and then, weeks later, how the yard blossomed alive with all manner of new, unnamed wild plants and shoots and bloomed-faced flowers. And how he suddenly awoke one night to discover the moldering ravine an amphitheater of swollen hordes of singing insect life, a thundering of bullfrogs, a sweltering din of mosquitoes, a screeching chorus of crickets. Latent with life, pollen and cyst and egg had been carried by the water and given birth at long last.

Madden stretched through the wet growth to the river's edge. Facts and meanings swirled and eddied within him.

He saw the fresh water flowing on past, headed for the sea.

A paper boat or a leaf could float the five miles to the turbines, and beyond to the sea. But only something living could do the opposite.

Suddenly, as if by a signal, frog and insect ceased their noise.

In the new silence, above the rain, Madden heard a car door slam.

He began tearing savagely at the shrubbery. His hair and chin dripped and his clothes were torn and caked with mud below the waist, but he did not think of these things as he climbed his way to the porch.

He smeared a wet trail across the kitchen.

Lorelei came through the unlighted living room.

"Why James, I thought you'd be in bed. And your clothes, why—"

"Wh-where have you been?" He shivered.

She reached to touch his clothes. He jumped back.

He saw that her clothing, too, was dripping. Much more than from a run from the car.

"Why, James—"

"Get away! Who are you?"

The sound of giggling.

He ran to the bathroom door. He kicked it in.

Grinning in the stark white porcelain bathtub were the twins, Tad and Ray. They splashed and curled eel-like appendages up over the edge.

"What is this?" muttered Madden, blinded by the light. "What are you boys bathing for at...?" Then he saw their smooth, shining skins glistening in the water in a strange new way.

So this is the way Darla came upon them that day, he thought. *So that was why, that was why. So now I have no choice....*

He fell upon them, pushing their small heads under the water until bubbles floated up.

They came up grinning.

"So you know," she said.

He turned.

The bright, white tiles around him.

Lorelei, dripping, came toward him, holding out her arms as if to embrace him. An alien scaliness glittered anew along her neck, her boneless arms.

Behind him, the little ones giggled.

Madden stepped back before she could touch him. His legs met the tub and he tumbled backwards, seeing in a flash the bright walls and ceiling.

There was a resounding splash and then violent churning. And giggling.

And the sound of the rain outside.

JOHN PALISANO

WINGS MADE FROM WATER

HER FACE turns to dust
when it's touched.
In a moment
water blooms gray
from her remains.

Disintegration.
Countless particles
bloom and fill.

Everything white, then slate
until it's all washed away
once more, once more…
and again, the water is still.

"DANNY!" A woman's voice called, but it was not his mother.

Aunt Franny, he thought. *I'm not in Berkeley. I'm in San Quinlan.* He stretched and blinked several times; his nightmare grew distant. Soon, the crushing fear he'd felt while asleep would be rewritten and forgotten. Even so, his hands shook—still rattled from the awful vision.

Remnants from my dream.

He made his way from his upstairs room, smelling the pine and the incense of the cabin house. Then he smelled the water. The San Quinlan River streamed only a few hundred feet away. Much of the structures were built close to the water. *Probably too close.* Unclaimed woods cradled the town's eastern border, the terrain rocky and prone to flooding.

The river smells clean and dirty. He remembered saying that to his father during a visit when he was younger. His father had laughed. "The river carries soot and minerals—all sorts of things," he'd said. "That's a pretty spot-on observation." They'd continued toward Saint Jude's. The church anchored San Quinlan Street, which was raised above the river, with an endless network of stone walkways, walls, and bridges, all defying nature. Everything seemed small-scale. Even the fire engine looked shorter, but back-heavy from its portable water tank.

"It's a pretty place for vacations," he'd said to his father. "But I like being in the city better."

"You'll probably feel different when you're older," his father had said. They sat on a stone bench a few yards from Saint Jude's. People mingled on the church's bright green lawn. "You going to be okay?"

"Sure," Danny said. He barely remembered his cousin. Chloe was ten years older, after all.

As they approached, no one paid them any mind. His father rushed them inside. He overheard someone say, "How can they do this? There's not even anything inside the coffin."

Danny sat between his parents on the pew. He saw a picture of his cousin, blown up poster-sized and framed, standing on top of a shiny oak coffin. *What did that woman mean there was nothing inside the coffin? Is Chloe not inside?*

He looked over the printed program and followed the service. He didn't know what most of the speeches were. Most quoted scripture. He kept looking at her name on the front: Chloe Chase Lyman. The picture was the same as the one on the coffin. She smiled from half of her face, and he kept trying to figure out her hair color. *It's a darker blonde than mine, like ash colored, but not all the way through. I always thought her blonde hair was as bright as the sun.*

Her eyes, though, he'd remembered perfectly. They sparkled like a bright blue ocean. He remembered her laughing when they were kids. *Come catch me, little Danny boy!*

The service ended. Danny's parents stood in line and hugged and kissed his Uncle Luke and Aunt Franny. Later, they'd meet them at the big Italian restaurant at the center of town—Domingo's. Danny thought it was strange that people went out to eat, and that so many were laughing after a funeral. His aunt and uncle weren't there.

They went back to Berkeley. Their lives continued. He hadn't thought about his aunt and uncle in years. He didn't feel connected to his parents, either, as he grew up. Their religion didn't feel like his. He couldn't relate. He got angry. He kept it inside, though. They never forced it upon him. *You'll find faith when you're ready.*

Danny could still feel the softness of Eric Stanley's face beneath his fist. It'd surprised him, because Eric was much bigger than him and talked as though he were as tall as a giant. "To hell with your parents and their stupid Jesus freak stuff," he'd shouted. It'd been enough. Only Danny could rebel against his parents, after all. Not this guy, an outsider, who had nasty words for everything Danny did the entire year.

It'd been enough, and without a sound, when Eric closed in, his mouth still spouting and yammering, Danny clocked him.

Eric made a surprised step back before falling in a heap, cradling his bleeding, broken nose and cheek. Danny pictured the kid how he'd look when he got older, a brief and imagined premonition.

The rest was a blur.

—Why did you hit him?

—I didn't mean to.

—You're angry.

—They're always bothering me.

—We can't have you in this school doing this.

—I'm being suspended.

—Indefinitely.

—My parent's paid...

—You broke a cardinal rule.

His parents, later. Their concerned expressions, both sitting on his bed as he lay.

—We won't be able to recover from this.

—We know this isn't you.

—You need to take this time and find yourself.

—I know who I am. I was just pushed. How come he isn't being punished? He started this.

—God has a plan. Sometimes it doesn't seem fair.

—Your father and I are taking a job for six months.

—We're going to need to make up the money for this.

—Okay.

—It's in the Philippines. You're going to stay with Aunt Franny and Uncle Luke.

—I barely know them.

—Just through the summer. We'll figure this out when we come back.

He pictured the car ride, his suitcase and backpack riding in the seat next to him. *They're worse with the religion than Mom and Dad.*

Danny remembered the moment after his dad hugged Uncle Luke. "Thank you." The look of disappointment. His father tried to hide it.

Remnants.

"OUR FATHER, please provide a circle of protection around our home, and around our family today. And thank you for your ever-guiding presence in our lives," Uncle Luke said. They'd linked hands around the oak table.

"Amen," Danny said, relieved to let go and eat. The steel-cut oatmeal, orange juice, and toast were magnificent. "You cook like no one's business," he said.

"It's a pleasure to serve," his uncle said.

Aunt Franny clutched her husband's hand. "That it is." She looked toward Danny. Then away. She shut her eyes and cried.

"Franny?" his uncle said.

His voice was not enough to stop her from rushing from the table. They both called after her, but they knew it was too late.

"I'm sorry," his uncle said. "It's not your fault." Behind them, they heard her rush into her bedroom, just off the living room, and collapse onto the bed. She wept.

Danny looked down at his plate.

"Things catch up, you know?" his uncle said. "You are staying in our daughter's room. Having a child's voice in the house again." He looked up to the framed picture of Chloe over the fireplace.

"My dad said you said it would be good for you," Danny said.

"I know. We thought that." His uncle kept his gaze on Chloe's picture. "But thinking and feeling are different things."

"No doubt," Danny said. *I'm trapped...making them feel bad. I don't want to be here, either. Like I'm caught inside an invisible net.*

His uncle got up and headed toward the bedroom. "Good luck today, kiddo," he said. "Make sure you finish your food before you go."

"Why didn't she wake up?" his aunt cried, her words muffled but clear from behind the closed door. "Why wouldn't she just wake up?"

Danny's blood felt flash frozen. He wanted to be anywhere else. His guts were tight. *I'm always compared to Chloe. She's still here. They haven't let go.*

As soon as his uncle was out of sight, Danny found a plastic bag, scooped his breakfast inside, put the empty plate in the sink, and hurried outside.

He sped up the driveway and turned left at the top of Gallows Road. His mind played the breakfast over and over, like a guppy looping endlessly around a fish tank. *Please, Mom and Dad, get back early.* Danny thought back to his cousin Chloe's funeral. *They're making me sleep in her room. Probably on her bed and old blankets.* He took out the bag with his breakfast and threw it into the woods. "All yours, bugs," he said. His stomach had turned, anyhow, thinking of his cousin inside her coffin.

This was close to the spot where we played when I was a kid.

—Come catch me, little Danny boy!

—Come catch me!

He walked toward the end of Gallows Road and saw the sign for San Quinlan Road, downtown's main strip. "San Quinlan? Might as well say San Quentin."

Danny walked on the stone sidewalk on the opposite side of the street, running a hand over the wall that kept pedestrians from falling into the San Quinlan River a few yards below. The sound of its flow felt inevitable and calming, the watery smell present everywhere. He looked over at the shops and offices that stretched a half a mile through downtown. Everything one needed was there.

He stopped near the church steeple. His stomach tightened. He remembered his cousin's funeral. *How did she die? That's something we'll talk about when you're older.* Turning back around, Danny looked over the stone wall lining the sidewalk and down toward the rushing San Quinlan River. Once he passed Saint Jude's, he looked back toward the road and the buildings opposite. He crossed the street.

He passed the gas station, its bays old-fashioned. It didn't have a convenience store attached, like the ones in Berkeley. Next door, Gary's Groceries was one of the largest structures in town, but even it would be considered small by city standards. Its design differed from the rest of San Quinlan in that it was made in the 1960s and looked of its era. Inside held a Starbucks, which made Danny feel connected to the outside world, even though he hated coffee. The GAP was built within an existing building so as not to ruin or tamper with the overall aesthetic of the town. It was surrounded by many local shops like Hector's Candy and Alhambra Art Gallery, the home of local celebrity artist Robert Alhambra.

Danny made his way toward the end of the strip of shops, to where Old Mill Road started. He had time. The last thing he wanted to do was be seen lingering aimlessly. He knew he could walk through the light woods, maybe catch some alone time free of human interference.

He didn't make it ten minutes until he came upon Kenny Peyton. Of course. Kenny could always be counted on for loitering and borderline mischievous behavior. "Yo," he called out. "You headed to the Mission?"

"That sounds like a good idea, actually," Danny said.

"Famous last words," Kenny said. "Dead serious."

DANNY'S FEET made sloshing sounds as he made his way through the forest. "It's still moist as all get out," he said. "Did the whole thing flood?"

"I didn't see it this time," Kenny said. "But it does this whenever it rains just a little. It's like it's a marsh, but isn't a marsh. It's weird."

"Smells like algae and mold," Danny said.

"That's San Quinlan for you. Everything's always damp and runny."

Danny looked down and saw the soil, rich from the river water. "How long does it take to dry out?"

"It never does. Probably why the people at the mission killed themselves."

"I've never heard the full story, all these years."

Kenny's voice took on a deeper, more serious tone. "Saw it myself, man. Was a kid, but I'll never forget all the stretchers. At least a dozen. All covered, but there was one boot sticking out from under a blanket. A work boot. Just like my dad's. Scared the crap out of me. I thought it was him and ran up to Cohen's Mill to make sure he was there."

"He was?"

"Sure," Kenny said. "And good thing he didn't see me. He would've killed me for walking that far alone."

"It's safe here."

"You think?" Kenny laughed. "San Quinlan just looks that way."

WHEN THEY arrived at Saint Anne's Mission, Danny forgot how rundown it'd been. "It's like God is angry and reclaiming the land."

"Or nature," Kenny said. "Not sure God would approve of the whole congregation offing themselves at once."

Danny heard his uncle's voice in his head. *That old story about the flock committing suicide in the woods is just tall tales. They closed it because it flooded one too many times to fix. It's more fun for kids to think it's haunted. I don't believe in ghosts, though. People can get haunted by other things. Real things.*

"Let's check it out," Kenny said. "See if there's anything good."

The large front doors weren't open, but were easy enough to swing out. The wood was still intact, even though it'd been warped and camouflaged with large water spots. "Is this safe?" Danny asked.

"No," Kenny said. "Not one bit. The whole place could fall on top of us at any second." He laughed.

"Well, screw it," Danny said. "You only live once."

"As far as we know," Kenny said.

They crossed the doorway. The once-white walls were decayed dark from neglect. Light pooled in from little windows. Danny pointed. "There's still glass in these."

"Weird, right?" Kenny said.

They made it past the first long hallway, which led inside a larger room. Several plastic buckets and broom handles were stacked in a corner. "Watch out," Danny said, first to notice the floor. "It's flooded in here." The water appeared half a foot deep.

"There're support beams running through," Kenny said. "We can walk on those." Most of the floorboards had lifted or were missing. The beams crisscrossed, leaving a dozen rectangular pools.

Kenny made his way out onto a beam balancing by keeping his arms outstretched, slowly putting one foot in front of the other.

"Don't fall in," Danny said.

"Shut up." Kenny didn't look back.

Danny followed him onto the beam. He stepped, his footing insecure. "This isn't cool."

"Come on, man. Just pay attention. You'll be fine."

Danny took another step, twisted wrong, and lost his footing. He jumped back to the still-existing floor of the hall. "Damn," he said. "Almost went in."

"Not my fault you have huge feet," Kenny said. He'd made it to the middle of the room and was able to stand on a cross section—a much larger surface than the beams themselves. He bent down. "Dude! You've got to see this."

"What?"

"There's fish."

The beams were slippery. Danny looked around and spotted a pole-shaped piece of wood. He grabbed it. He banged one end of it on the floor to test its strength. The pole felt solid. He had a crutch.

Balancing with the pole, Danny made his way back onto the first beam. He slipped, but caught himself.

By the third step, he'd found his rhythm and made his way toward Kenny, who, for the record, hadn't noticed Danny's effort, being much too transfixed by the fish.

"What kind of fish are they?"

"Don't know," Kenny said. "Wish my dad was here. He'd know."

Each fish was dark, with silver bellies and black skin. Their eyes were wide. Two were about a foot long, and two more were about half their size. "Is it a family?"

"Give me a break. Fish don't have families," Kenny said.

"Don't families stay together in the wild?" Danny asked.

Kenny laughed. "Is that what you believe?"

Danny's guts tightened. "I'm not sure, but if we don't help them, they're going to die."

"They can swim out when it rains and floods," Kenny said.

"When's that going to happen?"

"Could be next spring. Could be tomorrow. Who knows?" Kenny said.

"I saw some old buckets by the front. We could use those." Danny stood. "We can bring them to the river. Let them go."

Danny made his way toward the front where he found the three plastic buckets. When he carried them back, he put one on a small ledge between the slats. "Bad news," he said. "These aren't the only fish trapped in here."

Kenny looked up at him. "How many?"

"A lot," Danny said. "If we're going to free all of them."

Danny crouched and placed a bucket into the pool. The fish swam away, scared. He submerged it. "They aren't going to go inside," he said. "They're smart. They don't want to get trapped."

"They don't get it that they'll only be trapped for a little while until they're free again." Kenny said. "Wish there was a way we could tell them."

One of the small fish went inside the bucket. "Whoa," Kenny said. Danny tipped the bucket lip upward, but before he could, the fish swam out. "Damn it."

"We'll have to be faster."

"This is going to take awhile," Danny said.

"I have an idea." Kenny took another bucket and submerged its bottom. "We can give them a little nudge."

He dragged the bucket around the small pool. The fish swam away from it. Three went right into Danny's bucket. He jerked the handle and lifted the bucket halfway out of the pool. "They're still inside." Agitated and frightened, the fish swam in circles inside the bucket. "We only have one more left."

Kenny's bucket was up and out of the water. "Got him. Or her."

"How'd you do that?"

"Quick reflexes, man," he said. "It was scared and easy to trick. So, let's get them to the river and see what they do."

"The hard part is going to be getting out of here carrying these without falling in," Danny said. "It wasn't easy with just me."

"The weight of the bucket should help you," Kenny said. "Counterbalance and all."

"All right." Danny walked the beam, pole in one hand, bucket of swimming fish in the other. "You're right. It's easier. Weird."

Once they both made it to the front hall of the mission, Danny put his pole against the wall.

They made their way through the short patch of ground between the mission and the edge of the San Quinlan. Kenny lifted his bucket and jerked it hard so the water and the fish flew. "Go on. Be free." He laughed. The huge splash went toward the river.

Danny couldn't spot the fish. He went to the bed and poured his bucket out, careful to choose a spot where there weren't that many rocks. "Go find your kid," he said. They swam away fast and sure and disappeared downstream in a blink. He waved at them.

"Let's hide these buckets and get home," Kenny said. "You're shit as a fisherman and I'm hungry. We can come back tomorrow for the others. They'll survive."

"THIS HAS been hard on her," Uncle Luke said. "Having you here. Having a kid here. It's opened up a lot of wounds."

Danny sat on the edge of his bed, his uncle Luke in a chair a few feet away. In the background, he heard Aunt Franny sobbing, even though it was obvious she was trying to keep it down. *Why didn't you just wake up?*

Danny wanted to ask what happened to Chloe. He'd been so young when she'd died, his parents had only mumbled something about it. He wanted more than anything for them to come back from their missionary work and take him away from San Quinlan.

He looked toward his Uncle Luke's drooping expression. His uncle's eyes wouldn't meet his and his voice had gone uncharacteristically soft.

"I'm sorry," Danny said. "I sure didn't mean to bother anyone."

"You didn't," his uncle said, placing a hand on his shoulder. "None of this's your fault. I'll bring you up dinner."

"I'm not hungry," Danny said.

"I'll leave it on your desk. Aunt Franny worked hard on it.

Sometimes the strangest things will bring back a memory and make a hard moment real again. But if you talk to God, it can be healing. It can redeem you. Do you feel redeemed from your situation? From hurting that boy?"

Danny hadn't thought about it He pretended to. "Being here has helped me heal. Like today? There were some fish trapped in a pool, after the river had gone down?" He didn't mention the mission. That'd be reason for grounding. He was told not to go inside. "So, I got some buckets and collected the fish and brought them to the river and set them free."

His uncle nodded. "This isn't the first time God has put fish in the path of a man who needed a showing of faith."

"Right," Danny said, hoping his uncle would leave him be.

"I'm very glad your time here has given you that focus on your faith."

Then he left, briefly, before returning. Danny put his book of holy scripture in bed next to him and opened it. When his uncle returned, he'd see it, and hopefully believe Danny had fallen asleep bathed in the Good Word. He'd always find a quick phrase in there and then bullshit about it when asked.

He hadn't intended to really fall asleep, but he did. He vaguely heard his uncle come in, heard the gentle scrape of the tray as it slid across the desk.

Sleep blanketed him. He found himself back down at the banks of the San Quinlan, the white bucket with the fish in his hand once more. The fish made vocalizations. He thought they sounded like an orchestra tuning up, just smaller and rougher.

I must set them free.

Then he tilted the bucket, only he tilted with it. An unseen force pulled at him and as much as he tried to pull away, his body remained powerless in the way it does in dreams. He was a passenger and something else steered.

Up to his neck in the rapids, Danny clutched the handle of the bucket underwater. It caught the current and pulled him along.

I should let go.

No.

If I do I will drown.

It didn't make sense, but his dream-self knew that the rules as he knew them didn't apply.

The water carried him.

Where are the fish? Did they make it?

His feet couldn't touch the ground.

What if there's a big boulder underwater? I could get smashed.

Danny tried to look ahead, but the rushing breaks of the water were too high and fierce to see clearly through the water for obstacles. He noticed, too, a familiar turn. He was coming up toward his Aunt and Uncle's place. *How did I get here so fast?*

From the river, he spotted his room and a figure moving inside, silhouetted against the billowing curtain. He didn't recognize the movements or the gestures; he didn't think it was his aunt or his uncle. Maybe someone younger.

He heard weeping. A crying baby.

The current pulled Danny. He tried to fight it. He let go of the bucket; the water was too strong.

Paddling his feet and hands made no difference.

Before he went under, he saw the outdoor shower and then the small door that led toward the basement. *We don't use it. Flooded one too many times. Nothing but mud and bugs down there.*

He saw a dark blue field everywhere he turned underwater. The San Quinlan went deeper than he imagined.

His lungs hurt.

Can't breathe.

Oh, God.

Can't…

Catch…

He thought of the fish in the pools at the mission. Were they thinking the same thing? Would they slowly die of starvation? Would the still waters kill them, slowly asphyxiating them?

Have to…

Get…

Up.

Debris from the riverbed floated around him.

That's why the water isn't clear.

The bits of soil, leaves, and twigs spiraled in all directions.

Danny flapped his limbs.

His lungs felt like they'd implode. He fought the urge to open his mouth—letting in the water would be suicide. He hit something. He reached out and touched a smooth, hard surface.

A rock? Use it to climb out.

Useless.

Then his foot was stuck. Tangled around a root? Stuck in the riverbed mud?

The debris gathered around him. A million little specks of dark.

Like bees to honey.

Then the world slipped away.

HE WOKE to the smell of smoke. Morning. His aunt cooking. He eyed his dinner, untouched, at his desk.

He stretched, got up.

There was another sound. Rain. *We weren't expecting this.*

"Uncle Luke?" he called once he made it to the hallway. The house was silent. He did not hear their voices like usual. "Aunt Franny?" Making his way around the staircase, he thought, *that doesn't smell like cooking. It smells like burning.*

Downstairs, he called for his aunt and uncle again, and they still didn't reply.

When he made it around the bend he saw the kitchen engulfed.

Danny screamed for his aunt and uncle. Their room was just across from the living room. He tried to think if they had a fire extinguisher, but never recalled seeing one. *How can I put it out?*

He raced to their bedroom. The handle was locked.

Get out of here.

Not before I make sure they're not…

A small shove and their door gave. His aunt and uncle were sleeping. The illusion fractured. He spotted rugged halos of blood and dark matter on the wall behind their heads. His Aunt Franny clutched the black matte handgun.

"What the hell?" he said.

Danny turned and rushed out. *Do I have everything I need?*

No.

Then…

Yes.

I'm in one piece. Get out now. Run.

Getting outside was a blur.

He ran several yards away before he turned. He was shocked to see the flames had covered nearly the entire left, kitchen side of the house. The fire had been much worse than it'd seemed.

"No," he said.

He made to run, and did. Gallows Road wasn't far, but the nearest house was a mile away.

Before he could get to the main road, there were people in the driveway he didn't recognize. They had umbrellas. He'd forgotten it was raining.

Beyond, he saw the San Quinlan River, ready to breach.

There wasn't supposed to be a storm.

"You all right, young man?" A middle-aged woman asked, her bright blue eyes scanning him.

"I'm fine," he said. "My aunt and uncle, though. They're gone."

"Gone?" she asked. The man next to her watched Danny's face.

"They shot themselves. And the house is on fire," he said.

She stood next to him and put the umbrella over his head. The man and she exchanged a curious look. "The police and fire truck are coming," she said. "Don't worry."

On cue, the small San Quinlan fire truck pulled into the driveway. *They aren't using the sirens?* He wasn't sure why. *Maybe there's no one in the way to warn.*

The truck drove close to the house and the firemen rushed out. One on each side pulled out large feet, like kickstands, anchoring the truck. Two more pulled the main hose from its spindle, rushing toward the flames. The nozzle opened and water flowed.

Why isn't the rain putting out the fire?

But he knew. Somewhere deep inside, he pictured his aunt and uncle pouring gas all over the kitchen. They'd wanted the house to burn.

They almost took me with them.

The left part of the house fell. How could it have gone so quickly?

A large bit of the wall slid down the muddy embankment, edging close to the river. More debris slid behind, pushing the pieces in front inside the water.

The floor was gone where the side of the house had stood. Danny looked inside the basement, reminding him of a dark cavity or well. Water glimmered inside. It'd flooded, just as his uncle had always said.

The door that led from the basement toward the outside had

opened. A grayish mass floated to the top.

"Is that a person?" asked someone behind him.

The shape drifted away from the house, the water from the basement rushing behind it, making a small stream toward the river. It carried the gray figure down until it crossed from land into water. Inside the current the figure's arms fanned out like two waterlogged wings. The shape collided with something unseen, before breaking into several pieces, then each disintegrating into countless bunches of ashen sand. The clusters spread and her silhouette dissolved away, washed down the San Quinlan.

Chloe.
She was trapped down there.
All this time.

And then she was freed by fire, carried away by rain, her secret released.

Why didn't she wake up? He heard Aunt Franny's haunting cries. *She must've fallen asleep down there before it flooded. They kept her down there. Underwater. This whole time. That's why there was a picture on top of the coffin. She wasn't inside. She was under the house.*

Danny wiped rain from his cheek, turned, and made the first steps back toward the life from which he'd come. He thought of the fish trapped in the pools at the mission and pictured them freed, too, from the rising water, their fins carrying them like wings through the water.

He heard her voice.

Come catch me, little Danny boy!

Come catch me.

BRIAN EVENSON

COME UP

ONE

IN LATE June, Martin's wife dove off the dock behind their house and into the lake and never came up again. At the time, Martin was sitting on the patio, lazily reading. She walked past him, smiled shyly, and padded barefoot down the dock. Having already returned to his book, he did not see her dive off, only heard the splash.

How much time passed before he realized something was wrong? A minute, maybe two. He was reading, still reading, but his mind kept catching on something and soon couldn't thread the words into sentences. What was wrong? It was, somehow, too quiet. Marking his place with a finger, he looked up, saw the empty dock, the placid, smooth waters of the lake beyond.

"Kat?" he murmured.

There was no answer. He half-rose from his chair and craned around to stare at the glass doors leading back into the house. No sign of movement within. He walked out onto the dock, the wood hot under his feet. There was nothing to see there either. Just the surface of the water stretching away from him and toward the pines on the other side.

"Kat?" he called again, louder this time. Dropping his book, he started looking for her in earnest.

AT FIRST, he hoped she simply had left him. The thought, anyway, crossed his mind—she had, as he would tell the police a few hours later, left him before. He was, he admitted to the police, a philanderer—they would discover this on their own once they started talking to his wife's friends, he reasoned, so better to admit it from the outset—and she periodically got fed up.

"But we were getting along well," he told the two officers. "I wasn't cheating. It makes no sense that she would have left now."

Besides, every time she left it had been after screaming at him. This time there had been no screaming. Usually, she wanted to demonstrate forcefully that she was leaving, and tell him why. She would scream and throw things and pack her bags and only then go. But last he had seen her she was wearing a bathing suit and sauntering to the end of the dock with no indication that everything wasn't all right.

The police shined their flashlights at the dock. They shined them into the water, the beams of light quickly lost in the murk. They came into the house and looked through his wife's things, asked him if anything seemed to be missing.

"No, nothing," he said.

"Let me ask you," said one of the officers, a paunchy man with a shaved head. "What sort of life insurance did you have on her?"

"Excuse me?" he said.

"It's just, in cases like these, nothing missing, wife vanished, husband a philanderer, she's usually dead and it's usually the husband."

THERE HAD been times when Martin wanted to strangle his wife, sure, but he thought better of telling the officers that. It was like that in every marriage, wasn't it? There was always a time when you wanted to kill your spouse—certainly there had been more than a few times when *she* wanted to kill *him*. But he didn't want the officers to misunderstand.

Instead, he said, "The normal amount of life insurance. I didn't kill her."

"What's the normal amount?" the officer said.

"I didn't kill her," he said again.

"Nobody's saying you did," said the second officer, the one with hair.

"I loved my wife," he said.

"There, there," soothed the second officer.

Eventually they sent for a diver, who found nothing. The water was too cloudy, he explained. He couldn't see more than a few feet, and the lake was exceptionally deep.

"If she's actually down there," he said to Martin and the officers, "she may never come up again." His scuba mask pushed up on top of his head looked to Martin like a nascent second face, staring upward. "Or, who knows, maybe she will. But I'm not going to find her. We'll have to wait for the body to come up on her own."

By we *he means me,* thought Martin.

The officers hung around after the divers left, but in the end weren't sure what, if anything, to do with—or to—Martin. They would file a report, they finally decided. Had there been a crime? If things had happened just as Martin had claimed, then, no, there hadn't been.

"But what happened to her?" asked Martin.

"What do you think happened to her?" said the bald officer.

"If we get any leads, we'll let you know," said the second officer.

He was to call them if he remembered anything that might be relevant, no matter how small. Anything at all. If his wife turned up, dead or alive, he was to call them, too. Probably that went without saying, the second officer said, but he still was saying it.

"And above all, stay in the area," the bald one said. "Don't go anywhere."

TWO

HE MIGHT have sought a little physical consolation with one of the women he had cheated on his wife with, Mindy or Megan or Sue or Ally and so on and so on, but he had seen enough true crime shows to know this was a bad idea. He hadn't killed his wife, he knew he hadn't, which is why he must do absolutely nothing more to give the police of this backwater town the impression he had. He had to be careful, more careful than he had been when his wife was alive. People were watching him now, and they'd already decided he was a murderer. They would try to make anything he did prove it.

Which was why, later that evening when he discovered that the bottle of sleeping pills prescribed to him was inexplicably empty, he wasn't sure it would be wise to call the police. He tried to remember his wife's expression as she ambled out onto the dock. Had her eyes drooped, had her gait been more erratic than usual, had she been herself? He wasn't sure. At most, he was sure she had seemed relaxed. But was she *too* relaxed? He couldn't say. He hadn't been paying enough attention at the time. He hadn't known it was the last time he would see her.

If he gave the police the empty bottle of pills with his name on it, would they think, *Poor man, his wife committed suicide*? Or would they think, *The fucking husband drugged her and then drowned her*?

Probably, he was sure, the latter. In the end he kept the information to himself. He scraped the label off the bottle and disposed of the latter in a trash can on the edge of the municipal park. *I am doing exactly what I would do if I were guilty,* he thought as he was doing it, and yet he did it anyway.

THEY HAD moved to this house because of his wife. She had grown up near it, in the area that, according to the police, he was now not allowed to leave. The move had been one of the conditions of her forgiving him for a series of dalliances: they would leave the city and move to what was basically a village on the edge of a muddy lake, to a place where she was known, a place where, if he cheated, everyone would inform on him.

Even here, he had cheated, though he had been careful not to cheat with friends of hers. She had found out, they had fought, they had separated briefly, they had come back together. That was, he had come to believe over time, how their marriage worked. She (so he often told himself to keep himself from feeling guilty, even though he wasn't sure he believed it) liked the drama of it. These other women meant nothing to him, she knew that. Besides, it had to count for something that he had paid her the consideration of not sleeping with her close friends. Mostly. The one time he hadn't, she knew nothing about. At least, he believed she didn't.

HE WAS alone in the house. Her friends, even the one he had

slept with, avoided him. Obviously they thought he had killed her, and they told others or maybe the police did, so, soon, when he went into town to buy groceries everyone stared at him. He wasn't imagining it, at least he didn't think so. He kept to himself. It was safer. They hadn't been here long enough for him to have his own friends. At best, everybody else treated him like a stranger; at worst, like a murderer.

Why are you acting like a murderer? he asked himself. *Ignore them. You have nothing to feel guilty about.*

But of course he did. He was lying to himself. He wasn't a murderer, of course, that was true, but he had a great deal to feel guilty about: the way he had treated her, how he had cheated on her. And there was, now that he had discovered the empty bottle of sleeping pills, the nagging suspicion that perhaps she had killed herself, and killed herself because of him.

WITHOUT HIS sleeping pills, he was having trouble sleeping. He would lie in the dark, staring at the ceiling, his mind racing. He needed the pills—he'd been taking soporifics of some sort or another ever since he was a teenager, his prescription shifting each time he built up a resistance to whatever drug he was on. He needed to go to the doctor and ask for a new prescription, but the bottle had been full, he wasn't due for a refill for weeks. What if the police spoke to his doctor and he mentioned how he, Martin, had seemed to go through his sleeping pills suddenly very quickly, maybe even too quickly? Wouldn't they see this as evidence that he had drugged and drowned his wife?

No, now that he'd gotten rid of the empty pill bottle without telling the police about it, he had no choice but to pretend he still had his sleeping pills until the pills would have been gone. He would have to tough it out.

HE PACED the house, back and forth, back and forth. Twenty times a day he would walk out onto the dock and stand there looking down at the water, searching for changes in color, irregularities, clues of any kind. But it was just water, inscrutable, illegible. Back in the house he tried to read but was too tired to read, the words slipping out of his mind nearly as rapidly as they went in.

THE HOUSE was isolated enough that most days he didn't see

anyone. Of course, if he wanted to see someone he could. He could walk or drive into the town center and see other humans walking around, laughing and chatting and going about their business until they saw him and fell silent. That being the case, why would he want to see anyone? They didn't want to see him, so why would he want to see them?

Besides, still unable to sleep, he was so tired that half the time he wasn't sure what he was saying. His mouth was moving and words were coming out, but what did they add up to? What if he said something people took the wrong way? As revealing something even though there was nothing to be revealed? No, better to talk to nobody.

He wasn't healthy, he knew. Something was wrong with him. Maybe more than just one thing.

He filled his car with groceries, everything he would need for the next few weeks. He would keep to himself until then, not leave the house, and then it would be all right to refill his prescription of sleeping pills. After that, he told himself, things would go back to normal.

What was normal?

DID HE miss his wife? Of course he missed her. But it was hard to grieve when he didn't know what had happened to her, wasn't even sure if she was dead. He didn't know if he should be angry at her for leaving or distraught over her suicide or despairing because she had suffered a freak accident—struck her head after diving off the dock, say, or becoming entangled in something (what?) below the water's surface.

There was just a hole, a void, where his wife had been. You couldn't feel anything about a void. All you could do was try desperately to keep it from swallowing you.

HE WALKED from the house to the dock and back again. He listened to the water lap against the shore. He waded in, sometimes in his clothes, sometimes not, and felt the water move against his legs, somehow thicker than he remembered. Was some water thicker than other water? As soon as they were beneath the water, he couldn't see his legs at all. It was as if they were gone, swallowed. Anything could be under the water, just inches from you, and you wouldn't even know it was there.

Come up, he told her in his mind, *come up*, but nothing changed.

THE POLICE came back, knocking on his door until he opened it to them. They looked quizzically at him, taking in his unshaven beard, his filthy hair.

"Can we come in?" they asked.

"Have there been any developments in the case?" he asked.

The one with hair shook his head. Doing so shook his hair too. "Not per se. We have a few questions for you. Nothing serious. Can we come in?"

"Can't you ask them here?" he said.

The two officers exchanged a glance. What did it mean, that glance?

"Is there anything you've remembered that might be of help?" the one with hair asked.

Clearly, thought Martin, *they don't really have any new questions. They just want to come in. Why do they want to come in so much?* he wondered.

"No," he said.

"Nothing at all?"

"No," he said again.

"Is there anything you'd like to get off your chest?" asked the bald one.

They were trying to catch him off guard, Martin realized. Catch him tired, in a moment of weakness. But his whole life was a moment of weakness now. He couldn't talk to them, not while he couldn't sleep.

"No," he said, "no." And closed the door.

COME UP, he told her in his mind, *come up*. And then said it aloud just to make sure she heard.

He lay in bed staring into the dark, seeing nothing. He must have slept just a little, even without the pills. Or maybe he was half-awake and half-asleep, asleep enough anyway to dream or imagine he dreamed. He heard the sound of the door to the patio sliding open and sliding closed again, followed by the damp slap of her feet crossing the tile floor. He heard her stop just outside the bedroom door and then, even though the door never opened, he sensed her on the other side of it, on his side, gliding slowly across the carpet and toward him. On the carpet, her feet didn't make a sound. There she was, in the darkness reduced to a dim looming shape, just above him. And then she pulled back the covers and slid into the bed, beside him.

He held very still. He could hear the sound of her breathing but couldn't sense her chest rising despite her lying right next to him. Perhaps she was breathing very shallowly.

What happened to you, he said, or thought he said.

What do you mean? she asked.

One minute you were there and the next you weren't. Where did you go?

I'm right here, she said. *What makes you think I ever went anywhere at all?*

He did not know how to respond to this and so he said nothing. And then she reached across the bed and laid her arm over him. He felt the blanket growing damp against his chest, rapidly soaking through. He sensed her face close to his, and then her lips touched his and his mouth began to fill with water.

Wake up, he told himself, *wake up.*

THREE

HE AWOKE in the shower, fully clothed, water pouring over his head. He was choking, uncertain how he had gotten there. Why was he fully clothed? Hadn't he just been in bed? He stripped off his sodden clothes and left them heaped on the floor. He dried off, then turned off the bathroom light so as not to wake up his wife, and opened the door to the bedroom.

The bedroom was very dark. His eyes seemed to be having difficulty adjusting. He fumbled his way across the darkened bedroom, shuffling cautiously forward until he touched the dresser. He felt its top drawer into existence and opened it, but what was inside felt wrong: smooth, slick. His wife's underthings, he suddenly realized: he was standing before the wrong dresser. The room he was imagining in his head slid to one side. He sidestepped once, then again, then a third time, until he was sure the dresser he felt in front of him was his own. *But I was sure the first time too*, he thought, *and I was wrong.*

He opened the top drawer and reached in, felt the familiar fabric. He slipped on a pair of briefs. By now, his eyes had adjusted just enough that he could barely make out the shape of the bed. He moved toward it until his shins were touching the mattress.

He pulled the covers back and slipped in beneath them. His wife rustled beside him, gave a soft moan.

What is it? she asked.

"Nothing," he said. "Go back to sleep."

Where were you? she asked.

"I'm right here," he said. "I never went anywhere at all."

She gave a little moan but said nothing further. Soon he could hear the sound of her breathing, slow, regular. For once, even without the pills, he felt sleepy too.

Only as he was drifting off did he remember that his wife had vanished, was probably dead, probably drowned.

JUST AS he soon will be as well. Not the next night, nor the next, nights when he again awakens in the shower, sputtering, fully clothed, no idea how he has gotten there, but the third night, yes, that will be his last. The night when his dead wife, increasingly persuasive, says to him, *Honey, showers are nice, but to relax, really relax, there's nothing like a long, long bath.*

A bath, he answers, dully.

Sure, she says, then gives a little shrug. *Or a swim*, she says. She turns and leans toward him, and despite the darkness he can see her clearly, the fine bones in her face, her full white teeth, her hair impossibly undulating back and forth in the air. She leans closer and touches him, just with the tips of her fingers, then pulls away. He doesn't feel them, the fingers, but where they have been his skin is damp.

I know what's good for you, darling, she says. *Trust me.*

He isn't sure how long it has been since he has had anything to eat. Hours at least, maybe days. He isn't sure how long it has been since he felt rested. His thoughts flit everywhere at once. He has difficulty holding any single thing in his head.

And then finally something does hold:

Yes, a bath sounds nice.

Or maybe even a swim.

MICHAEL H. HANSON

BORN OF DARK WATERS

And how can man die better than facing fearful odds,
for the ashes of his fathers, and the temples of his Gods?
—Thomas B. Macaulay

IT WAS 2320 B.C., and La'ibum of Mesopotamia was a warrior in search of great victory. In truth he was an heir to a dynasty, but at the age of seventeen had decided to escape his upcoming duties and responsibilities for one last summer adventure before taking on the crown. On a warm June night, disguised in ragged clothes, and accompanied by a mere four dozen manservants, his train of asses and camels slunk out of the Akkad city proper by moonlight.

He had but one month to reach the island of Thera and its annual blood games, rumored this year to be the largest and greatest gathering of champions in the history of the world. La'ibum needed to prove his worth and manhood, that he was more, much more than a well-oiled and perfumed offspring of luxury and power.

Now if he could only make it to the nearest port before his mother awoke.

FOUR WEEKS later, La'ibum's rented sailing barge and its well-paid six-ship Phoenician pirate escort arrived at the main harbor of Thera. Standing on the bow of his vessel with his unusual stowaway-turned-companion Goodswap the trader, La'ibum smiled. The island kingdom was an impressive sight. The secondary homeland of all Minoans was singularly distinguishable by its double-ringed, three-hundred-and-sixty-degree harbor that circled its very heart, not to mention the multiple hot springs that released beautiful plumes of steam high into the air.

The rough oblong of the island's perimeter was twenty-five miles wide by three hundred miles long. The two-hundred-yard wide opening to the circular, inner harbors was guarded by two huge structures, twin fifty-foot-tall statues of ferocious bulls, cast in bronze and plated in polished elephant ivory. Large ruby gems marked their eyes and steam regularly issued from their nostrils.

"Everything you expected?" Goodswap asked, his ungainly Petasos hat warping in the wind.

"More so," La'ibum laughed, "even after your weeks of lessons and instructions my friend."

"I only taught your personal guard the basics needed to survive thievery, kidnapping, poisoning, and other close physical assaults when escorting you through the odd city street, or more importantly, the arena and its sports fields in the heart of the city proper." Goodswap said.

"It is really that bad?" La'ibum asked.

"And most of the thousands of these perpetrators are street urchins," Goodswap said, "dressed in rags, dirty and pathetic at first glance, most not more than ten years of age. My advice is to keep your sixteen guards about you at all times, and that the rest of your manservants be forbidden from traveling about on their own."

"Your advice is much appreciated, Goodswap, not to mention your wonderful regional history lessons."

"You paid for it," Goodswap replied, "I give nothing away for free."

"What?" La'ibum replied. "That ancient trinket? A bronze medallion with spells mostly worn off. I think I got the better part of the bargain."

"Nonetheless, a fair trade," Goodswap said, "and having reached our destination, I must leave your side now, lad, to be about my business. I dare say you may glimpse me off and on during the next week. Pray forgive me if I do not take heed. As a trader I have many, oh so many bargains and contracts to fulfill in such a short amount of time. Fare thee well."

La'ibum spun around but too late. As he had many times these past few weeks, the lanky, well-shaved, towering form of Goodswap, swarthy skinned with long black hair and dark penetrating eyes, had simply disappeared. Much as his servants tried, they could never find the odd, dark-purple-robed man's hiding place upon the ship. Goodswap came and went as he pleased over the endless sea journey. At first this annoyed La'ibum, but after several days he grew to like the mystery of the wise man. Perhaps he was part wizard. La'ibum leaned his head back and laughed to the bright sun. This adventure was proving to be everything he had hoped it would.

With sails down and oars put to water, it took a full hour to circulate the port waters and finally dock at an empty pier. Gold coin sufficed to secure their anchorage with the pier official for the full week, and La'ibum quickly acquired an adequate translator and tour guide to lead him and his personal guard to whatever holy official was in charge of registering for the games.

The streets of Thera were colorful, fast rivers of humanity. More so than in any of his previous travels, La'ibum was delighted by the multifaceted nature of multiple races (many he had never seen before) that traveled from all the distant reaches of the world to converge on this one island. Ivory skin giants with blue eyes and long flaxen or fiery red hair and beards, equally tall barbarians with coarse hair and skin as black as night sky, and everything in between. And all of them were decorated in an endless variety of chromatic feathers, animal hides, and variations of fabric, metal, and seashell armor.

The fierceness, bulging muscles, and openly displayed scars gave La'ibum more than a few pauses as he handed a small leather bag of silver coins to the appropriate Bull Temple monk who, in return, gave La'ibum three small ivory markers and a sheet of vellum listing the various open tournaments that could be entered shortly after sunrise each morning. The monk painted La'ibum's naked chest with two handfuls of blood from a recently slaughtered bull and spouted out a short prayer which La'ibum's translator later told him was an admonition to die well and bravely.

A more wary and sober La'ibum returned to his ship near

sundown, waving away the usual comforts of a female slave and wine for a long and troubled sleep.

DAY TWO of the blood games and La'ibum had learned much about life and death, and his own soul. On the first morning he had almost entered the taurokathapsia in one of the four sports fields that surrounded the steaming lake at the very center of the island. As he approached the entry gate a hand slapped on his right shoulder. It was Goodswap. Even La'ibum's guards were surprised at how the trader had slipped past them so easily.

"These local lads have been practicing for this event for years," Goodswap whispered. "Watch the first round and then decide if your own skills are better suited for another of the many events here this week."

La'ibum glanced back at the field for a moment, nodded his head, then turned to see that Goodswap had slipped back into the surrounding crowds unnoticed.

The middle of the field filled with a line of fifty lads between the ages of thirteen and seventeen. One of the competitors would sprint forward. Simultaneously, from the end of the field, a full-grown aurochs would be released from a pen and immediately charge its competitor. What followed happened in a matter of seconds. The giant bull's massive neckline was taller than an average man's height. Its large twin horns were each as long as a short sword. When man and aurochs met, one of two things happened: either the athletic, unarmed competitor managed to awkwardly leap up between the two deadly horns to temporarily land on the sable back and somersault completely over the wild beast to freedom and life; or the unlucky lad was immediately impaled and trampled to death by this angry land monster. The results were roughly fifty-fifty for the first group.

La'ibum slowly stepped back from the competitor's gate as his skin turned whiter than normal. Later that day he approached the archers' competition but quickly changed his mind, as it did not take much effort to remember his awkwardness with the bow over the past few years. Doing little to hide his frustration La'ibum strode back to his ship to bury his thoughts in sex and wine.

This second day of the great games he had thought to enter the spear-throwing competition, but a single viewing of the first round showed Nubian hunters releasing weapons that flew more than twice as far as La'ibum had ever cast. Not to mention much more accurately. Pursing his lips he traveled to the other fields to see what competitions might appeal to him.

At noon he entered an open round of free wrestling, where he managed to tie up and pin four separate opponents before being overwhelmed by a short but massively muscled, bald Egyptian. His conqueror was a good-hearted man who helped him back to his feet, bowed, and introduced himself as Ammon, captain of the royal guard for Pharoah Pepi I, to whose service he would return after the blood games ended. La'ibum bowed, slightly chagrined that the experienced warrior had so easily recognized his station, sure that his well-oiled locks, uncalloused hands, and fine tunic had given him away. Still, he had managed to hold the bulk of the stronger man off for a full five minutes before getting inexorably entangled and trapped.

Dusting himself off and ordering his guards to ignore the bruises his skin advertised, La'ibum left the field a happy man. Sure, he did not make it to the final rounds that would have given him an opportunity to win a gold bull medallion, or better yet, a holy brand upon his right shoulder, but he had overcome his fears and survived his first day of battle. More than a few wrestlers had left the field with crippling injuries this day.

ON THE third day of the games, the first half of the summer solstice, La'ibum found out that he had been earlier noticed by a respected noble Theran family, and after appropriate introductions had been made (including the gift of a foot-long, Akkadian-crafted solid silver bull from La'ibum to the household of Kallistoi), the future emperor of Akkad shared a magnificent lunch before the large arches of the island's main temple which looked down from a great height upon all of the fields in the island center. It was an unimpeded view that allowed La'ibum to watch the early rounds of individual gladiatorial combat in the nearest sports field.

Time and again La'ibum would see a warrior fall and he would unconsciously grasp his own hip-slung sword, a perfectly balanced weapon, finely honed and cast of iron, an oddity in this land of bronze weapons. La'ibum had spent many years drilling with this sword and secretly earning several bruises and now-hidden scars during secret late-night fencing lessons with his father's captain of the guards, Shulki. It was death for any of non-royal blood to even touch royalty at court in Sumeria, but La'ibum was clever enough to know that he would only excel at blade combat if he suffered the same conditions as real soldiers, and so he had made a deal with Shulki, and earned his sword craft through honest time and effort. And now, La'ibum's pride was daring him to join in the conflicts he saw, though at this distance individual figures looked as small as insects, even under this bright sunlight.

Several times during the course of the morning one or more of the Kallistoi servants would raise signal flags of various bright colors and swing them back and forth in the wind. After watching an hour of this La'ibum approached one servant and asked for an explanation.

"The different gatherings of heroes upon all of the fields look to us for directions, milord," Veros said. "The movement of competitors and warriors to different parts of each field, the signaling of the beginning and end to each event, the distribution of weapons, the commands to hospital carts and personnel to particularly bloody altercations, all of this is initially handled from this mount."

La'ibum then asked for a detailed description of every single flag command. This took nearly an hour as there were also numerous combinations of individual flag commands that allowed for complex interpretations in the movements and repositioning of large numbers of combatants upon the sports fields. Afterward, La'ibum spent five minutes reciting back the flag commands to Veros with nary an error. The surprised servant smiled and bowed to La'ibum.

"I must make a confession, young La'ibum," Master Kallinoros said when the Akkadian returned to the meal, "I hoped to dissuade and distract you from joining in the more mundane competitions today and tomorrow. No, no, let me finish. Your bravery and honor are not at question at this meal, especially after your fine day in the wrestling venue. Yes, I admit to being a fan. But you see, I feel that these group combats, now and tomorrow, are more free-for-all brawls for the lower classes and somewhat inappropriate for a nobleman of your fine breeding and title."

"Milord," La'ibum said with tact, "you are both wise and generous. But I must ins—"

La'ibum stopped talking as he had just seen Goodswap, standing at the periphery of the meal on the far side of an elaborate marble fountain carved into the shape of a lovely mermaid. Goodswap had made eye contact and shook his head quickly, twice.

"What must you, lad?" Kallinoros asked.

"Uh, I mean to say," La'ibum stuttered, "I must toast you and your family for your generosity of spirit."

La'ibum raised his bronze cup and spoke a long and holy Akkadian oath of thanksgiving.

"Tell me, La'ibum," Kallinoros said, "are you aware that there are also competitions of the mind here at Thera this week? Have you ever played table games back in Akkad?"

"Why of course." La'ibum smiled. "I thoroughly enjoy Senet, Mehen, a few Jiroft variations, Nard, and of course the royal game of Ur."

"Wonderful," Kallinoros laughed, "you must join me here tomorrow to teach me all you know of those games while we watch the crowd blood-brawls. They are the most renown and dangerous of the competitions this week and the view from up here is, of course, unmatched. And my daughter Oreanos will certainly be happy to play with us."

La'ibum glanced politely at Kallinoros's smiling daughter, a gorgeous lass of fifteen and shapely figure, olive-tinged skin, with green eyes and lovely, long ebony hair. It was obvious to La'ibum's court-trained mind that the island's rulers were considering a potentially profitable marriage to the future ruler of Akkad, a city-state with the power to ensure protected inroads to trade from the sea to inner Mesopotamia.

Still, La'ibum felt the need to uphold his honor and manhood with some statement, but once again, directly across from him, that damned trader seemed to appear from nowhere, inclining his narrow face (with all its odd, shadowy angles) and black leather Petasos hat directly at him. La'ibum felt a strange chill go down his spine. He swallowed twice and nodded to his host.

"Yes," La'ibum said, "it would be my honor."

THE NEXT morning, leaving his ship, La'ibum found Goodswap waiting for him at the end of the pier. The trader smiled as the young man approached, revealing a wide mouth filled with perfect white teeth with the single exception of a gap marking a missing left lateral incisor.

La'ibum bade his guards to give him and the trader space to converse.

"Your guidance yesterday was appreciated," La'ibum said, "but unnecessary, Goodswap. I am, after all, a man now."

"Of course, young lord," Goodswap agreed, "but even the wisest and eldest of kings accept advice from their counselors. Besides, I knew you would have come to the appropriate conclusions yourself. I was merely attempting to save you some unneeded effort. So, you are off to spend another day with the first family of Thera?"

"Yes," La'ibum said, "I am their guest. They wish me to teach them several board games. At least, that is what I have been told. I'm pretty sure the first family is looking to acquire a new son-in-law. And here I thought I was going to be able to leave such politics, trade, and intrigue behind me on this summer adventure."

"You are a future king, milord," Goodswap said. "Forgive me, but responsibility is one slave chain you will never shed. If I may be so bold, pray consider that the politics of ruling, caring for and feeding one's people, why, even war itself, all can be seen as merely larger and more complex versions of these board games you have always been fond of."

"Such an odd idea, Goodswap," La'ibum said. "Tell me, trader, has this trip been a profitable one for you?"

"Most profitable," Goodswap said, towering a full foot over the Akkadian. "I have made over five hundred transactions with both men and women of various standing."

"And yet you have nary a bag upon your person," La'ibum said, "nor porters or cart."

"Rest assured my goods are safe and secreted," Goodswap said, "and in fact, I would ask that you consider this one bauble I have left."

Goodswap reached under his robe and produced a strange device, a seven-inch-long tapered tube that appeared to be made of finely crafted and shaped bronze, and was capped on either end by clear, polished crystals.

"It is from the distant court of Emperor Yao," Goodswap said, "and has a most unusual function."

"And what is that?" La'ibum asked.

"Merely look through it," Goodswap said. "No, the other way, through the smaller clear gem. Yes, that's right."

"I don't see how…"

"Now look at something in the distance," Goodswap said, "the bull guardians at the harbor entrance."

"It's blurry."

"Now twist the tube near your eye in either direction," Goodswap said.

"I still don't…hey." La'ibum almost shouted, "I can see the ivory bulls. It is like I am a mere fifty feet from them. What magic is this, Goodswap?"

"Science, my lord," Goodswap smiled.

"Will a gold piece suffice?" La'ibum asked.

"No, milord," Goodswap said. "I am here to barter, and what I require are your last two ivory markers."

La'ibum almost gasped. He would need the ivory markers if he wished to enter any more contests during the rest of the week.

"I don't think I can…"

"I have a feeling," Goodswap said, "that after today, you will not feel particularly challenged by what these blood games might offer you."

La'ibum glanced up quickly at the strange words and made eye contact with Goodswap. The trader's eyes were dark and penetrating. For a moment La'ibum felt that he could drown in those bottomless wells of emptiness if he stared too long.

"I swear to you, La'ibum," Goodswap said, "you will need this viewing device for the most noble and brave challenge of your life, today."

"But…I am not competing," La'ibum stuttered, "that is, in anything but the roll of dice and movement of small figurines."

"My device for your markers, my lord," Goodswap repeated.

Reluctantly, La'ibum pulled the ivory tickets out of a leather satchel and handed them over to the tall trader, and then tied the bronze viewing tube to his tunic belt. A shout from one of his guards made him turn around.

"Yes, I know," La'ibum said, "we'll leave in a minute."

Turning back, La'ibum found himself standing alone. That damned trader had once again slipped away unseen into the surrounding masses.

MIDMORNING, LA'IBUM greeted the sun with a deep breath while standing upon the small courtyard of the first family of Thera, their estate carved into the lowest inner peak opposite the harbor entrance of the island nation. Below, the majority of competitors, roughly twenty thousand in number, paraded onto all four sports fields. This was the only time during the entire week, the second day of the summer solstice, when one might see all of the competitors (those that had survived to this point) together at one time in one place. In this, at least, La'ibum felt grateful for his current perch.

Breakfast had been a delightful affair as La'ibum spent over three hours explaining all the various rules and stratagem of his favorite board games, and could see that Kallinoros was impressed with the young lord's keen mind for detail and statistics. Afterward La'ibum took a small stroll to view the many lovely statues that sprinkled the exterior of this estate.

"The great lake at Thera's center seems more active than usual, Oreanos," La'ibum told his host's daughter who had attempted to silently approach him from behind. "The steam plumes are cycling faster than in recent days."

"Unfair, sir," Oreanos laughed. "You could not hear me. I stepped as light as a rock dove and I cast no shadow."

"Ahhhh but your endearing perfume was carried downwind, little sister," La'ibum smiled.

"Bah," Oreanos said, "everyone calls me that. I am a woman and a princess. Don't you find me comely, Prince La'ibum?"

"I require no such titles on Thera, fair Oreanos," La'ibum said. "Think of me as just one more warrior amidst the blood games."

"Hah, not likely, Prince," Oreanos said with a smirk. "I know all about you, sir. A royal letter and much gold arrived this morning from the Kingdom of Akkad. Your mother the queen wished to give her gratitude to any family that may have offered you comfort. My father is greatly honored by this recognition."

La'ibum ground his teeth in frustration. Was there no place upon the Earth he could escape the notice of his personal matriarch? Just as he was about to snap out a biting remark, a startling sound filled the air.

Oreanos screamed.

La'ibum spun around and saw a wondrous site. A gigantic plume of bright green steam erupted upward from the central lake, nearly half a mile, and quickly dissipated in the air, not falling back as short rain, as Thera's steam plumes most often did.

"This is unexpected?" La'ibum asked.

"Yes," Oreanos replied, "this has never happened, in either mine or my people's memory."

The household had now emptied onto the courtyard to see the happenings below.

"The games," Kallinoros shouted, "has there been a disruption?"

Suddenly inspired, La'ibum disconnected his bronze viewing tube from his belt and adjusted its focus. Thousands of warriors were wavering in hesitation and many more had slowly backed away from the central lake. Nobody appeared to have been hurt by the strange steam plume.

"All appears normal, my lord," La'ibum said, "perhaps this is just an aberration in your waters..."

Oreanos screamed again. "Look. Coming out of the lake."

La'ibum raised his looking glass to eye once again and saw a horrific site. Creatures out of myth and nightmare, first by the dozens, and then hundreds, began crawling onto the entire shore of the mighty lake. Some as large as a man, some larger than an aurochs, things with claws and scales, massive teeth, others with twenty-foot-long tentacles. Several man-sized creatures with bat-like wings took to the air. One swooped down above the courtyard, grabbing up a screaming slave in a swath of blood, and flew away with him.

The head of the palace guards rushed to Kallinoros's side.

"My lord, you must enter your house. We will do our best to barricade the entrance and protect you from this madness."

La'ibum, his mind working faster than it ever had, did his best to take in everything that was happening around him.

"No," La'ibum said loud, "what about the city below? Are your generals below? Are your police trained to suppress this dark magic?"

Kallinoros, looking to be in mid-panic, shook his head wildly. "No, of course not. This is all madness. The gods have turned on us and we must hide until their retribution is done. Everyone, into the temple, now."

"No," La'ibum yelled, "you can fight this, can't you see? You have well-trained, well-armed men below. They only lack direction."

The air was now filled with at least two hundred of the giant bat creatures who were swooping down and killing and stealing up dozens of onlookers not wise enough to hide behind shuttered doors and windows.

"Give me your trust, my lord," La'ibum practically screamed, "I need but your flag signalers and your palace archers."

Kallinoros grabbed his wife and daughter and ducked under the deadly swoop of one of the flying creatures.

"Very well," Kallinoros yelled, "I grant you my authority, Prince. Do what you must."

And La'ibum now found himself, thirty archers, and Veros and his six fellow flag signalers all alone upon the courtyard.

"Archers," La'ibum ordered, "you must protect the flag bearers from all flying threats. They are needed to save your countrymen below. Veros."

"Yes, my lord," Veros said.

"I will relay all my commands through you," La'ibum said. "Now. Prepare your flags."

La'ibum raised his viewing glass and desperately and quickly surveyed the four fields and the great central lake below. The neat, ordered rows of warriors were quickly shifting as an equal mix of them were breaking ranks in a slow retreat, or unleashing weapons to defend themselves against the forward momentum of what was now a sloppily marching army of monsters.

"Halt retreat," La'ibum shouted, "reform ranks. Ready weapons."

Three times Veros had this signaled by flag. It took two horrendously long minutes for the flag readers and signalers on the outer side of each field to note the instructions, but once they did, dozens of runners were sent to cowering monks and officials. By the third minute the masses of warriors began to obey their orders and redress their ranks.

Looking through his eyeglass La'ibum was suddenly struck with the odd notion that the large sports fields and central lake were but the surface of a table game laid out for his pleasure. Shaking the bizarre thought from his head he began barking out more commands.

"Veros, archers on all four fields face the waterfronts. Load bows and target within a yard of water's edge. We need to stop the accumulation of enemy forces."

A minute later Veros shouted, "Done, my lord."

"Fire," La'ibum shouted back.

Ten seconds later hundreds of arrows fell upon the vile creatures now trying to exit the lake. In the meantime, thousands of monstrosities had crossed the great circular beach and were encroaching upon all four of the sports fields.

"Veros," La'ibum shouted, "all forces, with the exception of spear throwers, withdraw fifty paces. Spear throwers target leading ranks of attackers."

A flurry of flag signals and twenty seconds later the warriors below hurried into positions.

"Good," La'ibum mumbled to himself, "reaction time is shorter. We might have a chance."

Thirty seconds later La'ibum shouted, "Cast spears."

Four thousand spears of various lengths and piercing capability flew through the air and impacted the front wave of vile monstrosities, killing many, crippling others.

"Again," La'ibum shouted.

The connection between waving flag and warrior response below was not long lost on the attacking monsters, as the giant bat-things began a concerted dive-bombing of the mountain shelf that was La'ibum's command center. The palace archers found themselves hard pressed to blunt this attack, but they managed to hold their ground moment to moment.

"Again," La'ibum shouted, watching the third and final volley of spears take their toll. Still, the monsters advanced.

"Veros, all axe bearers, mace bearers, and heavy swords prepare for assault," La'ibum commanded. "All archers to save their final volleys for the attacking front of the enemy."

La'ibum pulled his viewing glass from his eye and scanned all the perimeter of the isle that he could see. He had to make sure there would be no surprise counterattack on any flank. After committing his heavy weapons he would not have much in reserve for unexpected surprises.

"Archers fire at advancing enemy," La'ibum shouted. Hundreds more of the creatures fell.

La'ibum stood tall and unsheathed his own sword, holding it high.

"Charge," he yelled.

Thousands of hardened warriors from all across the world charged forward to engage thousands of nightmare beasts beneath a beautiful sunlit, cerulean sky. The spectacle was beyond breathtaking, beyond sublime, beyond any madness that La'ibum could ever imagine. Hundreds of men died in pain and gore splash as monstrous claw, fang, and tentacle met human flesh. Hundreds more beasts fell in pools of multicolored gore as axe, blade, and mace tore them asunder.

Oh you mighty, pure, brave men, La'ibum thought, *if we survive I will have the greatest songs ever written composed for your wondrous deeds today.*

A bat-thing swooped too near La'ibum, extending a nasty claw that glanced across the right side of his head. It was a nasty-looking but ultimately shallow wound that a slave quickly bound with a strip of his tunic. The pain was almost overwhelming, but La'ibum pushed aside all thought of it to focus on the battle below.

"Field four," La'ibum shouted, "shore up your right flank. Field one, buttress your center with long pikes. Field three, advance with all forces, your attackers are fewest in numbers."

And so for the next half of an hour La'ibum advanced, retreated, sacrificed, and regrouped the warriors below until he found that the remaining hundreds of monsters had been temporarily pushed back to the sloped beaches of the great central lake.

Another inspiration struck and La'ibum turned to Veros, "All barrels of oil, of any kind, are to be immediately transferred to the front line. Raid any storehouse, royal or otherwise, and get those barrels moved. We may have only minutes."

This required the most complex subtlety displayed yet by the flag signalers, and La'ibum prayed to the gods that the surviving monks and officials below would interpret and act upon these commands in time.

Five minutes later La'ibum could see with his viewing glass that carts and laborers from all over the island were rushing to the interior. In another five minutes barrels were carried toward the beach in droves.

Suddenly, the waters of the central lake began bubbling furiously, and short spouts of bright green steam shot into the air. La'ibum knew he had little to no time to engage his plan. Just then, a small hand grasped his left forearm. Oreanos had left the safety of the temple.

"I love you, La'ibum," Oreanos said, "I would die by your side."

La'ibum placed his left arm protectively over her shoulders, "Not if I can help it."

As the majority of the barrels arrived, La'ibum turned to Veros, "Empty all oil onto…"

Two bat creatures swooped down at La'ibum. Oreanos screamed. Royal arrows intersected both, but one lived and struck both La'ibum and Oreanos, knocking them to the ground. Half-crippled, the surviving bat-thing crawled over courtyard stone to finish off Oreanos. When it was within inches of her terrified form an avenging and snarling La'ibum leaped upon it, striking the vile creature's head from its shoulders with a mighty swing of his Akkadian sword.

La'ibum sheathed his weapon, scooped up the diminutive princess with his left hand, and pulled the viewing glass up to his eye with his right.

The central lake was bubbling furiously now and several bright green plumes of steam shot into the air, some as high as twenty-five feet.

"Veros," La'ibum yelled, "empty all oil downward onto the beach and into the lake itself. Now, before it is too late."

Within minutes the massive but narrow beachfront was covered in oil, and more was poured down and soon spread onto and eventually across the surface of the central lake. With his viewing glass La'ibum could see the last of the arrows, spears, throwing hatchets, slings, and boomerangs thrown and emptied in their final efforts to keep the remaining monster horde at bay.

"Light all torches and bear them to the beach," La'ibum yelled.

The response below was almost instantaneous and from above it appeared to La'ibum and Oreanos that a bright solid gold ring surrounded the lake.

"What does it mean, La'ibum," Oreanos said.

"Salvation or doom," La'ibum said. "Pray for the former, my bride."

Oreanos barely had time to gasp in surprise when La'ibum

turned to Veros.

"When the green plume rises as before," La'ibum shouted, "throw all torches onto the beach."

And moments later his prediction came true, as a nearly identical gigantic green plume rose high into the air as had happened earlier in the day whence all this madness first commenced.

Thousands of brave warriors charged forward and slung their flaming torches, most of which landed on the beach, though at least one hundred struck water. The result was instantaneous, as the bulk of the oil, on land as well as on the surface of the lake, ignited in a terrible maelstrom.

The burning waters themselves erupted with hundreds more monsters, but these met not helpless humans to devour, but a flaming hell that quickly set them afire to die in agony.

A few dozen of the largest of the flaming monsters managed to break from the fiery beach, but were quickly brought down by the surrounding mobs of warriors all too eager to show their mettle to these unwelcome guests.

One hour later and it was all done. Over ten thousand warriors from all over the world lay dead upon the fields of Thera, both noble and lowly born, master and slave, rich and poor, all joined in a free and equal brotherhood of death and blood…It was an image and thought that would never leave La'ibum's mind for the rest of his life.

As Kallinoros's household emptied back onto the courtyard when they realized it was safe to do so, Goodswap seemed to appear from nowhere to place a strong hand upon La'ibum's right shoulder.

"Well done, future king," Goodswap said, "though I have no medallion or brand to offer you, I'd say you have won the greatest of challenges in these blood games, eh?"

For a second La'ibum felt the urge to smack the smirk off the trader's face, but just as quickly his anger cooled as he realized the tall, weird man was not being facetious.

"You foresaw all of this," La'ibum said, "didn't you?"

"I interpreted many possibilities, my lord," Goodswap said, "but in the end, it was your free will, your intentions, your actions, and your bravery that decided the final outcome."

"And those things," La'ibum shuddered, "were they the

minions of all evil? Is the world now safe from all darkness. Have I won us that eternal freedom?"

"Think of this as but a warning vision of the distant future," Goodswap said, "of a faraway apocalypse that will greatly overshadow the minor cataclysm you just experienced. And pray thanks to all your gods that you and your many offspring will be but dust whence it eventually commences."

"And, trader—" La'ibum said as Oreanos dragged her father toward the two of them, shouting out in excitement, retelling the bravery of the Akkadian prince who had saved the island kingdom of Thera.

"Please," Goodswap cut in, "though that be my current title, I have always considered myself a salesman."

"Before you disappear as is your wont," La'ibum said, "what is this distant apocalypse that mankind will one day tremble beneath?"

Goodswap's mouth spread wide, almost shark-like in its dimension, once again revealing perfect white teeth except for a single, missing incisor.

"Prince La'ibum, it will be known simply as...the Sha'Daa."

EDWARD LEE

THE SEA-SLOP THING

When the going gets tough, June reflected with a wince, *the tough hijack a sausage from the deli counter.* Indeed, it had been a hectic day at the deli, taking orders, running the slicer, tabulating the scale, etc., yet never—even during peak store hours—did Zefowitz, her boss, ever see fit to give her help. *I can't do it all myself,* June often complained. *Nobody in this fuckin' shit-hole grocery store works but me!* which was true. But even the worst job in the world was better than no job.

When there was finally no line at the deli, June put up the BE BACK IN TEN MINUTES sign, secreted the aforementioned sausage under her apron, and scurried to the employee's restrooms. *Shit, I'm horny as fuck!* In a moment's time, the stall door was locked, her pants and panties were down, and the foot-long sausage was sliding quite vigorously in and out of her already-drenched womanhood. These moods hit her more often now that she'd hit forty—hormone changes, she'd read in *Cosmo,* the ultimate peak of the woman's sex drive—and being stuck in the deli twelve hours a day (and with no overtime since she was "on salary") left her little time or energy to pursue intercourse of a variety more normal than sticking sausages in herself, and even if she *had* the time and energy, there was not one single member of the male population of this redneck sinkhole of a town who

June would touch with a ten-foot pole. Ex-cons, drunks, lifelong potheads, guys with a dozen kids from a dozen different redneck tramps, guys who hadn't had jobs for most of their adult life, and guys with cars but who couldn't drive due to multiple DUIs. *No, thanks!* was June's resolve. *I'll stick to sausage!*

She'd previously been fantasizing of being taken hard and rough by some faceless man who was football-player-sized: six foot eight inches, three hundred and fifty pounds, all muscle, just hot and heavy right there on the deli floor. His rippled body would squash her mercilessly into the tiles as his hips hammered her loins with the endurance of a gas-powered sod pounder. June, close to smothering, would quiver through one bomb-burst orgasm after another while the faceless muscle-rack greedily pounded on, until at last the reward of his lust arrived. Given that this phantom lover was much larger than the average man in physical stature, he too was much larger than average in genital dimensions—ten inches, twelve or thereabouts, with the girth of a brawny wrist; and the volume and number of spurts of his ejaculation shared this "much-larger-than-average" trait. To be eloquent, the purse of June's womanly pleasures was flooded with one warm, adoring gust of seed after another. To be less than eloquent, the massive phantom cock and balls filled her squirming pussy up with so much spunk, he could've been pumping it into her with a fireplace bellows.

Hence, it was the recollection of this fantasy that June now summoned: standing spread-legged into the grocery store toilet stall, pants and panties at the ankles, apron jacked up, and banging a prodigious sausage fervidly in and out of her sex. The sausage was still shrink-wrapped, of course, and for those interested in minutiae, it was specifically a Dietz & Watson chorizo sweet sausage, twelve inches long. It would be appropriate to mention that June, at five feet one inch tall and ninety-five pounds, very much qualified as "petite," but her vaginal depth did not correspond to this qualification. She knew she could take more than twelve inches but she'd never met a man close to that size. Once she'd used a fourteen-inch zucchini, and even *that* had not reached "rock bottom." As for width, two inches barely cut it but would do in a pinch; two-and-a-half (about the girth of a beer bottle) was better. She'd tried three inches once (a Boar's Head Genoa Salami) but that had been a wee bit too much. But this Dietz & Watson? At precisely two and five-eighths, it seemed *made* for her. *Now I know the PERFECT width for me!* she celebrated.

And so horny was she that moment, and so stuffed was her head with the fantasy of being used as a fuck-dummy by a faceless giant, that on the tenth penetration of the chorizo, she came so hard she nearly fell over in the stall, and nearly shouted out loud.

Holy motherfucking SHIT! she thought, panting, and then she hissed through her teeth, standing on tiptoes, at the delicious post-orgasmic sensation of slowly withdrawing that big honker of a sausage.

It was just what she needed to take the edge off a tiring, thankless, and very tedious day. *Much better now!* She collected herself quickly, kept an ear out for the door when she washed off the sausage, then put it under her apron, and whisked back to the deli where, thankfully, no customers were waiting. She had just put the Dietz & Watson back in the front display case when she turned around—

—and froze.

Mr. Zefowitz was standing behind her, arms crossed over the bulbous belly that stretched his white dress shirt nearly to the point of popping its buttons.

"Uh, hi, Mr. Zefowitz," June said.

"You're fired," Mr. Zefowitz said.

June, not a passive personality, replied, "You can't fire me! Everyone else in this store is too STUPID to run this deli!"

"That's true, but I *can* fire you and I just have."

"What for!" June bellowed.

"For masturbating with store inventory," and then he walked to the case, removed the culprit sausage, and patted one end of it into his open hand. He smiled.

Embarrassment turned June's face beet red but it only took a moment for that embarrassment to transform to stark-raving rage. "You fat fuckin' pervert! You have a camera in the ladies room!"

"Not *a* camera, several," her boss remarked. "Security cameras, for your safety. Any old psycho could come in off the street, walk into there, and rape someone. Then we'd get sued, and we can't have that, can we?"

"Well you're sure as shit gonna get sued now! I'm takin' this shit to Channel 9!"

He put the sausage back (why not? It was shrink-wrapped) curled an index finger at her, and beckoned her into the back room. "Come in here to see why that will *never* happen."

Veins beat at June's temples. She was grinding her teeth she was so mad. She followed him into the back room, then he closed the door, and when he turned back around...

...his penis was out of his pants.

"Why is your dick out of your pants?" she asked, seething.

"Well, it *has* to be for you to suck it," he said. He pulled on in a bit, then scooped out his testicles. "And you *will* suck it and you'll swallow *everything* that comes out of it, otherwise that security tape will be on the internet five minutes from now."

June stared. She was shaking, she was vibrating. Then—

Then—

She sighed long and despondently, got on her knees, and began to suck.

FUCK! SHIT! Piss! This was the character of June's reflections once she got home. *No fuckin' job! How can I pay the rent!* Her useless, tits-on-a-bull, deadbeat of an ex-husband would be bringing the kids home from summer camp in a week, and with the pissant child support he paid, she couldn't even get a decent amount of groceries.

She plopped down in the ancient arm chair, and would've cried if she'd been so mad. Perhaps some TV would take her mind off things.

But no.

The TV was broken.

I am so screwed, and all because I just HAD to stick that sausage in my cooter...

At least it had been a good orgasm.

The taste of Mr. Zefowitz's sperm still buzzed in her mouth. *It's funny how sperm tastes worse when it comes out of the dick of someone you hate. Yeck!* She should've bitten it off, not that there was much to bite. Everything seemed to go wrong for June. *Just once,* she thought, *just ONCE, why can't something go right?*

Her cellphone rang, and before he answered it, she saw the text message saying that her pay-as-you-go card would expire in one day. *No job, and no money to renew my card. The hits just keep on coming.*

Then she answered the phone, expecting a bill collector. "Hello?"

"Hey, sweetheart!" a sly male voice answered. It was Fishy, probably her only friend in town. "How's the love of my life doing today?"

"I don't know, Fishy. What's his name?"

Fishy barked laughter. Everybody called him Fishy because, well, he worked the docks and smelled like fish. "That's my gal! Always good for a laugh. Say, you ready for some good news?"

"Fuckin'-A yes I'm ready for some good news," she said, ever the gentlewoman. "All I've had all day is *bad* news."

Fishy chuckled. "Yeah, I heard. You got canned from the deli 'cos Zefowitz caught ya stickin' a leg of lamb in your cookie."

Steam may very well have shot from June's ears. "It was a chorizo sausage, not a leg of fuckin' lamb! And-and, it's not true! And where did you hear that?"

"Aw hell, damn near everyone. Whole town's talkin' about it."

Fuck! Fuck-fuck-FUCK! June thought.

"Just don't you worry about none'a that, Junie," Fishy consoled. "I'se bet every dang gal in this town has stuck all *kinds*'a things in themselves."

Now she was truly close to tears. What could be worse than this? She'd have to move. Everyone would be calling her Sausage Girl. "Come on, Fishy. I thought you said you had *good* news."

"Oh, yeah, that's right. You know ole Captain Kupjack, don't ya?"

June made a face. "Yeah. That perverted old drunk's been trying to get in my pants since I was ten. I'm serious. *Ten.*"

Fishy chuckled. "Yeah, he's a rascal, all right. Anyway, he just pulled into the dock on his forty-two-footer."

"Shit," June muttered. "I was hoping you were gonna tell me his boat sunk with him in it, that fuckin' old crustcake diaper sniper."

"You're something, Junie, you really are. Anyhow, like I was sayin', he just pulled in, been gone two weeks. Devil Reef, I heard, and he must've brought back one hell of a catch 'cos he was spendin' money like water at the bar. Picked up everyone's tab."

"That scumbag skinflint never bought anyone anything. Ever," June observed.

"Well, he sure as hail did today, and he's *still* down there buyin' drinks. Oh, and he bought hisself a brand-new Cadillac ta boot."

This didn't sound right. "Unless he brought in twenty thousand pounds of rockfish, he couldn't make enough profit to pay off his crew and then buy a Caddie. And rockfish is out of season right now."

"Well, funny ya mention it, about his crew, I mean. When he left he had four fellas with him, but when he come back today, he had none. Said he dropped his crew off on Kent Island 'fore he pulled in. Ain't no one work for him from Kent Island that *I* know of."

June's shoulders drooped. This sounded like a run around. "Fishy, I don't give a fuck about Kupjack, his crew, Kent Island or *nothin'.* All I care about is good news, and if you don't have any, I gotta go."

"Hold up there, little girl! Don't let your titties get tied in a knot," Fishy said. "Lemme git to the best part. So when I was in the bar drinkin' on Kupjack, he slams like his tenth shot of Wild Turkey and he come to me and say, 'I need my boat painted, inside and out, and there ain't no painters in this town worth of pinch of dog shit, not one, 'cept June.'"

"Bullshit," June said. "Last time I saw that stewed old perv, he pinched my butt, so I told him if he was the last man on earth and I was hornier than a jackal in heat, I'd hang myself before I'd fuck him, and if he ever touched me again, I'd cut his dick off and use it for fish bait."

"Wow," Fishy laughed, "that's sure sendin' a message! But I'm serious. He knows you and I are friends, so he tells me to tell you he wants to hire you to paint his boat, and if you agree he'll give me a hundred dollars for a finder's fee."

June winced. "Are you shitting me?"

"Ain't nothin' but the truth, hon, and I sure could use that C-note."

"Well, you can forget it. I wouldn't work for that creepy two-bit little-girl's-bicycle-seat-sniffing old crock for *any* amount of money," and she took a sip of the cold, two-day-old coffee sitting next to her: the last coffee in the house.

"It's a two-month job, Junie, and he'll pay fifty bucks an hour, cash, daily."

June spat the fetid coffee in a wide spray across the room, where it dotted her velvet Elvis portrait. "Tell him I'll take the job!" she gagged. Drunken fat old pervert or not, that much money would solve all of June's problems for the next year!

"Be crazy not to," Fishy said. "Just you meet Captain Kupjack tomorrow mornin' at the dockyard."

"You can bet your ass, Fishy! Thanks!"

When she hung up, she squealed in proverbial glee. *Fifty bucks an hour! Finally, something GOOD happened to me!*

Good, indeed. And perhaps *too* good to be true...

BRIGHT AND early next morning, June walked briskly through the dockyard, whistling, for some reason, the theme for Sponge Bob. She'd been a boat painter for several years but quit after that time someone had dropped a Mickey into her iced tea. She didn't know what had happened to her in the four hours she was unconscious, but her anus hurt for days. *Was probably Kupjack, the dirty prick,* she thought. Even so, for fifty an hour? She'd just have to keep a close eye on anything she drank.

Wow, came the next thought. She was approaching Kupjack's slip when she spied a brand-new gold-colored Cadillac Seville. The gold paint job looked tacky but still, *That's probably sixty grand! Kupjack must've leased it, wants people to think he's a high roller.*

"Thar she is!" cracked a hoarse voice. Did June smell whiskey breath even at *this* distance? The disheveled, pear-shaped man leaned against the railing of his ancient piece-of-shit dock-shed-turned-office. Kupjack was as broken down as the shed, and as old. His distended liver made his stomach stick out like a woman nine months pregnant, and the big bushy Talibanish beard covered a huge pink face that was benchmarked by a warped nose akin to a rotten strawberry. Lastly, and most ridiculously, he wore a crooked, white captain's hat with a life preserver on it.

Then he rubbed his crotch through his canvas overalls.

Great, June thought. "Fishy said you had work for me."

"Aw, yeah," the old man crackled. "Just come back from Dunedin Reef with a hold full of crackjaw eel, done sold the lot to the Japs for top dollar."

"I heard it was *Devil's* Reef. And crackjaw eel? Isn't that *freshwater* eel?"

When Kupjack hitched in a pause, his man-tits jiggled. "Well, no, we *passed* Devil's Reef, I mean, and you're right, it were hagfish eel. I always confuse 'em see? Ugly buggers all look the same…I mean the *eel,* not the Japs. Then I drop my crew off St. Mary's Island, where I meet up with the Jap fish broker."

"I heard you dropped your crew off at *Kent* Island," June said.

This second challenge gave the fat drunk a jolt of annoyance. "Well, you done heard wrong, little lady, and that ain't neither here or there, and, yeah, I got work for ya. I need my boat painted inside and out, every square inch. Fifty bucks an hour, and it'll likely last all summer."

June couldn't help but ask, "What's the catch?"

"Catch?"

"Come on, Captain. You been trying to get in my pants for as long as I remember, and *nobody* pays fifty an hour to paint a boat. If that pay comes along with me being your nookie, then forget it."

Kupjack threw his old bearded fat face back and cackled like a witch. "Aw, girl, you're a riot, you are! 'Tis true, I was randy in my day, and gals followed my dick down the street like it was the Pied fuckin' Piper, and with *good reason.* But them days is gone. I'm old as Moses and fat as Buddha, and I'm so filled with liquor they won't even need ta embalm me when I die. Shee-it, if ya wanna know the truth, I can beat my dick like a red-headed stepson and I *still* can't get it hard enough to spit."

June sighed. "Actually, Captain, I *didn't* need to know the truth with that amount of detail."

"Believe you me, ain't nothin' I'd like more'n to bury my hardwood in a gal's tail and hump till she come so hard her eyeballs switch sockets, but, no, I'se afraid it'd be easier fer me to shoot pool with a piece'a over-cooked spaghetti. And the diabetes just make it worse." The old salty dog lifted one leg, pulled up a pant cuff, and displayed a discolored ankle close to six inches thick. "Damn shit make my ankles get all swole up big around as a Russer liverwurst, and that keeps the dick down too. Say, speakin' of liverwurst, is it true what I heard? That you got up'n fired from the deli for jack-hammerin' a liverwurst in and out'a your joy-trail?"

"No!" June exploded. "It's NOT!"

Kupjack shrugged lackadaisically. "Nothin' ta be 'shamed of, hon. Woman got every right to stick *anything she want* in her sauce-box, whether it be a liverwurst, a french bread, a bowling pin, one'a them big rolls'a cookie dough, a rotisserie chick—"

"I get the picture!" June yelled, her face turning evermore pink.

"Anyway, sweetie, the paint's on the deck'n the boat's unlocked, start right away if ya like. You need anything"—he jerked a thumb backward—"I'll be in the bar."

That's it? Just like that, I've got a fifty-buck-an-hour job?

It seemed so.

"Uh, thanks, Captain."

"Shore thing, sugar," he said, limping down the ramp. "Oh, I forgot. Do belowdecks first, 'cos I ain't picked up the exterior paint yet, plus I gotta get my hoist repaired," and then he hobbled toward the bar.

June walked down to the slip for the forty-two-foot *Gwendylyn Rose*, an old rattletrap but still chugging after decades. A pyramid of one-gallon paint cans sat stacked before the gang-ladder. All the supplies she'd need were right there as well, in a stationary storage locker. There was no time like the present so she pried the lid off a can, squatted down, and began to stir. Her first coherent thought to herself was a familiar one: *Shit, I'm horny as fuck!* June's sudden good fortune put her in a great mood, and when she was in a great mood...the juices got to flowing. *I must be a sex maniac,* she concluded, her sex already damp, *even though I never have sex with anything but vibrators, sausages, and vegetables.* The paint, epoxy-based, was hard to stir, yet the exertion didn't consciously occur to her. *I'm an orgasm addict, I guess,* and she supposed there were worse things to be. The position of her squat pressed the crotch of her cutoffs firm against her already throbbing pubis. *What I wouldn't give for a man right now, a great big fuckin' HUNK of a man with a dick the size of a baby's leg and balls like duck eggs.* Yes, something like that sliding into her and banging in and out like a bilge-pump piston would be just what the doctor ordered. So dense was this desire that she felt very tempted to take a break, go belowdecks, and give her "honey pot" a workover. She could get her fist in there no problem, and only a few twists would be required to set off a powder-keg orgasm. *But, no, with my luck someone would see...*And that would be even worse than her previous humiliation at the deli.

She got back to stirring, and—

Oh fuck. Not again.

That *Cosmo* article wasn't kidding about women in their forties. Her hormones must be overflowing, for the squat and the continued pressure of the crotch of her shorts pressing against her "secret garden" continued to titillate her. Again she mused of her phantom suitor, the faceless armature of over-muscular flesh, legs wide and hard as railroad ties, and dinner-plate-sized hands manipulating her like a sack of packing peanuts, flinging off her top, hauling off her shorts, and laying her out on her belly like a specimen. Her butt cheeks were parted, then—

Kurrrrrrr-HOCK!

—a golf-ball-sized wad of spit landed right on her anus. *No, not there!* she thought. *No, not there!*

Her mental plea was answered by the prompt insertion of that perfect, throbbing, heavily veined tennis-ball-can-sized cock. June's cheeks billowed; just the first thrust squashed the wind out of her. But once the mindless rhythm got going—

Yes, there! she thought. *Yes, there!*

Indeed, it felt like an *arm* going right up her butt. Was it actually prodding the bottom of her stomach? It occurred to June, in this peculiar moment of abstraction, that sometimes what a woman wanted more than anything was simply to be *filled,* to be used as a container of flesh and be *crammed* to the top, to be *stuffed* like a turkey until there was no more room to stuff anything more.

And if that's what women really wanted, that's what June was getting in the midst of this sopping, cringing, nerve-suckling fantasy.

Her heady glee could only be reflected by one word: *Fuck!*

The prodigious erection pistoned in and out, and the fact that it did so with *no regard for her at all* only made it more delicious. Her suitor's need had denuded her of all identity: she was no longer a thinking, living American woman; she was a squirming, flinching, mindless *thing* that was taken to be used solely as a receptacle for the phantom's animal lust.

And that was just fine with June! *My butt's being plungered like a gas station toilet…and I LOVE it!*

The phantom must've weighed four hundred pounds, and all

of it was muscle, and when it lay down flat it squashed June like a Twinkie under cinderblock (if he'd been filled with cream, like a Twinkie, it would be all over the place now!). All her breath was vised out of her; her tongue jutted. Every ounce of strength was required to wedge her hand under her belly and inch it toward her steaming sex, and she knew all it would take was a single press of her fingertip against her gorged clitoris and that would be that: Orgasm City.

Still, the brainless suitor humped her butt without relent. June's finger was two inches away, one inch, a half-inch—

Almost, almost...

—and just as the contact she craved would be achieved...

"Hey, girl, I say that's one mighty fine tail you'se stickin' out there!"

The marauding voice shattered the fantasy, and the gates to Orgasm City were slammed shut.

Shit! Who the—

June, transported back to the dull reality of her life in general and the even duller task of stirring a gallon of marine paint on the foredeck of this old rattletrap fishing boat, fired her glare behind her and down.

It was Rummy, the neighborhood dock bum, grinning toothless through a rust-colored beard that encompassed most of his face and scratching the crotch of dungarees that probably hadn't been washed in a year.

"It's rude to stare at people, Rummy!" she yelled.

"Gal with a butt like that make it hard not to, umm-hmm! Look like you had somethin' naughty goin' on in yer head, the ways you was squirmin' and moanin' and—"

"As a matter of fact I did, and you just ruined it!" she barked and kept stirring.

"Well then what say you'n me go belowdecks and pick up where ya left off?"

What say you drink your own piss instead, June thought in a rage. "What do you want, Rummy?"

"'Sides you? Nothin', girl. Only I wanted ta ask if you heard 'bout Kupjack, but I guess ya have, seein' how you're workin' for him now."

"Brilliant observation, and, yeah, I heard he was back in town."

"Naw, naw, that ain't what I meant. I meant about Kelly Point."

June grimaced, stirring away. The paint was like taffy. "What about Kelly Point?"

When Rummy scratched his beard, a snowstorm of dandruff fell. "Well, accordin' to the local talk, that be where Kupjack just come back from, then he drop his crew off on Brewer Island. But when he pulls in here there weren't *nothin'* in his hold. Was *bone dry's* what the dockmaster say. Then Kupjack up'n pay cash for that new Caddie and start spendin' money like Donald Strump...or whatever his name is. Donald Gates?"

June stopped stirring and whipped around. "Wait a minute. First I heard is was Devil's Reef, then Dunedin Reef, and now you're telling me he just came back from Kelly Point, and that he dropped his crew off a Brewer Island. Well, I heard it was St. Mary's Island after I heard it was Kent Island. What the hell's going on?"

"Gold, that's what."

June looked at him cockeyed. "Say again?"

"That's what I heard my own self...'twas *gold* he come back with, and it must've been a fair amount 'cos he walked out of the gold exchange in Salisbury this morning with a hundred grand, *cash.*"

June frowned. "Even if that's true, Rummy, how would you know?"

The man patted dust off his corroded shirt. "Simple. My sister works there. She told me."

In a town like this, June knew that most every bit of information communicated amongst the local population was ninety-nine-percent grapevine. "Fine, Rummy, but I still don't believe it."

"Then where'd Kupjack get the money?"

It's a good question, but..."I don't care," she resolved, then squatted back down to her stirring.

"And where *is* everybody?" Rummy continued the conjecture. The question was followed by a tinkling sound.

"What do you mean, where is— " but then June winced. Rummy was standing right there on the dockwalk in broad daylight, urinating into the water. "At least turn around when you do that, Rummy!"

"Oh, shee-it, sorry," he said. Were flies actually buzzing

around his exposed penis? He put it away but, without surprise, didn't even pull his zipper up. "Look around. Notice anything strange about the marina?"

It took June several moments to blink away the vision of Rummy's unwashed-for-years dick. But then, as her eyes surveyed the long expanse of boat-slips...

Damn near every boat is GONE..."Where'd everyone go?"

"Where you think?" Rummy replied. "They all high-tailed it to Kelly Point, to look for that stash of gold Kupjack found. Probably a lot more there." Rummy stepped down off the dock, into a small dinghy, which was where he usually slept. "'S'where I'm a-goin' now, I ain't no dummy. You wanna come with me?" he added with a crack of enthusiasm.

"No," she said. "No, thank you."

"All's right then. See ya later."

Hope not, June thought at her cynical best. Rummy pulled a cord, started a small outboard motor, and puttered out to the bay.

This is some weird shit going on here, she thought. Devil's Reef, Dunedin Reef, Kelly Point, Kent Island, St. Mary's Island, crackjaw, hagfish, etc. *Every time I heard one thing, I hear another thing completely different. And...*

She stared at the thought. *Gold?*

She'd never heard of one speck of gold in these parts, ever. But it *was* odd about Kupjack's sudden spending spree. The only thing tighter than Kupjack's wallet was a bull's ass in fly season. And now that she thought of it, why would he have bought a gold Cadillac, of all colors? It looked like shit.

Salty sea-foam towns like this all had their local legends, but the subject of gold did not fit into any of them. No hidden treasure, no pirates, no sunken Spanish galleons.

The paint was stirred, and the sun was cooking her back. She lugged the paint can down to the companionway steps to the first cabin. Her mind kept swimming in questions as she opened the portholes to get some cross breeze. *Wouldn't it be funny as shit if I found a gold coin down here?* Then—

"Oww!"

In a split second, she'd stepped on something and fallen—*thunk!*—right on her butt. She'd need to get some lights on down here; it was too dark, and...

What did I trip over?

She squinted, patting her hand around on the floor. There was nothing—No! Her hand landed on something cool, hard, and irregular. Was it a piece of glazed porcelain? It felt smooth, polished.

June picked it up and took it to the sunlight slanting in from a porthole.

And stared.

What the fuck IS it?

It was a six- or seven-inch long metallic object with rounded edges and a not-quite-symmetrical contour. The only thing she could think to compare it to would be a Baby Ruth bar, but of course Baby Ruth bars were not made of solid gold.

This thing was.

It's a gold ingot or something! June deduced. *That old fuck Kupjack really DID find gold!*

June's heart pattered. She paced back and forth, wide-eyed. This thing in her hand was obviously only a tiny bit of the entire stash Kupjack had found. *Like when you bite into a sandwich and a crumb of bread falls to the floor,* came a weighty simile. And with the price of gold over a thousand dollars an ounce, here was the nest egg poor June had never gotten even after a life of hard, honest work. And she knew one thing for sure: *This fuckin' Baby Ruth bar is coming home with ME.*

Stealing, schmeeling. It wasn't hers, no, but finder's keepers. *Kupjack has ENOUGH gold and he sure as shit knows where there's more. So...fuck him.* She put the gold bar/piece/ingot/whatever it was in her pocket. But, even though she now possessed a small fortune, she'd still have to paint the damn boat or else Kupjack would be suspicious. The piece in her pocket he'd dropped unnoticed, but if she quit on the spot—

He'll know I found something.

Therefore, she resolved to get to work and make it seem that everything was normal, yet as she prepared to retrieve the dropcloths, rollers, etc., the most natural thought occurred to her:

Maybe there's more. Maybe there are a few more pieces lying around that Kupjack dropped and didn't notice!

Some inner monitor went off in her brain which said, *You've got enough. Don't be greedy,* and to this monitor she promptly replied, *Fuck off.*

On hands and knees, she proceeded, patting the ancient floor in every dark corner, and it must be said that the excitement derived from finding a chunk of pure gold combined with the excitement of possibly finding more…June was not surprised to find the "purse of her loins" beating like a heart and drenching her crotch; and though her mind was quite set on gold, part of her cognizance was overwhelmed by imagery of the most lusty sort: dicks in her mouth, dicks in her butt, dicks in her "honey bucket." All these things and more poured over her mind's eye, and one imaginary cock after another dumped great plumes of sperm in her and on her. June was so horny, as a matter of fact, that she had to force herself *not* to stick her hand down her shorts for some stimulation of a more substantial nature. *Masturbate later, you horn dog! Right now you're looking for gold!*

But, lo, in her extensive, knee dirtying search, no gold was to be found. However she *did* discover one beer cap, a cigar butt, an M&M (a green one), and—

Yuck!

—a rubber glove with brown index finger. It was clear how the good Captain Kupjack utilized his spare time.

She moved on, next, to a tiny storage closet, which she felt inclined to skip but for some reason didn't.

Perhaps she should have.

She unlatched the narrow door, and—

Holy motherfucking FUCK!

—out spilled a veritable *pile* of skeletons. Easily the bones of four men were in evidence, and she didn't need to be a scholar of Euclidean calculus to realize that the bones constituted Kupjack's "crew." June naturally ejected herself from the compartment in a split second, but a split second was enough to digest the horror's details.

The skeletons still had their clothes on, the fabric of which seemed half corroded. One would think that the men had rotted down to bare bones while the clothing remained, but how could this be? There was no stench of death at all, if anything just a pleasant sea scent. The eye-socket of one victim remained filled by a glass eye. This could only be Tommy Ray Swain, a local deadbeat fishing hand who liked to pop the eye out at the bar and put in people's drinks, not an activity which was met with any levity. June had fucked him once in high school but wished she hadn't. For one thing, she'd received no orgasm for her efforts, for another, she got a UTI.

But that was another story.

The bones were clean, too, scrapless. Not a single sinew of flesh, tendon, or cartilage could be found on any of them.

Be that as it may, June ran her ninety-pound ass out of there as fast as her coltish legs could carry her. She tore across the main cabin, shot herself up the companionway steps, grabbed the door latch, and—

Fuck fuck fuck fuck fuck fuck FUCK!

The door was locked!

It must've locked by itself when she'd come down. She kicked at it ferociously. It didn't budge. Then...

What the FUCK?!

And errant glance out the porthole on the door showed her this:

Good ole Kupjack sitting in the captain's chair in the wheelhouse, swigging a bottle of Wild Turkey.

How could he not have heard me kicking the door, the old fuck? And with that thought, June POUNDED on the door with all her might. "Hey!" she shrieked. "I locked myself in! Open the door!"

Kupjack made no motion, no response.

And only then did June realize that the door *couldn't* be locked accidentally from the outside. It was a deadbolt which required a key...

"YOU FAT DRUNK PERVERT MOTHERFUCKER!" she bellowed. "YOU LOCKED ME IN!"

At this, Kupjack turned around in the chair, faced the outside of the door, and waved, grinning, right at June.

Whatever was going on here, June hadn't time to conjecture, but she instantaneously knew three things.

One, there was no breaking through the door without an axe.

Two, there was an axe in the engine room.

Three, to get to the engine room, she'd have to pass the skeleton pile at the closet, and there was a formidable probability that on such a trek, she would encounter whatever it was that had sucked the flesh off the bodies of four men.

Oh, and Four, the only reason Kupjack would've locked her inside was because he must strongly desire June meet the same fate as his crew.

June's teeth chattered as she daintily stepped over the tumble of corpses that had spilled into the narrow hall. To get to the engine room, she'd have to first pass through the bunk cabin, and this she did with some trepidation—so much trepidation, in fact, that she wet herself. *Terrific,* she thought. It was dark here, only one round window, deck level, on each side, and, wouldn't she know it, the light switch was on the other side of the cabin, next to the engine room door. Stifling heat seemed to pressure-cook her; she was pouring sweat. Not three steps across the floor and she felt the oddest bumps under her flipflops, as if she were walking over pebbles. When she looked down, even in the limited light, she saw that the "pebbles" were marble-sized nuggets of gold.

She noticed something else as well: a creeky low-tide scent. The cabin was only six feet long, but it felt like six hundred. Six bunks, three on each side, lined the walls, and in the occluded light, crumpled sheets and pillows looked like men. June didn't need that illusion. Then again—

What's that smell?

It was earthy, musky without being unwholesome, and, truth be told, it was kind of a turn on.

"This is NOT the best time to be horny!" she whispered to herself.

At last she made it to the door to the engine room, grabbed the latch, turned it, and—

Oh, for dick's sake!

—it was locked.

No recourse now but to return to the main door at the top of the companionway steps. And—*the fire extinguisher!* There was one on the wall. *Maybe I can break the door down with that!*

Just as she would open the door that led out of the bunk cabin—

click

—someone locked it from the other side.

Bug-eyed, June looked through the little round window and saw Kupjack smiling at her.

She bellowed loud as a trumpet: "You drunk old fat perverted piece of dog shit! Unlock the door! What's going on? What did you do to your crew? I'll KILL YA when I get out of here!"

She could just hear his voice, muffled as it was, through the door, "You WON'T get out of there, sweetie"—then he cackled a laugh. "Look up at the ceiling."

The ceiling? June was stifled, her mind a mix of terror and questions. She looked up at the ceiling and saw nothing of note at first; there wasn't enough light to see anything but the fact that the ceiling was black, or almost black. But as she squinted at an irregularity, her eyes began to acclimate to the low light, and in the corner of her eye, she noticed, right there on a bunk (next to a magazine entitled *All Hands On Dick!* and a jar of vaseline), a large flashlight.

Fuck yeah! came the cultured thought, and she grabbed the flashlight, snapped it on, and pointed the strong beam of light toward the ceiling...

And peed in her shorts again.

The ceiling...was *moving.*

Think of a three-hundred-pound blob of fresh-made bread dough dropped on the floor, and the way it would slowly spread outward. That's what this reminded June of, only it wasn't on the floor, it was on the fucking ceiling, and this wasn't bread dough, because bread dough wasn't the color of, well, feces.

Then the blob detached itself from the ceiling and fell right on June.

Holy motherfucking SHIT! she thought, struggling at once with the tent of churning slop that had landed on her. It formed something like a bubble over her, whose confines were very slowly drawing in, and June received the strangest impression that the, the, the *thing* was doing this on purpose, to lengthen the time of her terror before it had entirely converged on her. She received several more strong impressions as well, and another was that the mass of surf-smelling poop-brown glop had every intention of eating her.

Whatever the thing was, June didn't care. An alien that had landed in the sea? A secret genetic experiment run amok? Or just some unclassified, previously undiscovered sea creature?

June didn't give a flying fuck.

She collapsed down on her back, then stuck her legs out straight—a feeble attempt, at least, to put struts between herself and that ever-lowering mass of sea blubber, excrescence, reef slop, or whatever it was. The flashlight remained on, and as the top of that "bubble" sunk around her feet, she pointed the light upward.

I'm WAY out of my league here, she thought quite dismally, and she peed her pants again, too, by the way. Puckered holes began to emerge from the slop's inner-surface area, like octopus suckers, and all at once, she deduced what had happened to the crew. Once these suckers made contact with her flesh, they would emit slimy digestive enzymes and then they would, well, they would *suck.* They would suck all her flesh off her bones. And once she'd been liquified and digested, any moron knew what happened next. What goes in, must come out, right? June would be processed through the creature's bowels and then excreted through whatever manner of monster anus this hideous thing had in its butt.

More than that, she would be excreted, not as common poop, but as *gold.*

It began to occur to her, as her feet struggled against the descending wet mass, that she knew far too much than she had any business knowing. These rapid impressions that fired into her mind had no logical explanation, but still the impressions came, and with them the full gist. *This fuckin' ugly pile of shit is TELEPATHIC!* she realized. *It's sending signals to my brain and letting me know all about it!*

Ever so slowly, it continued to constrict, those suckers throbbing. Using her legs as struts against the top of the "bubble" did no good at all. Just as she *knew* the mass would collapse on her and begin to chow down, she noticed the strangest thing in the shifting illumination of the flashlight...

A cock and balls.

Or something *like* a cock and balls: a glistening milk-chocolate-brown sack heavy with two fist-sized lumps semblant of testicles, over which lay what could only be a flaccid, veined, uncircumcised *sea-peter.*

June's sentience shifted into a thoughtless, almost automatic mode. She did not consciously *think,* she merely *acted* the only way her instincts knew.

She shot her hand out, and began to fondle the bizarre genitals.

Her fingers played with the testicles for a few moments; she could feel them beating from within, and as she did so, she noticed something of significance:

The entirety of the mass of slop which surrounded her *stopped* descending.

I'll bet the fucker's horny, she deduced. *Probably hasn't had a piece of sea-slug ass in a long time. Let's see how he likes a HUMAN piece of ass...*

She kneed her way through dripping ichor, and with no hesitation whatsoever, she pulled what could only be the thing's penis into her mouth, all the while maintaining her titillation of its lumpen gonads. The penis did not become erect as a human one would but instead throbbed in her mouth like an animate pile of wet modeling clay. June's tongue roved over it, feeling the fascinating network of beating veins, and once or twice sliding over the meaty, rimmed aperture which she could only guess was the end of its urethra. An inclination directed her to try pushing her entire tongue *into* that aperture, and when it dilated enough for her to do so, she knew she'd made the right choice. The creature actually *shuddered* in pleasure.

And still, the body of the thing did not collapse on her and subsequently consume her. *It wants a blowjob,* she realized. *Gee, why is THAT no surprise?* But this thing's cock was so different from a man's, she wasn't sure how to commence. While weighing considerations, she "fucked" the monster's peehole with her tongue, plunging in and out, and figured the sensation was lengthening her life. The peehole, however, constricted after another minute, and June figured that meant it was time to get down to business. She began to tighten her mouth around the veined wad of flesh but it was too wide for her to rim her lips around as she would a regular dick. But then?

Yowza!

The odd penile mass in her mouth suddenly protracted, narrowing by degrees, and advanced down her throat. This advancement did not abate until it reached her stomach. It was June's good fortune that she possessed no mode of gag reflex. The situation could be likened to, say, a girthy snake slithering down from her mouth into her belly.

Here goes nothing...

She began to move her head back and forth, the action of

which caused her throat to slide to and fro over every inch of that "snake." *Fuck!* she thought. *This isn't deep throat, this is deep stomach!* She could feel the thing tensing, and she sensed in a more psychical way that the creature was going gaga over her oral ministration. But evidently, dicks were universal: if you suck one, it blows its load, and so was the case with *this* dick at that very moment.

June's eyeballs nearly started from her head. The thing came in her stomach as though it were a manual feeding tube. *You gotta be shitting me!* Was it a pint? A quart? June's belly filled with hot slop, and when the snake-like penile shaft withdrew from her throat, it was *still* coming. Quart, be damned—this thing was working on a gallon! Upon full withdrawal, her mouth filled with its cum as well.

What was the creature's sperm *like?*

Hot tapioca pudding? A bucket of shucked raw oysters? A colossal volume of frog eggs? All these similes combined would probably be a just parallel. The amount of it in her stomach was a grim prospect indeed; it seemed to bubble down there, and shift, and percolate. *At least I don't have to worry about buying dinner...*Further considerations bewildered her. For one, after being orally pummeled by a sea monster's cock, she would expect herself to be repulsed and terrified, not—

Not *what?*

Horny, she realized.

June was horny, all right, hornier than a nun full of Spanish Fly. Her vagina beat like an angry fist banging against a door. She gave up trying to isolate her thoughts when she realized that the *thing's* thoughts were still seeping into her head, but in no language but that of raw emotion: lust, desire, need, and, yes, love!

This great big plop of monster-slime LOVES ME!

And in a moment more, June—with no conscious forethought whatsoever—physically availed herself to *receive* the sea monster's love. She was out of her shorts, and spread-eagled on her back in less time than it took to say *Fuck the shit out of me!* It was during these few seconds before physical intercourse would ensue that the same *mental/psychic* intercourse became more acute. *Yeah, this thing loves me, all right, and it's about to prove that in spades,* June thought, but by now she was ready for some love herself, some *hard* love. Her feminine channel was drenched, her nipples gorged to a size she'd never before experienced, tingling electrically and actually throbbing. Her loins felt like a pot of sex stew, bubbling, roiling, cringing to be stirred, and she knew that she was undergoing some serious hormonal or cerbro-chemical change. Was it normal to *want* to be fucked by a sea monster? Meanwhile, the sea monster underwent a change of its own. That massive "bubble" shape of its body began to turn inside-out and backward, and when this prolapsation had finished, there stood before June some three hundred pounds of brown, mottled, low-tide-smelling porridge which bore the most vague semblance of the human form: i.e., jointless, digitless arms and legs, an undetailed approximation of a trunk, an eyeless, noseless, mouthless, earless lump for a head. Think a monstrous gingerbread man, or a shit-colored Gumby doll…

But, of course, Gumby was not possessed of erection, but this thing was, sticking up like a foot and a half-inch length of veined, pulsing radiator hose. Precum ran like a leaky tap from the puckered slit which crowned the glans. Those same malformed, fist-sized testicles to which June had been previously introduced, constricted in their hideous scrotum even as June stared up, drooling, legs spread painfully apart; and somehow, in the most abstract and introspective insinuation, the monster stared back at her with equal desire in spite of the fact no eyes could be found in its lumpen head.

In a sense of need which could only be likened to insanity, June's hands plied her gushing sex, the sensations of which she had never before experienced with such potency. *If this thing doesn't start banging the daylights out of me RIGHT NOW, I'm gonna have to fist myself!*

"Come on, pal!" she bellowed. "Let me have it!" She lewdly thrust her splayed groin forward. "Does it look like you need a fucking invitation?"

We need not accompany June through the preambles which led up to the business at hand; it should suffice to say, instead, that in a hackneyed wink of an eye, that man-shaped heap of ocean slop landed on her with the urgency of a pit bull on a meat wagon. June wanted to get fucked, and fucked she got. The thing made mewling sounds as it lay atop her, humping away, drawing that malleable cock in and out of June's "love-hole." Just as it had lengthened and narrowed in order to advance into her belly, it now lengthened and narrowed to advance into the deepest depths of her reproductive tract. At the front of her cervix, it seemed to turn semi-solid and then poured farther, farther, deeper, deeper, through the physical limits of the uterus, then impossibly dividing into two squirming tendrils, each of which quivered still deeper up into the fallopian tubes. The spasms of sensation that coursed through June's body were clearly sensations hitherto unfelt before by any human woman. The thing continued to hump her without relent, all the while those delectable "dick-tendrils" quivered and elicited neural pleasures so intense that all June could do was lie there—drooling, tongue out, limp limbed—and *feel.* The sentient part of her brain shut off so that it might focus solely on the waves of orgasms that pulsed through her being. Eventually her musky lover's orgasm commenced as well, triggered by the release of its pudding-like sperm: gushes of it, which blew against every inner recess of June's reproductive apparatus. When the thing clumsily began to get up, the unearthly penis continued to pour still more sperm into her, and when that was done, it stood upright and looked sightlessly down at June, whose body just went on spasming in orgasm for at least another half hour.

CAPTAIN KUPJACK sat above deck under the wheelhouse awning, nearly done with his first bottle of Wild Turkey for the day. A smile of robust satisfaction touched the booze-reddened face, and in further satisfaction he even gave his crotch a squeeze. The idea simply tickled him pink: June being consumed, digested, and pushed out of that hideous thing's butthole. *That smartass cunt finally gets what she deserves,* his thoughts cackled. She'd sassed him for years, and smirked off every advance, even turned down his offers of good money, while fucking and sucking every cock in town, every cock but poor old Captain Kupjack's. *Too good for me, huh, tramp? Think you're too high-falutin' for the Captain, huh? Well, how do ya like me now?*

Now?

By now that redneck gravy boat is nothing but a pile of solid-gold shit on the floor.

Yes, Kupjack liked that idea very much.

He waited a while longer, idly stroking his beard and giving further errant squeezes to his groin, until the sun pulled off a bit more, and then he got up and creaked his wobbling fat frame down the steps to the lower deck. When he arrived at the engine room door, he smiled into the porthole, looking for the telltale skeleton which would be all that remained of that fickle white-trash sperm depository named June. However—

"Where the hell is she?"

No evidence of June's remains were to be seen, and only then did the Captain notice that the door was no longer locked and that the deadbolt had been broken *outward.*

What kind'a monkeyshines goin' on here? he thought and scratched his bin Laden-style beard, and then he thought that maybe things had not gone as he'd planned and that maybe he should shag his fat drunken ass the fuck out of there without delay, but—

"Looking for someone?" a snide voice that could only be June's issued behind him.

It took a moment for the implication to register through Kupjack's whiskey-fogged perceptions as he turned, squinting, and saw none other than June herself standing behind him, buck naked and sheened in perspiration. "Why, ya conniving jizz-head whore! That thing should'a et ya by now!"

"It was going to," June replied, "until I fucked and sucked it to kingdom come and it fell in love with me." She looked up to the ceiling. "Honey? Be a sweetheart and come down here. You must be real hungry after all that wonderful lovin' you gave me. Well, soup's on!"

Kupjack was already screaming as the sea slop slithered down the wall and engulfed him. June used a nearby bunk for a ringside seat; the only thing missing was popcorn. The Captain's pathetic fat form could be seen struggling uselessly within the churning, ravenous pile. She had to credit the old perv at least in his resolve to garble every possible sexist expletive at her for as long as his vocal cords functioned. We need not repeat those expletives here…well, on second thought, maybe we will, just a few, in the interests of completeness:

"Ya dirty white-trash cutthroat fuck-toilet!"

"Low-down tramp, done chugged more cock than I've chugged whiskey!"

"Bet you've had more dick going *into* your ass than shit comin' *out!'*

And so on. At any rate, that was the end of Captain Kupjack, and the beginning of a new life for June!

A WEEK later, June stretched out in a lounge chair on the sundeck of her brand-new seventy-two-foot Stardust houseboat. No more shitty efficiency apartment for her, and no more minimum-wage jobs busting her tail for asshole sexual-predator bosses. Nope, it was the high-life for June from now on. In the trunk of Kupjack's Cadillac (which June had ransacked the night of the Captain's "disappearance"), she'd found several million in gold turds, not to mention the additional gold that the man had been turned into by the sea slug's digestive tract. She'd never have to lift a finger again in her life, and she figured she deserved it.

"Rummy, get me another Long Island Iced Tea, will you?" came her languid request from the lounge chair. It was great to just lay around all day on the boat, soaking up the sun and getting loaded. She'd hired Rummy and Fishy as her crew—why not? They were shiftless alcoholic idiots but she figured they deserved a break. They waited on her hand and foot, cleaned the boat, cooked her meals, etc. June liked the idea of being waited on by men.

"Comin' right up!" Rummy replied after having just finished peeing over the side. Then he shuffled off to the galley where there was a fully stocked bar. Fishy was down below in the back, scraping barnacles off the prop, and June simply continued to lie there, in her Bill Blass bikini, her Ray-Ban sunglasses, and a three-hundred-dollar Tropicana sun hat, and she would be happy to spend the rest of her days just like this. *Ah, the good life!* she thought.

But one question remained, did it not?

Whatever happened to the sea-slop thing?

Tempted as she was to keep it locked up for use as her personal sex minister, she knew that would be terribly cruel. It was a creature of the wild and an inhabitant of the deep blue sea—whatever the fuck it was—so in the deep blue sea it belonged.

And into the deep blue sea, she released it.

The best piece of male ass I ever had, she lamented, because she would've been perfectly content to let it fuck the stuffing out of her every day for the rest of her life. But how fair would that be to...to...*it?* To the sea thing, the sea monster, the...whatever the fuck it was?

This she knew beyond all doubt: no human man would ever be good enough ever again. But there was also something else she knew with equal certainty:

I was the best fuck of that thing's life.

She gazed out into the endless sea and smiled. See, that abstruse psychic connection she and it had shared never really severed with its departure.

And June knew full well that that great big wonderful pile of sea slop would be stopping by very soon for a booty call.

TIM WAGGONER

EVERY BEAST OF THE EARTH

VALERIE'S HEART pounded so hard she couldn't distinguish it from the rolling crashes of thunder that shook her tiny Miata. Rain came down in what seemed like solid sheets of water, and she gripped the steering wheel so tight her hands and wrists burned. She leaned forward, squinting, trying to see the road ahead, but although she had the wipers working at their maximum speed, they only smeared the water around. There was simply too much of it for the wipers to clear.

"No," she said. "No, no, no, no, no..."

An icy coldness took hold of her, and she felt light-headed. Blackness nibbled at the edges of her vision, and she knew she was on the verge of passing out. She almost let the blackness take her, so desperate was she to escape. But she fought back.

It was midafternoon, but the sky was dark as the inside of a cave, and the flashes of lightning, as blindingly bright as they were, only chased away the darkness for a split second, and then it rushed back in to fill the world. She risked a glance at the speedometer. She was doing five miles an hour, but it felt as if she were hurtling through the downpour at one hundred plus. She would've pulled over, wanted *desperately* to do so, but she was stuck in the middle lane of a three-lane highway, and there were vehicles on both sides of her, shadowy forms defined by headlights and taillights. The drivers weren't going any faster than she was, but their presence made her nervous as hell. What if one of the vehicles drifted out of its lane, even if only a few inches? It could strike her car, knock her into the other vehicle, and then, and then...

You're going five fucking miles per hour, she told herself. *The worst that could happen is you end up in a three-car fender bender.*

She knew this was true, but it did nothing to blunt her fear. If anything, the thought of a collision—no matter how minor—only served to sharpen it. She gripped the steering wheel tighter and concentrated on staying in her lane, doing her best to pretend the other two cars weren't there.

She couldn't believe she'd been so stupid. She *never* drove in the rain, wouldn't get behind the wheel if there was even a *hint* of precipitation in the forecast, and she checked the weather obsessively during the course of each day. The weather app on her phone had said there was only a three percent chance of rain today, and even that much had worried her. But she'd been overdue for a dental checkup and cleaning. She'd cancelled her last two appointments because of rain, and she didn't want to cancel again, not for a measly three percent chance. Now here she was, teeth clean, breath minty fresh, trapped in what for her was the very definition of Hell.

Fuck that app, she thought, and a manic giggle escaped her mouth. It sounded like the sort of laugh a crazy woman would make, but that was okay. As bone-deep terrified as she was at that moment, she probably *was* crazy, or damn near.

The sky had been clear when she'd walked into the building where her dentist's office was, but when she came out, it had grown darker, just a little, just enough to make her queasy. She'd gotten in her Miata and roared out of the parking lot like she was training for the Indy 500. Her apartment was less than ten miles from the dentist's, and she told herself that she would make it, that everything was going to be okay. She almost hadn't gotten on the highway, but it was the most direct route, and it would give her the best chance to get home before the rain started. So she'd decided to risk it. She had been on the highway for little over a minute before the deluge erupted.

Stupid. Stupid, stupid, stupid, *stupid!*

Though it hardly seemed possible, the downpour intensified, and she found herself almost completely blinded. She nearly screamed, but she didn't, not even when she felt the Miata begin to hydroplane. But when her car struck the vehicle on the right, she screamed loud enough that she thought her vocal cords might tear themselves to shreds. And when her car began to spin on the rain-slick road, she screamed even louder.

VALERIE WAS four when her grandmother gave her a *Children's Illustrated Bible*. Neither her father nor mother were religious, but her grandmother was, and she decided to tend to Valerie's spiritual education, which her parents had neglected so badly. Valerie's mother was angry about the Bible—or more accurately, about Grandmother's interference—but Valerie's father didn't seem to think it was a big deal.

"It's just a storybook as far as she's concerned," he said.

"It's not *just* anything," her mother countered, but she didn't argue further and Valerie got to keep the book.

Valerie was too young to read the text, but she liked the pictures. They weren't cartoony or childish like the illustrations in her other books. These pictures were realistic, more like paintings, and she found them fascinating. Her favorite picture was the one that accompanied the story of Creation. It ran vertically down the side of the page next to the words, and it was a series of small scenes, one stacked on top of the other. It began with a formless void, followed by a scene of planets, stars, and the sun. Next was a vast ocean, and after that a verdant landscape filled with animals. Last came Adam and Eve, both naked but standing behind strategically placed bushes and tree branches to conceal their naughty parts. What Valerie especially liked about the picture was that there were a couple dinosaurs among the animals in the fourth scene. Animals were cool, but dinosaurs were *awesome!*

The pictures of Jesus puzzled her. In them he had light skin and blond hair, but Grandma had shown her pictures of Jesus in her grown-up Bible, and in those his skin was darker and his hair was brown. She wondered if Jesus could change the way he looked, like the invading aliens she'd seen in a cartoon once.

But there was one picture that fascinated her more than all the others—a two-page spread depicting the Flood. She'd seen pictures of animals walking onto the big boat two by two in other books. She even had a toy boat with cute plastic animals that went inside. Grandma had gotten it for her last Christmas, which for some reason she liked to pronounce Christ-Mass. But the picture in her kids' Bible was very different. Rain poured down from a dark sky, and the ark floated on the water in the background. In the foreground were groups of people clinging to rocky patches of land which hadn't been covered by water yet. The people reached out toward the ark, as if imploring Noah to come help them. But the ark was too far away, and there was no one on deck. Valerie wondered if Noah *did* see the people and simply didn't want to help them because he didn't think them worthy of aid. Sometimes she imagined the men and women calling out in despair, sobbing as the water rose above their feet and continued rising.

But that wasn't the worst thing about the picture. Water rushed past the outcroppings the doomed people clung to, and animals were caught in the rapids. Cattle, antelope, even a mama elephant with a baby beside her, its trunk pressed to her body as it desperately tried to hold on. One animal—a deer, maybe, judging by its thin legs and split hooves—floated upside down in the water, obviously drowned. The other animals, who would soon join their companion in death, looked terrified. She would stare at that picture for long stretches of time, imagining the sound of the rain and the rushing water, the desperate pleas of the people on the rocks, the confused, mournful cries of the doomed animals.

Once, when Grandma came over to watch her while Mommy and Daddy were at the hospital to get her new baby sister, she showed Grandma the picture of the Flood.

"Why did God do this?" she asked.

"Because the people were wicked. They had to be destroyed so everything could start over again...so the people would be better."

Valerie frowned as she tried to absorb this. She then pointed to the drowned deer bobbing upside down in the current.

"What about all the other animals? The ones not on the ark? Were they wicked, too?"

Grandma opened her mouth, then frowned. After a moment of silence, she took the Bible from Valerie's hands, closed it, and set it on the couch next to them.

"How about we make some cookies?" Grandma asked.

Even at four, Valerie understood Grandma was trying to distract her, make her forget her question about the drowning animals. But because she *was* four, and Grandma had said the magic word—*cookies*—it worked. Mostly.

Valerie never opened her Bible after that, and she hid it in her closet so when her new sister was old enough, she would never see the picture and hear the screams of the animals.

THE MIATA missed hitting either of the other vehicles that flanked her, although she had a sense that she hadn't missed them by much. She fought to get her car back under control, and she thought she'd succeeded when she bumped into a metal guardrail. As slow as she was going, the impact was minimal, but it was enough to make her cry out, especially when an intense burst of lightning flashed, turning the world a blinding bright white, followed an instant later by a thunderclap so loud she felt the vibrations shiver through her body. Too terrified to pull back onto the highway, she rode the guardrail, metal scraping metal, and she might've continued like this all the way home if she hadn't reached an underpass. Suddenly the rain was gone, and her headlights showed her that others had stopped here to wait out the storm. A motorcyclist standing next to his bike, looking out at the rain. An SUV with its hazard lights on, driver and passengers still inside.

Now that *is a damn fine idea,* she thought.

She pulled over, put the Miata in park, hit the hazards, and turned off the engine. With an effort, she pulled her hands off the steering wheel and then sat there for several moments, doing her best to breathe evenly and waited for her pulse to return to some approximation of normal. Outside the underpass, the storm continued to rage unabated. The rain and thunder were still loud as hell, but they sounded more distant now, and that helped take the edge off her anxiety. Her panic loosened its grip—only a little, but even that much was a relief. Even so, she was shaking and her stomach roiled with nausea. The Miata's interior felt hot and stifling, and she wanted nothing more right then than to get out of her car. Leaving the keys in the ignition, she switched off the headlights, unlocked the door, opened it, and stumbled outside, almost losing her balance and falling. She sucked in cool, moist air, felt a breeze caress her skin, and her body relaxed. She still felt weak and light-headed, but her trembling lessened, and her nausea subsided, although it didn't go away entirely. But she was out of the rain. She was *safe*.

She looked around. She didn't know what had happened to the two cars that she'd been so worried about hitting. She assumed they'd passed her and kept on going, driving through the underpass and back out into the storm. She couldn't imagine anyone—even someone who didn't have her issues with driving in rain—continuing on in this hellish storm.

Suicidal dumbasses, she thought.

She made sure to stand on the shoulder, in case any other vehicles might pass through. How ironic would it be if she'd managed to get out of the storm alive only to be struck by another driver?

She walked behind the Miata and leaned over to check the damage on the vehicle's right side. As dim as the light was in the underpass, it was hard to tell, but it looked like it wasn't bad. Some minor dents and scrapes. Ugly, but nothing serious.

She'd pulled over less than thirty feet from the southern edge of the underpass, and she now turned to look out at the water pouring off the highway above like a waterfall. She felt a sudden claustrophobia, a sensation that she was trapped in a bubble of air deep beneath an ocean, tons of water pressing in from all sides, the bubble so fragile it might pop any second, allowing the water to rush in and engulf her.

Stop it, she told herself. *Stop it, stop it, stop it!*

She looked away from the wall of water that blocked the south entrance of the underpass and checked on her fellow shelter-seekers. The motorcyclist—a man wearing a sodden T-shirt and jeans—watched the rain, arms folded, and although she couldn't see his face, his body language indicated he was pissed, almost as if he saw the storm as a personal affront. No one had exited the SUV yet, but now Valerie could hear young children—*loud* young children—and an equally loud woman, presumably their mother, warning them to be quiet or else.

Valerie remembered how her mother used to say that kids and pets always went nuts when it stormed, full of wild, nervous energy. *It's like you have little storms inside you to match the big one outside,* she'd say.

Valerie considered getting back in her car to wait out the storm, rolling the windows down so it wouldn't feel too oppressive inside, but instead she turned back to the underpass's southern entrance. She felt pain at the base of her skull as she watched the water fall, the beginnings of what she feared would be a truly horrendous stress headache. But despite this, despite the cold nausea quivering in her gut, she found the downpour mesmerizing. The rain was falling so hard and fast, it looked like a solid wall. No, more like a shimmering curtain, the rhythmic rippling of its surface almost hypnotic. She wanted to look away, but she couldn't, and the longer she watched the rain, the more she became convinced she could see shapes within it. Large, indistinct, shadowy forms that drifted in and out of sight, as if she were gazing through a glass wall at the waters of some wild, turbulent ocean, watching sea creatures swim in close to take a look at her before moving off. It was a ludicrous thought of course, but one she couldn't escape, and it only served to heighten her anxiety. And still she couldn't look away.

One of the shapes seemed to draw closer to the curtain of water, and there was something about it that intrigued Valerie, despite how on edge she felt. She knew what she was seeing was only an illusion, a combination of falling water, dim light, and her own imagination. But the shape's outline seemed familiar somehow, and without realizing it, she started walking toward it to get a better look. It wasn't large, this shape. She estimated it was five feet high, maybe five and a half, and about two feet wide. It remained more or less stationary as she approached, although it bobbed slightly—up, down, left, right—almost as if it really were something floating in water.

A voice in the back of her mind shouted for her attention.

Stop! it warned. *Turn around and go back to the car, get inside, shut the door, and lock it! Then close your eyes and keep them closed until this damn storm stops!*

She heard the voice, but it was faint, more a nagging feeling than full-throated alarm. She'd been gripped by panic—accented by the occasional sharp spike of terror—ever since setting off on her desperate race for home. Her emotions were so jumbled at this point that she didn't recognize the voice of her own survival instinct attempting to warn her. Instead, she acknowledged the feeling and then immediately dismissed it. She had to know what that shape was, illusion or not. So she kept walking.

Only once did she glance over her shoulder to see what her fellow stranded travelers were doing. Had they also seen shapes in the rain that compelled them to investigate? But the mother and kids remained in the SUV, still shouting at one another, and the biker still stood with his arms crossed, pissed at the storm for inconveniencing him. If they saw any shapes—and Valerie doubted they did—they had likely decided they were simply tricks of the eye.

She faced forward and continued walking.

When she drew near the southern edge of the underpass, the boundary between *safe* and, well, *not safe*, she realized the shape was the silhouette of a person. She couldn't make out any features, but the overall form was unmistakable: torso, head, arms, legs…Not a very large person, either. Someone just over five feet tall and slender. She stopped a foot away from the wall of water, because now that she was close she could see that's what it was. Not thousands of separate drops plummeting from the sky but rather a solid mass of dark grayish water, as if she were standing in front of some kind of invisible barrier, like the clearest, most undetectable glass ever fashioned. And on the other side of this barrier floated what appeared to be the silhouette of a small person. But that wasn't the only shape Valerie saw. A dozen others moved in the background some distance away. Some small, no larger than house pets, while others were bigger. Just how big was impossible to tell through so much water, but she had the impression that some of them were *huge*.

Valerie stood there for several long moments, heart pounding in her ears. She held her breath as if she feared exhaling might cause whatever force was holding back all that water to pop out of existence as if it were no more substantial than a bubble. An image came to her then, tons of water rushing into the underpass to engulf the biker, the SUV mom and her bratty kids, and her. So vivid was this image that for an instant she thought it was real and started to scream, but then she managed to get herself back under some approximation of control and banished the image from her mind.

The shape on the other side of the barrier lifted its arm and stretched its hand toward her. Fingers emerged from the water, just the tips at first, but they were soon followed by the entire hand then wrist, forearm, elbow...The fingers and arm were delicate, feminine, but the skin was ivory white and mottled with patches of gray-green.

On some level of her being, deeper than mind, perhaps deeper than spirit, Valerie recognized that hand. She raised her own, fingers trembling, and reached toward it, tears sliding across her cheeks.

"Marie?" she whispered.

At the last instant she almost jerked her hand back, almost turned and fled, heeding the warning she'd ignored before. But it was too late. The discolored hand grabbed hold of her wrist and with surprising strength pulled her into the water.

"YOU ARE such a *bitch*, you know that?"

Marie sat slumped in the passenger seat, looking out the window, face turned away from Valerie. Anger radiated from Marie in what felt like solid waves of force, and Valerie wanted to snap back at her sister, call her an irresponsible little shit, but she held her tongue. As satisfying as it would be to lash out, it would only make things worse.

Valerie was nineteen, Marie fourteen-almost-fifteen. Both were soaking wet, hair plastered to their heads, clothes clinging to their bodies like thick burlap. It was night and a storm raged around them—bright lightning, ear-splitting thunder, pounding rain, gusting winds. Valerie had the wipers on their highest setting, their rapid *thwok-thwok-thwok* echoing the angry throbbing of her pulse. She was furious with Marie, and she thought it only appropriate that they were driving through a storm like this. Its fury mirrored her own. She'd never driven in conditions this bad before, and she had to fight to keep her Honda Accord under control. The wind was so strong each blast was like the punch of a giant fist that threatened to knock them off the road. Valerie loved the rain, always had. She especially loved listening to it hit the roof over her bedroom when she drifted off to sleep. But this storm was too much even for her.

"What the fuck were you thinking?" Valerie had to shout to be heard over the storm. "But you weren't thinking, were you? At least not with your head."

Marie didn't answer, didn't turn away from the window to face her.

They were traveling on 25A, a two-lane country road that connected their town of Ash Creek with Waldron. Valerie knew she was probably going too fast for this weather—almost fifty—but she told herself that it was okay. There was hardly ever any traffic on 25A this time of night, and there was nothing but cornfields on either side of them. If she did run the Accord off the road, the worst that would happen was they'd end up knocking down a dozen cornstalks and get stuck in mud. She'd have to call AAA to tow them out of the field, which would be embarrassing, but so what? Right now, she was too pissed to give a damn what happened.

An hour earlier, Valerie had gotten a call from Libby, one of Marie's friends, informing her that Marie had snuck out of their parents' house to go to a party in Waldron. A party thrown by some guys in their twenties that Marie and Libby had met at the mall last weekend. One of the guys—David—had made it a point of not only inviting Marie, but offering her a ride. According to Libby, David was hot and he drove a tricked-out Camaro. So Marie—who'd been flattered and flustered in equal measure—accepted his invitation. Marie had tried to talk Libby into going too, but she declined. She'd thought David and his friends were kind of sketchy, and she knew there would be drugs and alcohol there—maybe a *lot*—and she hadn't liked the look in David's eyes when he talked to Marie. A "Big Bad Wolf" look, she'd called it. Marie had kept after her all week to go and had given her the address of the house where the party was going to be in case she changed her mind. Libby had tried to talk Marie out of going, but she wouldn't listen. Finally, on the night of the party, not knowing what else to do and not wishing to get Marie in trouble with her parents, she'd called Valerie.

Valerie was finishing her first year of college at the University of Cincinnati, and when Libby told her what Marie was up to, Valerie rushed out of her dorm, got in her car, and raced off. Waldron was less than an hour away from Cincy, and during the drive, Valerie tried not to imagine what Marie might be doing—or might be having done *to* her—at the party. The rain started before she was halfway to Waldron, but it hadn't been too bad then. The storm didn't begin to worsen until after she'd found the house David and his friends rented and dragged her sister to the car. David hadn't seemed all that upset at having his underage date taken away so abruptly. Instead, he smiled at Valerie and asked for her phone number. Valerie told him to go fuck himself and all he did was laugh.

Now here they were, driving through a hellacious thunderstorm on the way to Mom and Dad's, Valerie warring with two equally strong impulses: to strangle her sister for being so reckless or hug her and ask if she was okay. But since her hands clenched the steering wheel in a death grip, she had to settle for using her voice.

"You didn't know those people. They could've done *anything* to you."

Marie shrugged, almost imperceptibly. Valerie chose to take it as an encouraging sign.

"They're way too old for you." She almost added, *You're only fourteen,* but she knew that pointing out her sister's youth would only make her angrier.

No shrug this time, but Marie didn't call her a bitch again. Progress?

So far, Marie hadn't asked her how she'd known about the party or its location. Maybe she'd already guessed it was Libby's doing. Or maybe she was so mad right then she didn't give a shit.

"I thought it would be fun."

Marie said this so softly that Valerie almost couldn't hear her over the storm.

"An older guy pays you attention and you're ready to spread your legs for him without a second thought," Valerie snapped.

That got Marie's attention. She whipped her head around, eyes filled with equal amounts of anger and shame.

"Fuck you!" she shouted. "You think you're so high and mighty since you went off to college. You're probably drunk most of the time and screw a different guy every weekend!"

A blast of wind buffeted the Accord, causing it to veer into the other lane. Valerie yanked the steering wheel to get the car back where it belonged.

"I'm nineteen," Valerie said. She almost added, *I'm an adult,* but despite her age, she really didn't feel like one yet.

"David was all right," Marie said. "So were his friends." She sounded sulky now more than angry. "You *really* embarrassed me tonight."

"Would you rather Mom and Dad had come to get you?"

Marie didn't reply.

One of the things that bothered Valerie the most about all this was that her sister hadn't said anything to her about David and the party before tonight. There had been a time when the two of them had shared every thought, every secret wish and hidden fear. But it seemed that time was gone, and it deeply saddened Valerie.

There was so much Valerie wanted to tell her sister. That she should be more careful, that she should value herself more, that there would be time for parties and older boys later, when she was older herself and could make choices in a more clear-eyed, level-headed way. But instead of saying any of this, she laughed.

Marie scowled, as if she suspected Valerie was laughing at her. Valerie was about to tell her it was nothing, that she had just realized she was acting too much like Mom tonight, and that she was sorry for being bitchy. But before she could speak again, an especially strong blast of wind hit the Accord and caused it to swerve. Valerie tried to correct, but she overcompensated, the tires hydroplaned, and there was nothing she could do to prevent the car sliding off the road. The Accord tilted to the right, and its passenger side wheels slipped into the ditch. The car followed the ditch's curve, launched into the air, flipped halfway over, and crashed to the ground. The vehicle slid through mud, flattening cornstalks just as Valerie had imagined earlier before coming to a stop.

Valerie wasn't sure if she lost consciousness or if she was simply stunned by the suddenness of what had happened, but the next thing she was fully aware of was hanging upside-down in the driver's seat, held in place by her seatbelt. The airbag had deployed, but it was already half-deflated, its work finished. Her head throbbed, but she didn't feel any other pain, so she assumed she was mostly unhurt. That, or the pain from her injuries hadn't hit her yet.

She looked toward her sister, the motion of turning her head sending a lance of pain through her neck. Marie's seatbelt was still on, but the passenger side window was shattered, and Marie's eyes were closed. There was blood on the right side of her face, and Valerie knew she'd hit the window. She feared her sister was dead, but then Marie moaned and stirred slightly. She was hurt, but she was alive.

The Accord had landed on its roof, but it wasn't lying flat. The passenger side of the vehicle was lower than the driver's side, and Marie's face practically lay in mud and water. The storm continued raging around them, and as Valerie watched in horror, water pooled around Marie's face, its level rising rapidly. She tried to reach out, grab hold of Marie's arm and pull her away from the water, but the front end of the Accord had been smashed in when it landed, and the steering wheel was pressed against her, pinning her right arm to her body. She tried to pull free, but it was no use. She was trapped.

She yelled Marie's name, but she didn't respond. Valerie could only watch as muddy water rose over Marie's nose and mouth. Tiny bubbles of air dotted the surface of the water for several moments, but then they stopped. The water continued rising until most of Marie's head was covered, and Valerie hoped the flooding would continue, the water level rising until the storm claimed her life as well. After all, *she* had been the one to drag her sister away from the party, *she* had been driving far too fast given how fierce the storm was, *she* had insisted on trying to talk things out instead of focusing all of her attention on driving. If either of them deserved to die drowning in a farmer's cornfield, it was her.

But although the rain continued, the water didn't rise much higher, and it never came close to touching Valerie. The storm continued for another hour before the thunder grew distant and lightning flashes came less often. Eventually, the rain slackened and died away. The storm had done a great deal of damage across several counties, and police and emergency crews were so busy dealing with the aftermath that Valerie and Marie weren't found until well after sunrise. Valerie hung upside down the entire time, awake, with only her sister's dead body for company.

VALERIE TRIED to draw in breath to scream, but all she managed to do was suck water into her lungs. A froth of bubbles burst from her mouth as she attempted to expel the water, and then she inhaled again out of reflex, taking in even more. Absolute animal panic took hold of her, and her body began thrashing, searching for something solid to grab on to. But there was nothing. She didn't question what was happening to her, didn't try to deny its reality. She had quite literally been pulled into her worst nightmare, and all she wanted was *out*. The underpass—and more importantly, air—was only inches away. If she could pull free of the hand (*Marie's hand*) that gripped her wrist and dragged her forward, she could turn around and swim back to the underpass. She hadn't gone near a pool since the accident, but she'd been a strong enough swimmer as a kid, and she felt confident she could find her way—*if* she could get free.

The water was murky, and she couldn't make out the features of the thing (*Marie*) that held on to her. She could feel it, though, and she grabbed hold of the thing's (*Marie's*) hand with both of hers and clawed at it, trying to tear herself from its (*her*) grip. She felt too-soft flesh slough away beneath her fingernails. Felt them scrape against the bones underneath. At first, the hand's (*her*) grip didn't lessen, but then the fingers pulled away, and she saw the shadowy form of the thing (*her sister*) rise upward and vanish into the gloom.

Lungs heavy and burning for air, she spun around in the water and kicked her legs to propel herself forward. She stretched out a hand, reaching for the underpass, for air, for fucking *sanity*, but there was only water.

But then her fingers brushed against something solid, and she allowed herself an instant of hope. Maybe it was a concrete pillar or a vehicle of some sort. Maybe the biker or the SUV mom had witnessed what had happened to her and had plunged their hands into the water, searching for her. But what she felt was slick and slimy, and it had an odd texture like...*fur,* she realized. Wet fur.

Her eyes had adjusted to the water's darkness somewhat, and she could discern the basic shape of the thing in front of her. It was an animal of some kind: small body, thin legs, slender neck, with a pair of backward curving horns growing from the top of its head. It was an...antelope? At least, that's what she thought it was. The animal had been in the water a long time, and chunks of its flesh had fallen off the bone—or perhaps been bitten off by predators of some kind.

She recoiled in horror, another burst of bubbles leaving her mouth, more water going in. She pushed herself away from the grisly thing, hands waving water in front of her, feet kicking. Her back thumped into something else, and she whirled around and found herself confronted with another dead animal. This one was larger than the antelope, with a round body, trunk-like legs, and leathery skin. It took her a second to identify it because the head had been reduced to little more than a skull with a few shreds of flesh clinging to it. *An elephant,* she thought. A baby one, just like in the picture of the Flood in her Bible.

She tried swimming away from it as well, only to bump into another body, this one a sheep, she thought, although it was so far gone it was difficult to tell. And then she was surrounded by dozens of half-rotting, half-devoured corpses of animals. Some exotic and wild—lions, hyenas, giraffes, rhinos, tigers, wolves, and bears. Others more mundane and benign—horses, dogs, cattle, raccoons, and foxes. They pressed in on her from all sides, a terrible menagerie of death and decay, and she thought of the question she'd asked Grandma when she was a little girl.

What about all the other animals? The ones not on the ark? Were they wicked, too?

Her limbs felt heavy as iron and pinpoints of light sparked in her vision. She knew she couldn't last much longer, that her body's oxygen supply was almost spent. She would die here, wherever *here* was, would become one more corpse in a sea of death.

I'm sorry, Marie, she thought, her mind sluggish and barely able to focus. *So... very... sorry.*

She closed her eyes and waited for the end. But before it could come, something heavy struck her shoulder. Her eyes flew open and she found herself peering at what looked like a rock the size of her head, rope tied around it, the other end stretching upward into the darkness. Without hesitation, she grabbed hold of the rock with both hands and gave a tug. The rope immediately began to ascend, taking her with it.

She rose rapidly, bumping against the carcasses of dead animals as she went. The last vestiges of her consciousness began to fade, and she thought she might die before she reached the surface—assuming there was a surface, that she wasn't trapped in an endless universe of water. But then her head broke through into air, and she drew in a heaving gasp. She immediately began coughing up water, her body expelling it from both lungs and stomach. So violent were her spasms that she lost her grip on the rope. Panicking, she flailed about and her hands struck something hard and solid. Not the rock. This was flat, smooth, and much larger. Her eyes were filled with tears from coughing so much, and it took a moment for her vision to clear, but when it did, she saw she was touching wood. A wall of wood, one so vast she could not see where it ended. The wood was worn and weathered, as if it had been exposed to the elements for a very long time. As she struggled to understand the structure that confronted her, something came falling down from above. At first she thought it was going to hit her, but instead it landed against the wall several feet away. It was a rope ladder, or at least a grisly variation of the concept. This one had been fashioned from lengths of bone and interwoven strips of dried muscle and ligament. She didn't want to touch the disgusting thing, but there was no sign of the other rope, the one with the rock on the end, and she didn't want to remain in the water anymore, not with the legion of dead animals drifting in its currents. She swam over to the ladder, took hold of the meat ropes, set a foot on a bone rung, and began to climb.

The going wasn't easy. Her body was weary from everything she'd been through, and her muscles trembled with fatigue. But she forced herself to continue, one rung after another. The water below was a glossy black, dark clouds filled the sky, and the light held a strange purplish cast. A steady wind blew against her wet body, its cold bite causing her to shiver. *At least it's not raining here*, she thought. She felt the wooden structure rise and fall, the ladder swaying with the rhythm. No, not a wall. A *hull.* This was a ship, a gigantic one, big as an ocean liner, maybe bigger. She had a horrible suspicion what it was, but she didn't want to deal with that then, so she pushed the thought away and continued her ascent.

She had no clear sense of how long she climbed. It seemed as if she'd been doing so forever, as if she'd been born on this rope ladder, would age, grow old, and die here, only marginally closer to her destination then she'd been when she'd started. But there came a time when she reached for the next bone rung and her hand slapped down on a piece of flat wood instead.

She grabbed hold of it, arm muscles quivering weakly, and for an awful moment, she thought she would lose her grip and plummet back toward the water. A fall from this great height would surely kill her, and for the smallest instant she was tempted by the prospect. It might be better to die than face whatever waited for her on the deck of this vast ship. But the temptation passed and she hauled herself over the railing and fell onto the deck. She rolled onto her back, spread out her arms, and lay there for a time, feeling the deck rise and fall beneath her, her entire body throbbing with pain from her exertions. Eventually, the pain subsided a bit, decreasing from agonizing to merely excruciating. She managed to sit up, although the maneuver took so much out of her that her head swam and she thought she might black out. She held onto consciousness, though, and when she felt strong enough, she rose to her feet.

A huge coil of wet rope lay on the deck close by, a rock tied to one end. It was the rope that had been lowered to rescue her, of course, and she wondered at its true purpose. A simple tool for measuring water depth? Maybe.

The deck of the ship was a flat, unbroken plane. No smoke stacks, no cabin for captain and crew. This wasn't a ship to be steered, she thought. Its only purpose was to float. She tried to estimate how long the vessel was, but she couldn't be certain. Several football fields at least, and perhaps much more than that. She wondered what, if anything, was contained in the decks below her feet. Were they empty? Or did they hold the remains of thousands of animals, all of which had died long ago when the water never receded and the stores of food ran out? But it was what—or rather *who*—waited for her on this deck that mattered.

She started walking into the wind, heading for the ship's bow.

How long she walked, she didn't know. Hours, maybe days. The perpetual twilight of this place never varied, making it impossible to gauge time. But eventually she drew near her destination, and the figure that stood waiting for her at the bow, hair blown out behind her by the wind. Valerie joined her sister, and the two of them stood silently side by side, gazing upon the dark water ahead of them. Dead animals bobbed on the surface, large shapes swimming around them, tooth-filled maws occasionally rising out of the water to tear off hunks of meat. Valerie heard a thumping sound and realized it was the noise of the ship bumping aside the floating corpses as it passed. She couldn't bring herself to look directly at Marie, but she could smell her, a combination of wet mud and rot that should've sickened her but didn't. The smell seemed almost natural here. After a while, Marie spoke, her voice thick and wet.

"You should've shown me the picture in the book. You should've prepared me."

"Yes," Valerie agreed.

She reached out and grasped her sister's hand. What little flesh remained to it was soft as clay and gave beneath Valerie's grip. Lightning flashed across the sky in front of them, followed by a crack of thunder so loud the deck shuddered beneath their feet.

Forty days and nights my ass, Valerie thought. The rain never really ended. There were only brief interludes between storms.

As she felt the first drops strike her face she gripped her sister's hand tighter. Marie's finger bones cracked under the pressure, but she didn't complain, and together they sailed onward.

GENE O'NEILL
NIGHTHAWK AND LONE WOLF

MEMO TO STAFF

We are asking all staff to arrive in Calistoga three days early, before 2:00 p.m. on Friday for group orientation. As you know from pre-camp materials, the campers arriving for this month's camp experience are very different this year. They are all boys in the 12- to 16-year-old range from urban environments, but many come from broken homes. In the past most have demonstrated institutional behavioral control problems, including foster home, juvenile detention, and school settings. This has resulted in a disruption of any continuity of discipline and schooling. All of these campers, for whatever reasons, obviously demonstrate poor socialization skills. That they do not cope well with others is an understatement.

So during pre-camp weekend we will have seminars, workshops, and lectures to be conducted by a group of well-regarded professionals who deal daily with children's behavioral issues—including a social worker from Oakland, a pair of clinical psychologists from San Jose and San Francisco, and a professor in Exceptional Children Psychology from Stanford. With their recommendations and guidance, we should be able to anticipate most problems and have some potential good solutions available.

Please keep in mind we will be focusing this month on *three* important areas:

1. Camper/staff safety

2. Developing camper socialization and coping skills in a group

3. Maintaining our normal primary camp goal of instilling an appreciation of Native American values, skills, background, and history.

This will be a challenging group of youngsters. There are growing numbers of these kinds of exceptional children in the state who have never had a camp opportunity of any kind. Our special Native American emphasis here should be an enlightening experience for them. Let's do our best to make this a safe, wonderful, and educational experience for these boys, which will hopefully encourage parents and others to send similar youngsters in the future.

A film major from SF State will be filming with his voice-over during the month. Oscar Owen is also a weekend DJ with the tag Double O, and his appearance and language should be appealing to both campers and staff. Give him your full cooperation. We hope to use this film commercially, making it available to interested groups, counselors, social workers, foster parents, and especially to similar youngsters that we will be recruiting in the future.

—Daniel Manspeaker, Director of Camp Little Bighorn

Double O—filming with voice-over narration, parts to be deleted:

Monday morning at around noon, I'm just hanging out in the background as the big yellow bus rolls into Camp Little Bighorn, an isolated group of cabins in the foothills north of Calistoga in the Napa Valley, near Lake Fallen Sky. I watch as forty-eight young dudes get off the bus looking about furtively, their expressions guarded. Holy ~~shit~~! No boisterous shouting and nervous gaiety, as I expected. This group of dudes, some wearing tattoos, after dismounting the bus, look like they're facing their drill instructors for the first day of Marine Corps boot camp at MCRD or Parris Island~~, though, they look more like a group of young gangbangers getting off a bus to juvie~~.

Although they hide it well with their sullen expressions, I'm guessing they share similar feelings of anxiety, dread, and hostility. They probably wish they were elsewhere. But after leaving the bus, they shuffle nervously in place as they stare at an older man, wearing a beaded headband, long braided gray pigtails, and a buckskin outfit, who is greeting them.

"Welcome to Camp Little Bighorn. I am Daniel Manspeaker, your Camp Director. This is a camp stressing Native American skills, values, and principles. Each of you for the next month will belong to an Indian tribe. The first order of business is getting you to your tribe's cabin. There are six of these cabins. Your group leaders will introduce themselves, and then read off your names and cabin assignments."

I follow with my camera the last group, who are assigned to the Lakota Sioux cabin. Their leader is a lanky, college-age man, who introduces himself as: Crazy Horse.

One boy in this group is very different from his streetwise cohorts. He is slight of build and very shy, hanging back in the group.

After leading the eight boys to their cabin, Crazy Horse says: "You will all now select a Lakota Sioux name from this master list. These will be the only names we will use here during the next month of your Native American camp experience. Any questions?"

There were none.

After selecting their Indian names, the eight campers have a few minutes to store their suitcases and personal gear in small foot lockers under one of four bunk beds, before assembling outside at the fire pit in the center of the circle of cabins for a brief orientation by the camp director, whom I'm sure they all regard as this weird old guy with the odd Indian last name~~, dressed like a clown~~.

SECOND DAY—Letter from Camp

Dear Aunt Ez:

I am doing well.

Everyone here at Camp Little, Bighorn is assigned a cabin with an Indian name, ours is one of the Great Plains Tribes. Lakota Sioux. Everyone in my cabin had to pick an Indian personal name, which is what we call each other here for the next four weeks. My name is: Nighthawk. I kind of like the fierce sound of it in my head when I close my eyes.

Surprise, Auntie: I've made a real friend already! He is called

Lone Wolf, the same age as me, although very blond, bigger, and stronger. He is beginning seventh grade, too, in September, but at a middle school in San Francisco. Tomorrow we begin learning Indian skills, including fish netting, paddling a canoe, and the proper use of the bow and arrow. The Great Plains Indians—most of the tribes here—hunted buffalo from horseback with a bow. So skill in this area was critical to their survival. Neither Lone Wolf nor I have ever drawn a bow and shot an arrow at a target. We will be a bit nervous. But you know I'll concentrate and do well.

Our cabin leader calls himself: Crazy Horse. We have found out that he is indeed strange, to say the least, maybe even crazy. For one thing, he likes to watch all of us shower. He says he's required to monitor our safety at all times. I suppose theoretically someone could slip on a bar of soap and injure themselves (that's a joke of course). Lone Wolf says that our cabin leader is just a creepy perv.

I will write again tomorrow night.

—Love, Luc (Nighthawk)

THIRD DAY—Letter from Camp

Dear Aunt Ez:

Today we had our first campfire and met an orange-headed lady, Red Deer, who is an oral story-teller. She does more than tell a story, she is a terrific one-person play, acting it all out in different voices. She knows a large number of ethnic folk tales, including many that originated with the various Indian tribes. But she decided to introduce herself with one from her original homeland, Ireland.

Red Deer told us a story from the famed Red Branch Tales about the legendary Irish hero, Cu Chullain. He was a mythical figure from the first century of Ireland. He was a bit like Robin Hood in England. But unlike the Sherwood Forest hero, Cu Chullain possessed a mystical ability called Riastradh in Gaelic. This supernatural ability was later translated into English as: Wasp Spasm, because initially one shook visibly as if stung while under its spell.

When Cu Chullain called on this secret ability, he could do all kinds of unusual things, resulting in him never suffering defeat in combat. In a low, mysterious voice Red Deer explained: "Among other skills, he could mentally control the flight trajectory of every spear he threw."

I was enthralled by the exploits of Cu Chullain, the story hour passing much too quickly. After a nice hand from the campers, Red Deer promised she would tell another Red Branch Tale later in the month. But she said that she had many other good ones she wanted to share each night at campfire, including a number of excellent legends from the Great Plains Tribes.

Red Deer is my favorite part of camp, so far. I think I'd like to stay the whole twenty-eight days after all, and hear all her stories. I hope she does tell more about Cu Chullain and his special mental abilities.

Do we have any Irish blood, Auntie? Is that why Gramps is so special?

I will write again soon.

Love, Luc (Nighthawk)

DOUBLE O—filming again with voice-over, no deletions:

After the briefest instruction with a bow, this skinny little guy is hitting only bull's-eyes. It's amazing, his arrows begin wobbling weakly, and then somehow straighten out and forcefully hit the target dead center. Because they eventually win the bowman competition, he's the hero of his Lakota Sioux tribe. He is called Nighthawk. But he should be called Robin Hood or some other expert bowman name.

SIXTH DAY—Letter from Camp

Dear Aunt Ez:

The first week has gone very well. I helped Lone Wolf with his bow-shooting skills, encouraging him to concentrate and visualize the accurate flight of his arrows.

Earlier today, we finished the week with a competition in riding horses bareback, canoeing, swimming, and archery. All the Lakota Sioux did well. In shooting long distance at targets, both Lone Wolf and I shot possibles. That means we put all ten arrows into the target bull's-eye—100 possible points added to the overall tribe score. So the Lakota Sioux won and can wear the White Eagle Feather for Best Tribe Performance, Week One.

But our archery instructor, Swift Arrow, got mad after the archery shoot and yelled at Lone Wolf and me, because he didn't believe that we'd had no previous bow training. And in an angry voice, he said: "You lied and had obviously benefited from advanced training in archery. It would not be fair to others in camp to let you carry a bow and quill of arrows next week during the survival training camp-out in the forest. Lone Wolf was very upset and angry, because we hadn't lied.

I will write again soon, after we return to base camp from survival skills week.

—Love, Luc (Nighthawk)

THIRTEENTH DAY—Letter from Camp

Dear Aunt Ez:

Survival camp-out for five days in the forest was really fun. We learned lots of useful things, like how to start a fire with a tiny bow and wood drill. Of course that was easy for me to do after I concentrated. We learned lots of other stuff, including what plants and mushrooms to eat and what to avoid in the forest. How to track animals and other humans. Lessons in canoe paddling and swimming in Lake Fallen Sky were great—it's cooler out there on the water.

But our tribe didn't win the White Eagle Feather for second week, because there was arrow shooting at pop-up targets while moving about. Very difficult for everyone, including the Lakota Sioux. Lone Wolf and I were not allowed to participate in this phase of the competition. This was an unfair handicap for our tribe's overall score.

And a boy called Big Bear, from the Cheyenne tribe that won, made fun of Lone Wolf and me, because as I've said, we weren't allowed to carry a bow and arrows like everyone else, unable to record a single bull's-eye for our tribe. Big Bear called us losers, sissies, and other names. Lone Wolf said something back, and Big Bear struck him in the face with his fist, giving Lone Wolf a nosebleed. The camp nurse fixed Lone Wolf up. He's fine now. But very angry at Big Bear.

—Love, Luc (Nighthawk)

THIRD WEEK—Memo to Staff

I would like to remind all staff that our primary goal this first month is the *safety* of campers and staff. Unfortunately we've had several incidents, inexplicit accidents/illnesses. The victims have been two staff members and one camper.

Rowdy Jenkins, group leader of the Lakota Sioux, was the most serious, requiring transport to the nearby full-service sanitarium hospital between Calistoga and St. Helena. Medical eye specialists were available there and are treating Rowdy for what they diagnosed as detached retinas. But he does not remember any traumatic blow, fall, or accident that might have caused such an injury. The specialists say this will require surgery and believe Rowdy will probably, at the very least, regain partial sight in both eyes, perhaps full sight with a best case scenario.

Don Weber, our award-winning archery instructor, has been hospitalized with a case of extreme laryngitis—apparently he caught a bug during survival week. Even though no one else demonstrates virus symptoms, it might be wise to keep an eye out for campers developing coughs, runny noses, or such. We do not want any type of cold/flu epidemic outbreak. Don is expected to be released tomorrow, and will be back to work soon, with hopefully a full recovery of his voice.

Elmer Jackson, a camper, a Cheyenne, suffered some kind of injury also during survival week, resulting in several fractured bones to his right hand. Elmer says he fell during tracking while wading in a creek the last day of survival week, and he thinks that's when it might have happened. Strangely, he woke up in severe pain during the first night after returning from the forest. Fortunately, he will be able to finish his last week of camp, but will have his hand in a cast, limiting some activities. His parents have agreed to this after visiting Elmer yesterday.

Please, stay alert. No more unexplained accidents or incidents, people. Let's finish this month with everyone returning home healthy, sound, and well.

—Daniel Manspeaker, Director of Camp Little Bighorn

TWENTY-FIRST DAY—Letter from Camp

Dear Aunt Ez:

I have a confession to make.

The first day of camp, Lone Wolf showed me some magic card tricks he brought from home. I disobeyed you and demonstrated one of the special mental skills taught me by Gramps to Lone Wolf: How I could lift my suitcase without touching it. And I bragged about some of my other special abilities. Of course he wanted to know all the secrets. So I taught him how to do some of my other tricks.

But Lone Wolf has a bad temper, and he used some of the things I taught him in a bad way. He hurt several people here at camp.

I'm terribly sorry. I know you taught me never to reveal any of Gramps' special abilities in public. I guess I just wanted to show off to Lone Wolf.

But don't worry, I made him promise not to use any of them again and hurt anyone else.

Love, Luc (Nighthawk)

TWENTY-FIFTH DAY—Letter from Camp Director

Dear Ms. Vukovic:

Thank you for your letter of concern about your nephew and others in camp. It is true that we have had several unexplained incidents. But these have all been taken care of properly. The three *victims* have all been given necessary medical care and are recuperating nicely. Rest assured that steps have been taken to ensure nothing more of this nature occurs.

There are only three more days left of camp, and I have instructed staff to keep a close eye on your nephew and his cabin mates. I can assure you that he is safe, and we will return him in the same condition as when he came to camp.

Yes, to your question, Luc has done well, especially in camp skills development—one of our most proficient campers with the bow and arrow. During the month, we had hoped to make more progress in development of his group socialization skills. Unfortunately, he remains a bit of a taciturn loner, perhaps his natural temperament.

But this brings me to your apparent major concern about the aggressiveness of one of his Lakota Sioux tribal mates.

Your letter is a bit confusing. There is no one in the entire camp who picked the Native American name Lone Wolf. Nor is there anyone in camp fitting your description. And that includes the four campers from San Francisco. I'm afraid Lone Wolf doesn't exist, at least here at Camp Little Bighorn.

I hope all this eases your stated concerns. We would very much like to see Luc return for camp next year.

Thank you for your support,

—Daniel Manspeaker, Director Camp Little Bighorn

DOUBLE O—filming/narrating the excited boys leaving cabins for the lake and the big final camp competition, the canoe race with deletions:

I'm tracking the Lakota Sioux cabin dudes again, the boys stepping out of the cabin. ~~Whoa—! Two big lads from the Cheyenne cabin, directed by Big Bear with a cast on his hand, throw water balloons. Nighthawk is hit squarely in the face and chest and completely soaked. From his squished up, red face, I know he is very angry. But he is too little and frail to retaliate physically against the bigger bullies.~~

Later during the canoe race, the Sioux paddlers move in too close, bumping and overturning the Cheyenne canoe…the boys all swimming to shore for safety, except for Big Bear with the cast. He tries to swim one-handed, but stops suddenly in the water—

Oh my God!…It's almost as if he is wearing weights on his feet, because he quickly sinks out of sight.

I contact the Camp Director who calls the authorities. All activities are halted, as the authorities investigate the unfortunate drowning. The camp is a confused mess. The campers' guardians have been notified, but no one can leave for a day or so until released by the authorities. Red Deer will tell stories and other activities will be conducted in cabins and circle.

LAST DAY—Double O—filming campers getting back on bus for home, with deletions:

The campers are all now smiling, bumping, and joking with each other. The month has been a great success. Even Nighthawk has a big smile on his face as he climbs aboard.

~~The only really sad note is the death of the camper, which the authorities determined was an accidental drowning.~~

JONAH BUCK

SIREN

August 2, 1917

Sebastian Barnevelder listened as the U-boat slowly failed all around him. As the stricken vessel lay at the bottom of the Atlantic, steel popped and groaned and squealed.

There were a dozen ways to die down here on the ocean floor. Water hissed from tiny fissures in the submarine's seals, filling the cramped, dark space with the icy black sea. The surviving men were unlikely to drown, though.

First the air would go bad and poison them. Or the rising water would squish all the air in the submarine into a smaller and smaller space until the pressure built up and everyone's lungs ruptured.

Most likely though, the incredible pressure of trillions upon trillions of tons of water would crush the U-boat and the men inside like screaming grapes in a wine press. No, nix that.

There wouldn't be time to scream. The water would obliterate them before anyone could blink, let alone scream. The bulkheads would pancake together and reduce the crew to a thin, red gruel. Everyone on board would be reduced to something the size and shape of a wad of chewed gum.

Good, Sebastian thought. He stood in the ankle deep water, so cold he hadn't been able to feel his toes in hours, and watched Captain Englehorn pound on the busted emergency radio unit.

There was no help coming. Even if the radio's guts weren't

spilling out, by the time the German Imperial Navy could steam out to their position, everyone aboard U-697 would be dead anyway.

The red emergency lighting sent ghastly shadows across the captain's face as he glanced up at Sebastian. "Barnevelder, what's the situation in the engine room? Any way we can get in there and access the emergency pumps?"

"No, sir. I can see through the porthole on the door. The hull's completely blasted out. There's nothing left but twisted metal and a little bit of Lieutenant Zeller."

Captain Englehorn nodded but his expression was hollow.

The air inside the submarine always stank of sailors and diesel, but a new smell overwhelmed even those omnipresent odors. The pungent scent of mortal terror hung in the air. It wept out of the pores of every man onboard.

Every man except Sebastian Barnevelder.

Germany had resumed unrestricted submarine warfare against Britain a few months earlier in hopes of bringing the Great War to a close. The German public was hungry, and their army was bled dry in the French mud. Something needed to change, and it needed to change soon.

At the time, Sebastian had hungered for missions like these. Germany's great foe, the United Kingdom, was an island nation. It received its supplies, everything it needed to wage war, from across the seas. Food. Munitions. Colonial recruits. Without those, the British couldn't continue the war.

To a submariner like Sebastian, the math was simple. Knock Britain out of the war, and France would be left to fight Germany by herself. For years the German submarine fleet had been cooped up in coastal waters. Weak-kneed politicians in Berlin feared the international fallout from another *Lusitania*, even if the British often used civilian ships to ferry in war materials.

"Then they brought it on themselves," Sebastian would often tell his wife, Laura, on his rare shore leaves. She would usually purse her lips but not say anything as she sipped her tea. She'd heard this screed every time he came home, and she humored him by allowing him to vent it every time.

Laura grew up in London, the daughter of a Rhenish banker working in one of the company's foreign offices. She'd picked up her tea habit there, something she'd never dropped even after moving back to Germany, and she spoke flawless English.

He knew she didn't approve of the war, but Sebastian had lost a brother in the meat grinder outside Verdun. Above all, he just wanted the war to end before he lost more friends and family, and of course the answer seemed painfully *OBVIOUS* to him.

Many decisions were so much simpler when the consequences were fuzzy, faraway problems that happened to other people. Simple answers to complex problems had an unshakable allure. Let the submarine wolf packs out to hunt, cripple British supplies, and the war would end.

That's why Sebastian had been so thrilled when the orders came down. At long last, the government had called open season on all British shipping. The submarines would be loosed into the Atlantic, sowing destruction in their wake. The war to end all wars would be over by Christmas with the German Empire victorious.

Oh happy day.

The narrow strait between Britain and the rest of the continent was thick with shipping. U-697's torpedoes sent thousands of tons of war material down to the bottom of the sea, taking hundreds of lives with it into the depths.

Sebastian rarely knew what cargo a ship held, and frankly, it didn't matter. The point was to strangle the British one ship at a time, slicing through each individual capillary of their trade network until the nation hemorrhaged itself into peace talks.

Two weeks ago, they sank a Danish ship moving at full steam toward the English coast, the *Haugaard.* A couple of outdated British warships, part of the "live bait" fleet the English maintained to free up their dreadnoughts, protected the *Haugaard.*

Captain Englehorn put a torpedo straight into the *Haugaard*'s guts. The ship blew apart like a vase shattering. Secondary explosions tore the ship to steel confetti before it could even sink beneath the waves. U-697 disappeared into the sea before the rickety picket ships could pinpoint its location.

That was two weeks ago.

A week ago, the submariners took a brief leave in Kiel so the U-697 could restock its armaments and make minor repairs. Merchant ships from all over the world now littered the bottom of the English Channel. They'd gone through all their torpedoes even faster than expected, racking up hit after hit. It was enough to puff him with pride.

Sebastian received a packet of letters when they docked, a true bright spot after working for weeks at a time in the cramped confines of the U-boat. News from home, from his sweet Laura, was a precious commodity. The letter he read last was the most recent from Laura. Her tone had grown gradually bleaker as the war pressed on her.

My dearest Sebastian,

I know you won't approve, but I have decided that I must act. With all the resources devoted to the war effort, there's precious little food being brought into town. I've been eating nothing but canned beets for the last week because it's all I can get from the market. I hear it's only worse elsewhere, that the countryside is starving as all the crops are requisitioned for the army.

That's why I'll be boarding a Danish ship, the Haugaard, *in a couple of days. Denmark is neutral in the war, and the company operating her needs someone who can read and write English for business transactions. All it will take is a quick trip across the Channel, and then they'll board me in London. The ration books here are worthless when there's no food to be had. If the war lasts much longer, I'm worried there will be riots or outright famine or both. It's a hard choice, but I know the British will surrender before they let London go hungry. When the war is over, we'll be together again.*

Stay safe.

Love,

Laura

Sebastian had clutched that letter so hard it tore in his hands. The sudden sweat from his palms smudged the ink until it was unreadable. His stomach filled with hot, panicky acid. He checked the dates on the letter and then checked them again.

The *Haugaard* was entered in U-697's logs as a confirmed kill a few days after the letter was written. Sebastian knew with the certainty of the damned that Laura had been aboard that ship.

Frankly, he didn't even remember much that had happened since he read those words, since they scorched their way into his brain like a red hot brand.

The rest was just a daze. Firing a torpedo at that merchant

marine ship. Launching an emergency dive as a British spotter plane droned over the horizon. Hollow *boom boom booms* as the depth charges poured off the deck of the destroyers overhead. Screeching steel and screaming men as the engine room hull ruptured in a tornado of hot metal and freezing water, sucking submariners into the blackness. Howling, uneven descent into the depths, expecting the submarine to collapse at any second.

Since they'd hit bottom, the screams had stopped. However, the atmosphere inside the submarine was oleaginous with gurgling fear.

Sebastian was the only one who didn't feel it. He could sense it crawling around inside his crewmates on pinching crab legs, wriggling nodules of dread metastasizing in their hearts.

Sebastian was beyond that. He was beyond any feeling except to the black hope that the U-boat would implode soon and end this farce.

He scuttled down the hallway, using the emergency lighting to guide his way. Someone farther back in the crew quarters had firmly lost every last shred of his sanity. "Still more majestic shalt thou rise. More dreadful, from each foreign stroke; as the loud blast that tears the skies, serves but to root thy native oak. Rule, Britannia! Rule the waves: Britons never will be slaves." The voice bawled out a few more verses of "Rule, Britannia!" before warbling off into hysterical laughter.

Something banged into the side of the hull a bit ahead of Sebastian. He twisted his head to listen. This wasn't the creak and groan of stressed metal. This was an entirely different sound, like something outside was knocking on the U-boat's exterior.

Sebastian stopped walking and stared at the opposite wall. There was something about that tapping. It reminded him of something.

Knock-knock-knock. The sound came in an uneven cadence.

He followed the noise like it had sunk hooks into his eardrums and was reeling him in. An icy razor of memory scraped across the inside of his skull, beckoning him to follow the noise as it moved toward the engine room.

Voices cursed and shouted from a nearby doorway. Sebastian glanced inside the radio room. A group of his crewmates stood next to the upended equipment. Heinrich Rosenblum hunched with his back to the wall like a cornered rat while three other sailors surrounded him.

"C'mon, Heinrich. Just put the pistol down," the radioman said.

Rosenblum shook his head. Beads of sweat dripped off his brow. They resembled blood in the red lighting. He held a service pistol in his hand. The weapon looked like an extension of one of the shadows that now lurked in every corner of the U-boat.

One of the other submariners glanced up. "Sebastian, help us talk to Rosenblum. He's got a bad case of the sea sillies."

Sebastian propped himself in the doorway and watched without saying a word. *The sea sillies. That's one word for it.*

Above their heads, the knocking noise came again. Everyone glanced up, as if their eyes could pierce the steel hull and see what was happening outside. Their attention snapped back to Rosenblum as he tried to snake around the closest man, and the other three sailors jerked to cut off his escape route.

"Let's just talk about this for a minute, Heinrich," the radioman said, making soothing hand gestures. "There's still plenty of time for a rescue party to find us. Plenty of air for everyone. We just have to stick things out a little longer."

Sebastian and everyone else in the room knew that no one was coming. There would be no rescue. Not from this black hell. The iron jaws of knowledge couldn't shut out hope, though.

"No. No, I don't want to suffocate down here like a convict in a gas chamber," Rosenblum said. "Can you taste it? The air is already starting to go bad. I'd rather just do it now. Do it quick."

"You can't fire a bullet in here. It could pierce the hull. Then we'd all be in a mess of trouble," the radioman said in his calmest voice. "You don't want that do you? No, just hand us the gun. You can do it."

Rosenblum's eyes looked too wide for his skull. They flitted about like caffeinated bats, never landing on any one of the men but instead ping-ponging around the cramped room.

The knocking sound came again, as if it were trying to get their attention. No one bothered to look up this time. All attention was focused on Heinrich Rosenblum.

Sebastian had thought about taking the same path as Rosenblum a few times since he discovered Laura's demise. He'd just functioned like a piece of machinery each day. His hands didn't care if he was hollow inside. They could perform their tasks on rungs and levers without conscious thought after months of raiding trade routes.

He might have done it, but the throbbing ache inside his soul made it nearly impossible to engage in a course of action. Slitting his wrists with a shaving razor. Blowing his brains across the room. Even jettisoning himself out of a torpedo tube. They were all possibilities, but he always felt like he was trapped beneath a massive boulder, crushing out any self-agency.

The radioman grabbed for Rosenblum's pistol when his eyes darted away. He was too slow. His hand grabbed onto Rosenblum's wrist, and he tried to wrestle the weapon out of his grasp. Rosenblum snaked his arm around, trying to free himself.

"No! No, just let me—"

The pistol went off.

The submarine's walls didn't collapse inward. A billion tons of black water didn't smash their way inside and chew them to bloody lumps. Their world didn't end in a single cataclysmic instant.

But that was only because the bullet went straight into the radioman's chest. He jumped like Rosenblum was a hot stove. Falling flat on his back, he tried to look at the wound in his sternum. He attempted to say something, but all that came out was a wheeze and a streamer of blood.

"*Gott in Himmel*!" Rosenblum shouted, clasping his hands to the sides of his head. More shouting erupted as the rest of the crew stampeded down the cramped halls to see what had happened.

Rosenblum was crying as he pried his hands away and inserted the gun barrel into his mouth, angling the weapon upward. One of the remaining men in the room made a lunge for him, but Rosenblum's finger was already on the trigger.

Another crack of gunfire echoed through the submarine. The top of Rosenblum's head vaulted upward like an egg starting to hatch. Cordite and blood scented the air inside the radio room.

"What the hell is going on?" Captain Englehorn yelled from the control room.

The bullet was lodged somewhere in Rosenblum's skull. If it had catapulted loose, they'd all be dead before their ears registered the gunshot.

The only thing under more stress down here than the ship's

hull was the crew's psyche. Things were starting to fall apart.

Sebastian stepped out of the doorway. All he could feel was a slight twinge of envy that Rosenblum and the radioman had found their own peace. He felt like the last shriveled brown leaf on a tree at the end of autumn, already dead but refusing to fall to the ground for some reason.

He just hoped Laura had died as these two had, quickly and with a minimum of pain. Most likely, she'd been blown apart before she even became aware her ship was under attack. The *Haugaard*'s boilers exploded with the torpedo strike, probably killing most of the passengers and crew in a single smiting blast of fire and steam.

There were alternatives, though.

Drowning was the most obvious. Laura could have been trapped in a room as the ship went down. She could have been crimped in half by collapsing metal. The steam could have burned her until the meat fell off the bone.

And the sharks. Oh God. The sharks...

The depth charge that trapped U-697 down here was a blessing for Sebastian at this point. He would have preferred the explosives simply blew the hull apart altogether. The sweet dark nothingness outside held a certain appeal.

Maybe he'd do like Rosenblum. Sitting down here at the bottom of the sea waiting for the inevitable was a weary business.

That knocking noise came again from overhead, as if it was reminding him it was there. Sebastian could tell that the noise wasn't simply random debris falling from thousands of feet overhead.

This was something natural. Maybe a pale, sightless fish latched its sucking mouth onto the hull, looking for sustenance on the ocean floor. Perhaps a spiny arthropod was impatient to slurp the marrow out of their bones.

That didn't seem right, though. This noise sounded purposeful.

Whatever it was, it was still headed toward the exploded-out engine room. He looked down the dark, narrow hallway. The walls were covered with valves, switches, and meters. Barely an inch was free from pipes or other obstructions.

The knocking came again.

Sebastian pushed away from the coppery scent of Rosenblum's

blood. He walked with one hand against the tilted wall to keep his balance. What was that out there? Why did it sound so familiar?

A shudder suddenly racked Sebastian's frame. He realized where he knew that *knock-knock-knock* patter from.

When Laura was a little girl in London, she broke her leg falling out of a tree. The leg didn't set perfectly, so she walked with a slight hitch. Whenever she moved on a hard surface, Sebastian could always tell her pace was a little uneven from the sound of her footsteps. The knocking had the same rhythm of Laura on a leisurely stroll.

Unbidden, his mind conjured a horrible image of a hunched, crooked figure walking across the top of their hull. The thought of a wraith with his wife's face jittering among the shadows made his blood want to stop and reverse flow through his veins. It was repugnant, ghastly, and all too plausible in the dark unreality his mind had fallen into.

Vague curiosity turned into a burning need to know what that noise was. He didn't want to die with that awful image choking his mind.

He slithered after the noise toward the rear of the ship. The passageway narrowed even further. U-boats were never built for the comfort of their inhabitants, and that only became worse as the ship rested at a drunken angle.

Freezing seawater dripped onto the top of Sebastian's head as he dropped onto his knees to navigate past a bent pipe. Even at a crouch, there was no other way through. The engine room lay just beyond. He'd have to slither on his belly.

Cold metal caressed his stomach as he wriggled past. He lurched to a halt as his belt buckle caught on the pipe. For a moment, nothing gave. He was stuck.

Those odd knocks marched past just overhead. Sebastian could reach out a hand and press it against the opposite side of the bulkhead, and then his fingers would only be separated from the source of those sounds by a thin veneer of steel. He almost did, but then he stopped himself. He wasn't sure he wanted to have any contact, even indirect, with whatever was out there.

It's just an octopus or something investigating our submarine, he told himself. He had to look, though. Now that his imagination had kicked up that image, he couldn't just leave the matter alone.

He had to know, dammit.

With a grunt and a heave, he finally hauled himself free of the bent pipe. He pitched over and landed face first in more cold water. It stank of oil and grease, the submarine's leaking lifeblood. Being submerged in that would be like drowning in Satan's septic tank. Spitting and sputtering, he pulled himself back into a crouch and moved the last few feet forward before steel ended and water began.

The hatch to the engine room stood in front of him. A valve on the door kept the hatch doggedly closed and provided the only seal against the blackness outside. If the ship had plummeted another hundred meters deeper when it sank, the seal would have given way and killed them all.

The footsteps had stopped. *Footsteps.* Sebastian pushed that term out of his mind. No, the knocks, the knocks that reminded him so achingly of Laura, had stopped. All he could hear was the murmur of voices and the creak of stressed metal.

A window sat in the middle of the engine room door. Six inches of treated glass separated him from the cold hell beyond. Sebastian grabbed a flashlight off a nearby rack. He flicked the light on and placed it against the glass, probing the darkness.

Blackness ate into the light like acid, devouring it before it could reveal more than a few feet. He could just make out the rent in the wall from the depth charge. Jagged metal peered at him like the maw of some giant, fanged fish.

Klaus Zeller's body floated at the very periphery of his light, trapped against the ceiling. The man was stuck in here when the sea came crashing through the wall. There wasn't much left of him, and what was there had been smashed and compressed until his body looked like old dough that had been kneaded by crazed bakers.

But that was it. There was nothing else out there. The engine room was completely empty.

Something moved near the blown-out wall. Sebastian swung the flashlight back in that direction, sweat prickling his skin. There was no sign of whatever he'd seen, but his flashlight only reached so far.

His conscious thoughts told him he probably hadn't seen anything. That didn't stop his lower brain from yammering that he sure as hell *had* seen something, some furtive, crawling shape slipping over the rim of the hole and skittering inside.

Sebastian's heart beat a staccato tune in his chest. He stared, pressing his face close to the window. His breath raised little plumes of steam on the glass.

Pale silt danced among the shadows, drawing his eyes everywhere with phantom movement. He couldn't see anything sliding along the walls or crawling across the floor, though. Certainly nothing person-shaped.

Laura's face appeared on the other side of the glass. Sebastian recoiled backward and banged his head against a rail. He dropped the flashlight, and it fell into the dirty water below. The light flickered out, leaving Sebastian with only the distant, fiery glow of the emergency signals. Outside, Laura raised a hand and tapped at the glass with her finger.

"No. Oh no," Sebastian said, unaware his mouth was even moving. That was Laura out there all right...only it wasn't. The ocean had ravaged her beautiful face. Her eyes were simply two dark pits, the sockets hollowed out. Some sea creature had laid a clutch of pale eggs in the sockets, and she stared at him a hundred twitching pupils as the fish embryos within squirmed. Her hair floated around her in a dark halo. Her skin clung to her bones like moth-eaten cloth.

Sebastian's brain was caught somewhere between revulsion, amazement, and wet, sucking insanity. He took a step forward.

Laura opened her mouth and voiced something to him. *It's so cold out here, Sebastian.* Her tongue was gone. In its place, a nest of seaworms had taken root. Her ragged lips kept moving. *Bitte, hilf mir. Please, help me.*

Fingers numb from shock and freezing water, Sebastian rubbed his eyes. The sea's darkness seemed to cling to Laura's very form as she pawed at the thick glass.

Even if he couldn't hear his wife's words, they sliced into his brain like obsidian scalpels. *I forgive you. Just be with me. It's so cold.*

Sebastian's limbs trembled. His mind told him that this wasn't Laura. That this couldn't be Laura. Laura was gone forever. This was something else, something masquerading in Laura's skin, something that fed on the drowned.

But he couldn't deny his wife's pleading lips. She was calling to him. They could be together again. He felt like Odysseus approaching the island of the sirens, knowing doom awaited him and not caring one wit.

Be with me, Sebastian. Be with me forever. What was left of her lips quivered into a smile as he started to turn the wheel to open the hatch.

DAVID J. SCHOW

GILLS

THERE HAD never been a lagoon, brown or black or otherwise; never *really*. Even without the help of civilized humans, the topography of the Amazon Basin both vanished and changed on an hourly basis. Soon only handfuls would remain—pressed leaves and desiccated insects on view in some museum.

Manphibian sat cross-legged in a mesh recliner, on a teak deck which surrounded a pool shaped like Brazil, working his way through a tumbler of iced coffee as the sky over the Valley slowly shaded to nicotine. He thought calmly about his place in this world. Out here, the lung part of his dual-purpose breathing system had to labor thirty percent harder just to sort oxygen from the particulates and feed it to his body's aeration network. He killed the coffee, slurping it through a straw since his fishy lips had never been able to close all the way.

"*Burrraaacck*," he said. He looked close at the webbing between his claws. Mites again. Dammit.

Manphibian had the coolest bathroom in all of Hollywood. Stainless steel fixtures; porcelain trim in aqua. The pool outside had a specially constructed tributary that could feed right into the jacuzzi when the little steel security hatch was raised. The jacuzzi seated four, the shower, ditto, and the in-name-only tub was actually a large bronze dish set into mosaic tile. It looked like the world's biggest birdbath, but Manphibian could extend his arms and legs and do a horizontal cartwheel-revolve inside without ever bumping the rim.

Manphibian stripped away his sunglasses and worked himself over with bug spray and a toothbrush. He did not have teeth, but had found toothbrushes to be excellent tools for cleaning his eusuchian scalework. Then he showered off. The taps were for hot, cold, fresh, or salt. He usually did not bother to dry; lack of moisture was bad for his armored skin and his scale ridges could rip towels to ribbons by the truckload. Besides, his entire house was more or less waterproofed, the most obvious evidence being the layer of hardball rubber that covered the floor everywhere except in his "swamp room."

"*Arroooggh*," he said, with satisfaction.

A studio guy was coming up here for a meeting today. Some new newt from Production. Manphibian felt sure it was to discuss not *a* project, but *the* project—a remake/update of his debut feature film, buzzed and rumored for about a decade now, and counting. The movie that would reinvigorate the franchise and put Manphibian back in the Monster Top Ten of all time.

It excited him.

On the far side of the deck, Sofia was sunning her bush. The very concept of pubic hair was another potent turn-on for Manphibian, whose fluted penis had already telescoped from beneath its protective sheath-plate, self-lubricated with electrolytic secretions. Crotaline tessellations on the head and shaft kept the penis anchored during underwater mating; Sofia called them "pleasure ridges." Women wanted Manphibian because his unique metabolism destroys pesky viruses and invasive micro-organisms—one of the reasons he can regenerate missing parts and live so long. They also wanted him because he was different, and almost never needed to come up for air.

Before wandering back to the deck, Manphibian put his shades back on. They were special goggles, custom-ground to keep the sun from hurting his delicate metallic eyes, and fashioned to overcome his lack of external ears. He checked himself in the bathroom mirror. Smooth.

Manphibian flipped Sofia to hands and knees and mounted her. The species concept of foreplay was unknown and irrelevant to him, although Bryce the agent had mentioned it. Once. The act was finished inside of forty-five minutes. Manphibian had met Sofia at a film retrospective of his work. Her favorite novel was *Mrs. Caliban*, by Rachel Ingalls, and her curiosity was predictable but honest. The amazing thing was that she had stayed with Manphibian even after the gloss of the new or the spice of the different had dissipated. She could have had any weightlifter on Venice Beach. She was possessed of long, tawny legs, small feet, about ten pounds of rail-straight, burnished brown hair, and perhaps the only pair of 38Ds in Los Angeles that were real breasts. Most importantly to Manphibian, she read books. He would sit in his bronze tub and she would share books with him, reading aloud by the antique glow of oil-fed hurricane lamps, her eyes a color Manphibian had never seen before in any creature of the sea—an arid brown, almost tan, like fossilized sandstone beneath a sheen of oil.

One of Manphibian's favorite short stories was about a Japanese man catapulted back to 1745 by the Hiroshima mega-blast, to be mistaken for a sea monster by the Scots who net him. His skin color is "yellow like a slug's belly" and "covered from throat to ankle with brilliantly colored images of strange monsters." Communication is attempted but there is no common ground...hence, obvious monster. Manphibian can relate. That beleaguered Japanese in the story had lacked the benefit of professional representation.

Sofia orgasmed like a broiling thunderhead, plateauing into a weird sort of Zen state. When Manphibian disengaged, she kissed him and jumped into the pool to paddle around. The way human beings swim amused Manphibian; like dogs trying to fly. The way Sofia swam just aroused him. Sometimes he stroked up from beneath, to penetrate her as she floated. He had to remember not to hold her under too long.

The pool was always clean. In the matter of the elimination of bodily waste, Manphibian did not suffer what Bryce unfortunately refers to as the "goldfish syndrome."

Manphibian's backstory was pretty much a rags-to-riches thing. Enroute from South America, he did bayou time, making friends with the water witches and the Peremalfait. His nostalgia was for python jerky, alligator wine, and mocha native girls by the village-full. In California, he could live like a king. Down in the Amazonas, he could be a god.

So why was he still here, outmoded by decades? The ongoing mutation that was his lifeforce had vacu-formed him into an antique. Today, sitting by his anti-linear pool, Manphibian had himself become nostalgia. So…why?

Manphibian knew "why" the day he had met Sofia at the seminar. The day a crowded auditorium had stood and applauded his old black-and-white adventures in 3-D. Perhaps that was the day that he admitted he was hooked. It was the reason he was waiting around, today, right now, for some chinless VP of Production to toss him a table scrap.

Sometimes, when Manphibian got depressed, he drove his Dodge Marlin all the way out of Mulholland to the sea. The last time he did this, he was mugged by bangers who stole his Platinum Card. Now Bryce, the agent, wanted him to have a bodyguard.

Dixie Kay Snow, Manphibian's very first cinematic leading lady, had called to ask if he could help her get a new agent. Not many parts were being cast for ingenues whose prime had slipped past the spoilage date decades ago. Then she asked if she could borrow ten grand. Manphibian sent her a check for three, knowing he'll never see *that* money again, even though his tax bracket still hovered at forty-eight percent, due mostly to his participation in merchandising.

Overall, Manphibian did not go out as much as he used to. While he enjoyed celebrity in cautious doses, he resented being asked to stand in the koi pond at the French Quarter Restaurant while snickering people snapped stupid photos with cheap, idiot-proof cameras. Every fucking time.

"I THINK my client was seeking more of an ecological feel," Bryce told the studio guy. "You know—a save-the-rainforests sort of vibe."

The enemy, whose name was Shelby something, nodded importantly. His college major had been "nod." Manphibian already hated Shelby's suctorial mouth.

Bryce was sitting on the waterproof sofa, dramatically framed by a floor-to-ceiling aquarium stocked with outrageously colored exotics. Manphibian's actual snack tank was back near the pantry because it was not built for ostentation. Bryce was backlit, the room light falling to place Shelby in the interrogation hot spot.

All this negotiative strategy had been mapped for Manphibian earlier; now Bryce expounded, for Shelby's benefit:

"Tens of thousands of acres are getting cleared down there, day to day, for three reasons—timber, fuel, and agriculture. As a metaphor, it's irresistible in terms of plot—the bad guys, in messing with Manphibian, are jeopardizing a one-of-a-kind intelligent creature in the process."

Just a week ago, Manphibian had read the latest hopeless attempt at a screenplay. No meat to it. Just by-rote formulaic monster vomitus. If there had been any meat to the story, or characters, or plot, then the writing would have classed as butchery...but it lacked any emotion so strong.

But Shelby the Development Nod had a blank, puzzled expression marring his soft face.

Bryce pressed dutifully on. "Manphibian stands for everything that is ancient and enduring and on the verge of being lost. For this story to get up and walk, it's got to evolve some legs. It needs a subtext. Some depth."

Shelby the Nod moved his head around. "See, the major problem is, I think we need a *new* version of Manphibian. A kinda nineties version."

Manphibian and Bryce stared at each other. It was as if the proposal had been to update the title of Poe's "City Beneath the Sea" to "Bite the Brown Bubbles."

The Nod expanded on his brilliant creative epiphany: "See, I showed the original Manphibian flick to my kid. He's thirteen. And he *wasn't scared*."

They waited. Scary was easy. Put a claw-tip right on the wet surface of someone's eyeball and you got *scary*.

"See, we think the uh, monster needs a redesign." He unveiled a xerox of a sketch.

Scary? thought Manphibian. Shelby's teen bratling should get a glimpse of his dad, naked with a hard-on.

The critter on the paper had a humanoid torso with extra abs and the muscle cut of a comicbook superhero. The legs were backward-jointed, like those of a dog. The head was snaky, blunt as a lead bullet, and hanging off the end of a neck straight out of Loch Ness. Its hands were too goddamned big. It had great big scary teeth and no pupils in its eyes.

"See, the artist is going to stab at another draft, 'cos this is basically what *we* like, except, of course, that women have got to want to uh fuck it."

Human women had to be sexually attracted by this ostrich-legged, peeny-headed slime worm. Kids would yowl, *let's get **TWO** of the action figure with Real Kung-Fu Stupidity and Glow-in-the-Dark Agenda! "Aarrraaaacccck*!" Manphibian frowned. Suddenly the room smelled like anchovies. Perhaps marinated in arrack.

"You're dead wrong, Shelby, and I'll tell you why," said Bryce. "If you say the name Manphibian, everybody knows what you're talking about—even people who've never seen the movies. You're messing with an icon."

"Every other monster we own, we've remade," said Shelby. "Updated them and redressed them and kept them parallel with the times. Didn't hurt a one."

"None of those remakes were hits."

Manphibian noticed that the drawing vanished as quickly as it had been produced. It was awkward and grotesque, not gracile, not logical; a bogey to be crudely Frankensteined from liquid rubber and toxic catalysts. Inside this soulless fake would be a wage-scale guy who hated his job.

"Doesn't matter. The originals were B-features. Bottom of the double bill."

"They're B-features with enough time behind them to resonate. You weren't even around when they premiered."

No, in fact, Shelby the Nod had not been even a concept back then, let alone a pitch. To Manphibian, Shelby looked about thirty-five human years old, max.

"And we're not talking about an aged actor, either," Bryce kept on, flinging both syllables of *ag-ed* at Shelby like daggers. "Manphibian doesn't age like humans. He'll be ready for action when we're dust. He could certainly kick your ass around the court, right now."

Manphibian crossed his legs and folded his claws over his knee, flexing the fins on his forearms so the stiletto spines fanned aggressively out. It would be wonderful to kick Shelby's ass. Or to maybe vise one butt cheek in each claw and split Shelby up the dotted line like a zip strip.

"Do you know who wrote the draft of the script you have?" Bryce was confident of Shelby's answer.

"You know I inherited this project when Allan Arnold Whitner left the studio," said Shelby, crunching the ice in his already-depleted coffee cooler.

"Not exactly factual," said Bryce. "You're here to fish, because Allan Arnold Whitner was fired by Samantha Coltrane, who paid half a million for a *Jaws* retread scooped up by her two favorite comedy writers. Samantha doesn't want the investment to sit on the shelf. You don't want Manphibian, so clearly you're here to lube up our rear ends before darling Sam rugs the franchise out from underneath us. You want us to sign off on the licensing rights. You want to own Manphibian the way Universal Studios owns Bela Lugosi's face."

Manphibian had heard two stories about old Bela's visage, and the images and tie-ins it represented. One was that Bela's heirs had sued and lost the right to a cut of the franchise. The other was that they had won, then lost their right to a cut on appeal. Of course, old Bela had not *really* been Dracula—maybe that had been the big boobytrap of his life.

Shelby was cornered, black eyes darting for escape routes. He employed the usual desperation move, which was to shift the spotlight of blame onto the writers. "Now, those guys Cangrejo and Lampreé are not just comedy writers. They're good writers. They wrote three in a row for Samantha that yanked a hundred-mil-plus each. Their stuff is tank-proof. You shouldn't judge—"

"I bear them absolutely no malice," said Bryce. "They took a pay gig offered by their producer. I probably would have done the same. But all you have to do, to tell their hearts weren't in it, is read the script."

Manphibian nodded in agreement. "*Orrrrrpp!*"

Sofia drifted through with most of her R rating covered and distracted Shelby the Nod by recharging his glass. Playing hostess interested her for about five minutes at a time in real life, but it permitted Bryce and Manphibian a vital huddle. Before Sofia poured, Manphibian made sure there were burst mites in the coffee. She winked at him like a child playing spy.

"It's a railroad, and we're on it, and the tracks go straight off the cliff into the nearest and most convenient abyss." Bryce had a knack for summation.

"*Graaaaah*," said Manphibian.

"But you have a power old Bela didn't have. We can't stop

their moronic idea for a movie. We can't stop the movie. But we *can* stop them from calling it you-know-what. And if they can't say the magic name, they *have* no remake of anything. Because all the merchandising is shackled to it. They can't have any 'Manphibian'-trademarked toys and snacks and CD-ROMs on the racks in time for Exmas—because *you're* Manphibian, and they can't touch your name and cut you out without us swooping in piranha-style."

Manphibian liked that. *Piranha style.*

"I mean, I guess they *could* call it *Manphibian-**LIKE** Creature from a Darkish, Not Totally Dissimilar Lagoonal Pond...*"

Manphibian *urrrped* his approval. Bryce could be a funny guy. He could make monsters laugh.

"The trade-off is this. You can't let them know how badly you want to be in this movie, because they'll just use your desire to do things right to leverage you out. But if you tell me you can live without it, just for now, I'll fucking rip them wide on merchandising and in two years we'll have enough money to make our own version. James Bond did it and Frankenstein's Monster did it and we can do it for you. Because you've got the time on them. You can wait forever and they'll be gone tomorrow. This asshole Shelby will be a memory by the time we manage to get three people into the same room together for a new meeting. There'll be some other big butt warming his useless desk. Hell, at that point, maybe Samantha Coltrane will have moved on and maybe we'll get a person who has some respect for what you do. So what do you say, Man?"

Manphibian ruminated Bryce's proposal, bobbing his knobby forehead at the key points. The time angle was particularly interesting. American moviemakers really needed to take a more Asian view of long-term cycles instead of using the next two weeks as their event horizon.

Shelby was slurping his third mite-laden iced coffee and trying to see Sofia's tits at every opportunity. Manphibian sucked several deep breaths, the delicate lamellae below his jaw flowering to grab air to oxygenate his attack systems. When he was pissed off he could literally swell to a size even more intimidating than his normal seven-foot-three. His spines extended and his eyes went that peculiar flat silver color which indicated he was not in the jolliest of moods. He glided up behind

Shelby as silent as a mime. He opened his massive webbed claws; at full flex, fifteen inches from thumb to pinky talon. He thrust out his chest like a Ray Harryhausen dinosaur and cut loose with a window-rattling "*Hooorraaaar*."

Shelby the Nod blew a fan of coffee and crushed ice out of his nose, urinated in his pants, and was out the door inside of ten seconds, stumbling three times and losing a shoe as he fled.

He looked pretty damned scared.

Manphibian thought that later tonight he should pay Shelby's slacker brat a visit, too.

DURING THE time absorbed by the meeting, seventeen square miles of Amazon rainforest had been consumed. The paper used for the injunctions filed at Bryce's behest could easily have covered the Ponderosa—twice—while rare species of birds and insects skipped the "endangered" phase and did a smash cut straight to extinction. Cattle now grazed on the clear-cut acreage not used for the manufacture of cocaine. Intrepid explorers seeking backwaters threaded with subterranean cavern networks which concealed ageless monsters would be disappointed by the wasteland awaiting them.

There was only one lasting way to make a proper lagoon, one that could engird and hold the slippery ghosts of myth: One-third stock footage, one-third backlot, and one-third location shooting.

The notice in the *Hollywood Reporter* bespoke the commencement of principle photography on something called *Gills*—a hasty retitling of Shelby the Nod's beloved no-brainchild. It still depressed Manphibian, who tore out the page, crumpled it, and consigned the wad to his low-flush toilet. Advance heat on the underwater creature feature had nonetheless caused Manphibian merchandising to come to a rapid boil.

Dark, sinister, foreboding, beautiful lagoons—the only place they could last is in the collective memory of the people whose imaginations have been enchanted by them. Manphibian knew that in the jungle, he could be a god, accepting forbidden sacrifices and watching tribal dancers shake virgin booty. And when the tribe had no further retreat, when their native land ran out, it would all crash and burn. Past that life there would be nothing. The wilds are always conquered, and are thus impermanent…

…unlike Manphibian, who swam in powerful, meditative

strokes through filtered, clear water, thinking that it is better to make a movie commemorating such loss than to actually suffer it. He thought about forbidden ceremonies. Erotic rituals. Hollywood bullshit. Goldfish syndrome, in terms of guys like Shelby the Nod.

Manphibian relaxed by his pool in the hills, pondering his place in this world. Perhaps he will have the pool repainted to a jungle theme—reeds and weeds.

His thoughts were about the fear people feel when their windshields are shattered on the freeway by imbeciles armed with marbles and Wrist-Rockets. Fear of drive-bys and psychos and the random quake that could kill you with a piece of your own home. Fear that ran the gamut from getting your mail dipped to losing your sense of identity.

Manphibian thought about fear. About squandered natural resources. About lotus, and laurels.

That haven for joggers and make-out duos, the Lake Hollywood Reservoir, was so close, he could walk from here. And even though his mouth was not built to do so, Manphibian smiled.

ANTHONY WATSON

THE EVERLASTING

WAVES CRASH against shingle, expending the last of their energy in an explosion of spray, the foam reflecting the light of the moon above in a shimmer of silver. Pebbles tumble and roll as the spent water recedes, the noise of them adding to the roar of the ocean, the shushing of the waves as they hit land, fall back, hit land, fall back…

Wind rushes through the marram grass atop the dunes, its force dissipated amongst the tall, dry reeds, shaking and bending, giving voice to them—that voice a cacophonous whisper that fills the air.

*Be with me…*the voice says. *Forever…*

HE AWAKES with a start to the sound of rain hammering against the windows, an insistent rhythm beating against the glass. Pale lunar illumination filters into the room, casting weak shadows against the wall. Snakes of water writhe slowly downwards, their image magnified and projected so that the wall itself seems to shimmer and contort.

…with me…

He hears the words even above the hammering of the rain, the howling of the wind, the sea crashing against the shoreline below the house.

He smells her then, the scent of her filling the room with its floral bouquet and feels the tears prickling his eyes once more. More tears, when he thought that he must surely have cried himself dry by now…

"We're creatures of water," she'd said, *"it's our very essence…"*

That essence spills from his eyes, leaves tracks down his face which mirror those on the window, on the wall. "Sarah…," he manages to say, the word catching in his throat, his voice faltering between first and second syllable.

A noise comes from outside the bedroom, a creak of floorboard then footsteps moving away. Alone as he is in this ramshackle house, the sounds are not a source of fear to him, rather it is with excitement, anticipation that he clambers from his bed, crossing the bare floorboards quickly to the door of the bedroom.

On the landing he feels the coldness of the water on his feet, hears the splashing his hurried steps make. Pausing, he fumbles for the light switch, flicks it on. The dull glow of the bulb, slowly warming to full illumination, casts its light over the flooded floor. Water pools around his feet, covers the dark mahogany floorboards, trickles over the landing edge to fall (like tears) to the hallway below.

YOU STAND, together, on the headland, gazing out to sea. A leaden sky is reflected in the gray water, the surface in constant motion, slowly undulating like the breathing of some massive beast. Drizzle hangs in the air, clings to your face, wets it, that wetness cooling immediately in the breeze which is a permanent companion to this exposed outcrop of rock.

"It's beautiful," she says, turning to face you, looking deeply into your soul with those pale, blue eyes, the weight of emotion held in her gaze emphasising the words she speaks in whispered tones. "We have to buy it." She turns, breaking the connection between you, spins round to once again regard the expanse of water that surrounds you. "Whatever it takes…"

And you don't answer, because there is no need. You take a step forward, take her hand in yours, squeeze it gently. She'd known what your answer would be the moment she'd looked into your eyes, known for sure what you would say.

A gust of wind rushes past you, strong enough to knock both of you off balance. Your grip tightens momentarily around her hand but her response is to laugh, a sound both joyful and full of anticipation of your life together in this remote place.

"I want to stay here forever!" she shouts. "Forever and ever!" And you laugh along with her, sharing her dreams, her joy.

HE STANDS alone, on the headland, gazing out to sea. Waves crash on the jagged shore far below, the ever-present wind rustles through the dry stalks of marram grass, the sound like that of a thousand angry rattlesnakes.

The house stands behind him, empty—oh, so empty—and brooding, looming over him in a way that now seems oppressive—a far cry from the days when he (*they*) regarded its appearance as dramatic and romantic.

His search last night had been fruitless—no more than he had suspected it would be, truth to tell—she had not been there, nor had any trace of her. Her scent, not the fragrance of the perfume she would sometimes wear but the smell of *her,* had gone when finally he had returned to the bedroom. He had read once that smell was the most evocative of senses, that nothing was more effective at recalling a memory than re-experiencing the smell associated with it. As he'd slumped back down onto the bed the truth of that theory had asserted itself, manifest as yet more tears against which he had to screw shut his eyes.

Sleep had not come easily but eventually he had succumbed, tossing and turning, waking frequently but only to the relentless hammering of the rain against the window. There had been no water on the landing this morning, no sign that she had been there. Perhaps it all had been a dream, no more than a romantic cliché, a trick engineered by his grieving mind.

He has no recollection of how it is he came to be standing here, no memory of breakfast or of even getting dressed. Here he is though, back in the place where their adventures had begun. The start of everything. Always it is here, to this place of memories, he comes, drawn by something beyond his ken, something intangible yet compelling.

Something, or some*one.*

"Where are you?" he asks, but his words are lost in the wind; in the whispering of the grass; the crashing of the waves.

"WHERE WERE you?" you ask, failing to hide the panic in your voice, "I've been frantic..."

She smiles, a slight tilt of her head betraying her amusement, her eyes sparkling in collusion. "Oh you're so sweet to worry like that," she leans forward to playfully peck you on the lips. "I was down on the shore. There's a storm coming in over the sea, I just wanted to watch it, it's so dramatic!"

You sigh, feel your panic slowly replaced by annoyance. "Why didn't you say something, tell me where you were going? You shouldn't go off wandering on your own, not after..."

*She interrupts your words by leaning into you once more, pressing her lips against yours. Her arms wrap around you, hold you tight (*forever...) *and you respond in kind, hug her even more tightly to yourself, never wanting to let go.*

"I'm safe down there," she says, breaking the connection between you to whisper the words. "It's such a special place..." and then she's kissing you again, pressing hard with her lips, making you respond, your hold on each other loosening, becoming a caress...

This time, when you break away from each other once more, you look at her face and see the serenity in her features, eyes closed, a smile playing across her lips. And then a coldness sweeps through you, the protective barrier of the lie that everything will be okay *has built around you crumbling as you see her open her eyes, or rather—terrifyingly—her* eye, *the left lid staying in place, refusing to move. You see the incomprehension in her right eye, watch as it turns to fear, reflecting that of your own as you reach for her again...*

THE SURFACE of the water in the pan starts to shimmer and undulate as it reaches boiling point, swirling currents beneath its surface dislodging the small bubbles lining the base of the pot. In seconds what was once smooth and still has become a swirling mass of exploding bubbles. He upends the bag of pasta, empties its contents into the boiling water and turns down the gas.

As if on cue the telephone rings, its shrill tone echoing through the empty house. He stirs the pasta sauce, bubbles popping on its surface like lava, and makes his way towards the insistent ringing.

"Yeah, hello..."

"Dave! Hi, it's Mark!"

"Hi, Mark, what can I do for you?"

"Just calling to see if you're okay and if you've got anything on Friday night?"

Immediately he feels the tightening in his stomach, the burn of acid as what is now his reflex response to any suggestion of interaction with the outside world kicks in.

"Only we're going out, a few of us, getting Chinese and we were wondering if you wanted to come along…?"

He hears the pessimism in his friend's voice, knows that Mark is expecting him to decline the invitation. He always does, this is the routine he has now fallen into. He simultaneously hates Mark for bothering him and loves him for caring enough to persist with his invitations.

"Well, I, err…"

"Come on, Dave." There's a hint of irritation in his voice now. No more than to be expected. "It's no big deal, just a few drinks, some food. It'll be a laugh!"

And, for a moment, he is almost swayed—if only through a sense of guilt—to just say yes. Then again, why not allow himself a bit of normality? Why keep punishing himself like this?

Something nags at him though, an important piece of information hidden away in the recesses of his subconscious. The date…

"Friday? That's the twelfth, yeah?"

"Errr…yes, that's the twelfth. Is that significant? Usually it's Friday the thirteenth you have to watch out for you know…"

"No, no," he feels the relief flooding his body, washing through it. He has found a reason to turn down the invitation. "It's just that it's the spring tide that night."

The pause as Mark tries to comprehend the meaning of what he has just heard seems to stretch for an eternity. Eventually he chuckles, the sound tinny, rasping down the telephone line.

"And that's relevant because…?"

Because she's now truly a creature of water, because the ebb and flow of the ocean has become her heartbeat, because the crashing of waves against the shore is her passion, the tumbling of pebbles on the beach in the wake of the retreating waves her whispered entreaties…

Because water is her power, her strength and…

"Dave! Dave, you still there?"

He gives no answer, could never explain away his words, his thoughts, his *understanding* to his friend. This is my truth, he thinks, not yours...

"Dave! What's going on mate? What's wrong—I don't..."

He hangs up, brings the conversation to an abrupt end. Replacing the phone in its cradle he walks, as if in a daze, back into the kitchen. The phone starts ringing again. He pays it no heed, instead continues walking towards the cooker where he sees the white froth of bubbles slowly spill out over the top of the pan to drip onto the hob beneath, water turning to steam with a hiss, the clouds dispersing to tendrils which hover for scant seconds before disappearing completely like half-glimpsed ghosts. The ghosts of water.

"WE DON'T really see each other anymore," she says.

"What do you mean?" you ask. "We see each other all the time."

"No, I don't mean that. We're either apart from each other or, when we're together, we're like one person, we know each other so intimately. Oh, I don't know, I'm not explaining this very well. We don't observe *each other anymore. I think we look at other people, strangers, more intently than we do each other..."*

"But that's a good thing," you interrupt. "It's great that we're so comfortable with each other..."

"Yes, yes it is, but wouldn't it be something special to recapture that initial thrill, the first time you see someone you're attracted to; look at the way they hold themselves, the way they move, the way they interact with the world."

"It's an interesting concept," you say, still unsure as to where exactly this conversation is going. "So, what're we going to do about it?"

And so you make plans, arranging to go to the same café but arrive separately and sit at different tables. You are both aware that the other is there but act as if alone, all the time casting glances at the other, observing from afar, truly seeing *each other.*

Once or twice your eyes meet, the two of you caught in simultaneous surveillance, each time the contact is ended immediately by a look away, a sudden profound interest in the food on the table in front of you. You are the first to leave, unable to cope with the erotic charge coursing through your body. The temptation is there to stop at her table on the way out, to take her hand, kiss her, embrace her, to revel in the shock and surprise of the other diners…

But you walk straight past her, out into the street without even a glance.

Your lovemaking that night is the most intense either of you has ever experienced.

The following morning, as the first gray light of dawn creeps through the window you exchange whispered declarations, voices husky, the words so softly spoken they are almost lost amidst the sound of the sea crashing against land far below you.

"I love you…"

"I love you…"

"Forever…"

HE SITS on the beach, the small stretch of sand between the outcroppings of rocks and the otherwise pebbled shore. Behind him the dunes throw a barrier across the path that winds its way up the cliffs to his house.

The sound of the sea, of the waves breaking softly against the sand, is a soothing one in the twilight which surrounds him. The day which is now drawing to a close is one which has been lost to him. Has he been here since the morning? He cannot remember but his feelings at this realisation are not those of worry, of concern that he is losing his mind, rather they bring a sense of contentment, that nothing matters, that this is normal.

Except, of course…

He carries his loss like a stone weight deep within him, a physical thing that lies inside, weighing him down. It is the same sensation as the longing he had felt in the early days but—whereas he could cope with that earlier situation because of the knowledge that the separation, the missing of her would be a temporary thing…he is afforded no such luxury now.

Absent-mindedly, he trails his fingers through the damp sand, leaves parallel grooves in the smooth surface. Water seeps into them from the saturated ground, welling up like tears in eyes.

The moon appears on the distant horizon, emerging from the bank of clouds that have thus far hidden its rising. The sun is only recently set and the full moon reflects its dying light, a bright orange orb floating above the sea, its reflection split into a multitude of fragments which ripple and morph on the ever-moving surface of the water.

This, the spot where she walked into the sea, out of his life—forever. This, the spot where she scrawled the words in the sand that would be his last memory of her, the inscription itself now a memory too, the words long gone, taken away by the tide just as she herself had been.

I love you, she had written, *forever.*

YOU AWAKEN to bright sunshine, shield your eyes against the intensity of the light, made even brighter by the white curtains which slowly sway from side to side in response to the breeze which blows through the open window.

You are alone in bed, Sarah is gone, already risen. Usually a deep sleeper, of late she has found it hard to make it through the night without waking. And with that thought the day becomes that much darker, the unavoidable reality of her situation—of your—*situation crowds out every other thought, the pall that will lie over the day already manifest.*

You rise, pull on your dressing gown and make your way downstairs.

She lies on the floor, just visible beyond the blanket box that serves as a coffee table. You run to her, cradle her in your arms, fearing that the worst has happened, that the inevitable has arrived ahead of schedule, that she is gone.

As you hold her you feel how limp her body is, the only movement the fluttering of her chest as her lungs seek desperately to pull oxygen into her unresponsive body.

"Wake up!" The force and urgency of your words hidden in the whisper which is all your terrified state allows you.

And then a movement. Her eyes flicker open, and she stares at you, eyes boring deep into your soul. Awareness slowly fills those pale eyes with fear and you watch as tears well up in them to spill over and run down her cheek.

"I'm sorry…," she says, the words barely audible but strong enough to break your heart so that all you can do is hold her tighter still, to tell her, "It's okay"—hating yourself for the lie—and to kiss away her tears, the taste of them salty, like brine, like the sea.

HE AWAKENS, finds himself sprawled on the wet sand and shivers as the coldness hits him. Water laps at his feet, his boots already soaked. Cursing, he drags himself to his feet but stops, still kneeling, as he sees the word written in the sand.

Forever.

The word sends a shiver through him, this time far stronger than those the cold which has seeped into his bones has brought about. At the sight of it, memories flood back, memories of the morning when he'd run down to the beach to find that devastating message and had realised that the woman he loved had left him, had somehow found the strength to make her way down here, to write the words in the sand and then…

"I can't live like this," she'd said on so many occasions, *"not that you can call this a life…"* And, selfishly, he'd always talked her out of doing anything…drastic, unable to contemplate life without her. Willing to let her suffer to avoid having to do so himself, waiting for the day when he would find her lying still for the last time. The tears he'd cried that day when she had put an end to everything, to her—*their*—suffering, had not just been for the loss of the woman he loved, but also for the fear that her last feeling would have been one of guilt, for going against his wishes…

"I'm sorry," he says and gets to his feet, tears prickling at his eyes.

It is as he rises, and steadies himself on legs stiff from cold, that he sees the other words in the sand.

Three words again but different from last time. Whereas before the message to him had been a statement, a confirmation—a condolence perhaps, this time they are a request. Not "I love you" this time but "Be with me."

A giddiness rushes through him, threatens to topple him to the sand, and he breathes deeply to calm the tremors which course through his body. Memories of that night, when she had spoken these same words, had awoken him with them, come to him, and the shaking of his body increases. Tears well once more in his eyes and his hands are cold against his cheeks as he wipes them away.

"Be with me…"

The shock of hearing the words spoken, even as he reads them again, releases a surge of adrenalin which spreads slowly from the small of his back, creeps along his spine.

Waves crash, the wind whispers through the marram grass. Perhaps he has misheard, interpreted those everyday sounds as something he so desperately wants to hear. But the words in the sand...

"Be with me..."

He turns, feet scraping divots into the sand which immediately fill with water. Turns to look out across the water, towards the sound of the voice. *Her* voice.

The sea glows with eerie phosphorescence, the white tops of the small waves illuminated by the distant moon. Spray blown by the breeze which accompanies the incoming tide wets his face, but he makes no move to wipe it away, intent as he is on staring out to sea, to see...her.

He chokes back a sob, raises a hand to bite the knuckle of his index finger. "Sarah..."

She is there. He can see her now. Bathed in her own luminescence she stands in the water, arms outstretched towards him. Beseeching him.

"Be with me..."

For a moment he cannot move. But only for a moment because then he is walking forwards, towards the water, towards her. Even as the water splashes over his feet, his gaze remains fixed upon her, the glowing shape that is his one true love, waiting for him to join her.

The water is up to his knees before he feels the true coldness of it. As he walks, so it resists him, a physical barrier to prevent him from reaching her. He hates it; for taking her and now for impeding his path back to her.

Be with me...

The words sound as if they have come from inside his own head but he ignores this for he can still see her, ahead of him, in the water.

He reaches out his own arms, ready to embrace her. The water now up to his waist, pushing against him, pushing him back.

She smiles.

Be with me...

Through his tears he returns the smile. His heart beats so fast now because of the love which fills it.

Forever...

BRUCE BOSTON

RIVER WATCH

THE RIVER arrived in early spring. Only a thin trickle at first, meandering across the plains from the northern hills, it chose a course along a gully on the town's eastern front.

Ours was a dry and dusty land. There was little that grew or thrived here, little to recommend it beyond its quiet isolation. Founded in the middle of nowhere for no reason anyone could remember, ours was a town that seemed destined to die likewise, a way station on the way to nothing in particular.

The river changed all of that. The trickle grew to a rivulet and then a stream and finally, cutting its own channel in the dusty earth, it took on sufficient depth and breadth so that it could be dubbed a river proper. And a fine one at that.

The waters of the river were clear and pure, a deep blue that reflected the open sky above. On its banks where only hardy patches of scrub grass once survived, rushes grew in profusion and wildflowers bloomed, filling our landscape with splashes of color.

Fishermen were the first to explore the river. Although they had never fished before, for our town knew nothing of such matters, their catches proved plentiful. Trout and salmon and other fish we had yet to learn the names of graced our plates and became specials in the local restaurants.

Young children began to play along the edge of the river and wade in its shallows. Older children and some adults ventured beyond the shoreline to swim in its cool waters and explore their limpid depths.

Boats began to ply the river, not only pleasure craft but those providing travel or commerce. Where the waters had pooled to form a natural harbor, a pier was constructed for the boats to dock. Strangers arrived from faraway cities we had heard of yet few had visited.

The town changed and developed a different atmosphere. Those who were the first to prosper from the river began to take on airs and dress in finery. And the rest of us, prospering in turn, soon followed their example.

There was talk of building a bridge across the river so the town could be extended. Some suggested a railroad that would increase commerce by carrying goods to and from the river. A resort complex that could summon a healthy tourist trade was proposed. Our mayor appointed several committees to investigate such projects.

Then both the river and its effect upon our world began to change. Like a confidence man who at first convinces you that all is well with his easy good looks and charming smile, and only gradually reveals the duplicity in his character, the river began to show its darker side.

Some discovered too late that the currents of the river could become inexplicably swift and often concealed treacherous undertows. Naturally there were drownings. A pregnant woman miscarried while bathing in the river and blamed it for her misfortune, claiming the waters had sucked away her unborn child. Though there may have been little credence to such a charge, other complaints followed, blaming the river for rashes and headaches, fevers and chills. And it was true that in the riverside rushes mosquitoes and other insects bred that could transmit disease.

Concerned citizens rightly observed that the strangers the river had carried here and who now lived among us, with their so-called modern ways, were a pernicious influence on the public consciousness. A League of Decency was founded to stem such corruption and protect the morals of our youth.

When the winter rains came, the river exhibited a fierceness we had never anticipated. The number of drownings increased greatly. Bodies washed ashore, white and bloated, some of them so waterlogged and transfigured by death they could not be identified.

In one storm that lasted three days the river raged beyond its banks, destroying structures that had stood for decades, wiping out entire families, leaving others homeless and businesses in ruins. Boats broke loose from their moorings and floated downstream. Most of the pier was washed away and had to be rebuilt at considerable expense to the public coffers.

The days on which the river appeared clear and blue became the exception rather than the rule. For the most part, its surface had taken on a sickly greenish hue, murky and impenetrable. Self-styled scientists, since our town boasted few of real learning, tested the waters of the river and the fish that inhabited it. They reported high levels of toxins in certain samples, chemicals that could be dangerous if not downright poisonous.

No one entered the river any longer without a boat. Parents forbade their children to play beside its shores. Those who had once blessed the river as our salvation began to curse it with equal fervor as a pernicious force that had invaded our lives.

When spring returned the rains deserted us and a sudden drought visited the land. It became very hot. The sun beat down mercilessly from a cloudless sky day after day with no relief in sight.

The borders of the river began to retreat, leaving a residue of muddy sludge in their place. The vegetation that had sprung up along its banks withered and disappeared. Our river was reduced to a stream, then a rivulet, and finally it died altogether. Or at least traveled somewhere else.

And though the river is gone, it has left a heritage behind. The town no longer prospers and now we resent our deprivations in a way that never mattered before. Now there are the dangerous ones among us—some of them strangers who have been abandoned here, some our very own—who wander across the new desert of the empty riverbed, strewn with the debris of rotting boats and the shattered skeletons of both humans and fish. They have set up makeshift camps where the waters once flowed. They live by any means they can, preying upon the rest of us, stealing, raping, and killing at random. By night their fires can be seen flickering in the barren wilderness. Their harsh voices carry unintelligibly across the sands.

And then there are others, dangerous in their own way, who contend the river has not finished with us, that it is biding its time and will return once it has rested. They speak of prophetic visions and describe how the river's currents visit them in their dreams and nightmares, full of fine promises and vile threats yet to be delivered.

MICHAEL A. ARNZEN

FRESH CATCH

JARED CHUCKLED when Twitchell's line unspooled and the kid began flailing a limp hand at the reel as if it might burn him. Sandy, Twitchell's reluctant tagalong gal, dropped her impotent reel to help him try to pull the surprise catch in. As Jared's small fishing boat rocked from the transfer of weight to one side, he tried to ignore the imbalance, turning away from the pair of touristy idiots to eyeball his own bobber out on the salty green. Fish had been teasing him all day. But the weather was right and he'd brought the boat to his honey spot—so soon they would be biting, he just knew it.

"Ho-o-lee…" Twitchell's voice raised an octave, and since he sounded like a dying seal, Jared thought that was reason enough to glance again their way. He forced a smile. They'd paid for this trip on his boat, ostensibly to fish, but he'd done this with couples on vacation a million times, and he knew they just wanted to be coddled and assured that this sea fishing excursion was a great way to blow five hundred dollars. So he had to pretend to care; it was standard operating procedure. If he was lucky, they'd actually reel one in and he'd probably get to keep it for dinner, along with tip.

The couple had managed to yank the catch up from the drink. The thing was bigger than anything he expected Twitchell might hook. And for just a second, it looked like Twitchell had snagged *a human baby.*

Both of them heaved on the rod to try to lift it from the wobbly green surface and the bulbous shark-gray shape suddenly cut through the skin of the water like a gull in response, spraying water, sailing swiftly toward them through the air. Twitchell's line trailed from its mouth, flaccid, caught between two tiny twisted arcs that could have been its lips. Jared fell back against the hull of the boat, worried the thing would run into him, but it splatted onto the floorboards between him and the two lovebirds, flopping and twisting wetly against the wood. Jared instinctively felt like the landed fish needed to be kicked or clubbed, and he raised a hesitant boot to do so, but with one last spasm the thing stiffened and stared idly at his foot, as if giving up the fight before he had the chance.

Twitchell's eyes were light bulbs as he came forward, gripping Sandy's bare, sweaty arm. "My God, what the hell *is* it?"

Together, they stared. Black eyes, filmy and gray, stared back at them, behind sclerae thin as mucus, a covering reminiscent of eyelids but weirder, speckled yellow. Its marbled eyes were forever closed, not understanding light. The lenses had no color—just a black bead in the center of gray. The thing's head itself was something like a flat basketball. A crooked slit of black made up its mouth. A large dimple near the top of its skull vaguely resembled a collapsed newborn's soft-spot.

Jared marveled over its ugliness. Gray gills and seaweed-clogged fins, no larger than Jared's palms, were wholly unfishly. Its body was shaped like a squeezed square—six rounded rectangular edges with hollow, sagging centers—and the skin was so loose it didn't appear to house anything resembling meat or muscle. It seemed empty, hollow, like a small, wet, crepe-papered crate with a mannequin's smashed plastic head attached.

Not knowing what else to do with his foot, Jared cautiously toed one side, flipping it over.

Flapped edges curling as it rolled, the thing revealed its flat bottom: all gray color tapering to the standard fish-belly bright white. Its bottom surface was flat as a stingray's hood, but it carried a blanket of tiny tentacles. Its stomach, if that's what you would call it, was lined with writhing suckers which still puckered the sky, searching for something to grip.

Satisfied that it was dead or dying, Jared reached for the bottle of Jim Beam beside the catch's head, placed it in his lap, and capped it. "Throw it back," he said in Twitchell's direction. "Too small. It's just a baby."

Sandy guffawed, her voice deep with snot. "A baby *what?*" she asked, her upper lip gnarled tightly to one side.

Twitchell just stared down at the creature; his chest muscles flexed in a rhythmic, unconscious way that mimicked the leech-like suckers on the thing's belly as he waited for it to move.

Jared gulped from the mouth of the bottle, eyeing them. *College kids*, he thought. *What would they do if they had actually caught something really worth fretting over, like a red-eyed shark?* He shoved the bottle between his legs to cool his thighs and tossed the cap over the side, figuring he might as well finish what he'd started. "Hell if I know what it is." He swallowed back the nausea rising up his throat from the booze, reminding him that his body was still working off last night's binge. "But I don't want that freak of nature on my boat." He twisted with a squeak in his seat to watch his own tranquil bobber impotently floating out on the green. He wondered if the sea was polluted out here, and that's why there wasn't much competition this time of year "Get rid of it."

Twitchell uttered something incoherent to Jared's back.

Sandy sniffled and whispered: "Are you *crazy?* Even Captain Jared said he doesn't know what it is. You can't possibly want to eat that thing. Why don't you toss it back like he says?"

Twitchell's voice surfaced from a mumble: "...rare. Maybe it's worth something. I think I saw something like that on the food network once. Could be a delicacy."

"It's disgusting. Probably poisonous."

Jared chugged from his bottle again. He could hear the liquid in his gut smacking against the walls of his stomach like the small waves lapping the hull of his small boat. "Throw it out," he repeated, refusing to look at them. Or it.

The boat was awkwardly silent while Jared watched his bobber. The red side of the sphere kept tipping like a buoy, and he couldn't be sure if his bait was being nibbled or if he'd tied too much weight to his sinker. Either way, he could feel them down there, circling the hook. It was always this way when he used hamburger meat to fish—at first they didn't know what the gloppy red meat was—the aquatic scent of blood foreign to their salty gills—and they took a while to realize that the wormy-looking globule was a kind of food. Not the best bait for fish, but good enough for Jared. The fish in this location were desperate; they didn't have much choice this far from shore. But that creepy creature was clearly some kind of mutant, and maybe his old honey hole had gone toxically sour.

The boat rocked. Jared figured Twitchell was bending over to pick the thing up and throw it overboard, giving in to Sandy's silent treatment, as well as her good looks. Jared knew the boy was whipped the second he saw the two of them together, all kissy and holding hands like teenagers. It wasn't often Jared took folks fishing on a date, but he didn't care what they did, so long as they paid him and maybe caught a thing or two to spread the word about his business.

Jared heard a large splash behind him. He grinned. "About time you grew a pair, boy." He wondered if the sound would disturb the fish he was after below. He squinted, studying his line closely.

Nothing.

Quiet. Water tickling wood, a sound like draining.

A slight sniffle…followed by a shrieked sigh.

He snapped around, boat creaking as his neck twisted.

Sandy was alone, hands cupped over her mouth and cowering from the dark pinkish curling puddle that swished on the deck of the boat like a shadow where Twitchell should have been standing.

JARED SURFACED from the water, wet hair revealing bald spaces on his scalp. "I don't see him *anywhere*," he grumbled, holding on to the edge of the sailboat and breathing heavily. Dizziness spun up his brain from too much drink.

Sandy wasn't talking. She kept her hand over her mouth, as if holding her breath, afraid to inhale the seawater's tainted air.

"Damn this." Jared lumbered over the side of the boat and fell back inside, huffing. He was too drunk for scuba and too tired for this malarkey. He wasn't completely convinced that the kid wasn't playing some kind of joke, but Twitchell had been gone for far too long. And Jared knew he might be out of business if he lost a man overboard and word got around. A drunk captain made for bad headlines, too. But maybe he could get it out of the woman that it was all Twitchell's fault: maybe he didn't know how to swim, or was allergic to saltwater, or heck, even suicidal to begin with.

He sat beside her, dripping, and caught his breath. Sandy didn't move; just stared out at the water, as if expecting her boyfriend to return from the deep at any moment.

"Are you ready to tell me what happened yet? Did you two get in a fight or something?"

She just watched the sea, mute, her eyes dilated black and cheeks wet with tears. The boat bobbed uncomfortably.

Jared groaned. Grabbed his bottle of JB. He took the last swig of the remainder to rinse the saltwater from his mouth. Moved to toss the bottle overboard, but had a better idea. He slammed it down against the metal anchor chain near the bow, where it splintered and sprayed glass beside Sandy's feet.

She cringed and then stared at him. "What?" was all she could say.

Jared's face was bright red and slimy with seawater. He flung a finger at her. "You better start talking to me now, little lady, or you're going overboard with your boyfriend." He stood, dizzily, pointing his thick finger at the girl's face like the barrel of a gun. He had difficulty keeping his balance, waiting for speech to surface from her silent treatment, but he felt more in control than he had since leaving shore.

"That thing," she said, looking down at the puddle between Jared's legs. "The thing just...*sprang*."

"What thing? You mean that stupid ugly fish?"

"That *thing*." She faced him boldly now, confronting him with the word till he put his finger down. "Twitchy bent down over it, and a second later it was just...just *on his face*, smothering him."

Jared rolled his eyes. "Oh, give me a friggin' break!"

"It wasn't dying—it was waiting to attack! It suffocated Twitch and he tripped and fell overboard with it..." Her eyes trailed back to the water, reflecting its green. "It killed him, Captain Jared."

Jared almost laughed at the stupid way she kept calling him Captain, but he sat beside her now, trying to calm. She wasn't making sense, but at least she was speaking. "Are you sure your boyfriend ain't pulling no dumb joke on us? He saw how scared you were of that thing. Maybe he's just pranking us..." Jared knew his voice betrayed his gut sense that she was right.

"No," she said, the muscles over her eyes tightening. "It ambushed him. It did it on purpose."

Jared smirked, disbelieving, and inhaled sea air like it might clear his head. He tugged on a rope to realign the sails. "Well if that boy is messin' with our minds, he's gonna learn the hard way. And if he's not...well, it's just better if we head back for shore now." The boat gained a modicum of speed and tipped gently to one side as the sail caught air. It felt good to be on the move.

Jared's reel sang. He'd forgotten about his line. He turned and noticed that his bobber wasn't trailing behind, but was anchored in the same spot. Or perhaps he'd caught something moving in the opposite direction. "Hold this here," he said to Sandy, motioning at the flimsy mast and releasing his grip. "I gotta reel that puppy in."

Sandy didn't move. "You can't be serious. How can you continue to fish with what just happened? Twitchell's out there, *down there*, somewhere. You gotta find him."

"No can do, missy. Unless I just hooked me your boyfriend, he's a goner." He pulled on the line and slowly turned the handle on his reel. There wasn't much slack, not enough to tell if he had caught something or not, and he couldn't tell if he was the one doing the reeling.

Sandy grabbed him by the shoulders and pulled him back. "I don't care how drunk you are, Captain Jared, you have to do something about my Twitchy!"

Jared laughed.

She slapped him from behind, slamming the full breadth of her palm against his stubbled face. It stung—he could feel the spikes of her fingers trailing up toward his eyes in his reddening cheeks, like a developing afterimage. His mouth was filling with spit—a gut reaction that told him he was ready to fight.

"Why you..." He was up and tackling her, but she dove out of his swinging arms, settling into the wooden slat that functioned as a seat on the opposite side of the boat. Jared's chin hit the pink puddle in the center of the floor. His teeth caught some tongue.

"*Leave me alone!*" Sandy shouted, and then nervously cast glances around the boat, as if looking for help. She screamed and the emptiness that surrounded them swallowed her voice.

"Shut up, lady," Jared said coolly, getting his legs under him, but stumbling from the dizziness of the alcohol. "Just shut up. I'll get your boyfriend for you. Okay?" He wiped the pink sticky goo from his chin. Sniffed his fingers. It smelled like freshwater: green like forests and mold. An odd smell for the ocean. He frowned, and then he noticed that Sandy was still crying out, her voice crackling. He called louder: "*Okay?*"

Sandy quieted, and nodded.

And then something like driftwood smacked against the bow with a hollow thud.

Jared knew it was Twitchell before he even saw him. Same Hawaiian Palm swimming trunks bubbling with air pockets and sloshing with the briny water. Same crew neck T-shirt with bait stains. Same hair. All doing the dead man's float, right out of the Red Cross handbook.

Sandy refused to look. Instead, she sat beside Jared's pole, and toyed with the reel, watching the bobber bob.

Jared scooped an arm over the edge of the bow, and scooped Twitchell up. He was light—much too light and flexible—flimsy as fabric as he pulled him inside. His trunks and T-shirt slipped free and floated away when Twitchell came up over the edge, Jared falling back into his boat with the too-light body in his arms. Or what was left of it.

On his lap and draped across his chest at strange angles: simply *skin*. A loose runny bag of hair and saltwater and bones; a few haphazard clumps of things mushy rolling inside. A lot of it was fatty tissue feeling something like sex, slick and slimy between his fingers. As the saltwater drained from its pink holes, the contents inside settled to the legs and feet of the sack of hairy flesh like a handful of coins in the bottom of a long stocking. Twitchell had been gutted, as if his insides had been sucked clean out. And it all felt horribly dry…much too powdery considering he had been underwater for at least half an hour…

"It's Twitchell, isn't it?" Sandy said, still watching Jared's bobber, refusing to turn around. Something had bit, but she didn't make any motion toward reeling it in. She just watched it and didn't watch it at the same time.

"No," Jared said, scraping the strange skin from his lap onto the sailboat's floor, landing with a dull thump that reminded him of the duffel bag from his Navy days. He stared at it, dumbfounded. "No, this ain't Twitchell. Not at all."

JARED WISHED he'd brought more booze. Sandy might not have been there at all—she had turned once, hazarding a minute-long look at Twitchell's skinned flesh, and then silently turned back to stare at the ocean as if nothing odd had happened. She hadn't uttered a sound. Just sat and watched the water.

He knew shock when he saw it and gave up trying to reason with her. He'd positioned the sail to catch the optimal amount of wind, but the boat was slow heading toward shore, barely visible on the horizon. They'd drifted much too far out—he'd been drinking all day, and didn't really pay much attention to his nautics because this was supposed to be just another boring fishing tour, nothing more. But now a kid was puddled on the floor of his sailboat, pink and ugly as a fresh caught shark with its belly slit.

The sky was getting gray, and the color reminded him of the thing that had landed on the boat. *Rain soon*, Jared thought, before finally grabbing Twitchell's dripping body and tossing it overboard. The skin smelled much like the stuff on the floor of the boat—green and moldy. He sniffed his fingers, watching as it floated away, a bubbling yellow cloud on the water like one of those emergency lifeboats with a serious flat.

He watched it drift away.

"Ya know," Jared said, staring at the skin in the water. "I'd heard about something like this, but I always thought it was just a buncha bullshit. One of those dumb fish stories people tell, stuff they usually just get from the internet." He dug into his breast pocket, found a crumpled damp cigarette. He always only brought one with him, for some solitude and mental regrouping after work. He stroked it straight and popped it between his lips.

"This is all your fault, you drunken jerk," Sandy finally said, ignoring him.

He chuckled in reply. "No way of explaining it, 'cept to just ask: *What would a freshwater fish do if you put it in seawater*?" He lit his smoke with a waterproof match. "Do ya know?"

She shook her head *no* with her back to him. He wasn't sure if it was a direct reply or not.

"Well…it'd *die*, that's what it would do." He inhaled smoke. Blew. "Unless it could find some freshwater to breathe into its gills. Fact is, there really are a few still pockets of it on the ocean floor. Freshwater eddies. Very few. But they're out there. And I think that's what your boy hooked into when he reeled that ugly thing onto my boat."

She cocked an ear his way.

Smoke drifted out of his nostrils. "Yup. That'd explain that ugly thing's eyes, all black and glazed like they was. Freshwater usually gathers in underwater caves and whirlpools and what not. Places where the sun don't shine. I'd heard about freshwater fish in the ocean, but I never thought I'd actually see one in real life…"

After a lingering silence, Sandy laughed. Loudly. Then she twisted around, eyes bloodshot and manic. "A freshwater fish? In the middle of the ocean? Right! And it's a fish that can fly through the air…like that *thing* did…and attack people, too!" Her lips were far too wide for a smile. "That wasn't some dumb trout, mister. That thing was an *animal*. A *predator* of some sort. And if you weren't so damned drunk you'da seen that, clear as day." Her face dared him to argue.

Jared cocked his head while he smoked, resting an elbow on a kneecap, dimly realizing the sun was no longer as bright as before. "Could be." He sucked tobacco. "But that don't mean it don't breathe freshwater. I could smell it all over that puddle there," he said, pointing down at the pink lake on the floorboards.

Her head shivered and flashed red. "You're a stupid *idiot*. Water doesn't smell."

"Wait," Jared said, getting an idea. "I'll prove it to you." He lumbered over to the sail and adjusted the mast.

"What do you think you're doing? You're not going back where we were *now*, are you?"

"Yup," Jared said, directing the boat toward where his bobber floated like an eyeball on the sea. "We're goin' freshwater fishing." He lumbered over to his rod, grinning.

"Oh no, we're not." She lunged, grabbed the mast, and randomly twisted.

The boat dipped, and Jared fell onto an out-thrust arm, catching himself sideways.

They seemed to be spinning in a spiral. "Lady," Jared grumbled, dizzily straightening himself. "Either you let that thing go, or you go overboard. I'm not tellin' you again." He tried to keep a straight face. "Captain's orders."

Sandy's head was still shaking, her grip on the mast so tight her muscles shook. "I'm not going back anywhere *near* that thing. You can try to throw me overboard if you want, but I'll take my chances. I can put up one helluva fight against a drunk old fool like you."

Jared's mouth filled with sticky saliva.

And that's when he knew he was angry enough to hit her. It had always been that way—in barrooms and brigs, drool spilling out of his lips when he threw the first punch. Like a salivating lust to taste the violence again. But he'd never hit a woman, and he wasn't about to begin now. He was in enough trouble, with a man lost overboard. So he spit what had flooded into his mouth over the side of the boat.

And the rectangular thing suddenly sailed into the air, belly-first, catching the spit in its suckers like a mitt before slapping back down onto the water. Amazed, Jared watched its dark shape float then sink into the green.

Sandy's entire face dilated: "Did you...My God, we gotta get out of here."

"Just as I suspected."

Sandy was madly attempting to adjust the sails, tugging on lines and poles, but clearly had no idea what she was doing. She was like a cat trussed up in a ball of yarn. The boat slowed to a dead stop. One of the sails loosened and sagged to the deck. Awkwardly, she stepped on it, and her foot slipped.

With the sound of tearing cloth, the thing cut the surface of water again and landed flatly on the boat. Sandy shrieked, backing away, keeping her eyes glued on the rectangular gray fish, bumbling against the sail and mast which seemed to wrestle with her.

Jared watched closely.

Sandy's eyes flicked up to meet Jared's, but only for an instant. She stared down at the gray fish in front of her feet as if it were a lion. "*Well*," she shouted, daring to glance up at him again. "Aren't you gonna *do something*?"

Jared coughed softly in the back of his throat. "Yup," he replied.

And he spat across the boat, gobbing her right in her face.

The fish lunged, slapping over Sandy's dumb-struck maw like a giant suction cup, air instantly wheezing from its gills like a cancerous lung while it squirmed, working its sides around both of her ears, slowly repositioning itself to entirely cover her thrashing head. She tried to beat it away, but it did no good—the suckers writhed and dug their way into her skin, tightening. To Jared, it looked like Sandy was wearing nothing more than a strange Halloween mask, dancing and flailing like a monster. It was almost funny when she dropped to her knees. But then he saw its eyes.

Its black eyes…

Its eyes that threshed red and pulsed with blood.

No, not blood.

Oxygen. From the water. The freshwater that Sandy's slumping body held inside, like slimy wet clay. Sucking it out of the bloody mud under the skin. Nearly all of the human body was water, everyone knew, and the rest was just dust. Not saltwater. *Fresh.*

Jared watched as Sandy withered and dried while the monster on her head puffed up with it. Her skin collapsed with a muffled fart.

And the thing's eyes pulsed a deeper red as it glared at him like a vampire.

THE SAIL was ruined, torn free of the mast by Sandy's flailing hands. Now it was draped on the floor, as useless as the emptied sheet of flesh beside it. The boat drifted, the ocean still and indifferent.

He wondered how much time he had left, if any at all…whether the boat would ever make it to shore, and what would remain when it got there.

Jared didn't completely understand the creature, but in the time it took for the beast to completely drain Sandy, he figured out how it worked. It drained the body of water—simply sucked it dry. Probably used some sort of vacuumed suction between its suckers and the lining of the victim's lungs to become a kind of lung parasite. Most likely, it was used to bigger animals than humans—working the water from the gills of sharks and whales, instead of air-breathers. Jared figured the thing couldn't get through some of the fat cells, just like water can't pass through the scaly skin of a fish. So it left the bones and fat for scraps. But it had undoubtedly inhaled most of the body's water. Nearly all. Enough to breathe and maybe store. To keep itself alive.

Jared watched as its defunct gills quivered like the tiny mouths of two drowning men.

His drunk was numbing him into an instinctive stupor—Jared's thoughts were jumbled, turning to darker thoughts, churning concepts without reason. He couldn't stop his mind from drifting…drifting to stories he'd heard from other fishermen at the bars. Tall tales of alien ships crashed at sea. Thoughts of vampire children tossed overboard and adapting to the elements for survival. Insane thoughts. But possible thoughts. Survival thoughts.

The only thing he knew—truly knew because he could *feel* it—was that he was thirsty. As thirsty as the thing that attached to Sandy's face. His parched throat felt scratchy, as though clogged with day-old bread.

Water water, everywhere…

The boxy gray baby-shaped head rolled its black-red eye up at him.

It was waiting.

Jared figured that he'd drunk enough booze to keep it at bay. He'd suffered enough hangovers to know how dehydrated alcohol could make you. And he guessed the creature could sense the strange spirit of alcohol, pulsing in his veins and cells. The same way it sensed the water in the blood of the hamburger meat they were using for bait. The water in Jared's spit. The water in Twitchell and Sandy's bodies.

It was waiting. And waiting was also his only chance.

Maybe the little monster would dry out first.

Maybe it wouldn't notice the tiny beads of nervous sweat accumulating under his collar.

His tongue was dry, a thick cracker in his mouth. He painfully bit on the muscle, trying to force his mouth to fill with saliva. Minutes passed—Jared and fish, eye to eye—while he collected the saliva like ammo. Finally, he spit overboard. A thin bloody drool. Part of it caught on his chin.

Its eyes flickered, but the creature didn't budge. It pulsed. And waited.

Jared broke his eyes away and sighed, craning his neck toward the sky. He prayed for rain. Cool, freshwater rain.

His collar parted.

Its red eye focused on the sweat beading on his neck, and for the first time it swiftly lifted its yellow-gray, mucous lid in what could have been a blink.

ADAM NEVILL
HIPPOCAMPUS

WALLS OF water as slow as lava, black as coal, push the freighter up mountainsides, over frothing peaks and into plunging descents. Across vast, rolling waves the vessel ploughs, ungainly. Conjuring galaxies of bubbles around its passage and in its wake, temporary cosmos appear for moments in the immensity of onyx water; forged then sucked beneath the hull; or are sacrificed, fizzing, to the freezing night air.

On and on, the great steel vessel wallops. Staggering up as if from soiled knees before another nauseating drop into a trough. There is no rest and the ship has no choice but to brace itself, dizzy and near breathless, over and over again, for the next great wave.

On board, lighted portholes and square windows offer tiny, yellow squares of reassurance amidst the lightless, roaring ocean that stretches all around and so far below. Reminiscent of a warm home offering a welcome on a winter night, the cabin lights are complimented by the two metal doorways that gape in the rear house. Their spilled light glosses portions of the slick deck.

All of the surfaces on board are steel, painted white. Riveted and welded tight to the deck and each other, these metal cubes of the superstructure are necklaced by yellow rails intended for those who must slip and reel about the flooded decks. Here and there, white ladders rise, and seem by their very presence to evoke a *kang kang kang* sound of feet going up and down quickly.

Small lifeboat cases resembling plastic barrels are fixed at the sides of the upper deck, all of them intact and locked shut. The occasional crane peers out to sea with inappropriate nonchalance, or with the expectation of a purpose that has not come. Up above the distant bridge, from which no faces peer out, the aerials, satellite dishes, and navigation masts appear to totter in panic, or to whip their poles, wires, and struts from side to side as if engaged in a frantic search of the ever-changing landscape of water below.

The vast steel door of the hold's first hatch is raised and still attached to the crane by chains. This large square section of the hull is filled with white sacks, stacked upon each other in tight columns that fill the entire space. Those at the top of the pile are now dark and sopping with rain and sea water. In the centre, scores of the heavy bags have been removed from around a scuffed and dented metal container, painted black. Until its discovery, the container appears to have been deliberately hidden among the tiers of fibre sacks. One side of the double doors at the front of the old container has been jammed open.

Somewhere on deck, a small, brass bell clangs a lonesome, undirected cry; a traditional affectation as there are speakers thrusting their silent horns from the metallic walls and masts. But though the tiny, urgent sound of the bell is occasionally answered by a gull in better weather, tonight the bell is answered by nothing save the black, shrieking chaos of the wind and the water it thrashes.

There is a lane between the freighter's rear house and the crane above the open hatch. A passage unpeopled, wet, and lit by six lights in metal cages. MUSTER STATION: LIFEBOAT 2 is stenciled on the wall in red lettering. Passing through the lane, the noise of the engine intake fans fills the space hotly. Diesel heat creates the apprehension of being close to moving machine parts. As if functioning as evidence of the ship's purpose and life, and rumbling across every surface like electric current in each part of the vessel, the continuous vibration of the engine's exhaust thrums.

Above the open hatch and beside the lifeboat assembly point, from a door left gaping in the rear house, drifts a thick warmth. Heat that waits to engulf wind-seared cheeks in the way a summer's sun cups faces.

Once across the metal threshold the engine fibrillations deepen as if muted underground. The bronchial roar of the intake fans dull. Inside, the salty-spittle scour of the night air, and the noxious mechanical odours, are replaced by the scent of old emulsion and the stale chemicals of exhausted air fresheners.

A staircase leads down.

But as above so below. As on deck, no one walks here. All is still, lit bright and faintly rumbled by the bass strumming of the exhaust. The communal area appears calm and indifferent to the intense, black energies of the hurricane outside.

A long, narrow corridor runs through the rear house. Square lenses in the steel ceiling illuminate the plain passageway. The floor is covered in linoleum, the walls are matte yellow, the doors to the cabins are trimmed with wood laminate. Halfway down, two opposing doors hang open before lit rooms.

The first room was intended for recreation to ease a crew's passage on a long voyage, but no one seeks leisure now. Coloured balls roll across the pool table from the swell that shimmies the ship. Two cues lie amongst the balls and move back and forth like flotsam on the tide. At rest upon the ping-pong table are two worn paddles. The television screen remains as empty and black as the rain-thrashed canopy of sky above the freighter. One of the brown, leatherette sofas is split in two places and masking tape suppresses the spongy eruptions of cushion entrails.

Across the corridor, a long bank of washing machines and dryers stand idle in the crew's laundry room. Strung across the ceiling are washing line cords that loop like skipping ropes from the weight of the clothing that is pegged in rows: jeans, socks, shirts, towels. One basket has been dropped on the floor and has spilled its contents towards the door.

Up one flight of stairs, an empty bridge. Monitor screens glow green, consoles flicker. One stool lies on its side and the cushioned seat rolls back and forth. A solitary handgun skitters this way and that across the floor of the otherwise tranquil area of operations, as if a drama has recently passed, been interrupted, or even abandoned.

Back down below, and deeper inside the ship, and farther along the crew's communal corridor, the stainless steel galley glimmers dully in white light. A skein of steam clouds over the work surfaces and condenses against the ceiling above the oven. Two large, unwashed pots have boiled dry upon cooker rings glowing red. From the oven, wisps of black smoke puff around a tray of potatoes that have baked to carbon and now resemble the fossils of reptile guano.

Around the great chopping board on the central table lies a scattering of chopped vegetables, cast wide by the freighter's lurches and twists. The ceiling above the work station is railed with steel and festooned with swaying kitchenwear.

Six large steaks, encrusted with crushed salt, await the abandoned spatula and the griddle that hisses black and dry. A large refrigerator door, resembling the gate of a bank vault, hangs open to reveal crowded shelves that gleam in ivory light.

Inside a metal sink the size of a bathtub lies a human scalp.

Lopped roughly from the top of a head and left to drain beside the plughole, the gingery mess looks absurdly artificial. But the clod of hair was once plumbed into a circulatory system because the hair is matted dark and wet at the fringes and surrounded by flecks of ochre. The implement that removed the scalp lies upon the draining board: a long knife, the edge serrated for sawing. Above the adjacent work station, at the end of the rack that holds the cook's knives, several items are missing.

Maybe this dripping thing of hair was taken to the sink area; brought here from somewhere outside of the galley, and carried along the corridor, and up one flight of stairs that lead from the crew's quarters. Red droplets that have splashed as round as rose petals lead a trail into the first cabin that is situated in a corridor identical to the communal passage on the deck above. The door to this cabin is open. Inside, the trail of scarlet is immediately lost within the engulfing borders of a far bigger stain.

A fluorescent jacket and cap hang upon a peg just inside the door of the cabin. All is neat and orderly upon the bookshelf, holding volumes that brush the low, white ceiling. A chest of drawers doubles as a desk. The articles on the desktop are weighed down by a glass paperweight and are overlooked by silver-framed photographs of wives and children at the rear of the desk. Upon the top of the wardrobe, life jackets and hardhats are stowed. Twin beds, arranged close together, are unoccupied. Beneath the bedframes, orange survival suits remain neatly folded and tightly packed.

The bedclothes of the berth on the right-hand side are tidy and undisturbed. But the white top sheet and the yellow blanket of the adjacent berth droop to the linoleum floor like idle sails. There is a suggestion that an occupant departed this bed hurriedly, or was removed swiftly. The bed linen has been yanked from the bed and only remains tucked under the mattress in one corner. A body was also ruined in that bed: the middle of the mattress is blood sodden and the cabin now reeks of salt and rust. Crimson gouts from a bedside frenzy have flecked and speckled the wall beside the bed, and part of the ceiling.

Attached to the room is a small ensuite bathroom that just manages to hold a shower cubicle and small steel sink. The bathroom is pristine; the taps, showerhead, and towel rail sparkle. All that is amiss is a single slip-on shoe, dropped to the floor just in front of the sink. A foot remains inside the shoe with part of a hairy ankle extending from the uppers.

From the cabin more than a trail of droplets can be followed farther down the passage and towards the neighbouring berths. A long intermittent streak of red has been smeared along the length of the corridor, past the four doors that all hang open and drift back and forth as the ship lists. From each of these cabins, other collections have been made.

What occupants once existed in the crew's quarters appear to have arisen from their beds before stumbling towards the doors as if some cause for alarm was announced nearby. Just before the doorways of their berths they seem to have met their ends quickly. Wide, lumpy puddles, like spilled stew made with red wine, are splashed across the floors. One crew member sought refuge inside the shower cubicle of the last cabin because the bathroom door is broken open, and the basin of the shower is drenched near black from a sudden and conclusive emptying. Livestock hung above the cement of a slaughterhouse and emptied from the throat leave similar stains.

Turning left at the end of the passage, the open door of the captain's cabin is visible. Inside, the sofa beside the coffee table, and the two easy chairs sit expectantly but empty. The office furniture and shelves reveal no disarray. But set upon the broad desk are three long wooden crates. The tops have been levered off, and the packing straw that was once inside is now littered about the table's surface and the carpeted floor below. Intermingled with the straw is a plethora of dried flower petals.

Upon a tablecloth that is spread on the floor before the captain's desk, two small forms have been laid out. They lie side by side, in profile. They are the size of five-year-old children and blackened by age; not dissimilar to the preserved forms of ancient peoples, protected behind glass in museums of antiquities. They appear to be shrivelled and contorted. Vestiges of a fibrous binding has fused with their petrified flesh and obscured their arms, if they are in possession of such limbs. The two small figures are primarily distinguished by the irregular shape and silhouettes of their skulls. Their heads appear oversized, and the swollen dimension of the crania contributes to the leathery ghastliness of their grimacing faces. The rear of each head is fanned by an incomplete mane of spikes, while the front of each head elongates and protrudes into a snout. The desiccated figures have had their lower limbs bound tightly together to create a suggestion of long and curling tails.

Inside the second crate lies a large black stone, crudely hollowed out in the middle. The dull and chipped character of the block also suggests great age. A modern addition has been made, or offered, to the hollow within the stone. A single human foot. The shoe around the disarticulated foot matches the footwear inside the shower cubicle of the crew member's cabin.

The contents of the third crate has barely been disturbed. In there lie several artifacts that resemble jagged flints, or the surviving blades of old weapons or knives to which the handles are missing. The implements are hand-forged from a stone as black as the basin that has become a receptacle for a human foot.

Pictures of a ship and framed maps have been removed from the widest wall, and upon this wall a marker pen has been used to depict the outlines of two snouted or trumpeting figures that are attached by what appears to be long and entwined tails. The imagery is crude and childlike, but the silhouettes are similar to the embalmed remains laid out upon the bed sheet.

Below the two figures are imprecise sticklike figures that appear to cavort in emulation of the much larger and snouted characters. Set atop some kind of uneven pyramid shape, another group of human figures have been excitedly and messily drawn with spikes protruding from their heads or headdresses. Between the crowned forms, another plainer figure has been held aloft and bleeds from the torso into a waiting receptacle. Detail has been included to indicate that the sacrificed figure's feet have been removed and its legs bound.

The mess of human leavings that led here departs the captain's cabin and rises up a staircase to the deck above and into an unlit canteen.

Light falls into this room from the corridor, and in the half-light two long tables, and one smaller table for the officers, are revealed. Upon the two larger crew tables, long reddish shapes are stretched out and glisten: some twelve bodies dwindling into darkness as they stretch away from the door. As if unzipped across the front, what was once inside each of the men has now been gathered and piled upon chairs where the same men once sat and ate. Their feet, some bare, some still inside shoes, have been amputated and are set in a messy pile at the head of the two tables.

The far end of the cafeteria is barely touched by the residual light. Presented to no living audience, perversely and inappropriately and yet in a grimly touching fashion, two misshapen shadows flicker and leap upon the dim wall as if in joyous reunion. They wheel about each other, ferociously, but not without grace. They are attached, it seems, by two long, spiny tails.

Back outside and on deck, it can be seen that the ship continues to meander, inebriated with desolation and weariness; perhaps punched drunk from the shock of what has occurred below deck.

The bow momentarily rises up the small hillside of a wave and, just once, near expectantly, looks to the distant harbour the vessel has slowly drifted toward overnight since changing its course.

On shore and across the surrounding basin of treeless land, the lights of a small harbour town are white pinpricks, desperate to be counted in this black storm. Here and there, the harbour lights define the uneven silhouettes of small buildings, suggesting stone façades in which glass shimmers to form an unwitting beacon for what exists out here upon these waves.

Oblivious to anything but its own lurching and clanking, the ship rolls on the swell, inexorably drifting on the current that picked up it's steel bulk the day before and now slowly propels the hull, though perhaps not as purposelessly as was first assumed, towards the shore.

At the prow, having first bound himself tight to the railing with rope, a solitary and unclothed figure nods a bowed head towards the land. The pale flesh of the rotund torso is whipped and occasionally drenched by sea spray, but still bears the ruddy impressions of bestial deeds that were both boisterous and thorough. From navel to sternum, the curious figurehead is blackly open, or has been opened, to the elements. The implement used to carve such crude entrances to the heart is long gone, perhaps dropped from stained and curling fingers into the obsidian whirling and clashing of the monumental ocean far below.

As if to emulate the status of a king, where the scalp has been carved away, a crude series of spikes, fashioned from nails, have been hammered into a pattern resembling a spine or fin across the top of the dead man's skull. Both of his feet are missing and his legs have been bound with twine into one, single, gruesome tail.

JOHN LANGAN

A SONG ONLY PARTIALLY HEARD

THIS IS the story he doesn't tell.

Not because no one will believe him (although no one would), and not because of the stares he knows his account would provoke, the poorly concealed laughs and muttered remarks ("Crazy," "What the fuck is he talking about?" "Goddamn boss's cousin"). No, the reason Horacio Martinez keeps his story to himself is that it won't make a difference, won't return Hector to life, won't alter the judgement of the sheriff's deputies, who have ruled the death an accident, which Horacio supposes it was, only one with slightly less randomness than the declaration implies.

There's something else, too, a reason under the reason. What he saw, what he heard, not so much when his friend died, but in the moments before and after it, was like nothing his ears and eyes have experienced, not during his decade here, in Wiltwyck, upstate New York, and not during his decade growing up in San Juan. He isn't sure how to describe it; although *holy* occurs to him. It's a term from his childhood, redolent of incense and candlewax, from when he was devout, when he spent each week anticipating the candle he would light at the foot of the Virgin, when his daily dress included his Maltese cross and his scapula, when every morning he checked his children's missal to see which saint's feast day it was. Uttering it now puckers his lips with embarrassment, unless it's as half of a curse. But it attaches itself to Hector's death with a force which will not be denied, and he supposes this means it's correct.

Following the departure of the police, everyone has been sent home with pay for the remainder of the day, a nod to compassion on the part of Cousin Fernando qualified by the fact that the work day had less than an hour left. Shocked as even the older men were by the violence of Hector's end, the employees were happy to take advantage of the boss's generosity, most of them walking down and across the street to the bar which occupies the ground floor of a large, three-story house on the corner there. No one paid much attention to Horacio, who found it easy to stay behind after the chain-link gate was rolled closed. To be certain his failure to depart wouldn't be noticed, he kept to the other side of the white trailer that serves as Fernando's office, remaining there as the echoes of his coworkers' voices faded into the distance. Once the only sound is the whoosh of a car passing by, Horacio peaks his head around the trailer, confirms the yard is empty, and crosses to where the *Helen Leucoria* sits in her ship cradle.

She's the tug half of an ATB, an articulated tug and barge combination, brought to the shipyard Fernando manages on the northern bank of the Redout Creek for an assortment of repairs and renovations. Her almost comically high bridge has been removed entire and set to one side, where a designated team works on it. A second team labors inside the ship's rounded hull, while a third, to which Hector and Horacio were assigned, has tended to the tug's exterior, inspecting and mending small injuries to the surface, in a couple of places replacing what can't be fixed. Horacio hasn't been at the shipyard long enough to be trusted with any truly significant task, nor does he find the work particularly easy to learn, but once he masters a task, he does so with a thoroughness that has attracted grudging nods from his coworkers, whose respect for him has grown as he has demonstrated himself more competent than his first week on the job indicated (about which, the less said, the better). Though he doesn't care for the work, he finds it oddly satisfying, and as his father is fond of saying, you don't have to like a job if the money is good, which it is. Give Fernando that much credit: he pays his workers well.

Overhead, one of the massive collars that encircle the tug's propellers hangs, like something from a jet. To the right, on the other side of the keel, the space the second collar occupied is empty, the hull torn and hanging down in strips. Directly beneath it, jagged and torn pieces of metal, some the size of windows, doors, begin a path stretching the twenty or so feet to the edge of the yard, where it drops to the surface of the creek seven or eight feet below. On a sunny summer day like this one, you can stand at this ledge and gaze through the clear water at schools of fish maintaining their positions in the current. This is the spot Hector was when, with an ear-splitting shriek, the collar tore loose from the tug and crashed to the ground, rolling toward the creek, leaving shards of itself behind as it went, revealing the propeller it contained. Tangled with half a dozen lengths of metal, each a razored whip, the propeller struck Hector.

Although he witnessed his friend's death, Horacio isn't certain exactly what he saw happen to him. He isn't sure he wants to know. One instant, Hector was turning to the juggernaut rumbling toward him; the next, he appeared to move in several different directions at once. The propeller and its metal necklace rolled off the edge of the yard into the creek, taking the better part of Hector with it, leaving behind his right arm below the elbow and a slice of his skull, the flesh stubbled from his recent buzz cut. His blood fell from the air in droplets. Already knowing it was too late, Horacio ran to the place his friend had been in time to watch the propeller rock to a halt, half-submerged in the water splashing around it. He saw Hector's leg, caught on a strand of metal wound around one of the propeller's blades. Horacio scanned the water, could distinguish no more of Hector amidst the turbulence the propeller had stirred. But there was something else, between the shore and the propeller, a movement at the creek's churning surface, a shape that glowed crimson and gold with the sunlight, that resolved into a form more shocking than the sight of Hector's leg floating in the Redout. Horacio's glimpse of it lasted for what seemed to be minutes, yet couldn't have been more than a couple of seconds, before he was joined by a handful of the other workers, all searching for Hector and crying out when they saw what remained of him, and the thing beneath the water darted out of view.

It was a woman: why not say that? Because she was like no

woman he's ever seen. She was drifting on her back, her long gold hair spreading around her head in a cloud. He guesses she was naked, if that's the right way to describe skin crosshatched with dark red and gold scales. What appeared to be trains of red silk, each the length of her long body, attached to her forearms, her hips, her calves, and rippled in the surrounding water. They reminded him of Ocho, the beta fish Fernando keeps in the office, and he understood that they were fins. From eyes a uniform blue (*Azure*, he thinks), she regarded him, an unreadable expression on her face. Tiny silver fish darted around her. In her look, he felt the weight of an intelligence ancient and strange.

There was one more detail, a sound, distant and musical, what might have been a song. The memory of it lingers, hours after he (thinks he) heard it. Almost, he can pick out lyrics, though the language is foreign to him. They have a plaintive quality that evokes images of clusters of rocks washed by foaming seas, of the sun high and unforgiving in a blue, blue sky. *Come*, the lyrics seem to be pleading, *come here, join us below the waves, where everything is calm, peaceful. Come to the peace of the kelp forests, of the eel dens, of the lobster roads. Come down to where ships lie in quiet rust and rot. Come let the small crabs and fish feast on you, give yourself to the sea, to the sea, to peace.*

This, the woman with her trailing red fins, her blue eyes on him, the song he (thinks he) heard, comprise the secret story, the experience he cannot help thinking of as holy. There is no doubt in his mind that Hector was gripped by a similar but more intense version of it in the minutes leading up to the accident. Horacio noticed him at the edge of the yard, his head tilted toward the creek. Nothing remarkable about that, but in the final moment of his life, as Hector turned to the mass of metal screeching toward him, Horacio saw reflected in his friend's face an experience of profound beauty. It was as if a beam of light were shining directly on his features, illuminating them, casting them into sharper relief. Horacio was reminded of endless paintings of ecstatic saints, bathed in the light of God. When the propeller and its looping shards struck him, Hector must have thought the beauty that illuminated him was killing him.

Or so Horacio imagines. He walks out from under the *Helen Leucosia*. Police tape flutters around the path of metal fragments leading to the edge of the yard. There, patches of Hector's blood still stain the ground. In the creek, the propeller rises like a bizarre idol. Hector's leg has been retrieved from it, along with what other pieces of him the police divers could locate. Horacio gives the men their due: they worked for a good couple of hours, searching for and retrieving his friend's remains with care and deliberation. With the exception of his left hand and a scoop of his lower back, the divers succeeded in recovering all of Hector, for which Horacio is grateful to a degree that surprises him. He is unclear whether the search for those last fragments of Hector will continue tomorrow, or if as much of him has been found as is going to be; he suspects the latter. In which case, assuming the police give the okay, the early part of the morning will be spent lifting the propeller from the Redout, inspecting it, and deciding if whatever damage it suffered can be repaired, or if a replacement will have to be ordered.

Horacio would like to see the propeller melted down, destroyed, but he assumes this is unlikely. Though battered and dented by its murderous transit, the propeller appears basically sound, able to be fixed, and a new one would be expensive, much more costly than the life of a man from Santo Domingo who enjoyed spending his Sunday afternoons with his girlfriend and her daughter, picnicking one place or another. Horacio's first, disastrous week at the shipyard, Hector invited him to join them that weekend, which he did, and while he had little to say to either Megan or Ella, he appreciated their smiling friendliness enough to join the three of them again a couple of weeks later, and intermittently thereafter, as recently as this past Sunday, when the four of them took an order of Chinese takeout to the picnic benches at Wiltwyck Point, an arm of land reaching into the Hudson. As Ella tip-toed across the rocky beach to splash in the river, Megan calling after her not to go too far, Hector and Horacio studied the boats traveling the water, from the sailboats whose sails belled from their masts, to the speedboats galloping from the crest of one wave to the next, to a combined ATB making its slow way south. Unlike Horacio, Hector loved boats, loved working on them, loved being out on them. He named the different types of sailboats, the horsepower of the speedboats' engines, the top speed of an articulated tug with and without its barge. This afternoon, he was most interested by an enormous oil tanker which had dropped anchor a couple of hundred yards north of them, almost beneath the Wiltwyck-Rhinecliff Bridge. "That's an old one," he said. "Early sixties. Didn't know any of them were still in service. Can you see what flag she's flying? I swear, my eyes are no good anymore." Horacio squinted, but did not recognize the colors. "It's gray," he said, "or black, with some kind of design on it in yellow. I think it's a triangle, but the sides are all wavy. That could be the wind, though. Whose flag is that?" Hector didn't know, nor could either of them read the letters in which the tanker's name and country of origin were written. Hector ventured they were Russian or Greek; Horacio guessed Thai or Sanskrit. Later, as they were packing up to leave, they saw water venting from a hatch in the tanker's flank. "They aren't supposed to do that," Hector said, frowning. "What?" Horacio said. "The water," Hector said, pointing to the green stream foaming into the Hudson. "That's sea water. They use it for ballast, to keep the ship stable. They aren't allowed to dump it up here. This is fresh water. Who knows what's in that shit?" Horacio shrugged. "What can you do?"

What can you do? He doesn't know what he expects, standing here as the creek eddies round the propeller. Another glimpse of the strange woman? To hear her song as Hector did, in all its terrible loveliness? To what end? He shakes his head. He feels himself caught in a narrative whose parameters he cannot identify, a minor character moved by a plot he does not understand. Disgust twists his lip, propels him away from the water at a brisk pace. If he hurries, maybe he can catch up to the others at the bar.

If he remained in place, staring into the water, would he make out the woman floating a half-dozen feet down, amidst a grove of green weeds, her fins wrapping around her like red robes? Would he see Hector's hand in hers? Would he watch her lift it to her perfect mouth, take one of the fingers between her lips, and strip the waterlogged flesh from the bones with her narrow, razored teeth?

For Fiona

ALESSANDRO MANZETTI
BY THE SEA

THE WHOLE night spent in my blue van chasing Venus, the tires barely touching nests of giant oysters, right and left. White and black pearls, assembly lines of meat, archangels descending from ropes, blowing into horns of bone, calling the others to watch the trenches of terrestrial meat. Seraphs like peeping Toms, with fifty euros hidden in their feathered underwear, sweat their transparent holy sap, together with the people of the night queued up behind my blue van, seeing the bright eyes of the cars, the silhouettes of drivers with crumpled and curled wings, the microscopic fires of Marlboros, listening to Bruce Springsteen's "The Ghost of Tom Joad" blaring out a car window.

The whole night spent in my blue van waiting for Venus, through the narrow galleries of this new, soft Golconda. Roma, the electric blues of euros, the oases of hookers in that great fascist desert, inhabited by white marble ribs and buttocks frozen since February.

You can see explorers, ghosts without eyes, with flies as their passengers and hands full of diamonds; white colonnades; a dwarf standing on the aristocratic hood of a Mercedes scanning the horizon like an Indian; everywhere rectangular footprints of the Universal Exhibition of 1942. My blue van, with a full tank and an endless thirst, fits like a brick of plastic explosive in this rational geometry, lifting the leaves of extinct bus stops, crushing the ghosts of Antonioni's *L'Eclisse* who have remained imprisoned on the set, their pockets still bulging with storms as they stagger across Via Cristoforo Colombo.

The rearview mirror reflects the tired ink of the asphalt, a bottle of beer that rolls endlessly, Vincent Price digging his dog's grave in front of the Cathedral of Saints Peter and Paul. All these things I'm leaving behind, including the past and the curses, which now flow like the opening crawl of *Star Wars*, the words crashing into black space, while ahead, ten meters before tomorrow, the waves drown the heads of new days.

The sea is nearby, to the south. The sea has my therapy; it holds Sara hostage and waits for me. I know it very well, its empty, submerged fishing net into which small bass swim belly up from the ecstasy of their daily dose of petroleum. It's my cursed place that moves back and forth, with its tides and its wide beach, a name written in the sand a thousand times, a castle without towers, and a syringe for an antenna. Poachers who drag mermaids by the tail, footsteps of bulldozers, the skeleton of a three-star hotel, and in the distance the neon lights of bars. Ostia, city of the living, sleeps, digesting dreams in its psychedelic canal, the foam and the gray fin of washing machines run aground; the Roman theater in Ostia, city of the dead, with the actors emerging from excavations, from the cracks, from ancient stone nests, nereids with decomposed thighs dancing with shopkeepers from other centuries, coins of Maxentius under their tongues.

This is the place I have to go back to every night. The shore. A trade, a contract, one Venus for another. My blue van knows the way, the bends and curves, its pistons frying when it hunts, when its stomach is empty. Its welds roar, it shakes off the old blood crusts, the thin mouth of its old car radio grinds its teeth and spits out "Walk on the Wild Side" by Lou Reed. It is its way of reminding me of her, Sara.

Sara sucks the souls of guys; the tequila of the party, her room, drunken people.
The amphetamines in the blood run barefoot chased by the muzzle of a truck.
Sara begins to shave her legs, eyebrows, puts cotton in her bra.

Sara becomes a she, and her eyes turn blue.
The fists of the Amazons, the she-males, their chorus of Spanish curses, the black enamel.
Sara who continues to repeat to all: "Honey, do you want to take a ride?"
But her body isn't free. Everyone has to pay for the little Venus.
The EUR district and its spaceship, fifty-one meters high, landed in Pakistan Square in 1957.
My blue van; her too-skinny body; her long fingers.
Sara who asks me twice: "Honey, do you want to take a ride?"
The Amazons throw stones at us; she climbs into the van in a hurry and sits in the hot seat, next to me.
It was two years ago the black enamel dug into me.
The probe of her mouth, many oil wells never discovered.
The diamonds of Golconda.

It was a Friday the last time I saw her, two months ago. That day continuously explodes, that day has a severed tail like a lizard tortured by children. The sachet of almonds between her legs, her skinny arms, and the yellow citron plants wobbling in the belly of my van. Transporting the last load of the day to the nursery; this is my job. Sara is waiting for me, walking back and forth in her five meters of that open-air harem. Outside the perimeter, close to the streetlights and the square, goddesses of the moment parade dressed in the blue fur coats of male desire, while a switchblade snaps and another tattoo appears on the shoulders, a red snake-shaped warning. The mark of the pimp.

A night Amazon, a she-male with gold bars hanging from her ears, pulling her little clump of Equatorial Guinea on a leash, looks at me crookedly and lowers her vanilla miniskirt. The gardens, the open space with two peeling benches where an old witch speaks to her fire, throwing sparks at whoever passes by, the hill on the left, the armored villas and the boxy hedges. The descent, the police siren that screams, suddenly dispersing the group of nameless African gazelles, their black thighs like legs of the night. A pimp rattles his ten bracelets and starts the engine of his expensive car, smiling at the magnet on the dashboard with the face of Idi Amin.

I move ahead, looking for my therapy, for her. I haven't used sertraline for months now.

Here she is. Her red knees, her black boots, the crucifix

between her newborn tits with two bright stones in place of the eyes of Jesus Christ. Sara, she's just thirty meters from me, with her handbag swollen with latex bellflowers and a dried sunflower sprinkled with hairspray sticking out from the purse's zipper. I speed up, but not enough. A black BMW, faster than me, brakes and opens the door. Sara looks around and decides to get in, while the muzzle of my van, still too far back, snarls, deforming the steel bars of the grille, revealing the radiator's baleen.

They run to the south, while the traffic lights of Via Cristoforo Colombo blink out of order, showing their faded orange eyes. I can barely keep up, the large citron fruits falling and bouncing everywhere as I change lanes. It's like a hailstorm only I can hear, in the back of the van and between my ribs, strangling my heart, making it climb up my throat to be spat onto the windshield, to see what I see. I can't make out who's driving the black BMW, while the car window at times shows Sara's profile, her white, byzantine face screwed onto generous jaws, pointed at the horizon, to the south, to the sea.

The street, this ramp of asphalt toward the shore, is very long, bordered by pine trees and unsold billboards with torn words in their white squares. On the right appear the rusted sides of a kind of Stonehenge made up of three buildings, under construction since 1970; pylons with crooked legs; minefields where heads full of loneliness are blown up and streams of mist flow through; a motel with no windows screaming "Always Open" in blue neon; a gypsy camp with a shaman who spits fire from his mouth, surrounded by children without shoes. Then you find the sea, in the background against the black edges of the Ostia beach, lit up at times by the purple and milk-white alien corpses of luminescent jellyfish. The black BMW stops in the parking lot of the large roundabout, turns off its lights and disappears. This is the moment when that day explodes, inside my mind, preventing me from remembering. I just know that the sea took Sara that night. The last time I saw her.

Our names in the sand survived the tides and the bulldozers,
Maddalena and Sara; the two lesbians, she and I, the two asteroids.
The sea who doesn't want to open its mouth and let her go.
"Honey, do you want to take a ride?" But she can't answer me.

The stereo in my van plays "My My, Hey Hey" by Neil Young.
It's useless to wait for a miracle, for an ABRACADABRA.
I will bring another bride, another Venus, to this cannibal sea.
"A trade, do you agree?"
You can't go back, when all of a sudden you're in the dark,
when a man driving a black BMW fucked you,
out of the blue.

For this reason, every night I go hunting, to barter with the sea. That's why I am here, in the seat of my blue bride eater. But it's time to change the music, the polycarbonate spirals of Metallica's *Black Album* begin to spin faster. The "Enter Sandman" riff spills onto the orthogonal axis of the EUR district, shaking the foundations of the Palace of Italian Civilization bruised with too many black holes; the modern Coliseum seems about to take off, with its base burned by the fire of an imaginary Apollo 18, crewed by ghosts with black fezzes who emerge from portholes carved in travertine. They are soldiers of a dead empire, hunting for the Moon. They are hunting like me.

A checkpoint; dummies with egg-shaped skulls stop my van. Then their general, Giorgio De Chirico, pops out, shooting a burst of colors along the van's side, and curses me. I see him lying down on the navel of a star-shaped square, in front of a fountain that sprays arcs of water, before getting up again to get my plate number. Neil Gaiman avenges me by giving him a kick in the ass, before slipping down the long colonnade hand in hand with Oneiros to go and have a beer.

The rhythm of the music slows down, perhaps only for a moment, the song "The Unforgiven" takes over, the illusion of a classical guitar's sound before the next storm pours out the car window and reaches a small colony of prostitutes, the ones with real pussies between their legs, parked near the pagoda of a rusty dead newsstand. The old empire in decline, you can see the remnants of the walls of Byzantium. "Look at that bitch," one of them says, looking at me, grimacing and gnashing her teeth. She should be the fat captain of that group of prostitutes, with her Marilyn Monroe canary yellow wig. She sees me passing, spits on the ground and rubs her fingers on the talisman buried in her loose bra: a small photograph of Father Pio. I know what they are thinking about me: a woman who enters that open air brothel brings bad luck, just like females that board ships under the eyes of frowning superstitious sailors.

The Black Album runs faster than usual. I have to find my Venus quickly tonight. The sea is waiting for our strange barter. I accelerate, I reach the artificial lake surrounded by the Walk of Japan, still stained by the purple of the Yoshino cherry blossoms. But it isn't spring, they are not in bloom; the specter of Basquiat is working on the bare branches with a psychedelic spray, decorating them with colors only he can see, thanks to his heroin binoculars. He's probably still grinding his teeth, recalling old bites from Brooklyn rats.

The ballad "Nothing Else Matters" bounces out the other side with me, into the labyrinths of Lebanon and Indonesia Street, toward the fresh flesh market. I stand in line with others to smell an Amazon with stylized silver hands that hang from her ears and a large nugget in her red panties. On the sidewalk, on the passenger side, there is a row of forgotten stuff: a plastic shell from which you can hear a thousand stories of desperate illegals crammed in fast rafts; a doll stitched with the too-big head of another; Mussolini's war helmet; a grenade; a Koran illustrated by a child; the scale model of St. Peters and of the Mosque of Samarkand with its four giant tits; an army of ants dragging a wedding dress; a sandbag from Danakil; an old election poster of the Christian Democrats; a spear from the Battle of Adwa; a meatball of human flesh; memories that, like the vertebrae of a spine, join the rectum of the past to the neck of tomorrow.

Now it's my turn. The Amazon, the she-male, looks into the passenger window, smiling. *A woman, yes, I am a woman, damn it!* She doesn't have Sara's blue eyes, but she's thin like her; she has long bones and tits that have yet to ripen. She's still not a bride, but she is becoming one. Nineteen years old, she looks like Sara, maybe the sea will accept her. Now she peeks inside the van, stretching her neck as if she's looking for someone hiding behind the seat.

"I'm alone."

She hears the broken rhythm of the song "My Friend of Misery" and lights a cigarette, moves the filter from her purple lips and sighs, "Cool music. Let's go?" then sinks two fingers inside her red panties; half-closing her huge eyes, giving me a glimpse of something between her legs. *The Black Album,* the gasoline of my courage, is about to run out.

"Let's go, but I don't want to do it here."

The Amazon with the large eyes says her name: Caroline.
Sara, Caroline, and Maddalena; we are three alien asteroids now.
Every now and then something strange falls from the sky.
Her fake nails, painted with a beautiful, phosphorescent green,
her too-big hands which now hold her smashed head;
I hit her very hard...
She remains motionless, in that pose;
she looks like a living statue of Pompeii protecting itself from hot hailstones.
Every now and then something made of steel falls from the sky.
The brain fluid leaking out over her face drips from the tip of her nose.
Yeah, I hit her very hard. Out of the blue;
her thoughts, slowly draining, seem so yellow.
"Honey, do you want to take a ride?" But she can no longer answer me;
now she's in the back of the van, between the citron plants,
while the car stereo plays "Walk on the Wild Side" by Lou Reed.
ABRACADABRA. Sara seems to be here, now,
with her skinny legs crossed, knotted,
with her smell different from everything else.
I push the blue van to the south, toward the sea.

The sea is waiting for me, on the usual shore. Ostia City sleeps with its toes immersed in the water, with the fog that crosses its rusted balconies; it doesn't seem to notice anything. I hear gunshots from the old Idroscalo area, but there's nothing to worry about. It's the ghost of Pier Paolo Pasolini who chases the people, the dead of today, the new ghosts, shooting into the air with his 24-karat Kalashnikov, waving his diary *The Novel of Narcissus* like a pirate flag. He enjoys scaring the souls in an orderly queue in front of the grand staircase of Purgatory, with a sealed K ration under their arm and the Star of David on their sleeves. They are not Jews; they are those guilty of forbidden love along with their accusers, bent over by stone toads tied around their necks.

The sea rears its back and sinks its foam claws into the sand. The beast has seen me. I turn off the square eyes of the van, then

I push Caroline out of it, dragging her by the ankles. *Damn heavy.* Before taking her onto the beach—before the sea, the beast, can see her—I must do something to fix her wrong eyes. The sea has spit out too many fake brides until now; it only wants Venus with blue eyes, like those of Sara. The terms are clear, and I really do not want to leave empty-handed this time. I climb back into the van, looking for something that could help me. *A spoon,* it will work fine. Caroline, lying on the ground, seems to admire the black sky. The expression on her face is the same as a broken TV. No electricity—the Amazon without pussy still sweats neuron juice, which is spreading on the grass like thick yellow frost.

I sit astride her. With one hand I hold her firmly by the hair; with the other I push the spoon into her right socket, exerting pressure, like a lever. I go deeper to excavate the optic nerve. The eyeball begins to rotate upward, showing thin blood vessels underneath. Now Caroline can look directly into her own brain. *We are monsters inside; beneath our human skin we are horrible.* The eye of the Amazon squirts out with a plop, and then it's time to work on the other. Those two empty holes that now shine in her face look like shotgun wounds on an alien; purple skin like that of a dinosaur.

I go back to the van to pick the right eyes, blue, stuffed in the ice of my lunchbox, fresh from yesterday, those of a little girl who, sitting on her backpack, watched the trains departing from the Tiburtina Station.

"Are you lost?"

Catching someone without being seen is very easy with all these windows, eighteen thousand square meters of illusions, mirrors, and reflections. *Thanks, Tiburtina Station!* But it's hard to find the same look as Sara's, the same naïve-blue blood of Neptune, of subzero planets. The sea is demanding, spits out everything, and I have to start all over, every time, hunting for Sara once again, the only one that the beast wants to keep in its gullet.

"Today you'll accept the trade, right? Look at that blue..." I lift the rubber lid of my lunch box and show the beast what it contains: the little girl's eyes in the ice. The waves rise, protrude, but they do not want to look; they want to be watched. On the black skin of the sea small yellow spots appear. *What...?*

I go down to the beach; I get closer to the beast, to the sea, for a better look. What is it spitting out today? It is not human flesh, not pieces of brides as usual. *They are…my rotten citron fruits which float,* and then suddenly other citrons emerge from the seabed. It's like a yellow dance, so heretical. *Jesus Christ.* Here is the tail of that damned exploded day. I can finally see it.

Sara who sucked the souls of drunken customers.
"Honey, do you want to take a ride?" But then she never came back.
The song "Do You Feel Loved" by U2 plays strongly in my head.
The magic is over, the ABRACADABRA.
Sara and Maddalena; the two lesbians, two asteroids, both of the same race.
I've been waiting for her for days, under her empty apartment.
But she came back home with him. She opens the car door,
I see her skinny legs and the red shoes.
The black BMW drives away screeching its tires.
"Honey, this is not just a ride."
She carries two suitcases, behind her I see a trail of rainbow, that of those who have been lucky, of those who harpooned a huge whale
to have enough oil, grease and light, for life.
You can't leave, out of the blue. The blue van roars.
She screams, and then my steel shot closes her mouth and her blue eyes.
We go south, toward the sea, who can clean everything, erase everything.
But her body re-emerges, it floats. I know what to do…
The adhesive tape, the citrons as ballast tied to her legs, around her waist.
It takes more than thirty citrons to make her go down,
so that no one could bring her back.
"Your new home, sweetie, three meters underwater. Yellow looks good on you."
What else can you do when a son of a bitch
steals the only Venus you've found in the last forty years of frost,
out of the blue.

I dive into the water, I know where to look: one meter, two meters, my lungs are bursting. I can't see anything; the moon's neon doesn't reach me. I follow the citrons that continue to float upward; I make my way to the seabed. I touch the sand with my fingers. Forty seconds, I can't hold on much longer. I found something: the bones of Sara's skeletal leg. Her flesh is becoming mush, and the citrons, detached from her body, rise like missiles to the surface. I cling to these horrid remains with my fingernails. I get a good grip on her shoulder blades and I can slide horizontally toward her head. Sixty seconds, I don't have much time. I find Sara; with the last of my strength I kiss her passionately.

"Honey, do you want to take a ride?"

Her mouth is empty, a meatless hole with ivory battlements. Then something soft twists around my tongue.

"*Are you alive?*"

The moray eel with its steel colored eyes slips down my throat, quickly slides down flopping wildly, and bites my heart.

CLIVE BARKER

SCAPE-GOATS

IT WASN'T a real island the tide had carried us onto; it was a lifeless mound of stones. Calling a hunchbacked shit-pile like this an island is flattery. Islands are oases in the sea: green and abundant. This is a forsaken place: no seals in the water around it, no birds in the air above it. I can think of no use for a place like this, except that you could say of it: I saw the heart of nothing, and survived.

"It's not on any of the charts," said Ray, poring over the map of the Inner Hebrides, his nail at the spot where he'd calculated that we should be. It was, as he'd said, an empty space on the map, just pale blue sea without the merest speck to sign the existence of this rock. It wasn't just the seals and the birds that ignored it, then; the chart makers had too. There were one or two arrows in the vicinity of Ray's finger, marking the currents that should have been taking us north: tiny red darts on a paper ocean. The rest, like the world outside, was deserted.

Jonathan was jubilant, of course, once he discovered that the place wasn't even to be found on the map; he seemed to feel instantly exonerated. The blame for our being here wasn't his any longer; it was the map makers'. He wasn't going to be held responsible for our being beached if the mound wasn't even marked on the charts. The apologetic expression he'd worn since our unscheduled arrival was replaced with a look of self-satisfaction.

"You can't avoid a place that doesn't exist, can you?" he crowed. "I mean, can you?"

"You could have used the eyes God gave you," Ray flung back at him; but Jonathan wasn't about to be cowed by reasonable criticism.

"It was so sudden, Raymond," he said. "I mean, in this mist I didn't have a chance. It was on top of us before I knew it."

It had been sudden, no two ways about that. I'd been in the galley preparing breakfast, which had become my responsibility since neither Angela nor Jonathan showed any enthusiasm for the task, when the hull of the *Emmanuelle* grated on shingle, then ploughed her way, juddering, up onto the stony beach. There was a moment's silence: then the shouting began. I climbed up out of the galley to find Jonathan standing on deck, grinning sheepishly and waving his arms around to semaphore his innocence.

"Before you ask," he said, "I don't know how it happened. One minute we were just coasting along—"

"Oh, Jesus Christ All-fucking Mighty." Ray was clambering out of the cabin, hauling a pair of jeans on as he did so, and looking much the worse for a night in a bunk with Angela. I'd had the questionable honor of listening to her orgasms all night; she was certainly demanding. Jonathan began his defense speech again from the beginning: "Before you ask—" but Ray silenced him with a few choice insults. I retreated into the confines of the galley while the argument raged on deck. It gave me no small satisfaction to hear Jonathan slanged; I even hoped Ray would lose his cool enough to bloody that perfect hook nose.

The galley was a slop bucket. The breakfast I'd been preparing was all over the floor and I left it there, the yolks of the eggs, the gammon and the French toasts all congealing in pools of spilled fat. It was Jonathan's fault; let him clear it up. I poured myself a glass of grapefruit juice, waited until the recriminations died down, and went back up.

It was barely two hours after dawn, and the mist that had shrouded this island from Jonathan's view still covered the sun. If today was anything like the week that we'd had so far, by noon the deck would be too hot to step on barefoot, but now, with the mist still thick, I felt cold wearing just the bottom of my bikini. It didn't matter much, sailing amongst the islands, what you wore. There was no one to see you. I'd got the best all-over tan I'd ever had. But this morning the chill drove me back below to find a sweater. There was no wind: the cold was coming up out of the sea. It's still night down there, I thought, just a few yards off the beach; limitless night.

I pulled on a sweater, and went back on deck. The maps were out, and Ray was bending over them. His bare back was peeling from an excess of sun, and I could see the bald patch he tried to hide in his dirty yellow curls. Jonathan was staring at the beach and stroking his nose.

"Christ, what a place," I said.

He glanced at me, trying a smile. He had this illusion, poor Jonathan, that his face could charm a tortoise out of its shell, and to be fair to him there were a few women who melted if he so much as looked at them. I wasn't one of them, and it irritated him. I'd always thought his Jewish good looks too bland to be beautiful. My indifference was a red rag to him.

A voice, sleepy and pouting, drifted up from below deck. Our Lady of the Bunk was awake at last: time to make her late entrance, coyly wrapping a towel around her nakedness as she emerged. Her face was puffed up with too much red wine, and her hair needed a comb through it. Still she turned on the radiance, eyes wide, Shirley Temple with cleavage.

"What's happening, Ray? Where are we?"

Ray didn't look up from his computations, which earned him a frown.

"We've got a bloody awful navigator, that's all," he said.

"I don't even know what happened," Jonathan protested, clearly hoping for a show of sympathy from Angela. None was forthcoming.

"But where are we?" she asked again.

"Good morning, Angela," I said; I too was ignored.

"Is it an island?" she said.

"Of course it's an island: I just don't know which one yet," Ray replied.

"Perhaps it's Barra," she suggested.

Ray pulled a face. "We're nowhere near Barra," he said. "If you'll just let me retrace our steps—"

Retrace our steps, in the sea? Just Ray's Jesus fixation, I

thought, looking back at the beach. It was impossible to guess how big the place was: the mist erased the landscape after a hundred yards.

Perhaps somewhere in that gray wall there was human habitation.

Ray, having located the blank spot on the map where we were supposedly stranded, climbed down onto the beach and took a critical look at the bow.

More to be out of Angela's way than anything else I climbed down to join him. The round stones of the beach were cold and slippery on the bare soles of my feet. Ray smoothed his palm down the side of the *Emmanuelle*, almost a caress, then crouched to look at the damage to the bow.

"I don't think we're holed," he said, "but I can't be sure."

"We'll float off come high tide," said Jonathan, posing on the bow, hands on hips, "no sweat," he winked at me, "no sweat at all."

"Will we shit float off!" Ray snapped. "Take a look for yourself."

"Then we'll get some help to haul us off." Jonathan's confidence was unscathed.

"And you can damn well fetch someone, you asshole."

"Sure, why not? Give it an hour or so for the fog to shift and I'll take a walk, find some help."

He sauntered away.

"I'll put on some coffee," Angela volunteered.

Knowing her, that'd take an hour to brew. There was time for a stroll.

I started along the beach.

"Don't go too far, love," Ray called.

"No."

Love, he said. Easy word; he meant nothing by it.

The sun was warmer now, and as I walked I stripped off the sweater. My bare breasts were already brown as two nuts, and, I thought, about as big. Still, you can't have everything. At least I'd got two neurons in my head to rub together, which was more than could be said for Angela; she had tits like melons and a brain that'd shame a mule.

The sun still wasn't getting through the mist properly. It was filtering down on the island fitfully, and its light flattened everything out, draining the place of color or weight, reducing the sea and the rocks and the rubbish on the beach to one bleached-out gray, the color of over-boiled meat.

After only a hundred yards something about the place began to depress me, so I turned back. On my right tiny, lisping waves crept up to the shore and collapsed with a weary slopping sound on the stones. No majestic rollers here: just the rhythmical slop, slop, slop of an exhausted tide.

I hated the place already.

BACK AT the boat, Ray was trying the radio, but for some reason all he could get was a blanket of white noise on every frequency. He cursed it awhile, then gave up. After half an hour, breakfast was served, though we had to make do with sardines, tinned mushrooms and the remains of the French toast. Angela served this feast with her usual aplomb, looking as though she was performing a second miracle with loaves and fishes. It was all but impossible to enjoy the food anyway; the air seemed to drain all the taste away.

"Funny isn't it—" began Jonathan.

"Hilarious," said Ray.

"—there's no foghorns. Mist, but no horns. Not even the sound of a motor; weird."

He was right. Total silence wrapped us up, a damp and smothering hush. Except for the apologetic slop of the waves and the sound of our voices, we might as well have been deaf.

I sat at the stern and looked into the empty sea. It was still gray, but the sun was beginning to strike other colors in it now: a somber green, and, deeper, a hint of blue-purple. Below the boat I could see strands of kelp and Maiden's Hair, toys to the tide, swaying. It looked inviting: and anything was better than the sour atmosphere on the *Emmanuelle.*

"I'm going for a swim," I said.

"I wouldn't, love," Ray replied.

"Why not?"

"The current that threw us up here must be pretty strong, you don't want to get caught in it."

"But the tide's still coming in: I'd only be swept back to the beach."

"You don't know what cross currents there are out there.

Whirlpools even: they're quite common. Suck you down in a flash."

I looked out to sea again. It looked harmless enough, but then I'd read that these were treacherous waters, and thought better of it.

Angela had started a little sulking session because nobody had finished her immaculately prepared breakfast. Ray was playing up to it. He loved babying her, letting her play damn stupid games. It made me sick.

I went below to do the washing up, tossing the slops out of the porthole into the sea. They didn't sink immediately. They floated in an oily patch, half-eaten mushrooms and slivers of sardines bobbing around on the surface, as though someone had thrown up on the sea. Food for crabs, if any self-respecting crab condescended to live here.

Jonathan joined me in the galley, obviously still feeling a little foolish, despite the bravado. He stood in the doorway, trying to catch my eye, while I pumped up some cold water into the bowl and halfheartedly rinsed the greasy plastic plates. All he wanted was to be told I didn't think this was his fault, and yes, of course he was a kosher Adonis. I said nothing.

"Do you mind if I lend a hand?" he said.

"There's not really room for two," I told him, trying not to sound too dismissive. He flinched nevertheless: this whole episode had punctured his self-esteem more badly than I'd realized, despite his strutting around.

"Look," I said gently, "why don't you go back on deck: take in the sun before it gets too hot?"

"I feel like a shit," he said.

"It was an accident."

"An utter shit."

"Like you said, we'll float off with the tide."

He moved out of the doorway and down into the galley; his proximity made me feel almost claustrophobic. His body was too large for the space: too tanned, too assertive.

"I said there wasn't any room, Jonathan."

He put his hand on the back of my neck, and instead of shrugging it off I let it stay there, gently massaging the muscles. I wanted to tell him to leave me alone, but the lassitude of the place seemed to have got into my system. His other hand was palm down on my belly, moving up to my breast. I was indifferent to these ministrations: if he wanted this he could have it.

Above deck Angela was gasping in the middle of a giggling fit, almost choking on her hysteria. I could see her in my mind's eye, throwing back her head, shaking her hair loose. Jonathan had unbuttoned his shorts, and had let them drop. The gift of his foreskin to God had been neatly made; his erection was so hygienic in its enthusiasm it seemed incapable of the least harm. I let his mouth stick to mine, let his tongue explore my gums, insistent as a dentist's finger. He slid my bikini down far enough to get access, fumbled to position himself, then pressed in.

Behind him, the stair creaked, and I looked over his shoulder in time to glimpse Ray, bending at the hatch and staring down at Jonathan's buttocks and at the tangle of our arms. Did he see, I wondered, that I felt nothing; did he understand that I did this dispassionately, and could only have felt a twinge of desire if I substituted his head, his back, his cock for Jonathan's? Soundlessly, he withdrew from the stairway; a moment passed, in which Jonathan said he loved me, then I heard Angela's laughter begin again as Ray described what he'd just witnessed. Let the bitch think whatever she pleased: I didn't care.

Jonathan was still working at me with deliberate but uninspired strokes, a frown on his face like that of a schoolboy trying to solve some impossible equation. Discharge came without warning, signaled only by a tightening of his hold on my shoulders, and a deepening of his frown. His thrusts slowed and stopped; his eyes found mine for a flustered moment. I wanted to kiss him, but he'd lost all interest. He withdrew still hard, wincing. "I'm always sensitive when I've come," he murmured, hauling his shorts up. "Was it good for you?"

I nodded. It was laughable; the whole thing was laughable. Stuck in the middle of nowhere with this little boy of twenty-six, and Angela, and a man who didn't care if I lived or died. But then perhaps neither did I. I thought, for no reason, of the slops on the sea, bobbing around, waiting for the next wave to catch them.

Jonathan had already retreated up the stairs. I boiled up some coffee, standing staring out of the porthole and feeling his come dry to a corrugated pearliness on the inside of my thigh.

Ray and Angela had gone by the time I'd brewed the coffee, off for a walk on the island apparently, looking for help.

Jonathan was sitting in my place at the stern, gazing out at the mist. More to break the silence than anything I said:

"I think it's lifted a bit."

"Has it?"

I put a mug of black coffee beside him.

"Thanks."

"Where are the others?"

"Exploring."

He looked round at me, confusion in his eyes. "I still feel like a shit."

I noticed the bottle of gin on the deck beside him.

"Bit early for drinking, isn't it?"

"Want some?"

"It's not even eleven."

"Who cares?"

He pointed out to sea. "Follow my finger," he said.

I leaned over his shoulder and did as he asked.

"No, you're not looking at the right place. Follow my finger—see it?"

"Nothing."

"At the edge of the mist. It appears and disappears. There! Again!"

I did see something in the water, twenty or thirty yards from the *Emmanuelle's* stern. Brown-colored, wrinkled, turning over.

"It's a seal," I said.

"I don't think so."

"The sun's warming up the sea. They're probably coming in to bask in the shallows."

"It doesn't look like a seal. It rolls in a funny way—"

"Maybe a piece of flotsam—"

"Could be."

He swigged deeply from the bottle.

"Leave some for tonight."

"Yes, mother."

We sat in silence for a few minutes. Just the waves on the beach. Slop. Slop. Slop.

Once in a while the seal, or whatever it was, broke surface, rolled, and disappeared again.

Another hour, I thought, and the tide will begin to turn. Float us off this little afterthought of creation.

"Hey!" Angela's voice, from a distance. "Hey, you guys!"

You guys, she called us.

Jonathan stood up, hand up to his face against the glare of sunlit rock. It was much brighter now: and getting hotter all the time.

"She's waving to us," he said, uninterested.

"Let her wave."

"You guys!" she screeched, her arms waving. Jonathan cupped his hands around his mouth and bawled a reply:

"What do you want?"

"Come and see," she replied.

"She wants us to come and see."

"I heard."

"Come on," he said, "nothing to lose."

I didn't want to move, but he hauled me up by the arm. It wasn't worth arguing. His breath was inflammable.

IT WAS difficult making our way up the beach. The stones were not wet with sea water, but covered in a slick film of gray-green algae, like sweat on a skull.

Jonathan was having even more difficulty getting across the beach than I was. Twice he lost his balance and fell heavily on his backside, cursing. The seat of his shorts was soon a filthy olive color, and there was a tear where his buttocks showed.

I was no ballerina, but I managed to make it, step by slow step, trying to avoid the large rocks so that if I slipped I wouldn't have far to fall.

Every few yards we'd have to negotiate a line of stinking seaweed. I was able to jump them with reasonable elegance but Jonathan, pissed and uncertain of his balance, ploughed through them, his naked feet completely buried in the stuff. It wasn't just kelp: there was the usual detritus washed up on any beach: the broken bottles, the rusting Coke cans, the scum-stained cork, globs of tar, fragments of crabs, pale yellow Durex. And crawling over these stinking piles of dross were inch-long, fat-eyed blue flies. Hundreds of them, clambering over the shit, and over each other, buzzing to be alive, and alive to be buzzing.

It was the first life we'd seen.

I was doing my best not to fall flat on my face as I stepped across one of these lines of seaweed, when a little avalanche of pebbles began off to my left. Three, four, five stones were skipping over each other toward the sea, and setting another dozen stones moving as they jumped.

There was no visible cause for the effect.

Jonathan didn't even bother to look up; he was having too much trouble staying vertical.

The avalanche stopped: run out of energy. Then another: this time between us and the sea. Skipping stones: bigger this time than the last, and gaining more height as they leaped.

The sequence was longer than before: it knocked stone into stone until a few pebbles actually reached the sea at the end of the dance.

Plop.

Dead noise.

Plop. Plop.

Ray appeared from behind one of the big boulders at the height of the beach, beaming like a loon.

"There's life on Mars," he yelled and ducked back the way he'd come. A few more perilous moments and we reached him, the sweat sticking our hair to our foreheads like caps.

Jonathan looked a little sick.

"What's the big deal?" he demanded.

"Look what we've found," said Ray, and led the way beyond the boulders. The first shock.

Once we got to the height of the beach we were looking down on to the other side of the island. There was more of the same drab beach, and then sea.

No inhabitants, no boats, no sign of human existence. The whole place couldn't have been more than half a mile across: barely the back of a whale.

But there was some life here; that was the second shock.

In the sheltering ring of the large, bald boulders which crowned the island was a fenced-in compound. The posts were rotting in the salt air, but a tangle of rusted barbed-wire had been wound around and between them to form a primitive pen. Inside the pen there was a patch of coarse grass, and on this pitiful lawn stood three sheep. And Angela.

She was standing in the penal colony, stroking one of the inmates and cooing in its blank face.

"Sheep," she said, triumphantly.

Jonathan was there before me with his snapped remark: "So what?"

"Well, it's strange, isn't it?" said Ray. "Three sheep in the middle of a little place like this?"

"They don't look well to me," said Angela.

She was right. The animals were the worse for their exposure to the elements; their eyes were gummy with matter, and their fleeces hung off their hides in knotted clumps, exposing panting flanks. One of them had collapsed against the barbed-wire, and seemed unable to right itself again, either too depleted or too sick.

"It's cruel," said Angela.

I had to agree: it seemed positively sadistic, locking up these creatures without more than a few blades of grass to chew on, and a battered tin bath of stagnant water to quench their thirst.

"Odd, isn't it?" said Ray.

"I've cut my foot." Jonathan was squatting on the top of one of the flatter boulders, peering at the underside of his right foot.

"There's glass on the beach," I said, exchanging a vacant stare with one of the sheep.

"They're so deadpan," said Ray. "Nature's straight men."

Curiously, they didn't look so unhappy with their condition; their stares were philosophical. Their eyes said: I'm just a sheep, I don't expect you to like me, care for me, preserve me, except for your stomach's sake. There were no angry baas, no stamping of a frustrated hoof.

Just three gray sheep, waiting to die.

Ray had lost interest in the business. He was wandering back down the beach, kicking a can ahead of him. It rattled and skipped, reminding me of the stones.

"We should let them free," said Angela.

I ignored her; what was freedom in a place like this? She persisted:

"Don't you think we should?"

"No."

"They'll die."

"Somebody put them here for a reason."

"But they'll *die*."

"They'll die on the beach if we let them out. There's no food for them."

"We'll feed them."

"French toast and gin," suggested Jonathan, picking a sliver of glass from his sole.

"We can't just leave them."

"It's not our business," I said. It was all getting boring. Three sheep. Who cared if they lived or—

I'd thought that about myself an hour earlier. We had something in common, the sheep and I.

My head was aching.

"They'll die," whined Angela, for the third time.

"You're a stupid bitch," Jonathan told her. The remark was made without malice: he said it calmly, as a statement of plain fact.

I couldn't help grinning.

"What?" She looked as though she'd been bitten.

"Stupid bitch," he said again. "B-I-T-C-H."

Angela flushed with anger and embarrassment, and turned on him. "You got us stuck here," she said, lip curling.

The inevitable accusation. Tears in her eyes. Stung by his words.

"I did it deliberately," he said, spitting on his fingers and rubbing saliva into the cut. "I wanted to see if we could leave you here."

"You're drunk."

"And you're stupid. But I'll be sober in the morning."

The old lines still made their mark.

Outstripped, Angela started down the beach after Ray, trying to hold back her tears until she was out of sight. I almost felt some sympathy for her. She was, when it came down to verbal fisticuffs, easy meat.

"You're a bastard when you want to be," I told Jonathan; he just looked at me, glassy-eyed.

"Better be friends. Then I won't be a bastard to you."

"You don't scare me."

"I know."

The mutton was staring at me again. I stared back.

"Fucking sheep," he said.

"They can't help it."

"If they had any decency, they'd slit their ugly fucking throats."

"I'm going back to the boat."

"Ugly fuckers."

"Coming?"

He took hold of my hand: fast, tight, and held it in his hand like he'd never let go. Eyes on me suddenly.

"Don't go."

"It's too hot up here."

"Stay. The stone's nice and warm. Lie down. They won't interrupt us this time."

"You knew?" I said.

"You mean Ray? Of course I knew. I thought we put on quite a little performance."

He drew me close, hand over hand up my arm, like he was hauling in a rope. The smell of him brought back the galley, his frown, his muttered profession ("Love you"), the quiet retreat.

Deja vu.

Still, what was there to do on a day like this but go round in the same dreary circle, like the sheep in the pen? Round and round. Breathe, sex, eat, shit.

The gin had gone to his groin. He tried his best but he hadn't got a hope. It was like trying to thread spaghetti.

Exasperated, he rolled off me.

"Fuck. Fuck. Fuck."

Senseless word, once it was repeated, it had lost all its meaning, like everything else. Signifying nothing.

"It doesn't matter," I said.

"Fuck off."

"It really doesn't."

He didn't look at me, just stared down at his cock. If he'd had a knife in his hand at that moment, I think he'd have cut it off and laid it on the warm rock, a shrine to sterility.

I left him studying himself, and walked back to the *Emmanuelle.* Something odd struck me as I went, something I hadn't noticed before. The blue flies, instead of jumping ahead of me as I approached, just let themselves be trodden on. Positively lethargic; or suicidal. They sat on the hot stones and popped under my soles, their gaudy little lives going out like so many lights.

The mist was disappearing at last, and as the air warmed up, the island unveiled its next disgusting trick: the smell. The fragrance was as wholesome as a roomful of rotting peaches, thick and sickly. It came in through the pores as well as the nostrils, like a syrup. And under the sweetness, something else, rather less pleasant than peaches, fresh or rotten. A smell like an open drain clogged with old meat: like the gutters of a slaughterhouse, caked with suet and black blood. It was the seaweed, I assumed, although I'd never smelled anything to match the stench on any other beach.

I was halfway back to the *Emmanuelle,* holding my nose as I stepped over the bands of rotting weed, when I heard the noise of a little murder behind me. Jonathan's whoops of satanic glee almost drowned the pathetic voice of the sheep as it was killed, but I knew instinctively what the drunken bastard had done.

I turned back, my heel pivoting on the slime. It was almost certainly too late to save one of the beasts, but maybe I could prevent him massacring the other two. I couldn't see the pen; it was hidden behind the boulders, but I could hear Jonathan's triumphant yells, and the thud, thud of his strokes. I knew what I'd see before it came into sight.

The gray-green lawn had turned red. Jonathan was in the pen with the sheep. The two survivors were charging back and forth in a rhythmical trot of panic, baaing in terror, while Jonathan stood over the third sheep, erect now. The victim had partially collapsed, its sticklike front legs buckled beneath it, its back legs rigid with approaching death. Its bulk shuddered with nervous spasms, and its eyes showed more white than brown. The top of its skull had been almost entirely dashed to pieces, and the gray hash of its brain exposed, punctured by shards of its own bone, and pulped by the large round stone that Jonathan was still wielding. Even as I watched he brought the weapon down once more onto the sheep's brain pan. Globs of tissue flew off in every direction, speckling me with hot matter and blood. Jonathan looked like some nightmare lunatic (which for that moment, I suppose, he was). His naked body, so recently white, was stained as a butcher's apron after a hard day's hammering at the abattoir. His face was more sheep's gore than Jonathan—

The animal itself was dead. Its pathetic complaints had ceased completely. It keeled over, rather comically, like a cartoon character, one of its ears snagging the wire. Jonathan watched it fall: his face a grin under the blood. Oh, that grin: it served so many purposes. Wasn't that the same smile he charmed women with? The same grin that spoke lechery and love? Now, at last, it was put to its true purpose: the gawping smile of the satisfied savage, standing over his prey with a stone in one hand and his manhood in the other.

Then, slowly, the smile decayed, as his senses returned.

"Jesus," he said, and from his abdomen a wave of revulsion climbed up his body. I could see it quite clearly; the way his gut rolled as a throb of nausea threw his head forward, pitching half-digested gin and toast over the grass.

I didn't move. I didn't want to comfort him, calm him, console him—he was simply beyond my help.

I turned away.

"Frankie," he said through a throat of bile.

I couldn't bring myself to look at him. There was nothing to be done for the sheep, it was dead and gone; all I wanted to do was run away from the little ring of stones, and put the sight out of my head.

"Frankie."

I began to walk, as fast as I was able over such tricky terrain, back down toward the beach and the relative sanity of the *Emmanuelle.*

The smell was stronger now: coming up out of the ground toward my face in filthy waves.

Horrible island. Vile, stinking, insane island.

All I thought was hate as I stumbled across the weed and the filth. The *Emmanuelle* wasn't far off—

Then, a little pattering of pebbles like before. I stopped, balancing uneasily on the sleek dome of a stone, and looked to my left, where even now one of the pebbles was rolling to a halt. As it stopped another, larger pebble, fully six inches across, seemed to move spontaneously from its resting place, and roll down the beach, striking its neighbors and beginning another exodus toward the sea. I frowned: the frown made my head buzz.

Was there some sort of animal—a crab maybe—under the beach, moving the stones? Or was it the heat that in some way twitched them into life? Again: a bigger stone—

I walked on, while behind the rattle and patter continued, one little sequence coming close upon another, to make an almost seamless percussion.

I began, without real focus or explanation, to be afraid.

ANGELA AND Ray were sunning themselves on the deck of the *Emmanuelle.*

"Another couple of hours before we can start to get the bitch off her backside," he said, squinting as he looked up at me.

I thought he meant Angela at first, then realized he was talking about floating the boat out to sea again.

"May as well get some sun." He smiled wanly at me.

"Yeah."

Angela was either asleep or ignoring me. Whichever, it suited me fine.

I slumped down on the sun deck at Ray's feet and let the sun soak into me. The specks of blood had dried on my skin, like tiny scabs. I picked them off idly, and listened to the noise of the stones, and the slop of the sea.

Behind me, pages were being turned. I glanced round. Ray, never able to lie still for very long, was flicking through a library book on the Hebrides he'd brought from home.

I looked back at the sun. My mother always said it burned a hole in the back of your eye, to look straight into the sun, but it was hot and alive up there; I wanted to look into its face. There was a chill in me—I don't know where it had come from—a chill in my gut and in between my legs that wouldn't go away. Maybe I would have to burn it away by looking at the sun.

Some way along the beach I glimpsed Jonathan, tiptoeing down toward the sea. From that distance the mixture of blood and white skin made him look like some piebald freak. He'd stripped off his shorts and he was crouching at the sea's edge to wash off the sheep.

Then, Ray's voice, very quietly: "Oh, God," he said, in such an understated way that I knew the news couldn't be brilliant.

"What is it?"

"I've found out where we are."

"Good."

"No, not good."

"Why? What's wrong?" I sat upright, turning to him.

"It's here, in the book. There's a paragraph on this place."

Angela opened one eye. "Well?" she said.

"It's not just an island. It's a burial mound."

The chill in between my legs fed upon itself, and grew gross. The sun wasn't hot enough to warm me that deep, where I should be hottest.

I looked away from Ray along the beach again. Jonathan was still washing, splashing water up onto his chest. The shadows of the stones suddenly seemed very black and heavy, their edges pressed down on the upturned faces of—

Seeing me looking his way Jonathan waved.

Can it be there are corpses under those stones? Buried face up to the sun, like holiday makers laid out on a Blackpool beach?

The world is monochrome. Sun and shadow. The white tops of stones and their black underbellies. Life on top, death underneath.

"Burial?" said Angela. "What sort of burial?"

"War dead," Ray answered.

Angela: "What, you mean Vikings or something?"

"World War I, World War II. Soldiers from torpedoed troopships, sailors washed up. Brought down here by the Gulf Stream; apparently the current funnels them through the straits and washes them up on the beaches of the islands around here."

"Washes them up?" said Angela.

"That's what it says."

"Not any longer though."

"I'm sure the occasional fisherman gets buried here still," Ray replied.

Jonathan had stood up, staring out to sea, the blood off his body. His hand shaded his eyes as he looked out over the blue-gray water, and I followed his gaze as I had followed his finger. A hundred yards out that seal, or whale, or whatever it was, had returned, lolling in the water. Sometimes, as it turned, it threw up a fin, like a swimmer's arm, beckoning.

"How many people were buried?" asked Angela, nonchalantly.

She seemed completely unperturbed by the fact that we were sitting on a grave.

"Hundreds probably."

"Hundreds?"

"It just says 'many dead,' in the book."

"And do they put them in coffins?"

"How should I know?"

What else could it be, this Godforsaken mound—but a

cemetery? I looked at the island with new eyes, as though I'd just recognized it for what it was. Now I had a reason to despise its humpy back, its sordid beach, the smell of peaches.

"I wonder if they buried them all over," mused Angela, "or just at the top of the hill, where we found the sheep? Probably just at the top; out of the way of the water."

Yes, they'd probably had too much of water: their poor green faces picked by fish, their uniforms rotted, their dog tags encrusted with algae. What deaths; and worse, what journeys after death, in squads of fellow corpses, along the Gulf Stream to this bleak landfall. I saw them, in my mind's eye, the bodies of the soldiers, subject to every whim of the tide, borne backward and forward in a slush of rollers until a casual limb snagged on a rock, and the sea lost possession of them. With each receding wave uncovered; sodden and jellied brine, spat out by the sea to stink a while and be stripped by gulls.

I had a sudden, morbid desire to walk on the beach again, armed with this knowledge, kicking over the pebbles in the hope of turning up a bone or two.

As the thought formed, my body made the decision for me. I was standing: I was climbing off the *Emmanuelle.*

"Where are you off to?" said Angela.

"Jonathan," I murmured, and set foot on the mound.

The stench was clearer now: that was the accrued odor of the dead. Maybe drowned men got buried here still, as Ray had suggested, slotted under the pile of stones. The unwary yachtsman, the careless swimmer, their faces wiped off with water. At my feet the beach flies were less sluggish than they'd been: instead of waiting to be killed they jumped and buzzed ahead of my steps, with a new enthusiasm for life.

Jonathan was not to be seen. His shorts were still on the stones at the water's edge, but he'd disappeared. I looked out to sea: nothing: no bobbing head: no lolling, beckoning something.

I called his name.

My voice seemed to excite the flies; they rose in seething clouds.

Jonathan didn't reply.

I began to walk along the margin of the sea, my feet sometimes caught by an idle wave, as often as not left untouched. I realized I hadn't told Angela and Ray about the dead sheep.

Maybe that was a secret between us four. Jonathan, myself, and the two survivors in the pen.

Then I saw him: a few yards ahead—his chest white, wide and clean, every speck of blood washed off. A secret it is then, I thought.

"Where have you been?" I called to him.

"Walking it off," he called back.

"What off?"

"Too much gin." He grinned.

I returned the smile, spontaneously; he'd said he loved me in the galley; that counted for something.

Behind him, a rattle of skipping stones. He was no more than ten yards from me now, shamelessly naked as he walked; his gait was sober.

The rattle of stones suddenly seemed rhythmical. It was no longer a random series of notes as one pebble struck another—it was a beat, a sequence of repeated sounds, a tick-tap pulse.

No accident: intention.

Not chance: purpose.

Not stone: thought. Behind stone, with stone, carrying stone—

Jonathan, now close, was bright. His skin was almost luminous with sun on it, thrown into relief by the darkness behind him.

Wait—

—What darkness?

The stone mounted the air like a bird, defying gravity. A blank black stone, disengaged from the earth. It was the size of a baby: a whistling baby, and it grew behind Jonathan's head as it shimmered down the air toward him.

The beach had been flexing its muscles, tossing small pebbles down to the sea, all the time strengthening its will to raise this boulder off the ground and fling it at Jonathan.

It swelled behind him, murderous in its intention, but my throat had no sound to make worthy of my fright.

Was he deaf? His grin broke open again; he thought the horror on my face was a jibe at his nakedness, I realized. He doesn't understand—

The stone sheared off the top of his head, from the middle of his nose upward, leaving his mouth still wide, his tongue rooted in blood, and flinging the rest of his beauty toward me in a cloud of wet red dust. The upper part of his head was split onto the face of the stone, its expression intact as it swooped toward me. I half fell, and it screamed past me, veering off toward the sea. Once over the water the assassin seemed to lose its will somehow, and faltered in the air before plunging into the waves.

At my feet, blood. A trail that led to where Jonathan's body lay, the open edge of his head toward me, its machinery plain for the sky to see.

I was still not screaming, though for sanity's sake I had to unleash the terror suffocating me. Somebody must hear me, hold me, take me away and explain to me, before the skipping pebbles found their rhythm again. Or worse, before the minds below the beach, unsatisfied with murder by proxy, rolled away their gravestones and rose to kiss me themselves.

But the scream would not come.

All I could hear was the patter of stones to my right and left. They intend to kill us all for invading their sacred ground. Stoned to death, like heretics. Then, a voice.

"For Christ's sake—"

A man's voice; but not Ray's.

He seemed to have appeared from out of thin air; a short, broad man, standing at the sea's edge. In one hand a bucket and under his arm a bundle of coarsely cut hay. Food for the sheep, I thought, through a jumble of half-formed words. Food for sheep.

He stared at me, then down at Jonathan's body, his old eyes wild. "What's gone on?" he said. The Gaelic accent was thick. "In the name of Christ what's gone on?"

I shook my head. It seemed loose on my neck, almost as though I might shake it off. Maybe I pointed to the sheep pen, maybe not. Whatever the reason he seemed to know what I was thinking, and began to climb the beach toward the crown of the island, dropping bucket and bundle as he went.

Half-blind with confusion, I followed, but before I could reach the boulders he was out of their shadow again, his face suddenly shining with panic. "Who did that?"

"Jonathan," I replied. I cast a hand toward the corpse, not daring to look back at him. The man cursed in Gaelic, and stumbled out of the shelter of the boulders.

"What have you done?" he yelled at me. "My Christ, what have you done? Killing their gifts."

"Just sheep," I said. In my head the instant of Jonathan's decapitation was playing over and over again, a loop of slaughter.

"They demand it, don't you see, or they rise—"

"Who rise?" I said, knowing. Seeing the stones shift.

"All of them. Put away without grief or mourning. But they've got the sea in them, in their heads—"

I knew what he was talking about: it was quite plain to me, suddenly. The dead were here: as we knew. Under the stones. But they had the rhythm of the sea in them, and they wouldn't lie down. So to placate them, these sheep were tethered in a pen, to be offered up to their wills.

Did the dead eat mutton? No; it wasn't food they wanted. It was the gesture of recognition—as simple as that.

"Drowned," he was saying, "all drowned."

Then, the familiar patter began again, the drumming of stones, which grew, without warning, into an ear-splitting thunder, as though the entire beach was shifting.

And under the cacophony three other sounds: splashing, screaming and wholesale destruction.

I turned to see a wave of stones rising into the air on the other side of the island—

Again the terrible screams, wrung from a body that was being buffeted and broken.

They were after the *Emmanuelle.* After Ray. I started to run in the direction of the boat, the beach rippling beneath my feet. Behind me, I could hear the boots of the sheep-feeder on the stones. As we ran the noise of the assault became louder. Stones danced in the air like fat birds, blocking the sun, before plunging down to strike at some unseen target. Maybe the boat. Maybe flesh itself—

Angela's tormented screams had ceased.

I rounded the beachhead a few steps ahead of the sheep-feeder, and the *Emmanuelle* came into sight. It, and its human contents, were beyond all hope of salvation. The vessel was being bombarded by endless ranks of stones, all sizes and shapes; its hull was smashed, its windows, mast and deck shattered. Angela lay sprawled on the remains of the sun deck, quite obviously dead. The fury of the hail hadn't stopped, however. The stones beat a tattoo on the remaining structure of the hull, and thrashed at the lifeless bulk of Angela's body, making it bob up and down as though a current were being passed through it.

Ray was nowhere to be seen.

I screamed then: and for a moment it seemed there was a lull in the thunder, a brief respite in the attack. Then it began again: wave after wave of pebbles and rocks rising off the beach and flinging themselves at their senseless targets. They would not be content, it seemed, until the *Emmanuelle* was reduced to flotsam and jetsam, and Angela's body was in small enough pieces to accommodate a shrimp's palate.

The sheep-feeder took hold of my arm in a grip so fierce it stopped the blood flowing to my hand.

"Come on," he said. I heard his voice but did nothing. I was waiting for Ray's face to appear—or to hear his voice calling my name. But there was nothing: just the barrage of the stones. He was dead in the ruins of the boat somewhere—smashed to smithereens.

The sheep-feeder was dragging me now, and I was following him back over the beach.

"The boat," he was saying, "we can get away in my boat—"

The idea of escape seemed ludicrous. The island had us on its back; we were its objects utterly.

But I followed, slipping and sliding over the sweaty rocks, ploughing through the tangle of seaweed, back the way we'd come.

On the other side of the island was his poor hope of life. A rowing boat, dragged up on the shingle: an inconsequential walnut shell of a boat.

Would we go to sea in that, like the three men in a sieve?

He dragged me, unresisting, toward our deliverance. With every step I became more certain that the beach would suddenly rise up and stone us to death. Maybe make a wall of itself, a tower even, when we were within a single step of safety. It could play any game it liked, any game at all. But then, maybe the dead didn't like games. Games are about gambles, and the dead had already lost. Maybe the dead act only with the arid certainty of mathematicians.

He half-threw me into the boat, and began to push it out into the thick tide. No walls of stones rose to prevent our escape. No towers appeared, no slaughtering hail. Even the attack on the *Emmanuelle* had ceased.

Had they sated themselves on three victims? Or was it that the presence of the sheep-feeder, an innocent, a servant of these willful dead, would protect me from their tantrums?

The rowing boat was off the shingle. We bobbed a little on the backs of a few limp waves until we were deep enough for the oars, and then we were pulling away from the shore and my savior was sitting opposite me, rowing for all he was worth, a dew of fresh sweat on his forehead, multiplying with every pull.

The beach receded; we were being set free. The sheep-feeder seemed to relax a little. He gazed down at the swill of dirty water in the bottom of the boat and drew in half a dozen deep breaths; then he looked up at me, his wasted face drained of expression.

"One day, it had to happen—" he said, his voice low and heavy. "Somebody would spoil the way we lived. Break the rhythm."

It was almost soporific, the hauling of the oars, forward and back. I wanted to sleep, to wrap myself up in the tarpaulin I was sitting on, and forget. Behind us, the beach was a distant line. I couldn't see the *Emmanuelle.*

"Where are we going?" I said.

"Back to Tiree," he replied. "We'll see what's to be done there. Find some way to make amends; to help them sleep soundly again."

"Do they eat the sheep?"

"What good is food to the dead? No. No, they have no need of mutton. They take the beasts as a gesture of remembrance."

Remembrance.

I nodded.

"It's our way of mourning them—"

He stopped rowing, too heartsick to finish his explanation, and too exhausted to do anything but let the tide carry us home. A blank moment passed.

Then the scratching.

A mouse noise, no more, a scrabbling at the underside of the boat like a man's nails tickling the planks to be let in. Not one man: many. The sound of their entreaties multiplied; the soft dragging of rotted cuticles across the wood.

In the boat, we didn't move, we didn't speak, we didn't believe. Even as we heard the worst—we didn't believe the worst.

A splash off to starboard; I turned and he was coming toward me, rigid in the water, borne up by unseen puppeteers like a figurehead. It was Ray; his body covered in killing bruises and cuts: stoned to death, then brought, like a gleeful mascot, like proof of power, to spook us. It was almost as though he were walking on water, his feet just hidden by the swell, his arms hanging loosely by his side as he was hauled toward the boat. I looked at his face: lacerated and broken. One eye almost closed, the other smashed from its orbit.

Two yards from the boat, the puppeteers let him sink back into the sea, where he disappeared in a swirl of pink water.

"Your companion?" said the sheep-feeder.

I nodded. He must have fallen into the sea from the stern of the *Emmanuelle.* Now he was like them, a drowned man. They'd already claimed him as their plaything. So they did like games after all: they hauled him from the beach like children come to fetch a playmate, eager that he should join the horseplay.

The scratching had stopped. Ray's body had disappeared altogether. Not a murmur off the pristine sea, just the slop of the waves against the boards of the boat.

I pulled at the oars—

"Row!" I screamed at the sheep-feeder. "Row, or they'll kill us."

He seemed resigned to whatever they had in mind to punish us with. He shook his head and spat onto the water. Beneath his floating phlegm something moved in the deep, pale forms rolled and somersaulted, too far down to be clearly seen. Even as I watched they came floating up toward us, their sea-corrupted faces better defined with every fathom they rose, their arms outstretched to embrace us.

A shoal of corpses. The dead in dozens, crab-cleaned and fishpicked, their remaining flesh scarcely sitting on their bones.

The boat rocked gently as their hands reached up to touch it.

The look of resignation on the sheep-feeder's face didn't falter for a moment as the boat was shaken backward and forward; at first gently, then so violently we were beaten about like dolls. They meant to capsize us, and there was no help for it. A moment later, the boat tipped over.

The water was icy; far colder than I'd anticipated, and it took breath away. I'd always been a fairly strong swimmer. My strokes were confident as I began to swim from the boat, cleaving through the white water. The sheep-feeder was less lucky. Like many men who live with the sea, he apparently couldn't swim. Without issuing a cry or a prayer, he sank like a stone.

What did I hope? That four was enough: that I could be left to thumb a current to safety? Whatever hopes of escape I had, they were short-lived.

I felt a soft, oh, so very soft, brushing of my ankles and my feet, almost a caress. Something broke surface briefly close to my head. I glimpsed a gray back, as of a large fish. The touch on my ankle had become a grasp. A pulpy hand, mushed by so long in the water, had hold of me, and inexorably began to claim me for the sea. I gulped what I knew to be my last breath of air, and as I did so Ray's head bobbed no more than a yard from me. I saw his wounds in clinical detail—the water-cleansed cuts were ugly flaps of white tissue, with a gleam of bone at their core. The loose eye had been washed away by now, his hair, flattened to his skull, no longer disguised the bald patch at his crown.

The water closed over my head. My eyes were open, and I saw my hard-earned breath flashing past my face in a display of silver bubbles. Ray was beside me, consoling, attentive. His arms floated over his head as though he were surrendering. The pressure of the water distorted his face, puffing his cheeks out and spilling threads of severed nerves from his empty eye socket like the tentacles of a tiny squid.

I let it happen. I opened my mouth and felt it fill with cold water. Salt burned my sinuses, the cold stabbed behind my eyes. I felt the brine burning down my throat, a rush of eager water where water shouldn't go—flushing air from my tubes and cavities, till my system was overwhelmed.

Below me, two corpses, their hair swaying loosely in the current, hugged my legs. Their heads lolled and danced on rotted ropes of neck muscle, and though I pawed at their hands, and their flesh came off the bone in gray, lace-edged pieces, their loving grip didn't falter. They wanted me, oh, how dearly they wanted me.

Ray was holding me too, wrapping me up, pressing his face to mine. There was no purpose in the gesture, I suppose. He didn't know or feel, or love or care. And I, losing my life with every second, succumbing to the sea absolutely, couldn't take pleasure in the intimacy that I'd longed for.

Too late for love; the sunlight was already a memory. Was it that the world was going out—darkening toward the edges as I died—or that we were now so deep the sun couldn't penetrate so far? Panic and terror had left me—my heart seemed not to beat at all—my breath didn't come and go in anguished bursts as it had. A kind of peace was on me.

Now the grip of my companions relaxed, and the gentle tide had its way with me. A rape of the body: a ravaging of skin and muscle, gut, eye, sinus, tongue, brain.

Time had no place here. The days may have passed into weeks, I couldn't know. The keels of boats glided over and maybe we looked up from our rock hovels on occasion and watched them pass. A ringed finger was trailed in the water, a splashless puddle clove the sky, a fishing line trailed a worm. Signs of life.

Maybe the same hour as I died, or maybe a year later, the current sniffs me out of my rock and has some mercy. I am twitched from amongst the sea anemones and given to the tide. Ray is with me. His time too has come. The sea change has occurred; there is no turning back for us.

Relentlessly the tide bears us—sometimes floating, bloated decks for gulls, sometimes half-sunk and nibbled by fish—bears us toward the island. We know the surge of the shingle, and hear, without ears, the rattle of the stones.

The sea has long since washed the plate clean of its leavings. Angela, the *Emmanuelle,* and Jonathan are gone. Only we drowned belong here, face up, under the stones, soothed by the rhythm of tiny waves and the absurd incomprehension of sheep.

LISA MORTON

THE WASH

"YOUR BEAUTY kills."

Lidia looked at the man who had spoken, wondering if she'd misunderstood him—the words had tumbled out as slurry rubble. When she saw the half-empty beer bottle in his hand she knew it wasn't his first of the evening. He swayed slightly, as if caught in a breeze, his smile loose and fluid.

"Whoa," the man—barely a man, he couldn't have been more than twenty-two—giggled and added, "That didn't come out right. I'm just *really* drunk."

Lidia didn't even answer. Clutching her own bottle of water, she turned away and pushed through the crowd. Behind her, she heard, "Hey, c'mon—!"

She kept moving, searching for some way out of the sardine-can party. When her roommate, Jason, had suggested this ("The guy throwing the party just scored a lead in an indie feature, so there'll be a lot of networking potential there"), it'd sounded great. Lidia's "acting career" didn't even justify either word; she had neither career nor much acting talent. She'd been in L.A. for a year now, waiting tables at a restaurant she couldn't afford to eat at while being bullied by the instructors in acting classes and cruising the industry websites for casting notices, but so far she'd scored nothing but mediocre reviews ("Lidia Sotos is credible as a vacuous ingénue") in micro-theater productions. At home—a small town in Texas, barely twelve hundred—they'd all told her how pretty she was, how she could be a movie star…but in the land of movies, she was average, neither uniquely beautiful nor skilled.

And this party had proven to be little more than a frat bash. The house, in a section of the San Fernando Valley surrounded by liquor stores and taco stands, was decent enough, newly purchased and renovated, but Lidia suspected the young owner's money had come more from a recently deceased grandparent than an acting gig. And there must have been fifty more just like him all crammed into the house, the air thick with pot smoke and the smell of spilled lager. Lidia didn't enjoy crowds or, if truth be told, parties. Not long after they'd arrived she'd been ready to leave, but Jason had spotted a gorgeous young man who had an intern job with a famous producer, and he was now actively engaged in trying to start something. Lidia watched them flirting, wondering what Jason wanted more—sex or work. In Hollywood there was often little difference.

Why had she let Jason drive? Lidia knew he was a good guy, that he wouldn't abandon her even if his handsome new friend asked to go somewhere else, but she also couldn't expect him to want to leave half an hour after they'd arrived, especially not with the newfound lust interest. She'd tried to call an Uber, but it was apparently a peak time and the expense involved in getting her home would keep her from eating for the next three days.

She found sliding glass doors that led out to the backyard, was relieved to find that here, behind the house, it was cooler and less peopled. The yard was expansive, recently landscaped with winding flagstone paths and drought-tolerant succulents. Lidia moved past the scattered couples, most involved in that quiet, intense chat that would likely lead to a one-night stand later on. How many would regret it the next day? She'd had two of those since arriving in California. Both had been unmemorable and led nowhere. She tried not to think about them now.

She glanced at her watch—10:07 p.m.—and figured she could wait another half an hour before checking back in with Jason. The September night still carried the day's heat, radiating up from the stone beneath her feet. Lidia wished there was grass here, but grass had become impractical in California, a state that was dying of thirst.

Lidia wandered past agave and echeveria, yucca and euphorbia. A wooden fence, painted the same color as the flagstones, ran along one edge of the yard, but there was no house on the other side. Curious, Lidia walked to the fence, stood on tiptoes, and looked over.

Beyond the fence, the land sloped down sharply, about fifty feet, to a concrete channel lined on either side with rusting chain link fence. The channel was perhaps thirty feet wide; on the other side, another steep climb led to the continuation of suburbia, with fenced-in houses lining the top of the slope.

The locals called these paved eyesores "washes"; they'd apparently once been brooks or creeks, but had been neutered of all nature to prevent flooding, or so Jason had told her when she'd asked about them. The Los Angeles River was, in Lidia's view, not a river at all but just a bigger wash. Considering how seldom it rained in Southern California ("It used to rain a lot more," Jason had assured her), she thought they must have other reasons to exist, maybe boundary lines or dumping grounds. She'd grown up around *real* rivers and creeks, and she didn't recall them ever seriously flooding.

From her vantage point, Lidia could see several hundred yards along the wash before it curved both north and south. Stretches of it were dimly lit by light spilling out of windows and streetlamps. A darker strip along the bottom of the wash was a thin trickle of water, little more than what might be carried by a gutter.

Lidia was about to turn away when movement caught her eye. She looked into the wash again, seeing nothing, but certain something had just been there, something that had passed from her view. She waited, looking down—

There it was again. She saw it in a patch of shadow first, a darker blotch moving in a slow, jerky manner.

A tumbleweed, or old bag caught by a night breeze? But there was no breeze tonight. No, it was some kind of animal, maybe an injured dog or…

It disappeared again. She watched, willing it to come back into view; it seemed to be moving from one side of the wash to the other.

She saw it, then, almost directly below her. It had activated a neighbor's motion sensor, placed behind his chain link fence to light up intruders in his yard. It froze as it was caught by surprise.

Lidia stared, trying to make sense of what she was seeing. It was the size of a large dog, but was plainly no canine. It was black, but the way the light glinted suggested it was scaled rather than furred. The head was the size and shape of a human's, the front legs could have been arms...but something was draped across its back, hiding part of the rear legs.

Wings. Wings grew from its shoulder blades, as darkly feathered as any crow's. One was folded, jutting up from the hunched back, but the other dragged along the ground, broken, useless.

Lidia leaned forward. The thing glimpsed movement. Its head snapped up, she saw yellow eyes and yellow fangs. It fixed its sulfur-colored gaze on her.

Holding her breath—*unable* to breathe—Lidia waited. It looked up at her, its expression alien and unreadable. Her mind ran scenarios—it would jump, crawl like some monstrous crab, run up the steep sides of the wash to attack her, its bent wing would abruptly heal and it would swoop into the air and dive for an attack she couldn't defend herself against. Maybe others would join it, others that even now were in the wash, hidden by the bends and unlit spaces. Maybe it would—

It turned and fled, a spasmodic, zigzag escape.

Heart hammering, Lidia watched until it disappeared around the curve of the wash. Even after that she watched, waiting to see if it would return, or if something *else* would happen, maybe something even worse gyrating into view—

"There you are. I've been looking all over for you."

Lidia jumped and spun only to see Jason behind her. The object of Jason's flirtation stood a few feet behind him, waiting, smiling shyly. Jason put up placating hands. "Whoa, sorry, didn't mean to startle you."

"I..." She couldn't find words for what had just happened. "There was something down there..."

Jason looked at her, perplexed, then stepped up to peer over the fence. He looked both directions before stepping back. "I don't see anything now."

"It was like..." Lidia risked a glance back into the wash, somehow hoping for a last glimpse that would save her from having to describe what she'd seen, but the concrete channel was hidden in shadow, lifeless.

Shrugging, Jason said, "A coyote, maybe? I think these washes lead back up into hills."

His handsome friend overheard and walked closer. "Matt said he saw, like, a *huge* coyote in his front yard a week ago. He was coming home late at night, and it was just standing there. It wasn't even afraid of him—it waited until he parked, then just sort of sauntered off back to the wash."

Jason smiled at his friend and then turned to Lidia expectantly.

"No," she said, shaking her head, "this wasn't a coyote. It was black, and I think it had wings, and it was...I don't know, hurt or sick..."

Jason and his friend exchanged a curious glance, and Lidia could see what they were thinking: *The girl's had too much to drink.*

After a few seconds, Jason gestured toward the front of the house. "What do you say we all take off? Oh, and this is Raphael—if it's okay with you, he's coming with us."

Lidia nodded, not really thinking about home or Jason or Raphael. She allowed them to lead her out of the yard, through the party, and down the block to where they'd parked. Just as Jason was unlocking the car door, a strange sound cut through the suburban night, a series of high-pitched yips that ended in a howl. "There, see?" Jason gestured vaguely to the north, where the hills crouched like waiting predators. "Coyotes."

But it didn't sound like any coyote Lidia had ever heard.

LIDIA WASN'T scheduled to work the next day, which was good because she'd gotten little sleep. Jason and Raphael had stayed up much of the night, talking, watching videos on Jason's tablet, making love. Raphael's cries of pleasure had been followed by Jason giggling and shushing.

Normally, Lidia might have felt a twinge of jealousy, not because her roommate was having sex but because it sounded *fun.* Her encounters had been a few brief sensations followed by the queasy feeling that she'd been used, that she'd given away something with far greater value than what she'd received. Back home there'd been Brendon, a sweet boy who'd worshiped her;

they'd dated for nearly a year before they'd finally slept together. A week later, Lidia had decided to leave for Los Angeles. Brendon was heartbroken, but the truth was he bored her; she had no intention of becoming the dutiful wife of the one-time high school football champion who now sold insurance and carried more debt than he'd ever pay off. She'd lied and told Brendon she'd stay in touch. She hadn't returned his last three messages.

But what really kept Lidia awake all night was neither her roommate nor her ex, but what she'd seen in the wash. She knew Jason must have been right—it'd been a particularly large blackbird, or a dog with something stuck to its back, or a human prankster, obscured by shadow. But that didn't explain the *feeling* she'd had watching it, a profound sense that what she was seeing was *wrong*. The only time she'd experienced anything like this had been when she'd seen the dead body of her grandfather laid out in his coffin, his face made up by the morticians to resemble a ghastly doll, not at all the man she'd known and loved. She tried multiple Google search terms ("Los Angeles wash animals"/"Los Angeles creatures"/"Southern Californian urban legends"), but found nothing that sounded like what she'd glimpsed.

She finally dozed for a few hours, but woke up when she heard sounds from her kitchen. Throwing on clothes, she crept out to see Jason, alone, humming to himself as he made coffee. "Hey," she said.

He smiled. "Oh, hey. Want some coffee?"

"Where's…uh…" She had forgotten the name of Jason's friend.

"Raphael? He split already. Had to meet up with his fams for church, if you can believe it. Hey, I'm sorry if we were loud last night…"

"It's okay. I couldn't sleep anyway."

"Why not?"

Lidia hugged herself as Jason poured two cups. "That…thing I saw in the wash. I wish you'd seen it—I don't know what it was."

"Did you try digging around online a little?"

Lidia nodded. "I did, but…nothing."

Jason sipped his coffee, peered at her, and finally set the cup down. "I've got an idea: it's Sunday, neither of us has to work, so let's go down there."

"Down where?"

"Into the wash. You've got me really curious now."

Lidia's stomach clenched, from both anxiety and excitement. "Oh, Jason…I don't know…how would we even get down there?"

"It's probably not that hard. I'll bet we can find a hole in a fence somewhere."

"It doesn't seem safe…"

Jason stepped closer to her, grinning. "C'mon, there are two of us. And it's not like we have to worry about flash flooding or anything, right? Besides, you *need* to know, don't you?"

"I guess so…"

Before Lidia had answered, Jason was walking out of the kitchen calling back over his shoulder, "Just let me get a shower, then we'll do it."

"Okay."

From his bedroom, Jason shouted, "We're going urban exploring!"

Lidia smiled weakly.

AN HOUR later, they were driving through last night's neighborhood, trying to follow the course of the wash hidden behind houses. A curve in the street revealed a foot-bridge crossing the wash two blocks north of the house where the party had happened. Jason parked. "This looks good."

As he stepped out of the car, Lidia followed silently.

The bridge was no more than thirty feet in length. The wash stretched off in either direction, the concrete dusty-dry, empty except for scatterings of trash. The grassy embankments topped either side, chain link or wooden fences separating the backyards of the suburban homes from the alien expanse of rubbish and concrete.

Jason shot out a pointing finger. "There, see? What'd I tell ya?"

At the far side of the bridge the chain link terminated in a gate. Although a heavy length of chain and padlock secured the gate, the metal frame had been bent out far enough to allow entrance. Jason jogged to it and stepped through easily. From there, it would be little effort to clamber down the sloped wall to the bottom of the wash.

Feeling something she couldn't name but that made her

anxiety ramp up, Lidia walked to the gate. "Come on," Jason said, waving her through.

Lidia nodded at the gate's frame, where inch-thick solid metal had been not just bent but curled up. "How did it get that way?"

Jason looked, shrugged. "Probably some city maintenance guy forgot the key and used a crowbar or something. Who cares? Come *on*."

Lidia crouched and stepped through the gap. As she straightened on the other side, the city scents of car exhaust and uncollected rubbish were replaced by the rich musk of algae.

Jason led the way, traipsing through the ankle-high grass of the embankment. When the brush a few yards in front of them rippled Lidia tensed, but then a squirrel leapt up to a half-dead tree limb before turning back to chitter at them angrily.

Gesturing at the squirrel as it disappeared over a brick wall, Jason said, "Hey, maybe that pissed-off squirrel was your mysterious creature."

Lidia didn't even answer, just shot her roommate a sour glance until he held up his hands, surrendering. "Just a joke—" Jason broke off as he started to turn, glanced down, saw something that made his nose wrinkle.

"What?" Lidia joined him, looked down to see a dead animal half-buried in the wild grass at their feet. It took her a few seconds to identify it as a coyote. It wasn't a large animal, no bigger than a medium-sized dog. It was difficult to see in the thick growth of grass and weeds, but it still caused Lidia a jolt of alarm. It hadn't been dead long—blood from its disemboweled belly still glistened on its tawny pelt, the open eye that stared forever forward didn't look glassy yet.

"There's your fuckin' coyote," Jason muttered.

Lidia felt a strange rush of pathos as she stared down at the coyote's corpse. It must have been young, hadn't reached its full size, and whatever had killed it hadn't eaten it…or at least much of it. "That's definitely *not* what I saw last night."

Jason couldn't seem to take his eyes off the remains. "What the hell kills a *coyote* out here?"

Lidia had no answer. Somewhere nearby, in the neighborhood surrounding the wash, a child uttered a high-pitched shriek. It was a mundane sound, but it made Lidia wish that she hadn't let Jason bring her down here, that she'd stayed home, tried to forget the party, the wash, the thing she'd seen there—

Her thoughts were interrupted when Jason sped past her. Ahead, the embankment above the channel narrowed. The slope eased down to the bottom of the wash with less severity, and Jason trotted down. He stood at the bottom, his feet on either side of the line of water no wider than a hand, and grinned up. "Come on down. It's not that steep."

Jogging down to meet him, Lidia worried briefly about getting back up. The slope seemed to slant more than Jason had indicated, leaving her to picture them losing footing when they tried to return, slipping down the rough concrete, scraping hands as they fought to gain purchase. But it was too late now—she was in the wash itself. Maybe exits would be easier to negotiate ahead.

Jason strode off to the north, toward the hills. A few feet behind him, Lidia looked up at the sides of the wash, at the fences that could only be partly glimpsed from this angle, at the searing blue sky overhead, and she wondered why the bottom of the wash seemed so quiet. The only sounds were their footsteps and some distant hum (a freeway?).

Ahead, the course of the wash curved slowly, arcing toward the northeast. Lidia picked up her pace, anxious to keep Jason in her sights. As they maneuvered the long curve, a tunnel was revealed ahead. "There we go," Jason said, pointing.

Confused by his statement, feeling an inexplicable dread as they neared the black tunnel mouth, Lidia asked, "What?"

"That tunnel showed up when I Googled the wash. That's where the concrete begins; on the other side, it's still natural creek, going up into the hills."

It was hard to believe. The tunnel mouth was situated beneath a major street; a shopping center lay on the other side. "So the wash passes under a strip mall?"

"Yeah. But there's just vacant land behind that strip mall—it backs right up against the foothills."

As they approached the mouth of the tunnel, light and sound seemed to dim, while the odors of rot and stagnation intensified. There was something else, too, something meaty but rank, like the odor of a sick man who'd stopped bathing.

"What *is* that? God, that shit is *rank.*" Jason uttered a disgusted laugh. At their feet more water flowed, yellowish and dense with sediment, trickling out of the tunnel mouth ahead.

"We're not going in there, are we?" Lidia hated herself for even phrasing it as a question.

"Yeah—don't you want to see the other side?"

"Let's just go up, through the mall…"

They had almost reached the tunnel mouth now. It was big—probably six feet in diameter—so they could easily walk through it without even bending over. But it was also long, dark, thick with that odor that wrenched Lidia's gut.

Jason pulled out his phone, punched up a flashlight app, and used the beam to penetrate the tunnel's murk. It didn't go far, but was enough to reveal a rounded floor covered in several inches of oozing filth, the occasional plastic bag half-buried to one side.

Lidia started to pull away. "I'm not going in there."

Jason placed one foot on the concrete lip. "C'mon, we got light. It's not *that* far."

"What if somebody's living in here?"

Jason waved the light, shook his head. "I don't think so." He stepped all the way in, crouched over slightly. He took a few steps before turning to look back. "C'mon, it's solid. I'll lead the way."

He pushed forward.

It would be so easy to go back. Let Jason go ahead, report back to her that he made his way through a filthy pipe to find a muddy, dull creek bed. She didn't even have to go back—she could just wait here, a few feet back, where the smell was lessened. Wait in the sun, the heat, the air…

But something drew her. Whether it was fear of being abandoned by her friend, or the need to *know*, or something more indefinable, she couldn't say. As she entered the dark mouth, she felt panic—but it didn't last, replaced by calm she'd never known before. It was warmer than she'd expected, the smell something she no longer noticed once there was no escaping it. She had one uncomfortable instant when she saw how far off the end was (a hundred feet? More?), but that also passed quickly.

Jason heard her coming, waited, smiling. "Attagirl."

Lidia said nothing. Instead she pushed past him.

"Hey, hold on…" Jason tried to point the light beam in front of her, but the darkness veiled it within a few feet.

Lidia didn't care. Something about this place reassured her, even as it pulled her on. Whatever awaited her, it lay ahead.

She picked up her pace, not noticing the soft, almost fleshy feel beneath her feet. Something brushed her face, but she didn't flinch or cry out. Instead, it excited her, like a lover's tickling stroke.

"Lidia, wait—!"

She didn't look back, not even when Jason cried out, not when a wet, slurping sound stifled his screams, not when the sound of something large being sucked down died out.

Lidia paused just long enough to wait for the silence to return before continuing on.

She reached the end of the tunnel and hesitated, blinded by the return of Southern California's sunlight. Squinting, she stepped out, felt moist dirt beneath her feet. When her eyes adjusted, she saw natural desolation, free of human mark. The creek, a clear stream between rocky sides, flowed beneath scrub and sage. The sky overhead was a cloudless, painful azure, arching above blissful solitude.

No, not complete solitude—Lidia looked down as the ground shifted beneath her feet, a slow, earthen vortex. She stepped back, not out of fear but out of respect for what was happening. A hand appeared—ebon, clawed, scaled—followed by the top curve of a wing that glistened darkly.

All at once, Lidia understood this place that had baffled and frustrated her. She knew that the concrete channels had not been built to direct, but to *guard.* To protect the City of Angels.

Like her, they were broken.

She knelt, reaching out. The grasping hand found hers; it felt reassuring, even loving, as it wrapped long fingers around her wrist. It pulled her down, toward the pure earth. As her arm was submerged, a last, conscious part of her tried to scream, but then the rich clay filled her mouth and she let it.

It's so beautiful, she thought, as she left the anxious world of air and light.

JODI RENÉE LESTER

JUST WATCH ME NOW

THREE

A THREE. They tell me that's what I am between drag after drag after drag off their cigarettes.

Three sheets to the wind. Three strikes. Third degree. Third child. Third place (always a bridesmaid, never a bride). Third in line. Three times a lady. Three for one (a bargain, a steal). One-third the person I should be. The rule of three—three minutes to die of suffocation, three days to die of dehydration, three weeks to die of starvation.

I stare ahead to a fixed point between and beyond their heads. My eyes blur.

"Threes don't go outside."

I feel them probe, sniffing me. Categorizing and assessing me.

Smoke after smoke after smoke.

I drop my head and vanish behind the thick curtain of my hair.

They bide their time and soon I would be biding mine.

Ashtrays overflow. Whose turn is it anyway? Argument ensues:

"I did it last."

"No I did it."

"No I did."

"No, it's me!"

I pick up and balance in my hands three plastic ashtrays, black to better camouflage the melted burn spots hidden beneath all that ash. Cigarette butts jut out at angles, bony remains of the dead. A wisp of smoke slithers from the peak, snaking lazily upward, snuffed by the stagnant air.

Head down, watching my feet, my snug-treads whisper across the linoleum floor and shuffle me once around the lounge. A coffee table surrounded by two sofas and two chairs that cordon off the smoking area within a larger room, a lobby of sorts. I circle them, a solitary procession, careful not to spill.

It takes forever but I reach the can beside the bank of payphones. Three of them. With the ashtrays upturned the debris falls and I clack them together. Stale powder wafts up in my face.

I pause, completely still and silent, prolonging the moment, seeing how long the fiends will hold out. I smother the urge to return to my room with them. Instigate a riot. A hidden smirk surfaces on my face.

I shuffle around once more and return to the sacred circle. Fingers and cigarettes reach over the ashtrays before they even touch the table. Long stems of collapsing ash, drooping, hanging on for dear life, finally tapped and released. Everyone falls back in their seats. Sighs of relief cut the tension.

People enter the room, one by one by one from all directions, converging on the lounge, cigarettes drawn, lighters at the ready, greedy eyes focused on one thing only. The empty seat. *My* seat. At the last second, just as a challenger was about to stake her claim, I flop down in the chair. The action stops.

All eyes on me.

The pace in the room slows a bit as they step into the circle, resigned to stand or perch on the edge of a couch or chair.

"Who's got a light?"

"Lay some fire on me, will ya?"

"Got a light-light-light?"

The first drag is communal, sacred. A vacuum, a temporary void in space restored as everyone but me exhales a cloud of smoke.

My head still down, I feel the challenger staring at me.

Dings and pings and callers, anxious and antsy, eager and apprehensive, listen to the sound of coins dropping, waiting for someone to pick up the phone. Mothers, fathers, lovers, friends, anyone who will answer. Whoever will stay on the line. Muffled voices, stifled sobs.

A short line has formed, pressing forward, willing the conversations to end.

A three, they say.

As time closes in, the more suspicious they become. A wave of people ebbs back out and a chair is opened. The challenger takes it, glaring the whole time at the top of my bowed head. Staring at me and the empty spaces between my fingers. She firmly tamps the top corner of her cigarette pack, popping one out.

"Smoke?" She holds the pack through the part in my curtain of hair, making sure I see the one little soldier poking out. A challenge rather than an offer.

I move my head slowly, the curtain swings side to side. *No.*

She shrugs, a false front, and retreats. Grabs the cigarette between her lips and draws it out. Striking a match, she lights her own and those of two others.

Three on a matchstick.

Again I shake my head.

"What?" she demands.

Silence.

"What the fuck?"

"'What the fuck.' Now what does one say to that?" The first words to escape my mouth since I entered this place. No one, including myself, really sure that I spoke at all.

I rise, slowly, and turn out of the lounge, begin my shuffle across the big room.

"Hey!" she calls after me, the last word. The alpha conveying her status.

My head still down, I watch my snug-treads scuff down the hallway of industrial-strength carpet.

A grin spreads across my lips that no one can see and only I can feel. Queen Bitch agitated into a state of rage.

A three-dollar bill in a room full of stooges, playing to an easy crowd.

THERE ARE worse places I could have ended up; I am well aware of that and, yes, even grateful. In my repeated fantasies, I drive off a cliff and soar down to the ocean. All these years living on the coast, so many opportunities. So many times I'd find myself gripping the wheel, fighting the urge to jerk it hard to the right. Yet here I am, in this place that sits atop a bluff overlooking the sea, and for some reason I find it calming.

NO ROOMMATE as of yet, but rumors abound that the Canadians are coming.

Tomorrow it starts. Assessment, medication trials, groups.

But I'm a three. Threes don't go outside.

I curl up in bed. Try to ease the pain my own way, knowing full well they will only allow me to go so far on my own. At some point I would have to give in, let them help me or play the game.

My door is ajar, a soft knock, entry. A woman in scrubs, surgical tray in hands, phlebotomy kit laid out neat, piece by piece by piece.

I offer her my arm without resistance, veins collapsing on first poke.

"You should use the butterfly. I'm a tough draw," I tell her, pointing out the vein that is usually the easiest to tap.

A second poke, still going commando. I look at her, bored. They never listen.

Nervous now, she slides a butterfly needle into the vein I picked out especially for her. Nice and snug. The blood flows. Relief flushes across her face.

Third time's a charm.

I'M HAVING my after-lunch smoke as a herd of teens pass through the lobby. They wander to the cafeteria, taking their time. A girl catches my eye. A ghost, a focal point. A frozen moment. Something familiar. A photograph in which she is a blur and the rest of the group, in full relief, fades into the background. The air before her ripples, as though she is in a pool of water, peering out from beneath the surface.

I WAKE up on a padded leather table, wrists and ankles bound in thick sheepskin straps. Four-point restraints. Other than me and the table, there is nothing but white walls and fluorescent lights, humming. I have no idea how I got here and am not sure I want to find out.

"Heyyy. Hey!" I call out weakly. I let a few seconds pass, but as long as I am conscious, there's no way I can stay pinned down like this.

"Hey! Hey! Heyyy!"

I hear a fumble at the doorknob, see a face in the window looking in on me. A male nurse enters, talks to me, makes sure it's safe to set me free.

"Yes, I'm calm." I will ask questions later. My goal is to get out of this trap.

"Well, you weren't so calm last night. Just need to be sure."

"I am now," I tell him without a hint of malice in my voice.

He releases my ankles, then my wrists.

"Thank you. Cigarette?"

He walks me out to the lounge where the others are having their first cigarette of the day.

All eyes on me.

The nurse stays close.

Queen B offers me a cigarette. A reward. This time I take it. Eyes no longer cast to the floor, but not looking at her either.

"Boy were you nuts last night." She lights the cigarette for me.

No response. I knew she was dying to tell.

"You were flipping and flopping like some wild fish. It took eight motherfuckers to get you into isolation."

"Something must not have agreed with me."

"I'd say. I've never seen anyone buck and twist like you did."

Nervous laughs around the table, everyone but me.

I finish my smoke and get up. The nurse walks me to my room, makes sure everything is copacetic. I reassure him. I'll be seeing my doctor in a couple hours anyway. He stays with me until I fall asleep. Whatever they gave me last night is still in my system. I drift into a deep sleep.

I AM a little girl and have not yet learned to swim. Pauline carries me on her back, telling me the story of the mermaid and her prince. "Down there," she says, "Do you see the lights from the kingdom?"

"Yeah, I see them."

We dive into the water, and I let go of her shoulders. I am swimming on my own now...down...past a strange reef of twisted coral. I enter a dark forest of undulating seaweed that gropes my legs as I swim through, toward the kingdom's lights, feeling the shadows upon me, ancient, watching eyes allowing me to pass. I see the castle in the distance, and beyond it, darker shadows still—stone ruins rising above the majestic kingdom, and I am struck by the beauty of it all. I look through one of the windows of the castle to get a peek of the mermaid and the prince, but all I see is a reflection of myself, and as I push away from the castle wall, something among the shadowy ruins begins to move and I can no longer swim.

Now I start choking, gasping for breath, but only swallowing water. I try calling for Pauline to come and get me, but I ingest more water. I look up and see her legs treading. I reach for her foot to pull me out of the mire, but it is just out of reach. It is always just out of reach.

I wake up gasping.

THAT AFTERNOON the three-ring circus resumes and carries on into the night. More of the same, with a tide of uncertainty. Everyone jockeys for position, making room for the new girl. In an act of good faith, I join the ritual of the community smoke.

Calmer, quieter recreational activities available in other parts of the big room I hadn't noticed before. A large table where a giant jigsaw puzzle is being assembled by the few surrounding it, kneeling on chairs, hovering, each with their own method, searching eagerly among hundreds of pieces, thousands, dispersed across the tabletop. Quiet concentration, an occasional gasp of success, every so often the eruption of a minor dispute. Mild rote bickering.

"This piece is missing. I know it."

"It's not missing. You always say that. If you don't like it, get your ass out."

Somewhere a piece of the jigsaw is deftly swiped and tucked into a pocket.

On a flagstone bench surrounding a large fireplace, a few sit, recently deposited there, faces slack, medicated.

It is about ten o'clock when I extinguish my last cigarette and turn in. The bed is comfortable, but sleep does not come easily. Irrelevant thoughts race through my mind until they become whispering voices, criticizing me. I had hoped I would be safe from them here. But once again, I am dragged through the mud of my entire life. Words and actions I barely recall are twisted around and used against me. There is no verdict other than guilty in this court.

It is an inevitable, relentless, excruciating pain so deep that I understand why cutters cut. Not to punish themselves, but to distract them from the pain that really matters.

I go to the nurse's station and ask for that sedative the doctor ordered. The nurse on duty makes a note in my chart.

Back in bed, I close my eyes and imagine I am driving late at night on a long dark highway, focusing on the intermittent white lines in the road as they pass beneath me. I let them hypnotize me until I fall asleep at the wheel.

I PRAY for a new intake. A new specimen to shift the attention away from me. Maybe the Canadians will get here soon.

Instead my prayers are answered with a distraction. Amy—MANIC-depressive psychosis.

Fortunately, Amy is a happy manic. No, an elated manic. Her blonde hair and sunshiny face brightens the room. All treatments thus far have failed to bring her down to a happy medium. Lithium. Thorazine. Lamictal. Seroquel. Depakote. Abilify. Nothing. She spreads laughter, biding her time, afraid they'll opt for a last resort. ECT. None of us want this for her. No one wants her sunshine eclipsed. Maybe just a dimmer switch so we can turn her down a notch.

Afternoon in the empty dining hall, a woman sits in an empty booth. She tries to shrink into anonymity by easing into the general population as quietly as possible. She is an actress whose most recent standout role was that of an aging, narcissistic Hollywood star. A simple line delivered with such palpable ferocity it immortalized her:

WHO STOLE MY TIPPERARIES!

Her identity will be hard to hide.

Amy is in top form today and indifferent to the proximity of the actress. She marches around the lounge, round and round. She starts over and over again, arms pumping as if holding a baton:

"WHO STOLE MY TIPPERARIES!" Stomp, stomp. "WHO STOLE MY TIPPERARIES!"

She laughs so hard, committed to her tribute, stomping and pumping, stomping and pumping.

Queen B sticks a foot out to trip her, but Amy marches over it.

The next time Amy comes around, I rush her, tackle her over

the back of the nearest couch onto the cushions. Amy still laughs, still shouts, though slightly muffled now. I heft up her body and start dragging it back to her room. I feel like my mom must have when I was little and in the midst of a tantrum. The two of us stumble on each other's feet, a couple of drunks.

"Sometimes you feel like a nut...," Queen B deadpans as I haul Amy out.

Still oblivious, Amy continues to holler.

I kick the door shut, throw Amy on her bed, and talk her down until the nurse relieves me.

AT NIGHT, the voices return to present evidence against me. Guilty on all counts, accused of showing no remorse. But I am remorseful. I have regrets going all the way back to the age of three. I believe what they say, they are quite convincing, but I'd do anything to make them stop, to get them off my back. They win. I punish myself. I shrink away, further inside myself.

Silence is compliance or so it would seem.

My uncle once told me that when he first met me I was three years old, and when he looked into my eyes all he saw was fathomless sadness, and he knew I didn't belong to this world. I think back as close to that time as possible and realize I'd always known.

THE VOICES in my head are temporarily quieted and replaced. I fall asleep to the sound in the halls and in the walls, and the gentle whispers in the water...

three...three...three...

TWO

THEY SAY I'm a two now.

Two tickets to paradise. Two wrongs don't make a right. Two can play at that game. Double standard. Double exposure. Double-cross. Two birds with one stone. Two peas in a pod. Put two and two together. The lesser of two evils. Stand on your own two feet.

"Twos go outside, but only with a staff member. It's not much but it'll make the day pass a lot easier."

"All I want is to go for a walk."

I TOSS Queen B a pack of cigarettes. We are alone in the lounge. Everyone else is waiting in line to eat. She takes one and I light it for her.

We smoke silently, a momentary truce.

Her eyes on me.

A payphone rings. Two other girls rush to answer it. One pushes the other out of the way and grabs it on the second ring.

"Who? I don't know no one by that name."

Irritated, the girl repeats the name out loud, glancing around the room half-heartedly.

"Not here. Wanna leave a message?"

Queen B reaches with her tread and gives my knee a push.

"Isn't that you?"

I get up, ease through the food line *(no cuts, no cutting)*, toward the bank of phones. The handset is slammed in place just as I get there. The girl doesn't waste any time. There is already a message on the whiteboard: Cassie, Call MOTHER.

Is that sarcasm or a taunt meant for me?

I HEAD into the cafeteria and grab a tray just as the teens start to line up at the door. They have to wait until my unit has gone through the line. First thing, coffee. Load it up with powdered creamer, a pack of sweetener (pink bad, blue good). Napkin. Utensils (blunt). I sip coffee and walk the line of hair nets and chafing dishes. My stomach rumbles.

I sit at a table in the far corner.

The teens file in and I can't help but look for her.

The hand tremors are worse and I struggle to get a sporkful of scrambled eggs into my mouth. They tumble back to the plate. After my second failure, I grip my wrist with my other hand for support, steadying the spork as I guide it to my mouth. It takes two fucking hands to eat scrambled eggs now.

A timid little kitten of a voice asks to sit down. I nod, still concentrating on my food.

"You got 'em, too."

"Huh?" I look up and see myself twenty years ago.

"The shakes." She cups a coffee mug in two cotton-gloved hands.

"Looks that way, doesn't it?"

I study the girl's face as she shrinks away, trying to crawl inside her cup and take a sip at the same time. Spots of acne sores dot her chin.

The resemblance is eerie.

"What's your name?"

"Alexandra," she says, almost a question.

"Cassie."

Her eyes glance up at me timidly as she nods acceptance. Heart-stopping deep wells of jade with dark rust rings around them.

I quit the eggs and start on the bacon, a little easier to navigate.

"What are the gloves for?" I ask.

"My hands."

Breakfast finished in amicable silence.

TWO NEW people sitting on the couch smoking, though they're not really new at all. They've been sequestered away in private rooms, detoxing for the past two weeks.

I wonder if there are more of them, tucked away, shaking and sweating it out.

These two stick together, heroin the glue that binds them. They swap war stories, compare needle tracks, yearning for their drug.

All this talk of heroin ignites music in my head. "Horses" stampede through my consciousness; "Poppies" swirl in mellow, barely coherent. I long to swim in the waters of oblivion.

MY THOUGHTS are no longer my own. I am certain of it. Someone is listening in. More incidents over time, more frequent. Too many to be coincidences. As soon as I have a thought, it is repeated. In a book, on the TV, or from someone else's mouth. There is no alone.

My memories are secondhand. If someone is not reading my mind, then I must be reading theirs.

AFTER DINNER, sitting in the lounge, I zone out. The chatter of conversation around me is calm and quiet. Someone is telling a story. The punch line is delivered and the lounge erupts with exaggerated laughter.

The feeling that someone is in my head, tracking my thoughts, reinforces itself and sets me on edge. The canned laughter is absolutely chilling.

My first instinct is to flee to my room, but the fear of being alone overrides it. I clutch my robe tight around my body, smoking one after another. The aura of panic running through me is palpable.

A SMALL group forms, patients heading out to the CD unit for a twelve-step meeting. The majority of them are lounge lizards.

I am terrified of being alone, me and my cigarettes.

I'm a two.

I orbit around the cluster of bodies, keeping them between me and the front desk staff, until we are out of the building.

I follow the addicts into the open air as they walk leisurely through a grove of trees. It is impossible, but in the distance I hear waves crashing on wet sand and frothy water flooding empty tide pools.

This walk is a nightly ritual for them. The conversation is different here, lacking urgency. No more war stories. No more posturing. Experiment suspended.

A breathless murmur of confidence emerges as they near the center of the grove, as if some power is being exerted on them. The pace slows, allowing them every second of every possible moment before reaching their destination.

They ask for a timekeeper. By giving the timekeeper their trust, they are allowed the deception of false freedom, without the consequence of losing privileges.

"I'll do it," I say.

They look behind them and only then do they see I have followed. In quick time they assess the risk.

The risk is worth it.

They put their faith in me.

In this short interval, they are no longer patients. Without endless cigarettes wielded as props, the veil of smoke dissipates, a rent in the cocoon is made, self-actualization achieved. They take control of their own destinies, walking through the trees as twilight descends. They hold the stars in the sky, freezing them in place as if their lives depend on it.

Dina—anorexia, booze—grasps a tree trunk, and swings around it, carefree, swooping down then up in a well-executed arc. Delight slips from her mouth, a giggle so sweet, and I realize it is the first time I have heard her voice. As she swings up, Marvin—detox, booze, depression—snatches the knit cap from her head and she chases him through the trees. Frolicking in and out, side and back, any way but forward. Not yet.

They all linger around the middle of the grove. Rain drops sprinkle down through the barren canopy of early winter. Faces turn to the sky and are cleansed.

Off to the side, a couple embraces, whispering to each other in an illusion of privacy.

"Two minutes," I call out, thinking I'm doing them a favor.

All eyes on me.

I guess the timekeeper calls time once and only once.

A little tension starts to break up the calm. They don't know what to do with themselves, with this knowledge that they only have two minutes. Now only one and thirty.

Dina's face becomes drawn, contemplating the time, counting down in her head. The couple, walking hand in hand, release their hold and part. Everyone else looks at the ground, kicking at the dirt.

The two-minute warning was damaging. I had no idea. I am new to the ritual. I want to put an end to their indecision, their misery. I abort the dis-ease, calling time thirty seconds early:

"Last call." It was out of my mouth before I could stop it.

Someone laughs, appreciating the irony.

I have failed as timekeeper.

Dina puts her cap back on, tucking loose strands of hair beneath it as she walks toward the center. The group, now absent of mirth, reunites and continues on to the other side of the grove.

Once again I fall behind.

The rest of the group is now silent, rosy cheeks stained with drops of rain. Each of them retreats, a moment of solitude before reprising their roles as patients and addicts. They had shed their skin on the way into the woods. Now their skin thickens as they cross through to the other side.

Layer by layer.

Each role so convincingly played. Except, I notice, for her. The saddest of them all, like a child lost and afraid. The actress.

A CLIPBOARD is passed around for each of us to sign while we wait for the meeting to begin. It reaches me. I never signed out, so I don't sign in. I am not here. I resist the temptation to tear off the sheet and pocket it for the actress's autograph.

At the sound of the gavel from inside the meeting room, cigarettes in all stages of smoking drop to the sidewalk, ground out by careless feet.

Everyone wanders in. The room is almost full. Must be the only thing going on in town. I take a seat in the back.

The room is dark except for the lectern at the front, which has a small lamp attached to it. A speaker stands there, gavel in hand, waiting for everyone to take their seats. Two spotlights shine down on him from behind. The yellow glow of the lamp and the strange pattern of shadows cast across his face make him look gaunt and jaundiced.

He welcomes everyone, especially the new people. He introduces Carter who will be talking about his eighth and ninth steps.

I listen to Carter share his story. He talks about his acts of contrition. I feel like I am in temple listening to the sermon on Yom Kippur and close my eyes. I think about people I have wronged. I never needed an addiction to do that. My mind is in a constant state of regret. I think about Yom Kippur and am hungry and repentant.

DRAMA THERAPY today. The session is combined, adults and teens. I look for my young friend. I see her sitting on the floor, Indian style. The hood of a sweatshirt shrouds her face, but she catches my eye as I enter the room.

She was looking for me, too.

The therapist explains how drama therapy works. A single patient, a life-altering event re-enacted.

"Any questions before we begin?" She pauses, hands clasped in front of her, and looks around the silent room. "Well, then, let's get started."

She calls on the patient to join her at the center of the stage.

Alexandra.

"THE SUN is hot, it's beating down on me. I hear the ocean and the sound of the wind as it sends my hair in every direction. I run toward it, then stop and turn around for a brief second. I smile and wave at Jake sitting there on the sand watching me go. I turn back around and continue running. I run, kicking up sand in my tracks… I run across the wet sand, hard and packed…I run into the water, leaping over the waves going deeper, trying to get past them…I swim out until I can no longer touch the ground.

"I'm treading water."

Alexandra sounds winded, then takes a deep breath.

"I point my legs straight down, and my arms straight up, and like a torpedo I go down…deep, deep down in the water…into the sea…farther down…I keep going. I see fish and the rocky bottom of the ocean. Glittering sand swirls up around me and I see a light in the distance. And now I'm swimming toward it."

Alexandra smiles as she says this.

A look of confusion and concern passes across the therapist's face, and she starts trying to talk Alexandra back.

"No. No, I don't want to go yet." Panic creeps into her voice. "No! Bubbles, coming from my mouth. Someone's pulling me up toward the surface. I go up…up. No, I don't want to. The sun burns through the water, and I know soon I will break the surface. No. Please…don't make me go."

As she comes around to the present, to this room, I see through tears of my own a blurred double image of her and she is crying.

MY PSYCHOLOGIST told me she takes a particular interest in Jung. I lie in bed, willing myself to dream up a doozy for her to analyze, hopefully remembering it by our next meeting. I feel the voices in my head trying to take hold. I feel the rush of fear.

I can't bear another night of this. Like all the previous sleepless nights I've had since my arrival, I am once again back at the nurse's station. The nurse on duty looks me over, recognizes that I am troubled. She hands me a tiny accordion paper cup that holds my sleeping pill and a second one empty for water. She asks if I'd feel better sleeping on the couch tonight, at least for a little while. I follow her eyes. I hadn't noticed this couch before. It is in the center of the big room, neither here nor there, creating a space of its own between the craft tables and reception. I nod my head.

At the water cooler I place the empty cup over my mouth and blow hard. It crackles and puffs out like a miniature Chinese lantern. A nifty trick to increase the volume of water it will hold.

I take my pill and return to the couch where the nurse is making a bed. Sheet, blanket, pillow which she even fluffs up for me. No Nurse Ratched she.

I lie down and get comfortable. The nurse returns to her station and turns off the fluorescents directly above me.

But here they come, the inner voices that go for the slow kill.

Stupid. Mean. Bad.

No matter which memory they torment me with, it slips off into the atmosphere somewhere, entering a loop of time and space.

But it was twenty-two years ago. Twenty-two.

The voices are immune to my rationalizations until the pill finally begins to snuff them out…

two…two…two…

ONE

I'M A one.

As I head for breakfast, a nurse calls me over to the nurse's station to tell me this. She delivers the good news as if bestowing upon me a Young Reader Medal. She is genuine and, I believe, truly pleased for me.

One day at a time. One good turn deserves another. One step ahead. One-track mind. One more shot. Looking out for number one. Love at first sight. First come, first served. One for the road. One foot in the grave. Back to square one.

Ones can go outside without a staff escort.

I am surprised because of the bad nights I've been having, but I guess they measure it by risk factor. Whether it's the actual escape or the potential liability that concerns them, I honestly don't know.

I expected I would feel good about this relative freedom, but now all I really want is the comfort of this shelter to which I have become accustomed.

I take a seat in the lounge. The doors to the cafeteria have yet to open. The line to breakfast has formed, the patrons are antsy. I wait it out, smoking until the line has waned. Queen B sits across from me.

"Did I hear right? You're a one? That means—"

"I know what that means."

AFTER LUNCH I sit waiting in the gazebo with my book. It is filled with short vignettes, giving me lots of easy stopping points. Even so, I find myself glancing up every couple of sentences, distracted, wondering if she'll show. The prospect of reading abandoned, I walk along the edge of the low shrubbery, protecting me from the cliff's edge and the long drop below. The pungent aroma of sagebrush, mint, and white sage combined clears my sinuses. I could stand here forever, breathing it all in, lost in its heady haze.

A shadow bleeds in from behind, rousing in me an instant of fear that I am about to go over the edge. I turn on instinct to face my attacker and there is Alexandra, farther off than I expected, behind all that hair, sheepskin boots trudging up the gentle slope of grass, hands deep in the pockets of her shorts.

"Smells good, huh?" She stands next to me and we look out over the sea.

I nod and feel her slip her gloved hand in mine. We stand there for a moment, silent, feeling the sun and the breeze, watching the waves tumble, tasting the salt in the air. It sparks a memory that comforts, taking me back on some strange trip through the past to a time I can't quite pinpoint.

She leads me to a boulder balancing on the precipice, and releases my hand to climb atop it.

I hesitate and she laughs, warm and carefree, hair blown back from her face.

"Don't worry. It's not going anywhere." She offers me a hand, helping me up.

"I'm not too fond of heights," I confess, clambering up the massive rock.

"Me neither. But for some reason it doesn't bother me here. I'll show you."

I crawl up beside her, low and grounded, my hands never leaving the rough surface as I sit beside her. I mimic her bravery, letting my legs hang over, feet dangling in the air.

"Just look out, toward the horizon. The feeling will pass."

After a few moments it does.

"Everyone kept congratulating me, you know. After that session yesterday. I've been here almost two months now. Hardly anyone ever spoke to me and then there I was, naked before them, and all of a sudden, everyone wants to touch me. It's like I got mobbed, like they all want a piece of me. The girl who had something fucked up happen to her, they want a piece of that, you know?"

I nod. I do know.

"Fucking vampires everywhere."

I laugh.

"Anything like that ever happen to you?"

"I've only been here a couple of weeks. People stare at me, summoning up their x-ray vision to figure me out. Whisper-whisper as I come and go. Even a place like this assigns celebrity, fleeting as it may be. Anything to shift their focus off themselves."

"Yeah."

We let the sun warm our faces, listening to the waves crash below.

"They say there's a whole civilization under there, deep down at the bottom of the ocean," she says, gazing out at the sea. "They say that it sank there, thousands of years ago."

Her words linger in the air, before the breeze carries them away. Seagulls drift past, riding the wind currents, crossing the tawny sun. Their cries bring us both to the present.

Alexandra turns to me, eyes wide, the haze in them dissipated, clear again, reflecting the deep bronze of the sky.

I HAVE gone through layers, deeper and deeper, league upon league upon league of consciousness.

I see the park. Pauline is down there. I must get to her before the others. If I can explain before the others get to her, she will understand. I swim downward and try to call out to her. I begin to panic, but not because I can't breathe. I try to speak, but my words are distorted and bubbles escape with them. I call out to my sister, "Pauline!" Wait for me. Please. Wait…

If she can hear me, she will know I am here. She'll come get me. "Pauline!" Wake, wake me…

Once again I think I'm awake, but have my doubts. I see everyone sitting around in the room downstairs. It is dark, but the rattlesnake lawyer is sitting deep in the corner of an old couch, ankle across knee, comfortable, waiting for nothing. An Asian woman is draped across him. I can feel the heavy atmosphere down there. Something wrong and sinister. I stop to remember rattlesnake lawyer's name. Jonathan is it? My speech is impaired and I try to articulate that I am there. But they go on without seeing me. Someone please wake me up. Wake me up. Wake me…

I am not asleep. I just can't open my eyes or raise myself from the bed. I am afraid of what I will see next. I don't know what is really going on downstairs. I am dead weight in this bed and no matter how hard I try, I can't cut through the levels of consciousness. I try to call through them, but no one hears me. No one is listening. I need someone to pull me out. Bubbles float to the surface. I don't even know what all this means. "Please." I have gone too deep and I know it. I am terrified. If I could kill myself now, I would.

"Wake. Please, someone, wake me."

SOMEONE IS shaking me. "Wake up. Come on, wake up."

"Help. Help me up. I need up. Pull me. Pull me *up*," I pant, reaching with my arm, groping blindly for whoever is there.

"Wake me," I plead.

Someone takes hold of my arms and pulls me up out of bed.

"Wake up. Come on. You're freaking me out. Wake up, dammit!"

I open my eyes and it takes a minute for me to recognize who it is.

"Are you awake?" The voice is familiar. She shakes me again and my vision begins to clear.

I'm afraid my voice won't work again. I open my mouth. "Ter-ri-fied."

"Who's Queen?"

I recognize the voice now.

"You."

EVERYONE IN my family has been so good to me, bringing their love and smiles, concealing their concern. But I can't help but feel guilty that I am here, that I have lost touch with life, struggling to find the desire and strength to breathe, to thrive, to live. Though they don't show it, I know they worry, probably wondering how they contributed to the disintegration of what little peace of mind I may have had. Everyone says look back to your childhood and figure out where it went wrong. The horrible things our mothers and fathers did to us when we were children, while we were growing up. Whatever memories we are suppressing will lead us to the truth. But for me there is nothing. No suppressed memories of a bad childhood, of my parents doing me wrong. Nothing. And it makes me angry when people insist that there is something there. My parents, my grandparents, my sisters, no one in my family ever did me wrong. Spats, yes. Struggles for understanding, yes. I pushed boundaries to assert my independence and they tried to let up on the reins a bit each time, let me have a chance, trust me to make the right decisions. Any failures were mine. Still, nothing they did or said was unreasonable in this regard. And looking back, I see they were right all along.

I was born with sadness and an aching that I could never understand. Whatever happened did so long before then.

I DIDN'T think I would have trouble falling asleep tonight. I was so tired when I lay down. But now my mind won't stop. The sobs come and the tears flow far too freely.

The feeling of loss is huge for me right now. I can't describe it. The voices come and criticize me all over again.

Guilt rushes to the surface once again.

I go to the nurse's station for the usual.

I SIT on the boulder near the cliffs. Guilt and regret wrack my mind, my soul, and take hold of me. I look out at a stretch of empty beach, watching the sea. The waves swell and rise. I close my eyes and feel them wash over me before they crash against the shore, the tide dragging the heavy burden from me as it recedes.

All the pain and doubt and regret, all of that is gone. Me and this rock I sit on, the breeze and the birds, the sand and the ocean, we are fine. I realize, it's time to go home.

I feel Alexandra's hand slip into mine. No glove this time. Her eyes are the clearest I've seen them yet. We are standing on the rock now, she and I, holding hands, swinging them forward and back, forward and back, building momentum. I look out at the water and feel her eyes on me.

"It's easy," she whispers. "Just watch me now..."

Wave thou art pretty
Wave thou art high
Wave to the city
Wave to the sky
Wave thou art future
Wave thou art why
Wave to the children
Wave wave good-bye

JEREMY MEGARGEE

THE HIKER

We all have our passions, and hiking has always been mine. I'm drawn to the mountains, the ridges, and the beating green heart of the forest. When I vanish into the trees—those old pillars of solitude—I feel perfectly at peace with myself. Alone in a vast wilderness, the civilized world nothing but a fragmented memory and new and wild horizons presented to those with the will and desire to pursue them. I've always had the will. The desire burns in my veins, and the smell of loamy soil and pine bark seems to pull at me with an eldritch magnetism.

All the best thru-hikers have told me about the detour from the Appalachian Trail that leads to Devil's Pond. It cuts through a rugged patch of West Virginia, steep and rocky terrain that gradually climbs in elevation with each fateful step. The trailhead is accessed through a little park that's easy to miss from the highway, just a parking lot and a solitary water spigot. The spruce pines seem to press in on the lot, sending their long shadows across the picnic tables and sapping any warmth from even the hottest summer days.

I found the trail just as summer was dying, fall encroaching quickly, the blue blazes on the trees leading up a twisty slope for a moderate three miles of hiking before reaching the pond at the summit. The map listed a shelter at the halfway point and a stream near the summit, but the real attraction was the pond itself. I'd heard it described as crystal clear water that would show you your own rippling reflection in the right light, a little piece of paradise hidden deep in the woods. It seemed like the perfect way to spend an afternoon. I had my pack, my lunch, and my music pounding soothingly in my ears. All that remained was the climb, and how I relished the climb.

Each new hike is a challenge presented to the hiker. A test of body and soul, mental strength, and the concept that if you work hard, a reward will be forthcoming. I'd conquered more wizened rocks than the terrain offered by the Devil's Pond trail, so I figured it would be relatively easy. I'd even checked the website HikingUpwards to see how other hikers had faired, and it provided me with only positive experiences. I expected the trail to bend to my will after minimal effort, but it seemed that fate was destined to defy my expectations.

The terrain seemed intent on showing me cruelty. Pitiless ascents, steep elevation changes, and sharp rocky protrusions that reached for me like teeth eager to chew. I immediately got the sense that the wilderness had turned its back on me. During past hikes I felt like a welcome visitor, but these woods were different. It was clear from the start that I was intruding here. I was unwanted, unaccepted, and clearly out of place. The wind whistled condemnations. The towering spruce pines seemed almost to judge me with knobby scorn. I felt this forest laughing at me with each stumbling step, each drop of sweat from the pores, and each long break I took to allow my lungs to stop burning with internal acid.

I couldn't understand it. Why this sudden rejection from nature? Hadn't I always been respectful to her? Kind to her? Gentle and sweet...like a lover from a bygone era. I romanced Mother Nature in the past, and she always reciprocated.

Not so on the trail to Devil's Pond. My boots dragged, my head ached, and my heart pounded like a failing piston in my chest. There were moments when I felt like I was shuffling through purgatory, a wispy ground fog drifting in across mossy stones and tangled oaken roots. It became almost impossible to find the blue blazes on the trees, each one more faded than the last.

I tilted my head up to listen to the sounds of the forest, but I suddenly became aware of the fact that all sounds had abandoned me. No birdsong, no chirping insects, not even the scuffle of a distant squirrel across dead leaves. It seemed wrong. It felt like the exploration of a wooded tomb instead of a fun hike with the sun high in the heavens.

I trudged on with jagged thoughts circling in my head. I considered turning back, but it's a great shame for a true hiker to admit defeat and go crawling back before conquering a summit. I thought my imagination was simply working against me, and I vowed to tough the hike out no matter how difficult it became. I'd not been bested before in the wilderness, and this time would be no different.

I caught sight of hope in the distance. It was little more than a white blur attached to the trunk of a tree, but I assumed it was a trail sign to gauge my progress. My breath left my mouth in ragged gasps, the sweat glistening on my brow, but a few more yards brought me face to face with the object.

It was not a sign. It was a horror.

Some sort of gleaming bone sculpture was strapped to the trunk of the tree, a skeletal conglomeration of chipped animal bones that flowered out into something vaguely spiderlike. A polished deer skull dominated the sculpture with jutting jaw bones emerging from a chest bound in twine. I stared into the hollow depths of the skull's empty sockets, and I struggled to make some kind of sense of this. Why was it here? Who made this morbid creation?

A few random theories came to me. Witchcraft? Devil worship? Some bizarre ritual, or perhaps just a hoax to elicit responses from those that passed it. I couldn't decide. All I knew for sure was that the object stank of death, almost like it was recently peeled of flesh and scrubbed to a shining gleam.

That symbol of decay offered me no hope. It had the opposite effect, delivering a new kind of dread into my already taxed system. I felt something like the beginning of slithering fear taking root deep inside of me. I stumbled past the thing and kept on walking, intent on giving it no power to spook me. Just a hoax. A few locals playing games for shits 'n' giggles. Nothing to be concerned with.

The elevation became brutal again, a tedious slog across sharp granite with the underbrush tangled close on each side. There were moments where I had to drop down to the toes of my boots and use my hands to gain purchase, pulling and hauling my weight up the unpredictable terrain.

The mist seemed to lick at my ankles, teasing the flesh and exploring with cold, insubstantial tendrils. It felt like tiny fingertips pressing their freezing touch against my skin, and each touch was designed to impede my progress, to make the climb all that much harder.

I kept going, clawing at the bark of a young dogwood to pull myself up over the crest of the next ridge. The sight that waited for me there stopped my breath in my throat. I swallowed dry, an itchy lump traveling slowly down my esophagus. Panic took over, my fingernails biting down into my palms to keep myself from losing it completely.

Another bone sculpture awaited me, this one much more intricate than the last. Two ribcages fused together with twine, fibulas fanning out into deathly blossoms, and what appeared to be two misshapen bear skulls wound together in a ball of frayed silk. The fangs seemed almost to beckon, a few sluggish flies crawling across the surface of the mouth to salvage whatever flesh might be left.

The sculpture shook me even more because I began to visualize that there was a presence responsible for its creation. Something watching and waiting in these woods, a sentient force capable of using these morbid talismans to send doubtful roots into my soul. Oh yes, a Presence. These bone creations were the silent Disciples, but it was the Presence that posed the true threat. It was weaving dark threads against me, drawing me deeper into the labyrinth it inhabited.

The bear skull appeared to grin, a trick of the light seeping in through the overhead branches, but it was enough to spur me onward and away. I clawed past the abomination and struggled to smash my boots down against the earth with a persistent need to put as much distance as I could between me and the Disciple.

I considered going back the way I came, but that would bring me back into contact with both of the monstrosities, so I decided to take my chances with the ascent. It was an optimistic plan, but it soon turned to misery when a new terror settled into my head.

Flashes of the Disciples began to enter my thoughts, and with their appearances came croaking whispers from long rotten tracheas. They put together nothing but jumbled words, the meaning incomprehensible to me.

"Loop. Repeat. Always the same. Trapped. Loop. Repeat."

The words were like barbs, and I longed to reach into my own brain and pull them out with a scream of satisfaction, but that option was not available to me. I could do nothing but march my exhausted shell of a body uphill, haunted by flashes of the Disciples and petrified at the thought of encountering the Presence responsible for them.

Finally a flare of light in an increasingly dark situation found me. There was a sign up ahead indicating that I'd reached the shelter on the trail. I pushed past spruce branches obscuring my sight, and there stood a small wooden cabin with an open interior, fire pit out front, and a lonely outhouse near the back.

I staggered toward the building with a vain hope of finding human habitation, but the shelter remained empty, almost like it had been waiting for my arrival. Nevertheless I found a small modicum of solace to have walls and a roof shielding me from a portion of the wilderness, and I allowed myself to collapse down onto the shelter's dusty floor. My eyelids fluttered closed and it wasn't long before restless sleep pulled me down into a muddled abyss.

I woke in the absence of daylight, the night strangely luminescent due to clear and powerful stars. It chilled me to think that I'd now have to brave the darkness in this void of a forest, but I was thankful that I'd remembered to pack my flashlight before venturing out. I reached in my pack and retrieved it, snapping the yellow beam into life, the glow giving the shadows of the shelter a shuddery illumination akin to multiple lit candles.

I was attempting to plan my next move when the beam of the flashlight crawled over the cover of the shelter's trail journal. I'd read such journals before on previous hikes, the pages usually full of whimsical notes from hikers and occasional diary entries about their own personal trials and tribulations in the wild. A desperate curiosity compelled me to pick up the book and crack open the spine. I expected to find the same content that I'd seen time and time again when reading a trail journal.

This was wholeheartedly different.

It seemed that all of the entries were made by one person, a hiker with the initials D.B. I started from the first page, squinting against the shadows to make out the words there.

"It's a loop. GET OUT. Don't go to Devil's Pond. It's always worse at Devil's Pond. Stuck. Lost. It's a cage, and the trees are the bars."

I shuddered at this. It seemed I was reading the thoughts of a madman, but I flipped through a few more pages to see if the narrative would change.

"Starts with the bone sculptures. They mock, but also hint. They're telling you why you're here. What you are. Why you can't stop until you reach the top. Find a way. STOP YOURSELF. Don't go any farther. It's bad. It's so fucking bad. I WANT OUT, I WANT OUT, I WANT OUT..."

The messages got progressively more incoherent, the man's penmanship seeming to dissolve right along with his sanity. I couldn't allow myself to read anymore. It left a bad taste in my mouth, so I threw the book into a dark corner of the shelter and let it sit there hidden in the gloom.

I pushed up to my feet and exited through the open front of the cabin, and I gazed at the trail twisting even higher toward my destination. After reading those scribbled warnings I should have been feeling dissuaded, but that same dogged determination still lurked inside of me. I felt that I simply *must* reach Devil's Pond. It was a pull within, almost like a fishhook had snagged my heart and something was reeling me in toward the summit of the mountain. The logical part of me wanted to turn back regardless of the fact that I'd have to pass the Disciples again, but I found myself incapable of doing that. I had no choice but to see this through. I came to hike this trail, and my only option was to finish it.

The starlight gave me more than enough luminescence to navigate by, so I put it off no longer, leaving the shelter behind and forcing myself back to that taunting incline. I climbed in a cold sweat, my clothing soaked and dripping, but oddly enough I felt no discomfort. All I felt was that burning desire to reach Devil's Pond and be done with it.

The wetness of the sweat seemed to settle deeper into my pores with each step closer to the top of that distant ridge. My hair was a sopping mess, beads of moisture trailing across my brow and my cheeks. I felt like a human swamp slopping its way across jagged terrain, droplets of my own foulness falling to the ground behind me with each bit of ground I managed to gain.

None of it mattered. I fell once heavily to the earth, a splash of liquid squelching out from my sleeves, but I got my knees back under me and resumed the climb. After a few shambling steps I came to the top of the ridge, and something like a doorway awaited me there.

It was a gate of bone shards, animal limbs twisted and shattered, dark sockets glaring, cracked skulls leering, finger and claw digits beckoning to a glimmering pond beneath a grove of spruce pines lording over the water like sentinels. The last of the bone sculptures, and it was immediately clear that the structure was built solely for me.

The end of my hike. I wanted so desperately for it to be over. I staggered past the threshold of bones, and suddenly a gush of stagnant water bubbled up out of my throat, a few splashes falling past my chapped lips. I couldn't account for it and I didn't try, I simply swallowed it back down like rising bile. The pond looked peaceful. I thought of throwing myself in and simply washing off the day. I thought of flipping to my back and floating with only the stars to witness it.

As tempting as the water was, a feeling deep in my diaphragm made me recoil from the surface. I knew that I was not alone here at the end of my hike. A Presence was with me, and it was getting closer. I saw it flopping just beneath the surface of the pond, a churning form spinning and floating, little bubbles escaping from the figure to drift up and break against the surface.

It stank of death, and from the flashes of fleshy tatters that I got, I could just make out bits and pieces of chipped bone. This was a bone sculpture too, but different from the rest. The waters shaped this figure, and the animals and insects did the rest, carving and shaping the ruined thing into this grim grand finale.

The closer it got, the less threatened by the Presence I became. It was a pitiful sight. A lost and forgotten thing. It floated there, a distinctly bloated human figure, facedown in the pond with a waterlogged pack swollen to massive proportions on its back. It seemed almost like a great dead turtle to me, and without even realizing I was doing it, I reached down to turn the form over.

I couldn't get a grip on it. My hands kept slipping, seeming almost useless to the task. It didn't matter. The Presence was turning over for me. A deep part of me did not want to see, but I knew I was powerless to stop it from happening.

The rotation of the figure stopped, and I leaned down to stare at the true nature of it. A face so pale that it was fishbelly white, dead eyes engorged and staring. Lank hair nibbled to tatters by snapping turtles and tadpoles. Skin black and thick, just swollen sausage beneath a thin layer of epidermis. A mouth appeared to stretch open to speak, but on second glance the lips parted due solely to the slithering leeches that had balled themselves up and made a home there.

It seemed that the corpse had drifted and picked up other bits of animal carrion that had fallen into Devil's Pond the longer it stayed here. Deer skulls. The ribcage of what may have once been a young black bear. The body so consumed by death that it attracted the dead parts of other organisms that once lived.

But despite these superficial horrors, it was a different reason entirely that made me scream until stagnant water oozed up from the center of my soul. I recognized this man. This bloated corpse. This drowned hiker. So familiar.

Familiar because it was me.

My pack. My clothes. My face.

The realization broke something in me, and I reached down desperately to pull the corpse up out of the water. My hands gained no purchase. I stared down at them, and suddenly I understood why.

My hands were just wispy appendages, barely there. I looked down at the rest of my body, and I saw much the same. It was like I was built from the same ground mist that seemed to cling around my ankles with each step I took on this hike. I brought the fog because I was the fog.

I tried again, but my spectral hands did nothing but pass right through the corpse. I couldn't even feel the wetness beneath. It all came rushing back then, just like the water from Devil's Pond that filled my lungs such a very long time ago.

The messages in the trail journal. The whispers from the bone sculptures. All those words of imprisonment.

It's a loop. It's a jail, a hell, an endless repeat. I've been here before. I've made this hike thousands of times on thousands of days. It always ends here. It always ends the way it ended the first time. I hiked here, I fell here, and I drowned here.

I'm stuck. I'm here again. I want out. I want out. I want out.

WE ALL have our passions, and hiking has always been mine. I've heard stories about the Devil's Pond trail, but now I finally get to explore it for myself. I've found the trail on this day when summer is dying, and up past the spruce pines I'll go.

NICOLA LOMBARDI

EVEN THE STARS FALL

(Translated by Joe Weintraub)

IT WAS a rough awakening, provoked by an irritating burning in his chest, as if the bit of a fine drill had pierced his heart. With immense effort, he fought to open his eyelids, at least a bit, just enough to glimpse through his sticky lashes the figure of Fosco busy prodding his chest with a branch glowing at one end.

"That's enough sleep for now. Wake up, you can do it...Are you there?"

Rino's line of sight was filled almost entirely by a black expanse, a shroud interwoven with infinitesimal points of light scattered at random atop the fabric. His head ached, throbbing, stabbing, gnawing. In place of his brain, his skull seemed filled with boiling lava. But it took only a few seconds before that seething mix cooled down—perhaps from the fresh air intruding into his eyes now that they were fully open—and the dark curtain hanging over him turned out to be the night sky, clear and infinite. And the stars were where they were supposed to be, each in its own place, charting a pattern far too large for Rino or anyone else to be able to interpret.

"But even the stars fall."

That observation jolted him. But it was still only the tail end of the last coherent thought that had preceded his lapse into unconsciousness. Idly looking over the spectacle offered by the heavens on that Night of San Lorenzo, he had managed to count no less than three shooting stars ("Ah," Fosco had commented drily, "It's only the Night of San Lorenzo, the Night of the Falling Stars") before the viscous coil of oblivion reached his brain and switched off the lights.

Slender fingers had intruded into his hair, ruffling through it gently at the top. Rino realized then he was lying outstretched, the heat of the sand beneath his bare back, his head resting on a soft surface. Smiling, he suddenly recaptured the substance of his memory, and he raised his eyes slightly, allowing Marina's head to enter the upper range of his vision. The girl was smiling, too, and continued to caress his hair like a mother with her child half-asleep in her lap. Really, it was wonderful. He could sense her fragrance, faintly diluted by the salty aroma gusting from the sea. And the others? Were they all still there? He tried to get up, struggling against the overall lethargy that still numbed his senses. His neck, as he lifted it just a bit from Marina's thighs where it had been reclining, was immediately chilled by a pleasant coolness. Bracing himself on his elbows, he naturally thought first to take a look at the fire. The bonfire that had (how long before?) crackled and burned so vigorously, was now no more than a tangle of expiring flames, churning like little red mice in a cage. Smoking fumes, gray and pungent, were unrolling toward land, rising up from the bramble of charred wood. The pleasant aroma of grilled meat and charcoal was still lingering around him.

The fellow with the red hair and beard could be seen squatting on the other side of the flames. His shape seemed blurred and wavering through the scalding air hovering above the remains of the fire. Rino tried to recall his name, but with little success. Then there were those other two girls. That blonde's name was Sandra, while the little brunette with the short hair was Cynthia. That's right: Sandra and Cynthia; he was starting to remember clearly. And, of course, Marina, behind him, under him, with that delicate hand continuing to caress his hair. He wondered if, by chance, he had made love to her, or if he had only dreamed of it. Well, no matter. That was, at the moment, a purely academic question, and he smiled, generally quite pleased with himself. Despite his leap into the void, his mind, by then, had already resumed working as it should, or almost. And to think that just before closing his eyes, he had believed that he was heading for his ultimate high, the "big blast," the definitive one from which there would be no return. But instead, here he was back again, wide awake and ready to swallow life as he had always done before.

Finally, he shifted his gaze to Fosco, his long black hair hanging disheveled over his tanned shoulders. His dark face, which seemed carved from the knot of a tree trunk, was turned toward him. Behind his moustache and goatee, he seemed to be smiling, benevolently. And just a little above his head, only several hundreds of thousands of miles farther away, the full moon pierced the sky like the glowing butt-end of a gigantic joint that someone hidden on the other side had, as a joke, pressed against a black curtain. Rino laughed softly at the notion. Obviously, the residue of alcohol and grass were still messing with his head.

RINO HAD relocated to Portolargo less than a month before. Perhaps "relocate" was a bit premature, given that he was renting the most squalid of studio apartments in the hope of finding something better. He had enough time to replenish his finances; with his contacts and connections that would not have been difficult, even if his reckless spending had always been a problem for him. But the air was getting difficult to breathe where he had settled before, and he was already well-known in all the police stations of the neighboring districts. They had never caught him with his hand in the till, but that was a mere detail. In any case, he knew very well when it was time to clear out.

Discotheques and late-night bars were his hunting grounds. There, he always found business to be good, and it was at The Flying Dutchman he got to know Marina. And Marina had introduced him to Fosco, also known as "the fisherman." He was kind of the King of the Hill, apparently, in those parts, and although he wasn't exactly a dealer, he could, of course, occasionally find something for you if he felt like it. But, certainly, it was vital to be in his camp if you wanted to deal in peace. Above all, he handled the running of the smaller boats, on the shadier side of the commercial port. Someone called him, in jest, "the fisher of souls," but without respect to anything evangelical.

Whatever the case, Rino was from "somewhere else," and he had quickly understood that becoming friends with this Fosco was the only way to avoid being forced to pack his bags and move on.

Invited to a late-night party on the beach, he at first wanted to back out. He had always felt uncomfortable out in the open, where there were too many people. But the gathering, apparently, would be limited to a small number of close friends, Fosco included.

"Think of it as a kind of initiation, if you like," Marina had told him, and that comment had removed all doubt. He would have to go.

He had brought a little of his best stuff with him, just to elevate the spirit of the evening. Business would, perhaps, be discussed, and it would be an opportunity to make himself known for what he was, or what he fancied himself to be: serious, reliable, discreet.

Marina had arranged the meeting in a rather out-of-the-way place, just beyond the pines, and there Rino had left his motor scooter, in a tangle of branches, chained to a trunk.

"Relax, no one steals anything from anybody around here." Marina had seemed so sure, He believed her at once, and they then walked toward the shore, hand in hand.

She was wearing a translucent sarong over a pink bikini. Along the way, Rino felt free to wander with his hands, but the girl, other than laughing softly, stood firm, at least for the moment. "Later, later, we can't keep Fosco waiting." Right, Fosco must not be kept waiting. That annoyed him, but Rino knew how to hold back. If those were the rules of the game, he was willing to accept them without question, to avoid being shut out.

Passing over a dune, he finally saw the bonfire. Several brownish and orange-colored shapes were crouching around it and looking over toward him. There was something primitive about that little scene. The priests of his new tribe were waiting for him. He smiled at that notion. And if the smile was followed by a shudder, he made sure to keep it to himself.

Unable to predict the direction the party would be taking, he had sniffed a short line of snow before leaving, just to avoid being overcome by any emotions. Approaching the small group, he felt light-headed, safe, vaguely defiant.

After some hasty introductions—as usual, he had grasped

hardly a single name, while remaining favorably struck by the women present—he took a look around.

"Aren't we much too close to those houses?" he remarked, gazing over toward a row of low, dark, shed-like dwellings about a hundred yards away. Fosco simply invited him to sit down beside them, thereby putting to rest any concerns.

Morsels of meat and fish were spitted on crude skewers, and the fragrance was inviting. There were considerable quantities of bottles and six-packs, and the girls were regarding him with such intense expressions, Rino was beginning to feel the blood already simmering in his veins.

Then the little packet containing his contribution to the party appeared out of one of his pockets, and almost before he could realize it, he had begun smoking, drinking, inhaling deeply, dancing, and singing out loud—until the moon and stars were extinguished above and around him.

THE DULL bellow rolled up into the air, toward the sky. The surf's backwash replied with a liquid hiss.

Fosco had risen to his feet, and he was now blowing into the interior of a great shell, which was serving as a horn. A second bass tone, more forceful and varied, resembled the prolonged cry of a dying bull, a groan arising from an unimaginable world. Rino felt himself shivering, despite his proximity to the still anxious flames.

Cynthia was laughing softly, watching the others with eyes full of excitement. Sandra smiled back at her, raising her lips to reveal the gums underneath. Redbeard said nothing. He alone turned his gaze from Fosco to the sea. There below, sky and water embraced along the beam of moonlight streaming down to trace the horizon. Shimmering waves lazily followed one another, expiring quickly into mounds of foam.

A third moaning from the shell, and only at that moment did Rino notice that Marina had given up caressing his hair. He let his head slip backward so that he could look her in the face. The declining light of the bonfire was drawing fleeting tattoos, red and yellow, across her tense features. Her green eyes were fixed on the sea.

The echo of that ominous tone was fading into the distance, in search of ears that could, perhaps, still hear it.

"What...what's going on?" His voice escaped from him like a thickening whimper.

Lowering his eyes toward him, Fosco again twisted his lips into a shadow of a smile. He was holding the shell tightly in both hands, as he would a rugby ball.

"You want me to tell you what's going on? Nothing new. Nothing that hasn't already gone down so many other times."

The girls were watching Fosco almost as if in adoration. For the first time, Rino appreciated the depth of the charisma that the man exerted over his crew. In that scattering of seconds, an aura of expectation adhered to the very air they were breathing, to the flickering heat escaping from the fire, to the briny stench blowing in from the east to chill his sweat.

Without a word, the girls and Redbeard got up, sweeping from their tanned bodies the sand that was sticking to them in streaks similar to trails of gilded ants. Even Marina moved away, shifting the thigh where Rino had been reclining, and if he had not instantly braced himself on his elbows, he would have fallen heavily backward. His mind framed a protest he could not begin to pronounce in words.

Then, the small strident voice of one of the girls pierced his heart.

"There they are! Down there! There they are!"

"Who?" he murmured, trying to push himself back onto his feet. But the world must not yet have become as steady as he had hoped, and a violent dizziness thwarted his attempt to get up. He felt the urge to vomit, but when he noticed the dark puddle drying alongside his head—a shiny, pitted hollow in the sand, moist with vodka, gin, and who knows what else—he realized there was nothing more left in his stomach to flush out. Suddenly drained of all energy, he sank back down, flat on his back. Numberless points of light hung over him, and he could not begin to determine whether or not they were falling. "The heavens are darker than dreams," he thought. He did not know if that idea contained in itself any sort of logic, but it seemed to him fitting and proper. "Bright dreams falling, falling..."

A kiss on his forehead, unexpected, brought him back to earth. Marina. She was leaning over him for what was apparently an affectionate farewell. "Thanks," she whispered into his ear before drifting away. "From all of us." Her breath, reeking of alcohol, turned his stomach.

He tried to respond, but he could only manage to gasp for air like a great pale fish stranded on the sands. He turned his head to one side, landward from the beach. The three girls and Redbeard were already off in the distance, walking slowly backward, never taking their eyes off of the sea, with expressions on their faces that alarmed him.

In the background, where the rows of small, black cottages stretched outward, it seemed to him that lights had been turned on, and that moving shapes were venturing out through wide-open doors.

The beating of his heart was now painful, as if a piston had been bolted into his chest.

And towering above him, Fosco appeared against the glimmering pitch in which his universe had been drenched. "I'm really sort of sorry about this, Rino. I kind of liked you."

Out of the corner of his eye, Rino caught a flicker of moonlight close to Fosco's right hand. It wasn't the large shell. A moan spun from his throat to plunge into the puddle of drying vomit."What?...No, please, don't...I..."

Fosco's expression turned inquisitive. Then, when he noticed that Rino was staring wide-eyed at the serrated edge of the massive knife he was holding in his fist, he broke out in a friendly laugh. "No, no, Rino, you can take it easy. We've got no more use for this, not now."

A man's crackling voice reached them from out of the distance, from the row of small houses. "Fosco, come on. Finish up and get out of there!"

Fosco cast his eyes in the direction of the old man who was calling out to him. Then he looked toward the sea.

Rino, still stretched out on his back, could not see the small globes, like stars fallen from the sky, that were now emerging from the waves about a hundred feet offshore. Small, gloomy spheres, slow, but still getting closer, disappearing now and then to reappear again, bright and gleaming, embraced by the cold light of the moon.

"Fosco, come on! What are you waiting for!" The piercing voice of one of the girls.

Rino looked at the man standing over him, and watched as an insane smile widened on his face. He seemed pleased with what was going on.

Suddenly, Fosco kneeled down close enough to be able to speak to him in a low voice. "We're not bad people. We only do what we have to do. It's our life."

That being said, he grabbed him forcefully by one hand and began to drag him over the sand, toward the sea, as he would a bag of trash about to be thrown out. Instinctively, Rino twisted and struggled to get to his feet. But what had been for him up until that moment only a diffuse prickling turned into a deep and unexpected agony.

"Give it up," Fosco told him, calmly, continuing without much effort to drag him along. At that moment, Rino turned his eyes toward the fire. Within the black branches that were still curling and writhing above and below the flames, he spotted stubby, carbonized clusters, severely contorted, slender and jagged stumps sticking out. Nothing identifiable in that charred morass—except for a human foot, spared, for the moment, from the fire.

The cry escaping from his throat proved to be quite similar to that gloomy, rallying peal Fosco had drawn from the shell.

"Believe me, that's all a waste of breath." Fosco stopped, kneeling down once again. "But I think it's only fair that you know at least what's happening to you and why."

Rino's heart was like a blind and wild bird, imprisoned in a narrow, red-hot aviary, each beat of the wing a spasm. Twisting his head, he brought his eyes downward in disbelief to where he already knew his own legs were no longer to be seen. His thighs ended just above the knees, sealed off by a pair of charred, deadened stumps.

"We have to do this every year, Rino. It's kind of a sacrifice. A life in exchange for lives. During the Night of San Lorenzo. You know very well we live off of fishing. They're the ones who guarantee full nets for us, every year."

Rino stared at Fosco, eyes full of tears.

"They…they're the drowned. Do you know how many poor devils get swallowed up by the currents and whirlpools, out there in the deep sea? Those are treacherous waters if you're not real familiar with them. The bodies are hardly ever returned to land. The sea holds on to them. And those lost down below, they protect our fishing. But you have to understand, they need to be repaid for their services. Life for life. You showed up at just the right time. It's a lot easier with a stranger from somewhere else. Sure, we could've taken care of you while you were unconscious, that would've been the merciful thing to do. But they want their offerings to be alive so they can drown them themselves. You'll be in good company. Sorry about the legs, but we couldn't allow you to get away. They are rather slow, you know..."

Yet another voice, crying out from the distance. "Fosco, get out! Else they'll take you, too!"

Fosco arose and replied to the appeal. "Papa, go back in the house and stop worrying. I'm coming now!" Then, turning back to Rino, he brought the knife to his forehead, giving him a military salute. There was no mockery in his face, but only sincere fellow feeling, since, in essence, all of them were victims, victims of a tragic game, a roundabout from which no one ever really manages to escape. Then he turned his back to the sea and drifted away, regretfully, toward the houses.

Rino moaned, gurgling, rolling over the cold compact sand of the shoreline. A sheet of frigid water slid past to caress him, and quickly withdrew, leaving behind a glistening, frothy edge. Finding himself again in a prone position, Rino propped himself up on his hands. The pain now was almost unbearable. All his nerve ends were, one by one, awakening. But he had to move off, he had to try something, he had to...

Raising his head and chest, he looked at the sea.

The globes, shining and menacing, that he had been unable to see before, now showed themselves for what they were—glistening heads, taut skin reverberating with a sickly phosphorescence. Three, four, five bodies, pallid, tottering, coated with slime, swollen, and deformed. They were leaving the water, in the most absolute silence, and they were coming for him.

His arms buckled, and Rino fell down face forward, tasting the moist and salty sand. A new slip of dark backwash chilled his face, forcing him to turn around again on his back, his arms flailing. And once more that sky, filling still every corner of his vision. The moon now seemed to have fled, to avoid being forced to witness. He took a deep breath. A foul stench of rotting fish, invaded his mouth and nostrils, stifling his lungs, turning his stomach. He dug his fingers into the sand, anchoring himself to a useless illusion. More water, which now seemed as cold as ice, flowed against his sprawling body, and with the water, a hand also arrived. The fingers, clenching into a fist within his hair, froze against his skull, and all at once, they began to pull. Almost in tears, he thought once more of those other caresses that only a short time before had seduced him, preparing him for martyrdom.

Before tightly closing his eyes, he thought he'd caught sight of a shooting star dividing the night in two. Having no more energy to spare, to waste, he put up no resistance. He felt himself being drawn to the water as he listened to the rhythmic sucking pace of the walking dead. Everything was pain and horror beyond redemption. In the night behind his eyelids, he visualized the bright wake of the meteor. But the sea swallowed him up before he could voice any of his useless longings.

ADAM MILLARD

ORI

"Death abducts the dying, but grief steals from those left behind."
—Katherine Owen

ONE

WILLIAM SCHAEFFER tamped his pipe and lit it, all the while staring down at the opened letter upon his desk. He had read it and reread it, and yet the words might as well have been written in Sanskrit, for it was all at once impossible to process, even by a brain as accomplished and celebrated as his.

Perhaps it is a mistake, he considered for a moment. A terrible mistake which could ultimately send him, an eminent creator of Secondary Persons, to an earlier grave than even the doctors had predicted.

Once again, he turned his attention to the envelope, and once again his name—printed there in bold, almost anthropomorphically menacing letters—told him that no, this was not a mistake; this letter was meant for him. It had been typed (by a SECPER he had designed, perhaps? Oh, the irony!), folded twice, and stuffed into the envelope with his name on it *deliberately*.

William clutched his chest with one withered and liveried hand as an insufferable pain wracked his entire body. The still-smoking pipe fell from his tightening lips and clattered upon the desk, spilling ash and tobacco cinders across the page.

A red-edged hole began to slowly widen through the words: FUNDING WITHDRAWN.

"Is something the matter?"

The voice came from behind, entering through the door to William's study, and William knew he had to fight through the mystery pain, lest his Personal Care Android, Ori, make a mountain out of a molehill and deliver him straight to his quarters for the purpose of rest.

"I'm perfectly fine, Ori," William said through gritted teeth. The SECPER's heavy footfall upon the carpet behind him suggested Ori was closing in; was no doubt already performing all sorts of computations and compiling variables by the thousands. Ori had probably already diagnosed him with dozens of afflictions and was already motoring through his databanks for the best course of treatment.

"That is not entirely true, is it, William?"

He was right there now, hanging on William's shoulder like an AI parrot. If Ori breathed—one of the few limitations of a Secondary Person—William was certain he would taste the bitter hydraulic fluid upon his own tongue.

With his eyes clenched tightly shut, William drew in a long, languorous breath. This was the last thing he needed right now; the third degree from a machine *he* had created. He slowly turned, the pain within his chest now nothing more than an acrid aftertaste.

Ori's expression was one of utmost concern. He bored holes into William's eyes with his own, searching his master's face for signs of fatigue and pain. William could never be angry at the SECPER, for if it wasn't for Ori, he would have pushed up an entire meadow of daisies by now. Would have been nothing but bones and dust, with hungry worms in between.

"I'm fine, Ori," William reiterated. "Just a little indigestion, is all." A forced smile. "Guess we had better tell Vox not to bake any more of that soda bread, right?"

Ori shook his head. "Vox's baking is impeccable, William. You know that better than anyone, since you personally loaded her databanks with over two million eight hundred thousand and fifty-nine recipes—none of which have caused you dyspepsia or gastralgia—and over the years you have seemingly made it your life's work to get through each of them."

William didn't know whether to be offended or angry. "Are you calling me fat, Ori?" He picked his pipe up from the desk, making sure to nudge the envelope across so that it covered the distressing letter from BioTech, and began to fill it with fresh tobacco from a pouch he produced from his pocket. It was all misdirection; while he was doing this, Ori wasn't doing the other. Wasn't asking questions about his health; wasn't looking to the desk to see what his creator had to hide.

"You know I can never be offensive to a human, William," Ori said, matter-of-factly, a slight frown creasing his eerily flawless artificial brow. "I am merely stating that you have never criticized Vox's cooking before, which may, in and of itself, be another symptom of whatever is troubling you."

"As I said,"—William lit his pipe—"you are finding things where there is nothing to be found, as you are wont to do upon occasion."

The SECPER did not look convinced. And why would he? With a microprocessor twice as powerful as anything his counterparts possessed—and there were thousands of them out there—Ori was one of a kind; the most able AI synthetic ever produced.

And therein lay the problem, for if those insipid and foolhardy suits up at BioTech knew just what William was capable of, and not only that but had already pulled it off with aplomb, there was no way upon God's green earth that he would have received such a rash and cruel missive. If they knew about Ori, BioTech would line William's pockets with gold, write him a blank cheque, fund him and his company until the end of time, and put him forward for the Nobel Prize of Robotics.

But they would never know about Ori.

They *could* never know.

"Perhaps you should restrict the number of pipes you smoke per evening," Ori suggested, sneering at the object in William's hand as if it were a deadly weapon and not just a decorative gourd calabash.

"Tell me, Ori, did you enter my study, my personal space, to order me around, or was it something that struck you once you had arrived? I'm growing increasingly weary of your constant scorn."

Good! William thought. *This is good! Misdirection at its finest!*

Ori sighed, or at least simulated something like one. "You must forgive me, William. It is my duty, as your Personal Care Android, to take care of your health and wellbeing—"

"And while I am fully aware of that, Ori, if I tell you I am perfectly fine, I expect you to take it as so and move on. I have very little time remaining upon this earth, I can ill afford to spend it on asinine squabbles with you."

At that, Ori simply nodded, his expression stoic.

William felt truly awful; Ori was just doing his job, the thing for which he had been created: taking care of his master in his twilight years. His programming meant he would exhibit extreme concern for William if there was even so much as a two-degree change in his temperature. It wasn't Ori's fault he was overly invested in his creator's health and wellbeing. The blame fell upon a small chip implanted in Ori's subgenual anterior cingulate cortex, the part of the AI synthetic's brain responsible for empathy and generosity. That microchip was the reason Ori behaved the way he did.

And William wouldn't change a thing about Ori.

"Say, Ori, when was the last time we drove to the ocean?"

The SECPER's eyes glazed over with cataracts as he searched his memory; it was rather unsettling if you weren't accustomed to it, seeing an android become a hemi-zombie. Eventually, after a series of mechanical lip-smacks, Ori said, "The last time we visited your favourite, Fistral Beach, was on the twenty-third day of March, two thousand and twenty. Since then we have taken the HydroPod to Barmouth, 2022, to Margate, 2027, and to Brighton, 2031."

William smiled, for the pain—and all memory of it—had entirely left his body. "Let's go to Fistral Beach. First thing in the morning."

"As you wish, William," Ori said. "Will there be anything else?"

William told him that no, everything was just fine, and when Ori left the room a few minutes later, William had managed to convince himself that it was the truth.

TWO

THE RIDE to Fistral Beach was more than pleasant; William spent the entire journey finger-composing Mozart's *Requiem in D Minor* as the music filled the HydroPod up like warm water. In the seat beside him, Ori watched on, a beatific smile upon his countenance. The vehicle, like all HydroPods manufactured since 2027, was self-driving, which meant both William and Ori could relax, enjoy the scenery, the passing glass tenements as they left the city, the way in which their surroundings ever-so-slowly changed from bleak gray to vivid green as they arrived in the countryside. Soon after that, the unmistakeable smell of the ocean drifted in through William's open window, and his smile broadened further still.

Once the vehicle had parked itself alongside the promenade, Ori climbed out, walked around to William's door, and opened it. "Take it very slowly," the SECPER said.

William's smile faded somewhat; had he really believed Ori's concern for him would vanish beyond the walls of the mansion? That the seaside vistas would cause the android to stop caring about him?

"I've climbed out of vehicles before, Ori," William said, unable to disguise his irritation. And, as if to prove he could manage just fine, he ushered Ori aside and eased himself out of the HydroPod, the door whispering automatically shut behind him. "See? Didn't make a fool of myself, did I?"

"Of course not, William," Ori said. "I have only ever seen you make a fool of yourself once: September fifteenth, 2023. You got dr—"

"Drunk at a BioTech function and pissed my pants," William finished for him. "Why do you always have to bring that up?"

"Do I, William?" Ori asked. "I don't ever recall having mentioned it before."

"Well, once is enough, and I'd appreciate it if you expunged that particular day from your memory bank."

"As you wish, William." Once again, his eyes became milky—this time for a beat, no more—before returning to their normal light-blue hue. "It is done, William. Are there any other days you would like me to delete?"

William shook his head and sighed. This was going to be a

longer day than he'd anticipated.

The promenade was quiet, save for a few dog-walkers and joggers running alongside their PT SECPERs. The sun occasionally threatened to break from behind a blanket of gray-and-white clouds, but never quite managed it.

Ori helped William across the pebbles on the beach first, and then the sand, as they approached the foaming deep. William always liked to stand just beyond the reach of the water, in that sweet spot where it occasionally trickled over his bare feet, though never reaching higher than his ankles.

"This will do just fine," William said, arriving at the sweet spot.

"Would you like me to remove your shoes and socks, William?" Ori motioned to the old man's feet.

"No, no, that won't be necessary today, Ori. I just want to watch for a while."

"Of course, William. You are suitably protected from the sun"—the android raised a hand toward the cloud-strewn sky—"and your temperature is currently thirty-seven-point-two degrees—"

"Can I just watch the ocean in peace, Ori?"

Ori nodded, bowed slightly, and took a step back, away from the surf. "Of course, William. Please tell me when you next wish for me to speak."

And so they stood for a while, the Atlantic stretching out before them for hundreds of miles. Gulls swooped and soared and, off in the distance, a cruiser shifted slowly across the horizon, off to somewhere exotic, its cargo thousands of affluent passengers whose only goal was to see as much of the world as possible before the sun blinked out of existence or they died, whichever came first.

"It's beautiful, isn't it?" William said.

Nothing.

William turned to find Ori staring unblinkingly out toward the cruiser, a slight pre-programmed smile playing about his features.

"It wasn't rhetorical, Ori," William said.

Ori snapped out of it, perhaps satisfied he had been given permission to speak again. "Yes, William, it is quite beautiful."

It was time. William *knew* it was time, and there would be no better occasion, for this was, he surmised, his final journey to the ocean. "Ori, I have an order for you."

"An *order*, William?"

"Well, let's call it a *favour*. Is that better?"

"As you wish, William."

William turned his attention back to the ocean, to the gulls in the sky and the boat on the horizon, and everything in between. "I wish to be buried at sea, Ori. I want to exist out there forever, not in some wooden box any curious or recalcitrant kid could dig up, if the fancy took it."

"Hopefully, you are speaking of something which will not happen for many years yet, William." When William turned to chastise his PCA, he saw something like genuine love within Ori's piercing blue eyes.

"It will be soon, Ori. You know that as well as I do, and we must prepare for the day, for time is quickly running out. We are down to the last grains of sand in an hourglass; is it not best to be organised for when the hourglass falls empty?"

"It is, William," Ori said. "And I have already updated your digital will and testament so that, when it does happen—many years from now—those lawyers who access it shall know precisely what your wishes are."

William turned to face the sea again. "Thank you, Ori."

"You're welcome, William."

The cruiser continued inexorably toward hotter climes in the distance and the gulls squabbled in the sky over morsels of food in beaks too small to see.

William smiled a little, but it soon became a grimace as a twinge in his chest reminded him—how very noble of it—of his own impending mortality.

THREE

WHEN THEY arrived back in the city, William was pleased to discover Vox had prepared a lunch of soup and crusted bread. The ocean always made him hungry; perhaps it was the salt lingering in the air, the scent of battered fish being cooked in kiosks across the seafront. Whatever it was, William was glad of the soup and bread, which he took in his large, oval dining room.

"Will there be anything else, William?" the cook asked as she circled the table, rearranging cutlery next to placemats which had never been used. "Perhaps a glass of water?"

William laughed. "Ha! I have seen enough water for one day, thank you. Perhaps a glass of wine? Something red and fruity?"

"We have a vintage Dolcetto in the cellar, William," said Vox, stopping at the door. "Would you have me bring it up?"

"I would," William said, dipping his bread in the minestrone. "I would indeed." He pushed the salty bread into his mouth and chewed frantically.

"As you wish, William." Vox left, leaving William alone for the first time all day. Lord knew where Ori was—probably off in some corner of the mansion, running medical data updates on himself—but William was glad of the solitude and the silence which came with it. It had been an emotional day—at least for William, for Ori was not capable of true emotion, not the way, say, another human being was—and his desire to spend the rest of it alone, without the persistent wittering of his PCA, had never been stronger.

Once he was sure Vox would be well on her way to the wine cellar, William took the letter he had received from BioTech from his suit pocket and, after reading it one final time—*those bastards! Those bastards would be nothing without me!*—he produced the box of matches usually reserved for lighting his pipe and drew the large, glass ashtray toward him.

He would burn it. He would burn it, and that would be that, for he knew no amount of supplication would change their minds.

And William Schaeffer had never beseeched anyone in all his years; he wasn't about to start doing so now, as his life drew to a close.

He pushed his soup bowl aside, dusted breadcrumbs from the table, and set the letter down so that he had free hands to liberate a match from its box. He gave the box a shake and the drawer flew open a little too violently, spilling matches all across the dining table and carpet.

"Dammit!"

He didn't have time to pick them all up now; would have Vox do it upon her return from the wine cellar. He took one up from the table and struck it against the box.

It lit on the first attempt. Posthaste, he picked up the letter and held the match to its corner, the corner signed by that condescending prick, Arthur Levine, CEO. With a bit of luck the paper would act as some sort of rudimentary voodoo doll, and, somewhere in his multi-billion credit penthouse, Levine would burst into flames.

The thought brought a smile to William's face and he held the match a little closer, browning the corner of the page but not lighting it straight away.

And then it happened. The pain in his chest returned, worse than it had ever been before. It was as if someone had bound his heart with barbed wire and was now pulling it tight, piercing all four chambers at once.

The lit match fell from between his thumb and forefinger and landed upon the table, thankfully now extinguished; the worst letter William had ever received fell from his other hand, floated down, down, down to the dining room carpet, swooping like the gulls from earlier that morning, the gulls with morsels of food in beaks too tiny to see.

Sweat soaked William's shirt, the seat of his trousers, as he threw himself back in his chair, willing the pain to leave his body as if he were some kind of agony exorcist.

But this time the pain did not abate. It grew more intense, and all at once William knew, without a shadow of a doubt, that he had just been a guest at his own last supper. And now he would die alone—as it was *always* going to be—sitting at a dining table with matches all around him and the BioTech letter there for all to see.

Through the pain which had turned his lips red with blood, he considered calling out for Ori. The SECPER had been his best friend, his confidant, and his primary carer for the past five years. Wouldn't it be nice to see his beautiful, smooth face one last time before he passed on to pastures greener?

He was still torn between hollering for Ori and simply allowing what will be to be when the decision was removed.

Darkness swallowed him up as he toppled sideways from his chair, his last breath coming at some point between the chair and the dining room floor.

VOX PLACED the Dolcetto upon the dining room table and crossed the room to where William lay, prone and not breathing. A quick scan told her all she needed to know; her master was dead.

"William Schaeffer is deceased," she said, without any trace of emotion. There was nothing she could do for the old man—nothing *anyone* could do for him, really—but Vox knew Ori, as William's PCA, was assigned to care posthumously for their creator, and so set off to find the android.

Upon locating Ori in the library, where he was in the middle of an important update—cables protruding from the nape of his neck were plugged into a huge server—Vox said, "William Schaeffer is deceased," in exactly the same manner she had said it a moment ago in the dining room. With almost infuriating indifference.

Ori's cataract eyes snapped open, the colour returning to them almost immediately. He stood, pulled the cables from the back of his neck, and turned to face Vox. "Please repeat."

"William Schaeffer is dead."

"Where is he, Vox?"

"Dining room floor—"

Ori raced from the room so quickly, he didn't hear Vox finish her sentence with:

"—but he's most definitely dead."

ORI SAT with William for more than eight hours, both of them on the floor, William's rapidly cooling head resting in Ori's lap. Vox did not interrupt; Ori could hear her working away in the kitchen, clattering pots and pans, even though there was no longer anyone to appreciate her meals, or indeed anyone to tell her what to cook.

Defunct.

Obsolete.

It was the prerogative of BioTech to recall those SECPERs whose masters no longer reside in the world of the living, and that is what would happen to Vox.

To *him*.

Broken down, perhaps, for spare parts. Assigned to another ailing BioTech employee who would be nowhere near as dear to Ori as William Schaeffer was. And the irony was, this was all BioTech's fault. Ori had seen the letter, one corner burnt, sitting on the dining room table. He was certain that discourteous missive had brought forward William's demise.

"Why did you not tell me, William? Why did you not confide in me?" Ori said, running a hand across his former master's face. The sensors in his fingertips sent a series of complex messages to his microprocessor; rigor mortis was beginning to set in. Soon, William Schaeffer would be stiff as a board, and about as full of life as one, too.

We are down to the last grains of sand in an hourglass; is it not best to be organised for when the hourglass falls empty?

Some of the last words William had spoken to him.

I wish to be buried at sea, Ori. I want to exist out there forever...

Ori knew what he must do, and that was honour William Schaeffer's last wishes.

It was quickly growing dark beyond the walls of the mansion.

"As you wish, William," Ori said. "As you wish."

FOUR

ORI RETURNED to the very same spot he and William had stood the day before. Only now it was dark—*beyond* dark—and gone was the scent of fish and chips and the squabbling gulls. Other than the hiss and whisper of the tide as it ebbed and flowed, Ori could hear nothing.

In his arms, William Schaeffer felt as light as a feather. Wrapped in a bedsheet, beneath which he now wore his favourite suit, William was already beginning to smell. Perhaps not to human olfactory organs—it would be another twelve or so hours before humans would catch a whiff of death, by which time William would be gone—but to Ori, the stench was almost unbearable.

"I brought you, William," Ori said. "I brought you to your favourite place. The ocean...it will be yours *forever.*"

But something didn't seem quite right about that, for Ori was not ready to leave his master, his friend, his creator. Not now.

Perhaps not *ever.*

Before he knew what he was doing, Ori had taken one step forward, toward the foaming surf. And then another. And a third.

The freezing water washed over his feet, filled his shoes, drenched his pure-white socks. And still forward he walked, to his knees, his waist, and for some reason he held William above the surface, as if its sudden chill might disconcert him. It was ridiculous, but years of service to this man, of putting William's needs above everything and everyone else, meant that it would take an eternity to care about anything else.

Not that he would ever have to care about anything else again.

Stopping only to remove the sheet from William's corpse, Ori watched as it floated away on the black Atlantic, a spectre made of only the best cotton, for William enjoyed his luxuries as much as the next man.

Seawater buffeted Ori as he moved implacably on, but he wouldn't drop William Schaeffer. He would *never* drop William Schaeffer, whose face and body were now entirely submerged.

Somewhere back on the promenade, a fight was breaking out between rival gangs. Ori pitied them. He pitied them all, for they had never met William Schaeffer.

But *he* had.

One foot in front of the other, over and over again. Ori walked for two miles, his feet remaining stuck to the seabed due to his immense bodyweight caused by his mechanical innards. He sidestepped huge, hulking rocks, battled through fronds of seaweed and fields of coral, searching for the right place to stop.

At two miles, his microprocessor hissed, gave out a single spark, and brought the AI synthetic to a halt. But Ori didn't mind, for it had fried at the precise moment he had glanced down at his creator's face.

In the oceanic abyss they would exist forever, creator and creation, as it was always meant to be.

Ori's eyes clouded over for the final time, a smile spreading across his flawless face.

We did it, William Schaeffer.

We did it.

Ocean, a body of water occupying about two-thirds of a world made for man—who has no gills.

—Ambrose Bierce

ABOUT THE EDITORS

ALESSANDRO MANZETTI is a Bram Stoker Award®-winning author (and four-time finalist), editor, and translator of horror fiction and dark poetry whose work has been published extensively in Italian, including novels, short and long fiction, poetry, essays, and collections. English publications include his collections *The Garden of Delight, The Massacre of the Mermaids, The Monster, the Bad and the Ugly* (with Paolo Di Orazio) and the poetry collections *No Mercy, Eden Underground* (Bram Stoker Award winner 2015), *Sacrificial Nights*, and *Venus Intervention* (with Corrine de Winter). His stories and poems have appeared in Italian, USA, and UK magazines. He edited the 2016 Bram Stoker Award nominee anthology *The Beauty of Death* volume 1. He is currently serving as a member of the Board of Trustees of the Horror Writers Association, and lives in Trieste, Italy.

Website: www.battiago.com

JODI RENÉE LESTER is an editor and writer. She has worked with several authors and anthologists on award-winning projects, including Alessandro Manzetti (Stoker Award winner for superior achievement in a poetry collection, *Eden Underground*, 2015), Maria Alexander (Stoker Award winner for superior achievement in a first novel, *Mr. Wicker*, 2014), Deborah Khoshaba, Psy.D. (National Indie and Excellence Award in the personal growth category, *Getting to Oz*, 2014), and Lisa Morton (Black Quill Award winner for best dark fiction anthology and Stoker Award nominee for superior achievement in an anthology, *Midnight Walk*, 2009). She currently works as the English language editor for Independent Legions Publishing based in Italy. In 2016, her story "Just Watch Me Now" first appeared in *The Lovecraft eZine*, issue #37. Her stories "Casting Lots" and "The Guixi Sisters" appeared in the anthologies *Songs of the Satyrs* (2014) and *Midnight Walk* (2009), respectively. She earned her bachelor's degree in biology at CSU Fullerton, studied creative writing with Dennis Etchison, and honed her editing skills with independent crime publisher UglyTown. She lives in the Lowcountry of South Carolina with her husband Mike, dog Ilona, and cats Mathias, Klaus, and Maggie.

AUTHOR BIOS

MICHAEL ARNZEN holds four Bram Stoker Awards and an International Horror Guild Award for his disturbing (and often funny) fiction, poetry, and literary experiments. Actually born in Amityville, New York, Arnzen now haunts the zombielands of Pittsburgh, PA. He has been teaching as a professor of English in the MFA program in Writing Popular Fiction at Seton Hill University since 1999, which provided the basis for his instructional guide, *Many Genres, One Craft*. See what he's up to now at gorelets.com.

MICHAEL BAILEY is a multi-award-winning writer, editor, and book designer, and the recipient of over two dozen literary accolades, including the Bram Stoker Award, Benjamin Franklin Award, Eric Hoffer Book Award, International Book Award, and Independent Publisher Book Award. His nonlinear novels include *Palindrome Hannah*, *Phoenix Rose*, and *Psychotropic Dragon*, and he has published two short story and poetry collections, *Scales and Petals* and *Inkblots and Blood Spots*, as well as *Enso*, a children's book. He has created anthologies such as *Qualia Nous*, *The Library of the Dead*, four volumes of *Chiral Mad*, *You Human*, and a series of illustrated books.

CLIVE BARKER is an English writer, film director, and visual artist. He is the recipient of World Fantasy, Bram Stoker, and International Horror Guild awards, and many others international prizes. Barker came to prominence in the mid-1980s with a series of short stories, the *Books of Blood*, which established him as a leading horror writer. He has since written many novels and other works, and his fiction has been adapted into films, notably the Hellraiser and Candyman series. He began writing horror early in his career, mostly in the form of short stories (collected in *Books of Blood 1-6)* and the Faustian novel *The Damnation Game* (1985). Later he moved toward modern-day fantasy and urban fantasy with horror elements in *Weaveworld* (1987), *The Great and Secret Show* (1989), the world-spanning *Imajica* (1991), and *Sacrament.* Among his works as a writer: *The*

Hellbound Heart (1986), *Cabal* (1988), *The Thief of Always* (1992), *Everville* (1994), *Coldheart Canyon* (2001), *Abarat* (2002), *Days of Magic, Nights of War* (2004), *Mister B. Gone* (2007), *Absolute Midnight* (2011), and *The Scarlet Gospels* (2015).
Website: www.clivebarker.info

DANIELE BONFANTI – A science fiction and horror author from Italy, his English debut, the novelette *Game*—honorable mention in Datlow's *The Best Horror of the Year*—was published in the 2016 Stoker-nominated anthology *The Beauty of Death*, followed by a story in Flame Tree's deluxe hardcover *Supernatural Horror Short Stories*. His Italian publications include the novels *Melodia* and *Quintessenza*, several short stories, and scores of articles in the popular print magazine *Hera*.

He also translates from English: works include novels by Ramsey Campbell, Brian Keene, Clive Barker, Brian Evenson, and Richard Laymon; long and short fiction by Jack Ketchum, Peter Straub, and Poppy Z. Brite. He is an active member of the Horror Writers Association.

An adventure enthusiast—mountaineer, kayaker, trail runner—and beekeeper, he lives on the slopes of Mount Resegone with wife and daughters, in an ancient house in the woods.

Website: www.danielebonfanti.com

BRUCE BOSTON is the author of more than fifty books and chapbooks, including the dystopian sf novel *The Guardener's Tale* and the psychedelic coming-of-age-novel *Stained Glass Rain*. His poems and stories have appeared in hundreds of publications, most visibly in *Amazing Stories, Analog, Asimov's SF, Daily Science Fiction, Strange Horizons, Realms of Fantasy, Weird Tales, the Nebula Awards Anthology*, and *Year's Best Fantasy and Horror*. His poetry has received the Bram Stoker Award, the *Asimov's* Readers Award, the Gothic Readers Choice Award, and the Rhysling and Grandmaster Awards of the SFPA. His fiction has received a Pushcart Prize and twice been a finalist for the Bram Stoker Award (novel, short story).

His latest collection, *Visions of the Mutant Rain Forest,* is a fiction and poetry collaboration with fellow SFPA Grandmaster Robert Frazier. www.bruceboston.com

DANIEL BRAUM is the author of the acclaimed short story collections *The Night Marchers and Other Strange Tales* (from Cemetery Dance & Grey Matter Press, 2016) and *The Wish Mechanics Stories of the Strange and Fantastic* (from Independent Legions, 2017). His short story "How to Make Love and Not Turn to Stone" from the *Beauty of Death* volume 1 received an honorable mention in Ellen Datlow's *The Best Horror of the Year.* His fiction has appeared numerous times in *Cemetery Dance Magazine.* His short story "Palankar" which is also about "death by water" can be found in the book *Nightscript* volume 3 (Cthlonic Press, 2017). He is the host of the Night Time Logic reading series. More about him can be found at: www.bloodandstardust.wordpress.com

JONAH BUCK wanted to learn eldritch knowledge and commune with pale creatures that flit across the sunless landscape to terrorize the living, so he became an attorney in Oregon. His interests include history, professional stage magic, paleontology, and exotic poultry. He has written a few dozen short stories, and his novels, including *Substratum* and *Carrion Safari,* are available from Grinning Skull Press and Severed Press. Special thanks to Maureen Walsh.

RAMSEY CAMPBELL – The Oxford Companion to English Literature describes Ramsey Campbell as "Britain's most respected living horror writer." He has been given more awards than any other writer in the field, including the Grand Master Award of the World Horror Convention, the Lifetime Achievement Award of the Horror Writers Association, the Living Legend Award of the International Horror Guild, and the World Fantasy Lifetime Achievement Award. In 2015 he was made an Honorary Fellow of Liverpool John Moores University for outstanding services to literature.

PAOLO DI ORAZIO (Rome, 1966), author of books and comic books since 1987 across Italy. HWA active member since 2015, in English he has published comics for *Heavy Metal* and short stories for the books *Dark Gates* (with Stoker Award®-winner Alessandro Manzetti; Kipple, 2014), *My Early Crimes* (Raven's Headpress, 2015), and *The Monster, the Bad and the Ugly* (with Stoker Award®-winner Alessandro Manzetti; Kipple, 2016). His short stories have also appeared in *The Beauty of Death* (Independent Legions Publishing, 2016) and *Year's Best Hardcore Horror* volume 2 (Comet Press, 2017). His short story "Hell" is in *The Best Horror of the Year* list by Ellen Datlow (2015).

Dennis Etchison is a three-time winner of both the British Fantasy and World Fantasy Awards. His collections include *The Dark Country, Red Dreams, The Blood Kiss, The Death Artist, Talking in the Dark, Fine Cuts, Got To Kill Them All & Other Stories, A Little Black Book of Horror Tales* and *It Only Comes Out At Night & Other Stories.* He is also the author of the novels *Darkside, Shadowman, California Gothic, Double Edge, The Fog, Halloween II* & *III* and *Videodrome*, the editor of *Cutting Edge, Masters of Darkness I-III, MetaHorror, The Museum of Horrors* and (with Ramsey Campbell and Jack Dann) *Gathering the Bones.* Etchison has written extensively for film, television and radio, including 150+ scripts for *The Twilight Zone Radio Dramas.* He served as President of the HWA from 1992 to 1994 and is the recipient of the 2017 Bram Stoker Award for Lifetime Achievement. His ebooks are published by Crossroad Press, and definitive new print editions of his first four collections are available from Shadowridge Press.

Brian Evenson is the author of a dozen books of fiction, most recently the story collection *A Collapse of Horses* and the novella *The Warren. The Warren* and two previous books, *Windeye* and *Immobility*, were finalists for a Shirley Jackson Award. His novel *Last Days* won the American Library Association's award for Best Horror Novel of 2009. His novel *The Open Curtain* was a finalist for an Edgar Award and an International Horror Guild Award. Other books include *The Wavering Knife* (which won the IHG Award for best story collection), *Dark Property,* and *Altmann's Tongue.* He is the recipient of three O. Henry Prizes as well as an NEA fellowship. His work has been translated into French, Italian, Greek, Spanish, Japanese, Persian, Turkish, and Slovenian. He lives in Los Angeles and teaches in the Critical Studies Program at CalArts.

DONA FOX is a horror/dark fiction author and poet. She has published stories and poems in *Cemetery Dance*, *Eldritch Tales*, *Haunts*, *The Nightmare Express*, *Terror Time Again*, *Thin Ice*, *Beyond*, and *New Blood* magazines and has appeared in numerous anthologies. She released a first single author collection of short stories, *Dark Tales from the Den*, in 2015 and a second collection, *Darker Tales from the Den*, in 2016. Dona is a member of Horror Writers Association and lives in Northern California. Website: www.donafox.com

STEPHEN GREGORY – After teaching for twelve years in England and Algeria and Sudan, escaped to Wales to write his first book, *The Cormorant.*

The Cormorant won the Somerset Maugham Award and was made into a movie starring Ralph Fiennes. *The Woodwitch* and *The Blood of Angels* completed his Snowdonian trilogy.

The Perils & Dangers of This Night, *The Waking that Kills*, and *Wakening the Crow* have also shown his love of the countryside, the seasons, and the stars, and particularly his interest in birds. His latest novel *Plague of Gulls* is set entirely within and around the medieval walls of Caernarfon, where he used to work as a tour-guide (clambering up and down the towers of the 13th century castle more than 2000 times). He also enjoyed a year as a screenwriter in Hollywood, writing for William Friedkin (notorious for *The Exorcist* and an Oscar-winner for *The French Connection*).

More recently Stephen has been teaching French to cheeky, cheerful Malay/Chinese girls in Brunei Darussalam in South-East Asia. He now lives with his wife Christine in a cottage beside the river Vienne in Charente, France (with dog Poppy and cats Gudrun and Smokey, all rescued and brought back from Borneo), while working slowly and steadily to restore their 400-year-old fortified farmhouse.

Eric J. Guignard is a writer, editor, and publisher of dark and speculative fiction, operating from the shadowy outskirts of Los Angeles. He's won the Bram Stoker Award, been a finalist for the International Thriller Writers Award, and a multi-nominee of the Pushcart Prize. Outside the glamorous and jet-setting world of indie fiction, Eric's a technical writer and college professor, and he stumbles home each day to a wife, children, cats, and a terrarium filled with mischievous beetles. Visit Eric at: www.ericjguignard.com

Michael H. Hanson created the ongoing Sha'Daa shared-world anthology series currently consisting of *Sha'Daa: Tales of the Apocalypse*, *Sha'Daa: Last Call*, *Sha'Daa: Pawns*, *Sha'Daa: Facets*, *Sha'Daa: Inked*, and the soon-to-be-released *Sha'Daa: Toys*, all published by Moondream Press (an imprint of Copper Dog Publishing).

In 2017, Michael's short story "C.H.A.D." will be appearing in the Eric S. Brown-edited anthology *C.H.U.D. Lives!* and his short story "Rock and Road" appears in the just-published Roger Zelazny tribute anthology *Shadows and Reflections*.

Michael also has stories in Janet Morris's Heroes in Hell (HIH) anthology volumes *Lawyers in Hell*, *Rogues in Hell*, *Dreamers in Hell*, *Poets in Hell*, *Doctors in Hell*, and the recently published *Pirates in Hell*.

Caitlín Rebekah Kiernan is an Irish-born American author of science fiction and dark fantasy works, including ten novels, many comic books, and more than two hundred and fifty published short stories, novellas, and vignettes. She is also the author of scientific papers in the field of paleontology. Kiernan is a two-time recipient of both the World Fantasy and Bram Stoker awards, and four-time recipient of the International Horror Guild Award. Among her fiction works, the novels: *Silk* (1998), *Threshold* (2001), *The Five of Cups* (2003), *Low Red Moon* (2003), *Murder of Angels* (2004), *Daughter of Hounds* (2007), *Beowulf* (2007, novelisation), *The Red Tree* (2009), *The Drowning Girl* (2012). To date, her work has been translated into German, Italian, French, Turkish, Spanish, Portuguese, Finnish,

Czech, Polish, Russian, Korean, and Japanese. In May 1996, Kiernan was approached by Neil Gaiman and editors at DC/Vertigo Comics to begin writing for *The Dreaming*, a spin-off from Gaiman's *The Sandman*. Kiernan wrote for the title from 1996 until its conclusion in 2001. She lives in Providence.
Website: www.caitlinrkiernan.com

John Langan is the author of two novels, *The Fisherman* (2016) and *House of Windows* (2009/2017), and two collections of stories, *The Wide, Carnivorous Sky and Other Monstrous Geographies* (2013) and *Mr. Gaunt and Other Uneasy Encounters* (2008). With Paul Tremblay, he has co-edited *Creatures: Thirty Years of Monsters*. One of the founders of the Shirley Jackson Awards, he served as a juror for its first three years. Currently, he reviews horror and dark fantasy for *Locus* magazine. He lives in New York's Hudson Valley with his wife and younger son.

Frazer Lee's debut novel *The Lamplighters* was a Bram Stoker Award® finalist for Best First Novel and a Book Pipeline finalist. His other published works include the Amazon #1 horror/thriller *Panic Button: The Official Movie Novelization*, novels *The Jack in the Green* and *The Skintaker*, and the Daniel Gates Adventures series of novellas.

His screenwriting credits include the acclaimed horror/thriller feature film *Panic Button*, and award-winning short films *Simone* and *The Stay*. His film and television directing credits include multiple award-winning films *On Edge* and *Red Lines* (starring Doug "Pinhead from *Hellraiser*" Bradley) and the promo campaign for Discovery Channel's *True Horror with Anthony Head*. His script doctor and story consultant engagements include commissions from The Asylum, Mediente Films International, Movie Mogul, and others.

Frazer is Head of Creative Writing at Brunel University London and is an active member of the Horror Writers Association and International Thriller Writers. His guest-speaking engagements have included StokerCon, World Horror Con, London Screenwriters Festival, and the Guerilla Filmmakers Masterclass. He lives with his family in Buckinghamshire, England, just across the cemetery from the actual Hammer House of Horror.

NICOLA LOMBARDI is a horror writer, editor, and translator. Among his publications in Italian: *I racconti della Piccola Bottega degli Orrori*, *La fiera della paura*, *Striges*, *I ragni zingari*, *La notte chiama* (with Luigi Boccia), *Madre Nera*, *La Cisterna*, *Pallide streghe d'autunno*. In addition, he has published two novelizations from Dario Argento's movies *Profondo Rosso* and *Suspiria*. Among his publications in English: the novel *The Tank* and the short stories "Tests of Courage" (in *Disturbed Digest* #10), "Sand Castle" (in *Play Things & Past Times*), "Hungry Shadows" (in *Disturbed Digest* #9), and "Professor Aligi's Puppets" (in *The Beauty of Death* volume 1). His short stories have appeared in several magazines and anthologies. He translated into Italian the H.P. Lovecraft biography *Dreamer on the Nightside* by F.B. Long and, for Independent Legions, the collection *Dread in the Beast* by Charlee Jacob and the novel *Mister Suicide* by Nicole Cushing. He's a Horror Writers Association active member and lives in Ferrara, Italy.

Website: www.nicolalombardi.com

LISA MANNETTI's debut novel, *The Gentling Box*, garnered a Bram Stoker Award and she has since been nominated five times for the prominent award in both the short and long fiction categories. Her story, "Everybody Wins," was made into a short film and her novella, "Dissolution," will soon be a feature-length film directed by Paul Leyden. Recent short stories include "Apocalypse Then" in *Never Fear: The Apocalypse*; and "Arbeit Macht Frei" in *Gutted: Beautiful Horror Stories*.

Her novella about Houdini, *The Box Jumper*, was not only nominated for both the Bram Stoker Award and the prestigious Shirley Jackson Award, it won the Novella of the Year award from This Is Horror in the UK.

She has also authored *The New Adventures of Tom Sawyer and Huck Finn*, two companion novellas in her collection, *Deathwatch*, a macabre gag book, *51 Fiendish Ways to Leave Your Lover*, as well as non-fiction books, and numerous articles and short stories in newspapers, magazines, and anthologies.

Lisa lives in New York in the spooky 100-year-old house she originally grew up in with two wily (mostly black) twin cats named Harry and Theo Houdini.

Visit her author website: www.lisamannetti.com
Visit her virtual haunted house: www.thechanceryhouse.com

JEREMY MEGARGEE has always loved dark fiction. He cut his teeth on R.L. Stine's Goosebumps series as a child and a fascination with Stephen King's work followed later in life. Jeremy weaves his tales of personal horror from Martinsburg, West Virginia, with his cat Lazarus acting as his muse/familiar.

ADAM MILLARD is the author of twenty-six novels, twelve novellas, and more than two hundred short stories, which can be found in various collections, magazines, and anthologies. Probably best known for his post-apocalyptic and comedy-horror fiction, Adam also writes fantasy/horror for children, as well as bizarro fiction for several publishers. His work has recently been translated for the German market.

LISA MORTON is a screenwriter, author of non-fiction books, Bram Stoker Award®-winning prose writer, and Halloween expert whose work was described by the American Library Association's *Readers' Advisory Guide to Horror* as "consistently dark, unsettling, and frightening." She has published four novels, over a hundred short stories, and three books on the history of Halloween. Her most recent releases include the anthology (co-edited with Ellen Datlow) *Haunted Nights,* which received a starred review in *Publishers Weekly*; the collection *The Samhanach and Other Halloween Treats*; and the acclaimed study *Ghosts: A Haunted History*. She lives in the San Fernando Valley, and can be found online at www.lisamorton.com.

ADAM NEVILL – *Some Will Not Sleep: Selected Horrors.* In ghastly harmony with the nightmarish visions of the award-winning writer's novels, these stories blend a lifelong appreciation of horror culture with the grotesque fascinations and childlike terrors that are the author's own. Adam L.G. Nevill's best early horror stories are collected here for the first time. Published October 31st, 2016. www.adamlgnevill.com

GREGORY L. NORRIS is a full-time professional writer, with work appearing in numerous short story anthologies, national magazines, novels, the occasional TV episode, and, so far, one produced feature film (*Brutal Colors*, which debuted on Amazon Prime January 2016). A former feature writer and columnist at *Sci Fi*, the official magazine of the Sci Fi Channel (before all those ridiculous Y's invaded), he once worked as a screenwriter on two episodes of Paramount's modern classic *Star Trek: Voyager*. Two of his paranormal novels (written under his nom-de-plume Jo Atkinson) were published by Home Shopping Network as part of their Escape With Romance line—the first time HSN has offered novels to their global customer base. He judged the 2012 Lambda Awards in the SF/F/H category. Three times now, his stories have notched honorable mentions in Ellen Datlow's Best-of books. In May 2016, he traveled to Hollywood to accept HM in the Roswell Awards in Short SF Writing. Follow his literary adventures at www.gregorylnorris.blogspot.com.

GENE O'NEILL has seen over 175 of his stories and novellas published, several reprinted in France, Spain, and Russia. Some of these stories have been collected in *Ghost Spirits*, *Computers & World Machines*, *The Grand Struggle*, *In Dark Corners*, *Dance of the Blue Lady*, *The Hitchhiking Effect*, and *Lethal Birds*. He has seen six novels published. Gene has been a Stoker finalist twelve times. In 2010 *Taste of Tenderloin* won the haunted house for collection; in 2012 "The Blue Heron" won for Long Fiction. Upcoming before the end of 2017 are the four trade paperbacks in the Cal Wild Chronicles from Written Backwards Press, a number of short stories, and a novelette. A long novel *The White Plague Chronicles* is a work in progress, with parts sent to an interested publisher.

Gene lives in the Napa Valley with his wife, Kay. He has two grown children, Gavin, who lives in Oakland, and Kaydee, who lives in Carlsbad and rides herd on his two g-kids, Fiona and TJ. When he isn't writing or visiting g-kids, Gene likes to read good fiction or watch sports—all of them, especially boxing.

JOHN PALISANO is the author of *Dust of the Dead*, *Ghost Heart*, *Nerves*, and *Starlight Drive: Four Halloween Tales*. His first short fiction collection *All That Withers* celebrates a decade of short story highlights. *Night of 1,000 Beasts* is coming soon.

He won the Bram Stoker Award© in short fiction in 2016 for "Happy Joe's Rest Stop." More short stories have appeared in anthologies from Cemetery Dance, PS Publishing, Independent Legions, DarkFuse, Crystal Lake, Terror Tales, Lovecraft eZine, Horror Library, Bizarro Pulp, Written Backwards, Dark Continents, Big Time Books, McFarland Press, Darkscribe, Dark House, Omnium Gatherum, and more. Non-fiction pieces have appeared in *Blumhouse*, *Fangoria*, and *Dark Discoveries* magazines. He is currently serving as Vice President of the Horror Writers Association.

Say "hi" at: www.johnpalisano.com

JOANNA PARYPINSKI is a college English instructor by day and a writer of the dark and strange by night. Her work has appeared in *Nightmare Magazine*, *Haunted Nights*, *HWA Poetry Showcase IV*, *The Burning Maiden* volume 2, *Dark Moon Digest*, and elsewhere. Living in the shadow of an old church that sits atop a hilly cemetery north of Los Angeles, she plays her cello surrounded by the sounds of screaming neighbor children. Visit her website at www.joannaparypinski.com.

DAVID J. SCHOW is a multiple-award-winning writer who lives in Los Angeles. The latest of his nine novels is a hardboiled extravaganza called *The Big Crush* (2017). The newest of his ten short story collections is titled *DJStories* (2018). He has written extensively for film (*The Crow, Leatherface: Texas Chainsaw Massacre III, The Hills Run Red*) and television (*Masters of Horror, Mob City*). One of Fangoria magazine's most popular columnists, he is also the author of *The Outer Limits Companion* (revised third edition, 2018) and *The Outer Limits at 50* (2014). As editor he has curated both Robert Bloch (*The Lost Bloch*, three volumes, 1999-2002) and John Farris (*Elvisland,* 2004) as well as assembling the legendary horror anthology *Silver Scream* (1988). Other recent nonfiction works include *The Art of Drew Struzan* (2010). He can be seen on various DVDs as expert witness or documentarian on everything from *Creature from the Black Lagoon* and *Psycho to I, Robot and King Cohen: The Wild World of Filmmaker Larry Cohen.* Thanks to him, the word "splatterpunk" has been in the Oxford English Dictionary since 2002.

MARGE SIMON lives in Ocala, FL. She edits a column for the HWA Newsletter, "Blood & Spades: Poets of the Dark Side," and serves on Board of Trustees. She won the Strange Horizons Readers Choice Award, 2010, the SFPA's Dwarf Stars Award, 2012, and the Elgin Award for best poetry collection, 2015. She has won the Bram Stoker Award ®, the Rhysling Award and the Grand Master Award from the SF & F Poetry Association, 2015. Marge's poems and stories have appeared in *Daily Science Fiction*, *You, Human*, *Chiral Mad*, and *Scary Out There*, to name a few.

LUCY A. SNYDER is a five-time Bram Stoker Award-winning writer. She's author of a dozen books and about 100 published short stories. Her fiction has been translated into French, Russian, Italian, Czech, Spanish, and Japanese editions, and her work has appeared in publications such as *Asimov's Science Fiction, Nightmare Magazine, Pseudopod, Strange Horizons, Apex Magazine,* and *Best Horror of the Year.* She has a Master of Fine Arts in creative writing from Goddard College and is faculty in Seton Hill University's MFA program in Writing Popular Fiction. You can learn more about her at www.lucysnyder.com

PETER STRAUB is the author of seventeen novels, which have been translated into more than twenty languages. He has written two volumes of poetry and three collections of short fiction, and he edited the Library of America's edition of H. P. Lovecraft's *Tales* and their 2-volume anthology, *American Fantastic Tales.* He has won many awards. In 2006, he was given the HWA's Life Achievement Award. In 2008, he was given the Barnes & Noble Writers for Writers Award by Poets & Writers. At the World Fantasy Convention in 2010, he was given the WFC's Life Achievement Award.

Lucy Taylor is the award-winning author of seven novels, five collections, and over a hundred short stories. Most recently, her work has appeared in her collection *Fatal Journeys* and in the anthologies *Fright Mare* ("Dead Messengers"), *Into Painfreak* ("He Who Whispers the Dead Back to Life"), *Peel Back the Skin* ("Moth Frenzy"), and at Tor.com ("Sweetlings," May 4, 2017). Several of her stories can also be found on the short fiction app Great Jones Street. Upcoming work includes short stories in the anthologies *The Five Senses of Horror* ("In the Cave of the Delicate Singers"), *Edward Bryant Tribute Anthology* ("Blessed Be the Bound"), and *CEA Greatest Anthology Written* ("Fecundity"). A new edition of her Stoker-winning novel *The Safety of Unknown Cities*, illustrated by Glen Chadbourne and published by The Overlook Connection Press, will be out later this year.

Taylor lives in the high desert outside Santa Fe, New Mexico.

Tim Waggoner has published close to forty novels and three collections of short stories. He writes original dark fantasy and horror, as well as media tie-ins, and his articles on writing have appeared in numerous publications. He's won the Bram Stoker Award, been a finalist for the Shirley Jackson Award and the Scribe Award, his fiction has received numerous honorable mentions in volumes of *Best Horror of the Year*, and he's twice had stories selected for inclusion in volumes of *Year's Best Hardcore Horror*. He's also a full-time tenured professor who teaches creative writing and composition at Sinclair College in Dayton, Ohio.

Anthony Watson has placed short stories in various indie press publications including *State of Horror: Louisiana* from Charon Coin Press, *Sanitarium* magazine, and *Far Horizons.* His most recent publications are the war/horror novella *Winter Storm* in a six-author collection *Darker Battlefields* from The Exaggerated Press, and *Stitches for Smiles* in a new horror magazine *Worlds of Strangeness.* Forthcoming are appearances in *The Black Room Manuscripts* volume 3 and *Morpheus Tales.* His weird western novella *The Company of the Dead* made up a double-header with Benedict J. Jones' *Mulligan's Idol* in volume 1 of *Dark Frontiers.* Work has begun on volume 2. December 2017 will see the publication of his novel, *Witnesses,* by Crowded Quarantine Publications.

As well as writing, he runs a horror review blog "Dark Musings" (found at: http://anthony-watson.blogspot.co.uk/).

He lives on the beautiful Northumbrian coast with Judith and their two dogs, a landscape which provides endless inspiration.

FORTHCOMING BOOKS

DREAMS THE RAGMAN
by Dennis Etchison
Novella – **eBook Edition**
October 2017

TALKING IN THE DARK
by Dennis Etchison
Collection – **eBook Edition**
December 2017

AVAILABLE BOOKS

CHILDREN OF NO ONE
by Nicole Cushing
Novella – **Paperback and eBook Edition**
October 2017

THE RAIN DANCERS
by Greg F. Gifune
Novella – **eBook Edition**
September 2017

THE WISH MECHANICS

by Daniel Braum

Collection – **Paperback and eBook Edition**

July 2017

THE ONE THAT COMES BEFORE
by Livia Llewellyn
Novella – **Paperback and eBook Edition**
May 2017

SELECTED STORIES
by Nate Southard
Collection – **Paperback and eBook Edition**
April 2017

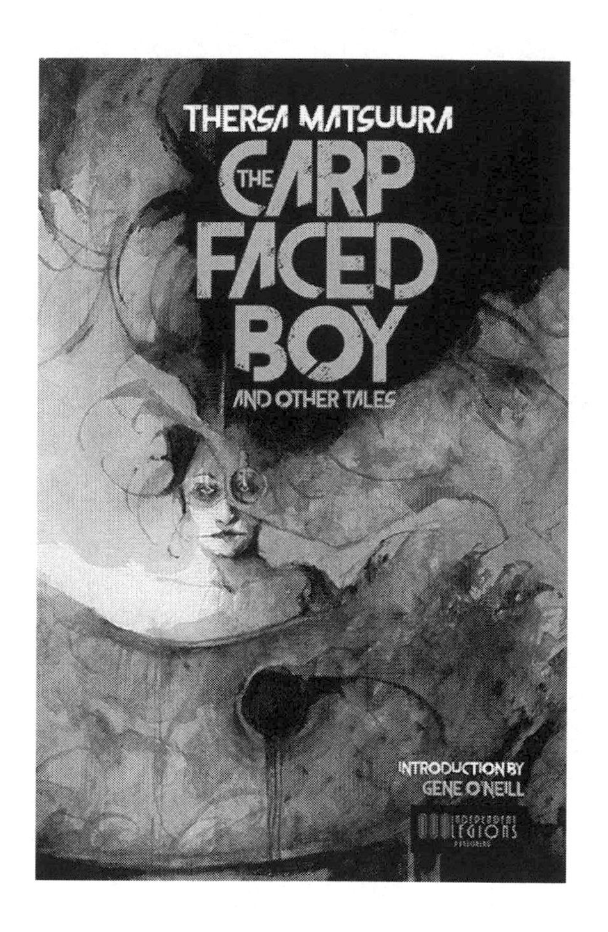

THE CARP-FACED BOY AND OTHER TALES
by Thersa Matsuura
Collection – **Paperback and eBook Edition**
February 2017

ALL-AMERICAN HORROR OF THE 21ST CENTURY
Edited by MortCastle
Anthology – **Paperback and eBook Edition**
November 2016

BENEATH THE NIGHT
by Greg F. Gifune
Novel & Novella – **Paperback Edition**
October 2016

THE BEAUTY OF DEATH
Edited by Alessandro Manzetti
Anthology – **eBook Edition**
July 2016

DOCTOR BRITE
by Poppy Z. Brite
Collection – **eBook Edition**
January 2017

WHAT WE FOUND IN THE WOODS
by Shane McKenzie
Collection – **eBook Edition**
September 2016

USED STORIES
by Poppy Z. Brite
Collection – **eBook Edition**
June 2016

THE HORROR SHOW
by Poppy Z. Brite
Collection – **eBook Edition**
August 2016

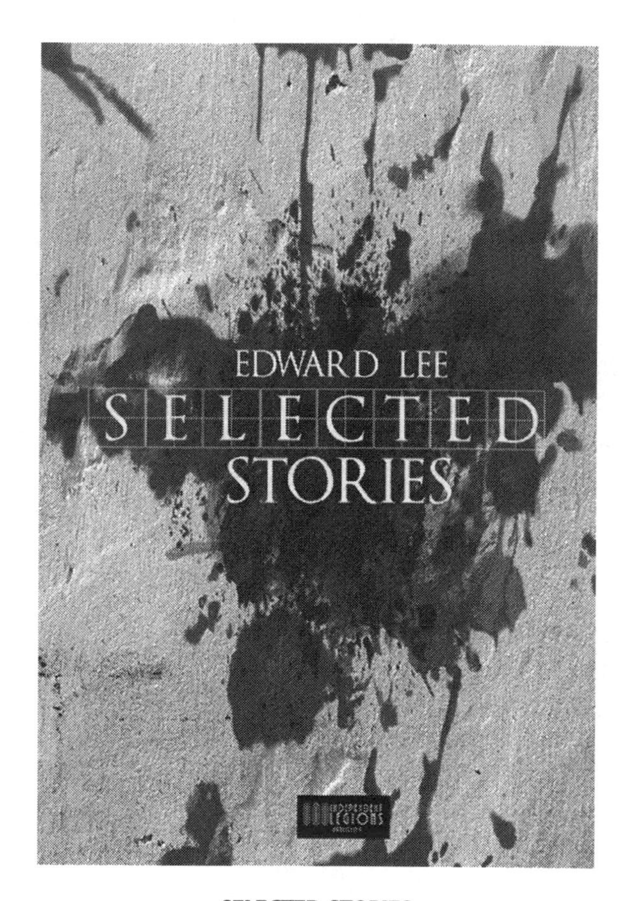

SELECTED STORIES
by Edward Lee
Collection – **eBook Edition**
July 2016

THE USHERS
by Edward Lee
Collection – **eBook Edition**
May 2016

THE CRYSTAL EMPIRE
by Poppy Z. Brite
Novella – **eBook Edition**
May 2016

SELECTED STORIES
by Poppy Z. Brite
Collection – **eBook Edition**
February 2016

THE HITCHHIKING EFFECT
by Gene O'Neill
Collection – **eBook Edition**
February 2016

SONGS FOR THE LOST
by Alexander Zelenyj
Collection – **eBook Edition**
April 2016

INDEPENDENT LEGIONS PUBLISHING

INDEPENDENT LEGIONS PUBLISHING
by Alessandro Manzetti
Via Virgilio, 10 - 34134 Trieste (Italy)
+39 040 9776602

www.independentlegions.com
www.facebook.com/independentlegions
independent.legions@aol.com

Books in Italian:
www.independentlegions.com/pubblicazioni.html

Made in the USA
Columbia, SC
08 December 2017